RIDE THE STAR WINDS

A. Bertram Chandler

BAEN

RIDE THE STAR WINDS

The Anarch Lords copyright © 1981 by A. Bertram Chandler. *The Last
Amazon* copyright © 1984 by A. Bertram Chandler. *The Wild Ones*
copyright © 1985 by A. Bertram Chandler.

Catch the Star Winds copyright © 1969 by A. Bertram Chandler.
"Chance Encounter" was first published in *New Worlds* March 1959.
"On the Account" was first published in *Galaxy* May 1973. "The Dutchman"
was first published in *Galaxy* November 1972. "The Last Hunt" was first
published in *Galaxy* March 1973. "Rim Change" was first published in
Galaxy August 1975.

A Baen Books Original

Baen Publishing Enterprises
P.O. Box 1403
Riverdale, NY 10471
www.baen.com

ISBN: 978-1-4516-3812-7

Cover art by Stephen Hickman

First Baen paperback printing, April 2012

Distributed by Simon & Schuster
1230 Avenue of the Americas
New York, NY 10020

Library of Congress Cataloging-in-Publication Data

Chandler, A. Bertram (Arthur Bertram), 1912-1984.
[Works. Selections. 2012]
Ride the star winds / A. Bertram Chandler.
    pages cm
  ISBN 978-1-4516-3812-7 (pbk.)
1. Science fiction, Australian. I. Chandler, A. Bertram (Arthur Bertram),
1912-1984. Anarch lords. II. Title.
PR6053.H325A6 2012
823'.914--dc23
                                          2012000208
Printed in the United States of America

10 9 8 7 6 5 4 3 2 1

CONTENTS

THE ANARCH LORDS

DEDICATION

For Vice-Admiral William Bligh R.N., one-time commanding
Officer of the H.M.S. *Bounty,* one-time Governor of New South
Wales, with belated apologies for the participation of an ancestral
Grimes in the Rum Rebellion of 1808 A.D.

☙ Chapter 1 ☙

"YOU GOT OFF LIGHTLY, GRIMES," said Rear Admiral Damien.

Grimes's prominent ears flushed angrily as he scowled at the older man across the vast, gleaming surface of the desk, uncluttered save for telephone, read-out screen and the thick folder that must contain, among other documents relating to himself, a transcript of the proceedings of the recent Court of Inquiry.

"You got off lightly, Grimes," Damien repeated.

His elbows on the desk, the tips of his steepled, skeletal fingers propping his great beak of a nose, he stared severely at the owner and erstwhile master of the star tramp (the privateer, the pirate) *Sister Sue.* Grimes thought irreverently, *If it weren't for that schnozzle his face would look just like a skull . . . Come to that, his uniform tailor must use a skeleton for his dummy . . .*

Briefly he entertained the ludicrous vision of a spidery tailorbot, fussily measuring and recording, scuttling around and over an assemblage of dry, articulated bones.

He grinned.

"What are you thinking, Grimes?" demanded Damien sharply.

"Nothing, sir."

"Ha. Of course. Nothing that you'd dare to tell me, you mean. May I remind you that the crime of Dumb Insolence, with its penalties, is still listed in Survey Service Regulations despite all the efforts of the Human Rights League to have it removed? And even though your Master Astronaut's Certificate of Competency was suspended by the court you still hold your Survey Service Reserve commission. And you have not yet been released from Active Duty."

"I was under the impression, sir," said Grimes stiffly, "that my Reserve Officer's commission was a secret."

"Was—and is. But *I* know your status. I can still throw the book at you if I feel like it." Then Damien allowed himself a grin and, briefly, looked almost genial. "But I didn't send for you so that I could haul you over the coals, although it has been like old times, hasn't it?" (That grin, Grimes decided, had become wolfish.) "Officially I'm supposed to be conducting a little inquiry of my own. The safe passage of merchant shipping is among my responsibilities— so, quite naturally, I'm interested in such activities as privateering. And piracy. But I already have your confidential report. And Mayhew's. I know what really happened—which is more than can be said for Lord Justice Kirby and his assessors, or for the boarding party that brought your ship in under arrest. That ex-girlfriend of yours—or not so 'ex'—did a good job of brainwashing your officers. My people thought that the apparatus she brought aboard *Sister Sue* was just an aid to interrogation, not for the implantation of false memories."

Damien laughed. "And it was a good story that the witnesses told the court, wasn't it? The wicked Kate Connellan and the even wickeder Countess of Walshingham seizing the ship at gunpoint and forcing you to embark upon a career of piracy . . . But somebody had to carry the can back. They didn't survive—and you did."

He opened the thick folder, found the right page. "And what did that old fogey Kirby say? Ah, here we are. 'Nonetheless I am of the strong opinion that the master, John Grimes, was not entirely blameless. He deliberately set his feet onto the downward path into violent crime when he placed his ship, his people and himself at the service of the notorious Commodore Baron Kane, as he is now known. John Grimes should have pondered the truth of the old adage, *He who sups with the devil needs a long spoon.* But John

Grimes was like too many in this decadent day and age, money hungry. Had his avarice put only himself at risk I should not think so hardly of him—but all of his crew, merchant spacemen and women, ignorant of the arts—if they may so be called—of war, were compelled, willy nilly, to share the perils to which their captain had deliberately exposed himself, persuaded by him that privateering is no risk and all profit . . . Sanctimonious old swine, isn't he? 'And some of his crew whom he deluded were not even experienced spacemen. His engineering officers, for example, young men recruited from industry and the Halls of Academe on the world of Austral, true innocents abroad . . .'"

"Those bastards!" exploded Grimes. "*They* were with the Green Hornet and Wally!"

"I know, I know. But they don't, not now. They have that fine set of false memories. They're little, woolly, innocent lambs, all of them, in their own minds, and in old Kirby's mind." He switched to his imitation of the judge's voice. "'It is obvious to me that John Grimes is unfit to hold command. I have considered the cancellation of his qualifications but have decided to temper justice with mercy, hoping that in the fullness of time he may come to see the error of his ways. Therefore I order that his Certificate of Competency be suspended for a period of ten Standard Years.'"

"And what am I supposed to be doing with myself for all that time?" asked Grimes.

"You still have your ship. We released her to you. We'll see that she finds employment. I've no doubt that your mate—your ex-mate, rather—will make quite a good master . . ."

"While I sit and sulk in the owner's suite when I'm not getting into his hair. No, sir. That wouldn't be fair to Billy Williams. Come to that, it wouldn't be fair to me. It'd be worse than just being an ordinary passenger." He got to his feet, began to pace up and down. He pulled his pipe from a pocket of his civilian slacks, filled and lit it. He said, speaking through an eruption of acrid fumes, "I think that the Service should do something for me in the way of employment."

"I didn't give you permission to smoke, Grimes. Oh, all right, all right. Carry on asphyxiating yourself. As far as the universe knows you're a civilian shipmaster—ex-shipmaster, rather—and I have no jurisdiction over you. *But* you're still on pay, captain's salary. We'll not let you starve even if *Sister Sue's* running at a loss."

"Thank you, sir. I'll not hurt your feelings by refusing my pay. I've earned it. But I want to be *doing* something."

"Why don't you write a book, Grimes? Your autobiography should make fascinating reading."

"And would the Survey Service provide legal defense if I were sued for libel? And if such a case were heard by Lord Justice Kirby the best lawyers in the universe couldn't save me."

Damien laughed. "All right, all right. If you wrote the book I'd probably be among those screaming libel. Now, Grimes, sit down and listen. I sent for you so that I could sound you out. I've an offer to make that I'd not be making if you'd indicated that you'd be quite happy bumbling around in that rustbucket of yours even if not in command of her.

"Have you ever heard of Liberia?"

"In Africa?"

"No. Not the province. The planet. The colony."

"Oh. That Liberia. Founded by a bunch of freedom-loving anarchists during the days of the gaussjammers. I've heard about it but I've never been there."

"How would you like to go?"

"Doing what? Or as what?"

"As Governor."

∽ Chapter 2 ∽

"YOU HAVE TO BE JOKING," said Grimes at last.

"I'm serious," Damien told him.

"Then this is another piece of dirty work for you."

"On the contrary, Grimes. If you take the job it will be in the nature of a clean-up operation."

"That sounds even worse. Sir."

"Grimes, Grimes, you have a suspicious mind."

"With very good reason."

"Do you want the job, or don't you?"

"Tell me about it first," Grimes said.

"Very well. Liberia is a Federated Planet but not now fully autonomous. I'll not bore you with a detailed history; you'll be able to read it up before you are installed in the Governor's Lodge. Suffice it to say that the original colonists, the idealistic Anarchists, after a bad start during which their settlement almost perished, became devotees of the goddess Laura Norder . . ." (*I'd better laugh,* thought Grimes, *to keep the old bastard in a good mood.*) "Their numbers increased and eventually they were able to exercise control over their environment. There was a resurgence of Anarchism and armed revolt against the authorities. The president—he was more of a dictator, actually—appealed for help to the Federation. After the mess had been more or less cleaned up it was decided that the Liberians would be far happier if governed by an outsider, somebody whom everybody, right, left and center, could hate. So now there's an elected president who, in effect, just does what the Earth-appointed governor tells him.

7

"Liberia is an agricultural planet. When it was first settled it was little more than a mudball crawling with primitive yet motile plant life. Now it is all, or almost all, wheatfields and beanfields and orchards. It has been called the granary of the Shaula Sector. There is only light, very light industry. In the past all heavy agricultural machinery has had to be imported. Now, as such equipment wears out it is not replaced."

"So they have their own factories?" asked Grimes.

"No. They're getting away from the use of machinery. They're using manpower."

"They must be gluttons for hard work."

"They're not. They import their labor."

"But who would ever emigrate to such a world, to sweat in the fields?"

"Quite a few, Grimes. Quite a few—although I doubt if they were expecting what they got. Have you ever wondered what happens to all the refugees? There was the so-called Holy War on Iranda, sect against sect. The losers—those of them who had not been slaughtered—were evicted. They were evacuated by Survey Service transports. Liberia, very nobly, offered to give a new home to those hapless people. And do you remember when the New Canton sun went nova?"

"Before my time," said Grimes. "But I've read about it."

"A large number of the New Cantonese finished up on Liberia," Damien said. "Wars, revolutions, natural disasters—all have contributed to the build-up of Liberia's vast pool of slave labor."

"Slave labor?"

"It's not called that, of course. It's indentured labor. It's got to the stage where the Liberians need no longer import expensive machines. It's got to the stage where they're pampered aristocrats, waited on hand and foot. (I wonder what their anarchistic ancestors would have thought!) The real ruler of the planet is not the governor, or the president, but the commanding officer of the peace-keeping force, Colonel Bardon, Terran Army. He's got the president eating out of his hand."

"And the governor?"

"The last governor—your predecessor?—met with an accident. It seems that he tried to put a stop to many of the abuses. The military didn't like it. His aircraft crashed when he was on the way to investigate conditions at one of the orchards. The Board of Inquiry decided that the disaster—killing the governor, his wife and his personal pilot—was attributable to pilot error."

"A not uncommon cause of such disasters, sir."

"The Board of Inquiry, Grimes, consisted of Major Timms, Captain Vinor and Lieutenant Delaney, all of them Bardon's officers. And there were witnesses who saw the aircraft—a helium-filled blimp with electric motors—explode and come down in flaming fragments."

"Oh. I'm surprised that they, too, didn't meet with accidents."

"Most of them did. The one who didn't managed to stow away aboard a bulk carrier and make it to New Maine. He told his story to our Sub-Base Commander there, who passed it on to Survey Service Intelligence."

"Then why isn't this Colonel Bardon relieved of his command?"

"Politics, Grimes. Politics. For quite some time now the Army has been the Lord Protector's pet. For some reason he despises the Survey Service. And Field Marshal von Tempsky refuses to believe anything bad about any of his people, especially when the complaint is laid by us. Nonetheless, it's a known fact that the Army sweeps all its misfits and bad bastards under the mat by shipping them off to outworld garrison duties."

"And the Survey Service is doing the same, sir?"

Damien chuckled. "You're a misfit, Grimes, but even I wouldn't call you a bad bastard. Your forte has always been giving bad bastards what they deserve. People like Colonel Bardon, for example. . . ."

"So you want me to become Governor of Liberia so that I can put a spoke in Bardon's wheel?"

"You could put it that way."

"But since when, sir, has the Survey Service been appointing colonial governors?"

"A good question, Grimes. We never have done so. But the

Protector of the Colonies—Bendeen—is a friend of mine. We were midshipmen together. He got as high as lieutenant commander, then married into a political family. Not long after he resigned his commission and went into politics himself. His wife's family found a safe seat for him and he was elected to the Assembly. Surprisingly, despite his idealism and an honesty more typical of spacemen than politicians, he attained ministerial rank. He has his sights set on the Lord Protectorship but I don't think he'll make it. He tramples on too many corns."

"And he wants to trample on Field Marshal von Tempsky's corns?"

"Yes. And those of the Cereal Consortium. He hasn't forgiven them for the engineered famine on Damboon, which resulted in the downfall of the Free Democrat regime."

"Mphm." Grimes knocked out his pipe in Damien's wastepaper disposer, refilled and lit it. "Mphm. So I'm supposed to be Protector Bendeen's cat's paw. If I take the job, that is. . . ."

"You could put it that way, Grimes."

"Mphm. But won't it look fishy? A Survey Service dropout, a master astronaut who's lost his ticket after a widely publicized inquiry, appointed to a governorship. . . . Won't there be questions asked, in the World Assembly, by the media, on every street corner?"

"Our rumor factory will be working overtime, Grimes. The El Dorado Corporation has its tentacles everywhere. It will be hinted that El Dorado is behind the appointment, that highly placed people on that world are pulling strings to find a soft, highly paid job for a man who was one of their officers, a Company Commodore, and who served them to the best of his ability. Bendeen will try to convey the impression that your appointment is not one that he would have made of his own free will."

"You should have become a politician yourself, sir."

"Whatever makes you think that I didn't?" asked the Rear Admiral.

~ Chapter 3 ~

GRIMES WATCHED *SISTER SUE* lift off from Port Woomera.

He stood there, on the stained and scarred concrete of the commercial spaceport apron, staring up at the dull-gleaming spindle that was the ship—*his* ship—climbing steadily until it was no more than a speck in the cloudless blue sky, listening to the cacophony of the inertial drive until it was no more than a faint, irritable mutter. And then the sky was empty and the only noises were those normal to a working spaceport at ground level—the whining of motors, the occasional clank and rattle from conveyor belts and gantries, now and again a shouted order.

Williams would do all right, he thought, despite his initial diffidence, even though the ex-mate had made it plain that he had hoped that Grimes would be along in an advisory capacity.

("The old ship won't be the same without you, skipper," he had said. Then, "I'll look after her for you. You'll be back. I know you will." And Grimes had thought, *But ten years is a long time.*)

And now *Sister Sue* was up and away, outbound for Caribbea with a cargo of manufactured goods, everything from robotutors to robutterflies, the beautiful little devices that had been developed to deal, lethally and expeditiously, with flying insect pests. (They would sell well enough, Grimes thought, while the craze lasted.) Her discharge completed she would go on Time Charter to the Interstellar

11

Transport Commission, carrying anything and everything anywhere and everywhere.

At least, thought Grimes, Williams had a good crew. Magda Granadu was still Catering Officer/Purser and the two old-timers, Crumley and Stewart, were still Reaction Drive Chief and Radio Officer respectively. The other engineers, Reaction Drive and Mannschenn Drive, were *real* space engineers, not refugees from universities and bicycle shops. (Their predecessors, together with their false memories, had been given passage back to Austral.) The Chief, Second and Third Officers were all young, properly qualified and actually employees of the Commission which, by the terms of the charter party, was required to supply necessary personnel.

So that was that.

Ex-Captain Grimes, ex-Company Commodore Grimes, soon-to-be-Governor Grimes climbed into the ground car that had been waiting to take him to the airport from where he would fly to Alice Springs to spend a few days with his parents before leaving for Liberia.

They met him in the waiting room at the base of the mooring mast.

Grimes senior, a tall, white-haired old man, greeted his son with enthusiasm. "I envy you, John," he said. "I really do. I just write about adventures; you have them!"

Matilda Grimes—also tall, red-haired and pleasantly horse-faced—frowned disapprovingly. "Don't encourage him, George. Ever since he left the Survey Service he's been doing nothing but getting into trouble, I hoped to see him become an admiral one day. I never dreamed that he'd become a pirate." She turned on her son. "And what do you intend to do now, John? You've had your Certificate taken from you . . ."

"Only suspended," said her husband.

She ignored this. "You'll never command a ship again, not even a merchant vessel. And after that trial. . . ."

"Court of Inquiry, my dear."

". . . nobody will ever employ you."

"As a matter of fact, Matilda," Grimes said, "I shall shortly be going out to take up a new appointment."

"What as?" asked Grimes's father.

"Governor, as a matter of fact. Of Liberia."

"I've always thought," said his mother, "that the standard of intelligence in the World Assembly is appallingly low. Now I am sure of it. And I've never trusted Bendeen. Any man who would give up a career in the Survey Service for one in politics must have something wrong with him. Appointing a pirate as governor. . . ."

"There are precedents," said George Whitley Grimes. "Sir Henry Morgan, for example." He realized that the other people in the lounge were looking curiously at the small family party and said, "I suggest that we continue this discussion at home."

The robutler brought in drinks. *The Old Man must be doing well,* thought Grimes. The machine was one of the very latest models, a beautifully proportioned and softly gleaming cylinder moving on silent treads rather than something unconvincingly humanoid. From a circular port midway up the thing's body a sinuous tentacle produced the drinks ordered—dry sherry, chilled, for Matilda Grimes, a pink gin for Grimes and beer for his father. A dish of assorted nuts, placed on the coffee table, followed.

"Here's to crime," toasted George Whitley Grimes, raising his glass.

"I'll not drink to that!" snapped his wife. Nonetheless she gulped rather than sipped from hers.

Grimes sampled his pink gin. He could not have mixed a better one himself.

He said, "You seem very prosperous, George."

"Yes. It was that *If Of History* novel."

"The Ned Kelly idea that you were telling me about the last time that I was here?"

"No. The one after that, based on the Australian Constitutional Crisis. *If* Gough Whitlam, the Prime Minister, had refused to relinquish office after the Governor General fired him. . . ."

"Don't go putting ideas into his head," admonished Matilda. "The last time that he was here the pair of you talked about privateering and piracy—and look what happened! The next thing we hear will be that he's fired the President of Liberia!"

"Perhaps I shall," murmured Grimes. "Perhaps I shall. . . ."

His father looked at him intently over the rim of his condensation-beaded glass. He said softly, "Tell me, John, did you really leave the Survey Service?"

"I did."

"Did they call you back?"

"Did they?" pressed his mother, suddenly alert.

It was useless, he knew, to try to lie to her.

He said, "No comment."

"And isn't it true," his father went on, "that after your piratical antics a bill was pushed through the Assembly making privateering illegal anywhere in the Federation of Worlds?"

"You read, watch and listen to the media, George."

"I do. And there have been some nasty rumors recently about Liberia. But you can't tell us anything, can you?"

"I can't. And I think that you'd both be wise to keep your suspicions to yourself."

"We shall," promised his father. "But I shall be tempted, mind you, to give them an airing in a novel."

"Please don't. The El Dorado Corporation might add two and two to make five and then be after my blood."

"All right." The older man finished his beer and, ignoring his wife's frown, demanded a refill from the robutler. "And now, young John, I am going to put an idea into your head—one that even Matilda will approve of. You're really a spaceman, aren't you? That's all you want to be, ever will want to be. And you don't want to wait ten years to get your Certificate back—especially when you've a ship of your own of which you should be the captain. You'll be governor, of a world called Liberia. When in Liberia do as the original Liberians did. . . ."

He talked, drawing upon his historical knowledge.

Grimes listened intently, as did his mother.

When his father was finished Grimes grinned happily. "It could work," he said. "By all the Odd Gods, I'll make it work!"

"But you will have to finish the job that you're being sent out to do," said his mother, frowning worriedly. "You'll have to finish that job first."

"Of course," Grimes assured her. "Of course."

Chapter 4

GRIMES TOOK ONE of the regular airships to Sydney and then a ramjet to New York. The World Assembly was housed in the old UN Building which, miraculously, had survived all the troubles that had plagued the city since the United Nations had taken up residence there. Staring down at Manhattan as the jet descended to the airport Grimes wondered what it had looked like during the days of its glory. He had seen photographs, of course, but would have liked to have been able to recognize, in actuality, such fabled towers as the Empire State and World Trade Buildings; the ornamental lakes that occupied their sites were all very well but, from the air, were no more than irregular puddles of blue water. But there was the Brooklyn Bridge, rebuilt only recently to the old design. And that must be the Chrysler Building. . . . It was too bad that this was to be a brief business visit only.

An official World Assembly car was waiting for him and whisked him swiftly to the Assembly's headquarters. He was expected there; a young officer in a smart, sky-blue uniform escorted him along moving ways and up escalators, delivered him to the office of the Protector of the Colonies.

Bendeen—a slim man, not overly tall, gray-haired and with a heavily lined face—came from behind his littered desk to greet Grimes. The WA lieutenant withdrew and the door automatically closed behind him.

"So you're the famous—or notorious—Grimes," said Bendeen. "All right. You can admit it. This office is bugproof—or so the experts loaned to me by Rear Admiral Damien assure me. We can talk. Officially, as you may have learned, I was pressured into finding you a job. In actuality you were strongly recommended to me by the Rear Admiral. Drink?" What Grimes had taken for just another filing cabinet detached itself from the wall, rolled up to them on silent casters. A tray was extruded from it; on it were two glasses of what looked like pink gin. "As you see, Governor, I share your taste in tipples. Your very good health."

"And yours, Protector," Grimes replied.

(His father's robutler, Grimes thought, was much better at mixing drinks than this thing of Bendeen's.)

"You're booked out, Grimes, on *Sobraon*. The VIP suite, of course. She lifts from Port Woomera tomorrow so that means another ramjet flight for you. Can't say that I envy you. I hate those things. If God had meant us to fly He'd have given us an ample supply of non-flammable, lighter-than-air gas. Which, of course, He did. But where was I? Oh, yes. Your commission as Governor. It's on the desk somewhere. Ah, here it is. A splendid example of the engraver's art with eagles and dragons and hammers and sickles and lions and unicorns and hammers and sickles and rising suns and . . . oh, yes, emus and kangaroos all over it. And the Grand Seal of the Assembly. No not a *seal,* but a seal. Red wax, you know. And your name, in Gothic script. It'll look fine when you have it framed on the wall of your gubernatorial office. . . ."

"Isn't there any sort of swearing in ceremony?" asked Grimes, at last getting a word in edgewise.

"You'll have to wait until Libertad—that's the capital of Liberia—for that. I'm told that the president likes to put on shows to impress the oppressed masses. And they are oppressed, you know. Not only is there the hard, manual work for precious little pay but there're all the lucrative rackets indulged in by Bardon's boys. I don't know what Bardon's got on von Tempsky but, as far as VT is concerned, the colonel can do no wrong. I've tried to have him replaced but the Field Marshal piles on more Gs with the Lord

Protector than I do. So I'm relying on you to catch Bardon with his hand in the till—or in the pocket of one of the indentured laborers. From what Damien has told me about you you're used to playing by ear. And you're a sort of catalyst. Things sort of happen all around you and, more often than not, you turn them to your advantage.

"There's a case waiting for you at the airport with plenty of light reading for your voyage—spools and spools of it. The VIP suite, of course, has a playmaster. You'll get a good idea of the world you're going to—history from the first settlement to the present. And now, finish your drink. The car's waiting to take us out to Kennedy. Don't forget the commission—there's a case for it somewhere. Ah, here . . ."

They emerged from the Protector's office into the corridor. Bendeen's manner changed, became stiff, hostile even. He said, as they passed through the door, ". . . this appointment was none of my choosing. But you are now the Governor—until such time as you are relieved."

Which will not be soon enough, implied the Protector's expression.

Grimes took the hint. This corridor must be well-covered by audio-visual bugs. He kept his distance from the Protector, set his face into sullen lines. The two men maintained their charade until they shook hands, with a marked lack of enthusiasm, at the airport and Grimes boarded the ramjet for Woomera.

⊰ Chapter 5 ⊱

THE MASTER OF THE TRANS-GALACTIC Clipper *Sobraon*
was well-accustomed to the carriage of Very Important Passengers
and to playing the urbane and courteous host. VIPs who were also
ex-pirates were, however, outside his normal experience. He had
heard of Grimes—who among the spacefaring community had
not?—and had never been among his admirers. Even as a small boy
he had not considered pirates and privateers glamorous; as a
shipmaster he regarded them as vicious and dangerous criminals.
When he had been shown his passenger list for the forthcoming
voyage, with the names of those worthy of special attention marked
with a star, he had stared at it incredulously.

"Not *the* Grimes?" he had demanded of his purser.

"I'm afraid so, sir," she had replied.

"But . . . A *governor* . . . Can't you be mistaken, Liz? Surely there
must be more than one John Grimes in this universe."

"Not with jug-handle ears. His photograph was among all the
others in the Security parcel."

"But he was on trial for piracy."

"A Court of Inquiry, sir, not a trial."

"Even so, he had his Certificate dealt with. The judge and the
assessors must have thought that he was guilty of something. And
with good reason. And am I supposed to have him at my table?"

"With all the other VIPs." She grinned. "At least he'll be less
boring than the others."

He scowled at her. "The man's a pirate, with blood on his hands. Get this straight, Liz, I don't want you and your tabbies fawning on him as though he were the latest tridi heart-throb. All that concerns us is that we're to deliver him from Port Woomera to Port Libertad with celerity and enjoying a far greater standard of luxury than he deserves. If I had *my* way I'd put him in one of the J Deck dogboxes!"

"You still could, sir. You're the master."

"Ha! And how long should I stay in one of the Line's senior ships if I did that? He must be treated correctly. Liz—with *icy* correctness. Convey subtly that any respect accorded to him is to his rank, not to himself. But subtly, Liz, subtly. Perfect service—but without the personal touch. The liquid hydrogen hand in the velvet glove . . ."

"Is velvet a good insulator, sir?"

"How the hell should I know? That will do, Liz; you've plenty to look after."

When the girl was gone he rang for his chief officer and then issued to that gentleman instructions as to how the VIP was to be treated.

Sobraon lifted from Port Woomera, slowly at first and then with increasing velocity as the thrust of her inertial drive built up. Grimes was a guest in the liner's control room, such courtesy often being extended to senior astronauts traveling as passengers and to civilian VIPs. He strongly suspected that the invitation had been extended to him in the second capacity. He looked out through the viewports at the fast receding scenery—to one side the semi-desert with its green rectangles of irrigated land, crisscrossed with silvery canals, to the other the dark sea with, far to the southward, the white glimmer of the Antarctic ice barrier. Twice recently he had been on Earth, he thought, and on neither occasion had he paid a visit to the Space Academy in Antarctica. The first time he might have done so, as a graduate who, despite the circumstances of his resignation from the Survey Service, was now a successful shipowner. On the second occasion it might not have been politic. A privateer-turned-pirate would hardly have been regarded by the Commandant as an Old Boy whose career should be emulated by the cadets.

He heard one of the officers whispering to another, "I wonder what he's thinking about? Is he working out how he could skyjack the ship?"

He looked around to see who it was. It must have been Kelner, the liner's chief officer, who flushed and turned away hastily as Grimes's eye caught his. The ponderously portly Captain Harringby must, too, have heard that whisper—but the expression on his heavy face was approving rather than otherwise. Then the shipmaster looked at Grimes who, although no telepath, could tell what he was thinking. *I invited you up here only because Company Regulations require that I give you the VIP treatment. But I don't have to like you.*

Grimes shrugged. So he was *persona non grata*. So what? It was not for the first time in his life, almost certainly would not be for the last. He would stick it out, seated stolidly in the spare chair. He would, after trajectory had been set, graciously accept the invitation, no matter how grudgingly offered, to partake of the ritual drink with the captain and his senior officers. Throughout the voyage to Liberia he would be the very model of a modern Governor General. *(All right, all right,* he told himself irritably, *I know that it should be Major General and, in any case, I'm only a Governor.* He looked at Harringby, smugly omnipotent in his command chair, and thought, *And I'd sooner be a shipmaster again.)*

Trajectory was set (competently enough, Grimes admitted) and *Sobraon* was falling down the warped continuum on the first leg of her passage, Earth to Liberia. (This was, actually, no more than a deviation; Trans-Galactic Clippers specialized in carrying rich passengers around the truly glamorous worlds of the Galaxy—to Caribbea, with its warm seas and lush, tropical islands, to Atlantia for the big game fishing and the ocean yacht races, to Morrowvia, with its exotic cat people, to New Venusberg, with its entertainments to suit all warped tastes, to Waverley, with its reconstruction of a Scottish culture that owed more to myth than to actual history, to Electra, where those of a scientific bent could feast their eyes on the latest marvels.)

Trajectory was set, the powerful gyroscopes pulling the ship around her axes until the target star was ahead, then making the necessary adjustment for galactic drift. (Grimes flexed his idle hands on the arm rests of his chair, for so long he had been doing what Captain Harringby was doing now, it seemed—it was!—all wrong that he was no longer doing it.) The Mannschenn Drive was actuated. Deep in the bowels of the great ship the rotors began to turn, to spin, to precess, to tumble down and through the warped dimensions as the temporal precession field built up.

There was the usual brief disorientation, the transient nausea and, for Grimes at least, a flash of prevision.

He saw, as plainly as if she had been standing there in person, one of his fellow privateers, Captain Agatha Prinn of the star tramp *Agatha's Ark*. She was dressed—how else?—in her uniform of severely cut, short-skirted business suit, gray, with minimal trimmings of gold braid. She was holding a paper bag. She dropped it. It burst when it hit the ground, releasing a cloud of fine, white powder. . . .

Colors, perspective and sounds snapped back to normal.

Grimes blinked, found that he was staring out of a viewport to an interstellar night in which the stars were no longer bright points of unwinking light but were amorphous nebulae.

Agatha Prinn and a flour bomb! he wondered. *What the hell was all* that *about?*

He realized that Captain Harringby was addressing him.

"Your Excellency," (but that's *me*! thought Grimes) "we are now on trajectory. Would you care to join me for liquid refreshment before lunch?"

It would make the old bastard's day if I said no, Grimes told himself.

"Thank you, Captain," he said as he unbuckled himself from his seat.

∽ Chapter 6 ∾

IT WAS A PECULIAR VOYAGE, not altogether unpleasant, with its mixture of ostracism and adulation and downright pampering. Governor Grimes took his meals at the captain's table—and Captain Harringby, presiding over this lavish board, accorded the governor the respect due to him while making it plain that he did not approve of Commodore Grimes, the pirate chief. Now and again he permitted himself a flash of unkind humor, such as when the wine stewardess was dispensing a vintage Burgundy to accompany the roast beef. "I suppose, Your Excellency, that you must, now and again, have acquired some very fine wines among your other . . . er . . . loot?"

"The Hallichecki," Grimes had replied stiffly, "do not use alcohol." He added, after sipping from his glass, "My privateering operations were against the shipping of the Hegemony."

"But didn't you seize a Terran ship? One of the Commission's liners?"

"That happened after a mutiny, Captain. It all came out at the Court of Inquiry." He added, "And, in any case, the attempted piracy was unsuccessful."

The others at the table were looking at him, some with disapproval and contempt, others with what was almost admiration. There was the fat Joachim Levy, one of the Dog Star Line's managers taking his Long Service Leave and bound for New Venusberg. He pursed his thick lips, then said, *"Our* ships are used to coping with piracy. When necessary they are armed—and their crews know how to use their weapons."

"I know," Grimes told him. "My Mate was ex-Dog Star Line. He was a very good gunnery officer."

Levy scowled and the plump, artificially blonde Mrs. Levy laughed. "So all the drills that the Dog Star Line officers have to go through are some use after all!" She smiled quite prettily at Grimes. "But wasn't it *fun,* Your Excellency? Sailing the seas of space with the Jolly Roger at the masthead and a cutlass clenched between your teeth?"

"Mphm," grunted Grimes.

"In the *good* old days," said Ivor Sandorsen, who was a Lloyd's underwriter, "you would have been hanged from your own yardarm, Your Excellency."

"As a matter of fact," said Grimes, "one of my ancestors was."

"Thus establishing a precedent."

"Another, better-known, pirate," said Grimes, "established another precedent. Sir Henry Morgan. He became a governor."

"Had Lloyd's been in existence in those days, sir, he would have paid the just penalty for his crimes."

"In any case," said Harringby with a superior smile, "I think that His Excellency will admit that the governorship of Liberia is hardly a plum as such appointments go. More of a rotten apple, perhaps."

"Have you been there, Captain?" asked Mrs. Levy, who seemed to have appointed herself Grimes's champion.

"No, madam. Nor do I want to. I shall place my ship in orbit about that world and a tender will rendezvous to pick up His Excellency. Then I shall be on my way."

"Rejoicing?" asked Grimes.

"I shall most certainly not be weeping."

"And you, Your Excellency," asked Dorothea Taine, tall, dark, intense, author of a best seller which Grimes's father had scornfully dismissed as *Womens' Weekly* rubbish, "will you be weeping or rejoicing?"

"That remains to be seen," Grimes told her.

"Sir—Your Excellency, I mean—what's it really like being a pirate? Sorry. A privateer. . . ." The young Fifth Officer made his diffident approach to Grimes as he was just dismounting from one of the exercise bicycles in the liner's gymnasium.

"There are better and safer ways of earning a living," Grimes said.

"Safer, perhaps, sir. But . . . Would you know if Commodore Kane is still trying to find volunteers for his privateer fleet?"

"Drongo Kane is better stayed away from. In any case, as you must have heard, the Survey Service is smacking down on all privateering operations."

"Mr. Barray!" The Chief Officer had just come into the gymnasium for his own exercise session. "Here you are. I thought that you were supposed to be checking the equipment in your lifeboat."

"I . . . I've finished that, sir. It's all in order."

"Then find Mr. McGurr and lend him a hand in hydroponics. This is his tank cleaning day."

Crestfallen, the young man left the gym. Shedding his robe and, clad only in trunks, the Chief Officer mounted the bicycle that Grimes had vacated. As he started to pedal he said, "Even you, Your Excellency, must know that young men often evince enthusiasm for the most unworthy people and causes."

"Are you implying that I'm unworthy, Mr. Kelner?"

"I never said so, Your Excellency."

"I can *use* you, Your Excellency. Or may I call you John? After all, I know your father; I've met him at Australian Society of Authors meetings . . ."

Grimes looked at Dorothea Taine over his coffee cup. He was taking this midmorning refreshment in the lounge; he did not see why he should be confined to his quarters, luxurious though they were, even though he was something of a social leper.

"Use me?" he asked.

The writer smiled. Her teeth were too large for her small mouth.

The heavy-rimmed spectacles that she affected made her big, black eyes look even bigger in her sallow face.

"I want to use you . . . John."

"How, Ms. Taine?" asked Grimes dubiously.

"Dorothea, please. Or you may call me Dot. I'm starting a new novel. One of those If stories. If Dampier, the buccaneer and privateer, had established a settlement on the West Coast of Australia, long before the one was established at Botany Bay. After all, he was there. . . ."

"And he didn't think much of it."

"But something could, just could, have made him change his mind. He could have fallen madly in love with a beautiful Aboriginal girl. Perhaps she could have saved his life, just as the Princess Pocahontas saved the life of Captain John Smith in Virginia . . ."

Grimes entertained a fleeting vision of a naked black girl getting in the way of a boomerang flung at the piratical Captain Dampier by her irate father.

"Mphm," he grunted around the stem of his pipe.

"You see, John, I want to make Dampier a *real* character. I can't go back in time to meet him. But there's one real life character, aboard this very ship, who could serve as a model. You. Dampier wasn't only a pirate and privateer, he was also an officer, a captain, in the Royal Navy. You've been a privateer and a pirate—and also an officer, commanding ships, in the Survey Service . . . If I could only get *inside* you . . ."

I don't want to get inside you, thought Grimes unkindly. *You're too skinny, for a start. And you gush.*

"Perhaps some evening, or evenings, after dinner . . . We could get away by ourselves somewhere and you could tell me all about yourself . . ."

"It would be very boring for you," said Grimes.

"It would not, John. It couldn't possibly be."

"I'm sorry," he told her, "but all my evenings are fully taken up. I've all the spools on Liberia to study. After all, I'm being paid to be governor of the damn place so I'd better know something about it before I get there. . . ."

"Do you mind if I join you, Your Excellency? Joe's gotten himself involved in a non-stop poker game and I'm just a bit lonesome."

"Please do, Mrs. Levy. What are you drinking? A Black Angel?" Then, to the bar stewardess, "Another pink gin, please, and a B.A."

"I *like* this little bar. . . . Your very good health, Excellency."

"And yours, Mrs. Levy."

"That sounds dreadfully formal."

"Vee, then."

"Only Joe calls me that. I prefer Vera."

"Your very good health, Vera."

"I only found this little bar a couple of days ago, John. (Do you mind?) It's so . . . private. Not like the main bars, always crowded and always that so-called music so that you can't hear yourself think. I guess that there're still parts of this big ship that I haven't seen. We—the Dog Star Line, that is—don't have anything in this class."

"But you are getting into the passenger trades."

"Glorified cattle boats," she sneered. "Nothing like *this*. But I don't suppose that Joe will ever be important enough to qualify for the VIP suite. I would so like to see how the VIPs live. . . ."

"I must throw an official cocktail party before we get to Liberia," said Grimes. "You're invited, of course. . . ."

After all, he thought, *I might want a job in the Dog Star Line some day. Mr. Levy, for all his apparent inattention to his wife, looked as though he might prove to be a very jealous husband. . . .*

"Never mind," she said with sudden coldness. "I'll just take my place in the queue. Goodnight, Your Excellency."

She finished her drink and left—and Grimes knew that he would never be employed by the Dog Star Line as long as she was the wife of one of that company's managers.

"Satisfied?" he asked sleepily.

"Yes . . . and no, darling. But we've several hours before Jane brings in your morning tea."

"You'd better be out of here before then, Liz."

"It's not important really. We tabbies stick together, even though some of us have gold braid on our shoulders and some haven't. Jane would never run screaming to old Herring."

"Herring?"

"Captain Harringby. Haven't you ever noticed the fishlike look he has sometimes?"

"What if he did find out? What would he do?"

"Nothing, darling. Nothing. He's all show and no blow. Like practically every other passenger ship master he's scared shitless of the Space Catering Officers and Stewardesses' Guild. We have the power to make any voyage a hell for all concerned."

"Mphm."

No matter how successful I am, he thought, *I shall never be fool enough to buy a big passenger ship.*

He persisted, "But you didn't answer my question properly . . ."

"About being satisfied? Well, you aren't exactly bad in bed, although you could be better. But I'll educate you, darling. What satisfies me is that I've won the sweep."

"The sweep?"

"Yes. We all put in twenty credits and the prize goes to the first member of *Sobraon's* female staff to go to bed with the notorious pirate. You. And I get the prize."

"So that's why the purser brought up my supper tray in person tonight instead of entrusting the task to one of her underlings! All right, Liz. You've won. But it's been touch and go." He laughed. "I wondered why my personal needs were being attended to by different stewardesses every day and night. A fair go for all, I suppose. I almost succumbed this morning when that little carroty cat . . ."

"Sue . . ."

". . . intimated that she'd just love to wash my back while I was taking my shower."

"And now I'll rub your front and hope that you'll rise to the occasion."

Chapter 7

SOBRAON was in orbit about Liberia.

Alongside her was one of that planet's meteorological satellite tenders, airlock to airlock and with the short gangway tube sealed in place, a means of transfer of personnel from spaceship to spaceship with which Grimes was unfamiliar. In the Survey Service spacesuits and lifelines were good enough for anybody, from admirals down. But now he was no longer a spaceman. He was a first-class passenger. And he was a governor.

He was dressed as such, in the archaic finery that must always have seemed absurd to any intelligent human being, a rig neither functional nor aesthetically pleasing. Starched white shirt, stiff collar and gray silk cravat . . . Black tailcoat over a gray waistcoat . . . Gray, sharply creased trousers . . . Highly polished black boots . . . And— horror of horrors!—a gray silk top hat.

He stood in the vestibule of the liner's airlock; at least Harringby had put the inertial drive back into operation so that Grimes was spared the indignity of floundering about clumsily in his hampering clothing. Nonetheless he was sweating, his shirt damp on his chest, sides and back. He derived some small pleasure from the observation that Captain Harringby was far from comfortable in his own dress uniform; obviously it had been tailored for him before he started to put on weight. The Chief Officer's black-and-gold finery fitted him well enough but his expression made it plain that he hated having to wear it. Liz, the Purser, carried her full dress far better than did the Captain and the Mate. She looked cool and elegant in her long, black skirt, her white blouse with the floppy black tie, her short, gold-trimmed jacket.

Also present were the Third Officer, who would be looking after the airlock, and two Cadets. The young men were comfortable in normal shirt-and-shorts rig. Grimes envied them.

Harringby saluted stiffly. Grimes raised his top hat. Harringby extended his hand. Grimes took it with deliberate and (he hoped) infuriating graciousness.

"Good-bye, Your Excellency," said the shipmaster. "It's been both an honor and a pleasure to have you aboard."

Bloody liar, thought Grimes. He said, "Thank you, Captain."

The Chief Officer saluted, waited until Grimes extended his hand before offering his own.

"The best of luck, Your Excellency."

Do you mean it? wondered Grimes.

Liz brought her slim hand up to the brim of her tricorne hat, then held it out to Grimes who, gallantly, raised it to his lips while bowing slightly. Harringby scowled and the Chief Officer smirked dirtily. Grimes straightened up, still holding the girl's hand, looking into her eyes. He would have liked to have kissed those full lips—and to hell with Harringby!—but he and Liz had said their proper (improper?) good-byes during the night and early morning ship's time.

"Good-bye, Your Excellency," she murmured. "And—look after yourself."

"I'll try to," he promised.

Harringby coughed loudly to attract attention, then said, "Your Excellency, I shall be vastly obliged if you will board the tender. It is time that I was getting back to my control room."

"Very well, Captain."

Grimes gave one last squeeze to Liz's hand, relinquished it reluctantly and turned to walk into the airlock chamber and then through the short connecting tube. The tender's airlock door was smaller than that of the liner and had not been designed to admit anybody wearing a top hat. That ceremonial headgear was knocked off its insecure perch. As Grimes stooped to retrieve it he heard the Chief Officer laugh and an even louder guffaw from one of the tender's crew. He carried his hat before him as he completed his journey to the small spacecraft's cabin. His prominent ears were burning furiously.

The crew of the tender—Liberia possessed only orbital spacecraft—were young, reasonably efficient and (to Grimes's great envy) sensibly uniformed in shorts and T-shirts and badges of rank pinned to the left breast. The Captain asked Grimes to join him in the control cab. He did so, after removing his tail coat and waistcoat, sat down in the copilot's chair. He looked out from the viewport at the great bulk of the liner, already fast diminishing against the backdrop of abysmal night and stars, saw it flicker and fade and vanish as the Mannschenn Drive was actuated. He transferred his attention to the mottled sphere toward which the tender was dropping—pearly cloud systems and blue seas, brown and green continents and islands.

"It's a good world, Your Excellency," said the young pilot. He grinned wryly. "It *was* a good world. It could be one again."

Grimes looked at him with some curiosity. The accent had been Standard English, overlaid with an oddly musical quality. The face was olive-skinned, hawklike. Native-born, he thought. The original colonists—those romantic Anarchists—had been largely of Latin-American stock.

"Could be?" he asked.

"That is the opinion of some of us, Your Excellency. And we've heard of you, of course. You're something of an Anarchist yourself . . ."

"Mphm?"

"I mean. . . . You're not the usual Survey Service stuffed shirt."

"A stuffed shirt is just what I feel like at the moment."

"But you've a reputation, sir, for doing things your own way."

"And where has it got me?" asked Grimes, addressing the question to himself rather than to the tender's pilot.

"You've commanded ships, sir. Real ships, deep space ships, not
. . . *tenders.*"

"Don't speak ill of your own command," Grimes admonished.

The young man grinned whitely. "Oh, I like her. She'll do almost
anything I ask of her—but if I asked her to make a deep space
voyage I know what her answer would be!"

"Fit her out with Mannschenn Drive and a life support system,"
said Grimes, "and you could take her anywhere."

"If I were qualified—which I am not. Master Astronaut, Orbital
Only—that's me."

"But you're still a spaceman, Captain. I'd like to have a talk,
spaceman to spaceman. But . . ."

"Don't worry about Pedro and Miguel, sir. They're like me,
members of the OAP, the Original Anarchist Party. We're allowed
by our gracious President to blow off steam as long as we don't *do*
anything. . . ."

"What could we do, Raoul?" came a voice from behind Grimes.

He turned to see that the other two crew members had taken
seats at the rear of the control cab.

He said softly, "What could you do? I don't know. Yet. I spent
the voyage from Earth running through all the official spools on
Liberia . . ." (He remembered guiltily that there had been times
when instead of watching and listening to the playmaster in his suite
he had been doing other things.) "Before I left I was given a briefing
of sorts. I still don't know nearly as much as I should. You have the
first-hand knowledge. I don't."

"All right, sir," said Raoul. "I'll start at the top. There's our
revered President, Estrelita O'Higgins. . . ."

"Mphm," grunted Grimes. He remembered how she had
looked in the screen of the playmaster. Tall, splendidly bosomed,
black-haired and with rather too much jaw to be pretty. But she
was undeniably handsome. In the right circumstances she might
be beautiful.

"Then there's your boy, Colonel Bardon. . . ."

"Not *my* boy," said Grimes.

"He's Earth-appointed, isn't he? Just as you are, sir. Most

people say that he's got Estrelita eating out of his hand—but it could well be the other way around."

"Or mutual," said Grimes.

They made a good pair, Estrelita and the Colonel, he had thought when he saw them in one of the sequences presented by the data spools. The tall, handsome woman in a superbly tailored blue denim suit, the tall, handsome man in his glittering full dress. Like her, he had too much jaw. In his case it was framed by black, mutton chop whiskers.

"Whoever is eating out of whose hand," Raoul went on, "it's the Terran Garrison that really runs Liberia. They get first pick of everything. Then the Secret Police get their pickings. Then the ordinary police. The real Liberians don't get picked on much. There's some grumbling, of course, but we aren't badly off. It's the slaves who suffer. . . ."

"The indentured labor," corrected Grimes.

"You're hair-splitting, sir. When an indenture runs out the only way that a laborer can obtain further employment is to sign up again. All his wages, such as they are, have gone to the purchase of the little luxuries that make life bearable. And not only luxuries. There are habit-forming drugs, like Dassan dreamsticks. . . ."

"They're illegal," said Grimes, "on all federated worlds."

The pilot laughed harshly. "Of course they are. But that doesn't worry Bardon's Bullies." He returned his attention to his instruments and made minor adjustments; the beat of the tender's inertial drive changed tempo. "I've time to tell you a story, sir, before we come in to Port Libertad. There was a girl, a refugee, from New Dallas. You must have heard about what happened there. An independent colony that thought that it could thumb its nose at the Federation and at everybody else. Then the Duchy of Waldegren wanted the planet—and took it. We took a few thousand refugees. A lot of the prettier girls finished up in the houses owned—not all that secretly—by Bardon. Mary Lou was one of them. That's where I met her, in a dive called the Pink Pussy Cat. And—don't laugh, please!— we . . . fell in love. I was going to buy her out of that place. But some bastard got her hooked on dreamsticks and. . . ."

"She withered away to nothing," said Miguel.

Grimes said nothing. What could he say?

Raoul broke the silence, speaking in a deliberately brisk voice. "There's Port Libertad, sir. That statue you can see, just to the north of the spaceport, is Lady Liberty. She was copied from the old Statue of Liberty in New York Harbor, on Earth. Those two big ships are bulkies, here to load grain. Some worlds, though, prefer to import the flour that's been milled here, on Liberia. Don't ask me why; I'm a spaceman, not an economist. Do you see that smaller ship? She's a fairly regular visitor. *Willy Willy,* owned by Able Enterprises. The master's Captain Aloysius Dreeble. A nasty little bastard on a nasty trade. He comes here to recruit entertainers—so called—for the brothels on quite a few of the frontier worlds."

"And New Venusberg," said Grimes. "That's where I last met him."

"You know him, sir?"

"All right, all right. I don't like him. And he doesn't like me."

Looking out and down Grimes could see the triangle of winking, bright, scarlet lights that marked the tender's berth. He picked up a pair of binoculars and stared through them. He could make out a body of men drawn up in military formation, flags streaming from portable standards, the burnished metal of musical instruments from which the afternoon sun was brightly reflected. A guard of honor and a band. . . .

From the speaker of the transceiver, through which the tender had been in communication from Aerospace Control, came a sudden blast of music, the drums almost drowning out the trumpets.

"They're warming up," said Raoul sardonically. "Be prepared to be deafened by our glorious planetary anthem as soon as you set foot on Liberian soil."

"And a twenty-gun salute?" Grimes asked, half seriously.

"No. I did hear some of the Terran Army officers discussing it before I boarded to lift off for the rendezvous with *Sobraon.* It seems that if you'd been landing in a Terran warship the Captain would have been able to accord the courtesy of a salute, in reply, to Madam

President. But as you've no guns to fire you get none fired in your honor."

"This protocol," said Grimes, "is a complicated business."

"Isn't it, sir? We should never have strayed from the simple ways of our ancestors. They'd have given a gun salute to an Earth-appointed governor—and not with blanks, either!"

Looking at Raoul's face Grimes saw that the words had been spoken only in jest—but Miguel, when he spoke, was serious enough.

"If all that we've heard of Governor Grimes is true, Raoul, Bardon's Bullies would love to give him his twenty guns, each one loaded with H.E.!"

"There are more subtle ways of getting rid of unpopular governors than that," Raoul Sanchez said with sudden bitterness. Then, to Grimes, "My brother was the late Governor Wibberley's personal pilot."

A man with motive, thought Grimes. A double motive. His girlfriend and his brother, both . . . murdered.

He asked, "Are you qualified for atmosphere flight, Captain?"

"Yes, sir. Both LTA and HTA." He grinned. "Are you offering me a job, Your Excellency? I already have one, you know."

"I'm offering you a job. I warn you that it mightn't be good for your health."

"It wasn't good for my brother's health, either. All right, I receive your signal, loud and clear. You think that I might be inter-ested in . . . revenge?"

"That thought had flickered across my mind."

"I am so interested. And now, sir, if you'll excuse me, I'll try to get this crate down in one piece."

And had he fallen into a trap? Grimes wondered. Wasn't it too much of a coincidence that these young men in the shuttle should all be OAP members, opposed to the present regime on Liberia? Were Raoul's stories, about his girl and his brother, true? (That could be checked.)

But he would have to employ some personal staff and he would prefer, whenever possible, to make his own choices. Any made for him by Colonel Bardon would be suspect from the start. And, thought Grimes, if Captain Sanchez were Bardon's man air travel, at least, would be safer for him than it had been for Governor Wibberley. Raoul didn't look the type to commit suicide just to help somebody else commit murder.

⁓ Chapter 8 ⁓

A BLAST OF SOUND assailed Grimes's ears as he stepped out of the tender's airlock, onto the top platform of the bunting-bedecked set of steps that had been wheeled into position. With an effort he identified it as music—the brass too strident and the drums too insistent—and with a further effort as the Terran Planetary Anthem, one of those forgettable songs with words and music composed to order by an untalented committee of lyricists and musicians. He stood to attention, his right hand holding his gray silk topper over his breast, his left hand grasping the cylindrical, gold-trimmed leather case in which was his Commission. It must look, he thought wryly, like a Field Marshal's baton. But would Bardon give him the respect that he would accord to a Field Marshal?

Sons of Terra, strong and free came to its blaring conclusion. Thankfully Grimes relaxed, put his hat back onto his head. Then there was a roll of drums, followed by more music—*Liberia's sons, let us rejoice* . . . He whipped off his hat, came again to attention. That anthem was over at last and he took a step towards the edge of the platform—and again froze. This time it was *Waltzing Matilda*.

The familiar words ran through his mind as he listened to the band.

Up came the squatter, riding on his thoroughbred.
Down came the troopers, one, two, three. . .
And there were the troopers, and there were more than three of

them. There were Bardon's Bullies, drawn up for his inspection, resplendent in their dress uniforms of blue and gold and scarlet.

Up jumped the swagman, sprang into the billabong . . .

Grimes thought, *And this is one helluva billabong that I've sprung into this time . . .*

After *Matilda* there were no more anthems, but Grimes was in no hurry to descend the steps to the ground. He made a slow survey of his immediate surroundings. That must be Bardon down there, waiting to receive him, even more splendidly attired than his soldiers, his finery topped by a plumed helmet. And the tall woman with him, in a superbly tailored suit of faded blue denim, had to be Madam President.

There was a crowd, but only a small one. There was a group of men and women, attired as was their President. There were the inevitable schoolchildren waving their little flags—the Federation star cluster on a black field, the Terran opalescent sphere on dark blue, the Australian national ensign with the British union flag in the upper canton and the Southern Cross constellation in the fly. There were spaceport workers in shabby, dirty, white overalls, small statured men and women, dark skinned and with Mongoloid features. There were officers from the ships in port. Grimes recognized one of these men—the weedy, ferret-faced Aloysius Dreeble, master of *Willy Willy*. Dreeble recognized him, grinned and raised two fingers in a gesture that would have been, had his palm been outward, V for Victory.

Grimes looked coldly at his old enemy and then turned away. He descended the steps with dignity. At the foot of them stood Bardon. The Colonel saluted smartly. Grimes raised his hat. The Colonel said, "Glad to have you aboard, Your Excellency." Grimes said, swapping lie for lie, "I'm happy to be here, Colonel Bardon."

"Your Excellency, may I introduce you to Madam President?"

Grimes removed his hat, put it to his chest and bowed. She inclined her head graciously. When they had both resumed normal posture they stood facing each other. Her eyes, gleaming black under heavy black brows, were level with his and looking at him appraisingly. The skin of her face was smooth and pale, her lips wide, full and very red. Her jaw was too heavy for a woman. But her smile, revealing strong white teeth, was quite pleasant.

She said, "I never dreamed that I should one day welcome a famous pirate as Governor of Liberia."

"Not a pirate, Madam President. A privateer."

"Pirate or privateer, Captain Grimes, you are bound to be an improvement over your predecessor."

"Indeed?"

"Yes. He was a psalm-singing do-gooder. You must know the type."

"I have met such people."

"Your Excellency," interrupted Bardon, "may I suggest that we inspect the Guard of Honor?"

The President shrugged and, with that well-fitting jacket of soft denim, the effect was spectacular.

She said with a smile that was not altogether malicious, "The Colonel wants us to help him play with his toy soldiers, Captain Grimes."

Bardon scowled, but not fiercely, and said, "My men are not toys, Madam."

It was, thought Grimes, very like an essentially light-hearted exchange of insults between husband and wife. But sometimes such apparently friendly gibes are symptomatic of well-hidden hostilities.

He walked with the President and the Colonel along the ranks of the Honor Guard, preceded by a Lieutenant with a drawn sword, with other officers bringing up the rear. At close quarters the men were not so impressive as they had seemed from a distance. Even so, Grimes could not fault the uniforms, well-tailored from spotlessly clean and sharply pressed cloth, with gleaming natural leather and brightly burnished metal. The archaic rifles, weapons brought out only for ceremonial occasions, held now at Present Arms, were beautifully maintained. On the features of each man the facial hair, a down-sweeping moustache, was brushed and trimmed into exact uniformity with the whiskers to right and to left. But even those tailored scarlet jackets could not hide the paunches or the wide, gleaming cross-straps and belts hold them in. And there were the sagging jowls and the shifty eyes, some of them bloodshot.

Bardon's Bullies, thought Grimes. *They look it.*

He said, "Thank you, Colonel. A fine body of men."

"I am pleased that you found them so, Your Excellency. You can rely upon them for loyal service."

"Thank you, Colonel."

"I prefer soldiers in undress uniform," said the President, turning her sultry gaze on Bardon. And then, to his rather embarrassed surprise, Grimes was treated to a similar, lingering glance. "And I am sure, Your Excellency, that you would feel far happier in something less formal."

"Too right," said Grimes.

She said, "You may dismiss your troops, Colonel Bardon."

Bardon turned to Grimes and asked, "Permission to dismiss the Guard, Your Excellency?"

Who gives orders to whom on this bloody planet? Grimes asked himself.

He said, "Dismiss the Guard, Colonel."

Orders were barked. Colonel to Lieutenant, Lieutenant to Sergeant, Sergeant to the enlisted men. Smartly, with a jingle of accoutrements, the detachment formed fours and, behind the band, stepping in time to the thud and rattle of the drums, marched toward the spaceport's boundary fence. Chattering shrilly, the schoolchildren followed their teachers in the wake of the departing military. The ground staff drifted back to their jobs. The spacemen strolled toward their ships.

Vehicles drove up—a huge, scarlet-enameled limousine for the President with the symbol of a clenched fist, holding a torch, in black, on each of its doors, an olive-drab-painted armored car for the Colonel and one of the Lieutenants, a superb RR Whispering Ghost, gleaming black and shining silver with the forward-leaning nymph on its bonnet holding a staff from which flew a Terran ensign, for Grimes. There was a civilian chauffeur, a young man with a full beard, denim-clad and with a scarlet neckerchief. Beside him, on the front seat, were two soldiers in drab battle dress.

Bardon said to Grimes, "Your ADC will look after you, Your Excellency, and will . . . er . . . show you the ropes at the Governor's Residence. Lieutenant Smith, please see that His Excellency is at the President's Reception, at 2000 hours. this evening."

Smith saluted. He was old for his rank, his face both pudgy and sulky. The decorations on the left breast of his tunic were of the variety that Grimes referred to as Good Attendance Medals. If he had ever been in a war, even a police action, he had failed to distinguish himself.

"Until this evening, Your Excellency," said Estrelita O'Higgins.

"Until this evening, Madam President," said Grimes.

"Until this evening, Your Excellency," said Bardon, saluting.

"Until this evening, Colonel," said Grimes, raising his hat.

He had to take it off again when he climbed into the car, through the door which the ADC had opened for him. Smith followed him into the vehicle.

∽ Chapter 9 ∾

RATHER TO GRIMES'S disappointment the drive out to the Residence did not take him through the city of Libertad but through countryside that, in a natural state, could have been beautiful but, with its too orderly orchards, was rather boring. He remembered that although cereals were Liberia's main exports here was also a considerable trade in various processed fruit products. Working in the aisles between the trees were the laborers, small, dark-skinned people, clad only in loincloths, picking the golden fruit and filling baskets with the gleaming globes. It was not the first orange plantation that Grimes had seen—but it was the first one in which machines had not been doing the harvesting.

Then there were terraced rice paddies, and more orchards and, eventually, a low hill on which stood the Governor's Residence. It was a low, rambling building, white-walled, its shallowly pitched roofs red-tiled. The main entrance was an imposing portico, with white pillars and a proliferation of intricately patterned iron lace. There was a wide, velvety lawn fringed with flowering bushes— plants indigenous to Liberia, thought Grimes, who was no botanist. There was a tall flagstaff at the peak of which the starry banner of the Federation stirred lazily in the light, uncertain breeze.

A small detachment of Terran Army troops—a Sergeant and six men—was drawn up before the portico. Unlike the Honor Guard at the spaceport they were wearing khaki, not full dress uniform, and were armed not with archaic, aesthetically pleasing rifles but with modern, ugly and viciously effective sprayguns. Like the Honor Guard, however, they looked far better from a distance.

Behind the soldiers were the liveried civilians, men and women in long, white trousers or skirts under high-necked, royal blue jackets. Some of these jackets were absolutely plain, others were decorated with silver buttons and varying quantities of silver braid. One man was wearing a chef's high, white hat. There was a civilian who was not in uniform, a short man, stocky, bald-headed, wearing a plain gray suit.

Grimes stared.

These, obviously, were the servants—but a mob like this to look after one man, even though he was a governor!

He voiced his disapproving surprise.

It was the chauffeur who made reply. He said smugly, "The Residence is a large building, Your Excellency. Even though there is only one level above ground there are three sub-surface ones. There is all the cleaning to do, and the cooking, and. . . ."

"And machines to do such work," said Grimes.

"Not here," said the chauffeur. "Not on Liberia. Not now. In order to create employment for the refugees whom we have accepted from all over the Galaxy we have reverted to the use of human labor wherever possible."

"I thought," Grimes said, "that this principle applied only to large-scale enterprises, such as agriculture. Not to menial work."

"Are you calling *me* a menial?" demanded the man.

"Of course not," said Grimes hastily. The driver already seemed more interested in the conversation than the handling of the car; if he got involved in a real argument he might forget to stop and plough into and through the reception committee.

He did stop; only just in time, it seemed to Grimes. The doors opened. The ADC was first out. Grimes followed, putting on his top hat. He raised it in response to the Sergeant's smart salute. The short, stocky civilian came forward and bowed, presenting his shiny, bald pate to the Governor's inspection. He straightened up and said, "Jaconelli, Your Excellency. David Jaconelli. Your secretary."

Grimes took his clammy hand, pressed it briefly.

He said, "I am pleased to meet you, Mr. Jaconelli."

One of the servants, the one with the most lavish display of braid and buttons on his tunic, presented himself and bowed far more deeply than had the secretary. His sparse gray hair, Grimes noted, was scraped back and plaited into a neat queue, a pigtail. He came erect and regarded Grimes from black, slanted eyes. His face was thin, the skin tightly stretched over the bone structure, his complexion ivory yellow. A wispy beard decorated his far from prominent chin.

He said, in a high-pitched voice that was not quite a twitter, "Welcome, Your Excellency, from myself and from all of your servants."

"Thank you," replied Grimes. Then, "You are . . .?"

"My name is Wong Lee, Your Excellency. I have the honor to be Your Excellency's majordomo."

"I am pleased to meet you, Mr. Lee." (Or should that have been Mr. Wong?) "You may tell the other servants to return to their duties." Orders were given in a high-pitched voice in a language that Grimes thought was Chinese. "And now, if you will be so good as to escort me to my quarters. . . ."

Led by Wong Lee, accompanied by Lieutenant Smith and Mr. Jaconelli, Grimes walked into what would be his happy home until such time as his gubernatorial employment was terminated. Would he be able to resign before he got fired? he wondered.

The four men marched through what seemed, to Grimes, like miles of corridors, over long reaches of gleaming parquetry, past a never-ending display, on either side, of works of art, copies—but excellent ones—of paintings of all periods, representative of every school since some inspired Cromagnard daubed his crude but enduring pigments onto a cave wall. There was a Turner—*Spaceship out of sight in a gas nebula,* thought Grimes irreverently—and a Picasso—*Portrait of a lady after a Mannschenn Drive malfunction.* And a Rubens . . . Grimes had no objection to naked blondes but preferred men less fat. A Norman Lindsay . . . None of his undressed ladies could be classed as skinny but they were far more to Grimes's taste than the models of the old Dutch master. Inevitably there was that famous woman who daren't smile properly—thought Grimes, cultural barbarian that he was—for fear of exposing her carious teeth. Then there were more Australian artists. There was Nolan, with his weirdly compelling perpetuation of a myth, the giant in his fantastic armor astride a horse that could have been borrowed (or stolen!) from Don Quixote. A myth? But there had been a Ned Kelly, whose name and fame had survived while those of countless far worthier citizens were long forgotten. And if the cards had fallen only a little differently at Glenrowan what might have happened? The course of Australian history, of Terran history, even, could have been changed.

Wong Lee noticed Grimes's interest in the Nolan paintings.

"A folk hero, Your Excellency?" he asked.

"Mphm. Yes, I suppose."

"Perhaps an honorable ancestor . . ."

"Not as far as I know."

They came to the Governor's suite.

There was a large, comfortable sitting room with, off it, an office—big enough, thought Grimes, for a full meeting of the entire Board of Admiralty. While the others watched respectfully he took his seat behind the vast, gleaming desk, enjoying the feeling of power. He had commanded ships and, recently, a flotilla—but this was different. Now he was boss cocky of an entire planet—on paper, at least. *De jure.* But *de facto*? That remained to be seen. He looked down to his reflection in the highly polished surface of the desk, saw behind his face the crossed flags, the banners of Terra and of the Interstellar Federation. He saw too, with something of a shock, that he was still wearing the absurd top hat. But he was the Governor, wasn't he? This was his Residence, wasn't it? If he couldn't make his own rules of etiquette, who could? Nonetheless he removed the head covering, skimmed it across the desk top to Wong Lee.

He got up then and, followed by the others, made a tour of his living quarters. There was a luxurious bedroom. He saw that his baggage had already been deposited there; it must have been offloaded and transported while he was inspecting the Guard of Honor at the spaceport. Somebody had begun to unpack and had laid out his civilian full evening dress on the bed. That somebody was a girl—tall, with glossy black hair swinging in a pageboy bob about her face, wearing a royal blue tunic and a long, white skirt that was slit to hip level, revealing a delectable length of smooth, ivory-skinned leg. She straightened up from what she was doing, turned to Grimes and bowed. Like the other servants she was of Mongoloid stock—a descendant, Grimes supposed, of those New Cantonese refugees. But there was some mixed blood—that wide mouth, the almost—but no more than almost—harsh angularity of the facial bone structure.

"This is Su Lin, Your Excellency," said Wong Lee. "She is to be your . . . handmaiden. I decided that you, as a space gentleman, accustomed to the ministrations of stewardesses aboard your ships, would prefer a personal attendant of the female sex."

"I like to make my own decisions," said Grimes.

"Then, Your Excellency, I will see to it that Peng Yuan, who was valet to your late, revered predecessor, performs the same duties for your honored self."

"I've already told you, Mr. Wong," said Grimes stiffly, "that I like to make my own decisions. I am sure that Miss Su will be quite satisfactory."

"It is not customary, Your Excellency, to use an honorific when addressing or referring to under servants."

Jaconelli and Smith exchanged glances, each permitting himself as much of a sneer as he dared.

Grimes restrained himself from saying that he was the Governor and that he made the rules. It would not do at all to cut the old man down to size in the presence of a subordinate and of the ADC and the secretary. As he knew from experience a wise captain does not unnecessarily antagonize his chief steward.

He looked at his wrist companion, the chronological function of which had been set to local time.

He said, "I think, now, that I'd like to get cleaned up and all the rest of it. What time should I leave the Residence for the Palace, Lieutenant?"

"1900 hours, sir."

"Thank you. And Mr. Jaconelli. . . ."

"Sir?"

"I take it that all of the late Governor Wibberley's papers will be accessible to me? In the office, perhaps. . . ."

"No, sir."

"No? Why not?"

"After the accident all documents were taken by Colonel Bardon. He said he was shipping them back to Earth."

"But there must have been copies."

"Yes, Your Excellency. But. . . ."

"But what?"

"He took them too."

"Why didn't you . . .?"

"Sir, I am only the Governor's secretary. Until your arrival the Colonel was the senior Terran officer on this planet."

"Mphm." Grimes glared at Smith, who had been listening to the exchange with interest and enjoyment. "You may go, Lieutenant. Be waiting for me in the car at 1900 hours."

"Very good, Your Excellency."

"And Mr. Jaconelli. . . . Please arrange with the Bureau of Meteorology for the release of Captain Raoul Sanchez, the shuttle pilot who brought me down from *Sobraon*, to serve as my atmosphere pilot."

"It was my understanding, Your Excellency, that Colonel Bardon was to second one of his officers to your service."

"Then tell the Colonel that I am making my own arrangements. Oh, and I'd like a crew list."

"A *crew list?*"

"A list of all the Residence staff. Age, sex, birthplace, national and/or planetary origin, qualifications, if any, etc., etc., and etc."

"Very good, Your Excellency. Will that be all?"

"Yes, thank you."

When the ADC and the secretary were gone the majordomo asked, "Will you require my services any further, Your Excellency?"

"No, thank you, Mr. Wong. You may leave. And you, Su Lin."

She objected. "But, Your Excellency, I am your body servant. I am to serve you in all ways."

"It is customary among our people, sir," said Wong Lee. "There is the help to be given to a great man in the removal of his formal attire and the donning of other ceremonial clothing. There is the bringing of refreshment when he so desires it. There is. . . ."

Meanwhile Grimes had succeeded in getting his pipe out of a pocket in his too-tight-fitting trousers and, after another little struggle, his tobacco pouch. He filled the vile brier and was patting his coat pockets in a vain search for a box of the old-fashioned matches that he preferred to other means of ignition.

And then Su Lin was holding a golden lighter, a miniature flame thrower from which issued a jet of incandescence. Grimes hated having his pipe lit for him but submitted to her ministrations. If he refused to submit to other, more intimate ones he would be likely to hurt her feelings. He would just have to see to it that the ministrations were not too intimate. During his Survey Service career he had always despised commanding officers who had engaged in liaisons with their personal stewardesses. (He was, in some ways, a snob; he had never shied away from the occasional affair with female shipmates who held commissioned rank.)

Wong Lee bowed deeply and glided away.

Grimes said to the girl, "Lin—or should it be Su?"

"Whichever pleases Your Excellency."

"All right. Su. Please wait in the sitting room while I get undressed and showered."

"But I am your body servant, Your Excellency."

Already she was helping him out of his tail coat and was loosening the cravat about his neck. He let her go ahead with it. After all, he thought, this was the girl's job, one for which she had been trained. And, he admitted, he liked being pampered, especially by attractive women. Her nimble fingers coped expeditiously with studs and buttons. (Why could not the items of formal dress be secured by seal seams?)

Surprisingly soon he was naked, unembarrassed but determined that things would go no further. He walked to the open door of the bathroom, into the shower cubicle. Before he could put a hand to the controls a slim, bare arm slid past his shoulder and a long, scarlet-nailed finger pushed the warm button. He felt smooth, soft nudity against his back. He turned to face the girl and said, "I am quite capable of washing myself. Su Lin. Please wait for me in the bedroom."

Then, lest the order be misconstrued, he added, "And get dressed."

She stepped away from him and bowed, saying, her voice expressionless, "As Your Excellency pleases."

She turned gracefully and glided away from him; her smoothly working buttocks were like peaches poised on the long, slender (but not too slender) stems of her legs.

Feeling excessively virtuous Grimes continued with his shower. The water temperature was just right. He pushed the detergent button, then the one labeled scrubbers. The soft brushes worked up a scented lather all over his body. He thought that her hands would have made an even better job of it. Although the feeling of virtue persisted he was beginning to feel something of a bloody fool. But one of his own rules, which he was determined not to break, was NEVER PLAY AROUND WITH THE HIRED HELP.

"You stinking snob!" he muttered.

And, talking of stinks, he would have to get the detergent dispenser charged with something less redolent of a whore's garret.

The blowers soon dried him and he returned to the bedroom. The girl was waiting for him, once again respectably attired. Her face, utterly devoid of expression, could have been carved from old ivory. Expertly she helped him into his full evening dress, the archaic white tie and tails, with decorations. When he was fully clad he surveyed himself in the full-length mirror of the wardrobe. The effect would have been better, he thought, had he been taller and slimmer, less stocky, but . . . *Not bad,* he thought. *Not bad.* He allowed Su Lin to make the final adjustments to the snowy white butterfly nestling on his Adam's apple.

"Thank you," he told her and walked through to the sitting room.

Lieutenant Smith, in his uniform mess full dress, was waiting for him.

He said, "The car is waiting for us, Your Excellency."

"Thank you," said Grimes.

He followed the ADC to the doorway. Before he could pass through it Su Lin came out of the bedroom carrying his hat, another topper, black this time. Grimes had deliberately forgotten the thing; he took it from her with a brief word of thanks that he hoped she sensed was insincere.

He let Smith pilot him through the labyrinth of corridors.

He thought, *I must tell Jaconelli to get me a chart of this bloody warren.*

⤳ Chapter 10 ⤳

THE GUBERNATORIAL CAR was waiting in the portico, the civilian chauffeur, in his livery of faded, frayed denim and red neckerchief, in the front seat and, beside him, two soldiers in khaki uniform. The rear doors of the vehicle opened. Grimes took off his top hat, climbed in. The ADC followed him. Wong Lee and Su Lin bowed deferentially as the Whispering Ghost purred away from the portico.

Grimes tried to make conversation.

"I'm not used to having an ADC," he remarked pleasantly to the Lieutenant.

"ADC, Officer Commanding the Governor's Guard, liaison with the Officer Commanding the Garrison. . . ." The officer's voice was surly. "I hope that you don't think up any other jobs for me, Your Excellency. If ever there was a penny-pinching operation, this is it. I'm surprised that they don't have me doing the cooking. . . ."

"Talking of cooking," said Grimes, hoping to switch the conversation to a topic dear to his heart, "what's the chef like?"

"Oh, all right, I suppose, if you don't mind mucked-up food. He's New Cantonese, of course. Like all the rest of the Residence mob, with the exception of my men and Jaconelli and myself." He laughed. "I'm surprised that they didn't appoint a New Cantonese as Governor. They'd be paying him much less than they're paying you, Your Excellency."

"Mphm." Grimes managed to make it sound like a reprimand. He didn't like and never had liked moaners. "Some people would think that being appointed ADC to a Governor was an honor."

"I . . . I suppose so, Your Excellency."

They sat in silence while the car sped down the winding road toward the city, taking a different route, Grimes noted, from that which had been taken during the journey from the spaceport. Dusk was falling fast but still work was continuing in the fields to either side of the highway. The last of the daylight was caught and reflected by metal implements, by sickles (sickles! in this day and age!) and the blades of hand-wielded hoes. A few of the laborers paused and straightened up to stare at the passing vehicle but most of them took no respite from their back-breaking toil.

Then there were no more fields but, to either side of the wide avenue, there were houses, each in its own garden. All of these buildings were low and rambling, the architectural style vaguely Spanish. Some—but only a few—of the gardens were well-kept; most of them were miniature jungles. The street lights were coming on but not all of them were working.

There was some traffic in the avenue. There was the very occasional solar-electric car. There was a sudden swarm of cyclists, skimming silently through the dusk. Motorized machines, thought Grimes at first, then saw that all the riders' legs were pumping vigorously. Workers, he decided, domestic servants possibly, returning to their compounds outside the city. And there were trishaws, tricycles with the passengers seated forward, flanked by the pair of leading wheels, with the operator on his saddle astern of them, pedaling hard. Most of the passengers were of Caucasian stock—and all the drivers Mongoloid. Grimes grunted disapprovingly. The use of such transport was justified only during periods of energy crisis—and such days were long past on all of man's worlds.

Ahead, now, was the President's Palace, a blaze of illumination, with its profusion of white pillars more Grecian than Spanish. The vast expanse of lawn surrounding the building was like dark green velvet, the drive along which the car made its approach was surfaced with well-raked yellow gravel. A flock of sheep drifted slowly across the headlight beams; the vehicle slowed to a crawl until the animals were past and clear. The driver turned his head to address Grimes.

"What do you think of our lawn mowers, Your Excellency? They're sort of cobbers of yours, Australian Merinos. Their ancestors came out with the First Fleet."

The ADC snapped, "Do not address His Excellency without permission, Garcia."

"Mr. Garcia to you, Mister. And, anyhow, this is *my* world, not yours."

Grimes shoved his oar in, hoping thereby to avert an acrimonious argument. He asked, "And do you have any other Australian animals here, Mr. Garcia?"

"Only yourself, Your Excellency."

Grimes laughed and the ADC growled wordlessly.

"Our beef cattle are Argentine stock," went on the driver, "and our dairy herds are from some little island back on Earth, Jersey. The pigs and the hens? From anywhere and everywhere, I guess."

The sheep were finally past and the car increased speed, passing a huge statue, a bronze giantess whose heroic proportions were revealed rather than hidden by her flowing draperies. She was holding aloft, in her right hand, a flaming torch. Clouds of flying insects—or insectlike creatures—attracted by the fatal lure of the flaring gas were immolating themselves by the thousand.

"I have often wondered," said the driver philosophically, "why the bastards, since they like the light so much, don't come out during the day. . . ."

An interesting problem, thought Grimes.

The vehicle pulled up in the wide portico. Waiting to receive Grimes was Colonel Bardon, in all the splendor of his mess full dress. With him was a group of local dignitaries—heavily bearded men in black velvet suits, in white, floppy-collared shirts with flowing, scarlet neckties, women in low-cut, black velvet dresses with scarlet scarves about their throats.

The ADC got out of the car first and stood to rigid attention. Grimes got out, putting on his hat. He raised it as Bardon saluted with a flourish, raised it again as the male Liberians swept off their own headgear—black, broad-brimmed and with scarlet bands—and as the ladies curtseyed. Then the party, Bardon and Grimes in the lead, passed through the huge double doors, held open by white-liveried servitors (more New Cantonese, thought Grimes) into an anteroom large enough to serve as a hangar for a fair-sized dirigible. The vast expanse of floor was local marble, highly polished, in which the multicolored veins were brightly scintillant. The high walls were covered with crimson, gold-embroidered silk. Overhead the huge electroliers glittered prismatically.

Attentive servants took hats, carried them away somewhere. Others swung open the enormous doors affording admission to the Reception Hall. This had a floor area that would have been ample for the apron of a minor spaceport. The decor was similar to that of the vestibule but on a much greater scale. Awaiting Grimes was the cream of Liberian society, the black-and-scarlet-clad Anarchist grandees and their ladies. At the far end of the vast hall were two platforms, red draped. On the lower but wider dais was a band, drums and gleaming brass. On the higher one Madam President was sitting in state; her chair was not quite a throne and the tiara adorning her glossy, black hair was not quite a crown. Behind her was a huge, gold-framed portrait of a heavily bearded worthy.

"Who's that?" whispered Grimes to Bardon. "Karl Marx?"

"Better not let anybody hear you say that, Your Excellency. That's Bakunin."

"Oh."

The music started. Grimes stiffened to attention, as did Bardon and the ADC. The Liberians also stood, but without rigidity. Nonetheless it was a mark of respect. Many of them sang. Grimes was both surprised and pleased that so many knew the words.

> Once a jolly swagman camped by a billabong
> Under the shade of a coolabahs tree,
> And he sang as he watched and waited till his billy boiled,
> 'Who'll come a-waltzing Matilda with me?'

Grimes wondered if those jumbuks, grazing on the wide lawns outside the Palace, could hear the national song of their long ago and far away homeland. And did they have an ancestral memory of the sheep-stealing swagman, a man who had been far more of an anarchist than these Liberians who attached that label to themselves.

Then it was the turn of the Terran anthem. Hardly anybody knew the words and the tune was not one to stick in the memory.

Sons of Terra, strong and free.
Faring forth through Time and Space,
As far as human eye can see
We run our sacred, fateful race . . .

Grimes wondered which was worse, the words or the music. Finally Liberia had its innings. Almost everybody sang.

Liberia's sons let us rejoice
For we are strong and free . . .

"Mphm," grunted Grimes. Who was free these days?

We sing our song with heart and voice
In praise of Liberty!
And praise we, too, our homeworld, so free from want
and care.
Stronghold of all the freedoms—
Advance, Liberia fair!

There was a final flourish of drums, then relative silence.

Bardon said, "And now, Your Excellency, I have to present you to Madam President."

"Lead on, MacDuff," said Grimes. He knew that he had misquoted but did not think that the Colonel would be aware of this.

"The name is Bardon, Your Excellency. Colonel Bardon."

The black-and-scarlet crowd parted like the Red Sea before the Israelites, opening clear passage toward the presidential dais along which Grimes, Bardon and the ADC marched, their heels ringing on the marble floor, keeping time to the rhythmic mutter of a single drum. The new Governor was acutely conscious that he was being observed, that he was being curiously regarded by all these bearded men and handsome women. (There may have been some ladies who could not be so categorized but he did not notice any.) He saw that Estrelita O'Higgins had risen from her thronelike chair, was making a stately descent of the short flight of red-carpeted stairs. If only she were holding a torch, thought Grimes, she would look just like one of those statues of Miss Liberty.

She stood there, at the foot of the stairs, waiting for him.

And who bowed to whom? Grimes wondered. Why had he not made a proper study of the protocol for such occasions? She was the (allegedly) elected ruler of a planet—but he was the appointed viceroy of Imperial Earth. Would she extend a gracious hand for him to kiss? At the spaceport they had bowed to each other, practically simultaneously, but this was the official reception, the state occasion.

She knew the drill (surely for this planet only!) even if he did not. She extended her long, smooth, pale arms and flung them around him, engulfing him in a powerful embrace. She must have been eating something with garlic in it, thought Grimes. But he returned her hearty kiss.

She released him, turning him around so that they were both facing the people.

"Comrades!" she cried in her deep contralto. "Comrades! I present to you our new Governor, John Grimes. The Federation, this time, has made a wise choice. John Grimes is a man of action. John Grimes is a man of the world, of many worlds, who knows that each and every planet has its own character. He knows that we, here on Liberia, have our own character. He knows that we have opened our world and our hearts to the poor, the distressed and the oppressed of many planets. There are people here, our guests, who, were it not for us, would be living lives of deepest misery—or who would not be living at all.

"Governor John Grimes, I am sure, will appreciate what we have done, what we are doing.

"I ask you, comrades, to welcome John Grimes and to take him to your hearts, just as you have taken so very many less fortunate outworlders."

A New Cantonese servant was bowing before them, extending a golden tray upon which were three tall goblets, each filled with a red wine. The President and the Colonel waited until Grimes had taken his before picking up theirs. Other servants had circulated through the hall. Soon everybody was holding a charged glass.

"Viva Grimes!" cried Estrelita O'Higgins, raising her goblet. (She was more than ever like those statues.)

"Viva Grimes!" sounded loudly from the body of the hall. "Viva Grimes!"

And everybody has had a drink but me, thought Grimes wryly.

He waited until the toast had been drunk, then made his own. "Long live Liberty!" He was probably more sincere, he hoped, than those who, so noisily, had drunk to his health. The wine wasn't bad, although a mite too sweet.

~ Chapter 11 ~

GUIDED BY ESTRELITA O'HIGGINS, accompanied by Colonel Bardon, Grimes made the rounds of the great reception hall. The ADC trailed behind for a while, then lost himself in the crowd. The new Governor was introduced to the people who—in theory—were now his subjects. He made and listened to small talk. Now and again he was able to initiate a discussion on more serious matters. He sampled snacks from the buffet tables and enjoyed the savory, highly spiced morsels. An attentive servant continually replenished his glass, even after only a couple of sips. On any other world but this, Grimes thought, a Governor would remain in one place and the people would be brought to meet him. Possibly this Liberian way of doing things was better. At least the newly installed dignitary did not go hungry or thirsty.

He met ministers of state and media personalities. He fended off searching questions about his recent experiences as a commodore of privateers. He asked questions himself, some of which were answered frankly while others were not. Politicians, he thought, were much of a muchness no matter what labels they had attached to themselves.

His conversation with Eduardo Lopez, Minister of Immigration was interesting.

"You must realize, Your Excellency, that I have little choice regarding the ethnicity of our immigrants. To deny any distressed person or persons sanctuary on racial grounds would be altogether contrary to our . . . constitution? Yes. Constitution. . . ."

"I thought," said Grimes, "that a society founded on the principles of Anarchism wasn't supposed to have such a thing."

"Contrary to our principles," said the President firmly.

"You are right as always, Estrelita," said the fat politician gallantly. "Principles. Of course, if I received a request for permission to enter from, say, an El Doradan, a representative of a society notorious for its devotion to capitalism, I should be obliged to refuse. But the poor, distressed and homeless, of whatever race or color, I must welcome with open arms."

"*We* must welcome," said the President.

"As I was saying—we must welcome."

"And can these immigrants become full citizens?" asked Grimes, although he already knew the answer to that question.

"Of course, provided that they show proof that they are fit and proper persons to become Liberians."

Grimes looked around him. Apart from the servants all those present seemed to be of Terran Anglo-Saxon or Latin stock. There were no Orientals, no Negroes.

"Have any outworlders yet achieved citizenship?" he asked.

"Er . . . no. You see, Your Excellency, the major qualification is freedom. As long as a person is in debt to the State he is not free. Once he has earned enough money to repay the debt he is free . . ."

"Debt?" asked Grimes.

"Resettlement is a costly business, Your Excellency, as you as a shipowner must know. Transportation between worlds . . ."

"The responsibility, I understand, of the Federation."

"Even so, there are costs, heavy costs. People come here. They must be fed, housed, found employment. . . ."

"Employment," echoed Grimes. "Menial work. Manual labor, for not very high wages. . . ."

"And would you pay a field hand, Your Excellency, the salary that you, highly trained and qualified, would expect as a shipmaster?"

"The laborer, in any field, is worthy of his hire," said the President.

Her hand firmly on Grimes's elbow she steered him away from Lopez, toward the flamboyantly red-haired Kitty O'Halloran, Director of Tri Vi Liberia. She was a large woman, fat rather than plump, and she gushed. "Your Excellency. Commodore. I'm dying to get you on to one of our programs. Just an interview, but in *depth*. Just the story, told by yourself, of some of your *outrageous* adventures. . . ."

"Outrageous?" parried Grimes. "I'm a respectable Governor. "

"But you weren't always. You've been a pirate. . . ."

"A privateer," he corrected her.

"Who knows the difference?" She tittered. "From what I've heard, you didn't know yourself. . . ."

Again there was the guiding pressure on his elbow. This time he was to meet Luigi Venito, Minister of Interstellar Trade, a tall, distinguished man with steely gray hair and—unusual in this company—a neatly trimmed beard.

"I thought, Your Excellency," said Venito, "that I might one day deal with you in your capacity as a shipowner. To meet you as a Governor is an unexpected pleasure."

"Bad pennies," said Grimes, "turn up in the most unexpected places."

"Ha ha. But I refuse to believe that the Terran World Assembly would appoint a bad penny to a highly responsible position."

"You'd be surprised," said Grimes. "And, in any case, governments are rarely as moral as those whom they govern." (*There are times,* he thought, *when I feel that I should have a Boswell, recorder in hand, tagging after me . . .*) "I hope that your government is an exception to the rule."

Venito chuckled. "Some say that we shouldn't have a government at all, not on this world. But after the first few years our founding fathers—and mothers, of course, Madam President—were obliged to admit that pure Anarchism doesn't work. A state of anarchy is not Anarchism. But we *are* free, unregimented, doing the things that we want to do as long as we do not infringe upon the rights of our fellow citizens. From each according to his ability, to each according to his needs. My own ability is trade, buying in the cheapest markets, selling in the dearest. All for the greatest good, naturally, of Liberia . . ."

He had been drinking, of course, not too much, perhaps, but enough to loosen his tongue. Grimes ignored the President's attempt to push him along to another group. There was one point that he wanted to clear up, a matter that had not been fully dealt with in the data that he had been given to study on the voyage out from Earth.

He said, "You must have made some interesting deals in your time. . . . Agricultural machinery, for example. . . ."

Venito laughed. "Yes. That *was* a good deal! The new colony on Halvan—and the ship carrying all their robot harvesters and the like months overdue! She's listed as missing, presumed lost, at Lloyd's. I think that the presumption still holds—but that's not important. . . ."

Only to the crew, thought Grimes, *and their relatives.*

"And we had still more refugees coming in and so I said to Lopez, 'Put these people to work in the fields—and I'll flog all our agricultural machinery at better-than-new prices!' And I did just that."

"Clever," said Grimes. "Ill winds, and all that. But it wouldn't have been so good for Liberia if you didn't have the indentured labor system, if your field workers were being paid decent wages."

"What is a decent wage, Your Excellency? Enough to buy the necessities of life—food, shelter, clothing—with a little left over for the occasional luxury. That's a decent wage. On this world nobody goes cold or hungry. What more do you want?"

"The freedom to change your job when you feel like it, for a start."

"But all our citizens enjoy that freedom."

"Yes. All your *citizens,* Minister."

"Citizenship has to be earned, Your Excellency."

The President not only had her hand firmly on his elbow; she pinched him quite painfully. He took the hint and allowed her to conduct him to a meeting with the Minister for Culture and the lady with him, the Chief Librarian of Liberia.

They knew his background, of course, and, talking down from their intellectual eminence, made it plain that they held spacemen in low esteem.

Chapter 12

THE RECEPTION WAS OVER.

The President and Colonel Bardon, very much like husband and wife getting rid of the guests after a party and looking forward to holding a post mortem on the night's doings as soon as they were in bed, escorted Grimes out to the waiting car, which was at the head of the queue of vehicles. Most of these were trishaws.

The ADC was there, with the two soldiers. All three of them made a creditable attempt at standing to attention. Grimes wondered briefly how the two enlisted men had spent their evening; obviously they had found congenial company somewhere. He knew how the ADC had passed the time; that officer had been mainly in the company of two not unattractive girls who seemed to have monopolized the services of one of the wine waiters. Surely ADCs, Grimes had thought disapprovingly, should always be at the beck and call of their lords and masters. But this was Liberia where all animals—unless they had the misfortune to be refugees—were equal. (But surely a Governor was more equal than the others.)

"Good night, Your Excellency."

"Good night, Madam President." Grimes clasped her extended hand. "Thank you for the party."

"It was a pleasure having you."

"Good night, Your Excellency."

"Good night, Colonel."

Grimes removed his tall hat before climbing into the passenger compartment of the car. The driver turned his head to regard him sardonically.

"Feeling no pain, Gov?" he asked. (He, too, must have spent a convivial evening.)

When in Rome . . . thought Grimes resignedly. He said, "I'll survive."

"More than your predecessor did . . ." muttered the chauffeur.

The ADC and the soldiers embarked. The doors slid shut. The car drove away.

Grimes drowsed most of the way back to the Residence.

Wong Lee was waiting there to receive him and so, in his suite, was Su Lin. As though by magic the girl produced a pot of fragrant tea and brought it to him on a lacquer tray as he went into his office and sat down at the desk. He sipped from the cup that she poured for him; the steaming liquid cleared his head. The old man and the girl watched impassively as he opened the first of the folders that Jaconelli had laid out for him.

This contained the information on the Terran staff of the Residence.

Jaconelli, Grimes read, had been born in Chicago. His solitary qualification was Bachelor of Commerce, the minimal requirement for any secretarial post. Surely a Governor, thought Grimes, should be entitled to at least a Master to handle his correspondence and affairs.

Harrison Smith, the ADC, was another Bachelor—of Military Arts. He was a graduate of West Point. His birthplace was Denver. His Terran Army career had been undistinguished; he had not played a part, however minor, in even a police action or a brushfire war.

The Sergeant of the Governor's Guard, Martello, was another American. Although seven years older than his officer he, too, had been lucky enough to avoid action during his Army service.

The privates were a mixed bunch—one New Zealander, three Poms, a Swede and an Israeli. That all of them had reached early middle age without attaining non-commissioned rank did not say much for them.

The New Cantonese file was a thicker one—but only because there were more names in it. Wong Lee had the biggest entry.

The majordomo was old, even older than his appearance and manner had led Grimes to believe. He had actually been born on New Canton, where his parents had been the owners of the Heavenly Peace Hotel and the Jade Dragon Restaurant. As had been the custom of his people he had commenced his training in hotel and restaurant management at a very early age. In spite of his refugee status he had easily obtained such employment on Liberia although he was never allowed to become the owner of his own establishment. He had applied for the post of majordomo to the Governor when the first of such appointments was made by Earth. He had got the job and for many years had kept it.

All the others had been born on Liberia, some of mixed parentage. Among these was Su Lin, with a New Cantonese father and an Irandan mother. And young enough, thought Grimes, to be his own daughter. He looked up at her from the typed pages. She looked back at him and smiled. He frowned back at her.

Finally he got to the transcript of the telephone conversation that Jaconelli had had with the Bureau of Meteorology. The Secretary, pulling rank as the Governor's personal representative, had received an assurance from one of the Deputy Directors (*the* Director had been among those at the reception) that Captain Raoul Sanchez would be released at once from his normal duties and instructed to report at the Residence at 0900 hours tomorrow morning. *Tomorrow* morning? Grimes looked up at the wall clock. *This* morning.

He said, "Thank you, Mr. Wong. Thank you, Su Lin. I shall not be needing you any more tonight. Please see that I am called promptly at 0700 hours."

The old man bowed deeply and then glided out of the office. The girl remained.

Grimes said again, "Thank you, Su Lin. Please call me at 0700 hours."

She said, "But you have yet to retire, Your Excellency. And my duties are to attend you at all times."

"I am capable of putting myself to bed," Grimes told her.

"But, Your Excellency, I have been trained . . ."

"And so have I, from earliest childhood—to undress myself and even to fold and hang my clothes properly."

She laughed at this and it made her even more attractive. If Grimes had not been so well looked after on the voyage out from Earth he might well have yielded to temptation.

"Good night," he said firmly.

"Good night, Your Excellency," she said softly.

A little later, wrestling with the fastenings of his archaic finery, he regretted not having retained her services if only to help him to undress.

⌢ Chapter 13 ⌢

SHE CALLED HIM AT SEVEN, placing the tea tray down on the bedside table with a musical clatter and then whispering softly into his ear, "It is morning, Your Excellency. It is morning."

Grimes ungummed his eyes and looked up at her. There must be, he admitted, far worse sights with which to start the day. She smiled at him and poured tea from the pot with its willow pattern decoration into a handleless cup on which was the same design. As soon as he had struggled into a sitting posture, propped by the plump pillows that she had arranged for him, she handed him the cup. He handed it back to her. When he first awoke it was not a drink that he needed but the reverse. With some embarrassment—normally he slept naked—he got out of the bed on the side away from her and padded through to the bathroom. The pressure on his bladder relieved, he returned to his bed and slid the lower portion of his body under the covers. This time he accepted the cup and sipped from it gratefully. He saw that she had brought his pipe from where he had left it in the office and had filled it. She put one end of the stem into her mouth, applied flame to the bowl from a small, golden lighter that she brought from the side pocket of her tunic. When it was drawing properly she handed it to him.

Even an Admiral, thought Grimes smugly, *wouldn't be getting service like this . . .* He wondered if he, as a Planetary Governor, outranked an Admiral. *De jure,* possibly, if not *de facto.*

He sipped and smoked, smoked and sipped.

She asked, "What does Your Excellency desire for breakfast?"

"What's on the menu?" Grimes asked.

"Whatever Your Excellency wishes," she said.

A roll in bed with honey, he thought. Then, *Down, boy, down!*

He said, after consideration, "Grapefruit, please. Then two eggs, sunny side up, with bacon and country-fried potatoes. Hot rolls. Butter. Lemon marmalade. Coffee. . . ."

"At once, Your Excellency?"

"No, thank you. I always like to shower and depilate and all the rest of it first. And dress. . . ."

"What will Your Excellency wear this morning?"

And just what was a Governor's undress uniform?

"I leave it to you. Something informal, or relatively so. . . ."

He put the almost empty cup down on to the tray with a decisive clatter, declined the offer of a refill. When she removed the tea things, carrying the tray through to the sitting room, he got out of bed. There was an old-fashioned bolt on the door to the toilet facilities; he shot it. He completed his morning ablutions, depilation and all the rest of it without interruption. On returning to the bedroom he found that the bed had been made and that clothing had been laid out on it—underwear, a ruffled shirt of orange silk, dark gray, sharply creased slacks. Highly polished, gold-buckled shoes stood by the couch.

He dressed and went through to where a low table had been set with crockery and cutlery, a covered dish of hot rolls, a butter dish and another with the marmalade. There was a pot of coffee, a bowl of sugar crystals and a jug of cream. A prepared half-grapefruit awaited his attention, as did that morning's issue of *The Liberty Star.* He sat down, propped the newspaper against the coffee pot and made a start on the grapefruit. He read the account of Madam President's reception for the new Governor the previous evening. He was amused to see himself referred to as "an officer who achieved great distinction whilst in the Federation Survey Service" and as "a successful shipowner who has put his great administrative and business talents at the disposal of both his home planet and of

Liberia." The piece on Grimes concluded with the pious hope that he, as an experienced captain both of spaceships and of industry, would not feel the urge, as had his predecessor, to meddle officiously in the smooth running of the world that he had been called upon to govern.

The attentive Su Lin—he had not noticed her return—removed the plate with the now empty grapefruit shell, replaced it with that occupied by his eggs and bacon. She asked him how he preferred his coffee. He told her that he liked it black. He held the paper in both hands as she poured.

The eggs, bacon and fried potatoes were just as he liked them. The rolls were crisp. The marmalade, when finally he got to it, was deliciously tangy. By this time he had turned to the INTERSTELLAR SHIPPING—ARRIVALS AND DEPARTURES Columns. *Sobraon's* arrival and departure were listed as *Orbital Only*. *Willy Willy*, with the obnoxious Dreeble commanding, had lifted off, with passengers for Isa—a world rich in metals, Grimes knew, with mining and smelting as the major industries—while the Governor had been enjoying himself at the reception. One did not need to be clairvoyant, he thought, to know what sex those passengers belonged to or for what employment they had been recruited. *Bulkalgol and Bulkvega* were due out very shortly, with grain, one for Waverley and the other for Caribbea. After that it looked like being a slack time, for some weeks, at Port Libertad. One name among the *Future Arrivals* caught Grimes's attention— *Agatha's Ark*. He remembered that old flash of prevision he had experienced while *Sobraon's* temporal precession field had been building up.

He filled his pipe, brought the stem to his mouth. Before he could strike a match Su Lin was holding the flame from a golden lighter over the charred bowl. Grimes hated having his pipe lit for him but submitted to the attention. He did not mind, however, having another cup of the excellent coffee poured for him.

The Liberty Star, he discovered ran to a daily crossword puzzle. He got up from the breakfast table and sat down in one of the easy chairs. Without being asked the girl brought him a slim, golden stylus from the office. But the puzzle was not to his taste; it was not of the cryptic variety. Furthermore it required of the would-be solver an encyclopedic knowledge of Terran political history—names, dates and all. And that, thought Grimes, was not a subject in which he would ever be awarded full Marx. He savored the pun, knocked out his pipe in a convenient ashtray (it had been burning unevenly), refilled it and, Su Lin being temporarily absent, clearing away the breakfast things, lit it properly himself.

He got up and, trailing an acrid rather than an aromatic cloud of blue smoke, wandered out into the corridor and, to his pleased surprise, found his way to the main doorway of the Residence without too much trouble. Servants bowed to him as he passed, the guard on duty at the entrance to the building saluted smartly.

It was pleasant outside, the morning sun warm but not too much so, the light breeze carrying the scent of the gaudy flowers from the big, ornamental beds. The closely cropped grass of the lawn was springy under the soles of his shoes. Su Lin joined him, walking respectfully to his left and half a pace to the rear. He was conscious of her presence and found himself wishing that their relationship was not one of master and servant.

She broke the silence.

"Your Excellency," she said, "someone approaches from the air."

"Thank you," said Grimes. He had already heard a distant clatter, looked up and seen a dark speck in the sky. He stopped walking and stared at it. Su Lin produced from a pocket a thin, round case, about twenty millimeters in diameter. She did something to it and it opened out into a tapered tube. She removed the covers from each end, handed it to Grimes. He realized that it was a telescope, a sophisticated instrument with a universal focus. He raised it to his right eye, managed to bring the approaching aircraft into the field of it. It was a minicopter, little more than a bubble-enclosed chair with two long skids under it as landing gear and over it the almost invisible rotating vanes.

Grimes recognized the pilot. It was Raoul Sanchez. He raised his free hand to wave. The young pilot returned the salutation, altered course slightly so as to come into a landing close to where Grimes and the girl were standing. Almost immediately the little aircraft was surrounded by a small crowd of indignant gardeners, gesticulating and shouting in high-pitched voices, pointing at the barely visible scars that the landing gear of the minicopter had made on the surface of the lawn. Sanchez grinned and shrugged apologetically. A door slid open in the surface of the transparent bubble.

"Better keep off the grass, Captain," said Grimes. "You'd better shift to the drive before we have a riot on our hands."

"Will do, Your Excellency."

The gardeners scrambled back as the vanes started to spin again. The machine lifted, drifted slowly over to the broad drive, settled down again, the skids crunching audibly on the gravel. By the time that Grimes had walked to it Sanchez had unstrapped himself from the chair and disembarked. He was wearing a suit of faded, deliberately frayed denim and a red neckerchief. He bowed formally to Grimes.

He said, "Your aerial chauffeur, Your Excellency, reporting for duty."

Lieutenant Smith who, accompanied by two soldiers, had come on to the scene achieved an expression that was both sneer and scowl.

Chapter 14

SANCHEZ LED THE WAY around the sprawling Residence to what was almost a minor airport. He had been there before, of course, while his brother had been atmosphere pilot to the late Governor Wibberley. There were hangars—two of them occupied and the third, the very big one, empty. Outside this, at a suitable distance, was a tripedal mooring mast.

Smith said, with, a gesture toward this construction, "Your airship will be delivered this afternoon, Your Excellency. One of the Army's Lutz-Parsivals. Colonel Bardon has appointed Lieutenant Duggin to be your pilot."

Before Sanchez could protest Grimes said, "I have made my own appointment, Lieutenant. Captain Sanchez will be flying me."

"But the Colonel . . ."

"Is not the Governor, *I* am."

"But Captain Sanchez is a spaceman . . ."

"And a qualified airshipman. Is that not so, Captain?"

"It is, Your Excellency," replied Sanchez as Smith said nastily, "So was his brother."

"That will do, Lieutenant Smith!" snapped Grimes while making a *pipe down!* gesture aimed at the other man. "That will do. Captain Sanchez is my pilot. And now, Captain, shall we look at what toys we have to play with?"

He walked to one of the occupied hangars, into it. The craft housed therein was a small pinnace of a type carried by the larger warships of the Survey Service, a spaceship in miniature. That, thought Grimes, he could fly himself—although legally he couldn't, his Master Astronaut's Certificate having been suspended. (Of course there was his Reserve Commission but that was supposed to be kept a secret.) Sanchez opened a door in the pinnace's side, into the little airlock. Grimes clambered on board, followed by Sanchez and Smith. He went forward first, to the control cab. With two exceptions the instrumentation on the console seemed to be in order. Certain switches, dials and screens had been removed and replaced by blank cover plates.

"No Mini-Mannschenn?" asked Grimes. "No Carlotti deep space radio?"

"They were removed, Your Excellency," said Smith, "when Colonel Bardon had this pinnace modified for the Governor's use."

"Modified *how!*" demanded Grimes.

"The space occupied by that equipment was required for the bar and for . . . for . . ."

"Mphm," grunted Grimes. He asked suddenly, "Does the Residence run to its own Carlotti transceiver?" (That was one of the many things, he thought, that he should have found out long before he arrived on Liberia.)

"No, Your Excellency," said Smith. "Surely you must have noticed that there are no Carlotti antennae on the roof."

"They could be in the cellar," said Grimes, "and work just as well!"

Smith made a show of ignoring this and continued, "The only Carlotti equipment is at the spaceport. It is manned and maintained, of course, by Terran personnel."

And so the Governor, thought Grimes, *can communicate directly with Earth only by courtesy of the Garrison Commander.*

He completed his inspection of the pinnace. He was not overly impressed. He could not refrain from using his memories of *Little Sister* as a yardstick. When he made his way out through the airlock Su Lin was there to help him down to the ground. He waved her aside irritably and then, when he saw her hurt expression, rather hated himself.

He said, "It's all right, Su. I'm a spaceman. I'm used to getting into and out of these things."

With the others he made his way into the second hangar in use. The aircraft there was a helicopter, a rather beat-up Drachenflieger, no doubt one of Bardon's cast-offs. Sanchez looked at the machine disparagingly.

"Governor Wibberley," he said, "never used this. My brother reckoned that it wasn't safe."

"And he, of course," said Smith, "was an expert on aeronautical safety."

"*You* . . ." the pilot growled, his fist raised threateningly.

"Lieutenant Smith," snapped Grimes, putting a control room crackle into his voice, "you will refrain from making provocative remarks." Then, his voice a little milder, "Captain Sanchez, I will not tolerate brawling among the members of my . . . family. And now, will you take luncheon with me?"

"Thank you, Your Excellency."

"And will you, Lieutenant Smith, please inform us when the airship is approaching?"

"Very good, Your Excellency."

The party walked back to the main entrance to the building, Sanchez beside Grimes, Su Lin the usual half-pace to the rear and Smith, sulking hard, well astern.

It was a leisurely and pleasant meal, with drinks before, served by the attentive Su Lin. The honeyed sand crawlers were especially good, reminding Grimes of the honeyed prawns that he had enjoyed in Chinese restaurants on Earth. With the meal there was rice wine, served warm in tiny cups. When it was over Grimes lit his pipe— waiting until the girl was out of the room—and Sanchez a slim, black cigar.

The pilot said, "I must apologize for having lost my temper with your ADC, Excellency."

"He asked for it," said Grimes. "I've been considering asking Colonel Bardon for a replacement, but . . ."

"Better the devil you know, sir."

"Precisely. You must have seen him, now and again, when you visited your brother here."

"Yes. I never did like him. He didn't like me. And my brother hated him. It was mutual."

"He's Bardon's man, of course."

"Of course," agreed Sanchez.

Su Lin returned with coffee.

"Is it switched on, Su?" asked the pilot.

"Yes, Raoul," she replied.

Grimes stared at them.

"Is *what* switched on?" he demanded.

"A device that I carry," she replied. "A—how shall I call it? A conversation modifier. It takes our voices and—scrambles? shuffles? To any listener you are telling Raoul about some of your deep space adventures and he is asking questions about them."

"And what are you saying?"

"I am urging Your Excellency to take at least one of these *chinrin* cakes with your coffee. *Chinrin* cakes, of course, were a great delicacy on New Canton. The refugees brought *chinrin* seeds with them when they came here and now we have our own little plantations of the shrubs."

"This modifier," asked Grimes curiously. "Does it have to be programmed?"

"Only in the most general of terms. It could almost be said to be intelligent. Perhaps it functions psionically. It could be a form of pseudolife but that I cannot say. I am not a scientist."

"Could I see it?" asked Grimes curiously. To his surprise she blushed embarrassedly.

"When Su Lin said that she carried the modifier," explained Sanchez, "she didn't mean that she carried it *on* her . . ."

"An implant?" asked Grimes.

"Yes, sir. But not a *surgical* implant. If you know what I mean."

"Oh. So am I to understand that as long as she's around, and along as she has *it* switched on, the bugs with which the Residence must be crawling will be sending absolutely fictitious reports to Bardon's monitors. I suppose that the bugs are Bardon's?"

"Of course, sir," said Sanchez.

"Mphm." He turned to Su Lin. "So you're rather more than my faithful handmaiden, it seems—just as Wong Lee is rather more than my faithful majordomo. But this . . . this *thing* of yours . . . where did you get it?"

It was Sanchez who answered.

"Shortly after the late Governor Wibberley's so-called accident there was a salesman here from Electra—not that he called himself a salesman. Trade Representative was his title. He was wined and dined by Estrelita but didn't make any sales. He was allowed to wander around without supervision—after all, what harm could a woolly witted scientist-engineer do? He enjoyed a liaison with one of our girls, an OAP member." He grinned. "She put the hard sell onto him and made a convert. Probably only a temporary one but still a convert. She told him about our problems and of the way in which the Governor, who had been taking too much interest in the state of affairs here, had been eliminated. . . ."

"Tanya Mendoza is a friend of mine," said Su Lin. "She came to visit me here. It was quite natural that she should bring her Electran friend with her and quite natural that I should show him around the Residence. He had a detector with him—although as far as Smith and Jaconelli were concerned he had nothing on him but the usual camera and recorder carried by tourists. He confirmed our suspicions that—as you have said—the Residence is crawling with bugs. He promised Tanya that he would do something about it, something that would not be obvious to the . . . the . . . buggers, is there such a word?"

"There is," said Grimes, "although its real meaning is not the one that you have given it."

Looking at her face he saw that she was making some sort of physical effort. He was about to ask what was wrong when Sanchez said, "Very interesting, Your Excellency. Very interesting. . . ."

Then, from behind him, Smith said, "Your Excellency, the airship is approaching now."

The device had been switched off, Grimes realized. So all

conversation from now on was being faithfully and truthfully recorded.

He turned to face his ADC.

"We'll be right out," he said.

～ Chapter 15 ～

THE LUTZ-PARSIVAL came in slowly and cautiously.

She was a graceful ship despite her chubbiness, her metal skin gleaming brightly in the sunlight. On her tail fins was painted the insignia of Bardon's regiment, a rampant golden lion. He would have to get that changed, thought Grimes. To a kangaroo? Why not?

"He's handling her like a cow handling a musket," muttered Sanchez disgustedly.

Grimes was inclined to agree. The approach was overly careful and then, in the final stages, clumsy. The ship dropped too fast as the helium in the gas cells was compressed and then lifted steeply as water ballast was dumped to compensate, drenching the gubernatorial party.

"If this," said Grimes furiously to Smith, "is a fair sample of the Army's airmanship it's just as well that I've appointed my own pilot!"

"Your Excellency," replied the ADC, "Lieutenant Duggin is a little rusty. . . ."

"If we were made of metal," said Grimes, "we'd be getting rusty!"

With his hand he wiped the water from his face. He would have liked to take his shirt off to wring it out.

"Your Excellency," said Su Lin, "you must go back inside to change into dry clothing."

"It doesn't matter, Su. I'll soon dry out. I want to see what other comic turns that clown up there is going to put on for us."

The airship circled slowly, once again losing altitude. This time her descent could be measured in millimeter per seconds. It was a long and painful process. By the time that the dangling lines had been picked up by the ground party—soldiers of the Governor's Guard supplemented by New Cantonese gardeners—Grimes's clothing was merely damp. And then the pilot did not use his engines for the final approach to the mast but was towed into position by the mooring crew. At last the nose cone was secure in the socket. A ladder was lowered from the control gondola and down it scrambled the plump figure of the pilot, handling himself as clumsily as he had handled the ship. He shambled rather than marched to where Grimes was standing and threw a casual salute in his direction.

"Lieutenant Duggin, Your Excellency. Reporting for duty."

"Lieutenant Duggin, you are relieved from duty," Grimes told him. "Lieutenant Smith will make arrangements for your transport back to barracks."

"But I'm your pilot, sir."

"You are not. But if ever I require a bath attendant I'll send for you."

"But, sir. . . ."

"That is all, Lieutenant. Captain Sanchez, do you wish Lieutenant Duggin to make a formal hand over?"

"It would be advisable, Your Excellency."

"Very well, Captain. See to it, will you?"

He stood with Su Lin and Smith watching as the two pilots walked to the dangling ladder and mounted it. As it took their weight the airship sagged down from the mast and then resumed her horizontal attitude. No further ballast was dumped; no doubt there was an automatic release of pressure from the atmospheric trimming cell or cells.

"Wait here, Mr. Smith, to look after Mr. Duggin after he's handed over," Grimes told the ADC.

He walked with Su Lin back to his quarters in the Residence.

～✥～✥～✥～

She brought him tea. He sent her away to get another cup so that she could join him in the taking of refreshment.

He asked, "Are you switched on?"

She said, "Yes, Your Excellency."

"And what are we talking about?"

"I am telling you about the New Cantonese festivals that we still observe on this world."

"Fireworks, processions of lanterns and dragons and all that?"

"Yes, Your Excellency."

"I hope to see at least one of your festivals."

"You will be an honored guest."

"Thank you, Su." He sipped from his cup. "Now you can tell me about the underground. What do you do, what do you hope to accomplish?"

"As far as we, and the other refugees, are concerned we want full citizenship. As far as Captain Sanchez and the OAP are concerned they want a return to the egalitarian principles of the original colonists of the planet. All of us are against the regime of Estrelita O'Higgins and Colonel Bardon and the vicious trades that they foster."

"Such as?"

"The shipping of girls—yes, and boys—to the brothels of various worlds where there is a demand for them, such as Isa and Venusberg. The pleasure houses—so-called—on this planet. The drug trade. And the profiteering in all the stores at which the refugees must purchase the essentials of life to ensure that nobody can possibly save enough money to become financially independent."

"So you want a revolution."

"Yes. Not necessarily an armed revolt, although it might have to come that." (And was this, wondered Grimes, his solicitous handmaiden with her limited but courtly English? She was reminding him more and more of a girl he had once known who had been President of the University of Kandral's Young Socialist Club and who had finished up as Vice President of the planet.) "We realize that once we take up arms against O'Higgins we shall also be taking up arms against Earth, against the Federation, as represented here by Bardon. If it is at all possible the change must be made by constitutional methods. The Governor is more than a mere figurehead. He has . . . How shall I put it? He has the power to hire and fire."

"Mphm?" Grimes knocked out and refilled his pipe. Su Lin reverted to her serving maid persona and lit it for him. He thought, *I shall have to try to break her of* that *habit.* "Mphm?"

"Governor Wibberley was conducting his own investigation of the state of affairs here. He had amassed considerable evidence of malpractices. He was almost ready to act. And then. . . ."

"So you want me, as Governor, to sack Colonel Bardon *and* President O'Higgins *and* all her ministers. . . ."

She said, "There have been precedents. There was one, in *your* country, on Earth, many years ago."

He said, "There's more than one Australian precedent. The Governor General, Sir John Kerr, sacked Prime Minister Gough Whitlam. Some years previously the Governor of New South Wales, Sir Philip Game, sacked Premier Jack Lang. . . ."

"You see."

He went on. "And many years before that the garrison in New South Wales deposed the Governor, Captain—as he was then—William Bligh."

"And wasn't Bligh," she asked, "the man who was always having mutinies? You've had a few yourself, haven't you?"

"Which doesn't mean that I like having them, Su."

She laughed. "I suppose not. But there must be ways of doing things constitutionally. And to do them without calling Earth first for approval—always supposing that Bardon let you get a message through."

"Messages did get through, after Wibberley's death," said Grimes. "That's why I'm here."

"As trouble shooter?" she asked. "Or as shit stirrer? In any case, Bardon's made sure that no more messages get through without his knowledge."

"Just who—or what—are you, Su Lin?" he asked.

"You have seen my dossier, Your Excellency."

"For what it's worth."

"There *is* a Su Lin," she told him. "But she is not on Liberia any longer. She was carefully selected out of all the New Cantonese as being almost my double. I required only minor body sculpture to make me her replica."

"Then what is your real name?"

"It doesn't matter. I rather like Su Lin, anyhow."

"Where are you from? You aren't from FIA, are you? Or are you? If you are I should have been told."

"I am not."

"The Sinkiang People's Republic?"

"No. The New Cantonese here are no worse off than they would be on New Sinkiang."

"Then where?"

There was a knock on the door. Grimes saw Su Lin's face go briefly tense as her vaginal muscles switched off the device that she carried.

Sanchez entered.

"I have taken delivery of the Lutz-Parsival, Your Excellency," he reported formally. "She seems to be airworthy in all respects, although I shall have to make a more detailed inspection later." *(To look for hidden bombs,* thought Grimes.) "I have left her at the mast, in the sunlight, to recharge the power cells."

"I think that I'd like to have a sniff round aboard her myself," said Grimes, "if you will be so good as to accompany me."

"Of course, Your Excellency," said Sanchez.

~ Chapter 16 ~

"WE SHALL HAVE TO GIVE HER A NAME," said Grimes to Sanchez as he and the pilot made their way along the catwalk running from stem to stern inside the airship. "LP17 is too . . . impersonal. Ships are more than just . . . *things.*"

"What do you have in mind, Your Excellency?"

Grimes thought hard. There had been quite a few ships for which he had felt a real affection, most recently *Little Sister* and *Sister Sue.* He grinned.

"*Fat Susie,*" he said. "She is rather plump, isn't she? I'll tell Mr. Jaconelli to organize painters for you to put the new name on the envelope. And at the same time they can change the insignia on the tail fins. I want a kangaroo instead of that tomcat of Bardon's."

"People might think," said Sanchez, "that you're naming the ship after Su Lin."

"She's not fat," Grimes told him. "But there was a fat Susie, not so very long ago."

(He wondered where she was now, how she was faring.)

He inspected the comfortable lounge with its wide out-and-down-looking windows on either side, the not-too-Spartan sleeping accommodation, the little galley with a standard autochef. This, if he was going to make much use of *Fat Susie,* would have to be modified to his requirements. He spent some time in the control cab, familiarizing himself with the instrumentation. It would not take him long, he thought, to learn how to fly this thing.

"She'll do," he said at last.

He was first down the ladder with Sanchez not far behind him. As he dropped to the ground he heard the air pump start up to pressurize the helium in one of the cells to compensate for the loss of weight.

Sanchez, who would now be living in the Residence, dined with him that evening, the two men taking their meal in Grimes's sitting room. (He had decided to use the dining room only for state occasions.) They were waited upon by Su Lin. The meal was a good one, traditional New Cantonese cookery. The pilot wielded his ivory chopsticks with as much assurance as did Grimes.

There was no need for Su Lin to activate what Grimes thought of as the anti-bug; conversation consisted mainly of generalities and of astronautical shop talk. Finally Sanchez said good night and left. Su Lin brought more tea, for herself and Grimes.

She said, "I am switched on."

"Indeed? And what are we talking about, Su Lin? I have to call you that as I don't know your real name."

She laughed. "As far as the bugs are concerned you're living up to your reputation. Casanova Grimes, the terror of the space ways."

"Do people really think of me like that?"

"Some of them do. Pirate, libertine. . . . Oh, you've a reputation all right."

"Mphm."

"If Bardon thinks that you're spending all your time womanizing he'll not be expecting you to start putting your foot down with a firm hand."

"Mphm."

He looked at her. It was obvious that she was enjoying being herself and not playing the part of a faithful handmaiden.

He said, "You were just going to tell me who you're really working for when Raoul came in."

"Yes, I was. Do you really want to know, Your Excellency?"

"As long as we're in private you can call me John."

"I am honored, John. I'm with Pat."

With Pat? Did she mean that she had an Irish boyfriend, Grimes wondered, and therefore out of bounds as far as he was concerned? But PAT was an acronym, he remembered. PAT. People Against Tyranny. He recalled the first time that he had heard of this organization; it was during a spell ashore between ships at Lindisfarne Base. A dictatorial planetary president had been assassinated and PAT had claimed the credit for this act of justice. There had been some discussion of the affair in the junior officers' mess.

"Aren't you running rather a risk telling me, Su?"

"I don't think so, Captain Grimes, Survey Service Reserve."

"My Reserve Commission is supposed to be a secret."

"It is—and PAT CC, Pat Central Committee, are among those keeping that secret."

"Do you mean to tell me that Admiral Damien is one of your members? If ever there was a tyrant, he's one!"

"So you say. But we have members everywhere. On Electra, for example. Silverman, the scientist/salesman, really came here just to check the bugs in the Residence and to supply me with the counter measure. But getting back to Damien—didn't it ever occur to you that, when he was O.C. Couriers and you a courier captain, he was always sending you on missions in the hope, usually realized, that you'd throw a monkey wrench into somebody's machinery at the right time?"

"You could look at it that way."

"And when it was necessary to put a stop to the privateering operations of Drongo Kane and the Eldorado Corporation—just who did Admiral Damien pressgang back into the Survey Service?"

"Me. All right, then. Since PAT seems to have been using me for the Odd Gods of the Galaxy alone know how many years, why have I never been asked to become a member?"

"Because you're an awkward bastard. You'd be as liable to throw a monkey wrench into our machinery as into anybody else's."

"Then why are you spilling all these beans?"

"Because I was told to do so. It was decided that you should know that there is a galaxywide organization behind you—as long as you're doing the right things. And that if you do the wrong things—there's a nasty, mercenary streak in your nature—you'd better try to make a get-away to the Magellanic Clouds."

Grimes got up from his chair and began to pace back and forth. He managed to light his pipe—on the run, as it were—before Su Lin could do it for him.

He said, "I don't like being manipulated."

"You haven't been manipulated all the time," she told him.

"And this nasty, mercenary streak you accuse me of having. . . ."

"What shipowner doesn't have one?"

"Some more than others. More than me."

"So you say." Her smile robbed the words of offense.

It did more than that, making her look very attractive. And, he knew now, there was no longer that master-servant relationship to deter him from entering into a relationship with her. But would she now renew the offer that she had made when, so far as he then knew, she was no more than a serving girl?

She was still smiling at him, on her feet and facing him. She did not break away when he took her in his arms—but she did not put her own arms about him. She did not turn her lips away from his— but she did not open them.

When the kiss—such as it was—was over she said, "As well as being mercenary, you're snobbish. You had the offer, your first day here, and you turned it down. And now that you know that there's no great social gulf yawning between us you think that we'll fall happily into bed together."

Now Grimes was really wanting her. He kissed her again, brutally, and, holding her to him, walked her backwards into the bedroom. He threw her on to the couch. She sprawled there, looking up at him. And was that contempt in her expression—or pity?

She said, "When I first met you, you were making the rules. Now I'm making them. You can have me when I'm ready—and not before. Once you've proven yourself to be as good a man as Governor Wibberley was. . . ."

"You mean that he and you. . . ."

"Try to get your mind off sex, John. He was a *good* man, a religious man. A Bible-basher you'd call him—but, unlike so many

Christians, he really tried to live according to his faith, to comfort and succor the helpless. Even agnostics such as myself could appreciate him, to say nothing of the mess of Anarchists, Confucianists, Buddhists and the Odd Gods alone know what on this planet. We—the various undergrounds and PAT—hope that you will carry on his work, the restoration of hope and dignity to the refugee peoples, the suppression of Bardon's rackets. . . ."

"Get off your soap box, Su," said Grimes tiredly. "I'm here to do a job and I'll do it to the best of my ability. I'll expect some pay for my work—after all, I have that nasty, mercenary streak in me—but, if all goes well, I'll arrange it myself. It won't cost PAT anything. It won't cost *you* anything. And now, if you'll excuse me, I'd like to go to bed. By myself."

"I certainly do not intend otherwise."

She got up from the bed and walked slowly out of the room.

"Call me at the usual time," Grimes called after her.

∿ Chapter 17 ∿

THE NEXT DAY Grimes had been looking forward to taking a test flight in *Fat Susie* but, while he was having his breakfast, Jaconelli brought him a list of the day's appointments. He was to be host at a luncheon, he learned, for Madam President and her ministers. After this he was to accompany her to the official opening of the new Handicrafts Center just outside Libertad. After that he was free—for what little remained of the day.

He spent the forenoon familiarizing himself with the Residence, guided by Wong Lee and with Su Lin and Lieutenant Smith in attendance. It was one of those buildings that seemed to have just happened, additional rooms and facilities being tacked on to an originally quite small house as required. The servants' quarters were underground, as was the kitchen. Grimes lingered here, using a pair of long chopsticks handed to him by the chef to sample tidbits from various cooking utensils. He did some more nibbling during his tour of the storerooms.

There were the vaults in which the records were stored—or had been stored. Filing cabinets were empty and the only information available from the read-out screens was purely domestic—food, light, heating and wages bills for the past decade and the like. Grimes found details of the last official luncheon given by his predecessor. Wibberley had been English and had fed his guests on pea soup, Dover sole (were there sole in Liberia's seas?), steak and kidney pie, trifle and a cheese board featuring Stilton, Wensleydale and cheddar. He wondered how the New Cantonese kitchen staff had coped with this feast. To judge by the two breakfasts that he had already enjoyed they had probably made a very good job of it—just as they would almost certainly do with the menu that he had ordered.

He returned to his quarters to change from shirt and slacks into an informally formal lightweight suit. Su Lin. the dutiful handmaiden, assisted him unnecessarily to dress. She walked with him out to the portico where, with Jaconelli and the ADC, he waited to receive the guests.

Bardon, wearing a dark blue civilian suit that was almost a uniform, rode in with Estrelita O'Higgins in the presidential limousine. The President was in superbly cut blue denim with scarlet touches. The ministers and their companions were similarly clad. Before luncheon there were drinks in one of the big reception rooms.

The Colonel cornered Grimes while the Governor was graciously circulating among the guests.

He said abruptly, "I hear that my Lieutenant Duggin isn't good enough for you, Your Excellency."

"Frankly, Colonel, he isn't," said Grimes. "In any case I'd already made my own appointment of an atmosphere pilot."

"I was hoping, Your Excellency," said Bardon, "that you, with a military rather than an academic background, would be more cooperative with the Garrison than the late Governor Wibberley was."

"A military background, Colonel? Piracy, you mean?"

"I was referring to your Survey Service career, Your Excellency."

"In the Survey Service, Colonel, we expected a reasonably high standard of ship-handling competence."

"Ship-handling, sir? An airship is not a spaceship."

"One did not need to be an airshipman to know that Duggin was not very competent."

"You are entitled to your opinion, Your Excellency." Grimes wandered on, chatting with the other guests. Most of them,

inevitably, asked him what he thought of Liberia and then, before he
could make reply, told him what he should think.

And then the sonorous booming of a gong announced that
luncheon was about to be served.

Grimes enjoyed the meal in spite of the company; he did not
like fat cats and most of the guests could be categorized as such. The
Residence chef and his assistants had done very well. Local Crustacea,
served simply with a melted butter dressing, could almost have been
the yabbies that Grimes remembered from his younger days in
Australia. The Colonial Goose—leg of hogget, well-spiced—could
not have been better. The tropical fruit salad, its components
marinated in wine, was a suitable conclusion to the meal. There
should have been kangaroo tail soup for the first course but the
necessary ingredients had not been available on this planet.

It was Estrelita O'Higgins, sitting at Grimes's right, who
brought the luncheon party to a close.

"Your Excellency, they will be waiting for us at the Handicrafts
Center. Oh, there is no *real* hurry." She smiled. "Everybody of any
importance is here. Nonetheless, we have our obligations. Our duties."

She asked for more coffee.

Finally the party made its collective way to the waiting cars.
Grimes rode in his own official vehicle, accompanied by his ADC
and with two soldiers sitting forward, with the chauffeur. Estrelita
O'Higgins led the motorcade.

The new Handicrafts Center was a big, single-storied hall, one of
those buildings that manage to show signs of dilapidation even
before their completion. It looked like an unprosperous factory.
Outside its main entrance, which was bedecked with wilted flowers,
was a small crowd. There was a band which, at the approach of the
official cars, struck up with a selection of Australian folk songs
which, at first, Grimes found it hard to recognize; every one of them
sounded like a military march. There were the schoolchildren with
their little flags. Most of them, Grimes noted, were New Cantonese.
There were older people—teachers?—and they, too, were mainly
representative of the refugee population.

The cars stopped.

Estrelita O'Higgins, squired by Colonel Bardon, got out of hers. There was some not very enthusiastic flag waving and a ragged cheer. Grimes, accompanied by his ADC, disembarked. Was it his imagination or was the cheering a little louder?

The President, accompanied by Grimes, Bardon and the Minister of Industry, mounted a temporary, bunting-covered dais. She spoke into a microphone and her amplified voice came from the speakers mounted on the street lamp standards. She told her listeners how Liberia—that generous host!—had supplied facilities for the fitting education of the children of those to whom refuge had been given.

God bless the Squire and his relations, thought Grimes, *and keep us in our proper stations.*

Manual Silvero, the Minister of Industry, said *his* piece. He extolled the virtues of labor. A fat, short, greasy man he looked, thought Grimes, as though he had never done an honest day's work in his life.

He concluded, "And now it is my honor to request His Excellency, Commodore John Grimes, to open this well-appointed, palatial, even, training establishment."

The President led the way down from the dais. Bardon indicated that Grimes should follow her. The others came after them. They walked to the entrance, which had a scarlet, silken ribbon strung across it. A young man—a native Liberian—approached them, bearing a plump, purple cushion. On it was a pair of golden scissors. Bowing, he presented the implement to the Governor.

Grimes took the scissors, worked them experimentally. They seemed to be in order. He walked the few steps to where the ribbon barred his way to the drab looking interior of the Handicrafts Center.

And was it accidental or did somebody possess both a sense of humor and an acquaintance with Australian folk music?

Click go the shears . . .

Click went the shears and the ribbon parted.

The children cheered (because they had to) and there was a patter of polite handclapping.

⫷ Chapter 18 ⫸

GRIMES RETURNED to the Residence.

Sanchez was waiting for him in the portico.

He said, as soon as Grimes was out of the car, "I've taken her out, Your Excellency . . ."

Grimes wondered who *she* was.

"She handles quite well . . ."

"Oh. *Fat Susie.*"

"Of course. What did you think I meant, sir?"

"Come with me to my office and tell me about it." Then, to the ADC, "I'll not be requiring you any more today, Lieutenant Smith."

"Very good, Your Excellency."

As soon as Grimes and the pilot were seated Su Lin materialized with a tea tray.

"Are you switched on?" Grimes asked the girl. He realized, too late, that this would be rather a foolish question, one that would cause the snoopers to wonder, to add two and two to make at least five, if she were not.

But she was.

Grimes said, "I want to wander around the city incognito. To see for myself without having to peer through a thick screen of officials, politicians and hangers on."

"Like that Caliph of Baghdad," said Raoul. "Haroun al Raschid or whatever his name was."

"Yes."

"Governor Wibberley used to do it," said Su Lin. "I would help him with his disguise. A denim suit, false whiskers. A voice modulator. . . ."

"But how did he—how do *I*—get out of this place unobserved?"

"Wong Lee has a car," she said. "It's a van, rather, with the back enclosed. He runs into the city now and again, in the evening. He goes to the Golden Lotus Club. This is one of his recreational nights."

"And mine," said Grimes, suddenly making up his mind. "Su, could you disguise me? Is there a denim suit that would fit? Can you still lay your hands on the other things?"

"Of course."

"And would you come with me, Raoul?"

"It will be my pleasure, sir."

"Then what are we waiting for?"

He went through to his bedroom and got out of his informal suit. When he was down to his underwear Su Lin came back with a bundle of clothing and other things. She unnecessarily helped him on with the floppy-collared white shirt and the scarlet neckerchief, the blue denim suit, the black, calf-length boots. There was a full-length mirror in the wardrobe door and Grimes admired himself in it. He rather liked this rig—but he was still him.

The girl told him to sit in a chair, went behind him to carry on the work of disguise. He felt the sticky coldness as some adhesive was dabbed on to his skull behind his ears and then her hands as she firmly pressed the prominent appendages to the fast-setting gum. She came around to stand in front of him and looked down at him.

She said, "That's better. Now, open your mouth, please . . ."

He obeyed.

Her deft fingers inserted a pad, a tiny cushion covered in slick plastic, into each side of his mouth, under each cheek. He was, of course, aware of their presence although they were not uncomfortable.

"Now look at yourself," she told him.

He got up from the chair and did so. He stared at the chubby-faced stranger who stared back at him from the mirror.

He asked, "Don't I get a moustache?"

His voice was as strange as his appearance, high, squeaky almost. He could see his expression of surprise.

She told him, "The voice modulator is incorporated in one of the cheek pads. The way you look and the way you sound nobody will recognize you."

"Perhaps. But just about everybody on this world has face fungus of some kind."

"All right." She went back to the things that she had laid out on the bed and selected something that looked, at first glance, like a large, hairy insect. "This is self-adhesive," she told him. "You'll need a special spray, of course, to get it off."

Grimes looked at himself again.

That heavy moustache suited him, he thought. It was a great pity that his modulated voice did not go with his macho appearance. He supposed, ruefully, that he couldn't have everything.

He took the broad-brimmed black hat, with its scarlet ribbon, that the girl handed him, went through to the sitting room. Sanchez got up from the chair in which he had been sitting when Grimes entered. At first Grimes did not recognize him; the tuft of false beard on his chin was an effective disguise.

Sanchez asked, "Ready, Joachim?"

"Joachim?"

"You have to have a name."

"Joachim, then," agreed Grimes. "I rather like it." He patted his empty pockets. "What do I use for money?"

Su Lin handed him a well-worn notecase and a small handful of silver and copper coins.

She said, "At first you'd better let Raoul do the paying, until you get the feel of the local currency."

"That shouldn't be long," Grimes told her. "As a spaceman I'm used to paying for things, on all sorts of worlds, in all sorts of odd coins and pieces of paper or whatever. And now, as soon as I've found my pipe and tobacco, I'll be ready to go."

"You will *not* smoke a pipe, Joachim," said Su Lin severely.

"I've seen people smoking pipes in Libertad."

"And everybody knows that *you* smoke one. There were cartoons in the newspapers when your appointment was first announced; in every one of them you had a pipe stuck in your face. Pipe and ears—those are your trademarks."

"Mphm."

"Here's a packet of cigars, and a lighter. And now, if both of you will follow me, I'll take you to the truck."

Grimes thought that he had already acquired a fair knowledge of the geography of the Residence; he soon discovered that he had not. There was a door that he had thought was just part of the paneling in the corridor; beyond this was a corridor of the kind that, aboard a ship, would be called a working alleyway. There was a tradesman's entrance. Beyond this was the rather shabby van, in the driver's seat of which the old majordomo was sitting. Wong Lee was not wearing his livery but was looking very dignified in a high-collared suit of black silk, a round black hat of the same material on his head. He ignored Grimes and Sanchez as they clambered into the rear of the vehicle. The door shut automatically as soon as they were aboard. There was a roll of cloth of some kind on which they made themselves comfortable. The only light came from ventilation slits and that—it was all of half an hour after sunset—was fading fast.

The van started, so smoothly that the passengers were hardly aware of the motion. Raoul offered Grimes a long, thin cigar from his pack, took one himself. The two men smoked in companionable silence, broken eventually by the pilot.

He said, "Wong Lee's letting us off on the corner of May Day Street and Tolstoy Avenue. On the outskirts of the city. From there it'll be easy to get a trishaw. He'll pick us up on the same corner at 0100 tomorrow."

"And how do we fill in the time until then?" asked Grimes.

"Easily, Joachim. I'll try to give you an idea of the way in which the refugees are exploited here. We'll do a tour of the pleasure district."

"Combining business with pleasure, as it were," said Grimes.

"You can put it that way," said Raoul coldly, very coldly.

Grimes remembered, then, what he had been told when the pilot's shuttle craft brought him down from the orbiting *Sobraon* to Port Libertad, about the New Dallas girl called Mary Lou who had been one of the entertainers in the Pink Pussy Cat.

He said, inadequately. "I'm sorry, Raoul."

"There's no need to be, Joachim. I know that you're not the sort of man who'll get much pleasure from what we're going to see. You're no Holy Joe—as Wibberley was—but you have your principles."

"You hope," said Grimes, adding softly, "and *I* hope."

The van stopped.

The rear door opened to a warm darkness that was enhanced rather than dispelled by the sparsely spaced, yellow street lamps.

Grimes and Sanchez got out.

Without a word to them Wong Lee drove away.

Chapter 19

IT DID NOT SEEM TO GRIMES to be a place at which to wait for a cab—or its local equivalent—but, after a wait of no longer than five minutes, an empty trishaw, its operator pedaling lazily, drifted along, halting beside them when hailed. Yet another New Cantonese, Grimes decided, a little man, scrawny in his sleeveless singlet and baggy shorts yet with muscles evident in his thighs and calves.

Grimes clambered into the basketlike passenger compartment, which was forward of the driver, followed by Sanchez who, before mounting, ordered, "Garden of Delights."

The trishaw operator grunted acknowledgment and, as soon as his passengers were seated, began pumping his pedals. The journey was mainly through quiet side streets and, Grimes decided, more or less toward the locality of Port Libertad, the glare of lights from which was now and again to the right and now and again to the left but always forward of the beam.

They came to a street that, by local standards, was fantastically bright and bustling. There were street stalls, selling foodstuffs, from which eddied all manner of savory aromas. There were brightly lit facades, establishments whose names were picked out in multicolored lights. *The Pink Pussy Cat . . . The Dallas Whorehouse . . . The Old Shanghai . . . The Ginza . . . The Garden of Delights . . .*

The trishaw stopped.

Grimes got out and began to fumble for money. Sanchez forestalled him, tossing coins to the operator, who deftly caught them. The two men walked into the vestibule of the Garden of Delights where, sitting in a booth that was like a miniature pagoda, an elderly Oriental gentleman who could have been Wong Lee's slightly younger brother was sitting in receipt of custom.

Again Sanchez paid and led Grimes through a doorway, through an entanglement of beaded curtains, into a large, dimly lit room, the air of which was redolent with the fumes of the incense burners standing on tripods along the walls and between the tables. The decor, thought Grimes, was either phonily Terran Oriental or fair dinkum New Cantonese—but he had never been to New Canton and never would go there. (Neither would anybody else; the planet was now no more than a globe of incandescent slag.) There were rich silken hangings. There were bronze animals that could have been either lions or Pekingese dogs. There were overhead lanterns, glowing parchment globes encircled by painted dragons. There was music—the tinkling of harplike instruments, the high squealing of pipes, the muted thud of little drums.

There was a stage at one end of the hall. On it was a girl, gyrating languidly and gracefully to the beat of the music. She was attired in filmy veils and was discarding them one by one. *(And what the hell,* wondered Grimes, *did Salome have to do with China, or New Canton?)* Nonetheless he watched appreciatively. The girl was tall, high-breasted, slender-limbed. Her dance *was* a dance, did not convey the impression that she was disrobing hastily prior to jumping into the shower or into bed.

Grimes's attention was distracted momentarily by a waitress who came to their table. She was wearing a high-necked tunic that did not quite come down as far as possible, golden sandals and nothing else. She had brought two bowls of some savory mess, one of rice, what looked like a tall, silver teapot, two small silver goblets, two pairs of chopsticks. She poured from the pot into the cups, bowed and retreated.

"Your very good health, Joachim," said Sanchez, raising his cup.

"And yours, Raoul."

Grimes sipped. He had been expecting tea, was surprised—not unpleasantly—to discover that the liquid was wine, a hot, rather sweet liquor. He put the cup down, picked up his chopsticks and with them transferred a portion of rice to the sweet-and-sour whatever it was in his bowl. He sampled a mouthful of the mixture. It wasn't bad.

On the stage the dancer was down to her last veil. She swirled it around her—partially revealing, concealing, affording more glimpses, concealing again, finally dropping the length of filmy fabric. She stood there briefly, flaunting her splendid nudity. She bowed, then turned and glided sinuously from the stage. The orchestra (if one could call it that) fell silent. There was a pattering of applause.

Grimes looked around. There were not, he saw, many customers. There were men, dressed as he and Sanchez were. At two of the tables there were obvious spacers. At one of these the waitress was being mauled. Obviously the girl was not enjoying having those prying hands all over her body but she was not resisting.

"You'll not get shows like this out in the country, Joachim," said Sanchez.

(And that, thought Grimes, was the pilot's way of telling him that there could be bugs here; it was very hard, these days, to find a place that was not bug-infested.)

He said, "That was a lovely dollop of trollop. On the stage, I mean."

"She'll not be that way long, Joachim. The signs were there. Her eyes—didn't you notice?"

Grimes admitted that he hadn't paid much attention to her face.

"That faraway look. Dreamsticks. Soon she'll start to wither. The waitresses, too. But there are plenty more where they came from. Don't tell me that you haven't had the recruiters around your plantation yet."

"I thought that they were selling encyclopedias," said Grimes.

"Ha, ha!"

The music had started again, a livelier tune. The dancer who came on the stage might have been beautiful once, still possessed the remains of beauty. But her movements were clumsy; her strip act was just that and nothing more. When she was completely naked she stood there, swaying, beckoning to various members of the audience. Grimes felt acutely ashamed when he, briefly, was the target of her allure. He was ashamed for his cloth when, finally, one of the spacers got to his feet and shambled to the stage.

"They aren't going to do it *here!*" he whispered to Sanchez.

"There are rooms at the back, Joachim. She'll want to go through his pockets in privacy. Her habit's expensive. But let's get out of here. It's not very often that you have a night on the town and there are more places to sample."

"Wait till I've finished my sweet and sour," said Grimes.

The Dallas Whorehouse was their next port of call. The girls there were all tall and blonde, the music a piano on which a tall, thin and very black man hammered out old-time melodies. He was far better than the instrument upon which he was performing. Grimes recognized "The Yellow Rose Of Texas" and, in spite of himself, was amused by the very well-endowed young lady who borrowed two twenty-cent pieces from a spacer sitting just under the stage and placed one over each nipple, after which she counter-rotated her breasts without dislodging the coins. When she was finished she deftly flipped them into the cupped hands of the spaceman.

"In a few weeks' time," said Sanchez sourly, "she'll have to use paper money—and stick it on with spit."

"A pity," said Grimes sincerely.

The pilot looked at his wrist companion. "Finish your beer, Joachim. I have to show you that the big city's not all boozing and wenching, otherwise you'll be going back home with a false impression."

"Give me time to finish the tacos and this chili dip," grumbled Grimes.

Chapter 20

THE NEXT PLACE that they went to was a very dowdy house, one of a terrace, in a poorly lit side street. As they approached it Grimes wondered what sort of entertainment would be offered in such a venue: something unspeakably sordid, he thought.

There was a doorkeeper, a burly man wearing the inevitable frayed denims and the almost-as-inevitable heavy beard.

"Your contributions, comrades," he growled, gesturing toward a battered metal bowl on the table before him. There was a clink and rattle of coinage as Sanchez paid for himself and Grimes.

The two men passed through a curtained door into a hall, took seats toward the back. Grimes looked around curiously. The room, he saw, was less than half full. There were both women and men there, some of them obviously Liberians, some New Cantonese, some Negroid, some blondly Nordic. As yet there was nobody on the platform, behind which were draperies of black-and-scarlet bunting, at the end of the room.

Grimes was about to ask what was going on when a tall, heavily bearded man mounted the platform. He was followed by a fat woman, by two other men of average height and, finally, by a girl who was more skinny than slim, whose protuberant front teeth gleamed whitely in her dusky face. She took her seat at a battered upright piano; the others sat behind a long table on which were water bottles, glasses and what looked like (and were) old-fashioned microphones.

The thin girl assailed the keyboard of her instrument. The people behind the table stood up. With a shuffling of feet and a subdued scraping of shifted chairs those in the body of the hall stood up. Everybody—excepting Grimes—started losing.

> The faith of our fathers lives on in our hearts,
> The flame of their courage burns on,
> Their banners still fly. let us lift them on high.
> In the light of Liberia's sun . . .

There was more, much more. Grimes hummed along with the rather trite music while he listened to the words. This was a political meeting to which Sanchez had brought him, he decided, a gathering of the Original Anarchists. At last the song was over. Everybody sat down but the big, bearded man on the platform.

"Comrades," said this person. "Comrades, and honorary comrades . . ." (The New Cantonese? wondered Grimes. The refugees from New Dallas and other devastated worlds? So even the OAP was capable of discrimination . . .)

"Comrades. Honorary comrades. Again there is hope. Again Earth has sent us a Governor, one who may take our part, as Governor Wibberley did, against the tyranny of O'Higgins and Bardon. But I must warn you, all of you, not to place too much faith in him. After all, the man is no more than a common pirate. . . ." (Piracy, thought Grimes, wasn't exactly a common trade.) "We will support him if and when he confronts O'Higgins and Bardon. We will stand against him when he attempts to re-impose the rule of Imperial Earth.

"But what manner of man is this new Governor, this pirate Commodore Grimes? With whom shall we have to deal when the time comes? What say you, Chiang Sung?"

One of the New Cantonese got to his feet.

"I am only an under-chef at the Residence, Comrade. I have little contact with him. I have seen him, of course. He has inspected the kitchens. He was very affable. He appreciates good food. It will be a pleasure to work for such a gentleman. But Su Lin, his maidservant, can tell you more than I."

"And where *is* Su Lin?" demanded the fat woman. "Where is the Pekingese Princess? The airs and graces that she puts on when she's no more than a governor's trollop . . . Come to that—where is the Lord High Mandarin Wong Lee? With all due respect to Comrade Chiang Sung, we should exercise far greater discrimination."

"And where," demanded one of the smaller men on the platform, "is *Captain* Raoul Sanchez?" He went on, sneering heavily, "Oh, he came crying to us after that wench of his died and after his brother was murdered—or so he says. But I suppose that now he's found himself a new girl and, as we know, he's inherited his brother's soft job he'll scrub us."

Grimes heard Sanchez growl softly and gave him a sharp nudge with his elbow.

He sat through a long and boring speech by the Comrade Chairman. The more he heard the less he was puzzled by the fact that the Liberian authorities tolerated the OAP. Probably many of the men and women at this meeting were government agents. Possibly these same agents, as dues-paying members, made quite heavy contributions to the OAP working expenses. He listened to horror stories from various refugees, men and women in domestic service whose masters and mistresses, according to them, were unduly harsh. Most of such tales left him unmoved. Those servants would not have lasted long in like capacities aboard any spaceship, naval or mercantile. Those who make a practice of insolence, dumb or otherwise, should not be surprised when their employers take counter measures.

The meeting came to a close just as Sanchez was beginning to fidget and snatch ever more frequent glances at his wrist companion. The pianist again battered the long-suffering keyboard. Everybody stood up.

> *Arise, ye prisoners of starvation.*
> *Arise, ye wretched of the world,*
> *For Justice thunders condemnation*
> *And the flag of Hope's unfurled!*
> *Then comrades come rally*

> *And the last fight let us face.*
> *Fraternity and Liberty*
> *Unite the human race!*

"Time we got going, Joachim," said Sanchez.

They made their way toward the door, accepting handfuls of leaflets as they did so. They were almost out and clear when they were accosted by a large, heavily moustached man.

"New here, comrades?"

"Yes, comrade," said Sanchez. "We're up from our plantation. Somebody told us that there was an OAP meeting so we thought we'd look in."

"Interested, comrades?"

"Yes. We have drifted away from the old ideals."

"I'd like to send you some more literature, comrades. Put you on our mailing list."

"We'd be pleased with that," Sanchez said. He pulled out his notecase, took out a card and gave it to the man. "And now, if you'll excuse us. We have a date. With two of the girls from the Whorehouse."

"But you're contributing to their degradation, comrades."

"Come off it, comrade. They like their work. Or they will with us—eh, Joachim? Come on, man. We mustn't keep the ladies waiting."

As they waited for a trishaw Grimes said, "Raoul, surely you could see that the man was some sort of undercover agent."

"Of course I did."

"But you gave him a card . . ." ,

"I didn't say that it was mine, did I?" He hailed an approaching trishaw. "Come on, Joachim. We mustn't keep Wong Lee waiting."

⨳ Chapter 21 ⨳

SITTING IN THE BACK of Wong Lee's truck they talked.

"What did you think of the OAP meeting, sir?" asked Sanchez.

"Not much," said Grimes frankly. "Just an occasion to blow off harmless steam under the watchful eye of the authorities."

"You're right, sir. And the other places?"

"I've seen worse on other worlds."

"Including the encouragement to drug addiction?"

"Even that."

"But not in the same way, sir. On other planets there are pushers—but surely they are not employed by the government. The policy here, on Liberia, is that the refugees shall become so dependent on dreamsticks and other drugs that they lack the drive to achieve full citizenship."

"Are there any emancipists?" asked Grimes.

"Emancipists?"

"It's a term from Australian history, Raoul. During the days when New South Wales was a penal colony the emancipists were convicts who had been granted their freedom. More than a few of them became wealthy and influential men."

"We do have the equivalent here, sir, but there aren't many of them. There's Calvin McReady, who's one of our minor grain kings and all set to become a major one. There's Sin Fat, who owns the New Shanghai. But they regard themselves as Liberians, not as refugees, or ex-refugees. They are as money- and power-hungry as any of the native-born Establishment."

"So it was, all too often, in New South Wales," said Grimes. "But tell me, Raoul, why are you in the GAP? Is it only for personal reasons?"

Sanchez fell silent for a while, quietly smoking one of his long cigars.

Then, "There are more than personal reasons, sir. When I was a child I was taught the history of Liberia. After I left school—before, even—I could not help but see the disparity between the ideals of our founding fathers and what we have—despite all the lip service—now. . . ."

"Mphm. You went into an odd trade, didn't you, for one of your political beliefs. A spaceman has to accept discipline, take orders. Once he becomes captain he has to give orders."

"But I wanted to become a spaceman," Sanchez said. "I want to become a *real* spaceman, not a ferry master. Oh, I could never stand Survey Service discipline and spit and polish, such as you were once used to—but merchant ships are run on fairly democratic lines."

"Mphm," grunted Grimes dubiously.

"Of course, sir, what would be ideal would be a *little* ship, with no crew, of which I was owner-master. Something on the lines of that *Little Sister* of yours. . . ."

"Either accumulate at least a million credits or hire yourself out as yachtmaster to a billionairess who'll give you such a ship as a parting gift." Grimes laughed. "I did it the second way. I certainly couldn't have done it the first."

"But you must *know* people, sir."

"I do, Raoul. I do, Hinting, are you? Well, if all goes well I just might—only might, mind you—be able to get you a berth as a very junior officer in a deep space ship. After that it'd be up to you—getting in your deep space time, passing examinations and all the rest of it. There are no instant captains in deep space. But forget that we're spacemen. I'm a planetary governor who's been traveling incognito among his people. You're my guide. Tell me about the dives we were in tonight."

"First, sir, the Garden of Delights. It's owned by Colonel Bardon and Estrelita O'Higgins. The manager is one Chiang Sooey. Chiang is not yet a citizen but hopes to become one. The turnover rate of entertainers is high—Chiang likes them to take their pay in dreamsticks and the like rather than in money. . . ."

"And the dreamsticks. . . . Where do they come from?"

"One of the main sources of supply used to be the ships owned by Able Enterprises but recently a dreamweed plantation was started by Eduardo Lopez. . . ."

"The Minister for Immigration?"

"The same. There was an influx of refugees from Bangla—there was some sort of Holy War there. Dreamweed comes from Bangla. The people there use it but they're immune to its worst effects. They were recruited to work on the Lopez plantation. The occasional leaves they smoke or chew will not reduce their capacity for hard work."

"And the other people, the customers, who get hooked have to work like bastards to feed their habit."

"Yes. And burn themselves out. And now, the Texas Whorehouse. Owned by a syndicate of Bardon's officers. Managed by Lyman Cartwell, of New Dallas origin. Like Chiang Sooey, not yet a citizen but hopeful of becoming one. It's not at all likely, he's become a dreamstick addict himself."

"I take it that the clipjoints—how much do I owe you, by the way?—that we didn't patronize are all very much the same insofar as ownership is concerned."

"With the exception of the New Shanghai, of course. And I'll let you have a detailed accounting as soon as possible, sir."

"Do that, Raoul."

"To date, sir, you've just seen the glamorous—*glamorous*, ha, ha!—side of the exploitation of the refugees. You've yet to see the conditions on the farms and plantations—the living quarters, the company stores . . ."

"It's time," said Grimes, "that you and I took *Fat Susie* out for an airing. A leisurely tour of my domain. . . ."

"I'd like that, sir."

Obviously the van was slowing.

It stopped and the rear door slid open.

Grimes and Sanchez jumped down to the ground, found themselves standing by the tradesmen's entrance of the Residence. Su Lin was waiting for them there. After a brief word of greeting she led them inside the building and through a maze of passageways to the Governor's quarters. She produced the inevitable tea. After this had been sipped she brought out a bottle of solvent and, applying it with gentle hands, removed Grimes's false facial hair. Sanchez attended himself to the stripping of his own disguise.

The pilot said good night and departed for his accommodation. The girl stayed with Grimes and insisted on preparing him for bed. She did not offer to share his couch with him.

~ Chapter 22 ~

AFTER A NOT TOO EARLY breakfast Grimes sent for Sanchez.

Su Lin was present while the two men studied charts spread on the desk in the Governor's office. Whatever the bugs picked up and reported would not be what was actually being said.

"I suggest, sir," said the pilot, "that we start by flying to the McReady estate. There are mooring facilities there."

"A surprise visit, Raoul?"

"More or less. We'll give him a call about an hour before we're due. That'll give him time to muster a few hands and to get his own blimp away from the mast and into the hangar."

"It sounds rather high-handed."

"You're the Governor, sir."

"But not an absolute monarch. Mphm."

"If we cast off at noon," said Sanchez, "we should arrive at about 0900 hours, McReady's time, tomorrow morning. The actual flying time will be seventeen hours, weather permitting. At this time of the year there shouldn't be much wind, either with us or against us. Would you mind standing a watch or two, sir? There's an automatic pilot, of course, but I'm old-fashioned. I feel that the control room should be manned at all times."

"So do I," said Grimes.

"I can stand a watch too," put in Su Lin. "I may not hold any licenses or certificates but I can handle lighter-than-air craft."

"Did you fly with Governor Wibberley?" Grimes asked.

"No. I learned . . . elsewhere."

"But what gave you the idea that you were coming with us?"

"The Lord High Governor must have his personal maidservant in attendance, mustn't he? Who's going to make your tea and cook your meals?"

"I can handle an autochef," Grimes told her huffily. "When I was by myself in *Little Sister* I fed quite well. I don't need a huge kitchen, such as here, with hordes of chefs and scullions."

"Three watches will be better than watch and watch, sir," said Sanchez.

"I suppose so. But you're the expert, Raoul. Shall we need any crew apart from the three of us?"

"What for?"

"As long as you're happy," said Grimes, "I am. I don't want any of Smith's nongs in my hair. Come to that—I don't want Smith himself, even though he is alleged to be my ADC."

"He hates flying," said Su Lin. "Whenever possible he found some excuse to avoid accompanying Governor Wibberley on his flights."

"He knew what was going to happen," said Sanchez bitterly.

"Could it happen to me?" asked Grimes interestedly. "To us?"

"*Fat Susie* is clean," the pilot told him. "So far. And I've set up an intrusion recorder that will let me know if anybody has been sniffing around her during my absence."

"One of *your* electronic toys, Su Lin?" asked Grimes.

"Yes."

"Then all right. Raoul, get *Fat Susie* ready for flight. I'll see Smith and Jaconelli and tell them that I shall be away from the Residence for a while."

"Perhaps you'd better tell Madam President and Colonel Bardon as well," suggested Su Lin.

Sanchez left.

Grimes picked up the telephone on his desk, was able to get in touch with the ADC and the secretary without any trouble. After a very short while they came into the office.

"Good morning, gentlemen," said Grimes.

"Good morning, Your Excellency," they chorused.

"Captain Sanchez and I are going to take *Fat Susie* out for a trial flight. I can't be sure when I shall be back."

"Will you require me, Your Excellency?" asked Smith.

"No, thank you. Somebody has to mind the shop during my absence, to maintain my liaison with the military. . . ." Smith looked relieved. "And you, of course, Mr. Jaconelli, will maintain liaison with the civil government. I'd like you both to pass out the necessary information regarding my temporary absence from the Residence."

"Will you be filing a flight plan, Your Excellency?" asked Smith.

"No. Captain Sanchez and I will just be swanning around, admiring the scenery, letting the wind blow us where it lists. . . ."

"It is a calm day, Your Excellency," said Smith.

"Just a figure of speech, Lieutenant."

"And should we wish to get in touch with you, Your Excellency?"

"*Fat Susie's* radio telephone system will be operative throughout."

Smith, Grimes noticed, was sneaking glances at the charts laid out on the desk. He wouldn't learn much. The one with the courses plotted on it was under all the others, the one on display was of the Lake Country, west of Libertad.

"I think that's all, gentlemen," said Grimes.

"Thank you, Your Excellency."

"And will you pack an overnight bag for me, Su Lin?"

"Very good, Your Excellency."

After having made sure that his tobacco pouch was full Grimes strolled out of the Residence and made his way to the mini-airport.

Fat Susie was swinging lazily at the low mast. The end of the ladder hanging from her control cab was just clear of the ground. Grimes caught hold of the side rails, got his feet onto the bottom step. He heard, above him, the air pump whine briefly as pressure in the atmospheric trimming cells was reduced to compensate. He climbed up to the cab, through the open door, went forward.

"Permission to board, Captain?" he asked Sanchez, who was feeding information into the auto-pilot.

"Glad to have you aboard, Commodore," replied the young man.

"What courses do you propose to steer?"

"With your permission, sir, north at first to make a circuit of Mount Bakunin. When it's erupting it's very spectacular—but it's been quiet for some years now. Of course, if it were erupting we shouldn't be going near it. After that we follow a great circle to the McReady place. That takes us over Rumpel's Canyon and, a bit farther on, the townships of Vanzetti and Princeps. . . ."

"Should be a scenic trip."

"Yes, sir."

Through an open window came the sound of a female voice.

"Ahoy, *Fat Susie! Fat Susie,* ahoy!"

Grimes looked out and down. Su Lin was standing there, two large suitcases on the ground beside her.

"Your Excellency," she called, "could you send a line down for the baggage?"

"I'll fix it, sir," said Sanchez.

Grimes watched with interest as the pilot opened a hatch in the deck of the cab, lowering through it a wire from a winch secured to the overhead. Su Lin hooked on both bags. By the time that they were inboard she was halfway up the ladder. She did not stay long in the control cab but went up into the body of the ship. Sanchez and Grimes were again discussing the navigational details of the flight when she came back.

"I've checked the autochef," she said. "It's very short on spices. No mace, no cumin, no turmeric. No . . ."

"You've time to get some from the kitchen, Su," said Sanchez. "But make it snappy." He turned to Grimes. *"Women . . ."* he said.

"Don't spoil the ship for a ha'porth of tar," Grimes told him. "Don't spoil the stew for a pinch of salt. Don't spoil the roast for a sliver of garlic. Don't . . ."

"Wasn't your Survey Service nickname Gutsy Grimes, sir?" asked Sanchez respectfully.

"It was. For some obscure reason people still find occasion to remind me of it. What time did you order the ground crew for?"

"They should be along now," said Sanchez.

And there they were, following in the wake of Su Lin, who was carrying a quite large bag. Again the winch was put to use and then, as soon as the girl was aboard, the ladder was retracted. Two soldiers clambered up the other ladder, that inside the metal tripod, to the head of the mast. Sanchez stuck his head out through a forward window of the cab, a portable loudspeaker to his mouth.

"Let go!" he shouted.

There was a faint clang as the quick release shackle at the end of the airship's mooring wire was given a sharp blow.

"Lift!" called Sanchez.

Grimes, who had been given instructions on the drill by the pilot, used the air pump to reduce pressure in the midship's trimming cell. *Fat Susie* drifted lazily astern, drifted and lifted, going up like an unpowered balloon. She cleared the Residence roof with ease. Grimes, looking out and down, saw that an almost horizontal part of it was being used as a sunbathing area by female members of his domestic staff. Apparently unembarrassed, one of the naked girls got to her feet to wave to the slowly ascending dirigible.

"Back inside, sir," ordered Sanchez. "I'm going to close the windows."

The transparent panels slid silently into place. Almost as silently the motors started. Sanchez put the wheel over, watching the gyro-compass repeater. When he was satisfied he switched to automatic.

Fat Susie, maintaining course and above-ground altitude, would find her own way to Mount Bakunin.

Su Lin came back into the control cab carrying an insulated container.

"I thought," she said, "that you would both like lunch here."

"The Governor," said Sanchez, "would like lunch anywhere."

"I resent that," said Grimes, but jocularly. From the steam that issued from the box when its lid was removed he thought that the girl had conjured up a meal of chili beef. He sat down on the settee, gratefully took the bowl and chopsticks that she handed to him.

~ Chapter 23 ~

GRIMES ENJOYED THE FLIGHT.

He had always loved dirigibles, maintaining that they were the only atmospheric flying machines that were real ships. And now he had one of his very own to play with—although it was a great pity that he was not master as well as being *de facto owner*. When he had time and opportunity, he thought, he would qualify as a pilot of lighter-than-air craft. Meanwhile • Sanchez was instructing him in the elements of airship handling, allowing him to take the controls during the circuit of Mount Bakunin.

The snow-covered upper slopes of the great, truncated cone were dazzlingly white on the sunlit side, a chill, pale blue in the shadow. The frozen-over crater lake was like cold, green stone. The lower slopes were thickly forested and even the old scars of lava flows were partially overgrown with scrub. As was to be expected in the vicinity of a high mountain there were eddies and updraughts and downdraughts. Sanchez watched alertly while Grimes steered and Su Lin, acting as altitude coxswain, turned her own wheel this way and that. He said little, just an occasional "Easily, sir, *easily. . . .*" or "Not so fast, Su, or you'll put us in orbit. . . ." *Fat Susie* made her own creaking protests at the over-application of elevators or rudder but these diminished as Grimes and the girl got the hang of their controls.

And then course was set and its maintenance left to the

114

automatic pilot. *Fat Susie* flew quietly and steadily into the darkening east, the flaming sunset astern. Dusk deepened into night and the stars, the unfamiliar (to Grimes) constellations appeared in the sky. Those directly overhead were, of course, obscured by the airship's upper structure but Su Lin was able to point out and identify those not far above the horizon.

"That's the Torch of Liberty," she said. "The bright red star at the tip of it is the Pole Star. . ."

"Mphm." (That constellation, thought Grimes, looked as much like a torch as that other grouping of stars, with Earth's Pole Star at the tip of its tail, looks like a Little Bear.)

"The Hammer and Sickle. . . ."

"I was under the impression," said Grimes, "that the founders of this colony were Anarchists, not Communists."

"They had to call their constellations something," put in Sanchez. "And that one does look like what it's called."

Su Lin went up and aft to the galley, returned after not too long with dinner for them all, a simple but excellent meal of lamb chops and some spicy green vegetable with a fruit salad to follow. Shortly after this Grimes retired to his cabin; he was taking the middle watch at the suggestion of Sanchez. "You'll want to see Rumpel's Canyon," the pilot had told him. "In the *dark?*" queried Grimes. "You'll see it all right, sir," Sanchez assured him.

Stretched out on the comfortable couch he had little trouble in getting to sleep, lulled by the slight swaying motion of the ship and by her rhythmic whispering. He awoke instantly, feeling greatly refreshed as Su Lin, calling him for his watch, switched on the cabin light. She had brought him a pot of tea.

"Rise and shine!" she cried brightly. "Rise and shine, Your Excellency!"

She put the tray down on the bunkside table and returned to the control cab.

Grimes poured and sipped tea, then got up and went into the tiny toilet facility. He finished his tea while he was dressing. He filled and lit his pipe, then went out into the narrow alleyway toward the control cab. Looking up at the gas cells, their not overly taut fabric rippling from forward to aft, he wondered how it had been in the early days of airships when the only buoyant gas available was hydrogen. It must have been hell on smokers, he thought.

He clambered down the short companionway into the cab. Su Lin turned away from the forward windows, through which she had been peering, binoculars to her eyes.

"The canyon's coming up now," she said.

She handed him the glasses. He adjusted the focus and looked. There was the hard, serrated line of the land horizon, black against the faintly luminous darkness of the sky.

"More to your left," she told him.

A spark of light . . . A town or village? But there was an odd quality about it. It was pulsing as though it were alive. The ship flew on and now there was more than just a spark to be seen. A stream of iridescence came slowly into view, a winding, rainbow river and then, most spectacular of all, a great cataract of liquid jewels.

At last the show was over, fading astern.

"Luminous organisms," said Su Lin matter of factly. "Found only in the Rumpel River. And now, sir, will you take the watch?"

"I relieve you, madam," said Grimes formally.

"She's on course and making good time. If any of the automatic controls play up the alarm will sound. Call Captain Sanchez— although that shouldn't be necessary. There's a bell in his cabin. Call him, in any case, at 0345. The clock's adjusted to McReady's time."

"So I see." Grimes lifted his hand and spoke into his wrist companion. "Advance to 0045 exactly on the word *Now.*" He watched the changing seconds on the clock. "Now."

"I'm an old-fashioned girl," said Su Lin. "I prefer old-fashioned watches—not contraptions that can do just about anything but fry eggs. Good night, sir. Or good morning, rather."

"Good morning, Su." said Grimes.

His watch passed pleasantly enough. He looked out at the dark landscape streaming past below with the very occasional clusters of light that told of human habitation. He studied the instruments— gyro compass, radar altimeter, ground, airspeed and drift indicators and all the rest of them. He looked into the radar screen and saw a distant target, airborne, and finally was able to pick it up visually, a great airliner ablaze with lights along the length of her, sweeping by on course, he decided, for Libertad.

Then, satisfied that all was in order and would remain so, he went briefly aft to the galley to make for himself a mid-watch snack—a pot of tea and a huge pile of thick ham sandwiches. He went to the galley again to make more tea, this time for Sanchez when he called him.

"You shouldn't have done that, sir," protested the pilot. "You . . . You're the Governor."

"Where are your Anarchist principles, Raoul? In any case—you're the captain and I'm only a watchkeeper."

Shortly afterward Sanchez relieved him in the control cab.

He said, "At least you and Su managed to keep your paws off the controls. I was half expecting that you'd go down for a closer look at the canyon."

"I'd have liked to, Raoul, but I was brought up to believe that the captain's word is law."

"And so, surely, is the Governor's."

"That," said Grimes, "I have yet to convince myself of."

All of *Fat Susie's* people were well-breakfasted, showered (and in the cases of Grimes and Sanchez depilated) when the airship made the approach to the McReady Estate. The morning was fine, almost windless, and below the dirigible the grainfields were like a golden sea. Reaping had been commenced and, like hordes of disciplined ants, the laborers, scythes flashing in the sunlight, were cutting a broad swathe through the wheat, the cut stalks being loaded onto hand-drawn carts. This sort of harvesting, thought Grimes, would be relatively inexpensive only if there were an abundant supply of slave labor—flesh and blood robots. And flesh and blood robots are superior to the metal and plastic ones in at least one respect; they are self-reproducing.

Ahead was what was practically a small town—the threshing sheds, the barracks, mess halls and the like. On a low hill was a sprawling building that seemed to be larger than the Governor's

Residence, tall by Liberian standards, all of four stories. In the center of its flat roof was a mooring mast from which a dirigible, smaller than *Fat Susie,* a clumsy looking non-rigid, was just casting off.

"McReady to *Fat Susie,*" came a nasal voice from the speaker of the transceiver. "The mast will be ready for you. The mooring crew is waiting."

"Thank you, Mr. McReady," said Grimes into the microphone.

He had little to do but watch as Sanchez brought the airship in. He thought that the pilot was maintaining full speed for too long—and restrained himself from backseat driving. But a dirigible, he realized, would lose way very quickly once power was cut. Such was the case. It was Su Lin who started, by remote control, the small winches that let down the weighted lines for the mooring crew to grab hold of and the other winch that paid out the stouter mooring, flexible wire rope, from *Fat Susie's* blunt nose.

The men on the roof worked efficiently.

A dozen of them held *Fat Susie* in position while two more of them clipped the end of her bow wire to the other wire from the tower. Winches whined, then there was a muffled clang as the airship's stem came into contact with the swivel cone.

"We're here," said Sanchez.

The door on the port side of the cab slid open, the ladder extended downward until it was just clear of the roof surface. Grimes looked out and down to the people awaiting him, to the tall, blue-denim-clad man with the broad-brimmed hat decorated with a silver band, to the almost as tall blonde woman in her denim shirt and full skirt. Both of them, he saw, were wearing riding boots, with silver spurs.

He thought, ironically, *Deep in the heart of Texas.*

✍ Chapter 24 ✍

GRIMES CLAMBERED down the ladder to the pebbled roof.

McReady removed his hat in a sweeping salute. The woman curtseyed. Grimes, bareheaded, acknowledged with a stiff bow.

"This is an unexpected honor, Your Excellency," drawled the man.

"I was passing," said Grimes, "and thought that I'd drop in."

The man chuckled and extended his hand. Grimes took it. The grip was firm but unexpectedly cold. And there was coldness, too, behind the pale blue eyes set in the darkly tanned, bluffly handsome features. And McReady's wife, thought Grimes as he shook hands with her, was cast from the same mold as her husband—handsome enough but a cast-iron bitch.

Su Lin came down, followed by Sanchez.

Grimes made introductions.

"This is Su Lin, my personal attendant . . ." The McReady couple nodded coldly to the girl. "And Captain Sanchez, my pilot . . ." There was more hand-shaking.

"And now, sir, how can we entertain you?" asked McReady.

"With your permission, sir, I'd like to look around your estate," said Grimes. "I want to get the feel of this world—just as a captain likes to get the feel of a ship to which he has been newly appointed."

"But why pick on *me*, Governor?"

"I want to see how outsiders, comparative newcomers, make

119

good on Liberia. After all, this entire planet is a social experiment—
and how things are turning out is of great interest to my lords and
masters on Earth."

"You've a fancy way with words, sir. And you've caught me at a
busy time: unless I get dug into my paperwork I'm goin' to be
suffocated under a pile o' bumfodder. But I can spare you Laura.
Laura, honey, will you give the Governor the five credit tour?"

"Surely, honey." Then, to Grimes, "Do you wish to start right
now, or would you like refreshment first?"

"Now, if you wouldn't mind," said Grimes.

The "five credit tour" did not include a look over and through
the McReady mansion. Grimes and his party were carried by an
elevator down to the ground floor and then out to where two
trishaws were already waiting. Laura McReady gestured and the
driver of the first one dismounted, went through the motions of
helping Grimes into the passenger carriage (he did not require such
assistance but did not wish to hurt the man's feelings) and then
assisted the woman to take her seat beside him. Su Lin and Sanchez
boarded the other vehicle unaided.

"Do you wish to see the village, sir?" asked Laura McReady.

"The village?"

"It's what we call where the laborers live."

"That will do for a start, Ms. McReady," said Grimes.

She turned her head and barked an order. The driver began
pedaling. The trishaws made their way along a rather narrow but
well-surfaced road along the sides of which tall bushes, blue-
foliaged and with huge scarlet flowers, were in luxuriant growth.
Gaudy insects, gold and crimson and metallic green, hovered in
clouds around each blossom. From somewhere came the
monotonous song of something that might have been a bird but that
probably was not.

The road wound through outcroppings of bare rock, rounded,
weatherworn, that gleamed whitely in the sunlight, then through an
orchard grown from seeds of Terran origin. The citrus scent was
heavy in the warm, still air.

They came to the village—a long street with buildings on either side, with cross streets that were little more than lanes. Bright banners—red, yellow, and blue, decorated with ideographs—depended from poles protruding horizontally from the ornate eaves of the single-storied structures.

"Shops," said Laura McReady. "Eating houses. And so forth."

Grimes sniffed the savory aromas that eddied from some of the establishments. "Eating houses? Do you think that we could look inside one?"

"If you wish, sir." Her voice was cold, disapproving. "I'm afraid that I can't recommend any of these places. Mr. McReady and I have always preferred to eat the kind of food to which we are accustomed."

The trishaws stopped. The driver of the leading one dismounted, opened the door of the passenger compartment on Grimes's side. Grimes jumped out before the man could extend a helping hand. Mrs. McReady, however, made a major production of dismounting from the vehicle like a great lady born to the purple. Even the Baroness Michelle d'Estang would not have put on such airs and graces. By the time that she had set her well-shod, silver-ornamented feet on the ground Grimes had been joined by Sanchez and Su Lin.

He led the way into the eating shop. There were a few customers there, seated around small tables. These, seeing who had come in, got hastily to their feet and bowed deeply. (To him, Grimes wondered, or to their mistress?) A middle-aged woman came out from the kitchen at the rear of the premises. She, too, bowed and murmured, "You have honored my humble establishment, Missy Laura. . . ."

"*Your* establishment? Surely it is owned by the McReady Estate, is it not?"

"I am the humble cook and manager, Missy Laura."

"And this gentleman here is the new Governor, Commodore Grimes. He wishes to sample your cooking."

"Please to take a seat, Missy Laura. This way, please . . ."

She led the party to a table, pulled out four chairs. Su Lin pushed back the one intended for her. Here she was no more than a servant. She accompanied the manageress into the kitchen. Before he took his seat Grimes looked around. The customers were still standing respectfully.

"Sit down, please," said Grimes to them.

They ignored him.

"Tell them to sit down, Ms. McReady," said Grimes to her.

"Yes, Your Excellency," she said sweetly—but her expression was not sweet.

She made a gesture and the customers resumed their seats.

She said to Grimes, "You must remember, Your Excellency, that these are only laborers."

"But human beings, nonetheless."

"You are entitled to your opinion, sir."

Su Lin and the plump manageress returned, bearing dishes of tiny spring rolls, bowls of rice and others of interesting looking pickles, chopsticks, a teapot and cups. Laura McReady condescended to take tea and, without speaking, implied that it was not to her taste. Grimes sampled a spring roll; it was delicious. He tried the pickles and liked them. Sanchez, too, was eating with a good appetite. Between them the two men cleared all the edibles on the table.

More tea was brought and with it a dish of small cookies. Grimes took the one nearest to him. It was still warm, hot almost. It must have been freshly baked. He broke the crust and was surprised to see a small square of folded paper inside. So, he thought, they had fortune cookies even on Liberia.

He unfolded the paper. The writing on it was in minuscule characters but very clear.

Pay heed to the manner in which people nourish others, and watch what they seek out for their own nourishment.

Wasn't that from the *I Ching?* He should have Magda with him here, he thought, to throw the coins and consult the Oracle of Change.

He tore the paper into tiny shreds, dropped them into the ashtray.

"What did it say, sir?" asked Raoul. "Mine says that there will be advantage in crossing the great water. I suppose that 'great water' is another way of saying 'deep space'."

Laura McReady sneered silently.

Their meal finished, the party walked out into the street, escorted to the door by the deeply bowing manageress. The question of payment wasn't mentioned; presumably the McReady Estate would be footing the bill. (They could well afford it.) Raoul Sanchez and Su Lin lagged behind, talking in low voices. Then the pilot overtook Grimes and Laura McReady, who were walking slowly along the footpath.

"Your Excellency. . . ."

"Yes, Captain Sanchez?"

"Perhaps we should inspect one of the other eating houses."

"His Excellency has already enjoyed a good lunch." said the McReady woman.

"We can inspect without eating," said Grimes. He suspected that there was some good reason for Raoul's suggestion.

"But when you have seen one you've seen them all," insisted Ms. McReady.

"Not necessarily," said Grimes.

She glared at him. Did he, he wondered, wield, as Governor, the punitive powers that he had possessed as a Survey Service commanding officer? Could he put this woman in the brig on a charge of Dumb Insolence?

Su Lin turned into one of the narrow cross streets. Sanchez followed her. Grimes and the McReady woman brought up the rear. She was almost literally seething with hostility. The girl paused outside the door of a place that was little more than a shack, waited until the others caught up with her. She lifted the bead curtain to allow Grimes, Sanchez and Laura McReady to enter before her.

The lighting inside was dim, the air musty. There were long tables and benches, most of them occupied. One of the diners saw who had come in, got to his feet, still holding his bowl in one hand, his chopsticks in the other, and bowed. There was a scraping and shuffling as other men and women followed suit. And it was not toward himself, Grimes noticed, that this obeisance was directed.

"Tell them to sit down, please," he said to Laura McReady.

She did so.

Su Lin went through to the kitchen. She returned carrying a steaming bowl and a pair of cheap, plastic chopsticks. These, with a bow, she handed to Grimes. He looked suspiciously at the mess in the bowl—like gray, slimy noodles it was, specked with green and yellow—and sniffed the sour vapor. It reminded him of the sort of mess on which he had been obliged to live, for far too long a time, during a voyage in a ship's boat, nutriment that was actually reprocessed sewage.

He lifted one strand with his chopsticks, brought it to his mouth and sucked it in. It was even worse than he had been expecting. He swallowed it, then handed the bowl and the eating implements back to the girl.

He said, "So this is how the poor live."

"Your Excellency," said Laura McReady, "the food served in this establishment satisfies the highest nutritional standards. If this were not so there would never be a good day's work done in the fields."

"Mphm." Grimes filled and lit his pipe, hoping that the fumes of burning tobacco would clear the taste of that . . . sludge from his mouth. "Once I had to eat stuff like this myself. I functioned quite well on it. But I didn't have to like it."

"These people, Your Excellency, are not like you and me. They don't know anything better."

"What about the ones in the first place?"

"Foremen and forewomen. Clerks and the like."

"More highly paid than the laborers in here?"

"Of course. You're more highly paid than . . . than a common spacehand, aren't you? But may I suggest, Your Excellency, that we continue this conversation outside?"

"Not in front of the children, eh?"

"You could put it that way," she said coldly.

They walked through the village, looking into shops in which both luxuries—sweetmeats, spices and pickles to lend savor to the staple diet, cheap jewelry to brighten drab clothing—and necessities were sold. They saw purchases being made and paid for by thumbprints on a screen-pad, recorded by some master computer. They visited a school, in which children, ranging in age from about four to fourteen, were being taught how to be good little field hands. They made the rounds of the barracks, the dormitories for males and females, the married quarters, the hospital. Somehow Su Lin had taken charge—and if Laura McReady's looks could have killed the girl would not have lived beyond that laborers' eating house.

Everything was well-maintained, spotlessly clean.

And everything was drab, drab.

For most of the people on the McReady Estate life was just a matter of going to work to earn the credited pay to buy the food to give them the strength to go to work to earn the pay, etc.

Grimes found no evidence to indicate that drugs such as dreamsticks were available to the workers—but there were shops selling a limited variety of alcoholic beverages, most of which seemed to be industrial alcohol with the addition of crude flavorings.

He sampled the so-called rum and even he didn't like it.

∽ Chapter 25 ∽

AT GRIMES'S INSISTENCE the party then went to the fields to watch the progress of the harvest. Laura McReady did her best to dissuade him but at last, sullenly, gave the necessary orders to the trishaw drivers. On the ride out they passed, bound in the opposite direction, a steady stream of large, steam-driven trucks bound for the threshing floors in the village.

Having observed the nature of the cargoes of these vehicles Grimes asked, "Why don't you thresh on the spot and just bring the grain in?"

"Why should we, Your Excellency?" asked Mrs. McReady. Then she condescended to explain. "The straw and the husks are . . . processed. They, too, have nutritional value. You, yourself, have just sampled some of the food made from such materials."

"Oh," said Grimes. "So that was the origin of the sludge we tasted. I thought that it came from something worse."

"Why should we waste good organic manure?" countered the woman.

Grimes pursued the subject.

"So your slaves get the husks and you get the grain. For export."

"Not slaves, Your Excellency. Indentured labor."

"Mphm."

They came to one of the fields, to where a line of steam trucks was awaiting cargo. They dismounted and watched for a short while the huge-wheeled handcarts being pushed in from the slowly receding line of reapers, each piled high with golden, heavy-headed stalks. Men and women, sweating in the afternoon sun, naked save for brief loincloths, tipped the loads out onto the road and then, gathering up huge armfuls of grain-bearing straw, staggered up ramps to the truck beds to restow the harvest. Human beings, thought Grimes, reduced to the status of worker ants. . . . But worker ants do not toil under the watchful eyes of overseers. And these overseers, men and women bigger and tougher-looking than the common laborers, were armed with whips, short-handled but with at least two meters of lash. Usually they just cracked these threateningly while shouting in high-pitched voices—and then Grimes shouted in protest when one of the overseers drew a line of blood on the sweating back of a frail girl.

"The lazy little bitch," said Laura McReady, "deserved it. Look at the load she's carrying!"

"Even so . . ." protested Grimes.

"Your Excellency, you are the Governor. Before you became Governor you were a spaceman. With all due respect to you, what do you know of the management of a large agricultural enterprise?"

"Very little," admitted Grimes. "But I'm learning. And I don't like what I'm learning, Mrs. McReady."

"We all have to learn unpleasant lessons, Your Excellency."

And I shall be teaching some, I hope, thought Grimes.

He led the way onto the field itself, walking between the furrows, his feet sinking into the soft soil. The incoming handcarts swerved to avoid him—or to avoid Laura McReady, who was walking close behind him. Her they knew but they would not know the new Governor. He came up to the line of reapers, stooped and sweating as they wielded their flashing sickles. He heard the cracking of the overseers' whips and their shouted orders. He saw a woman, not young, one of the gatherers, straighten up briefly from her labors and stand there, her face turned up to the uncaring sky. For some reason (and who could blame her? thought Grimes) she was weeping quietly.

She stood in tears amid the alien corn . . . Where did that come from? Not that it mattered. What did matter was that a woman was standing there, in tears, the helpless victim of a harsh economic system and of political hypocrisy.

"Su Lin," he said, "will you ask her what is wrong?"

"What does it matter, Your Excellency?" asked Laura McReady.

"It does to her, madam." said Grimes.

Su Lin went up to the woman and, in a soft voice, spoke to her in her own language. The answer came in a rather unpleasant whining voice, punctuated by sobs.

"She says, Your Excellency," Su Lin told him, "that her husband was promoted to threshing floor foreman. Now he has no time for her. He has taken up with one of the girls working under him."

"You can't blame *me* for that," said Laura McReady smugly.

Grimes ignored this.

"Tell her," he said to Su Lin, "that I am sorry. Very sorry."

And what the hell good will that do? he asked himself.

And what the hell good will that do? Mrs. McReady, to judge from the expression on her face, was obviously thinking.

She asked, "And now have you seen enough, Your Excellency?"

"For the time being," said Grimes.

"Then may I suggest that we return to the manor house?" She added, without enthusiasm, "You and Captain Sanchez will be dining with us, of course."

"Thank you," said Grimes. "And Su Lin?"

"Your servant, Your Excellency, will be able to take a meal with our own domestic staff."

And make sure that you keep your pretty ears flapping, Su, thought Grimes.

Following the line of furrows they made their way back to the waiting trishaws.

～ Chapter 26 ～

AFTER THEIR RETURN to the manor house Grimes, Sanchez and Su Lin went back briefly into the airship. There the two men showered and changed—not that they had much to change into, just fresh suits of blue denim enlivened by scarlet neckerchiefs. They held a brief conference in the control cab before making their way down to the roof.

"The setup here," said Grimes, "reminds me of what I have read of the plantations in the American deep South before the War Between The States. Instead of Negro slaves there are New Cantonese indentured labor—but the only essential difference is that of skin pigmentation. . . ."

"And nobody is strumming a banjo and singing Negro spirituals," commented Sanchez drily.

"But Commodore Grimes is right," said Su Lin. "The situation is analogous."

"Not exactly," Sanchez insisted. "Far from exactly. Where are the Yankee generals at the head of the Union armies, marching south to free the slaves?"

"It wasn't quite like that, Raoul," said Grimes. "In fact, according to some historians, the question of slavery was only a side issue. The major one was that of secession. And I don't think that Liberia has any desire to secede from the Federation." He got up from the settee, looked out and down from one of the control cab windows. "There's some sort of functionary down there. He seems to be waiting for us. We'd better go and join our gracious hosts at the tucker table."

The McReady butler, a tall, thin, pigtailed man in black-and-white brass-buttoned livery, bowed deeply to Grimes as he stepped from the foot of the ladder to the roof surface.

He said, "The Lord and the Lady are awaiting you, Your Excellency. Please to follow."

He led Grimes and the others into the elevator cage, scowled at Su Lin when she was standing too close to her master, scowled at her again when she moved to stand by him. The downward journey did not commence until the grouping of the passengers was to the butler's satisfaction—he standing in solitary state by the control panel, Grimes and Sanchez in one corner, Su Lin in another.

The downward journey was swift and smooth. The door opened. The butler was first out, bowing deeply to Grimes as he disembarked, saying. "Please to follow, Your Excellency." Then, to Su Lin. "Wait here, woman. You will be sent for."

She smiled submissively and bowed to the upper servant. She winked at Grimes.

The butler, with a slow and stately walk, led the way along a corridor the walls of which were paneled with some dark, gleaming wood, floored with the same material. There were no pictures or other decorations. They came at last to a hinged door which the butler opened with a flourish. Beyond this was a large room, paneled as was the corridor but with wall ornaments. There were the mounted heads of horned beasts and others ferociously fanged. There were highly polished firearms—antique projectile weapons, modern lasers and stunguns. There were, even, crossed cavalry sabers.

McReady and his wife got up from the deep, black-leather-upholstered armchairs in which they had been sitting. They were dressed for the occasion—the man in a silver-braided and -buttoned black jacket over a ruffled white shirt, a kilt in a tartan that Grimes could not identify (he was no expert in such matters), long socks in the same tartan, highly polished black, silver-buckled shoes. Laura McReady was in high-necked, long-skirted, long-sleeved black with a sash in the same tartan as that worn by her husband.

Both of them looked at the formally informal attire of their guests and allowed themselves the merest suggestion of a sneer.

"Your Excellency," said the woman, "we must apologize. We assumed that you, as the Governor, would be dressing for dinner."

"The rank is but the guinea stamp," quoted Grimes. "A man's a man for a' that."

"Indubitably," said McReady. He repeated the word, making it sound anything but indubitable. "But be seated, please. A drink or two before dinner, Your Excellency?"

"That will be a pleasure," said Grimes.

He and Sanchez lowered themselves into deep armchairs, facing the others across the black, gleaming surface of the low round table. There was a decanter already there, a bowl of ice cubes and, standing on ceramic coasters, tour glasses, two of which had already seen used.

"Whisky, Your Excellency? Captain Sanchez? On the rocks?"

"That will be fine," said Grimes.

"Thank you," said Sanchez.

The whisky, rather to Grimes's surprise, was not Scotch. It was bourbon. He didn't mind. It would have been improved by light conversation during its intake. Words were exchanged, of course, but it was obvious that the McReady couple were trying, without enthusiasm, to be on their best behavior and were annoyed that their guests, sartorially, had themselves made no great effort. After the second drinks—insofar as Grimes and Sanchez were concerned—had been disposed of a gong sounded somewhere outside.

The butler appeared and bowed.

"Lord McReady, dinner is served."

"Your Excellency," said McReady, "shall we proceed to the dining room?"

The dining room was a huge barn of a place, gloomy, the only lighting being from the candles set in ornate silver holders on the long, polished table. The McReady family, thought Grimes, must have a thing about black wood. McReady stood by his high-backed chair at the head of the not very festive board; Laura McReady indicated that Grimes should take one halfway down the table on McReady's right. She moved to her own chair at the foot of the table, leaving Sanchez to find his way to a position facing Grimes.

Everybody sat down.

Grimes, his eyes now accustomed to the near darkness, looked around curiously. There were paintings on the walls, ancient-looking oils, uniformly gloomy, horned beasts standing around drearily in a drizzle, another horned beast—a Terran stag?—understandably perturbed by the harassment of hounds. He had been expecting that the McReady estate would be Little Texas; it was turning out to be, inside the manor house at least, Little Scotland. And what would be for dinner? Haggis? He hoped not.

But there was no kilted piper to play in "the chief of all the pudding tribe." There was only the liveried butler supervising the activities of the New Cantonese maids, pretty little girls in short-skirted uniforms. Somebody, somewhere, had switched on music—and that had no Scottish flavor. Grimes recognized one of the tunes—"The Yellow Rose Of Texas." He wished that the local representatives of the Clan McReady would be consistent.

The first course was a soup that Grimes categorized as lukewarm varnish. The second course was some sort of flavorless fish, steamed, with a bland, uninteresting sauce. This was followed by boiled mutton accompanied by vegetables with all the goodness stewed out of them. Finally there was an overly sweet fruit tart smothered with custard. The wines, Grimes had to admit, were not too bad. Without them the meal would have been quite impossible.

Throughout there was desultory conversation.

"And what do you think of Liberia, Your Excellency?"

"I have hardly been here long enough, Mrs. McReady, to form an opinion."

"Have some more of this mutton, Your Excellency. It's from our own flocks."

"I don't think that I have room, Mr. McReady."

"Oh, but you must. Haven't I heard somewhere, Your Excellency, that your nickname in the Survey Service used to be Gutsy Grimes?"

"Just a slice, then."

"Governor Wibberley used to enjoy his visits here. It was on his way back to the Residence from our estate that he was so tragically killed."

"Oh."

Grimes looked across the table at Sanchez. Sanchez looked at him.

"That is an unusual name that you have given your airship, Your Excellency."

"How so, Mrs. McReady?"

"*Fat Susie* . . ."

"She's named after a girl I once knew," said Grimes.

"And did you *call* her Fat Susie? To her face?"

"No."

"And was she fat?"

"Well, she was . . . plumpish."

"And where is she now?"

Damn the woman, thought Grimes. *She sits there like a statue all through the meal and now, once the subject of my murky past crops up, she's putting me through the third degree . . . And what was the* official *story of Susie's disappearance?*

"I don't know," he said truthfully.

At last the meal was over.

The party retired to what McReady called the gun room for coffee and brandy and cigars. (Grimes refused the latter and stuck to his pipe.) Mrs. McReady made deliberately half-hearted attempts to stifle her yawns. Grimes said that it was time that he was getting on his way. He thanked his hosts for a very enjoyable day and evening. There was a brief session of not very warm handshaking. The butler escorted the Governor and his atmosphere pilot up to the roof where, black against the darkly luminous sky, *Fat Susie* swung at the mooring mast like an oversized windsock.

Su Lin was waiting for them aboard the airship.

She said, "Look what I found!"

She showed Grimes and Sanchez a small sphere of black metal.

"Where was it, Su?"

"Tucked in between the main gas cells."

"What is it?"

"Just a ball, an empty ball, not hidden very cleverly and bound to show up on the metal detector I used. Just a warning."

"I wish it were a bomb," said Grimes viciously, "so that I could drop it on those bastards!"

"Not selective enough," she told him. "There are quite a few nice people in the servants' quarters."

"And I suppose that you had a nice meal," said Grimes.

"Very nice, as a matter of fact. Satay, and . . ."

"Don't tell me. But if this . . . *thing* is just a warning how did they know that *you* were going to go through the ship with a fine tooth comb and find it?"

"Not me," she said, "but *you*. You are the ex-Survey Service Commander, the pirate Commodore. They're hoping that you will make a better job of cleaning up the mess here than your predecessor did." She laughed. "You know, I think that the dummy bomb was planted not by the baddies but by the goodies."

"A warning nonetheless," said Grimes.

"Too right," she said.

~ Chapter 27 ~

AS A MATTER OF COURTESY Grimes kept in radio contact with both President O'Higgins and Colonel Bardon. There seemed to be no great need for him in the capital—no schools or bridges to be opened, no official dinners or luncheons to attend. During his conversations he was deliberately vague about *Fat Susie's* flight plan. "Just swanning around," he would say. "Just letting the wind blow me wherever it listeth. . . ."

And that, for much of the time, he was actually doing. During his younger days on Earth he had acquired some expertise as a hot air balloonist and he found his old skills returning. Now he was the instructor and Raoul his pupil. With main engines shut down and only the air pumps in operation he would decrease or increase altitude in the search, usually successful, for a fair wind. The dirigible drifted over the countryside, going a long way in a long time and quite often in the right direction.

Her descents to ground were unscheduled, dropping down with very little prior warning onto the manor houses of the vast estates, her people receiving grudging hospitality ("What the hell is *he* doing here?" Grimes overheard on one occasion) from those whom Grimes, remembering his Australian history, categorized as squatters. In long ago Australia, however, there had been three classes of colonist—the wealthy squatters, the small farmers and the laborers who, in the very earliest days, had been convicts. More than one governor had sided with the little men against the big landowners. Some of them had been socially ostracized by the self-made aristocracy. One of them, the immensely capable but occasionally tactless Bligh, had been deposed by his own garrison, the New South Wales Corps, the officers of which were already squatters or in the process of becoming such.

On Liberia things were only a little different, although there were no small farmers. The status of the refugees was almost that of those hapless men and women who had been shipped out to Botany Bay in the First Fleet and its successors. Bardon's Bullies were not at all unlike the personnel of the New South Wales Corps. They were up to the eyebrows in every unsavory and lucrative racket.

There was the Lopez dreamweed plantation in the foothills of the Rousseau Ranges, an expanse of low, rounded hills covered with a purple growth that, from the air, looked more like the fur of some great animal than vegetation. The swarming, brown-skinned laborers, gathering the ripened leaves, could have been lice. There was the sprawling, red-roofed manor house with, at its highest point, a latticework mooring mast. There was a ship at this mooring, a large dirigible with military markings, crossed swords below the Terran opalescent sphere on its dark blue ground. It seemed to be taking on cargo of some kind, bales piled on the small area of flat roof space being hoisted, one by one, into its interior.

"And now, sir," said Sanchez, grinning widely, "we shall embarrass them by making our presence known. Give them a call, Su."

"*Fat Susie* to Lopez Control," said the girl into the transceiver microphone. "*Fat Susie* to Lopez Control. Do you read me?"

"Lopez Control here," came the answer at last in a very bored voice. "What do you want?"

"Request mooring facilities."

"You'll just have to wait, *Fat* . . ." There was a long pause, then, "What did you say your name was?"

"*Fat Susie.* And, in case you're wondering, the Governor, Commodore Grimes, is on board."

Loading operations had ceased, Grimes saw, looking out and

down through his binoculars. Loading operations had ceased but work had not. The remaining bales on the rooftop were being rolled into a large penthouse—from which, no doubt, they would hastily be taken down and stowed somewhere out of sight.

A fresh voice issued from the speaker of the transceiver.

"R273. Major Flattery commanding\ to *Fat Susie*. My compliments to His Excellency. I am casting off now so that you may approach the mast. May I ask how long you will be staying here?"

"Tell him," said Grimes, "that I don't know."

Su Lin passed on the message.

"*Fat Susie*," said Flattery, "please inform His Excellency that I am on urgent military business and have a schedule to keep. I would like to know how long I shall be delayed."

"Tell him," said Grimes, "that I am on governmental business."

"*Fat Susie*," said the major (he must have overheard Grimes's instructions to Su Lin), "please inform His Excellency that I shall be obliged to inform Colonel Bardon that my schedule has been disrupted. Over and out."

R273 cast off drifted lazily astern from the mast. Flattery was in no hurry to start his engines. Sanchez, coming in against the wind, passed closely to the larger ship. Grimes could look into the control cab, saw a ferociously moustached face scowling at him through one of the windows. Major Flattery, he assumed. He waved cheerfully. Flattery did not acknowledge the salutation.

The mooring party—dark-skinned men in startlingly white loincloths and turbans—was waiting for *Fat Susie*. She was brought to the mast smartly enough, hooked on. A tall, thin man, in a white tunic with a scarlet sash, white-trousered but barefoot, stood at the foot of the ladder, extended a hand to assist Grimes as he stepped down from the platform. Then he put his hands to his turbaned forehead and bowed deeply.

"Sahib. The Burra Sahib and the Burra Memsahib await you."

Aren't I a Burra Sahib? wondered Grimes.

He followed the man into the penthouse with Su Lin a couple of steps behind him. Sanchez was staying with the ship; it had been decided not to ignore the warning, dummy bomb that had been planted at the Me Ready estate. The rooftop shelter was a big one, being intended for the handling of freight as well as passengers. Grimes sniffed suspiciously. The air still carried a sickly sweet aroma. Dreamweed. It would not be wise, he thought, to inhale too deeply.

There was a large car for cargo, a much smaller one for passengers. Inside this cage the air was free of taint. The downward journey was smooth and swift. The vestibule into which they emerged had a tiled floor, black and white in a geometrical pattern which was repeated on the tiled walls. From somewhere came the tinkling music of a fountain accompanied by bird song. This could have been a recording but Grimes didn't think that it was.

The butler led Grimes and Su Lin through a succession of arches, bringing them at last to a large, airy room, the floor of which was covered with beautiful carpets. There were others, even more beautiful, on the walls, tapestries almost, with strutting peacocks, prowling tigers and brightly clad horsemen doing unkind things to fierce looking boars with their long lances.

At a low table Eduardo Lopez and Marita Lopez were sitting on piles of cushions, sharing a narghil. The fat little man, in white silk shirt and trousers, with crimson cummerbund and slippers, could have been an old-time Oriental potentate. His wife, in gauzy white trousers and bodice, could have been an overblown harem beauty.

"Lopez Sahib," announced the butler, "the Governor Sahib and . . ." He paused to look doubtfully at Su Lin. "The Governor Sahib and his servant."

Lopez put down the mouthpiece of the pipe onto the inlaid surface of the table. He got slowly to his feet. His wife remained seated.

"A good day to you, Your Excellency. Had we been expecting you we would have arranged a proper reception."

"I like to keep things informal," said Grimes.

Meanwhile Su Lin had collected more brightly covered cushions, had put them down by the table.

"Please be seated, Your Excellency," she said to Grimes.

Grimes sat, cross-legged. Lopez resumed his own seat. He, his wife and Grimes were the points of an equilateral triangle about the round table. Grimes sniffed the fumes that were drifting from the bowl of the water pipe. Mainly tobacco, he decided, but with some addition.

"You will smoke, Your Excellency?" asked Lopez. He clapped his hands. "Ram Das! A pipe for the Governor Sahib!"

"I'll use my own, thanks," said Grimes hastily. "And my own tobacco."

Su Lin made a major production of filling and lighting the vile thing for him. Mrs. Lopez went into a paroxysm of coughing.

When she was quite finished Lopez inquired, "And how may we serve you, Commodore Grimes? And may I presume to ask why you are honoring us with your presence?"

"A sort of captain's inspection," said Grimes. "A tour of spaceship Liberia. Just finding out what lives where and what does what. After all, this world is my new command."

"It could be argued," said Lopez mildly, "that Madam Estrelita O'Higgins is the captain of spaceship Liberia."

"A sort of staff captain, perhaps," Grimes said. "And, carrying on with the astronauticai analogy, Colonel Bardon is the master at arms. But I am the master. My name is on the register."

"I am not a spaceman," said Lopez, "but I think I see what you mean. I do necessarily agree with you."

For what seemed a long time the Lopez couple and Grimes smoked in silence, Su Lin and Ram Das watching them impassively. Then Grimes asked a question.

"What was that army dirigible doing here, Mr. Lopez?"

"Major Flattery is a personal friend, Your Excellency. He was paying a social call."

"Indeed? His ship seemed to be loading some sort of cargo."

"It is our custom," said Lopez, "to make small gifts to our departing guests."

"Indeed? And I suppose that these same guests make gifts to you in exchange. Like folding money."

"A plantation owner," said Lopez coldly, "expects to make some small profit."

"Talking of plantations," said Grimes, "I would like to inspect yours."

"I have nothing to hide, Your Excellency," stated Lopez. "Ram Das, ask Mendoza Sahib to attend me here. At the same time arrange for two trishaws to be waiting in the portico."

"To hear is to obey, Sahib."

The butler silently left the room.

~ Chapter 28 ~

GRIMES LOOKED CURIOUSLY at Mendoza when that gentleman eventually made his appearance. He could have been a survivor from the long defunct British Raj in India. He was tall and thin, deeply tanned, black-haired and with a pencil-thin moustache. His eyes were startlingly blue against the dark skin of his face. He was clad in spotless white—shoes, trousers with a knife-edge crease, a high-necked, gold-buttoned tunic. Under his left arm was a white sun helmet.

He stiffened to attention as he faced his employer.

"Sir?"

He could have been a subaltern of some crack Indian regiment of the old days called before his colonel to be given his orders.

"Ah, Mr. Mendoza. This gentleman is the new Governor, Commodore Grimes . . ."

Mendoza bowed stiffly in Grimes's direction. Grimes disentangled his legs and, with Su Lin's assistance, got to his feet. He extended his hand. After what seemed to be a long hesitation Mendoza took it. It was like, thought Grimes, getting a fistful of cold, wet, dead fish.

"The Commodore," said Lopez, "would like a tour of the plantation. I assume that his . . . er . . . servant will accompany him."

"Yes," said Grimes, "Su Lin will be coming with me."

"You spacemen!" chuckled Lopez. It was a dirty chuckle. He

flinched under Grimes's hostile glare then went on hastily, "I beg your pardon, Your Excellency, but members of your profession do have a reputation, you know."

"If a world such as New Venusberg," said Grimes coldly, "were obliged to depend upon spacemen for its prosperity it would very soon go bankrupt."

"Yes, yes. Of course. I was merely jesting. And now, if you will accompany Mr. Mendoza, he will show you everything that you wish to see. Dinner will be awaiting you on your return. Do you appreciate Oriental cuisine, such as Indian curries?"

Grimes said that he did. Then he and Su Lin followed Mendoza from the room, leaving Lopez and his consort to the enjoyment of their shared pipe.

The trishaws were waiting in the portico, each powered and piloted by a scrawny man, both of whom had an almost black, dusty skin. Two pairs of yellow eyes regarded Grimes and the girl incuriously, looked to Mendoza with a mixture of respect and fear. Fear was predominant.

"Will you ride with me, Your Excellency?" asked the plantation manager. "Your servant can bring up the rear."

Grimes would far sooner have ridden with Su Lin but the arrangement proposed by Mendoza made sense. He would be able, when sitting alongside the visitor, to point things out and to explain. (He would be able, too, to distract Grimes's attention from things that he should not be seeing.)

He climbed into the passenger basket of the leading trishaw while the driver sat impassively, his gnarled feet on the pedals. Mendoza joined him. The man was redolent of some male perfumery. Grimes sniffed disgustedly. He would much sooner have been smelling Su Lin's clean scent.

Mendoza gave orders in a language strange to Grimes. Then, "Jao!" he snapped. "Juldi jao!"

"Atcha, Sahib!"

The trishaw took off like a rocket, its spinning wheels spattering the loose gravel of the driveway to port and to starboard. Grimes turned his head to look astern. The vehicle with Su Lin was following.

"We shall pass, first, through the laborers' compound," said Mendoza. "As you will see, Your Excellency, our workers are well and adequately housed."

Well and adequately housed they may have been, although Grimes had his doubts. The trishaws sped between rows of barrack-like buildings, drab gray, of poured concrete construction. The windows were tiny, unglazed, some screened by dirty rags fluttering lethargically in the light breeze. There seemed to be children everywhere—black, skinny, naked brats of both sexes. But they were not running and shouting and screaming as children should. They were squatting silently in the dust, staring at nothing. There were a few adults abroad—withered, ancient crones shuffling on their various errands, old men sitting in doorways conversing among themselves in low voices.

These adults, despite their apparent age, seemed to be showing far more life than did the children. They stood up as the two trishaws passed, salaaming deeply. And Grimes thought that he read hate in their yellow eyes.

"Mr. Mendoza," he said, "shouldn't these kids be at school?"

"School, Your Excellency? What for? Whatever skills they will need when they join our work force they will learn from their parents."

"Shouldn't they be . . . playing?"

"Playing, Your Excellency?"

"Yes. I've seen children on more worlds than you've had hot dinners and, more than once, I've cursed the noisy little bastards. But these. . . . Anybody would think that they were doped."

"They are, Your Excellency."

"What!"

"It is their way of life. Their parents start them on the dreamweed almost as soon as they are weaned. By adolescence they have built up at least a partial immunity and are able to function as members of the work force."

"What a life!" exclaimed Grimes.

A. Bertram Chandler

"They have never known any better, Your Excellency. And who can say that they are not happy, sitting there and dreaming their dreams?"

"Would you want *your* children to grow up like that, Mr. Mendoza?"

"I have no children, Commodore Grimes. It is extremely unlikely that I shall ever be a father. To me the necessary preliminaries, undertaken with a woman, would be extremely distasteful."

His voice must have carried. From the following trishaw came Su Lin's scornful laugh.

The manager lapsed into sullen, haughty silence. The vehicles sped on, hardly slackening speed when, once they were clear of the compound, there were hills to negotiate. The road was now a winding one, threading its way between hillocks on each of which the fleshy stems and leaves of the dreamweed flourished. In this locality the crop was not yet ready for harvesting; the predominant colour of the vegetation was a greenish blue. As they progressed, however, Grimes saw an increasing number of purple leaves.

And then they came to an area in which the harvest was in full swing. On either side of the winding roadway rose the glowing purple mounds, over which crawled the small, dark-skinned people, their white loincloths in vivid contrast to the almost-black of their thin bodies. They were working in pairs—usually it was the man who wielded the knife, hacking the fleshy leaves from the thick, convoluted stems while a woman filled a basket with the yield. Filled baskets stood by the roadside, awaiting collection. Overseers moved among the workers. These wore white jackets and turbans as well as loincloths. Their skin was lighter than those of the laborers, their build heavier. They carried short whips.

The air was heavy with a sweet yet acrid aroma. Grimes wondered if it were safe to breathe. He asked Mendoza as much.

"Perfectly safe, Your Excellency," the manager told him scornfully. "The dreamweed has to be taken orally—chewed and swallowed. If you care to look you will see the fieldhands doing just that. Doesn't it say in the Bible, 'Thou shall not muzzle the ox that treads the corn'?" He barked an order to the trishaw driver and the vehicle slowed to a crawl, as did the one carrying Su Lin. "On the other hand, it is not desirable that the ox make a pig of himself. As that man there is doing."

The person indicated was working far more slowly than the others. The leaves that he was hacking from the stems he was stuffing into his busily chewing mouth while his woman, holding her almost empty basket, watched.

An overseer was making his way around and over the tangle of stems, shouting angrily. The man paid no heed, although his woman put out a hand to try to catch his wrist as he was raising another bundle of leaves to his mouth. He shook her off, went on chewing. The overseer was now within striking range. He raised his whip and used it, slashing the addict across the face. The laborer screamed shrilly. He brought up his long, heavy knife to ward off the whip that was descending for a second blow. And then there was a flurry of fast action, after which the whipwielder was staring stupidly at his right wrist from which the bright red, arterial blood was spurting, then at his hand, still clutching the whip, on the ground at his feet. The woman was wailing loudly; it seemed odd to Grimes that so loud a noise could come from so small a body. But she was soon quieted. The knife silenced her, slashing down onto the juncture of scrawny neck with thin shoulder.

There was blood everywhere.

On the hillock both workers and overseers were scrambling desperately away from the scene of the maiming and the killing. Down in the road the trishaw drivers were attempting to turn their vehicles so that they could return to the safety of the compound. The madman, purple froth spattering from his working mouth, his yellow eyes glaring, was jumping down the hillside toward them, miraculously avoiding being tripped by the tangled roots and stems.

Su Lin's trishaw was around, making off downhill. Grimes's trishaw was turning. As it did so it heeled over. Mendoza fell heavily against Grimes—and Grimes fell out on to the roadway. He scrambled to his feet. He would have run but, in his fall, he had twisted his right leg. He was weaponless. He looked around frantically. A stone to throw at the fast advancing homicidal maniac . . .

But there weren't any stones, and it was a very long time since, as a very junior officer in the Survey Service, he *had* taken a course in unarmed combat.

He decided that if he were to die all his wounds would be in front. He would not turn his back on his murderer. And perhaps—perhaps!—he might be able to cow the man into submission with his best quarterdeck glare . . .

The killer was down on the road now, loping toward Grimes. Grimes stood there, facing him.

"Stop!" he barked.

And the man did stop and momentarily—but only momentarily—the light of sanity gleamed in his yellow eyes. Then he came on again, the bloody knife upraised.

"Stop! Drop that knife!"

The man came on.

Grimes heard running feet behind him. So Mendoza, he thought, had returned to sort things out. Presumably he was used to such emergencies and, probably, armed.

But it was not Mendoza. It was Su Lin. She ran past Grimes as he shouted at her, "Get back, you stupid bitch! Get back!"

She had something in her right hand, something small that gleamed golden in the sunlight. Grimes recognized it. It was the lighter that she had used to ignite the tobacco in his pipe.

He staggered after her. He had to save her from the madman, even though it might cost his own life.

The maniac screamed dreadfully. Before he threw up his hands, his knife dropped and forgotten, to cover his face Grimes saw the two-meter-long flame, a thin pencil of intense radiance, that slashed across the mad, staring eyes, searing and blackening them. There was a sickening stench of burned flesh in the air. Then the man, hunched and moaning, turned and shambled blindly away. Sightless, he could not keep to the road. He crashed into the dreamweed plants, tripped and fell heavily. His thin, high whining was a dreadful thing to hear.

Su Lin, the lethal lighter back in a pocket, stopped to pick up the knife.

"What . . . What are you going to do?" asked Grimes.

"Finish him off quickly," she said. "It will be the kindest way."

She was right, of course.

Grimes made no attempt to stop her but did not watch.

∽ Chapter 29 ∽

THE TWO TRISHAWS RETURNED.

Mendoza got out of the leading one, walked past Grimes and Su Lin to where the huddled form of the dead maniac was sprawled face down, the hilt of his knife protruding from his back. Two of the overseers were squatting by the corpse, talking in low voices. The manager went to them, was obviously questioning the men. He returned to the governor and the girl. His expression, decided Grimes, was an odd combination of condemnation and disappointment.

He said, "This is a serious matter."

"Too right it is," said Grimes. Then, "And where were *you* when the shit hit the fan?"

"A man is dead, Your Excellency."

"For all the help that you were, I could be dead too. As for your dead man—he is responsible for one death himself. Possibly two."

"But this is a serious matter, Your Excellency. This woman may be your servant but she is a native of this world—and not a citizen. Only citizens may carry weapons."

"Only citizens, Mr. Mendoza?" Grimes gestured toward the dead man. "Was *he* a citizen? What about his knife?"

"A working tool, Commodore."

"And a murder weapon."

Mendoza ignored this.

He said to Su Lin, "Give me your flamethrower, girl. It will have to be produced as evidence when you are brought to trial."

Grimes thought hard and fast.

He said, "It is not hers to give to you, Mr. Mendoza."

"What do you mean?"

"It is *my* lighter. During my career as commodore of a privateer flotilla *I* found it convenient to carry on my person gadgets such as that lighter—seemingly innocent but capable of being used in selfdefense . . ." While he was speaking he was filling his pipe. "I had to use it once," he went on untruthfully, "to quell a mutiny . . ."

"Then what is *she* doing with it?"

By this time the bit of Grimes's pipe was between his teeth. Su Lin lit it for him, using a flame of normal dimensions and intensity.

"You see what she's doing with it," Grimes said through a cloud of acrid smoke. "She regards this as part of her duties."

"Like stabbing a blinded man in the back, Your Excellency."

"He would not have lived," said Su Lin. "Not only was he blinded but his brains were fried."

"This is a matter for Mr. Lopez," said Mendoza stiffly.

"Naturally," agreed Grimes. "After all, it was one of his employees—or slaves—who would have murdered me had it not been for Su Lin."

"It was one of his employees who was murdered by your servant, Your Excellency. At the very least there will be a heavy claim for compensation."

"Quite possibly," said Grimes. "I shall have to look into the legal aspects. I am not as young as I was and being attacked by homicidal maniacs puts a severe strain upon my nervous system. It is likely that I shall require the services of an expensive psychiatrist to undo the mental damage that I sustained." He drew deeply from his pipe and then exhaled the smoke. "But no doubt Mr. Lopez is rich enough to pay both the doctor's bill *and* the damages that I shall demand."

"Your Excellency," almost sneered Mendoza, "is quite a space lawyer."

"As far as this planet is concerned," growled Grimes, "I am the law—and the prophets. The members of my personal staff answer only to me, and don't go forgetting it. Come, Su Lin, we will share a trishaw back to Mr. Lopez's not so humble abode. Mr. Mendoza can do as he pleases."

The two of them clambered aboard one of the waiting vehicles.

"Home, James," ordered Grimes, "and don't spare the horses."

To his surprise the man understood. It was a pity as it meant that he and the girl were not able to compare notes during the ride back to the Lopez establishment.

Understandably Mr. Lopez was not pleased when he heard Grimes's story. He would have been far happier, Grimes could not help thinking, if Mendoza had returned alone with the news of the murder of yet another troublesome planetary governor. And yet, Grimes knew, the messy affair had not been planned. How could it have been? But Mendoza had been quite prepared to let nature take its course and would have been commended rather than otherwise if Grimes had been hacked to pieces.

"A sorry business, Your Excellency," sighed Lopez.

"It could have been sorrier still as far as I'm concerned," said Grimes coldly. And then—he might as well put the boot in while he had the chance—"I was far from impressed by the conduct of your Mr. Mendoza. Any officer of the Survey Service behaving as he did would face a court martial on the charge of cowardice in the face of the enemy."

"My trishaw driver bolted," Mendoza said.

"So did Su Lin's. But she managed to jump out and run back to help me."

"Ah, yes," murmured Lopez, "there is the matter of the weapon that she was carrying, quite illegally."

"Not a weapon," Grimes told him. "A lighter. *My* lighter."

"A very special sort of lighter," insisted Lopez.

"*Anything* can be used as a weapon," said Grimes. "You should see what the average petty officer instructor in the Survey Service, a specialist in unarmed combat, can do with a rolled-up newspaper.

And when I was privateering one of my officers could do quite dreadful damage with a pack of playing cards."

"You realize, Your Excellency," persisted Lopez, "that I shall be obliged to make a full report to President O'Higgins's chief of police and to Colonel Bardon."

"Report away, Mr. Lopez. I am Colonel Bardon's superior officer. And, legally speaking, I rank above the president. As far as I am concerned *my* servant took steps, effective steps, to save my life while yours, Mr. Mendoza, was rattling down the road as fast as his trishaw could carry him."

"The driver panicked!" almost shouted Mendoza.

"That's *your* story. Stick to it, if you feel like it. I could hardly care less."

There was what seemed to be a long silence, broken at last by Lopez.

"Well, Your Excellency, what has been done has been done. I suppose that now you will wish to return aboard your airship to freshen up before joining Madam Lopez and myself for dinner. . . ."

"I shall return aboard my airship," said Grimes, "and then I shall order my pilot to cast off."

"But I have instructed my chef to prepare a meal, a very special meal, for the occasion of your visit."

"You'll just have to eat it yourself. Come, Su Lin."

The butler escorted them from the oriental opulence of Lopez's reception room up to the roof. Grimes regretted having missed what probably would have been a superb curry. But, he consoled himself, there might have been some subtle poison in the portions served to him, or, possibly, a stiff infusion of dreamweed essence.

He was relieved when he emerged into the late afternoon sunlight, looking up to the gleaming bulk *of Fat Susie* swinging at the mast. Sanchez looked out from an open control cab window and waved cheerfully. Grimes raised a hand to return the salutation.

Now there would be that blasted ladder to negotiate. The wrenched muscles of his right leg were still painful and he could move the limb only by making a conscious effort.

"Your Excellency," said Su Lin, "I will ask Captain Sanchez to send down a cradle for you."

"You will not."

Slowly, painfully, he went up the ladder, taking as much weight as possible on his arms, Su Lin close behind him. He clambered at last into the control cab.

"What's wrong, Commodore?" asked Sanchez anxiously.

"Just a twisted leg, Raoul. It could have been worse."

"Very much worse," said the girl.

"But what happened?"

"I'll tell you later. Meanwhile, get us the hell out of here."

"The mooring mast is not manned, sir."

"You can actuate your release gear from the cab, can't you? As long as nothing fouls it, it's quite safe."

Sanchez did as ordered and *Fat Susie* drifted slowly astern, away from the roof of the Sanchez mansion, a winch whining as the short length of wire cable was reeled in. Only Ram Das, the butler, was there to see them go.

"You must rest now, Your Excellency," said Su Lin.

"All right."

"Where do we go, Commodore?" asked Sanchez.

"I'll leave it to you, Raoul. Surprise me."

Walking slowly and painfully he made his way aft to his quarters.

∽ Chapter 30 ∽

STRIPPED, prone on his bunk, Grimes submitted to the ministrations of Su Lin.

He murmured, "What did I ever do to deserve you? Devoted handmaiden . . . Highly efficient bodyguard . . . And now masseuse . . ."

Under her kneading fingers the soreness and stiffness were dissipating. But there was another stiffness, of which he was becoming embarrassedly conscious. *As long as she doesn't ask me to turn over . . .* he thought.

But she did not.

She slapped his naked buttocks and said cheerfully, "You'll survive, Commodore. But you usually do, don't you?"

"If I didn't," he told her, "I shouldn't be here." He flexed his legs experimentally. "Thanks to you, I shall be able to stand my watch."

"All part of the PAT service," she told him. "And, talking of watches, it's almost time that I was relieving Raoul. You'll be fit to take over at midnight, will you? Good. Then you had better get some sleep."

"I'll do just that," he said.

Sleep was a long time coming—and when it did he was plagued by nightmares—or, rather, by a recurring nightmare. In it he would be standing there, helpless, on the hot road, under a blazing sun, while the madman came at him with bloody machete upraised. Each time he woke up just as the sharp, gleaming blade was descending on his unprotected head.

And then Su Lin was there, switching on the light, putting the tea tray down on his bunkside table.

"Are you all right, Commodore?" she asked. "Do you feel fit enough to take over? If not, Raoul and I can manage between us."

"I'm feeling fine, Su Lin."

"You don't look it."

"I'm a little tired, that's all. The tea will perk me up. Get back to control like a good girl. I'll be with you shortly."

"As you say, Commodore," she said doubtfully.

The tea did refresh him.

He dressed, then made his way forward and down into the cab. *Fat Susie* was ambling along at cruising speed, almost silently, only the occasional click and whine of servo-mechanisms telling that the auto-pilot was functioning, maintaining course and adjusting attitude and altitude as requisite.

He looked at the chart and at the dotted line of the extrapolated track ahead of the airship's actual position, a trace that, astern of her, was unbroken.

"We're flying over the Unclaimed Territory, as they call it, now," said Su Lin. "No doubt, eventually, it will be tamed—with wheatfields and vineyards and . . . dreamweed plantations. It all depends, I suppose, on what sort of influx of refugee labor—slave labor—there is over the next few years. . . ."

"Assuming, of course," Grimes said, "that things continue going on as they have been going on. But aren't we supposed to be throwing a spanner into that machinery?"

She grinned. "We are, Commodore."

"Just what is down there, anyhow?" asked Grimes.

"In places, a jumble of rocks. Deep canyons. Savage animals. Even more savage plants."

"Savage plants? You have to be kidding, Su Lin."

"I'm not. I thought that you had been given a thorough briefing on this planet before you were sent here, *Governor.*"

"I was given a fine collection of spools to study on the way out. I studied them. But they were all concerned with history, politics, economics and sociology."

"I'll see to it that you get a briefing on Liberia's natural ecology when we get back to the Residence. Who knows? It might come in useful some day. It will be interesting, at least."

"As you say." Grimes was still looking at the chart. "I suppose that these names given to the various natural features should tell me something. Mount Horrible . . . Bloodsuckers Canyon . . . Shocking Valley . . . But that sounds more comic than sinister . . ."

He was interrupted by an insistent beeping from the radar. He went to the console, looked into the PPI. Yes, there was a target, an airborne target, just abaft the starboard beam, all of forty kilometers distant. He pushed the extrapolation button. The airship, as he assumed that it must be, was flying on an almost parallel course in the same direction. Su Lin had gone to the radio telephone transceiver. "*Fat Susie* to unidentified aircraft to my starboard. Do you read me?"

The reply came with no delay.

"*Citizen Marat* to *Fat Susie*. I read you loud and clear. Where bound, *Fat Susie*?"

"Cruising, *Citizen Marat*. Where are you bound? Over."

"Libertad to Rousseauville with mail and passengers. Over." Grimes, now, was staring out through the starboard window of the cab, binoculars to his eyes. He realized that he could not see the line of the land horizon against the dark luminosity of the sky. And, at this range, he should be able to see the other airship's running lights—but there was nothing there. And something seemed to have blotted out those stars at lower altitudes. He looked ahead. There the stars were dimming, were being obscured.

So *Fat Susie* had driven into a belt of cloud. So what? Radar and radar altimeter were working perfectly. The only traffic was bound in the same direction at the same speed. The extrapolated course was well clear of any mountains.

He heard Su Lin say, "A very good night to you, *Citizen Marat*. And *bon voyage*."

"*Bon voyage* to you, *Fat Susie.*" And then the male voice of the other watchkeeper chuckled. "Are *you Fat Susie?*"

"Just Su," she replied. "And not fat."

"I'd like to meet you some time."

"Good night." she said firmly. "Over and out."

"Wolves of the air," commented Grimes. "Off with you now, Su Lin. Get your head down. I have the watch."

Grimes, although he had done his share of atmosphere flying, was a spaceman, not an airman. He did not like this pushing ahead through thick fog. (Cloud, he told himself, cloud, not fog. The air would be clear enough at ground level, clear enough if he pushed *Fat Susie* up and through this vaporous ceiling.) He considered reducing altitude, then decided against it. Airships are not designed for hedge-hopping. Should he lift? But that would mean the dumping of ballast. And Sanchez had set the course, had set it in three dimensions, and might be annoyed, when called to take over the watch, to find that Grimes had been playing silly buggers all over the sky while he slept. All right, all right, Grimes was the pilot's employer. But he, Grimes, was not the master. Sanchez was.

Should he call Sanchez?

And then, Grimes told himself, *he'd have valid grounds for thinking of me as an old woman. Damn it all, I'm a shipmaster. I've commanded far bigger vessels than this little gasbag. As commodore, I've commanded a flotilla. (And,* he thought wryly, *made a jesusless balls of it.)*

Apart from the visually invisible *Citizen Marat* there was no other traffic. There would not be, Grimes knew, over this region of the planet. Grimes consulted the radar. The other airship was on a slightly converging course but she was drawing ahead. Furthermore, she was maintaining an altitude at least a thousand meters in excess of *Fat Susie's.* She would cross ahead of *Fat Susie* safely enough and without incident.

The watch wore on. The air in the control cab, from the fumes of Grimes's pipe, was almost as thick as the air outside. The airship maintained course and altitude without a human hand at the controls. In the PPI the glowing blip that was *Citizen Marat* was now ahead, still edging over to port. Grimes stared into the screen, drowsy, hypnotized by the steady rotation of the sweep.

But there was something wrong!

The range was no longer opening; it was closing fast. A glance at the auxiliary screen showed that the other ship was losing altitude rapidly. What the hell was she playing at?

It was one of those occasions when Grimes wished that he had three pairs of hands. Somehow he managed to push the General Alarm button and, a split second later, to initiate the process of switching from automatic pilot to manual control. *Fat Susie*—the stupid bitch!—seemed reluctant to yield the dominance of her functions to a mere human. It seemed ages before the illuminated sign, AUTO, over the wheel and the gyrocompass repeater flickered out to be replaced by manual. And all the time there was the urgent stridency of the alarm bells to engender panic.

Sanchez and Su Lin were in the control cab. Neither had taken time to dress. Sanchez stared out through the windows at nothingness, then went to the radar.

"Holy Bakunin!" he muttered. "How the hell did you . . .?" Then, "Turn away, man! Hard-a-starboard!"

Grimes, at the wheel, spun it rapidly to the right. He felt *Fat Susie* heel over, heard her creaking protests. From above and abaft the control cab there was a peculiarly muffled crash—and, almost immediately afterwards, a noise that could only be that of the discharge of at least one medium caliber automatic cannon. *Fat Susie* lurched, shuddered. Grimes, clinging to the now useless wheel, managed to keep his feet. He stared out through the port window, saw that the colliding airships had, fortuitously, found a pocket of clear air in the cloud blanket. By the crimson glare of his own vessel's port navigation light he could see a great hulk backing away, under reversed thrust, from its victim.

He could read the name . . .

No, not the name. The single letter and the three numerals.

Wherever the real *Citizen Marat* was, this was not her.

This was the army's *R273*, the rigid dirigible that had cast off from the Lopez mooring mast to make room for *Fat Susie*.

The clouds enveloped her once more and she vanished from sight.

Fat Susie, her main gas cells ruptured, fell almost like a stone.

⁓ Chapter 31 ⁓

"UP INTO THE SHIP!" shouted Sanchez.

"Why?" asked Grimes stupidly.

"Because the control car is going to hit first, you fool!"

Su Lin was already mounting the short ladder. Grimes followed her. Sanchez followed him. They reached the catwalk that ran fore and aft between the gas cells, these containers wrinkled now, collapsing upon themselves. There was no place else to run. The vertical ladder that gave access to the outside of the envelope was blocked by fold upon fold of limp fabric.

The lights were still burning, running from the emergency power cells. They gave some small comfort. The three members of *Fat Susie's* crew huddled together in their cave of wrinkled cloth, blocked now at either end, waiting for the crash.

"It can't be long now," said Sanchez at last.

His voice was oddly high, almost a soprano.

He's scared, thought Grimes. *I didn't think that he'd be the type to show such fear . . .*

He said philosophically, "What goes up has to come down, I suppose."

His own voice was high and squeaky, even in his own ears.

The helium, he thought. *There's a lot of it in the atmosphere we're breathing. It's making us sound like refugees from the papal choir . . .*

"She was a good little ship," said Sanchez regretfully. "I'd like to get the bastards who did this to her."

"I'd like to get the bastards," said Grimes, "who did this to us. Did you see the markings on the other dirigible before she backed away?"

"I did," announced Su Lin, her voice faint, almost as inaudible as a bat's sonar squeak. "I did. It was the Army ship that we saw at the Lopez plantation. It was no more *Citizen Marat* than I am."

"You're the wrong sex in any case," quipped Sanchez,

There was no doubt about that, thought Grimes. He was acutely aware of the girl's nudity pressed against him.

He said, changing the subject, "I wonder what premiums Lloyd's would charge to insure the life of a Liberian governor?" He was about to add. "Especially one who travels by airship . . ." when *Fat Susie* struck.

It was an amazingly gentle contact. The catwalk lifted beneath their feet, throwing them together but not violently. From somewhere beneath them there came the sound of a muffled crash. And then there was silence, broken only by the sound of their breathing and the hiss of escaping helium.

The lights did not go out but their illumination was dimmed by the layers of fabric through which it had to shine.

They were huddled together, the three of them, in a sort of cave, the walls and ceiling of which were formed by the fabric of collapsed gas cells. Luckily air was getting in from somewhere. At the same time the helium was getting out. Their voices were reverting to normal timbre.

"Where's that fancy lighter of yours, Su Lin?" asked Grimes. "We can use it to burn our way out."

"Unluckily," she told him tartly, "I don't have any pockets in my birthday suit. The lighter's where I left it when I turned in. On my bunkside table."

"And the door to your cabin," said Sanchez thoughtfully, "should be right behind where you are standing now . . ."

Wriggling, squirming, they managed to turn around. Su Lin's

body, Grimes realized, was slippery with perspiration. So was Sanchez's, on the other side of him. They were facing a featureless wall of limp fabric. They tried to lift it up and clear, but it was anchored somehow at its lower edge. They tried to pull it down, then to pull it sideways. Grimes was almost envying the nudity of his companions. His own clothing was becoming soaked. He could feel the sweat puddling in his shoes.

During their struggles with that impenetrable curtain Su Lin's hip was pressing heavily against his right side. There was something hard in his pocket of which he became painfully conscious. His pipe, of course. His pipe—and the old-fashioned matches that he preferred to other means of ignition.

"Raoul," he asked. "This fabric . . . Is it flammable?"

"Of course not."

"Will it melt, if heat's applied?"

"I don't know. I just fly airships. I don't build them."

"Then there's only one way to find out. Su Lin, can you shift a bit to your right? A bit more . . ."

"Normally I should appreciate this," grumbled Sanchez, against whom the girl was now pushing.

Grimes got the box of matches, after a struggle, out of his pocket. It felt damp to his touch. Had his perspiration made them useless? He got one of them out of the box, struck it. It fizzled sadly and went out. He dropped it, extracted a second one. He was careful not to touch either its head or the striking surface with his fingers. This one did burn, but unenthusiastically. The oxygen content of the air in their little cave must, thought Grimes, be getting low, depleted by their consumption of it during their exertions.

Carefully, carefully he brought the feeble flame into light contact with the fabric. It began to smoke and bubble. A vile, acrid stench assailed their nostrils. The match went out. Grimes let it fall, got a third one from the box. By the time that it had burned away there was a small hole with fused edge, just large enough for Su Lin to get her index finger into. She tried to tug downwards but achieved nothing.

Grimes used seven more matches to enlarge the hole in an

upward direction. (There were now only three left; he should have put a full box in his pocket before going on watch.) He could, now, get his right hand into the vertical slit. He pulled, sideways, with all the strength that he was able to exert in this confined space. The fabric was stubborn—but there was room, now, for Sanchez to get his left hand into the hole to join the struggle.

Suddenly there was a ripping noise. Slowly, slowly the rent was enlarging while the two men panted from their combined effort. Luckily fresh air, in appreciable quantities, was getting in now.

They paused, to breathe deeply.

Between them the girl said. "Give me a hand, you two. I think I can squirm through . . ."

She did that. With her gone there was room for Grimes and Sanchez to move with much greater ease. They could hear her scuffling progress on the other side of the curtain. They heard her grunt with effort. Was something jamming the door to her cabin? They heard, faintly, what they hoped was a sigh of relief.

At last she was back.

"Stand clear!" she called. "Stand clear!"

The jet of flame—not as long as when the lighter had been used as a weapon but still as glaringly incandescent—swept downwards, and then up. It went out.

She said, "Come in. This is Liberty Hall. You can spit on the mat and call the cat a bastard."

The ship—what was left of her—was theirs again.

They gained access to their cabins.

Sanchez and Su Lin got dressed, then they and Grimes sat in the little wardroom with stiff drinks. They felt that they deserved them but were careful not to overindulge. Grimes wanted to take a torch to go outside to assess the damage but the others vetoed the suggestion.

"We're still alive," Su Lin told him. "If we go outside the ship, at night, we very soon shan't be. This is the Unclaimed Territory. Remember?"

"And as for viewing the wreck," said Sanchez, "that can wait until daylight. One thing *is* certain—*Fat Susie* will never fly again."

"Mphm," grunted Grimes, filling and lighting his pipe. Then, "What time is sun up, Raoul?"

The pilot looked at his watch, just a timekeeper without any fancy functions.

"About an hour," he said. Then, with a wry grin, "Where *has* the night gone to?"

"I'll make some tea," said Su Lin briskly.

She got up from the settee, went from the wardroom into the adjoining galley. After a brief absence she returned.

"Raoul," she said, "there's no fresh water . . ."

Sanchez got up and went back with her into the airship's kitchen. They returned, eventually, to the wardroom. Their faces were grave.

"Commodore," said the pilot, "there's good news and bad news. The good news is that this was a crash that we shall be able to walk away from. The bad news is that we owe our soft landing to the fact that we lost considerable mass during our descent. Our fresh water tanks must have been holed."

"If our luck holds," said Su Lin, "we might find that we're not too far from a stream . . ."

"And that the stream doesn't harbor any life forms big enough to be a serious menace to us," Sanchez said.

"Meanwhile," the girl went on, "we have beer, and table wines, and lolly water. Even if there's no water handy it'll be at least a week before we die of thirst."

"You're a pair of cheerful bastards," grumbled Grimes.

"Don't complain," the girl told him severely. "We're alive. There's no reason at all why we shouldn't stay that way."

"I'm surprised," said Grimes, "that Major Flattery didn't stick around to make sure that we were all very dead."

"I was myself—but, thinking it over, I can see why he just made us crash, *here,* and then flew off," said the girl. "I can see what the official story will be. Steering gear failure and a midair collision, contributed to by the bad airmanship of the vessel sustaining major damage. Flattery's own ship was damaged too, so much so that he could not make an immediate search for survivors—if any . . . In the fullness of time a proper search will be organized—but everybody will be quite sure either that we were all killed at once by the crash or, shortly afterwards, by the local flora and fauna . . ."

"Why should Flattery make a report at all," asked Grimes, "except to his boss, Colonel Bardon? . . . As far as the rest of Liberia is concerned Governor Grimes will be enjoying himself flying hither and yon about his domain. Eventually there will be a public urinal or something to be ceremoniously opened and people will start to ask, 'Where *is* the Governor?' And Lopez Sahib will have been the last person to have seen me, and he will say that *Fat Susie* was last sighted proceeding east—whereas we were proceeding north. . . ."

"And years from now," said the girl, "when the Unclaimed Territory is opened up for exploitation, somebody will find what's left of *Fat Susie* and what's left of us. If anything."

"And I shall be blamed, posthumously," Sanchez said. "Pilot error. That's what they'll say."

"And what they'll say about me," contributed Grimes, "is that my famous luck finally ran out . . ."

They all laughed, enjoying, briefly, their indulgence in gallows humor.

Then Grimes asked, "Could we make our way back to civilization by foot?"

"Not if we're where I think we are—where I'm reasonably sure that we are—we couldn't. Not even if we had weapons. Did *you* bring any private pocket artillery with you, Commodore?"

"No."

"Su Lin?"

"Only my all-purpose lighter. And there are some quite useful knives in the galley—not that they'd be much use against the local predators. And you, Raoul?"

"There's a laser torch in the workshop. Normally it runs off the mains, although it has a power cell. But the power cell has a limited life."

"We could recharge—or could we?—from the power cells that are supplying juice for the emergency lights," said Grimes.

"And *they,* too, aren't exactly everlasting," Sanchez told him.

"Even so, once the sun is up they should be recharging themselves."

"Yes. Of course. Assuming that things weren't too badly damaged by the collision and the crash. As soon as it's light we'll go outside and see just how well off—or badly off—we are."

~ Chapter 32 ~

DAWN CAME, the light of the rising sun striking through but diffused by the tattered fabric that obscured the outside of the wardroom windows. Su Lin led the way into the galley where each of them selected a knife. Grimes did not like knives; he made no secret of his preference for doing his killing from a distance, lobbing missiles and directing assorted lethal rays at some enemy whom he would never meet face to face while, of course, this same enemy would be reciprocating in kind.

These sharp blades, however, were better than nothing—not as good as Su Lin's versatile lighter but the charge in that would not last forever.

The three of them made their way aft, frequently having to hack their way through the tough fabric of the collapsed helium cells. They cut their way into the workshop. They found not only the laser gun—it looked like a weapon, a pistol, but its range would be pitifully short—but also two long-handled spanners, a big screwdriver that might be used as a stiletto, and a hammer.

Egress would not be possible through the control car; comparatively gentle as their fall had been at the finish, that compartment had taken the brunt of the impact. The thin metal skin forming the envelope must, Grimes knew, have been pierced by the sharp prow of Flattery's airship and by the fire of the major's automatic cannon—but none of them could do more than hazard a guess as to where the bigger rents would be. So, even though they were conscious that they were using power which might be badly needed for defense, Sanchez cut through the metallic integument, burning what was, in effect, a large inverted U, a panel that was easily bent out and down.

Fat Susie had found her last home on top of a low, rounded hillock. No, not a hillock. It was an island in the middle of a river. It would be an easy swim to either bank. Furthermore, that stream would be a valuable source of fresh water.

Grimes was the first out through the improvised doorway although the others tried to restrain him. He stood there in the warmth of the morning sun, savoring the fresh air, the light breeze that carried the not unpleasant tang of some vegetable growth. He straightened up from his knife-fighter's crouch, an attitude which he felt must look more than a little foolish. He wished that he had a sheath into which to stick the long, sharp blade.

Su Lin joined him, her golden lighter, ready for action, gleaming in her right hand. Sanchez—the captain, last to leave his ship— jumped down. Unlike the others he did not stand admiring the scenery. He stared up at *Fat Susie,* a great, gleaming beached whale that had been run down and almost cut in two by some passing vessel. .

"The bastards!" he muttered with great feeling. "The *bastards!*"

"But not very efficient ones," commented Grimes. "They should have made sure of us."

"But they have, Commodore. They have. This is the Unclaimed Territory."

"All that I see," Grimes told him, "is a quite pleasant little island in the middle of a river, with the eastern and western banks within easy-reach of even such a poor swimmer as myself. The banks are well-wooded—and that looks like fruit on some of the trees. Is it edible, I wonder?"

Su Lin muttered something about Gutsy Grimes.

"We have to eat, don't we?" Grimes said. "*Fat Susie* wasn't stocked for a long voyage. We have to live off the land." He grinned. "Unless we resort to long pig," he finished.

"The Governor's talking sense, Su Lin," Sanchez admitted. "What do you know, really know, about the Unclaimed Territory? Apart from hearsay, that is. . . ."

"What do *you* know, Raoul?" she countered.

"Not much. Not one quarter as much as I should. It's a reserve of native lifeforms, some of them nasty. . . ."

"Like that?" asked Grimes.

He indicated with his knife something that, moving silently, was almost upon them. It didn't look like much to worry about. It could have been an almost deflated air mattress, garishly striped in blue, green and orange, flung carelessly down upon the mossy ground. But it was motile, flowing over the irregularities of the surface.

"Just a glorified amoeba . . ." he said.

Foolishly—as he was very soon to realize—he squatted, prodding the wetly glistening surface with the point of the blade. He wondered dazedly what had hit him as he was hurled violently backwards. He sprawled there, paralyzed. He was dimly aware that Su Lin had her lighter out, was directing its shaft of intense flame at the . . . *thing.* There was a strong smell of burning. Grimes was expecting it to be of seared meat but he was surprised. The smoke that irritated his nostrils, that made him sneeze, that made them all sneeze, was one that he would have associated with a grass fire.

He heard rather than saw the flurry of activity as the creature, flapping madly in its death throes, died.

Then Su Lin was beside him, kneeling by him, her strong, capable hands stroking him gently.

"Commodore! Are you all right?"

"What. . . . What hit me?"

"It was an electric shock. I should have remembered what these things look like. . . ."

"What . . . things?"

"Shockers, they call them . . ."

He managed to sit up.

"Then this must be the Shocking River that I saw on the chart. And the shockers themselves . . . Like electric eels and rays back on Earth, and similar animals elsewhere. . . ."

"Yes. But these aren't animals. They're plants. They use their chlorophyll to convert sunlight into electricity. . . ."

Grimes was recovering now, his interest diverting his attention from the pain that persisted in his cramped muscles.

"Plants, you say? Motile plants . . . But why motile?"

"So that they can move from shadow into sunlight to recharge their batteries, crawl back into the shade to avoid an overcharge." She laughed. "I gave this one an overcharge, all right! Too, very often, their victims are thrown away from them by the shock. Then they have to ooze toward them and over them to envelop and ingest them."

Grimes shuddered. He did not fancy being enveloped and ingested.

"But why," he persisted, "are their victims such mugs as to touch them in the first place?"

"Why were you such a mug, Commodore?"

"Mphm. And, come to that, why did I get a shock? The knife has a wooden handle. It should have been a fairly effective insulator . . ."

He was still holding the weapon. He dropped it to the ground, saw the metal studs that secured the hilt to the blade.

"Yes, Su Lin, I was a mug. But *why* are the local animals mugs too?"

"They are attracted by the gaudy coloration—which duplicates, almost exactly, the coloration of other plants, non-motile and without built-in solar power plants, which are very good eating. I hope that we find them so—as we might be here for a very long time."

"If you will excuse me from the natural history lesson," said Raoul, "I'll carry on with my survey of the ship."

"Do that," said Grimes. "Su Lin and I will explore the island, what there is of it, and see what it has to offer in the way of a balanced menu."

"We will keep together," said the girl firmly. "As far as I can recall, from what I have read, the shockers are the least dangerous of the life forms that we are liable to encounter. So, while one is poking around the wreckage, the other two will be keeping a lookout. I shall have my lighter and the Commodore will have the laser pistol."

"I wish it were a *real* pistol," said Grimes.

"We have to make do," she said, "with what we've got."

≈ Chapter 33 ≈

THERE WERE FLYING THINGS that sailed through the air with lazy, undulant grace—until they swooped. They were all great, flexible wing, long, sharp beak and huge, bulbous eyes. These creatures, the humans soon discovered, were attracted both by movement and by color. They saw one dive from the air onto a shocker, saw it stunned into immobility and, slowly, slowly enveloped by the crawling plant. They were attacked themselves, three times. On the first two occasions pairs of the creatures were easily driven off by the slashing jet of fire from Su Lin's lighter, set to maximum intensity. The third attack was by a solitary flyer, hungrier or more aggressive than the others. It came boring in, vicious beak extended, like some nightmare airborne lancer, until Su Lin, standing her ground, succeeded in blinding it. *(Her favorite technique,* thought Grimes with a shudder. *I'd sooner have her on my side than against me. . . .)* Whining shrilly the thing veered away, flapping clumsily, and fell into the river. Almost immediately its struggling body was attacked by the denizens of the stream—and very shortly thereafter a covey of aerial predators swooped down, not (of course) to rescue their mate but to prey upon the aquatic carnivores that were ripping its (?) body to shreds. Long, writhing, segmented, many-legged bodies were impaled on the sharp beaks, carried into the sky and then dropped from a great height to fall with armor-shattering impact onto a rocky outcrop on the far side of the water.

A. Bertram Chandler

"That could have happened to us," muttered Sanchez, at last tearing his eyes away from the distant, grisly feast.

"But it didn't," said Grimes. "Thanks to Su Lin. But I suggest that, from now on, we move *very* slowly. It might help."

It did—but working in slow motion was tiring. And although the flying things now seemed to be ignoring them (perhaps they were intelligent and had come to the conclusion that the strange, two-legged beings on the island were better left alone), there were other . . . nuisances. There was a sort of huge worm that, unexpectedly, would extrude its blind head from the mossy ground and attempt to fasten its sucker mouth upon their booted feet and ankles. There was a small army of crablike things, each with a carapace all of a meter across, each armed with a pair of vicious looking pincers, that marched out of the stream and up the hill in military formation, that milled about in confusion on finding the way blocked by the wreckage of *Fat Susie,* that finally made its way around the stranded airship and then down the hill and into the water.

There was a straggler.

This Grimes killed with the laser pistol. The smell of roast crab made his mouth water.

"That was very foolish, Commodore," chided the girl. "The rest of them might have come back to attack you."

"But they didn't, did they? And I'm very fond of crab."

"These things only look like crabs. Their flesh might be poisonous to us."

"There's only one way to find out. Standard Survey Service survival technique. You take only a very small taste of whatever it is you're testing. If, at the end of an hour, you're suffering no ill effects then it's safe and you can tuck in."

While he spoke he was using his knife to lever up the top of the carapace, like a lid. The smell was stronger, more tantalizing. He scooped out a pea-sized portion of the pale pink, still steaming, flesh with the point of the blade. He was raising it to his mouth when she put out a hand to stop him.

"No, Commodore. Not you. You're the Governor. I'm the

guinea pig." Her long fingers plucked the morsel of meat from the knife, brought it to her mouth. "Hm. Not bad, not bad at all. Now, I'll put this thing in the shade. If I'm still healthy at the end of an hour it will be our lunch . . ."

Slowly, painstakingly they continued to make their way about the wreck. They found that a relatively large area of the solar energy collecting screens on top of the envelope was undamaged. Power would be no problem. Hopefully neither food nor water would be— as long as they could fill buckets from the river without being dragged into it and eaten. (None of them had any desire to see the things that had attacked the downed flier at close quarters.) They might even, constructing a raft or canoe from the dirigible's metal skin, be able to get away from the island by crossing the stream or by drifting downriver. But what then? Could they hope to make their way overland or by water to human settlement? So far they had seen only a small sample of the Unclaimed Territory's flora and fauna, and only those creatures that operated by day.

What came out at night?

Yet, thought Grimes, there just could be a way. It all depended on what was in the workshop, what materials there were for making emergency repairs. Too, they would have to gain access to the wrecked control car so that they could study the charts.

"I'm still alive," said Su Lin, breaking into his thoughts. "It's lunch time. I can whip up some mayonnaise, and . . ."

But when they went to pick up the crab-thing they found that the worms had gotten to it first, sucking the shell dry and empty.

Chapter 34

BACK IN THE WARDROOM they took lunch, eating rather uninteresting sandwiches (Grimes bitterly regretted not having had the crab put in a safe place) and washing them down with mineral water. After the meal and a brief smoke Grimes suggested that they get in a supply of fresh water. There were buckets available; there were some large empty plastic bins that could be filled. Sanchez volunteered to do the actual bucket filling and insisted that it was his duty. While he stooped on the river bank, bending out and down and over, Su Lin and Grimes kept watch—she of the sky and he of the water. Her weapon had a far greater range than his, the laser tool.

The winged creatures did not bother them. The many-legged swimmers did, once they became aware of the humans' existence. Grimes drove off the first attack, by a single predator, without any difficulty. He discovered that if he kept the water boiling or almost so it was a good deterrent. The ugly, vicious things did not venture from the merely warm into the very hot. He was beginning to congratulate himself when, very fortunately, he took a glance upstream. The water centipedes—as he had decided to call them—were coming ashore, were advancing toward them, their two-meter-long bodies wriggling sinuously along the bank. Hastily he and the others retreated up the hill, temporarily abandoning the buckets. Luckily the aquatic predators could not stay long out of their native element. They returned to the river.

But they waited there, their writhing bodies gleaming just under the surface, stalked eyes upheld like periscopes.

Grimes had seen in the workshop some pairs of rubberized work gauntlets. Accompanied by Su Lin and Sanchez he went to get three pairs of these.

"A good idea, sir, now that it's too late," complained Sanchez. "I could have done with these when I was having to dip my hands into that near-as-dammit boiling water . . ."

"They're to insulate against more than heat," Grimes told him.

Su Lin laughed appreciatively; she was quicker on the uptake than the pilot.

They went in search, then, of shockers. It was quite easy to distinguish them from those other gaudy plants that they imitated. If a thing wriggled sluggishly when it was lifted, it was a shocker. If it didn't wriggle and was securely rooted to the ground it wasn't. They were able to build a barricade of the electric plants up-river from where the buckets had been left. Then Grimes, with the laser, heated the water to near-boiling point again, simmering a centipede that was evincing hostile attentions toward him. The other creatures, as before, came ashore upstream. They tried to cross the living, garish carpet to get at their prey. They twitched and died.

Grimes wondered if they were edible—but the motile plants had already made that decision. Very soon the long, twisted bodies were enveloped and the process of ingestion had commenced. Grimes shrugged. Those centipedes hadn't looked very appetizing. Hopefully, perhaps tomorrow, at the same time as today, there would be another procession of crabs. . . .

Anyhow, something had been accomplished. The wreck of *Fat Susie* was now well-stocked with water.

"What now, Commodore?" asked Sanchez wearily.

"We get down into the control car to fetch out the charts, Raoul."

"Come off it, sir. Can't it wait until tomorrow? We've put in a very busy day, and it will be advisable for us to keep watches all through the night. We've seen only the daytime beasties—Bakunin alone knows what the nocturnal ones are like!"

"Was Bakunin a xenobiologist?" asked Grimes interestedly.

"Just somebody to swear by, sir—the same as your Odd Gods of the Galaxy."

"We'll continue this theological discussion later," said Grimes. "Right now I want those charts. I want to see what chance we have of getting out of here."

"But we can't even get ashore from this blasted island!"

"Can't we?" asked Grimes gently. "Can't we?"

"Of course we can," said Su Lin, "as long as the Commodore's famous luck hasn't run out."

"I don't think that it has," said Grimes softly. "I don't think that it has. . . ."

They had to cut their way into the control car, using the laser tool. Fortuitously—a case of Grimes's luck!—the aperture that they burned in the deck was directly over the chart table. Fantastically none of the charts sustained fire damage. They took these to the wardroom, spread them out on the carpet, studied them.

"We're here," said Sanchez definitely, drawing a circle around the representation of an island in a wide river with a soft pencil.

"Are you sure, Raoul?"

"Yes, sir. It's not far from where Flattery attacked us. We made very little headway after that—for obvious reasons."

"Mphm. Now find me a small-scale chart, one with the Shocking River and this island on it but showing the terrain beyond the Unclaimed Territory."

"This one should do, Commodore."

"Good. Now, how was the wind today?"

"I . . . I didn't notice. . . ."

"Did you, Su Lin?"

"No."

"Well, I did. It's been northerly all the time—no more than light airs during the forenoon but, by now, quite a stiff breeze. Presumably—and hopefully—this weather pattern will persist. From where we are now the shortest distance to what is laughingly referred to as civilization is due south."

"But we still have to get off the island, sir!" protested Sanchez. "And then, when we do, we have to cross at least a thousand kilometers of broken terrain *crawling* with all manner of *things*. . . ."

"I know that, Raoul. Now, am I correct in stating that I saw, in the workshop some tubes of a very special adhesive?"

"Yes, sir."

"Used when you're slapping patches on to ruptured helium cells."

"That's what it's for, sir."

"And did I see some cylinders of compressed helium?"

"You did." Sanchez laughed. "I see what you're driving at, Commodore. A balloon with the envelope made from pieces of our burst gas cells glued together. And suppose we get winds with an average velocity of, say, twenty kilometers an hour . . . A fifty-hour flight—and we're out of this mess!"

"And probably into a worse one," grumbled Su Lin, but smiling as she spoke.

But the supply of adhesive, they discovered, was sufficient only for making the odd repairs. There was not nearly enough to gum together pieces of fabric to make a balloon large enough to support three persons. The helium situation was better—but what would they have to put the lighter-than-air gas in?

Grimes said, "With luck we might be able to make a reasonably airworthy one-man balloon. With luck that one man might make it, then come back to rescue the others . . ."

"A one-woman balloon," said Su Lin.

"After we've made the thing," said Grimes, "we'll decide who's to go."

⮐ Chapter 35 ⮐

SANCHEZ STOOD THE EVENING WATCH, Su Lin the middle and the morning watch was kept by Grimes. Before they broke up—two to go to their beds and the other to commence his tour of duty—they discussed procedure. Would it be better for the watchkeeper to stay inside the ship or should he go outside? They agreed that an open-air vigil could well be tantamount to suicide. Then there was another question. Should lights be rigged to illuminate *Fat Susie* from the outside, or not? None of them knew much about the flora and fauna of the Unclaimed Territory. Would night prowlers be scared away by lavish illumination or would they be attracted to it?

"We didn't have any unfriendly visitors last night," argued the pilot. "The only lights were those inside the ship—and most of the ports were well-screened by wreckage."

"Any nocturnal animals," said Grimes, "could well have been scared away by the descent of a huge monster from the sky. It might not be long before they accept *Fat Susie* as part of the scenery. If we rig lights outside it will make her look unnatural and delay acceptance. Too, if we do have to go outside to fight something we shan't be fighting in the dark."

"That makes sense," said Su Lin. "But the watchkeeper should stay inside the ship, on the catwalk handy for the cabins, and, on no account, go outside by himself. And the watchkeeper will have with him what seems to be our most effective weapon—my lighter." She grinned at Grimes. "And I hope that you, Commodore, will use matches to light your pipe. I don't want the lighter's charge reduced unnecessarily."

They found suitable and powerful lights and ran them, on wandering leads, outside the ship. They stood there, while the darkness deepened, waiting to see if anything would be attracted. They soon came to the conclusion that the gearing lamps would be useful in an unexpected way. Up the hill, from all sides, oozed the shockers, coming to recharge their solar batteries. They soon formed a tight cordon about the wreck, seemingly content to remain there, quiescent, soaking up the radiation. They were far more effective a barricade against intruders than anything that might have been constructed from the available materials could be.

After a not very satisfactory supper Grimes and Su Lin retired to their cabins, leaving Sanchez in charge.

The girl called Grimes at 0345 hours, bringing him the usual tea tray. After a sketchy toilet he dressed, then joined her on the catwalk.

She said, "It's been a quiet night. Either the lights have been scaring things off—or they've been electrocuted. If you don't mind, Commodore, I'll get my head down. We shall have a busy day."

"Off you go," Grimes told her.

He made his way through the ship to the hole that had been cut in her metallic skin, looked out. The external lights were burning brightly, the garish carpet of shockers was still in place. Here and there were sluggish stirrings, lazy undulations. A few of the carnivorous, mobile plants were bulging. They had fed, obviously. On what? On something quite big, that much was obvious. Something that, quite possibly, might have gotten inside the wreck and fed on its human occupants.

Would it be possible, wondered Grimes, to . . . to harvest? Why not? They were plants after all, not animals . . . to harvest the shockers, keep them in captivity and export them at a nice profit? The Survey Service would be a potential customer. Grimes recalled occasions in his own career when he had been involved in the exploration of newly discovered plants. Efficient sentries such as these creatures would have been very, very useful.

Get-rich-quick Grimes, he thought. *That's me.*

At the moment there was only one snag. As Governor of this world he could not, legally, engage in any profit-making enterprise. As Governor? He laughed aloud. If things didn't go as he was hoping he would soon be the late Governor Grimes.

He went back inside, smoked his foul pipe. He went into the galley and constructed a multitiered sandwich, made tea. He thought, as he was munching his snack, *we shall have to institute a system of rationing until we find out just what around here is edible.*

The watch wore on.

At 0600 hours he called Sanchez.

Shortly thereafter the two of them went to the hole in the envelope. They could not watch the sunrise as that was on the other side of the ship. They saw the shockers slowly oozing away from the shadow cast by the twisted hull. Artificial light they liked when there was nothing else—but they preferred the real thing.

"So we can get out," said Grimes, "without having to wear rubber boots . . ."

Until it was time to call Su Lin the two men busied themselves in the workshop, carrying the tools and some of the materials that they would need out of the ship. They did not think that any of the local lifeforms would be interested in gas cylinders, shears or tubes of adhesive. They kept a watch for fliers, some of which were already sailing through the sky like, Grimes thought, the manta rays that he had seen in the tropical seas of Earth. Only once did one swoop down upon them but it sheared off at once as soon as Grimes directed a jet of flame, from Su Lin's lighter, in its direction.

Then the girl was called and they had breakfast. She, officiating as cook, looked at Grimes suspiciously.

"I could have sworn," she said, "that there was more bread than this when we finished supper last night. And there were those hard-boiled eggs that I had plans for. And what's this in the ashbin? An empty sardine can . . ."

"I'll get you another crab this morning," promised Grimes.

"You'd better, Commodore. You'd just better . . ."

After the meal—fried eggs (there would be no more after this) and bacon (in. short supply but not finished)—they got down to work. Working mainly inside the ship they cut large sections from the fabric of the collapsed helium cells, trying to keep these as big as possible. Sweating with the exertion they—Grimes and Sanchez—lugged these out of the ship, spreading them on the mossy slope while the girl, her weapon once again in her possession, kept watch. They were troubled only by the great worms. Su Lin managed to kill one of these before it could withdraw its ugly, sucker-equipped head back into its burrow. They dragged it out of the hole, carried the still-twitching body— it was like a huge, greatly elongated sausage—into the wreck. There was a chance that its flesh might be edible.

Grimes, using his versatile wrist companion, and its computer functions, had made his calculations the previous evening, had drawn plans and diagrams on the backs of the charts salvaged from the control car. The workshop yielded rulers and tapes and sticks of crayon. Finally, making ample allowance for overlap, it was possible for Grimes and Sanchez to begin cutting out elliptical sections from the gas cell fabric. They worked slowly and clumsily. At last Su Lin could stand it no longer.

"Here, Commodore," she told him, "take this." She handed him the golden lighter. *"You* keep watch. Dressmaking, with the preliminary cutting, is one of my skills. Obviously it's not one of yours."

"I never said that it was," Grimes told her.

So, while the others, on their hands and knees, worked he acted as sentry, scanning the sky and the ground and the river. Right on time the procession of crabs emerged from the water, led by the crustacean whom Grimes was now referring to as The Grand Old Duke Of York.

"Why do you call it that?" asked Sanchez curiously. (He and the girl had stopped work to make way for the procession.)

Su Lin laughed. She recited, in a sing-song voice,

"The Grand Old Duke Of York
He had ten thousand men,
He marched them up to the top of the hill
And he marched them down again . . ."

Meanwhile Grimes had opened fire on the stragglers. This time he got two of them. Work on the balloon envelope was suspended while these were carried into the ship and stowed in the galley for future reference.

Eventually, leaving Sanchez to work by himself, Su Lin went to prepare the midday meal, calling the two men when it was ready. She had boiled one of the crabs, serving it with a sort of sweet-and-sour sauce. It was delicious. The only fly in the ointment was that with her method of cookery she had seriously depleted the fresh water supply. So more had to be brought up from the river, using the same technique as on the previous day.

Nonetheless the work progressed steadily. A wrinkled, empty sausage skin was taking shape. (Grimes found it hard to believe that it, when fully inflated, would be spherical—but each segment of the envelope had been cut according to the formulae presented by the computer function of his wrist companion.) The supply of adhesive was holding out better than he had expected. When sunset came upon them the job was almost finished. All that remained was to gum into place two more panels and to fit a valve cannibalized from one of *Fat Susie's* gas cells.

Sanchez wanted to go on working under artificial light. Grimes would not permit this. It would be far too easy, he said, for something to swoop down upon them from the gathering darkness overhead, unseen until it was too late to take defensive measures. Su Lin was in complete agreement with him. So the empty, almost-finished balloon was rolled up and placed just outside the doorway cut in the airship's metal skin. It was too bulky for them to lift it inside. It had been bad enough having to lug it from its original position.

The sun was well down when they were finished and dusk was fast deepening into night. The lights were switched on. From inside the wreck they watched the shockers, attracted by the harsh illumination, making their slow and undulant way up the slope. Did the things have a memory? Grimes wondered. Did they recall that they had fed well the previous night? But he just somehow could not accept the idea of a sentient plant.

Before long the castaways were partaking of their evening meal. Su Lin had found time during the day to test the flesh of the huge worm that Grimes had killed earlier. It was nonpoisonous but, even with the exotic sauce that she had concocted, not very palatable. Presumably it was nutritious and a strictly rationed one glass of red wine apiece took the curse off it.

As before, they kept watches. But this time, by arrangement, Grimes called the others earlier. They wanted to make an early start on the balloon construction. After a very sketchy breakfast they went outside, emerging from the ship a few minutes before sunrise.

Sanchez was first out and yelled loudly in horror and anger.

"What's wrong?" demanded Grimes.

The pilot pointed.

On top of the rolled up envelope were two of the shockers. Obviously they had eaten only very recently; their bodies bulged in the center like that of a boa constrictor immediately after a very heavy meal. And what juices would have been oozing from them, what corrosive digestive fluids and excretory matter?

Su Lin hurried back inside for the work gloves. The three of them put these on and, with rather more haste than caution, removed the carnivorous plants from the top of the roll of balloon fabric, throwing them to the ground. They were all expecting to find a ragged hole eaten through the material—but it seemed to be undamaged. They felt the surface of the tough plastic with their fingers, prodded it and pinched it. The real test, Grimes knew, would not be until the balloon was inflated. And if all was well insofar as gas-tightness was concerned there was a way in which the aerostat could be furnished with protection from aerial attack during its flight.

But he would not, he decided, say anything to the others until the process of inflation was initiated. A lot would depend on how much of the fast-setting, stick-anything-to-anything adhesive was left.

There was an assault by the fliers while the last panel was being glued into place. Grimes beat this off—but when the last attacker had been disabled (those bulging eyes were very vulnerable) he noticed that the lance of flame from the lighter was neither as bright nor as long as it had been.

He said as much to Su Lin.

She replied, "I warned you that the charge wouldn't last forever. When it's exhausted all we shall have is that almost useless laser and the knives." She added, "This balloon of yours had better work,Commodore."

Then the envelope was finished and the equatorial band, made from strips of gas cell fabric, carefully positioned, held in place by sparing dabs, little more than specks, of the adhesive. Above it was a criss-crossing of webbing. Other strips of material would descend from the band when the balloon was ready for flight. These were attached to one of the light, wickerwork chairs from the wardroom. The aeronaut would travel in something approaching comfort.

The two ends of the filling pipe were connected to their respective valves.

"All systems go!" said Sanchez, squatting by the gas cylinder.

"Not yet," said Grimes.

"But we have to fill this thing, sir." said the pilot.

"All in good time. But, first of all, *Little Susie* must be fitted with her defensive armament."

"*Little Susie?*" asked Sanchez.

"She has to have a name, hasn't she?"

"Defensive armament?" asked Su Lin.

"Yes. Shockers. We've found out that they can't harm the fabric. We've seen a flier killed by one of them."

"But with their bright coloring they'll attract the fliers, sir," the pilot said.

"The fliers, Captain Sanchez, are going to be attracted to anybody or anything invading their airspace. I don't fancy trying to fight them off with a galley knife. Come to that—even if I had a decent pistol I couldn't deal with anything up on top of the envelope. Not without shooting holes through my own means of support."

"Get your gloves on again, Raoul," said the girl. "We'll do as the man says and collect a few shockers." She asked Grimes, "Will the adhesive hold them in place?"

"I don't know," he said. "There's only one way to find out. If the glue won't work we'll just have to lash them on to the envelope somehow."

∽ Chapter 36 ∽

THE INFLATION of *Little Susie* was still further delayed. Grimes didn't like the way that the fliers were hovering not overly far overhead, circling watchfully, gliding and soaring against the rising wind, maintaining their position relative to the island. It seemed to him that the airborne predators were far too interested in what was going on.

He said, "It will take three of us to handle this operation. It should be more—but three bodies is all we have. Somebody will have to stand by the valve on the helium cylinder, ready to shut off immediately. The other two will be kept busy handling the lines. Nobody will be able to keep a proper lookout."

"We'll just have to carry on and take a chance, Commodore," said Sanchez.

Grimes looked at the young man severely.

"As a spaceman, Raoul, you should know that chances aren't taken, except when the circumstances are such that there's absolutely no option."

"As now, sir."

"No. I admit that we have not had time to explore this island thoroughly—but you must have noticed, as I did, that at the northern end there is quite a miniature jungle of low bushes. In spite of their proximity to the water they are *dry*-looking bushes. But not *too* dry. . . ."

Get on with it! said the young man's expression although he remained silent.

"All animals," went on Grimes pedantically, "fear fire. That holds good on every world that I have visited. I am sure that this one is no exception. My proposal is this—that we start a fire among those bushes, hopefully not too fast-burning but one with plenty of smoke. The wind will blow the smoke right over us. As we work we shall require goggles and handkerchiefs, well-wetted, to tie over our noses and mouths. The fliers—unless they are related to the legendary phoenix—will not be at all inclined to dive into the heart of an apparent conflagration. . . ."

"Not so apparent, Commodore," said Sanchez. "But it's a good idea. As long as *we* don't get barbecued."

"We'll try just a small sample of shrubbery first," Grimes told him. "And, at the same time, we'll make sure that this mosslike growth is not flammable. We don't want to have to work with flames licking around our ankles."

"Especially," said Su Lin, "since our getaway craft will carry only one person . . ."

Grimes's plan worked.

The undergrowth at the northern end of the island was flammable but not explosively so; in fact, even with the laser in use, it was not all that easy to start the brush fire. Once Grimes got it going, however, it kept on going. A column of black, almost intoxicatingly aromatic smoke arose, drifting up the slope to cover the activities of the balloon crew, rising into the cloudless sky at an acute angle. Overhead, the fliers departed downwind. Were they really frightened? wondered Grimes, or were they hopeful that land animals fleeing the conflagration could be swooped upon as they ran in panic? The other local predators were doing well for themselves. The shockers, incapable themselves of swift motion, trapped the little, many-legged things that ran over them; in the river the water centipedes were feeding well.

Luckily there were very few sparks. Even though helium, unlike hydrogen, is an inert gas, any large burning fragment could have melted a hole in the envelope fabric. But the slowly swelling balloon was unscathed.

Grimes and Su Lin tended the guy lines, straightened out folds in the slowly distending fabric. They had to work, he said later, like one-armed paperhangers. *Little Susie* slowly took shape, lifting from the ground as she acquired buoyancy. And, although dwarfed by the bulk of the wrecked airship, she was not so little. She was not beautiful either. Despite the careful calculations and the painstaking implementation of these during the cutting and gluing of the segments she was a sadly lopsided bitch. But she was, thought (and hoped!) Grimes, airworthy. She strained at her mooring lines, anchored to the ground by grapnels from *Fat Susie's* stores. She was eager to be off.

"Shut off and disconnect," ordered Grimes, his voice muffled by the wet handkerchief covering his mouth. "After all this trouble we don't want to burst her. And now, Su Lin, if you'll be so good as to pack me a tucker box I'll be off. Expect me back when you see me. I'll be as quick as I can mustering help."

"But you're not going, Commodore," said Sanchez. "I'm not going?" (All the time Grimes had assumed that he would be piloting the balloon.) "*I'm* not going? Damn it all, it's my job."

"It is not, Governor Grimes," Su Lin told him. "Raoul and I have talked this over. *You* are the Governor. You are the best hope we have, such as it is, of cleaning up the mess on this planet. You're too precious to risk."

"Me, *precious!*" Grimes exploded. "Come off it, girl!" He turned to Sanchez. "*You* know, Raoul, that I'm a quite fair balloonist. Didn't I teach you quite a bit about the art of free ballooning?"

"Yes, Commodore, and I learned from you. And I am, after all, a qualified airshipman."

"Even so . . ."

"There's another point," said the girl. "We don't know, we have no way of knowing, where the balloon is going to come down. With a little bit of luck it might be somewhere that's just lousy with OAP members and supporters. On the other hand, it might be somewhere crawling with police, police informers and staunch supporters of Bardon and O'Higgins. Even if the descent is made unobserved, by night, the balloon pilot will still have to feel his way around cautiously, to find people whom he can trust. What chance would you have of doing that, Commodore? For a start, you're an obvious outworlder with an Orstrylian accent that you could cut with a knife. Raoul's a native. He knows people. He knows his way around . . ." It made sense, Grimes had to admit.

But he didn't like it.

He and Sanchez stood in the billowing, eddying smoke through which the afternoon sun gleamed fitfully. They looked up at the misshapen *Little Susie,* bobbing fretfully at her moorings.

"A poor thing, but mine own," murmured Grimes. "Look after her, Raoul."

"I hope she looks after me," said the pilot.

"You know," went on Grimes, "this is the first time in my life that I've actually designed a ship. I really should be risking my own neck on her maiden flight, not yours . . ."

"You and Su Lin," consoled Sanchez, "will be running plenty of risks staying here."

"Mphm. Why remind me?"

"Sorry, Commodore. What will you do if I'm not back with help within, say, ten days?"

"Then we make a raft or a canoe and try to make our escape downriver. In fact, I think we'll make a start on the project tomorrow."

"And that will be a ship, designed and built by yourself, that you will have the pleasure of commanding. But I hope, sir, that it never comes to that." The pilot laughed. "You seem to have a *thing* about the name Susan. Your spaceship, the one in which you went privateering, is *Sister Sue.* The airship is *Fat Susie.* The balloon— *Little Susie.* What will you call the canoe or raft?"

"*Wet Sue,*" said Grimes after a moment's thought.

"That sounds Chinese. It should please Su Lin . . ."

"Were you talking about me?" asked the girl, coming out of the ship with a plastic bag of foodstuffs and a flagon of water.

"Not exactly," said Grimes.

"Oh. Well, here're your provisions for the voyage, Raoul. As long as this wind holds they should last you as far as the nearest cantina."

If you get there, thought Grimes.

"Bon voyage, Raoul," said Su Lin. She put the food and drink into the chair suspended below the balloon (the added weight didn't seem to worry it) and then threw her arms about the pilot and kissed him soundly. Grimes felt a stab of jealousy. *"Bon voyage,* and look after yourself." Grimes made a show of checking everything before liftoff. "Food . . . Water . . . Ballast . . . Now all we need is the crew. . . ."

"All present and correct, sir!" reported Sanchez briskly, saluting.

"Good. You know the drill, Raoul. That bag of assorted stones is your ballast. Don't throw it all away in one grand gesture. You'll probably have to jettison some weight after sunset when the helium cools and loses buoyancy. But don't be a spendthrift. Once weight has been dumped you'll not be able to get it back. Conversely, gas valved is lost forever . . ."

"Understood, Commodore."

"Then, good luck, Raoul." He extended his hand. Sanchez took it. "Good luck. You'll need it."

"We all need it, sir."

Sanchez hung the flagon of water from one arm of the chair, the bag of food—bread, cold meats and fruit—from the other. He took his seat, buckled on and adjusted the safety belt.

"Ready?" asked Grimes.

"Ready."

"Trip for'ard grapnel."

Sanchez yanked sharply on one of the three mooring lines. The grapnel flukes swiveled, came free of the soil. "Trip port and starboard grapnels!" This time it was Grimes and Su Lin who jerked upwards on the lines. The grapnels lost their grip. The balloon lifted. Su Lin did not jump back and clear smartly enough and a fluke fouled her clothing, catching in the loosely buttoned front of her tunic. She was lifted from the ground. Grimes caught her dangling legs, held her. Cloth ripped. *Little Susie* continued her ascent, taking with her Su Lin's upper garment.

Grimes actually ignored the half-naked girl whom he was holding tightly in his arms, stared up and after the rising balloon. She was rising steadily, carried along in the stream of smoke that was still coming from the brush fire. The fliers, well downwind, were staying clear of the reek of the burning. But would they continue to do so? The diminishing balloon was drifting into clear air. Su Lin disengaged herself from Grimes's arms—he was hardly aware that she had done so—and was absent from his immediate presence very briefly. Then she was pressing something into his hands. It was a pair of binoculars that she had brought from the ship.

Grimes thanked her briefly, then put the powerful glasses to his eyes. The hemisphere of the balloon that he could see was holding its shape. There were (as yet, anyhow) no leaks, no ripped seams. Sanchez was sitting stolidly in his chair. But, Grimes saw as he adjusted the binoculars to obtain a wider field at the expense of magnification, the fliers, the circling, soaring and swooping carnivores, were closing in. The only weapon that Sanchez had with him was a long knife—and that was supposed to be used in lieu of a ripcord rather than to ward off attack. Too, his view obscured by the bulging gasbag, the pilot quite possibly was not even aware of his danger.

And what use would the shockers be as defensive weaponry? Grimes could see them plainly enough, gaudy patches on the silvery gray envelope. He had applauded his own cleverness in having them attached to *Little Susie's* skin but now was having his doubts. Contact with them might well be lethal but their bodies would never be tough enough to stop a direct, stabbing assault by one of those long, murderous beaks.

So far there was no direct assault.

The fliers were making rings around the balloon with contemptuous ease, flying in ever diminishing circles. (Surely Sanchez must have seen them by now—but what could he do about them? Did Anarchists pray to Bakunin?) Closer they were coming to the helpless aerostat, closer and closer. And then a leathery wing brushed *Little Susie's* taut skin—no, not her skin but the garishly colored plant attached to it.

Grimes watched the airborne predator falter in its flight and then fall, its great wings still outspread but unmoving. Dead or merely stunned, it was parachuting down. It did not reach the ground. The others were upon it, tearing it to shreds as it dropped. Grimes was reminded of maddened sharks feasting upon the injured but not yet dead body of a member of their own species.

Little Susie drifted on, steadily diminishing in the field of Grimes's binoculars. Smoke was coming from her. *Smoke?* Yes. Grimes could just see that there was something dangling below the pilot's chair, a bundle from which the thick fumes were issuing. Clothing? Possibly. Perhaps Sanchez' jacket, probably Su Lin's shirt.

The pilot's ingenuity was to be commended, but . . . Weight was being sacrificed. As a result, gas might have to be valved. And then, with sunset not far off, ballast would have to be dumped.

Was Sanchez sufficiently proficient a balloonist to juggle his buoyancy and ballast and still stay aloft for long enough to complete his voyage?

Grimes, he admonished himself, *don't be a backseat driver.*

Then *Little Susie* was no more than a speck in the sky, and then she was gone. She had not fallen, Grimes told himself. She was still aloft, still flying steadily south. She was just out of sight, that was all.

"This wind is chilly," said Su Lin.

He turned to look at her. She had her arms crossed over her naked breasts. She was shivering. Her creamy skin was speckled with smuts, some of them large, from the dying fire upwind. Her handkerchief mask and her goggles were still in place.

The effect was oddly but strongly erotic.

"There is nothing more that we can do today," she said. "I am going inside. Are you coming?"

Why not? Grimes asked himself. *Why not?* He followed her into the ship.

ᔪ Chapter 37 ᔪ

SHE DID NOT MAKE her way to her own cabin but into that occupied by Grimes. She sat down on the bunk, stripped off her goggles and the improvised mask, dropped them carelessly to the deck. This was out of character; she was usually fanatically tidy. She . . . slumped. But her breasts were proudly firm, the prominent nipples erect.

She said, "Well, Grimes, this is it. The girl from PAT and the Survey Service's prize troubleshooter alone at last. And for how long? Until Raoul returns at the head of the United States Cavalry to rescue us from this howling wilderness. *If* he does return, that is . . ."

"He'll be back," said Grimes with a conviction that was not altogether assumed.

"But when, Grimes, *when?* And how do we pass the time until we're rescued?"

"We have to keep ourselves supplied with food . . ."

"You would say that."

"We can't live on fresh air and sunshine. And then we have to make a start on building some sort of raft or canoe to get us out of here, downriver, if Raoul doesn't come back."

"As far as I'm concerned," she told him, "mucking about in boats has never been one of my favorite pastimes. Especially in homemade boats on rivers *crawling* with large, vicious carnivores . . . Did it escape your notice that this stream runs through Bloodsuckers Canyon on its way to the sea?"

As she spoke she was easing her heavy boots off her feet—her slim, graceful feet with their crimson-lacquered toenails.

"We have to do something to pass the time," said Grimes.

"For a Governor, for a pirate Commodore, for a Captain in the Survey Service Reserve you're remarkably dim. Or are you putting me on?"

"The thought of that had flickered across my tiny mind," said Grimes.

She laughed. "So the man is capable of double entendres. There's hope for him yet. . . ."

Slowly Grimes was removing his sweaty shirt. It was not quite at the stage when it could be stood in the corner but it was not far from it. And, on the bunk, the girl was sliding her trousers down her long, shapely legs. Above the waist her body was besmirched with smoke and smuts; below her navel her skin gleamed with a creamy translucence. The lush blackness of her pubic hair was in vivid contrast to the rest of her and was the focus of Grimes's mounting desire.

But, even though now naked himself, he hesitated before joining her on the not-too-narrow couch.

"Are you still . . . bugged?" he asked. "Or should I say antibugged?"

"I've room for only one thing at a time," she told him. "And, right now, that one thing is you."

It was good, very good, but Grimes could not shake off a feeling of guilt. Here was he—and here was Su Lin—reveling in the release of tensions, the all-over skin to skin contact, the intimate moist warmth, the murmured endearments and finally—from the girl— the screamed obscenities. (This rather surprised him; he had expected that one of her race would be a *quiet* lover.) He could not help thinking of Raoul Sanchez, dangling from that crudely cobbled gasbag in the perilous sky, with no one to comfort him through the coming night.

Tenderly and skillfully Su Lin aroused him again.

This time he thought only fleetingly of the young pilot. After all, he was *there* (wherever *there* was) and Grimes was here. Worrying about Sanchez would not make his voyage any safer.

And then, looking up, they saw through the port that darkness had fallen. They did not bother to dress at once. More important was to switch on the outside lights and then to make sure that there were enough shockers, attracted by the illumination, to form a protective cordon about the ship. (To judge from their numbers, few, if any of the motile plants had been destroyed by the brush fire, which now seemed to be completely out.) Satisfied that they were about as safe as ever they would be they heated water, refraining from extravagance, and shared a sponge-down. Attired in clean clothing they had a not-too-bad dinner of what Grimes described as tarted-up bits and pieces, washed down with a quite decent local variety of claret. They drew up a watch-and-watch roster.

Grimes—who should have been drowsy but was not, who was feeling exceptionally fit and alert—took the first tour of duty while Su Lin slept in his bed.

~ Chapter 38 ~

THE NIGHT PASSED.

Grimes, who (thanks to his father's influence) was already something of a maritime historian, began to feel considerable sympathy for those long-ago Terran seamen to whom watch and watch had been routine. He recalled having read somewhere that Bligh—the much and unjustly maligned Bligh!—had been, by the standards of his time, an exceptionally humane captain. He had put his crews on three watches, four hours on and eight hours off. And now Grimes, following in Bligh's footsteps for the second time in his career, was having to revert to the bad old ways and, thereby, was missing out on his beauty sleep.

He didn't like it.

Neither did Su Lin. "Midnight already?" she complained.

"No," he told her. "It's one bell. 2345. You've fifteen minutes before you're on watch."

"At least you've made tea. Thank you." She sipped from the steaming cup and grimaced. "What did you do? If I weren't a lady I'd refer to this as gnat's piss."

"One for each person and one for the pot," he said.

"What! I'll not believe that you used three spoonfuls of tea to make this feeble brew!"

"Who mentioned spoonfuls? One tea leaf for each person, one for the pot. There's precious little dry tea left in the canister."

"I think I'll be able to find another packet or two. But you're right. We shall have to be economical . . . ."

Grimes would have liked to have stayed with her, to have watched her as she slid her elegant nudity from under the bed coverings. But he feared that if he did so there would be no middle watch kept. Regretfully he went back out into the alleyway. Before long, dressed in shirt, slacks and calf-length boots, she joined him there.

"All quiet," he told her. "All lights burning brightly. The shockers have been capturing occasional nocturnal beasties but I didn't see what they were. If you're happy, I'll get my head down."

"I have been happier," she told him. "On the other hand—I've been unhappier. . . ."

She kissed him briefly, then broke away before things could develop. He went into his cabin, stripped rapidly and slid between the sheets that were still warm from her body.

It seemed that only seconds had passed when she called him at 0345.

The pot of tea she brought was better—but only a little better—than the one that he had made. There was only one packet of tea remaining in the stores and they would have to make it last.

They shared breakfast—fried rice with the protein component being what was left of the worm. They knew that they must soon make a serious attempt at living entirely off the country but were inhibited from foraging by the activities of the fliers which, almost immediately after dawn, maintained a patrol over the island. And they were now almost weaponless. The charge of Su Lin's lighter was so depleted that it was now useful only for the ignition of the tobacco in Grimes's pipe. (And how long could he make his tobacco last?) The laser tool was effective only at very short range. Knives would not be of much use against something that could dive, without warning, from the sky with at least two meters of sharp, horny beak extended before it.

Water was not, yet, an immediate problem. There were still bottles of various mineral waters in the stores—but once these were gone they would have to go down to the river again. While there had been three of them, one could watch the sky, another keep an eye on the stream and the third one fill the buckets.

"Sometimes," said Su Lin, "I wish I were a mutant. One with eyes at the back of my head."

They spent the day mainly inside the wreck. Grimes, once again using the backs of the charts on which to make calculations and draw plans, tried to work out ways and means of using what wreckage was available to make some sort of boat or raft. A coracle would have been easy—had there been any of the adhesive left. But this had all been used in the manufacture of *Little Susie*. The sheet metal of the skin was very thin and could be bent into shape by hand. The laser pistol was actually a welding tool. Yet a canoe made this way would be almost as flimsy as a coracle and would offer hardly more protection against the aquatic predators.

At sunset Grimes had a sudden rush of brains to the head. Using the laser he killed—at least, he hoped that had killed it—one of the shockers when the creatures, attracted by the lights, took up their stations about the ship. Handling it with heavily gloved hands, careful not to let the still twitching mass touch any other portions of their bodies, they got the thing into the galley, put it onto one of the work surfaces. It overlapped considerably, the edges of it hung down almost to the deck.

Su Lin carved off a slice, then cut from this a very small portion. She chewed thoughtfully. When she spoke, Grimes saw that her teeth were stained green.

She said, "There's moisture here. And possibly—hopefully— some food value. Of course, there must be. The thing eats meat itself. . . ."

After an hour had elapsed she was suffering no ill effects. She and Grimes dined on shocker salad, washed down with shocker juice. (The thing's "battery" yielded a quite refreshing, only slightly acid fluid.) They were well-fed enough but they still felt hungry. Too, probably their diet, although rich in vitamins, would be deficient in many other essentials.

There was another night of watch and watch.

Just before sunrise, before the fliers resumed their diurnal patrol, Grimes was lucky enough to kill a shocker just after it had killed a thing that, he said later, looked like a cross between a spider and an Airedale terrier. He was able, at some risk, to get the animal's body into the wreck before any of the other carnivorous plants could reach it.

This provided them with meat for the day's meals.

The flesh was tough but Su Lin found that marinating it in juice squeezed from a dead shocker tenderized it. The meat was almost flavorless—but it was meat.

It would be possible for Grimes and Su Lin to hold on until Raoul Sanchez returned with help.

If he returned. . . .

If not they would either have to live out their lives as castaways or risk their lives on a hazardous voyage downriver in some cranky, homemade canoe.

Chapter 39

"DON'T . . . STOP . . ." SHE MURMURED. But Grimes's body, clasped to hers by her strong arms and thighs, had become motionless. He tried to raise his head from where it had been beside hers on the pillow. He demanded, "Do . . . you . . . hear . . . it?"

"Hear what? I can hear your heart thumping away like a runaway steam engine . . ."

"Not . . . my heart. Or yours . . . Listen!" She heard it then. It was very faint, coming from far away. It was the irritable mutter of an inertial drive unit. A small one, thought Grimes, such as are fitted to ships' boats and pinnaces. And there had been a pinnace in one of the hangars at the Residence.

The mutter was now more of an interrupted snarl.

The thing was getting closer.

So Raoul had made it after all.

Grimes tried to disengage himself.

She asked, rather tartly, "Aren't you going to finish what you started?"

He said, "My name is Grimes, not Sir Francis Drake."

She said, "I wasn't aware that we were playing bowls."

They laughed together.

And then doubt assailed Grimes. What if this approaching pinnace or whatever were not piloted by Raoul Sanchez? What if this were Bardon or some of his minions coming to make sure that the troublesome Governor was well and truly dead?

Then this might be the last time.

She said, "I thought you were in a hurry to rush out to repel boarders."

He said, "A man can change his mind, can't he?"

He completed the act—but it was not as good as it should have been. All the time he was aware of that rapidly approaching pinnace. He rolled off her, hastily pulled on a pair of trousers, picked up the almost useless laser pistol from the table on which he had left it, went out to the catwalk and then made his way to the hole that had been cut in the metal envelope. He was just in time to see the ship's boat coming in to land.

A ship's boat?

And what was the name on the bows?

No, not a name. Just letters and a number.

AA #1.

The boat touched ground, crushing at least half a dozen of the shockers. A scent like that of new-mown grass filled the air. The cacophony of the inertial drive unit abruptly ceased. Slowly the outer airlock door opened. From it stepped a woman, not young but far from old, with short, iron-gray hair and matching eyes, dressed in a uniform that was, essentially, a short-skirted business suit, well-tailored from some gray fabric that looked (and probably was) very expensive, with touches of gold braid at the collar and on the sleeves.

She looked at Grimes and at the scantily clad girl standing behind him.

She asked pleasantly, "Have I interrupted something, Commodore?"

And then she, herself, was interrupted as four of the fliers, briefly scared off by the racket of the boat's inertial drive unit but now, with that engine shut down and silent, returning in search of prey, swooped. She would have been skewered had not Raoul Sanchez, jumping out of the airlock, knocked her to one side and then delivered a dazzling exhibition of laser play.

Before the remainder of the circling predators could launch a fresh attack he yanked the woman to her feet, hustled her through the opening cut in *Fat Susie's* skin and then literally fell in after her.

"Who is your friend, Raoul?" asked Su Lin.

The pilot scrambled to his feet, then said courteously, "Allow me to introduce Captain Agatha Prinn, of *Agatha's Ark*. Captain Prinn already knows Commodore Grimes, of course."

"Of course," she agreed. "We're old flotilla mates. And now the Commodore is a Governor and I'm still a star tramp skipper. But didn't somebody say once, 'Uneasy lies the head that wears a crown'?"

"You're more of an absolute monarch aboard your ship, Agatha," Grimes told her, "than I am on this planet. But tell me, do you still have that young El Doradan officer, the Count von Stolzberg, with you?"

"You mean Ferdinand, your son. . . ."

"How did you know . . . ?"

"Everybody knew. But no, he's no longer with me. A pity. He was a good spaceman. But after the Inquiry into the privateering racket we were told that any El Doradan officers must be repatriated. . . ."

"Excuse me, sir and madam," put in Sanchez, "I really think that this old pirates' reunion can be deferred for a while. What's of pressing urgency is what's happening now on Liberia, not what happened when you were scouring the interstellar spacelanes under the Jolly Roger!"

Grimes glared at the young man, then laughed.

"All right, Raoul. Come into the wardroom and tell us your story. And is there any beer left, Su Lin? Good. This calls for a celebration. Raoul back in one piece, and Agatha with him . . ."

"It's thanks only to Captain Prinn that I am back," said Sanchez.

The flight of *Little Susie,* said Sanchez, had not been too bad an experience. The worst of it had been the way in which he had almost been kippered, sitting in his chair with the smoldering rags—Su Lin's shirt and then his own clothing—directly beneath him. But the smoke had scared off the fliers.

During the first night he had been obliged to drop most of his ballast. The next day, to prevent the balloon from rising to a dangerous altitude, it had been necessary to valve helium. But the wind had been stronger than anticipated and he had made good time. By late afternoon he was out of the Unclaimed Territory. He didn't know quite where he was but, sighting a village on the horizon, decided to make his descent before he was over the settlement. He came down in a wheatfield, one some weeks away from its future harvesting. There was nobody to see his landing.

He extricated himself, with some difficulty, from the smothering folds of the deflating gasbag. He was, he realized, armed only with a galley knife and practically naked; he had stripped himself to his underpants to keep his deterrent fire going. As long as he was airborne he had not felt the cold as he had been traveling at the same speed as the wind. Now that breeze on his bare skin was very chilly.

He made his way toward the lights of the village, finding the going difficult in the fast-gathering darkness. At last he stumbled onto a road. Then he made better progress.

There was nobody abroad. He walked past the slave barracks—the *refugee* barracks, he corrected himself—and heard the sound of voices and of Oriental music and smelled the enticing aromas of exotic cookery. Now he was hungry as well as cold.

He kept on until he was in the village itself. There was the inn. He saw the sign—THE TORCH OF LIBERTY. It was then that he thought that some of Grimes's famous luck had rubbed off on himself. The parents of Miguel, one of his crew aboard the Met. Service tender, were innkeepers. The name of their cantina was The Torch of Liberty. Like their son, they were members of the OAP, the Original Anarchist Party. Raoul knew that there must be many Torches Of Liberty throughout Liberia—but somehow he was sure that this was the right one.

He went round to the back door.

He knocked cautiously.

He went on knocking.

At last the door opened and Miguel was standing there, demanding, "Who is it? What do you want?"

"I still can't get over the fantastic coincidence," said Raoul.

"No fiction writer," Grimes told him, "would dare to use the coincidences that are always happening in real life. But go on."

Miguel was on leave.

Miguel saw to it that Sanchez was fed and clothed and plied with restorative drinks. He listened to the pilot's story. He was of the opinion that the planetary authorities should be ignored and that Grimes should be rescued from the island as secretly as possible. The best way of achieving this, he said, would be to "borrow" one of the Met. Service tenders from Port Libertad and fly directly to the site of the wreck.

Meanwhile, Sanchez learned, already the news had been put about that Governor Grimes and his small entourage had perished in an airship crash. Searches had been mounted—but not one of them had covered the Unclaimed Territory. The Met. Satellites were making continual photographic surveys of Liberia—but the processing of the films was being carried out by Bardon's people. Almost certainly the fire on the island had been seen from orbit but it was being ignored.

Miguel and Raoul flew to Port Libertad in Miguel's 'copter. Both of them in Met. Service uniform, they attempted to take over one of the tenders. But the spaceport guards—Bardon's people—were suspicious. One of them had recognized Sanchez. There had been shooting, a chase. The two men had split up. Perhaps Miguel had escaped; Sanchez hoped that he had. Raoul, by this time little more than a mindless, hunted animal, had run up the ramp into the after airlock of one of the deep space ships in port. . . .

Agatha Prinn took up the tale.

"I was just strolling ashore," she said. "I'd just gotten as far as the airlock, in fact, when I heard shooting. I wondered what the hell was going on. And then this young man came bolting up the ramp, brushing past me. I was curious, naturally. And, having been to this world before, I was inclined to think that anybody in trouble with the authorities couldn't be all that bad. So I told my second mate—

he was shipkeeping officer—to keep an airlock watch and to swear to any police or guards or whatever that no strangers had come aboard while, in my own quarters, I heard young Raoul's story.

"And what a story it was!

"As you know, Commodore, we tramp masters neither know nor care who heads the governments of the various worlds that we visit. We deal only with Customs, Immigration and Port Health officials. We never meet Prime Ministers or Presidents or Governors. At first I couldn't believe that *you* were the Governor Grimes of Liberia. But it all tied in. Jug-handle ears, ex-Survey Service officer, ex-owner-master, ex-commodore of privateers.

"I've already told you that I've been to this world before, more than once. On any planet, this one included, I like to take one of my boats for a sightseeing cruise around. I log it as Boat Drill, of course. So the Port Authorities didn't feel it worth their while to make close inquiries when, this morning, I told them that I was about to go on my usual sightseeing tour." She laughed. "As a matter of fact one puppy, laughing himself sick over his alleged humor, did ask me to keep my eyes skinned for Governor Grimes and *Fat Susie.*"

"And now you've found him," said Grimes.

"And now I take you and your people back to *Agatha's Ark*. I've plenty of spare accommodation. I'll keep you out of sight until we lift—and then you can use my Carlotti equipment to bleat to your bosses back on Earth about what's been happening."

"Why can't I bleat now?" asked Grimes.

"Because it's not legal for any ship to use deep space radio while in port. You should know that. You're Governor, aren't you?"

"Mphm. Well, if you don't mind, Agatha, I'd like you to take us back to the Residence. I'm still Governor—and I want to play hell with a big stick as long as I'm in office. There's Major Flattery for a start. I shall demand that he be arrested and put on trial. There's the dreamweed trade. There's . . . Oh, I could go on and on . . ."

"You can go on and on, Commodore, once you're up and clear from Liberia."

"But that wouldn't be the same, Agatha. Look at what happened in New South Wales. Governor Bligh was deposed—and then what could he do? He got no support from his Lieutenant Governor in Tasmania. He returned to England and was, to all intents and purposes, swept under the mat. Oh, Major Johnston was, eventually, brought to trial but received little more than a rap over the knuckles—and that after leading an armed mutiny!

"I have to stay here.

"I have to exert my authority. I have to show Estrelita and her boyfriend Bardon who's boss."

"As you please, Commodore," said Agatha Prinn. "I wish that I could be of some real help—but *Agatha's Ark* is no longer a privateer. The only arms aboard her are a few privately owned laser and projectile pistols."

"Just take me back to the Residence," said Grimes, "and I'll play it by ear from then on."

~ Chapter 40 ~

THEY MANAGED to scamper the short distance between the wreck and the ship's boat without being attacked by anything. Once inside the small craft they made a careful search and were relieved to find that no hostile lifeform had taken up residence while the boat had been left unattended. Then, with Agatha Prinn at the controls, they lifted from the island and set course for the Residence.

Captain Prinn wanted to deliver Grimes at his own front door but he talked her out of it. It would be better, he said, if he and the others were dropped within easy walk of the gubernatorial palace: that way they could make entry without their being expected by Jaconelli and Smith. Too, Agatha would not be liable to reprisal by the authorities if there were nothing to associate her with the Governor.

"But they must know," she protested. "They must know that I was one of your captains on the privateering expedition."

"They *should* know," he told her, "but they almost certainly don't. If they had associated you with me they would not have allowed you to go flapping off by yourself all over Liberia. Thanks to my father I'm something of a student of history—and I know that very often Military Intelligence has been a contradiction in terms."

They timed their arrival for the beginning of evening twilight. Raoul took the controls and dropped the boat to a field just off the

road running up the hill to the Residence. They disembarked—
Sanchez first, then Su Lin, finally Grimes. All of them were armed
with weapons supplied by Captain Prinn—laser pistols for the
pilot and the girl, a Minetti automatic for Grimes. Only Sanchez
was wearing anything approximating a disguise, a uniform (which
fitted quite well) borrowed from one of *Agatha's Ark's* junior
officers.

"Let me know if I can do anything more, Commodore," said the
tramp captain.

"You've done plenty already, Agatha. But if things go too badly
wrong you can put in a full report to Rear Admiral Damien once
you get clear of this world."

"I'll do that."

Surprisingly she took him in her arms and kissed him. He found
himself wishing that he could carry on from there but there was no
time. Besides, Su Lin was looking in through the open airlock doors,
an amused expression on her face.

He broke away.

"Thank you for everything, Agatha."

"It was nothing. And, good luck, John. The very best of luck."

Grimes jumped down to the damp grass.

He stood with the others and watched the boat lift, watched her
running lights dim and diminish as she continued her interrupted
voyage to the spaceport.

They walked up the road.

They met nobody.

They did not use the front entrance to the Residence but went
round to a back door, to what Grimes thought of as the tradesmen's
entrance. Surprisingly, there they were met. Wong Lee, the old
butler, seemed to have been expecting them. He bowed and said, "It
is good that you are back, Excellency."

"I'm pleased to be back," said Grimes. "Too right I am."

He followed the old man through the maze of corridors. They
came at last to the Governor's quarters. The sitting room was empty
but there were voices coming from the adjoining office. One

belonged to Smith, the ADC, the other to Jaconelli, the secretary. They seemed to be having a party. There was a clinking of glasses and the speech of each man was slurred.

"Flattery's got his step up to half-colonel," Smith was complaining, "but there's no hint that I shall get my captaincy."

"But *you* didn't actually *do* anything," said Jaconelli. "Flattery did do something. He got that bastard Grimes out of our hair for keeps. And that poisonous tart Sue Ellen or whatever her name was . . ."

"What've you got against *her?*"

"She wouldn't play, that's what. Anyhow, they're all out of our hair. Grimes, the uppity tart and that upstart of a ferry skipper . . ."

"No, they're not," said Grimes, stepping into his office with his Minetti out and ready.

That was just the start.

There were the soldiers of the guard to be disarmed and locked up. They were not so easy to deal with as Smith and Jaconelli had been. There was actually gunfire while Sergeant Martello, holed up in Smith's office, got through on the telephone to Colonel Bardon, quite bravely ignoring Grimes's finally successful attempt to shoot out the lock. (Sanchez's prior attempt, using his hand laser, had succeeded only in fusing this into a mass of metal that held the door as firmly as in its original state.)

Martello got up from his seat at the desk to face the intruders. He was a big, paunchy man, almost bald and with little, porcine eyes in his fat face. His hand went to his holstered weapon, then he thought better of it. He raised his hands reluctantly above his head.

"All right," he growled. "You've won—for the time being. But the Colonel will soon fix your wagon . . ."

"That will do, Sergeant!" snapped a voice from the telephone screen. "You have my permission to surrender to the pirate. You will be released very shortly."

Martello moved to one side, away from the scanner.

Grimes looked into Bardon's angry face.

"Colonel Bardon," he said, "you are to place yourself under

arrest. Before you do so, however, please see to it that Major—or should I say Lieutenant Colonel?—Flattery is clapped in irons."

"It's you who's under arrest, Grimes. Do you want to hear the charges? Whilst under the influence of drugs or alcohol you, in charge of a dirigible airship, deliberately collided with another such vessel owned by the Terran military establishment on Liberia, causing considerable structural damage. Returning to the Residence, you have threatened officers, non-commissioned officers and enlisted men of the Terran Army with firearms and illegally incarcerated them. A man in your employ, one Raoul Sanchez, attempted to steal a shuttlecraft from the Port Libertad spaceyard. A woman in your employ, one Su Lin, murdered a laborer under the protection of Senor Eduardo Lopez.

"A pirate, sir, is obviously no fit person to be appointed as governor of a civilized planet."

Grimes laughed.

"You must have suspected, Bardon, that I just might get out of the mess that your precious Flattery left me in—otherwise you wouldn't have been so ready with all those charges! But I must correct you on two points. One—I was a privateer, not a pirate. Two—I rather doubt that this is a civilized planet."

"Are you giving yourself up, Grimes?"

"Are you putting yourself under arrest, Bardon?"

"Don't argue with him!" There were two faces in the screen now; the other one was that of the President. "Send your soldiers to take the Residence. *Now*—or as soon as you can get them out of the whorehouses and grogshops!"

"I'll send Flattery to bomb the bloody place!" growled Bardon.

"You will not. The building—and it cost plenty!—is Liberian property. And what about your own men imprisoned there?"

"They wouldn't be much loss," Bardon said.

"I heard that, Colonel, *sir,*" put in Sergeant Martello. "Now, let me tell you that I've never liked working for you and your officers. If the Commodore will have me, I'll fight for him!"

Bardon cursed, then the telephone screen went blank.

Grimes stared at the big sergeant, who was still standing with hands upraised, still covered by the weapons held by Su Lin, Sanchez and Wong Lee.

Was the man sincere?

What was his motivation?

Grimes had . . . glimmerings. A lifetime in the Army, a failure to attain commissioned rank, a growing, festering resentment at having to take orders from officers no better soldiers than himself, quite possibly not even as good. Perhaps harsh treatment by Bardon or officers like him, unjust treatment . . .

Perhaps—it was possible although not probable—the uneasy stirrings of a conscience.

"All right, Sergeant," he said, "I'll believe you—with reservations. I'm not a soldier—so you shall be my advisor. But I'll be obliged if you'll hand your pistol—butt first—to Captain Sanchez. No, cancel that. Keep *very* still while Captain Sanchez takes the gun from its holster . . . Good. Now you can drop your hands. . . ."

They watched him, more than half-expecting an explosion of hostile energy. But the sergeant just stood there, grinning.

He said, "You'll not believe this, Commodore, but as a boy I used to read space stories, pirate stories especially. I wanted to be a pirate when I grew up. Now, whatever happens, I'll be able to say that I served under one of the famous pirate captains."

Grimes started to explain, for the thousandth time, the difference between a privateer and a pirate, then decided that he would be merely wasting his breath.

Out of earshot of the sergeant he had a few words with Wong Lee.

"Get word to the spaceport," he said, "to Captain Agatha Prinn of the ship *Agatha's Ark*. I can't use the telephone; Bardon will be monitoring any calls made from here. See that Captain Prinn is told just what's been happening since I got back. Then, as soon as she's off this world, she can make a full report to Earth."

"Very good, Your Excellency."

"How many of your people can use firearms?"

"Most of them, Your Excellency."

"How . . .? But no matter. Round up all the weapons you can and have men on the roof. That parapet is more than merely ornamental."

≈ Chapter 41 ≈

GRIMES STOOD with Su Lin on the small, railed platform that was at the highest point of the low-pitched roof. They had binoculars with them, powerful night glasses that converted infrared radiation into visible wavelengths. They swept the terrain on all sides of the Residence. Of one thing they could be certain—nothing big was out and moving, although there were small, glowing sparks representing tiny nocturnal animals.

"How is it," asked Grimes, "that so many of the domestic staff—if Wong Lee is to be believed—are expert in the use of weapons?"

She said, "You must have guessed by now that the Underground—or one of the many Undergrounds—has seen to it that the Governor's personal entourage are capable of defending him should the need arise."

"Mphm. But I thought that only full citizens of this world were allowed to own firearms."

"Ever since firearms were invented they've been falling into the wrong hands. Or—in this case—the right hands. Criminals or freedom fighters have always been able to get arms. When you went a-pirating it wasn't in an unarmed ship, was it?"

"For about the four thousandth time," growled Grimes, "I was a privateer, not a pirate."

"Sorry." The laugh following the word indicated that she wasn't.

Grimes broke the short silence.

"Isn't it time," he asked, "that I was put into the picture? After all, should things come entirely unstuck who'll have to carry the can back? Me, that's who."

"Too right," she said, in an imitation of an Australian accent. "But I agree. You have been kept in the dark—by everybody, from Admiral Damien on down. Liberia is on the point of blowing up. Not only is there the OAP but there are the secret organizations of the various refugees. The aim of PAT is that it shall be a *controlled* explosion. We may be People Against Tyranny—but we are also against Anarchy, using the word in its very worst sense, against mob rule and mindless violence. One of our requirements was a Governor who could stand as a figurehead for the rebels and who would recognize whatever sort of government is formed after the revolution.

"We had our doubts about your predecessor. He was a good man, but rather lacking in glamour. But you are a glamorous figure."

"Who? Me?"

"Yes. The people will rally behind a famous pirate, a man who was a pirate for the very best of motives. . . ."

"Mphm. Well, Su Lin, where do we go from here? What happens next?"

"Bardon sends a detachment here to arrest you. That will be the signal for rioting to break out in the city, for risings on many of the big estates and plantations. . . ."

"And if the detachment Bardon sends," said Grimes, "is a really powerful one, with hovertanks and aircraft, we stand a very good chance of winding up very dead."

"Bardon and O'Higgins want you alive, so that you can stand trial for your crimes. And then they'll crucify you. No, not literally. But you'll be crucified, all right. Deported to Earth in disgrace together with a curt note from the President. 'Please do not send us any more criminals as Governors.' But, of course, they will have to arrest you first. . . ."

Sanchez came up to the lookout point. Grimes handed him his night glasses and then, with Su Lin, went down to his quarters. He sent for Sergeant Martello. The big man soon made his appearance, escorted by two machine-pistol-toting chefs. He drew himself to stiff attention.

"Commodore, sir!"

"Sit down, Sergeant. And that'll do the rest of you. Oh, Su Lin, will you organize tea for us? Good. . . ."

"You sent for me, sir?" said Martello.

"Obviously, I want your expert advice. I know, of course, what forces the good colonel has at his disposal *on paper*. What's the situation in actual practice?"

"If any hostile power from outside tried to invade this world, sir, they could take it with an armed space tug and a platoon of Boy Scouts. One of the things that sickened me was the way in which equipment has been allowed to deteriorate. I was in charge of the maintenance of armored vehicles at the barracks—and I made such a nuisance of myself trying to get people to do their jobs properly that I was shifted to the Residence Guard, just to get me out of the way. It'd take all of a week to get the hover-tanks in order for any sort of real action. The wheeled vehicles, the armored cars, are in slightly better nick, but they're only lightly armed."

"Aircraft?" asked Grimes.

"Flattery's ship was damaged after that collision with yours. I don't think that anybody has gotten around to starting repairs yet. There's another dirigible but, the last I heard, all the helium cells were leaking badly. Three ex-Survey Service pinnaces, I suppose you'd call them. Inertial drive jobs. Light armament. Half a dozen little helicopters. . . ."

And I've a pinnace of my own, thought Grimes. *And a near-wreck of a helicopter. And, of course, Raoul's little flitterbug. . . .*

He asked, "If you were Colonel Bardon, Sergeant, what would you do?"

"Bardon," said Martello, "has always liked making arrests in the middle of the night or in the small hours of the morning. The same applies to the civil—if you can call those bastards civil!—police. But they've been arresting people who weren't expecting it. And they haven't had to be rounded up from the nightspots to go on duty.

"Believe me or don't believe me as you please, Commodore, but I think that the attempted arrest will be in the morning—and not too early in the morning, either. The approach, I think, will be made by road. Bardon was involved in a minor crash once and he's scared of flying. He'll not be expecting any armed resistance except that from you, your pilot and, possibly, Miss Su Lin. . . ." He looked admiringly at the girl, who had just come in with a tea tray. "However did you organize all the Residence Chinks, miss, right under our noses? I can see by the way they're handling their guns that they know how to use them."

She smiled coldly. "I suppose that I should thank you for the implied compliment, Sergeant. But in China, many, many years ago, there used to be a saying. Horseshoes are made from inferior iron—and soldiers from inferior men."

Amazingly Martello did not take offense. He laughed. "That certainly applies to Bardon and most of his officers!"

But not to the enlisted men? wondered Grimes, but said nothing.

He sipped his tea. So did the sergeant and Su Lin.

He said, "Since it doesn't seem that anything is going to happen tonight—what's left of it—I'll get my head down. You know where to find me if you want me."

He got from his chair, walked through to his bedroom.

He heard Martello whisper to the girl. "He's a cool customer, the Commodore. We could do with a few like him in the Army. . . ."

Nonetheless he was a long time getting to sleep. He was hoping that Su Lin would join him. But she, he reproached himself, would be doing all the work while he caught up on his rest.

~ Chapter 42 ~

GRIMES SHOULD HAVE GIVEN ORDERS that the prisoners be thoroughly searched before they were locked in a storeroom. He was awakened, shortly before sunrise, by the unmistakable clatter of an inertial drive unit. His first thought was that Bardon had mounted an attack by air after all, especially as there was also the rattle of automatic fire. Snatching the borrowed Minetti from his bedside table, pausing briefly to throw a light robe about himself, he ran into his sitting room, stared out through the wide window. He could see people on the lawn, could see the muzzle flashes of the guns that they were firing upwards. The noise of the inertial drive diminished. So the pinnace—as he assumed that it was—had been driven away.

He decided that it would be better if he stayed in one place rather than go running around, making inquiries. He collected his pipe and tobacco from the bedroom, went into his office and sat down behind the big desk. He had succeeded in establishing his personal smokescreen when Su Lin and Sanchez came in.

He grinned at them.

"So you repelled boarders," he said.

They did not grin back.

"We failed," said the girl, "to prevent the prisoners from escaping."

"They were only a liability," said Grimes.

"But they escaped in the pinnace," Sanchez told him. "*Our* pinnace. Worse—before they left they made sure that the two helicopters will never fly again."

"Who let them out?" demanded Grimes. "Martello? I was a fool to have trusted him."

"Come in, Sergeant!" called Su Lin, turning to face the open door into the living room.

Martello entered.

"It was my fault, sir," he admitted.

"So you released your cobbers."

"No cobbers of mine, Commodore. But I should have remembered that Levine was a professional thief before he joined the Army. Yes—and after. Burglar Levine they call him. He used to boast that he could pick any lock ever made. . . ."

"And now you tell me." He turned to Su Lin. "Any of our people hurt?"

"None badly. Two sentries knocked out, but they're recovering."

"So it could have been worse."

"But our aircraft, sir! We don't have any aircraft now!"

"And so what, Raoul?" asked Grimes. "What could we do with them if they were still operational?"

"They'd give us a chance to escape from here."

"*All* of us, Raoul? All the Residence staff? Cooks and gardeners and maids and scullions and . . . and . . . I'm surprised at you. What about the tradition that the captain should be the last to leave the sinking ship?"

Sanchez flushed ashamedly.

"It's just that, even now, I can't think of the refugees as being part of the revolution."

"But they are," said Su Lin. "And they've far more to rebel about than you romantic Original Anarchists."

Grimes got to his feet.

"Since I'm up," he said, "I might as well stay up. I'd like breakfast, Su Lin, in half an hour's time. But let me know if there's any sign of an attack."

After the others left his quarters he went through to his bathroom.

~ Chapter 43 ~

THERE WAS A UNIFORM that he had brought with him in his luggage—his own uniform, that of a Far Traveler Couriers captain. If there was any fighting to be done he would prefer to do it properly attired. So he dressed himself in the slate-gray shorts, shirt and long socks, flicked a few specks of dust off his gold-braided shoulderboards. He contrived a belt from a dressing gown sash, thrust the borrowed automatic pistol into it. He walked into his sitting room just as Su Lin entered with a laden tray.

"No morning paper?" he asked severely.

She looked him up and down with amused approval. She said, "Something seems to have gone wrong with the delivery, Commodore."

"I wonder what?"

He sat down to enjoy his meal. (The condemned man ate a hearty breakfast?) Su Lin sat down to talk to him, sipping coffee from her own cup.

"All quiet," she said. "Too quiet. The telephone's dead. On the credit side, there's no sign of any air activity. Back to the debit side— I'd have been expecting that there'd have been rioting in the city by now."

"How would we know if there was any rioting?"

"There would be fires, explosions. All I can think of is that the various rebel factions are waiting to see which way the cat will jump.

219

And there are so many rebel factions. The OAP and all the planetary organizations. The Texans, for example, would be quite happy to see the New Cantonese pulling the hot chestnuts out of the fire from them."

"And everybody would like to use me as a cat's paw."

"We're here with you, Grimes. Raoul, and all the New Cantonese, and even Sergeant Martello."

"I still can't make him out."

"It's simple. He just hates Bardon, is all. He had his rackets, as do all the Terran troops on Liberia. He was poaching on Bardon's preserves. Bardon became the heavy colonel and put a stop to the sergeant's little games. And then, when Bardon, during that telephone conversation, made it plain that he didn't give a damn about the safety of his own people in the Residence, that was it."

"So all his other talk, about playing at pirates and the rest of it, was just so much bullshit."

"Mm. Maybe. Maybe not. . . ."

Sanchez came in.

He, too, was in his own version of uniform—the faded blue denims, the scarlet neckerchief.

"Armored cars, Commodore," he announced. "Approaching from the city."

"ETA?" asked Grimes.

"Thirty minutes from now, sir."

"Good." Grimes broke another crisp roll, buttered it and then thickly spread the exposed surfaces with marmalade. "Then I've time to finish my breakfast in comfort."

"But we could ambush the armored cars, sir. There're low walls along the road as they approach the Residence."

"Captain Sanchez," Grimes told him severely, "*we* cannot afford to break the law, such as it is. *They* must be seen to fire the first shot. Besides," he went on, "our firearms won't make much impression on their armor."

"We could get the officers," said Raoul, "before they button up. And the kitchen staff has been making Molotov cocktails."

"Their intentions may be peaceful," said Grimes. "Mind you, I shall be surprised if they are. But, until we know for certain. . . ." He bit into his roll. He did not, now, feel much like eating but he had to consider his reputation—Gutsy Grimes, the man who would not miss a meal even though the Universe were crumbling about his ears.

"I'll get back on top, sir," said Sanchez at last. "I'll let you know what develops."

"Do that, Raoul," said Grimes through a mouthful of roll and marmalade.

Eventually he got up, patted his lips with his table napkin, filled and lit his pipe. Accompanied by Su Lin he took the elevator up to the roof. They joined Sanchez on the lookout platform. Grimes took the proffered binoculars, looked at the advancing armored column. There were a half-dozen of the drab-painted six-wheeled vehicles. Their hatches were open; in each one stood the begoggled car commander. It was all very pretty and, thought Grimes, remarkably archaic. From a staff mounted on the leading car flew a large, white flag.

So there was to be a parley first.

Oh, well, thought Grimes, *I might as well hear what the man wants to say.*

He went down to the portico, stopping off in his quarters to collect his cap. He glanced at himself briefly in the wardrobe mirror. In his rather shabby uniform, with his cap at a rakish angle, with that scarlet dressing gown sash into which the pistol was thrust, he looked like the pirate that many supposed him to be. Then, outside the main entrance, he was standing there, Su Lin and Sanchez beside him and behind him the Residence staff, all armed, their colorful liveries making them look like a smartly uniformed army.

The leading car came to a halt about twenty meters from the portico. The officer climbed down from the turret. He was a man whom Grimes did not recognize. He was carrying, on a stick, another white flag, a small one.

He came to attention before Grimes and then, it seemed, thought better of it. He fell into what could be described only as an insolent slouch.

"You are John Grimes?" he asked.

"I have that honor," Grimes replied.

"You are under arrest. I have to inform you that any resistance will make things all the worse for you and your people."

"You've come to the wrong shop this time, Major Johnston," said Grimes.

"My name is not Johnston," said the major, obviously baffled by the historical allusion.

"Maybe not. And this isn't Sydney, New South Wales. And now, sir, I'm ordering you off my premises. And take your mechanized tin cans with you."

"Very well, sir. You have been warned."

The officer turned, marched back to his armored car. Grimes and the others retreated inside the Residence. The big, solid doors slammed shut but they could not keep out the sound of the highly amplified voice that was shouting, over and over again, "Come out! Come quietly! Come out, or I open fire!"

This ceased when a marksman on the roof scored a hit on the sonic projector. Almost immediately there came the rattle of heavy machine-gun fire. The doors shuddered but held. Nothing came through them—but it could not be long before they were literally chewed away. The doors held—but windows shattered. "Down!" Martello was bawling in his sergeant's voice. "Down!"

People were dropping to the floor but none of them was a casualty.

Yet.

Grimes went up to the roof, found his way to the parapet that was little more than a low gutter rim. He crouched behind it, beside one of the chefs who was pouring automatic fire down on the cars. He tapped the man on the shoulder. "Hold your fire until it can do some good," he admonished. "Ammunition doesn't grow on trees. . . ." The man grinned at him cheerfully, inserted a fresh clip into his weapon and blazed away again. But if the defenders were the rankest amateurs the attackers were not much better. Had they continued to concentrate their fire on the main entrance they would have been through it in minutes. But they seemed to be playing at Red Indians attacking a wagon train, circling the Residence. And they were not using their laser cannon. That made sense, Grimes supposed. Lasers could start a disastrous fire and Estrelita O'Higgins had made it clear that she did not want the building too badly damaged. Meanwhile, these circling tactics ensured that nobody escaped. Perhaps the intention was to starve the defenders out.

Then Bardon would have a long wait, thought Grimes wryly. The Residence's larders were very well-stocked. There was a deep freeze that could almost have accommodated a herd of mastodons.

It was a situation approaching stalemate—until one of the armored cars broke down. Martello's tale of slovenly maintenance had been a true one. The defenders on the roof concentrated their fire on the stalled vehicle. There was a chance, just a chance, that a lucky bullet might find a chink in the armor. Eventually the major decided that he had better do something about it. Three cars moved into position to shield the disabled one from the fire from the roof while a fourth one moved into position just in front of it. A tow . . . thought Grimes. A tow. . . . That meant that hatches would have to be opened so that somebody could climb out to fix the towing wires. Where were those Molotov cocktails that he had heard about?

And somehow they were there, ready to hand, ten bottles with rag wicks, not yet ignited, filled with some clear fluid. An aroma more intoxicating than unpleasant was making itself known despite the reek of cordite. And Su Lin was there, her golden lighter in her hand. Grimes got recklessly to his feet, holding one of the bottles. "Light it!" he ordered the girl. She obeyed. The flame blowing back from the flaring wick scorched his arm as he threw.

The missile fell well short, bursting spectacularly but harmlessly.

"I should have played cricket when I was a boy," remarked Grimes glumly. He raised his voice. "Are there any cricketers here? Any fast bowlers?"

(If only the Residence staff were Indian and not Chinese . . .)

"Cricket?" Martello's rough voice was contemptuous. "Baseball

was my game, Commodore. Still is. An' I'm a pitcher, not a bowler
. . . Gimme!"

He snatched the bottle from Grimes's hand, waited until Su Lin
had ignited the wick, then threw. Neither range nor direction could
have been bettered. He threw again, and again. From the armored
cars there was screaming. At least one of the Molotov cocktails must
have found an open hatch.

He let fly with two more bottles.

He was a good target standing there, too good a target. A burst
of machine-gun fire caught him, threw him back onto the gentle
slope of the roof. Crabwise, Grimes scrambled to him but there was
nothing he could do. The entire front of the big man's body was . . .
shredded. Shredded and pulped. Even his face was gone.

I shall never know what really made him tick, thought Grimes,
gulping back his nausea.

Then he heard the explosions.

Crouching, he made his way back to the parapet. Two of the
armored cars were burst open, literally. Their ammunition must
have gone up. A third was on its side, its wheels spinning uselessly.
A fourth, its rear wheels gone, looked ludicrously like a circus
elephant trying to sit down.

The two survivors had turned and were retreating, fast.

The turret hatch of the down-by-the-stern car opened. From it
was poked a rifle barrel to which a white rag of some kind had been
tied.

"Hold your fire!" ordered Grimes.

Su Lin repeated the command in a language that the New
Cantonese could understand.

Slowly a man clambered out through the hatch, slid down to the
ground, stood there with hands upraised. He was joined, after a long
interval, by two others.

"We surrender!" shouted the first man, a sergeant.

"We don't want you!" called Grimes. "Just get the hell out of
here!" Then, "No! Stop! Look after your mates first!"

They managed, at last, to persuade those in the overturned car
to open up. Only two men crawled out.

"Where's the other?" shouted Grimes.

"Dead, sir. His neck's broken."

"I want to see him!"

"Why?" whispered Su Lin.

"Haven't you heard of the Trojan Horse?" he countered.

The corpse was dragged out. The man was obviously dead, his head almost twisted off his body. And, thought Grimes, nothing could possibly be living in the two still-smoking wrecks.

The five men shambled down the road.

"You're too soft-hearted, Grimes." said Su Lin. "You should have made them bury their own dead before you let them go."

"I never thought of it," admitted Grimes.

He was conscious of the smell of burnt meat drifting up from the destroyed cars. He thought ruefully that disposing of the mess left over after a space battle is so much easier than disposing of similar mess on a planetary surface.

~ Chapter 44 ~

THE GARDENERS formed the burial detail and seemed more annoyed at having to mar the beauty of the Residence lawn than by the true, gruesome nature of their work. Martello was laid to rest a little apart from the others. Someday, thought Grimes, the sergeant would have his monument, a statue depicting him in the uniform of a baseball player, not of a soldier, frozen in stone or metal in the act of pitching.

Grimes, as Governor, conducted a brief service, one that he modeled on that used by the Federation Survey Service, whose personnel observed a wide variety of religions or none at all, that was used for enemies as well as friends.

"These men," he said, "did their duty as they saw it. They will be missed by their friends and relations. Let us not dishonor their remains. May they rest in peace."

Then Sanchez, with a work party, set about salvaging weaponry from the wrecked cars. He hoped to be able to dismount both the heavy machine guns and the laser cannon from the two not too badly damaged vehicles. Su Lin and Grimes went to his sitting room to see what news programs, if any, they could find on the playmaster.

They were lucky.

Almost immediately they found a channel on which a grave-faced newscaster was keeping his listeners up to date on what had been happening.

". . . the criminal John Grimes. According to reports that we have received, Colonel Bardon, as instructed by President O'Higgins, sent a force of six armored cars, under Major Jackson, to arrest the ex-Governor. It seems that Grimes and his criminal associates have barricaded themselves in the Residence and are refusing to give themselves up to justice. Two of the military vehicles have returned to the city, to the barracks, where Major Jackson is making his report to Colonel Bardon. The remaining four are maintaining the siege, ensuring that the notorious ex-pirate and his gang do not escape to terrorize the countryside.

"A statement issued by Colonel Bardon assures us that the situation is well in hand."

There followed a report on a game of soccer. Su Lin switched channels. The commentator whom she found could have been an archbishop in mufti.

". . . must be made to realize that we, as a proud and independent planet, cannot, will not and must not accept as gubernatorial figureheads men of dubious character. . . ."

Su Lin switched channels again.

". . . minor rioting in the Vanzetti Plaza district . . ."

There were shots of police charging demonstrators, of demonstrators pelting police with rocks, bottles and other missiles. There was an explosion, after which the facade of a building crumbled in almost slow motion. A mist of tear gas hung over everything.

And there was the shouting: Grimes! Grimes! Grimes!

"Somebody is acting at last," said Su Lin happily. "I wish I could see who they are. Oh, hell! Here come the water cannon!"

And so that riot, thought Grimes, soon became a washout.

"We shan't get the real blowup," said Su Lin earnestly, "until there's a direct confrontation between you and Bardon, and you win. You've seen how O'Higgins and Bardon have handled the first engagement. Almost certainly there was TV coverage of the action; I shan't be at all surprised if Raoul finds cameras in the armored cars. But those shots will never be shown. Not unless—*until*—we win."

"And I can't see us winning until there's something better than that abortive riot we saw. And I can't see any sort of uprising until we show the people that we can beat Bardon." He thoughtfully filled and lit his pipe. "But why doesn't he use his ground-to-ground missiles? He must have some in his armory. . . ."

"Because he wants you alive. He's not fussy about the rest of us—but he wants *you*. There must be a show trial. And *he* will be on trial as well as you. He must be seen to have acted with moderation despite great provocation. He must present the image of statesman as well as soldier. And then, after you've been found guilty and deported, who will be Governor *de facto*, soon to become Governor *de jure*?

"Bardon, of course."

"I'd never have given him credit for that many brains," said Grimes.

"It's dear Estrelita that has the brains, not him."

"Estrelita may be the statesman, but not the soldier. What Bardon does next is our immediate worry. Mphm. My guess is another attack, by land, tomorrow morning. With full TV coverage—not to be released unless things go well. If I were him I'd use a squadron of hover-tanks. . . ."

"Sergeant Martelio cast doubts upon their serviceability."

"I hope he was right. I hope most sincerely that he was right. Meanwhile, we'll maintain full watches during the night and have all hands on deck at sunrise."

≈ Chapter 45 ≈

GRIMES—just in case Bardon did mount a bombing attack, either from aircraft or by rockets—ordered that bedding be shifted down from the ground floor into the basements of the Residence. He decided, however, that he would remain in his palatial quarters. Su Lin had almost convinced him that he would be more use to O'Higgins and Bardon alive than dead. He was willing to take chances with his own life—but not with the lives of others.

The armored cars had yielded two useful heavy machine guns and a good supply of ammunition. Their crews, however, had removed the crystals from the laser cannon before abandoning the vehicles, must have taken these with them. This was annoying, but Grimes felt a grudging respect for the men. They were not altogether devoid of the soldierly virtues.

The night was quiet.

The sentries, with their powerful night glasses, maintained their vigil on the roof. The only thing that they reported was a fire of some kind in the city. Grimes went up to look, it did not seem to be a very big conflagration. He and Su Lin caught a late night TV news session on the playmaster and there was no mention of it. There was no further mention of the riot that they had seen earlier. And, they learned to their amusement, Colonel Bardon's armored cars still had the Residence under siege. It would not be long, said the smug announcer, before the notorious pirate commodore was brought to justice.

Grimes turned in.

Su Lin turned in with him.

They knew, both of them, that no matter what the outcome would be they would not be enjoying much more time together. They had been thrown together by circumstances beyond their control—and other circumstances, inevitably, must soon send them on their separate ways.

They would enjoy what they had while they had it.

When Grimes awoke, in the early morning, Su Lin was no longer with him although her place in the bed was still warm. Had there been some kind of emergency? But had this been so he would have been called.

Then the lights came on as the girl entered the bedroom, bringing with her the tray with the steaming teapot, the cups, the sugar bowl and the lemon slices. They sipped the hot, fragrant drink in companionable silence, their naked bodies in close contact.

She said, at last, "You pirate chiefs do yourself well, don't you?"

"Only when they have pirate molls like you to look after them . . . ."

There was a gentle tapping at the door.

Wong Lee came in. He looked at the couple in the bed with an odd combination of regret and approval; certainly there was no censoriousness.

"Your Excellency," he said, "a body of troops approaches from the city."

"Hover-tanks?" asked Grimes.

"No, Your Excellency. There are vehicles, but they seem to be personnel carriers."

"See that all weapon posts are manned. Oh—and better get the galley staff to make plenty of tea and piles of sandwiches. We may have the chance to grab a bite before the shooting starts."

"All that is already in hand, Your Excellency."

"Good man!"

Grimes jumped out of the bed, ran through to the bathroom. He made a hasty toilet, despite the fact that he was joined there by Su

Lin. He even found time to depilate, knowing that a scruffy, unshaven commanding officer does not inspire the same confidence as one who looks clean and bright and on top of the Universe. He dressed again in his Far Traveler Couriers uniform, with the pistol thrust under the red sash. Followed by the girl, who was clad in form-fitting black blouse and slacks, he went up to the lookout platform.

The sun was just up.

The column of personnel carriers, led by a command car, was still a long way off, approaching slowly along the winding road from the capital.

Raoul Sanchez came to him.

He said, "I've set up the two heavy MGs to cover the drive."

"What makes you think they'll use the drive, Raoul? Those are foot soldiers. They have almost the same freedom of movement over any sort of terrain as a hover-tank."

"I had to put the guns *somewhere,* sir."

"Sorry, Raoul. And, after all, guests usually try the front door first."

He could see quite clearly now, with the aid of the powerful binoculars, the men sitting in the personnel carriers. They were wearing full battle armor. This would restrict their freedom of movement but would protect them from almost anything short of a direct hit by a heavy artillery shell. Too, a laser cannon would fry them inside their carapaces but Grimes didn't have any laser cannon, only a few pistols.

He absentmindedly munched a ham sandwich that somebody had brought him. There wasn't enough mustard.

"They're stopping," said Sanchez unnecessarily.

They were stopping, had stopped.

Two tall figures got down from the command car.

Bardon, decided Grimes. Bardon, and . . . ?

In spite of the all-concealing battle armor he knew that the other one was a woman by the way that she was moving.

So Estrelita O'Higgins was making political capital by being present at the kill.

Soldiers were disembarking from the troop carriers, forming up on the road. How many of them were there? Grimes swore under his breath. There must be at least five hundred of them. Five hundred well-armed (definitely), well-trained (possibly) professional soldiers against less than one-fifth that number of rank amateurs. Even Grimes was an amateur in this sort of warfare. The Residence was not a spaceship.

Somebody must still be in the command car, using a sonic projector.

"Surrender! Come out, all of you, with your hands raised! Show a white flag to surrender!"

There was a small flagstaff on the lookout platform; so far as Grimes knew it was rarely used. But the halyards were intact. He went to them, cleared them.

"A flag . . ." he muttered. "A flag . . ."

"Sir, surely not . . ." Sanchez sounded heartbroken. "You're not showing the white flag, sir?"

"Who said anything about a *white* flag? I want something, anything, that's as unlike a white flag as possible!"

"Here!" said Su Lin, thrusting a bundle of some black cloth at him. He took it from her and suddenly realized that she had removed her shirt.

But it would do.

The black flag—the black flag of piracy, Grimes's enemies would say—rose jerkily to the masthead, stirring lazily in the light morning breeze.

Bardon put on a show.

Grimes watched it with grudging respect. There was more to the man than he had thought. He must have made a study of Australian history. Perhaps he had gotten the idea from Major Jackson's report to him on his conversation with Grimes, when Grimes had said, "You've come to the wrong shop this time, Major Johnston . . ." The New South Wales Corps, with rattling drums and squealing fifes, had marched on Bligh's Government House to place him under arrest. A drum and fife band preceded

Bardon's Bullies, playing some derisory tune that Grimes could not identify.

And those musicians were unarmed. Bardon was trading on Grimes's decency, gambling that he would not open fire on the bandsmen.

Grimes at last recognized the tune. *Lillibullew.* It had never been one of his favorites. Nonetheless, he thought wryly, the bandsmen deserved to be shot for murdering it.

But how would it look, how would it look on TV screens throughout the planet—and, eventually, on Earth—when men whose only weapons were fifes and drums were mowed down by a man who had just hoisted, atop his castle, the black flag of piracy?

They were taking their time marching up the drive toward the main entrance of the Residence—the bandsmen in their colorful dress uniforms, Bardon behind them, with Estrelita O'Higgins striding, in step, beside him and, after them, the rank upon rank of robotlike troopers.

Down came the troopers, one, two, three . . .

And four, and five, and six, and . . .

Those drummers couldn't keep a tune. The beat was ragged, becoming more so. Men were having trouble keeping in step. But was that arhythmic throbbing coming from ground level? It was not. It was surging down from the sky in ragged waves.

Whistles shrilled.

The approaching army halted. Men looked upwards. Weapons were deployed to sweep the sky—but not fired. There was a ship there. A civilian ship, not a warship. An *Epsilon* Class star tramp. It would not be the first time in history that neutral onlookers had been present at a battle, as sensation-hungry voyeurs.

The spaceship steadily lost altitude. Was she going to land? Did Captain Agatha Prinn intend to rescue her one-time Commodore? *Keep out of this, you silly bitch!* Grimes was thinking, was saying aloud. *Keep out of it! If you do land you'll get shot up and Bardon's story will be that you were caught in the crossfire . . .*

But *Agatha's Ark* was not landing. She hovered there, the cacophony of her inertial drive deafening. And was that a cargo hatch opening in her dull, pitted side? It was. Things were falling out, tumbling earthwards, bursting as they hit the ground. Bardon's men stumbled through the stifling, white cloud, the machinery of their armor clogged by the fine particles. They looked like men caught in a sudden blizzard. Grimes was reminded of pictures he had seen of Napoleon's Retreat from Moscow.

There was a lull in the bombardment.

Grimes, accompanied by Su Lin and a half-dozen of the Residence's domestic staff, ran out over the flour-caked lawn and grabbed the dazed Bardon and Estrelita O'Higgins, hustled them inside the building. Sanchez, with another party, captured Bardon's command car without firing a shot. In it was the TV equipment that would be covering the taking of the Residence.

It was covering, now, the ignominious defeat of Bardon's Bullies.

Very shortly afterward other TV units in the city were covering the riots that immobilized the remainder of the Terran garrison and drove the members of Estrelita O'Higgins's police into hiding. Those who were lucky.

Chapter 46

"I DIDN'T THINK OF IT MYSELF," admitted Agatha Prinn. "It was my agent, actually, Mr. Dennison of Starr, Dunleavy and Bowkett . . ."

"Dennison," said Su Lin, "is one of us. But go on, Captain Prinn."

"Mr. Dennison's idea was that I lift off as scheduled and then just sort of drift over the Residence, make a landing and snatch Grimes to safety. I said that I didn't fancy landing on anybody's lawn, no matter how big. I like to have something solid under my tail vanes when I set down. Why, I asked him, couldn't I, sort of accidentally, drop something on Bardon's boys? 'But you don't have any bombs,' he told me. 'You're just a star tramp, not a warship. And, in any case, if you play any active part in a battle, no matter on whose side, you'll be as big a pirate as your pal Grimes.' "

" 'I've a cargo of flour,' I told him. 'In bags. And, while it was being loaded, some ill-intentioned person planted an incendiary device in the middle of it. Luckily this will be discovered while I'm hovering over the Residence, to play my last respects to my old Commodore. So I will have to jettison cargo . . .' "

"Which you did," said Grimes. "I'm eternally grateful to you."

"Gratitude isn't enough, Commodore. Who's going to pay for the delay while I load a fresh cargo? Who's going to pay for the cargo that's been destroyed?"

"Lloyd's of London," Grimes told her. "I imagine that the jettison will come under the heading of General Average."

"But as the owner of *Agatha's Ark* I shall still be held liable for my share of the expense involved."

"I'm sure that Rear Admiral Damien will see you right."

"Eventually. But the tide runs very slowly through official channels."

"Then, Agatha, would you accept a job on this world, a sinecure, for a very short time and at a *very* high salary? Terms to be negotiated."

"What is it?" she asked suspiciously.

"I'm the ruler of this world until things get sorted out. A new president has to be elected and approved. Until it's done I'm the only one with legal power. Liberia has no Examiner of Interstellar Masters and Mates. Yet. Do you want the post?"

"What's the catch?"

"There's no catch. All you have to do is supervise just one examination. Mine. As I read the law, a Liberian Master's Certificate of Competency will be good anywhere in the Galaxy. My real Certificate, issued at Port Woomera, was suspended by that Court of Inquiry.

"So . . ."

"You're an opportunistic bastard, Grimes," she said.

"Too right," he agreed smugly.

"So we have a farce of an examination, after which I issue a Certificate of Competency, autographed by myself. Are you sure that you wouldn't like to sign it too, as Governor? And then, just to oblige you still further, I put young Sanchez on my books as Fourth Mate so he can start getting in Deep Space time for *his* certificates. Is there anything else?"

"At the moment, no. But if there is, I'll let you know."

"Do just that." She grinned. "Well, Commodore, it was all an exciting break from the usual tramping routine, just as the privateering expedition was. But I have to get back to the spaceport to see what's happening to the *Ark*. I have a strong suspicion that Lloyd's surveyors will be sniffing around the hold, trying to find evidence of a fire. . . ."

"And will there be?" asked Grimes.

"Surely, Commodore, you would not expect me to defraud an insurance company?"

She finished her drink, got up and strode out of the Governor's sitting room. (Its windows repaired, the Residence was habitable again.) Grimes and Su Lin watched her go.

Agatha Prinn, thought Grimes, was one of the women whom he would always remember with affection. Just as—he looked at her, lounging gracefully in her chair—Su Lin would be.

"What will you do now?" she asked suddenly.

"I . . . I was thinking of resigning. As soon as they can arrange a relief for me. Once I have a valid Certificate of Competency I can take over command of my ship again. But . . . I'm not so sure. Suppose I don't resign. Suppose I stay here, as Governor . . ."

"If they let you."

He ignored this.

"Being Governor's Lady wouldn't be a bad life for a woman, Su Lin. And I'd need somebody like you, who knows the planet better than I do."

"I'm sorry," she told him. "Genuinely sorry. But PAT will be reassigning me. Dennison is arranging for my passage off Liberia now. But cheer up. We'll meet again some time. There's bound to be some complicated mess somewhere that will take the two of us to clear up. And I could never settle down on one world for keeps, any more than you could.

"You're lucky. Admit it. You'll soon be getting your precious *Sister Sue* back."

But I lost Fat Susie, he thought, *and even that lopsided apology for a balloon,* Little Susie. *And it will not be long before I lose Su Lin.*

Somehow, suddenly, his memories of the girl were more vivid, more real than her flesh and blood actuality. Their lovemaking in the wrecked airship . . . She standing beside him, proudly barebreasted, while he hoisted the piratical black flag on the flagstaff on the roof of the Residence . . .

Damn it all, he would even miss having her lighting his pipe for him.

Was he, after all, so lucky?

THE
LAST
AMAZON

DEDICATION
For Susan,
who makes me keep my nose to the grindstone.

~ Chapter 1 ~

THE BANDS PLAYED and the Federation Survey Service Marines paraded in their scarlet and gold dress uniforms and the children waved their little flags and the grown-ups lifted high their broad-brimmed black hats as Grimes, ex-Governor John Grimes, arrived at Port Libertad, there to embark aboard the star tramp *Rim Wayfarer*. With him, to see him off, were two people whom he did not regard as friends—but protocol demanded their attendance. One of them was Estrelita O'Higgins, still, despite all, President of Liberia. She was a survivor, that one. She had contrived to lay the blame for all of the planet's troubles, culminating in the armed revolt against the Earth-appointed Governor, Grimes, on the now-disgraced Colonel Bardon, lately commanding officer of the Terran garrison. The other was Captain Francis Delamere, of the Federation Survey Service, the new Governor.

Delamere should have a far easier time of it than either Grimes or his immediate predecessor. He had brought his own garrison troops out with him, a large detachment of Marines who—in theory at least—gave their allegiance to the senior Terran naval officer on Liberia, Captain Delamere. And almost immediately after his arrival (he was a notorious ladies' man) he had made a big hit with the President. For him the job should be a sinecure. Even he would find it hard to make a mess of it—as long as he did not try to interfere with the smooth running of the machinery of government that

Grimes—who was for a while, after the putting down of the rebellion, *de facto* dictator—had set up, with able, honest and dedicated men and women in all the key positions.

But Frankie, thought Grimes, would find it hard to keep his meddling paws off things. He had tried to take an officious interest in Grimes's own affairs even before the formal handing-over ceremonies, and had made it plain that he wanted his old enemy off the premises as soon as possible, if not before, so that he could bask in his new gubernatorial glory.

He had said, in his most supercilious manner, "There's no need for you to hang around here like a bad smell, Grimes."

"But I thought that you were keeping *Orion* here for a while," said Grimes. "Wise of you, Frankie. During my spell as Governor I could have done with a Constellation Class cruiser sitting in my backyard."

"Who said anything about *Orion*, Grimes? I came here with a squadron."

"A *squadron?*" echoed Grimes. "Two ships. One cruiser and one Serpent Class courier . . ."

"I was forgetting," sneered Delamere, "that you're something of an expert on squadrons. Didn't you command one when you were a pirate commodore?"

"A privateer," growled Grimes. "Not a pirate."

"And now an ex-Governor," Delamere reminded him. "As such, you're entitled to a free trip back to Earth . . ."

"Not in a flying sardine can."

"Beggars can't be choosers, Grimes. Anyhow, the sooner you're back the sooner you'll be able to find another job. If anybody wants you, that is. You can't hope to get another command, not even of that *Saucy Sue* of yours."

"*Sister Sue,*" Grimes corrected him stiffly.

"What's in a name? As far as I know your Certificate of Competency has not been restored—and you'd need that, wouldn't you, even as a bold buccaneer."

"I've already told you once that I was a privateer."

"Even so, you were bloody lucky not to be hanged from your

own yardarm for piracy. That judge, at the Court of Inquiry, was far too lenient. Did you slip him a backhander out of your ill-gotten gains?"

Grimes ignored this. "Anyhow," he said smugly, "I now, once again, hold a valid Certificate of Competency as Master of an Interstellar Vessel."

"What! Don't tell me that it *has* been restored to you!"

"No. It's a new one. Liberian."

"And you say it's valid? Oh, I suppose that *you* signed it, as Governor, after examining yourself."

"If you must know, it is signed by the Liberian Minister of Space Shipping. And I was examined, and passed, by the Examiner of Masters and Mates. I admit that she was appointed by myself, for that purpose. But it's a valid Certificate, recognized as such throughout the Galaxy."

"You're a cunning bastard," whispered Delamere, not without envy.

"I am when I have to be," Grimes told him. "And now all that I have to do is to catch up with *Sister Sue* and get my name back on the Register."

"I'm not letting you have that courier to take on a wild goose chase," snarled Delamere.

"I've already told you that I have no intention of traveling in the bloody thing. I'm quite capable of making my own arrangements. I know where I want to go and I know which ship, due here in a couple of days' time, will be heading in the right direction when she's finished discharging and loading."

And so the bands were playing and the Marines, in their full dress scarlet and gold, were drawn up to stiff attention with gleaming arms presented and the children were waving their little flags and the grown-ups were raising their broad-brimmed black hats high in the air as the big ground car rolled slowly up to the foot of *Rim Wayfarer*'s ramp.

Delamere's aide, a young Survey Service Lieutenant, got down from the front seat where he had been sitting beside the Marine corporal driver. He flung open a rear door with a flourish. Estrelita

O'Higgins was the first out, tall in superbly tailored, well-filled denim with a scarlet neckerchief at her throat. She was as darkly handsome as when Grimes had first met her, on his arrival at this spaceport (how long ago?) but then he had been prepared to like her, to work with her. Now he knew too much about her—and she about him. Some applause greeted her appearance but it was restrained.

Delamere was next out. He wore full ceremonial rig—the gray trousers, the black morning coat, the gray silk top hat—far more happily than Grimes ever had done. In uniform Handsome Frankie, as he was derisively known, looked as though he were posing for a Survey Service recruiting poster. Now he looked as though he were posing for a Diplomatic Service recruiting poster. He took his stance alongside the President. The impression they conveyed was that of husband and wife about to see off a house guest who had outstayed his welcome.

Again there was a spatter of applause.

Grimes disembarked.

This day he was dressed for comfort—and also in accordance with local sartorial tradition. He was wearing faded blue denim, a scarlet neckerchief, a broad-brimmed black hat.

The cheers, the shouts of "Viva Grimes! Viva Grimes!" were deafening. The Marine band struck up the retiring Governor's own national song, "Waltzing Matilda." Both Delamere and the President frowned. This was not supposed to be an item on the agenda—but Colonel Grant, commanding officer of the Marines, had known Grimes before his resignation from the Survey Service.

The people were singing that good old song.

And soon, thought Grimes, *there'll be only my ghost to haunt this billabong . . . .*

Estrelita O'Higgins extended her long-fingered right hand, palm down. Grimes bowed to kiss it. She whispered something. It sounded like, "Don't come back, you bastard!" Francis Delamere raised his silk hat. Grimes raised his felt hat. Neither man attempted to shake hands.

Slowly Grimes walked up the ramp to the after airlock of *Rim*

Wayfarer. At the head of the gangway the master, Captain Gunning, smart enough in his dress black and gold, was waiting to receive him.

He saluted with what was probably deliberate sloppiness and said, "Glad to have you aboard, Commodore."

"I'm glad to be aboard, Captain," said Grimes.

"I bet you are. It must be a relief to get away from the stuffed shirts."

"The era of the stuffed shirt is just beginning here," Grimes told him.

Gunning, looking down at the new Governor standing stiffly beside the President, laughed. "I see what you mean."

Grimes turned, to wave for the last time to those who had been his people. They waved back, all of them, native Liberians and those who, as refugees from all manner of disasters, had sought and found a new home on Liberia.

"Viva Grimes! Viva Grimes!"

"I hate to interrupt, Commodore," said Gunning, "but it's time that I was getting the old girl upstairs."

"She's your ship, Captain."

"But what a sendoff! Those people sound as though they're really sorry to lose you."

"Quite a few," Grimes told him with a grin, "will be glad to see the back of me."

"I can imagine."

The two men stepped into the elevator cage that would carry them up to the control room. The ramp retracted and the outer and inner airlock doors closed.

In less than five minutes *Rim Wayfarer* was lifting into the clear, noonday sky.

✺ Chapter 2 ✺

GRIMES AND GUNNING were at ease in the master's day cabin, enjoying a few drinks and a yarn before dinner. Trajectory had been set, all life support systems were functioning perfectly, the light lunch served as soon as possible after liftoff had been a good one and Grimes was looking forward to the evening meal.

It was good to be back aboard a ship again, he was thinking as he sipped his pink gin, even though it was only as a passenger. Still, he was a privileged one, being treated more as a guest.

"You know Sparta, of course," said Gunning.

"I was only there the once," said Grimes. "Years ago. When I was captain of the Federation Survey Service census ship *Seeker*."

Gunning laughed. "But you must know *something* about Sparta. Every time that I'm sent to a planet I haven't been to before I do some swotting up on it. There's not much information in the ship's library data bank—just the coordinates and a few details about climate and such. Rim Runners don't believe in paying good money for what they, in their wisdom, regard as useless information. But I found the Libertad Public Library quite informative. Historical details—from the time of *Doric*'s landing to the present. The way Sparta was dragged into the political framework of the Federation—and the way a certain Lieutenant Commander John Grimes initiated this process."

"I was just there when it happened," said Grimes. "Or when it started to happen. I was little more than a spectator."

"As you were on Liberia, Commodore, when things happened." Gunning laughed. "I'd just hate to be around when you were something more than just a spectator."

"But I was little more on Sparta," Grimes insisted. "One of my scientific officers, Maggie Lazenby, was the prime mover. She took a shine to Brasidus, who is now the Archon, and he to her." He laughed. "It was the first time that he'd had any dealings with a woman. He really thought that she was a member of some alien species . . . ."

"I've often thought the same myself about women," said Gunning. "But that must have been a weird state of affairs on Sparta when you landed there."

"It was," reminisced Grimes. "It was. An all-male population, with all that that implies. Babies—male babies only—produced by the so-called Birth Machine. A completely spurious but quite convincing biology taught in the schools to make sense of this. The planet was a Lost Colony, of course, founded during the First Expansion. You know, the Deep Freeze ships. They started off with an incubator and a supply of fertilized ova. Male ova. The first King, who had been master of the starship, made sure of that. He didn't like women. He tried to model his realm on ancient Sparta but with one great improvement. Men Only. I suppose that when the original supply of ova ran out the Spartans might have had to resort to cloning but, before this came to pass, the people of another Lost Colony, Latterhaven, made contact. Trade developed between the two worlds. Fertilized human ova in exchange for spices and such."

"I got most of that from the library at Port Libertad," said Gunning. "But what was it like? A world with no women . . . ."

"What you'd expect," said Grimes. "The really macho types, with their leather and brass, in the armed forces. The effeminate men working as nurses in the crèche and other womanly occupations. The in-betweeners were the helots; after all, somebody has to hew the wood and draw the water. But once the bully boys got a whiff of real pussy—*Seeker* had a mixed crew—all hell started to break loose. And there were, too, some women on the planet already. The doctors running the Birth Machine had their own secret harem."

"I expect that you'll find things changed, Commodore," remarked Gunning.

"I shall be surprised if I don't. To begin with, there's no longer a monarchy. The Archon is the boss cocky. And there has been considerable immigration from the Federated Planets—mostly people, as far as I can gather, who have their own ideas about what life was like in Ancient Greece. Billy Williams—who's been acting master of *Sister Sue* during my absence—has been sending me reports."

"That was a nice little time charter you got for your ship," said Gunning. "Earth to Sparta with assorted luxury goods, Spartan spices back. Did your early connections with Sparta help you to get it?"

"Possibly," Grimes told him. He did not add that the Federation Survey Service, in which he still held the reserve captain's commission that not many people knew about, owed him a few favors. He laughed. "But I never thought that *Sister Sue* would be earning her living as a retsina tanker. It's all those immigrants, of course. They must have *real* Greek wine—although the local tipple wasn't at all bad when I was on Sparta years ago—and olives and feta cheese and all the rest of it."

"But surely," objected Gunning, "the ancient Greeks didn't drink retsina. It was the Turks, when they occupied Greece in more recent times, who tried to cure the wine-bibbing Christians of their addiction to alcohol by making them put resin in the wine casks."

"True, true. But you must have found, Captain, that any attempt to revive an ancient culture on a new world is as phony as all hell. The aggressive Scottishness of the Waverley planets, for example. And New Zion—have you ever been there?—where all hands stop whatever they're doing at the drop of a yarmulke to dance the hora .... The original culture of the all-male Sparta was phony enough—but it was consistent. But now? Unfortunately Billy Williams isn't a very good letter writer but I've gained the impression that those new colonists have succeeded in reproducing an ancient Greece that never was, that never could have been."

"You'll have time to find out for yourself, Commodore. You told me that you'll have about three weeks there before your ship drops in. Unluckily I've only two days' work there—just a small parcel of bagged flour to discharge and a consignment of spices to load—and then I shall be on my way."

The sonorous notes of the dinner gong drifted through the ship.

The two men finished their drinks and got up from their chairs to go down to the dining saloon.

~ Chapter 3 ~

GRIMES QUITE ENJOYED the voyage.

Rim Wayfarer was a comfortable, well-run ship, her captain and officers good company. The food was good, even by Grimes's exacting standards. He was, he admitted to himself, rather surprised. Rim Runners were looked down upon by the personnel of such shipping lines as the Interstellar Transport Commission and Trans-Galactic Clippers and, too, by the officers of the Federation Survey Service. They were the sort of outfit that you joined when nobody else would have you.

But, thought Grimes, *you could do very much worse for yourself.*

The day came when the star tramp dropped from the warped dimensions engendered by her Mannschenn Drive into normal Space-Time. It was a good planetfall, with no more than twelve hours' running under inertial drive to bring the ship to Port Sparta.

Grimes was in the control room, keeping well out of the way, when Gunning made his landing. As far as he could see from the viewports and in the screen everything was much as he remembered it. There, on the hilltop, was the Acropolis, gleaming whitely in the rays of the morning sun. Sprawling around the low mountain was the city, laid out with no regard to geometrical planning, a maze of roads and alleys running between buildings great and small, none of them more than two stories high but some of them covering considerable acreage. Yes, there was the Palace . . . . Grimes supposed that Brasidus, as Archon, would be making it his residence. (The Spartan royal house had ceased to be after the revolution.)

And there was the spaceport. A real spaceport now, capable of handling at least twelve ships at a time. And what ships were in? Obligingly, Gunning's Chief Officer gave Grimes the use of a screen showing the area toward which *Rim Wayfarer* was making her approach. There was something big. Grimes stepped up the magnification. A Trans-Galactic clipper, probably a cruise liner. And something small, but not too small. One of the Survey Service's couriers, Lizard Class. An Epsilon Class tramp—but it couldn't be *Sister Sue*. She, as far as Grimes had been able to determine, must now be about halfway from Earth to Sparta.

Slowly, but not too slowly, *Rim Wayfarer* dropped to her berth, marked by the three scarlet flasher beacons. As always the Port Captain, like Port Captains throughout the Galaxy, had done his best to make the job an awkward one. With all the apron space there was to play with he still expected Gunning to set his ship down between the big cruise liner and the little courier. Luckily there was very little surface wind. The tramp master cursed good naturedly, as Grimes himself, in similar circumstances, had often cursed. He said to Grimes, "Fantastic, isn't it, Commodore? When a man is actually serving as a spaceman he will be a prince of good fellows. Once he takes up ground employment, as a stevedore or a Port Captain or whatever, he has absolutely no consideration for those who used to be his shipmates . . . ."

Grimes said, "I was a Port Captain myself once. On Botany Bay."

"And did *you* berth all the ships in a tight huddle so as to leave hectares of great open spaces?"

"I didn't have hectares of great open spaces to play with. Luckily only on one occasion did I have more than one ship in. And then one of them was a relatively small destroyer and the other a really small private yacht."

"So you were the exception to prove the rule," laughed Gunning.

He returned his attention to the controls and the *Wayfarer* dropped steadily down to a neat landing in the exact center of the triangle marked by the flashing beacons.

∾◡∾◡∾◡∾◡

The port officials boarded.

Grimes remained in his quarters until Gunning buzzed him on the intership telephone, asking him to join him and his official guests in his day cabin. He collected his passport and immunization certificates and made his way up to the captain's flat by the spiral staircase.

There were three visitors in Gunning's office. The captain was sitting behind his paper-strewn desk. Sitting in chairs arranged to face the shipmaster were two men and a woman. One of the men— a customs officer?—was in a kilted uniform that was all leather and brass and a plumed brass helmet was on the deck beside him. At least, thought Grimes, customs officers on this planet did not wear uniforms aping those of honest spacemen. The other man—tall, bald-headed—was wearing a dignified, long white robe. The woman, her back to Grimes, was attired in a simple green tunic that left her suntanned arms and most of her shoulders bare. Her hair, braided and coiled around her head, was a gleaming auburn with the merest touch of gold. There was, thought Grimes, something familiar about her.

"Ah, it's you, Commodore," said Gunning, looking up from the documents. "I thought that it was Melissa with the coffee . . . . But we'll get the introductions over before she brings it in."

The two men and the woman got to their feet, turned to face Grimes.

"Maggie!" he gasped.

"John," she said. (She was not surprised.)

He said, "It's been a long time . . . ."

She said, "It's not all that long since I got you out of that mess aboard *Bronson Star*."

"I mean," said Grimes, "that it's a long time since we were here, on this world, together."

Looking at her he thought, *But she still looks the same as she did then. The face still as beautiful in its high-cheekboned, wide-mouthed way, the figure, revealed rather than concealed by the short, flimsy dress, still as graceful . . . .*

"A long time . . ." he repeated.

"I suppose that it is, at that," she said matter-of-factly. "And here am I, still holding the exalted rank of commander in the Scientific Branch of the Survey Service, and here's you, who've been a yachtmaster, an owner-master, a pirate commodore, a planetary governor and the Odd Gods of the Galaxy alone know what else."

"A privateer," said Grimes. "Not a pirate."

"Whatever you were," she told him, "it's good to see you again."

He took her extended hand, grasped it firmly. He would have kissed her—she seemed to be expecting it—if Gunning had not coughed loudly.

"You already know Commander Lazenby," said the captain. "But may I introduce Colonel Heraclion, Chief Collector of Customs, and Dr. Androcles, Port Health Officer?"

Hands were shaken. Grimes took a chair next to Maggie. The ship's catering officer brought in a tray laden with a large coffee pot, sugar bowl, cream jug and cups. She departed and Gunning poured for his guests.

The colonel said, "I do not usually attend to such matters as the Inward Clearance of shipping myself. But I bear greetings from the Archon." From the leather pouch at his belt he withdrew a large envelope, handed it to Grimes. "To you, sir."

Grimes took it. It was, he noted, unsealed. He remembered having read somewhere that a gentleman, entrusting a letter to another gentleman for delivery, never seals the envelope. Did the ancient Spartans observe such a custom? (Did the ancient Spartans use envelopes?)

He pulled out the sheet of paper—it was more of a card, really. He read the stiff, unfamiliar calligraphy. *The Archon presents his compliments to His Excellency the Commodore Grimes and requests that he will accept the hospitality of the palace during his stay on New Sparta.* It was signed, simply, *Brasidus.*

Grimes passed the card to Maggie.

"Good," she said. "He told me that he would invite you."

"Are you staying there?" he asked.

"Of course." She laughed. "After all, Brasidus and I are old friends. I could be staying aboard *Krait*, of course, but, as you should know, Serpent Class couriers are not famous for their luxurious passenger accommodation."

"So you're here on Survey Service business," remarked Grimes.

"Of course. I'd not have gotten passage here—even if it is in a spaceborne sardine can like *Krait*—otherwise. Research. A study of the effects on a Lost Colony by its assimilation into mainstream Galactic culture. Or of the effects on mainstream culture when assimilated into a Lost Colony. Nothing serious, and all good, clean (for most of the time) fun. Perhaps you'd like to help me in my research. That ship of yours isn't due in for some time yet."

"It should be interesting," said Grimes. "But haven't you already found that New Sparta has been spoiled by contact with the rest of the Galaxy?"

"Far from it," she told him. "Anything would have been an improvement on the way it was."

"That," said Colonel Heraclion stiffly, "is your opinion, Commander Lazenby."

Grimes looked at the man with interest. *Yes*, he thought, *there are men to whom an all-male society, such as New Sparta had been, would be almost a paradise. Oh, well. One man's Mede is another man's Persian.*

"I am in agreement with Commander Lazenby," said Dr. Androcles. "Like the colonel, I was a young man when Commodore Grimes' ship, *Seeker*, gave us our first real contact with the outside universe. The people realized then that, for generations, they had been living a lie."

"In the opinion of your medical profession, perhaps," sneered the colonel. "But do not forget that you and your colleagues had been promulgating that same lie."

"Gentlemen, gentlemen," chided Captain Gunning. "I do not think that my day cabin is a fitting venue for a heated argument about New Spartan politics."

"It was the outworlders who started it," said Heraclion sourly.

"Outworlders," Maggie reminded him, "who just happen to be honored guests of your Archon."

The colonel was about to make a heated reply, then thought better of it. Dr. Androcles laughed.

"I'll help you to finish your packing, John," said Maggie.

⮦ Chapter 4 ⮧

WHEN THEY WERE ALONE in his quarters Grimes kissed her. She returned his embrace, then pushed him away.

"Not now," she said. "There'll be plenty of time for this sort of thing in the palace."

"Will there?" he asked. "Haven't you already said that you and the Archon are old friends? I ... assumed ...."

"Then you assumed wrong. Ellena keeps Brasidus on a tight leash."

"Ellena?"

"His wife. The Archoness, as many call her, although there's no such rank or title. She's from Earth. An Australian, of Greek ancestry. Very much the power behind the throne. But finish your packing and I'll fill you in." She took from its shelf the solidograph that she had given him—how long ago?—and held the transparent cube, with its lifelike, three-dimensional image of her face and figure, studying it before passing it to him. "You're something of a sentimental bastard, aren't you? That's one of the reasons why I'm rather fond of you."

"Thank you."

"And now for putting you in the picture. To begin with, my research project is only a cover. I was seconded to the Intelligence Branch, and by them put under the orders of Rear Admiral Damien."

"But he's not in the Intelligence Branch."

"Isn't he? There are intelligence officers whom everybody knows about and there are intelligence officers who, as it were, hide their light under a bushel. Like you, for example."

"*Me?*"

"Yes, you. The admiral told me that you had been pressganged back into the Survey Service with the rank of captain on the Reserve List. All very Top Secret, Destroy By Fire Before Reading and all the rest of it. What you did to break up Drongo Kane's privateering racket was no more—and no less—than Intelligence work. So was what you did on Liberia. Whether you knew it or not you were a member of the Department of Dirty Tricks."

Grimes sighed. "All right, all right. But just what dirty tricks am I supposed to be doing here?"

"Just shoving a spanner into the works."

"But Brasidus—from what I remember of him—is a nice enough bloke. I'm sure that he's a good Archon, whatever an Archon does when he's up and dressed. There's never been any talk of tyranny, so far as I know. People are still emigrating to New Sparta from Earth and other planets."

She said, "That's part of the trouble."

"How so?"

"One of our people was among those migrants. Under cover, of course. According to her papers she was a schoolteacher. She sent a few reports back to Earth—and then they stopped coming. Since my arrival here I've been able to make discreet inquiries. She was drowned in a boating accident."

"If it was an accident . . ." said Grimes. "Is that what you're driving at?"

"Of course. She was out on a river trip with other members of the New Hellas Association. Colonel Heraclion—although he wasn't a member of the boating party—is one of the Association's high-ups. Oh, I know what you're thinking. *New* Hellas, when what he wants is *Old* New Sparta. But the New Hellenes are a bunch of reactionaries. Some—like the good colonel—want a return to a womanless world, the way it used to be. Others—and they're mainly immigrants—want a return to the way ancient Greece used to be on Earth."

"The glory that was Greece . . ." quoted Grimes. "What's so wrong with that?"

"Ancient Greece," she told him, "was glorious, if you happened to be a member of the upper crust and male. If you were a slave, a peasant or a woman it wasn't so glorious."

"But there are women in this New Hellas Association. This murdered agent of yours—all right, all right, of ours—was a member and a woman."

"There are some women," she said, "who, in their secret hearts, would enjoy being human doormats. There are other women who would enjoy being glamorous *hetaerae* in a society where the other members of their sex were no more than drab *Hausfrauen*."

"*Hetaerae* and *Hausfrauen* in the same culture!" laughed Grimes.

"You know what I mean. Well, it wouldn't be so bad if the New Hellenes were just trying to attain their ends by democratic means but, according to our late agent, they're plotting a coup. A coup on classical lines. And then yet another unsavory dictatorship which, eventually, will have to be put down at great expense. If such things can be nipped in the bud . . . ."

"By whom?"

"Need you ask, ducky?"

"Damn it all," said Grimes, "I'm a civilian. A shipmaster and shipowner. All that I came to this world for was to rejoin my ship."

"You're not a civilian, John. Oh, you may have been for a while, but ever since you accepted that reserve commission you've been back in the Service. I've written orders for you from Admiral Damien—not with me at the moment but in the captain's safe aboard the courier. I'll get them out for you before too long."

The intercom phone buzzed. Grimes pressed the *Acknowledge* button. Gunning's face appeared in the screen.

"I hope that I'm not interrupting anything, Commodore, but Colonel Heraclion asked me to remind you that the car is waiting to take you to the palace. If you like I'll send somebody down to give you a hand with your gear."

"Thank you, Captain," said Grimes. "But don't I have to pass Port Health, Immigration and Customs?"

"The colonel informs me that all formalities have been waived in your case." The master laughed. "It's always handy to have friends in high places."

The screen went blank.

Grimes opened the door of his cabin in preparation for the arrival of the junior officer who would help him with his bags. Maggie continued talking but only on topics which, should she be overheard, would give nobody any ideas.

"Talking of friends," she said, "I met one of yours a couple of days ago."

"But the only person whom I got to know on this world, when I was here before, was Brasidus."

"This one's an offworlder."

"From Earth?"

"No. From Bronsonia. An investigative reporter, she calls herself. She works for that scurrilous rag *Star Scandals*. She's doing a series on sleazy entertainment centers on as many worlds as she can get to visit during the time allowed her. She's tailing along after some outfit calling itself Galactic Glamour, featuring exotic dancers from all over. They're doing a short season here before pushing on to Latterhaven.

"Anyhow, I met her when I was slumming, as part of my research. We had a couple or three drinks. She knew that I'm Survey Service. And you know how stupid people are . . ." She assumed a voice that was not hers but which was ominously familiar to Grimes. *"Oh, you're in the Survey Service . . . A commander. Do you know Commander Smith?"* She laughed. "What she said was, *Do you know Captain Grimes? He used to be in the Survey Service—he got as high as commander, I believe, before they threw him out . . .*"

"I resigned!" growled Grimes.

"So I said to her, *Who doesn't know Grimes?* And she grinned nastily and said, *So we share that dubious pleasure.* But don't you want to know who she is?"

"I know only one person who answers to your description of her," muttered Grimes. "But tell me, is she, too, a guest at the palace?"

"No. She did come calling around once, flashing her press ID, but Ellena took an instant dislike to her. The guards have strict orders never to admit her again."

"Thank All The Odd Gods of the Galaxy for that! With any luck at all I'll not be meeting her again."

"Then your luck's run out. You surely don't think, do you, that you'll be confined to the palace during your entire stay here? Apart from anything else you'll be helping me with my ethnographical research—and I've little doubt that our path will, from time to time, cross that of the fair researcher for *Star Scandals.*"

"I don't frequent low joints," said Grimes virtuously.

"Then you've changed!" she laughed.

He laughed with her. "Oh, well, I shan't really mind meeting Fenella again for a talk over old times. But it's a pity that Shirl and Darleen aren't here as well . . ."

"And who are they?" asked Maggie, with a touch of jealousy.

"Just girls," said Grimes.

And then the Third Officer appeared to help carry the baggage down to the airlock.

∾ Chapter 5 ∾

AT THE FOOT OF THE RAMP two of Heraclion's men loaded Grimes's baggage into the rear of the hovercar—a vehicle that was doing its best to look like an ancient Greek chariot—while the commodore said his farewells to Captain Gunning and the star tramp's officers. The colonel took his seat alongside the driver who, like his superior, was dressed in brass and leather although with much less of the glittering metal on display. Maggie and Grimes sat immediately behind the two Spartans.

The ducted fans whined loudly and raised eddies of dust. The vehicle lifted itself in its skirts, slid away from the spaceship, picking up speed as it did so. Soon it was clear of the spaceport environs, proceeding at a good rate toward the city. There was other vehicular traffic—chariotlike hovercraft, both military and civil, carts piled with produce and drawn by what looked like donkeys and mules, imports from distant Earth. There were, as there had been on the occasion of Grimes's previous visit, squads of young men, who appeared to be soldiers, on motorcycles but there were others on horseback.

Grimes remarked on what was, to him, archaic means of transport.

Heraclion, speaking back over his shoulder, said, "There are those among our new citizens, Commodore, who want to put the clock back to the time of the Spartan Empire on Earth . . . ." (*The*

Spartan Empire? wondered Grimes. He most certainly could not recall any mention of such during his studies of Terran history.) "Even so, I have to admit that a troop of cavalry mounted on horseback is a far better spectacle than one mounted on motorcycles."

The hovercar, its siren screaming to demand right of way, was now fast approaching the outskirts of the city. It sped along the narrow road between the rows of low, white houses and less privileged traffic hastily made way for it. A turn was made into what was little more than a winding lane. This, Grimes realized, must be the entertainment district. In the old days, during his first visit to Sparta, such a venue was undreamed of. Gaudy neon signs, dim on the sunny side of the street but bright in the shadow, advertised the delights available to those with money behind the heavy wooden doors, the shuttered windows. The lettering, although aping the Cyrillic alphabet, spelled out its messages in Standard English.

DIMITRIO'S LAMB BARBECUE—TOPLESS LADY CHEFS

(Grimes could appreciate the female cooks' need for aprons; barbecues are apt to sputter and spatter.)

HELEN'S HETAERAE

(And did one drop in there for intellectual conversation?)

ARISTOTLE'S ARENA

This was a much larger building than the rest. Under the flickering main sign were others:

GALACTIC GLAMOUR
EXOTIC WARRIOR MAIDS
OFFPLANET AMAZONS
LIMITED SEASON ONLY

Maggie had to put her mouth to his ear to be heard above the shrieking siren. "That's the outfit I was telling you about. The one that your old girlfriend is doing the series on." She laughed. "The trouble with Aristotle is that he's not a very good historian. His entertainment is more Roman than Grecian. I think that he'd even put on Lions versus Christians if he thought he could get away with it."

"Have you been there?"

"Yes. That's where I met Fenella Pruin. After I admitted that I knew you she laughed nastily and said, 'This is just the sort of show that *he'd* enjoy. A pity he's not here.' I didn't tell her, of course, that you were on your way to Sparta."

"Thank you. With only a little bit of luck she'll never know I'm here."

"She'll know all right. The local media have already bruited abroad that the famous Commodore John Grimes is to be the guest of the Archon."

"Then I'll just have to rely on you to keep her out of my hair."

They were out of the Street of the Haetaeri as the red-light district was called, making the ascent of the low hill on top of which stood the Archon's palace. Troops were drawn up before the long, pillared portico, weapons and accouterments gleaming in the afternoon sunlight. Short spears were raised in salute as the hovercar whined to a stop and subsided to the ground.

Grimes looked at the soldiers appreciatively. They were young women, all of them, uniformed in short white tunics and heavy, brass-studded sandals with knee-high lacings. The leather cross-straps and belts defined their breasts and hips sharply. Shoulder length hair, in almost every case glossily blonde, flowed from under their plumed helmets.

"The Lady Ellena's Amazon Guard," commented Heraclion sourly.

"I'd sooner have them than a bunch of hairy-arsed Federation Marines," said Grimes.

Maggie's elbow dug sharply into his ribs.

They disembarked then—Maggie, Grimes and the colonel.

The Amazon officer marched before them, her spear held high. Other girls fell in on either side of them, escorting them. They passed through the great doorway into the hall, dim after the blazing sunlight outside, to where the Archon and his lady, flanked by berobed dignitaries of both sexes, awaited them.

Grimes found it hard to recognize Brasidus. The young, clean-shaven sergeant whom he had known was now a portly, middle-aged man, his hair and full beard touched with gray. Perhaps it was the white robe with its broad purple trim that gave an illusion of stoutness but the commodore did not think so. Brasidus would never have been able to buckle on the simple uniform that he had worn in the old days.

And the large woman who stood beside the Archon was indubitably stout. She, too, wore a purple-trimmed robe. Her rather spuriously golden hair was piled high and elaborately upon her head but even without this added height she would have been at least fifteen centimeters taller than her husband. She looked down her long nose at the guests with very cold blue eyes and her full mouth was set in a disapproving line.

The Amazon guard grounded their spears with an echoing crash.

Brasidus stepped forward, both hands extended.

Grimes had started to bow but realized that this salutation would not be correct. He straightened up and extended his own right hand. The Archon grasped it warmly in both of his.

"John Grimes! It is indeed good to see you again, after all these years! My house is yours while you are on Sparta!"

"Thank you . . . Lord," said Grimes.

"And have you forgotten my name? To my friends I am, and always will be, just Brasidus. But allow me to present my lady wife. Ellena, my dear, this is John Grimes, of whom you have often heard . . . ."

"The famous pirate commodore," said the woman in neutral tones.

"And John, this is the Lady Ellena."

She extended a large, plump hand with scarlet fingernails. Grimes somehow got the impression that he was to do no more than touch it. He did that.

There were other introductions, to each of the assembled councilmen and councilwomen. There was an adjournment to a large room where refreshments were served by girls who circulated among the guests pouring the wine—a Terran retsina, Grimes decided, although he thought that it had not traveled well—from long necked *amphorae*. There were feta cheese and black olives (imported?) to nibble.

Finally the party broke up and Grimes was escorted to his quarters by one of the servant wenches. They could have been a hotel suite on just about any planet.

He was sitting down for a quiet smoke when Maggie joined him.

"Dinner's at 1900 hours," she told him. "No need to get out your penguin suit or a dress uniform. It'll be just a small occasion with Brasidus, you and me reminiscing over old times."

"What about the Lady Ellena?"

"She's off to a meeting. She's Patron of the Women's Branch of the New Hellas Association."

"But . . ." He hesitated. "Is it all right to talk?"

"It is. I was supplied with the very latest thing in bug detectors. When it's not detecting bugs it functions quite well as a wristwatch."

"What about Ellena and the New Hellas mob?"

"I don't think she's mixed up in any of their subversive activities. She's a silly bitch, but not that silly. She knows which side her bread is buttered. But she loves being fawned upon and flattered."

"I take it she's of relatively humble origins."

"Correct. She was an assistant in a ladies' hairdressing salon in Melbourne, Australia. She was proud of her Greek ancestry. When New Sparta was thrown open to immigration from Earth she scraped together her savings and borrowed quite a few credits—which she repaid, by the way; I give her credit for that—with the idea of setting up in the same line of business here, getting in on the ground floor. Of course, in the beginning ladies' hairdressers were something of a novelty and quite a few men wandered into them by mistake to get their flowing locks trimmed and their beards curled. Brasidus made that mistake. He didn't know much about women then and she knew who he was—he wasn't yet Archon but he was on the way up—and poured on the motherly charm. She was able to hitch her wagon to his rising star."

"So Cinderella married the handsome prince," said Grimes sardonically. "And they all lived happily ever after."

She said, "We have some living to do ourselves after all this time."

She led the way into his bedroom.

❧ Chapter 6 ❧

IT HAD BEEN A LONG TIME, as she had said, but after the initial fumbling there was the old, sweet familiarity, the fitting of part to part, the teasing caress of hands on skin, of lips on lips and then, from her, the sharp yet melodious cries as he drove deeper and deeper and his own groans as her arms and legs imprisoned his body, her heels pummeling his buttocks.

They did not—they were out of practice with each other—reach climax together but her orgasm preceded his by only a few seconds.

They would rather have remained in the rumpled bed, to talk lazily for a while and then, after not too long an interval, to resume their love-making but, after all, they were guests and, furthermore, guests in the palace of a planetary ruler. Such people, no matter how humble their origins (or, perhaps, especially if their origins were humble) do not care to be kept waiting. So they showered together—but did not make an erotic game of it—and resumed their clothing. Maggie, who, by this time, was well-acquainted with the layout of the palace, led Grimes to the small, private dining room where they were to eat with the Archon. They arrived there just before Brasidus.

The meal was a simple one, served by two very homely maid-servants. There was a sort of casserole of some meat that might have been lamb, very heavily spiced. There was a rough red wine that went surprisingly well with the main course. For a sweet there was not too bad baklava, accompanied by thick, syrupy coffee. "We do not grow our own yet," said Brasidus, "but we hope to be doing so by next year. Soon, John, there will be no need for your *Sister Sue* to bring us cargoes of such luxuries from Earth." He laughed. "And what will you do then to make an honest living? Return to a career of piracy or find another governor's job?" There was brandy, in warmed inhalers, a quite good Metaxa.

The serving wenches cleared away the debris of the meal.

Having asked the permission of their host Grimes lit his pipe and Maggie a cigarillo. They were expecting, both of them, to settle down to an evening of reminiscent conversation over the brandy bottle but Brasidus surprised them.

"Help yourselves to more drinks, if you wish," he told them. "I am going to change. I shall not keep you long."

"To change, Brasidus?" asked Grimes.

"Yes. I have heard much of that new show at the Arena—you, Maggie, told me of it. I have not seen it yet. Ellena does not approve of such entertainment. I thought that this evening would be an ideal opportunity for me to witness the . . . the goings on."

"You're the boss," said Grimes.

When he was gone Maggie said, "He likes doing the Haroun al-Raschid thing now and again. Strolling among his citizens incognito, keeping his finger on the pulse and all the rest of it. Ellena doesn't altogether approve, but when the cat's away . . . ."

"And we're among the mice this evening, I suppose."

"I'm afraid so. But *you* should enjoy the show at the Arena. As I recall you, you have a thing about the weirder variations of the female face and form divine. That cat woman on Morrowvia with whom you had a roll in the hay. That *peculiar* clone or whatever she was from whom the Survey Service had to rescue you when you were trying to get *Bronson Star* back to where she had been skyjacked from. There have been others, no doubt."

"Mphm," grunted Grimes through a cloud of acrid tobacco smoke. He refilled the brandy inhalers. "Mphm."

"I will have one too," said Brasidus.

Grimes stared at him. Had it not been for the man's voice he would never have recognized the Archon. Yet the disguise was simple enough, just a spray-on dye applied to hair and beard, converting what had been light brown hair with the occasional silver thread to a not unnatural looking black.

The Archon drained his glass, then led the way out of the small dining room.

They made their way to what Grimes thought of as the tradesmen's entrance.

Two men were waiting for them there, dressed, as was Grimes, in one-piece gray suits in a somewhat outmoded Terran style. Unlike Grimes, who liked a touch of garish color in his neckwear, they had on cravats that almost exactly matched the color and texture of the rest of their clothing. Their side pockets bulged, as did Grimes's. Were they, he wondered, also pipe smokers? The Archon himself was dressed in the clothing appropriate to a lower middle-class citizen on a night out—knee-length blue tunic with touches of golden embroidery, rather elaborate sandals with, it seemed, more brass (not very well-polished) than leather. Maggie had on the modified Greek female dress that had been introduced from Earth— a short, white, rather flimsy tunic, sleeveless and with one of her shoulders left completely bare.

Brasidus introduced his two bodyguards—or so Grimes thought they must be; they looked the part—as Jason and Paulus. They could have been twins—although, he found later, they were not even related. They were tallish rather than tall, stoutish rather than stout and wore identical sullen expressions on their utterly undistinguished faces.

Jason brought a rather battered four-passenger hovercar round to the portico. It looked like something bought, cheaply, from Army Surplus. But there was nothing at all wrong with its engine and Grimes noticed various bulges in its exterior paneling mat that probably concealed weapons of some kind.

Jason was a good driver.

Soon the vehicle was whining through the narrow streets of the city which, mainly, were illumined by deliberately archaic gas flares, avoiding near collisions with contemptuous ease, finally gliding into the garish neon glare of the Street of the Haetaeri. Parking was found very close to the entrance of Aristotle's Arena. The three men and the woman got out and walked the short distance to the ticket booth. Brasidus pulled a clinking coin purse from the pouch at his belt and paid admission for the party.

"It's a good show, citizen," said the ticket vendor, a woman who was disguised as a Japanese geisha but whose face, despite the thickly applied cosmetics, was more Caucasian than Asian. "You're just in time to see the cat girls doing their thing."

Maggie, who had been to this place before, led the way down a flight of stone stairs. At the bottom of these they emerged from dim lighting into what was almost complete darkness. An usherette dressed in what looked like an imitation of an Amazon guard's uniform—but the tip of her short spear functioned as a torch—led them to their seats, which were four rows back from the circular, sand-covered arena. She sold them doughnut-shaped pneumatic cushions—the seating was on stone benches—which they had to inflate themselves. As they settled down in an approximation to comfort the show started.

There was music of some kind over the public address system. Grimes didn't recognize the tune. Maggie whispered, "But you should, John. Apparently it's a song that was popular on Earth—oh, centuries ago. Somebody must have done his homework. It's called, 'What's new, Pussycat?'"

Brasidus muttered sourly, "Some Earth imports we could do without."

A spotlight came on, illuminating the thing that emerged from the tunnel that gave entrance to the arena. It was . . . *Surely not!* thought Grimes. But it was. It was a giant mouse. A robot mouse, its movements almost lifelike. There were no real mice on New Sparta, of course, although immigrants from Earth knew about them and there were now plenty of illustrated books on Terran zoology. And cats, real cats, had been introduced by the Terran immigrants.

The mouse made an unsteady circuit of the arena.

Two more spotlights came on, shining directly onto the naked bodies of the two Morrowvian dancers. Their makeup accentuated their feline appearance, striped body paint making them look like humanoid tigresses. Spiky, artificial whiskers decorated their cheeks and vicious fangs protruded from their mouths.

They did not make the mistake of dropping to all fours but they moved with catlike grace, in time to the wailing music. They stalked the mouse from opposite directions and whoever was at the remote controls of the robot managed to convey a quite convincing impression of animal panic, even to a thin, high, terrified squeaking. Every now and again one of the girls would catch it, but do no more than stoop gracefully to bat the robot off its feet with a swipe of a pawlike hand. Each time it recovered and made another dash, and then the other girl would deal with it as her companion had done.

Finally the audience was tiring of the cat and mouse game. There were shouts of, "Finish it! Finish it!"

The taller of the two girls pounced. She dropped to her knees and brought her mouth, with those vicious fangs, down to the neck of the giant mouse. There was a final, ear-piercing squeak. There must have been bladders full of some red fluid under the robot's synthetic skin; a jet of what looked like blood spurted out over the cat woman's face, dripped on to the sand. She made her exit then, still on all fours, the carcass hanging from her mouth. Either the robot was very light or those false teeth were very securely anchored.

Her companion trailed after her, also on her hands and knees, caterwauling jealously.

The applause could have been more enthusiastic but, even so, the audience wasn't sitting on its collective hands.

"Quite good," admitted Brasidus. Then, "You have been to Morrowvia, John and Maggie. Do the people there really hunt like that?"

"They are fond of hunting," Maggie told him. "But they hunt much larger animals than mice, and they use spears and bows and arrows. And their teeth, after all the engineered genetic alterations, are like yours and mine. And they don't have whiskers. And their skins aren't striped, although their hair, on the head and elsewhere, often is . . . ."

"Please leave me some illusions," laughed Brasidus.

But Grimes was not listening to them.

He was looking across the arena to where a tangle of audio and video recording equipment had been set up. In the middle of this, like a malignant female spider in her web, was a woman.

Even over a distance Grimes recognized her, and thereafter, while the lights were still on, tried to keep his face turned away from her. Eating one of the hot, spiced sausages that Brasidus had bought from a passing attendant helped.

∾ Chapter 7 ∾

"CITIZENS!" The voice of the master of ceremonies blared from the public address system. "Citizens! Now it is my great pleasure to announce the two boxing kangaroos from New Alice . . ." There was an outburst of applause; obviously this was a very popular act. Grimes could not catch the names of the performers. It would be too much of a coincidence, he thought, if they should turn out to be Shirl and Darleen. Those ladies had been in show business on New Venusberg but as quarry in the so-called kangaroo hunt. He knew that they could fight—first as gladiators in the Colosseum and then helping to beat off a Shaara attack—but their weapons had been boomerangs, not their fists. "And now may I call for volunteers? You know the rules. No weapons, bare fists only. Should any one of you succeed in knocking down one of the ladies she will be yours for the night. Stand up, those who wish to take part in the prize fight of the century! The usherettes will escort you to the changing room."

All around the arena men were getting to their feet. There was no shortage of volunteers.

"What about you, John?" asked Maggie. "Wouldn't you like to add a New Alician to your list of conquests?"

"No," Grimes said. "No." (He had no need to tell her that he and those two New Alicians, Shirl and Darleen, had been rather more than just good friends.)

"*I* am tempted," said Brasidus.

"It would not be wise," said Jason.

The last of the volunteers—there had been two dozen of them—had been led to the changing room. The house lights dimmed. There was taped music, an old Australian folk song that Grimes recognized. *Tie me kangaroo down, sport, tie me kangaroo down* . . . Some, more than a few, of the audience, knew the words and started to sing. Grimes joined them.

"Please don't," said Maggie, wincing exaggeratedly.

Then the song was over and the music that replaced it was old, old. There was the eerie whispering of the didgerydoo, the xylophonic clicking of singing sticks. Out of the tunnel and onto the sand bounded the two New Alicians, their hands held like paws in front of their small breasts. Save for the absence of long, muscular tails they could well have been large, albino kangaroos. As they hopped around the ring the lights over the arena itself brightened and some, but not all, of the illusion evaporated. But it was still obvious that the remote ancestry of these girls had not been human. There were the heavy rumps, the very well-developed thighs, the lower legs inclined to be skinny, something odd about the jointure of the knees. They were horse-faced, but pleasantly so, handsome rather than pretty, not quite beautiful. They were . . . .

Surely not! thought Grimes. This would be altogether too much of a coincidence. First Maggie (but his and her presence on this world together was perhaps not so coincidental), then Fenella Pruin, and now Shirl and Darleen. But he knew, all too well, that real life abounds in coincidences that a fiction writer would never dare to introduce.

The music fell silent. There was a roll of drums, a blaring trumpet. There was the voice of the announcer as the first pair of volunteers, in bright scarlet boxer shorts, came trotting out through the tunnel.

"Citizens! Killer Kronos and Battling Bellepheron, to uphold the honor of New Sparta!"

The men, both of them heavily muscled louts, raised their fists above their heads and turned slowly to favor each and every member of the audience with simian grins.

A bell sounded:

The men advanced upon their female adversaries, clenched fists ready to deliver incapacitating blows. Shirl and Darleen stood their ground. Kronos launched what should have been a devastating swipe, that would have been one such had it connected. But Shirl little more than shrugged and the fist missed her left ear by considerably more than the thickness of a coat of paint. And then she was on him, her own fists pummeling his chest and belly. He roared with rage and tried to throw his thick arms about her, to crush her into submission. She danced back and he embraced nothingness. What happened next was almost too fast for the eye to follow. She jumped straight up and drove both feet into his midsection. It was almost as though she were balanced on a stout, muscular but invisible tail. She and Kronos hit the sand simultaneously, she in a crouching posture, he flat on his back. He stirred feebly, made an attempt to get up and then slumped.

Meanwhile Darleen was disposing of her own adversary by more orthodox means, using fists only. It was a classical knock-out.

So it went on. Some bouts were ludicrously short, others gave better value for the customers' money. Some challengers limped out of the arena under their own steam, others had to be carried off.

Brasidus was highly amused. "These wenches," he said, "would make a better showing in a fight than the Lady Ellena's Amazon Guards. But I suppose that unarmed combat is all that they're good at."

"Not so," said Grimes. "Their real specialty is throwing weapons. With them they're lethal."

"You seem to know a lot about the people of New Alice," Maggie said. "Have you ever been there?"

"No," he told her. "I . . . I met some of them once, on another planet." (Perhaps someday he would tell her of his misadventures on New Venusberg. Had it not been for the inhibiting influence of Eldoradan investors in the more dubious entertainments available on the pleasure planet the galactic media would have given him and Fenella Pruin more than their fair share of notoriety. As it was, hardly anybody knew what had happened and the part that Grimes had played.)

"Javelins?" asked Brasidus, his mind still on weaponry.

"Not quite. For throwing spears they use something called a *woomera*, a throwing stick, which they use like a sling. It gives the spears extra range. But their most spectacular weapon is the boomerang . . . ."

"And what is that, John?"

Before Grimes could reply the voice of the announcer boomed over the auditorium.

"And now, citizens, the two wonder women from New Alice, the splendiferous Shirl and the delicious Darleen, will entertain you with an exhibition of the art of boomerang throwing. The boomerang is a weapon developed on their native world in Stone Age days, millennia before there were such things as computers and yet employing and utilizing the most subtle principles of modem aerodynamics . . . ."

"The boomerang was developed on Earth, long before New Alice was ever dreamed of," whispered Grimes indignantly.

All the lights came on and the auditorium was now as brightly illumined as the arena itself. Shirl and Darleen stood in the center of the ring, their naked bodies gleaming in the harsh glare. Despite their participation in twelve boxing bouts their skins were unmarked. Slowly they scanned the audience. At one time Grimes thought they were looking straight at him but they gave no sign of recognition. But, of course, they would not be expecting to see him here. After the show he would go around to the stage door, or whatever it was called, to give the girls a big surprise.

Two of the pseudo Amazons came onto the arena, each carrying a small bundle of wooden boomerangs. There were big ones, and some not so big, and little ones. They were decorated with bands of bright paint—white and blue and scarlet.

The attendants bowed to Shirl and Darleen and then strode away. There was the obligatory roll of drums. Shirl picked up a half-dozen of the little boomerangs from the sand. She handed the first one to Darleen, who threw it from her. Then the second one, then the third, then the fourth, and the fifth and the sixth. It was a dazzling display of juggling with never less than five of the things in the air at the same time, each one terminating its short, circular flight in Darleen's right hand just after the launching of another, resting there only briefly before being relaunched itself. And then the flight pattern was changed and it was Shirl who was catching, one by one, all six of the boomerangs, catching and throwing time after time again. Another half-dozen of the boomerangs came into play and Shirl and Darleen widened the distance between themselves, a boomerang-juggling duo.

Finally each of the things was thrown so that they came to rest in the center of the arena, forming a pile that could not have been neater had it been stacked by hand.

There was the big boomerang flung by Shirl (or was it Darleen? Grimes still had trouble distinguishing one from the other) that made several orbits of the main overhead light, like a misshapen planet about its primary, before returning to its thrower's hand. There were the medium-sized ones that were sent whirling over the heads of the audience, too high for any rash person to try to catch one at the risk of losing a finger or two. Most of these were directed to the vicinity of where Fenella Putin was sitting amidst her recording apparatus.

At last the girls decided that they had given her enough of a show and turned to face that part of the auditorium where the Archon's party was sitting. They scanned the faces of the audience and then they were looking directly at Grimes. They held a whispered consultation, then looked at him again. So they had recognized him. So he would not be able to surprise them in their dressing room when the show was over. It was rather a pity. He shrugged.

Shirl (or was it Darleen?) picked up one of the medium-sized boomerangs. She looked at Grimes. He looked at her. He raised a hand in a gesture of greeting. Both girls ignored it. Shirl assumed the thrower's stance. Her right arm was a blur of motion—and then the boomerang was coming straight at Grimes, the rapidity of its rotation about its short axis making it almost invisible. He tried to duck but he was jammed in between Maggie and Jason and unable to move.

There was a sudden rattle of automatic pistol fire; Paulus had pulled his vicious little Minetti from a side pocket. The boomerang disintegrated in mid-flight, its shredded splinters falling harmlessly onto the people in the front row. There were shouts and screams. There were two of the pseudo-Amazon usherettes making their hasty way to the scene of the disturbance—and they were not so pseudo after all; each was holding a pistol, a stungun but a weapon nonetheless and lethal when set to full intensity. Jason had his pistol out now and he and the other bodyguard were both standing, pointing their Minettis at the approaching Amazons.

"Put them down, you fools!" roared Brasidus.

Grimes hoped that they would have enough sense to realize that he meant the guns, not the chuckers-out.

The stunguns buzzed. They had been set at very low intensity, not even causing temporary paralysis but inducing a dazed grogginess. The two Amazons were joined by four more strapping, uniformed wenches and the Archon's party was dragged ignominiously to the manager's office.

Ironic applause accompanied their forced departure from the auditorium.

☙ Chapter 8 ❧

ARISTOTLE WAS A FAT MAN, bald, piggy-eyed, clad in a white robe similar to those worn by the professional classes, soiled down the front by dropped cigar ash and liquor spillage. He was smoking a cigar now, speaking around it as he addressed the prisoners who stood before his wide, littered desk, supported by the Amazon usherettes.

"You . . ." he snarled. "You . . . Offworlders by the look of you . . . At an entertainment such as mine some riotous behavior is tolerated, but not riotous behavior with . . . *firearms.*" With a pudgy hand he poked disdainfully at the two automatic pistols that had been placed on his desk. "I suppose you'll try to tell me—and the police, when they get here, and the magistrate when you come up for trial—that you didn't know that on this world civilians are not allowed to carry such weapons, by order of the Archon. You know now."

"But this . . ." Jason waved feebly toward Brasidus. "But this is the . . ."

The Archon raised a warning hand, glared at his bodyguard.

"And this is what, or who?" demanded the showman disdainfully. "Some petty tradesman enjoying a night on the tiles with his off-planet friends, at their expense, no doubt. Showing them the sights, as long as they're doing the paying. And, talking of the foreigners, which of them started the gunplay?"

"This one," said the Amazon supporting Paulus, giving him a friendly cuff as she spoke.

"So it was you," growled Aristotle. "And now, sir, would you mind satisfying my curiosity before the police come to collect you? What possessed you to pull a gun in a public place and, even worse, to interrupt a highly skilled act by two of my performers?"

"That . . . That boomerang thing . . . It was coming straight at the Commodore. I did my best to protect him."

"The Commodore? You mean the gentleman with the jug-handle ears? I do have a distinguished clientele, don't I? I know of only one visiting Commodore on New Sparta at this time, and *he* is a guest of the Archon. He'd be too much of a stuffed shirt to sample the pleasures of the Street of the Haetaeri."

"Little you know," said a familiar female voice.

Aristotle shifted his attention from the prisoners to somebody who had just come into the office. "Oh, Miss Pruin . . ." he said coldly. "I do not think that you were invited to sit in on this interview."

"I invited myself," said Fenella. "After all, news is news."

Grimes managed to turn his head to look at her. She had changed very little, if not at all. Her face with rather too much nose and too little chin, with teeth slightly protuberant, the visage of an insatiably curious animal but perversely attractive nonetheless. She grinned at him.

"Do you know these people?" he demanded.

"Not all of them, Aristotle. But the gentleman with the jug-handle ears is Captain Grimes, although I believe that he did, briefly, hold the rank of Company Commodore with the Eldorado Corporation. That was when he commanded a pirate squadron . . . ."

"Privateers," Grimes corrected her tiredly. "Not pirates."

She ignored this. "And the lady is Commander Maggie Lazenby, one of the scientific officers of the Federation Survey Service. Both she and Captain—sorry, Commodore—Grimes were on this planet many years ago and were involved in the troubles that led to the downfall of the old regime."

"Oh. *That* Grimes," said Aristotle. His manner seemed to be softening slightly. "But I still am entitled to an explanation as to why his friend ruined the Shirl and Darleen act."

"The boomerang," insisted Paulus, "was coming straight at the Commodore. It could have taken his head off."

"It would not," said two familiar female voices speaking in chorus. Shirl and Darleen, light robes thrown around their bodies, had come into the office which, although considerably larger than a telephone booth, was getting quite crowded. "It would not."

"It would not," Aristotle agreed. "Surely you know what that part of the act signified?"

"The boomerang," explained Shirl (or was it Darleen?), "would have stopped and turned just short of you, returning to my hand. It was a signal to you that you were to follow it—after the show, of course. I thought that everybody knew."

"It was announced," said Aristotle. "Just as it was announced that any boxer who succeeded in knocking down Shirl or Darleen would be entitled to her favors."

"It was *not* announced," said Grimes.

"It was *not* announced," said Jason and Paulus, speaking together.

"Well, it should have been," admitted Aristotle. "But all of my regular customers know of the arrangement."

"We are not regular customers," said Brasidus.

"But that, sir, does not entitle your friends to brandish and discharge firearms in my auditorium." He raised and turned his head. "Come in, Sergeant, come in! I shall be obliged if you will place these persons under arrest. No, not Commodore Grimes and Commander Lazenby, they are guests of the Archon. But the other three. Charge them with discharging firearms, illegally held firearms at that, in a public place."

"If you would please tell me who is which . . ." said the Sergeant tiredly.

He looked at Grimes. "Oh, I recognize you, sir. Your photograph was in the *Daily Democrat*. But which of the ladies am I supposed to take in?"

He stood there in his military-style uniform (but black instead of brown leather, stainless steel instead of brass), removing his plumed helmet so that he could scratch his head. The two constables, reluctant to enter the crowded office, remained outside the now open door.

"Just the men, Sergeant," Aristotle told him impatiently. "Just the men."

"All right." The Sergeant grabbed Brasidus by the arm that was not held by an Amazon usherette. "Come on, you. Come quietly, or else."

"But that is the Archon," objected Paulus in a shocked voice. He tried to break away from restraint so that he could come to his master's aid. "Take your paws off the Archon!"

"And I'm Zeus masquerading as a mere mortal!" The Sergeant pulled Brasidus towards the door. "Come on!"

"He *is* the Archon," stated Grimes.

"Come, come, sir. This lout is nothing like Brasidus. I did duty in the Palace Guard before the Lady Ellena had us replaced by her Amazon Corps. I've a good memory for details—have to in my job. His hair and beard are light brown, just starting to go gray. Besides—" he laughed—"Ellena would never allow him to come to a dive like this."

"My establishment is not a dive!" expostulated Aristotle indignantly.

"Isn't it? Then what's it doing on *this* street?" He called to the constables. "Come in, you two, and grab the other two lawbreakers."

"There'll be some room for us after you get out," muttered one of the men.

The Sergeant twisted Brasidus' right arm behind his back. It must have been painful.

"Take your hands off me!" growled Brasidus. "Take your hands off me, or I'll have you posted to the most dismal village on all of New Sparta, Sergeant Priam. I am the Archon."

Priam laughed. "So you think you can fool me by saying my name? Every petty crook in the city knows it."

"He *is* the Archon," said Grimes.

"He *is* the Archon," stated Maggie.

"He could just be," said Fenella. "There are techniques of disguise, you know. I've used them myself."

"Call the Palace," Brasidus ordered Aristotle. "The Lady Ellena will identify me."

The showman pressed buttons at the base of the videophone on his desk. Only he could see the little screen but all of them could hear the conversation.

"May I speak to the Lady Ellena, please?"

"Who is that?" demanded an almost masculine female voice, probably that of the duty officer of the Amazon Guard.

"Aristotle, of Aristotle's Arena."

"What business would *you* have with the Lady Ellena?"

"None of yours, woman. I want to speak to her, is all."

"Well, you can't."

"It is my right as a citizen."

"You still can't. She's out."

"She's still at her meeting," said Brasidus.

"What meeting?" demanded the Sergeant.

"Of the Women's Branch of the New Hellas Association."

"You seem to know a lot about her movements," muttered the police officer. He looked as though he were beginning to wonder what sort of mess he had been dragged into. If this scruffy helot were indeed the Archon . . . But surely (so Grimes read his changing expressions) that was not possible. "Get the New Hellas bitches on the phone," he ordered Aristotle. "Get the number of their meeting hall from the read-out."

Aristotle obliged.

Then, "May I talk with the Lady Ellena, please?"

"She is addressing the meeting still," came the reply in a vinegary female voice.

"This is important."

"*Who* are you?"

Before he could answer the Sergeant had pushed his way round to the showman's side of the desk.

"This is Sergeant Priam of the Vice Squad. This is official police business. Bring the Lady Ellena to the telephone at once."

"What for?"

"For the identification of a body."

There was a little scream from the New Hellas lady.

"Bring him round here," ordered the Sergeant, "so that he can look into the video pick-up. And then we shall soon know one way or the other."

Two of the Amazon usherettes obliged.

There was some delay, and then Grimes heard Ellena's voice.

"Is this the body that I'm supposed to identify? But, firstly, he's alive . . ."

"I didn't say a *dead* body, Lady."

"And secondly, I wouldn't know him from a bar of soap."

"It's me," said Brasidus.

"And who's 'me'? I most certainly don't know you, my man, and I most certainly do not wish to know you."

But she did not terminate the conversation.

"Have you any alcohol?" Brasidus asked Aristotle.

"Do you expect me to give you a free drink after all the trouble you have caused?"

"Not for drinking. And, in any case, I will pay you for what I use. Some alcohol, please, and some tissues . . ."

Grudgingly the showman produced a bottle of gin from a drawer and, from another, a box of tissues. He demanded—and received—a sum far in excess of the retail price of these articles. Everybody watched as the Archon applied the gin-soaked tissue to his beard which, after a few applications, returned to its normal color.

"So," said the Lady Ellena, "it is you. I did recognize the voice, of course. But where are you calling from? A police station? And why do you wish me to identify you?"

"I'm at Aristotle's Arena . . . ."

"Oh. Another of your incognito slumming expeditions. And you got yourself into trouble. Really, my dear, you carry the concept of democracy too far. Much too far. For a man of your standing to frequent such a haunt of iniquity . . . I suggest that you order the Sergeant to furnish you with transport back to the Palace. At once."

"You had better not come with me," said Brasidus as Grimes

and Maggie made to follow him and his police escort from the office. "The Lady Ellena regards spacemen as a bad influence. And as for the rest of you . . ." The note of command was strong in his voice. "As for the rest of you, I shall be greatly obliged if no word of tonight's adventure gets out. I am requesting, not ordering—but, even so, I could have your Arena closed, Aristotle, and your performers deported, just as you, Fenella Pruin, could also be deported, after a spell in one of our jails. I am sorry, John and Maggie, that we shall not be able to enjoy the rest of the evening together, but there will be other times. Jason will run you back to the Palace at your convenience.

"A good night to you all."

He was gone, accompanied by the deferential policemen.

"Could we have our pistols back?" asked Paulus.

"Help yourself," said Aristotle.

"Another good story that I am not allowed to use," grumbled Fenella Pruin. "At least, not on this world. But the evening need not be a total disaster." She turned to Grimes. "Perhaps an interview, John? I am staying at the New Sparta Sheraton . . . ."

"And *we*," said Shirl and Darleen, "are staying at the Hippolyte Hotel."

"And I," said Maggie sweetly, "saw him first. Come along, John. We'll find a place for a quiet drink or two before we return to the Palace."

"I'm supposed to be running you back," said Jason sullenly.

"So you are. Come with us, then. But you will sit at a separate table. Don't look so worried. We'll pay for your drinks."

~ Chapter 9 ~

THEY HAD THEIR DRINKS in an establishment where the almost naked waitresses made it plain that they were willing to oblige in more ways than the serving of drinks and who regarded the few female customers with open hostility. After having had a glass of ouzo spilled in her lap Maggie decided that it was time to leave. Jason, who had been getting on well with the hostess who had joined him at his table, sharing the large bottle of retsina that had been purchased at Grimes's expense, got to his feet reluctantly. His companion glared at him when he corked the wine bottle and took it with him.

"Waste not, want not, Commodore," he said.

"Too right," agreed Grimes.

"I thought that this wine was a present," complained the overly plump blonde.

"It is," said Jason. "To me."

They made their way to the parked hovercar, got in. The drive back to the palace was uneventful. They entered the building, as they had left it, by a back door. Amazon guards, or guards of any kind, were conspicuous by their absence. Security seemed to be non-existent. Grimes said as much.

Jason laughed. "If you'd tried to get in this way without me along with you there'd have been a few surprises. Unpleasant ones."

"Such as?" asked Grimes.

"That'd be telling, Commodore. Just take my word for it."

"You're not a native, are you?" asked Grimes, who had detected more than a trace of American accent.

"No sir. No way. Before I came here I was an operative with Panplanet Security, home office Chicago. Paulus and I brought all the tricks of our trade with us. And now good night to you, Commodore Grimes and Commander Lazenby. I take it that you know the way back to your quarters."

Maggie assured him that they did.

They went to Grimes's suite.

They sat down and talked, discussing the events of the evening, comparing notes.

Maggie asked, "However did you get to know those two New Alice wenches, or, come to that, Fenella Pruin?"

"It's a long, sad story," he said. "At the finish of it I had all three of them as passengers aboard *Little Sister*—the deep space pinnace of which I was owner-master before I bought *Sister Sue*."

"It must have been an interesting voyage."

"Too interesting at times. But there were . . . compensations."

"I'm sure. Knowing you." She sipped from the drink that he had poured her. "It's a pity that we have no power to recruit the Pruin woman. She impresses me as being a really skillful investigator."

"Only when there's a story with sex involved, the only kind of story that *Star Scandal* prints."

"There are other stories, you know, equally interesting, and other media with good money to pay for them. Perhaps if I could get her interested . . . Or if you could. You know her better than I do. Come to that, Shirl and Darleen could do some work for us . . . ."

"Shirl and Darleen? Oh, they'd make quite good bodyguards. They're at their best in a rough and tumble. But as intelligence agents? Hardly."

"As intelligence agents," she said firmly. "Not very high grade ones, but useful. They told you where they were staying."

"The Hippolyte Hotel. But what's that got to do with it?"

"The Hippolyte Hotel is owned by a company made up of

members of the New Hellas Association, mainly well-to-do female members. The Lady Ellena is a major shareholder. The name of the place is her choice. As you must have already gathered she has a thing about Amazons. In case you don't already know, Hippolyte was Queen of the Amazons."

"I'm not altogether ignorant of Terran history and mythology."

"All right, all right. But the Hippolyte is much frequented by NHA people. Too, I found out that the Hippolyte offered special rates to the stars now appearing at Aristotle's Arena."

"What's so sinister about that?"

"I . . . don't know. But there have been rumors. All those performers are alleged to be specialists in various offplanet martial arts. As far as your girlfriends Shirl and Darleen are concerned it's more than a mere allegation. Could Ellena be thinking of recruiting instructors in exotic weaponry and techniques for her Amazon Guards?"

"Terrible as an army with boomerangs," misquoted Grimes.

"Very funny. But our own Survey Service Marine Corps Commandos are trained to inflict grievous bodily harm with a wide variety of what many would consider to be archaic weapons."

"Mphm."

"Officially," she said, "you're in charge of this Intelligence Branch operation, whether you like it or not. Not only do you rank me, but you've had more experience in Intelligence work."

"But I didn't have the intelligence to realize it."

"You do now. Anyhow, although I'm officially subordinate to you, I can make suggestions, recommendations. I recommend that you exercise your influence on Shirl and Darleen—they seem to like you, the Odd Gods of the Galaxy alone know why!—and persuade them to accept the Lady Ellena's offer. If she makes it, that is. And if she does, and they do, then perhaps your other girlfriend might stay on here to do a story on their experiences instead of following the rest of the troupe across the Galaxy . . . ."

"This used to be an all-male planet," said Grimes. "But now . . . First you, then Fenella, then Shirl and Darleen. It never rains but it pours."

"You're not complaining, are you?" she asked.

"Certainly not about you," he told her gallantly.

They finished their drinks and extinguished their smokes and went to bed, the bed that Maggie would have to leave to return to her own before the domestic staff was up and about.

~ Chapter 10 ~

THE NEXT MORNING Grimes was awakened from his second sleep—he had drifted off again after Maggie had left him—by one of the very plain serving maids who brought him a jug of thick, sweet coffee and informed him that breakfast would be served, in the small dining room, in an hour's time. He had some coffee (he would have preferred tea) and then did all the things that he had to do and attired himself in a plain, black shirt and a kilt in the Astronaut's Guild tartan—black, gold and silver—long, black socks and highly polished, gold-buckled, black shoes. He went out into the passageway and rapped on the door to Maggie's suite.

She called, "Who is it?"

"Me."

"Come in, come in."

He was amused to find that she was attired as he was, although her kilt was shorter and lighter than his and the tartan was the green, blue, brown and gold of the Institute of Life Sciences.

"All we need," he said, "is a piper to precede us into the Archon's presence. I wonder if he'll give us haggis for breakfast."

She laughed. "Knowing you, you'll be wishing that he would. You'll be pining even for Scottish oatmeal. The Lady Ellena's ideas as to what constitutes a meal to start the day do not coincide with yours."

They most certainly did not. Grimes maintained that God had

created pigs and hens only so that eggs and bacon could make a regular appearance on the breakfast tables of civilized people. He regarded the little, sweet buns with barely concealed distaste and did no more than sip at the syrupy, sweet coffee.

The Archon was in a subdued mood. The Lady Ellena looked over the sparsely laden table at her husband's guests with obviously spurious sweetness.

"Do have another roll, Commodore. You do not seem to have much of an appetite this morning. Perhaps your party last night was rather too good."

Grimes took another roll. There was nothing else for him to eat.

"The Archon tells me," she went on, almost as though Brasidus were not among those present, "that you know two of the performers at Aristotle's Arena. Those rather odd girls called Shirl and Darleen. The boomerang throwers."

"Yes," admitted Grimes. "We are old acquaintances."

Maggie was trying hard not to laugh.

"You have no doubt already noticed," went on Ellena, "that I have formed a Corps of Amazons. I considered this to be of great importance on a planet such as this which, until recently, had never known women. Women, I decided, must be shown to be able to compete with men in every field, including the military arts and sciences."

"Mphm," grunted Grimes, pulling his pipe and tobacco pouch out from his sporran.

"Would you mind refraining, Commodore? I am allergic to tobacco smoke. Besides, the ancient Hellenes never indulged in tobacco."

Only because they never had the chance to do so, thought Grimes as he put his pipe and pouch away.

"I am interested," she said, "in recruiting instructors from all over the Galaxy. Brasidus has told me that Shirl and Darleen—what *peculiar* names—are proficient in boxing techniques, especially a sort of foot boxing, and in the use of throwing weapons. Boomerangs."

"The ones that they demonstrated last night," said Grimes, "were only play boomerangs."

"I know, Commodore, I know. After all I, like you, am an Australian. Or, in my own case, *was*. I am now a citizen of New Sparta. But I have no doubt that the young . . . ladies can use hunting boomerangs, *killing* boomerangs, with effect."

"I've seen them do it," said Grimes.

"You have? You must tell me all about it some time. Meanwhile, I shall be greatly obliged if you will act on my behalf and try to persuade the young ladies to enter my service as instructors."

"Rank and pay?" asked Grimes, always sensitive to such matters.

"I was thinking of making them sergeants," said Ellena.

"No way," said Grimes. "There will have to be much more inducement. As theatrical artistes they are well-paid." (Were they?) "They are members of a glamorous profession. I would suggest commissioned rank, lieutenancies at least, with pay to match and specialists' allowances in addition."

"Do you intend to demand a 10 percent agent's commission?" asked Maggie.

He kicked her under the table and she subsided.

Ellena did not appear to have a sense of humor. She said, sourly, "Of course, Commodore, if you wish a recruiting sergeant's bounty, that can be arranged."

He said, "Commander Lazenby was only joking, Lady."

Maggie said, "Was I?"

Ellena looked from one to the other, emitted an exasperated sigh.

"Spacepersons," she said, "consider things funny that we mere planet lubbers do not."

Such as money? thought Grimes.

"Nonetheless," she went on, "I shall be greatly obliged if you will endeavor to persuade Miss Shirl and Miss Darleen to enlist in my Amazon Corps. Need I remind you that you are a shipowner whose vessel makes money trading to and from this world? Perhaps if you could bring yourself to call upon them this very morning . . . ."

"I will come with you, John," said Brasidus, breaking his glum silence.

"But you have forgotten, dear, that there is a Council meeting?"

"I have not, Ellena. But surely such a matter as providing separate toilets for the sexes in the Agora does not demand my presence."

"It does so. The status of women on this world must be elevated and you, as my husband, must make it plain that you think as I do."

"I'd accompany you, John," Maggie told him, "but I'm scheduled to address the Terra-Sparta Foundation on the history and culture of my own planet. I can't very well wriggle out of it."

"I'll organize transport for you, John," said Brasidus.

"It might be better if I did," said Ellena. "It will look better if the Commodore is driven to the Hippolyte by one of my Amazon Guards rather than by one of your musclebound louts."

So Grimes, in a small two-seater, a hovercar looking even more like an ancient war chariot than the generality of military vehicles on this world, was driven to the Hippolyte Hotel by a hefty, blonde wench who conveyed the impression that she should have been standing up holding reins rather than sitting down grasping a wheel. She brought the vehicle to an abrupt halt outside the main doorway of the hotel, leapt out with a fine display of long, tanned legs and then offered Grimes unneeded assistance out of the car to the pavement. The doorwoman, uniformed in imitation of Ellena's Amazons but squat and flabby (but with real muscles under the flab, thought Grimes) scowled at them.

"What would you, citizens?" she demanded.

"Just get out of the way, citizen, and let us pass."

"But *he* is a man."

"And I am Lieutenant Phryne, of the Lady Ellena's Amazon Guard, here on the Lady's business."

"And *him*?"

"The gentleman is Commodore Grimes, also on the Lady's business."

"All right. All right." She muttered to herself, "This is what comes of letting theatricals in here. Turning the place into a space-men's brothel."

"What was that?" asked Phryne sharply.

"Nothing, Lieutenant, nothing."

"The next time you say nothing say it where I can't hear it."

Grimes looked around the lobby of the hotel with interest. All its walls were decorated with skillfully executed mosaic murals, every one of which depicted stern-looking ladies doing unkind things to members of the male sex. There was Jael, securing the hapless Sisera to the mattress with a hammer and a nail. There was Boadicea, whose scythed chariot wheels were slicing up the Roman legionnaires. There was Jeanne d'Arc, on horseback and in shining armor, in the act of decapitating an English knight with her long, gleaming sword. There was Prime Minister Golda riding in the open turret of an Israeli tank, leading a fire-spitting armored column against a rabble of fleeing Arabs. There was Prime Minister Maggie on the bridge of a battleship whose broadside was hurling destruction of the Argentine fleet. There was . . . There was too much, much too much.

Grimes couldn't help laughing.

"What is the joke, Commodore?" asked Lieutenant Phryne coldly.

"Whoever did these murals," explained Grimes, "might have been a good artist but he . . ." She glared at him. "But *she*," he corrected himself, "was a lousy historian."

"I do not think so."

"No?" He pointed with the stem of his pipe at the very imaginative depiction of the battle off the Falkland Islands. "To begin with, Mrs. Thatcher wasn't *there*. She ran things from London. Secondly, by that time battleships had been phased out. The flagship of the British fleet was an aircraft carrier, the other vessels destroyers, frigates and submarines. Thirdly, with the exception of one elderly and unlucky cruiser, the Argentine navy stayed in port."

"You seem to be very well-informed," said the Amazon lieutenant coldly.

"I should be. My father is an historical novelist."

"Oh."

The pair of them walked to the reception desk.

"Would Miss Shirl and Miss Darleen be in?" asked Grimes.

"I think so, citizen," replied the slight, quite attractive brunette.

"I shall call their suite and ask them to join you in the lobby. Whom shall I say is calling?"

Before Grimes could answer his escort said, "I am Lieutenant Phryne of the Lady Ellena's Amazon Guard. This citizen is Commodore Grimes. The business that we have to discuss is very private and best dealt with in their own quarters."

The girl said something about hotel regulations.

The lieutenant told her that the Lady Ellena was a major shareholder.

The girl said that Shirl and Darleen already had a visitor. A *lady*, she added.

"Then I shall be outnumbered," said Grimes. "I shall be no threat to anybody's virtue."

Both the receptionist and the lieutenant glared at him.

⊷ Chapter 11 ⊷

"**COME IN!**" called a female voice as Lieutenant Phryne rapped sharply on the door, which slid open. "Come in! This is Liberty Hall; you can spit on the mat and call the cat a bastard." Then, "Who's your new girlfriend, Grimes? You never waste much time, do you?"

Fenella Pruin, sprawled in an easy chair, her long, elegant legs exposed by her short *chiton*, a glass of gin in her hand, looked up at the commodore. So did Shirl and Darleen, who were sitting quite primly side by side on a sofa, holding cans of beer. Foster's, noted Grimes, an Australian brand, no doubt brought to New Sparta as part of one of *Sister Sue*'s cargoes.

"Lieutenant Phryne," said Grimes stiffly, "has been acting as my chauffeuse."

"And what are you acting as, Grimes? What hat are you wearing this bright and happy morning? Owner-master? Pirate commodore? Planetary governor?"

"Recruiting sergeant," said Grimes.

"You intrigue me. But take the weight off your feet. And you, Lieutenant. And find the Commodore a gin, Shirl, and his Amazon Guard whatever she fancies . . ."

After the drinks had been organized Grimes found himself sitting between Shirl and Darleen, facing Fenella.

"Here's to crime," she toasted, raising her refilled glass. "And now, Grimes, talk. What's with this recruiting sergeant business? Let me guess. You're an old boozing pal of the Archon's. The Archon's lady wife is building up her own private army, of which Lieutenant Phryne is a member. Lady Ellena is on the lookout for offplanet martial arts specialists to act as instructors. Right?"

"Right."

"And Shirl and Darleen are not only artists with the boomerang but expert in their own peculiar version of *savate*. Boxing with the feet. Right?"

"Right."

"What's in it for them?"

"Lieutenants' commissions. Standard pay for the rank, plus allowances."

"Should we accept, Fenella?" asked Shirl. "It would seem to be a steady job, staying in one place. We are becoming tired of jumping from world to world."

"Leave me to negotiate," said the journalist. Then, to Grimes, "At times I wear more than one hat myself. As well as being a star reporter I am a theatrical agent. Oh, only in respect of Shirl and Darleen. I sort of took them under my wing when you left them stranded on Bronsonia." She added virtuously, "Somebody had to."

"Is it an agent's hat you're wearing?" asked Grimes sardonically. "Or a halo?"

She ignored this and turned to Phryne. "What's lieutenant's pay in the Amazon Corps?"

"One thousand obols a month."

"And what's that in *real* money? Never mind . . . ." She used her wrist companion as a calculator. "Mmm. Not good, but not too bad. And the bennies?"

"Bennies, Lady?"

"Side benefits."

"Free accommodation, with meals in the officers' mess. Two new uniforms a year. A wine ration . . ."

"We do not like wine," said Darleen. "We like beer."

"I think that I could arrange that," Grimes said.

"All the more cargo for your precious ship to bring here," sneered Fenella. "But, anyhow, a generous beer ration must be part

of the contract. Imported beer, not the local gnat's piss." Again she
turned to Phryne. "What extra pay do instructors get?"

"I cannot say with any certainty. But junior officers often complain that instructor sergeants make more money than they do."

"And a sergeant's pay is?"

"In the neighborhood of six hundred obols a month."

"Which means that they must get at least another five hundred
extra in special allowances. Find out how much it is, Grimes, and
then argue that a commissioned officer should receive allowances
on a much higher scale than a non-commissioned one. And, talking
of commissions . . . . What about mine?"

"I do not think," said Grimes, "that the Amazon Corps needs a
press officer."

"I wasn't talking about that sort of commission. I was talking
about my agent's commission."

"Surely even you wouldn't take money off Shirl and Darleen!"

"I've no intention of doing so, but I expect something for myself
for handling their affairs. To begin with, I got some very good
coverage of the adventures of the rather tatty troupe that I signed
them up with. (Talking of that, I shall expect the Lady Ellena to buy
them out of their contract.) Now I shall want coverage of Shirl's and
Darleen's experiences in the Amazon Guard. *With The Woman
Warriors Of New Sparta* and all the rest of it. Which means that I
must be given rights of entry to the Archon's palace at all times . . ."

"I did hear," said Grimes, "that you were given the bum's rush
the one time that you came a-calling."

"I was. And I still resent it. Just see to it that it doesn't happen
again."

"That is a matter for the Archon."

"Or for the Archoness. But you'll just have to talk her round,
Grimes. If she wants Shirl and Darleen, those are the terms."

Grimes looked at her through the wreathing fumes from his pipe.
The nostrils of her sharp nose were quivering but he did not think that
this was due to the reek of burning tobacco. She was on the scent of
something. She could be a valuable ally. Although he and Maggie
were attached to the Intelligence Department the muckraking

journalist was far more skilled at ferreting out information than they, simple spaceman and relatively unsophisticated scientist, could ever be.

He got to his feet.

He said, "I'll do my best, Fenella."

She said tartly, "There have been times when your best has not been good enough." Then she grinned. "But you usually finish up with what you want."

He turned to Shirl and Darleen. "Thank you for the drinks. And I hope that I'll soon be seeing you in uniform."

Darleen said, rather wistfully, "We would like to be wearing your uniform, aboard your ship."

He laughed and said, "Unfortunately the Merchant Navy, unlike the Survey Service, doesn't run to Marines . . . ."

"Perhaps when you next go a-pirating . . ." said Fenella.

"Mphm," grunted Grimes. (Piracy, to him, was a very dirty word.)

Accompanied by Lieutenant Phryne he made his way out of the suite and then down to the parked hovercar.

Phryne drove back to the palace by a circuitous, sight-seeing route.

She said snobbishly, "Forgive me for speaking my mind, sir, but those . . . ladies are not, in my opinion, even good NCO material. To become a commissioned officer one must possess at least a modicum of breeding."

"And Shirl and Darleen do not?"

"No. You must have seen them. Drinking their beer straight from the can."

"I often do that myself."

"But you're a spaceman, sir. You're different."

"They're from New Alice. They're different."

"You can say that again. And I don't suppose that they'll even know the right knives and forks and spoons to use in the officers' mess."

"I shouldn't worry. That's an art that they've probably picked up since I last knew them. I remember that Miz Pruin tried to bully what she called civilized table manners into them when she and they were passengers on my ship some time ago."

"Miz Pruin . . ." muttered Phryne scornfully. "So now she's to be allowed the run of the Palace. I had the pleasure of being guard commander when she was evicted."

"What have you got against her?"

"She's a muckraker. I've had experience of her muckraking. I'm from Earth originally, as are most of the women on New Sparta, but for a while I was a member of an experimental, all woman colony on New Lesbos. I soon found out that, when it came to the crunch, I was more heterosexual than otherwise but I was stuck there, with quite a few others, until I'd earned enough to pay my passage back home—and a police constable's salary was far from generous. Dear Fenella came sniffing around. She did a feature on New Lesbos for *Star Scandals*. What got my goat was that a photograph of a quite innocent beach party was captioned as a Lesbian orgy. Damn it all, there are nude beaches a-plenty on Earth and other planets!"

"But very few, these days, reserved for the use of one sex only," said Grimes.

"There just wasn't more than one sex on New Lesbos," she said, "just as there wasn't more than one sex here before the planet was thrown open to immigration."

"She's a good reporter," said Grimes.

"The only good reporter is a dead one," said Phryne. "And boomerangs are toys for backward primitives and kicking should be confined to the Association Football field."

Grimes laughed. "I take it, Lieutenant, that you were featured in that famous photograph."

"I was, Commodore. I was wrestling one of the other girls. But men wrestle each other, don't they? And nobody accuses them of being friendly."

Yet another useful word stolen from the English language by an overly noisy minority, thought Grimes.

He said, "What does it matter, anyhow?"

She said, "It matters to me."

~ Chapter 12 ~

THE LADY ELLENA received Grimes in her office, listened to what he had to tell her.

She said, "You were overly generous, Commodore—but, of course, it is easy to be generous with somebody else's money. Even so . . . . Commissioned rank for that pair of cheap entertainers . . . ."

He said, "You wanted Shirl and Darleen. Now you've got them."

She said, "I most certainly did not want the Pruin woman. Now it seems that I've got her too."

Grimes told her, "She was part of the package deal, Lady."

Ellena made a major production of shrugging. "Oh, well. At least I shall not have to mingle with her socially. And I think that the Palace will be able to afford to treat her to an occasional meal in the sergeants' mess."

"Or the officers' mess," said Grimes. "Shirl and Darleen will be officers . . ."

"Thanks to you."

" . . . and they will wish, now and again, to entertain their friend."

"I cannot imagine her being a friend to anybody. But now, in *my* Palace, she will be free to come and go, to eat food that *I* have paid for, to swill expensive imported beer. But that, of course, is the least of *your* worries, Commodore. After all, it is *your* ship that brings in all such Terran luxuries, at freight rates that ensure for you a very handsome profit."

"Being a shipowner," said Grimes, "is far more worrisome financially than being a planetary ruler. I've been both. I know."

"Indeed?" Her thin eyebrows went up almost to meet her hairline. "Indeed? Well, Your ex-Excellency, I thank you for your efforts on my behalf. And now I imagine that you have business of your own to attend to."

Grimes could not think of any but, bowing stiffly, he made his departure from the Lady Ellena's presence. He was somewhat at a loose end; Maggie was still at her function, giving her after-luncheon talk and answering questions, and Brasidus was still presiding over the council meeting.

He found his way to his quarters. His suite possessed all the amenities usually found in hotel accommodation, including a playmaster. There were gin and a bottle of Angostura bitters in the grog locker, ice cubes in the refrigerator. He mixed himself a drink. He checked the playmaster's library of spools. These included various classical dramas in the original Greek and a complete coverage of the Olympic Games, on Earth, from the late Twentieth Century, Old Style, onwards. Unfortunately the library did not include anything else. Grimes sighed. He switched the playmaster to its TV reception function, sampled the only two channels that were available at this time of day. Both of these presented sporting events. He watched briefly the discus throwing and thought that these people would have much to learn from Shirl and Darleen. Then he switched off and got from his bags some spools of his own. He set up a space battle simulation and soon was engrossed, matching his wits against those of the small but cunningly programmed computer.

Eventually Maggie joined him there.

She flopped into an easy chair, demanded a drink. Grimes made her a Scotch on the rocks. She disposed of it in two gulps.

She said, "I needed that! What a bunch of dim biddies I had to talk to. Oh, it wasn't so much the talking as the stupid questions afterwards. Most of my audience knew only two worlds, Earth and New Sparta, and were quite convinced that those are the only two planets worth knowing. As a real, live Arcadian I was just a freak, to be condescended to. They even lectured me on the glories of

Hellenic culture and the great contributions it has made to Galactic civilization. Damn it all, Hellenic culture is only part of Terran culture, just as Australian culture is. Talking of Australians, and pseudo-Australians, how did you get on with Shirl and Darleen?"

"I persuaded them to accept commissions in the Amazon Guard. Unluckily—or was it so unlucky?—Fenella was part of the deal. She's staying on to do a piece on them, and part of the package is that she's to be allowed free access to the Palace at all times."

"Why did you say, 'or was it so unlucky'?"

"She might be able to help us. I gained the impression that she's on the track of something. Is there any way that she could be pressganged into the Intelligence Branch? After all, we were."

"But we were—and are—already officers holding commissions in the Survey Service. When admirals say, Jump! we jump. Even you, John, as long as you're on the Reserve List."

"Civilians can be conscripted . . ." said Grimes. "*I* was. I became a civilian as soon as I resigned from the Service after the mutiny."

"As I heard it from Admiral Damien," Maggie said, "you were offered the Reserve Commission that you now hold. You were not compelled to accept it."

"Mphm. Not quite. But there were veiled threats as well as inducements."

"Could you threaten Fenella?"

"I wish that I could. But as I'm not a major shareholder in *Star Scandals* I can't."

"Inducements?"

"I've already played one major card by getting her the permission to come calling round to the Palace any time that she feels like it. There should have been a *quid pro quo*. I realize that now."

"Now that it's too late. What we want is an I'll-scratch-your-back-if-you'll-scratch-mine situation. What inducements can we offer? Mmm. To begin with, I'm the senior officer of the Federation Survey Service on this planet . . . ."

"*I* am," said Grimes indignantly.

"But only you and I know it. As far as the locals are concerned, as far as Fenella is concerned, you're no more than an owner-master, waiting here for his little star tramp to come wambling in with her cargo of black olives and retsina. And *I* have a warship at *my* disposal. A minor warship, perhaps, but a warship nonetheless."

"A Serpent Class courier," scoffed Grimes, "armed with a couple of pea-shooters and a laser cannon that would make quite a fair cigarette lighter. Commanded by a snotty-nosed lieutenant."

"You were one yourself once. But how far could you trust Fenella? Suppose, just suppose, that you spilled some of the beans to her? Could she be trusted?"

"I think that she subscribes to the journalists' code of honor. Never betray your sources. Too, there's one threat that I could use. The Baroness Michelle d'Estang of Eldorado is a *Star Scandals* major shareholder. I was among those present when Michelle, wielding the power of the purse, killed a really juicy story that Fenella wanted to splash all over the Galaxy."

"I take it that Michelle is one of your girlfriends."

"You could call her that."

"And we've other cards to play. Both of us are personal friends of the Archon. And you, I have gathered, have been on more than friendly terms with Shirl and Darleen. Soon, I think, we must have a get-together with Miz Pruin and offer her our cooperation in return for hers."

"If you say so," said Grimes. "And now I suppose that we'd better get dressed for tonight's state dinner party."

"We have to get undressed first," she said suggestively.

⇜ Chapter 13 ⇝

SO THERE WAS THE STATE DINNER PARTY, as boring as such occasions usually are, with everybody, under the watchful eye of the Lady Ellena, on his or her best behavior, with the serving wenches obviously instructed not to be overly prompt in such matters as the refilling of wine glasses. The female guests, thought Grimes snobbishly, were a scruffy bunch, immigrants all, mainly from Earth, most of whom would never, on their home planets, have been invited to a function such as this. The same could have been said regarding the hostess, Ellena.

What really irked the Commodore was the ban on smoking. Not even when things got to the coffee and ouzo stage was he able to enjoy his pipe—and normally he liked to enjoy a couple or three puffs between courses.

He was seated near the head of the high table, with Maggie on his left and the headmistress of the Pallas Athena College for Young Ladies on his right. Maggie had gotten into a conversation with Colonel Heraclion, who was sitting next to her on her other side, leaving Grimes to cope with the academic lady.

"You must already have noticed changes here, Commodore," she said.

Grimes swallowed a mouthful of rather stringy stewed lamb (if it was lamb) and replied briefly, "Yes."

"And changes for the better. Oh, the first settlers did their best

305

to recreate the glory that was Greece but, without the fair sex to aid them in their endeavors, all that they achieved was a pale shadow . . . ."

She waved her fork as she spoke and drops of gravy fell on the front of her chiton. It was rather surprising, thought Grimes, that they succeeded in making a landing as the material of the dress dropped in almost a straight line from neck to lap. He categorized her as a dried-up stick of a woman, not his type at all, with graying hair scraped back from an already overly high forehead, with protuberant pale blue eyes, with thin lips that could not hide buck teeth. Why was it, he wondered, that such people are so often, too often prone to fanatical enthusiasms?

"The founding fathers—there were not, of course, any founding mothers—were spacemen, not Greek scholars," she went on. "They knew something, of course, of the culture which they were trying to emulate, but not enough. It has, therefore, fallen to me, and to others like me, to finish the task that was begun by them."

"Indeed?"

"Yes. For example, you should still be here when the first Marathon is run. It will be a grueling course, from the Palace to the Acropolis. A little way downhill, then on the level and, finally, uphill. The race will be open to *everybody*, tourists as well as citizens."

"Better them than me," said Grimes.

"Come, come, Commodore! Surely you are not serious. Taking part in such an event could be one of the greatest challenges of your career."

"Foot racing," Grimes told her, "is not an activity in which I have ever taken part."

"And I know why," she told him. "You are a smoker. I saw you puffing a pipe outside the banqueting hall before you entered. But, even so, you could enter. And—who knows?—you might be among those to finish the course. Think of the honor and the glory!"

"Honor and glory don't pay port charges and maintenance and crew salaries," said Grimes.

She laughed. "Spoken like a true cynic, Commodore. A cynic and a shipowner."

"A man can be both," he admitted. "And if one is the latter one tends to become the former."

"A cynic . . ." she trotted out the old chestnut as though it had been newly minted, by herself . . . "is a man who knows the cost of everything and the value of nothing."

"Mphm."

The meal dragged on.

Finally, after the coffee had been served, there was a display of martial arts in the large area of floor around which the tables stood. There were wrestling matches, men versus men, women versus women, men versus women. (The ladies, Grimes assumed correctly, were members of the Lady Ellena's Amazon Guard. He recognized Lieutenant Phryne, although without the leather and brass trappings of her uniform her body looked softer, much more feminine. Nonetheless she floored her opponent, a hairy male giant, with almost contemptuous ease.)

And then it was the turn of Shirl and Darleen. They were already in their Amazon lieutenants' uniforms. (Somebody must have worked fast, thought Grimes.) They had boomerangs, little ones, no more than toys, that, at the finish of their act, seemed to fill the banqueting hall like a flock of whirring birds.

At last it was over, with the boomerangs, one by one, fluttering out through the wide open doorway, followed finally, after the making of their bows to quite enthusiastic applause, by the two New Alicians.

The academic lady was not among those who clapped.

"*Boomerangs* . . ." she muttered. "But they're not Greek . . ."

"I suppose not," said Grimes.

"And those two women . . . If you could call them that. Mutants, possibly. But *officers* . . . . In the elite Amazon Guard . . . ."

"Instructors, actually," Grimes told her.

"Oh. So you know them. You have some most peculiar friends, Commodore. From which planet do they come?"

"New Alice."

"New Alice?" She laughed creakily. "And how did it get its name? Is it some sort of Wonderland?"

"Just one of the Lost Colonies," said Grimes. "Fairly recently rediscovered. A rather odd Australianoid culture "

"Most definitely odd, Commodore, if those two ladies are a representative sample."

"*All* transplanted cultures are odd," he said. "And some cultures are odd before transplantation."

"Indeed?" Coldly.

"Indeed."

The next time Grimes saw a demonstration of boomerang throwing was at the Amazon Guards' drill ground. He stood with Maggie, Lieutenant Phryne and Fenella Pruin. He watched Shirl and Darleen as they hurled their war boomerangs, ugly things, little more than flattened clubs, at a row of man-sized dummies, twelve of them, achieving a full dozen neat decapitations. More dummies were set up. This time Shirl and Darleen improvised, snatching weapons from a pile of scrap metal and plastic, speedily selecting suitably shaped pieces, hurling them with great effect. But there were now no tidy beheadings. There was damage, nonetheless—arms torn off, bellies ripped open, faces crushed.

"Not very effective against well-aimed laser fire," sneered Phryne.

"Better than bare fists," said Grimes. "And, come to that, more effective than your wrestling . . . ."

"Care to try a fall or two, Commodore?" she asked nastily.

"No thank you, Lieutenant."

Maggie laughed and Fenella Pruin sniggered.

And then all three of them watched the Amazons, under the tutelage of Shirl and Darleen, trying to master the art of play boomerang throwing.

"No! No!" Darleen was yelping. "Not *that* way, you stupid bitch. Hold it *up*, not across! Flat side *to* you, not away! And . . . And *flick* your wrist! Like *this!*"

An instructor officer she might be, newly commissioned, but already she was beginning to sound like a drill sergeant.

Grimes, Maggie and Fenella drifted away from the field. They stood in the shade of a large tree. Grimes was amused when Maggie went through routine bug detection; she was taking her secondment to the Intelligence Branch very seriously. There certainly would be bugs in the foliage, he said, but not of the electronic variety. She was not amused.

"Now we can talk," she said.

"What about?" asked Fenella Pruin.

"You."

"Me, Commander Lazenby?"

"Yes. You. You're after a story, aren't you?"

"I'm always after stories. Ask Grimes. He knows."

"And the story with Grimes in it you weren't allowed to publish. *I* know. Do you want to publish the story—if there is one—that you get on New Sparta?"

"Of course."

"Suppose you aren't allowed to?"

Fenella Pruin laughed. "Really, my dear! Even I know that a mere commander in the Survey Service doesn't pile on many Gs."

"A commander," Maggie told her, "with admirals listening to what she has to say."

"Am I supposed to stand at attention and salute?"

"Only if you want to. Anyhow, we can help you, and you can help us."

"*We*? You and Grimes, of all people!"

Maggie contained her temper. "Miz Pruin," she said coldly. "You know why I am here, on New Sparta. Making an ethological survey for the Survey Service's Scientific Branch. You know why Commodore Grimes is here. Waiting for the arrival of his ship so that he may, once again, assume command of her. We know why you are here. Sniffing out a story, the more scandalous the better."

"There's one that I've already sniffed out," said Fenella Pruin nastily. "You're sleeping with Grimes. And if you don't watch him like a hawk he'll be tearing pieces off Shirl and Darleen again."

"He'd better not," said Maggie. "Not while I'm around."

"Don't I get a say in this?" demanded Grimes.

"No matter who is sleeping with whom, or who is going to sleep with whom," went on Maggie, "we, the Commodore and I, could be of help to you. We are *persona grata* in the Palace, as old friends of the Archon. Too, I know my way about this planet. Both of us do."

"You could be right," admitted Fenella grudgingly.

"Of course I'm right. And, on the other hand, although you lack our local knowledge, although you don't have our contacts, you are quite famous for your ability to sniff out scandals. Political as well as sexual."

"Bedfellows often make strange politics," said Fenella.

"Haven't you got it the wrong way around?" asked Maggie.

"No."

It was Grimes's turn to laugh.

Maggie ignored him, went on, "It will be to our mutual benefit if we pool information. The Commodore and I have our contacts. You now have yours—Shirl and Darleen in the Amazon Guard. Too, if you made yourself too unpopular—as you have done on more than one planet—I could be of very real help to you."

"How?"

"You must have seen that Serpent Class courier at the spaceport. *Krait.* Her captain, Lieutenant Gupta, is under my orders. I could see to it that you got offplanet in a hurry should the need arise."

"You tempt me, Commander Lazenby. You tempt me, although I doubt very much that Lieutenant Gupta's flying sardine can is as luxurious as Captain Grimes's *Little Sister* . . . ." She turned to Grimes. "I was really sorry, you know, when I learned that you'd gotten rid of her. We had some good times aboard her . . ."

Grimes could not remember any especially good times, either on the voyage out to New Venusberg or the voyage back. But Maggie, of course, had taken the remark at its face value and was glaring at him.

"Never look a gift horse in the mouth," said Grimes to Fenella, adding, "That's one proverb you can't muck around with."

"Isn't it? Didn't a grazing cow once say, 'Never take a horse gift in the mouth . . .'?"

"Shut up, you two!" snapped Maggie. "Are you with us or aren't you, Miz Pruin?"

"I know what's in it for me," said the journalist. "Put what's in it for you?"

"I've told you. Just help in my research project."

"And for Grimes?"

"I'm just helping Commander Lazenby," he said. "Just passing the time until my ship comes in."

"If that's your story," she said, "stick to it. But all right, I'll play. And I'll expect the pair of you to play as well."

"We shall," promised Maggie.

~ Chapter 14 ~

FENELLA PRUIN was now allowed into the Palace although she was still far from welcome. Should she chance to meet the Lady Ellena while making her way through the corridors the Archon's wife would sweep by her as though she didn't exist. Brasidus himself would acknowledge her presence, but only just. She was tolerated in the officers' quarters of the Amazon Guard because of her friendship with Shirl and Darleen, both of whom had become quite popular with their messmates. And, of course, she was free to visit Maggie and Grimes any time that she so wished.

She joined them, this day, for morning coffee.

After the surly serving wench had deposited the tray on the table and left, after Maggie had poured the thick, syrupy fluid into the little cups, she demanded, "Well? Have you anything to tell me yet?"

"No," admitted Maggie. "I am still nibbling around the edges, as it were. The New Hellas people are up to *something*. But what?"

"It's a pity that you can't join them," said Fenella.

"It is. But they know that I'm an officer of the Federation Survey Service. And they know that both Commodore Grimes and I are personal friends, old friends of Brasidus." She laughed. "Although if it were not for that personal friendship they might try to recruit John."

"It'd be my ship they'd want," said Grimes. "Not me especially."

"Why not?" asked Fenella. "After all, you were slung out of the Survey Service in disgrace . . . ."

"I resigned," growled Grimes.

"And you were a pirate . . ."

"How many times," he demanded, "do I have to tell people that I was a privateer? And now, Fenella, do you have anything to tell us?"

She looked at him and said, "I was under the impression, Grimes, that the ethological research project was Commander Lazenby's baby, not yours."

"Commodore Grimes," said Maggie, "is helping me with it. Just out of friendship, of course."

"Of course," concurred Fenella, twitching her nose. "Of course. But the Commodore was quite recently a servant of the Federation, on the public payroll, as a planetary governor, no less . . . Are you really self-employed, Grimes? Or is it just a cover?"

"It is a known fact," snapped Maggie, "that Commodore Grimes is an owner-master."

"At the moment," said Grimes, "just an owner. I shall be master again as soon as I get my name back on *Sister Sue*'s register."

"It is the *unknown* facts that interest me . . ." murmured Fenella. "Such as the real reason for the appointment of a notorious pirate . . ."

"*Not* a pirate!" yelled Grimes.

" . . . to the governorship of a planet."

"You've trodden on corns in the past," said Grimes coldly. "You should know, by this time, that there are some corns better not trodden on."

Maggie sighed. "All this is getting us nowhere and has nothing at all to do with New Sparta. Would you mind telling us, Fenella, just what you've found out?"

The journalist finished her coffee, said, "No thanks, Maggie. One cup of this mud was ample. Potables shouldn't need knives and forks to deal with them." She took a cigarette from the box on the table, puffed it into ignition. "Now, I think I'm getting places, which is more than can be said for the pair of you. A Major Hera has taken quite a fancy to Shirl and Darleen. She is taking private *savate* lessons and, in return, is teaching the two girls her own version of wrestling. Now, now . . . I know that you have dirty minds, or I know that Grimes has, but there's nothing like what you're thinking. Not yet, anyhow, but I must admit that Shirl and Darleen are surprisingly innocent in some respects. Well, Hera is a high-up in the Ladies' Auxiliary of the New Hellas Association. She's already persuaded quite a few Amazon officers and NCOs to join. She's been trying to persuade the two new Instructor Lieutenants to join. I've advised them to yield to her blandishments and then to keep their eyes skinned and their ears flapping."

"I can't see them as spies," said Grimes. "They're too direct. Too honest."

"Who else have we got?" she asked. "Not me. Not either of you,"

"And they will report to you?" asked Grimes.

"Yes," she said.

"They will report to *us*," stated Maggie firmly. "After all, they are Commodore Grimes's friends. What could be more natural than that they should join him here for a drink or two?"

"As long as I am present," said Fenella.

"Talking of drinks," said Grimes, "I could do with a stiff one to wash away the taste of that alleged coffee."

The two ladies thought that this was quite a good idea.

∾ Chapter 15 ∾

"YOU KNOW, JOHN," said Brasidus, "I think that I was much happier in the old days. When I was a simple sergeant in the army, with authority but not much responsibility. Now I have responsibility, as Archon, but my authority seems to have been whittled away." He sighed. "Sparta—it wasn't called *New* Sparta then—was a far simpler world than it is now. We were happy enough eating and drinking and brawling. There were no women to tell us to wash behind the ears and watch our table manners." He gulped from his mug of wine. "I regard you as a friend, John, a good friend, but I have thought that it was a great pity that you ever came to this planet, opening us up to the rest of the Galaxy . . ."

"If it hadn't been me," said Grimes, "it would have been somebody else. The search for Lost Colonies is always going on. I've heard that 90 percent of the interstellar ship disappearances have now been accounted for. And, in any case, how many ships of that remaining 10 percent founded a colony? Possibly none of them."

"You are changing the subject, my friend. In the old days I should never have been obliged to disguise myself in order to enjoy, with a good friend, what you refer to as a pub crawl. I should never have had to wait for an evening when my wife—my *wife*—was out attending some meeting or other. There weren't any wives."

"As I recall it," said Grimes, "some of your boyfriends, your surrogate women, could be bitchy enough. And, in any case, the

315

King of Sparta would have done as you are doing now, put on disguise, if he wished to mingle, incognito, with his subjects."

"If he had mingled more," said Brasidus sourly, "he might have kept his crown. And his head. As it was, he just didn't have his finger on the pulse of things."

"And you have?"

"I hope so."

"Tell me, what do you feel?"

"I . . . I wish that I knew."

The two men looked around the tavern, which was far from crowded. They had been able to secure a table at which they could talk with a great degree of privacy. Even the two bodyguards, although not quite out of earshot, were fully occupied chatting up the slovenly, but crudely attractive, girl who had brought them a fresh jug of wine. Had he not already seen how swiftly Jason and Paulus could act when danger threatened Grimes would have doubted their value.

"But you have your Secret Service, or whatever you call it," pursued Grimes. "Surely they keep you informed."

Brasidus laughed. "I sometimes think that the State subsidizes the New Hellas Association and other possibly subversive organizations. They're packed with Intelligence agents, all of them dues-paying members. But do they tell me everything? Do they tell me *any-thing*?"

"They must tell you something, just to stay on the payroll if for no other reason."

"But do they tell me the truth?" demanded the Archon. "This way, mingling with my people in disguise, I can hear things for myself. There are grumblings—but what government has ever been universally popular? Need I ask *you* that? There are those who want a return to the Good Old Days, a womanless world, and who resent the influx of females from Earth and other planets. There are those who want a society more closely modeled on that of ancient Greece, on Earth, with women kept barefoot and pregnant." He laughed. "There are even those, mainly women, who hanker after some mythical society that was ruled by a woman, Queen Hippolyte, where men were kept in subjection. But that, as you would say, is the lunatic fringe . . . ."

"With the Lady Ellena as a member?" Grimes could not help asking.

Brasidus laughed again. "She is a good wife, I'll not deny that, although perhaps a shade overbearing. And I . . . humor her. She believes, or says that she believes, that the Hippolyte legends are true. Oh, I've tried to reason with her. I've imported books from Earth, Greek histories, and she's condescended to read them. And she says that there has been a conspiracy of male historians to suppress the Hippolyte story, to laugh it away as a mere myth . . ."

"Your scholars had done some ingenious tampering with history and biology before your Lost Colony was found," said Grimes.

"That was different," said Brasidus. "But Ellena . . . I've played along with her, up to a point. I let her form her Amazon Guard. Having toy lady soldiers to play with keeps her happy."

"Toy soldiers?" asked Grimes. "Oh, they probably wouldn't be a match for an equal number of Federation Space Marines, but against ordinary troops they'd give a very good account of themselves."

"You really think that?"

"I do."

There was a brief silence, broken only by the happy squeals of the serving wench who had been looking after Paulus and Jason. Of the serving wenches, rather. The original girl had been joined by another, equally coarsely attractive. The pair of them were sitting on the bodyguards' laps, fondling and being fondled. Grimes filled and lit his pipe, looking toward the door to the street as he did so. He saw the women enter, six of them. A fat blonde, a tall, skinny redhead, four very nondescript brunettes. They were dressed, all of them, in rather tawdry finery, with chaplets of imitation vine leaves intertwined with their tousled hair, latter-day bacchantes—or a sextet of working girls enjoying a night on the tiles. They did not seem to be sober, lurching and staggering as they made their way across the floor, giggling and nudging each other.

"Women," muttered Brasidus, "cannot drink with dignity."

Not only women, thought Grimes, although he was inclined to the opinion that drunken men are somewhat less of a nuisance.

The fat blonde failed successfully to negotiate the quite generous space between Grimes's table and that at which the two bodyguards were sitting. Her heavy, well-padded hip almost shoved Grimes off his chair. "Gerrout o' my way, you barshtard . . ." she slurred, glaring at him out of piggy blue eyes that, the Commodore suddenly realized, looked more sober than otherwise. Two of the other women had gotten themselves entangled with Brasidus. Wine bottle and glasses were overset.

Simultaneously, Jason and Paulus were having their troubles. Their chairs had gone over backwards and they were sprawled on the floor, their limbs entangled with those of their female companions. They were trying to get their pistols out from the concealed holsters, but without success.

The corpulent innkeeper came bustling up. "Citizens! Citizens! I must implore you to keep the peace!"

"Keep a piece of this!" snarled the redhead, cracking him smartly across the brow with a wine bottle.

Grimes tried to get to his feet but two of the brunettes pounced on him, bore him to the floor. They were surprisingly well-muscled wenches. Their hard feet thudded into his ribs and belly. He had enough presence of mind to protect his testicles with his hands—but that left his head uncovered. A calloused heel struck him just behind the right ear and, briefly, he lost consciousness. Then dimly he was aware of the scuffling around him and the voice of the fat woman— no trace of drunkenness now—saying sharply, "Now! While he's still out!"

But I'm not still out, thought Grimes, not realizing at first that she was not talking about him.

He was no longer out but those two useless bodyguards were, jabbed with needles loaded with some kind of drug by the tavern wenches. He was no longer out and he raised himself on his hands and knees, in time to see the six women—no, the eight women; they had been joined by the two serving girls—hurrying through the door to the street with Brasidus supported between them. None of the inn's patrons had made any move to interfere. Why should they? Drunken brawls were not uncommon.

Somehow he got to his feet. He started toward the door and then hesitated. Unarmed he was no match for no less than eight hefty, vicious wenches. He stumbled to where Paulus was sprawled, face down, on the floor. He fell to his knees, fumbled in the man's clothing. He found the concealed holster almost at once, pulled out the pistol. He checked that it was loaded, cocked the weapon. He had by now recovered sufficiently to run, albeit painfully, to the door.

To his surprise he did not have to look far to find the kidnappers. They were standing there, all eight of them, in the middle of the poorly lighted street, still supporting the unconscious Archon between them.

"Freeze!" yelled Grimes, waving the Minetti.

They turned to look at him but otherwise made no move.

"Release him! At once!"

"If that's the way you want it, buster," said the fat blonde.

The women stepped away from Brasidus. Fantastically his body remained upright. Even more fantastically it seemed to elongate, as though the Archon were becoming taller with every passing second. Grimes stared incredulously. He heard, then, the faint humming of a winch. He looked up and saw, at no great altitude, a dark gray against the black of the night sky, the bulk of a small airship. He started to run forward, to try to grab the feet of his friend. Somebody tripped him. He fell heavily but, luckily for him, retained his grip on the pistol. He sensed that the kidnappers were closing in around him and fired at random, not a full, wasteful burst but spaced shots. Surely, in this scrum, he must get somebody in the legs.

He heard a yelp of pain, then another.

He got to his feet.

Nobody stopped him.

There was nobody there to stop him.

He looked up.

The dirigible was gone, presumably with Brasidus a prisoner in its cabin.

He looked around.

The dirt of the road surface had been scuffed by the struggle. In two places there were dark, glistening stains. Blood. But the women had melted into the shadows, taking their wounded with them. He hoped that the fat bitch was among the casualties.

There was the sound of approaching, running feet. He turned in that direction, holding the pistol ready. He saw who was coming, three policemen, what little light there was reflected from their polished black leather and stainless steel.

Hastily Grimes put the gun into a pocket.

The leading police officer shone his torch full on Grimes's face, although not before the Commodore had noticed that he was holding a stungun in his other hand.

He said disgustedly, "*You* again." Grimes thought that he recognized the voice. He went on, "I heard shots. There has obviously been some sort of struggle here. What have you been doing?"

"I haven't been doing anything," said Grimes virtuously if not quite accurately. He tried to fit a name to the owner of the voice. "Sergeant Priam, isn't it? Would you mind not shining that light into my eyes?"

"Certainly, sir. Commodore, sir. And now would you mind telling me what in Zeus's name has been going on?"

"A kidnapping. The Archon. He was snatched by a gang of women, carried away in an airship. No, I didn't get any registration marks or numbers. The thing wasn't carrying lights."

The beam of the sergeant's torch was directed downward.

"And this blood. Whose is it? The Archon's?"

"There was a struggle, as you can see. One or two of the women got hurt."

"You shot them."

"It was better," said Grimes, "than having my head kicked in."

"Let me have the weapon, sir."

Grimes shrugged and passed the weapon over.

He said, "It's not mine. It belongs to one of the Archon's bodyguards."

"And where are they?"

"Inside the inn. Unconscious."

Sergeant Priam sighed heavily. "Why do these things always have to happen to me? You will have to come to the station, sir, to make your report." He laughed. "But you'll find it far easier to make your report to Colonel Xenophon than, eventually, to the Lady Ellena!"

～ Chapter 16 ～

GRIMES TOLD HIS STORY. Jason and Paulus, almost recovered, thanks to the administration of the antidote, from the effects of the drug with which they had been injected, told their story. The innkeeper, his head bandaged, told his story. Two witnesses, selected at random from the tavern's customers, told their stories. Colonel Xenophon, a tall, thin, bald-headed man looking more like a schoolmaster—but a severe schoolmaster—than a policeman, listened.

He said, "I have known, for some time, of the Archon's nocturnal adventures. I was foolish enough to believe that his professional bodyguards would be capable of protecting him."

"On a normal planet," said Jason hotly, "we should have been."

Xenophon's furry black eyebrows rose like back-arching caterpillars. "Indeed? How do you define normalcy? Is your precious Earth a *normal* planet? Among my reading of late have been recent Terran crime statistics. They have caused me to wonder why any citizen, male or female, is foolhardy enough to venture out after dark in any of the big cities.

"And now, Commodore, you are quite sure that the flying machine which removed the Archon was an airship? Could it not have been one of the inertial drive craft or helicopters that have been introduced from Earth?"

"It could not," said Grimes definitely. "I know an airship when I see one."

"Even in the dark?"

"There was enough light. And the thing was . . . quiet. Just a faint, very faint humming of electric motors."

"So . . . . And in what direction did this mysterious airship fly after the pick-up?"

"I don't know. Those blasted women jumped me. I was fully occupied trying to fight them off."

"Ah, yes. The women. Did you recognize any of them, Commodore?"

"No. But I shall if I run across them again. But, damn it all, Colonel, what are you doing about this crime, this kidnapping? Dirigible airships aren't as common as, say, motorcycles. There can be very few, if any, privately owned. Your Navy has a fleet of lighter-than-air craft. I'd have thought that you'd have started inquiries with the Admiralty, to find out what ships had been flying tonight."

Xenophon smiled coldly. "I should not presume, Commodore, to instruct you in the arts and sciences of spacemanship. Please do not try to tell me how I should do my job. Already inquiries have been made. All the Navy's ships are either in their hangars or swinging at their mooring masts. All Trans-Sparta Airlines' ships, passenger carriers and freight carriers, have been accounted for. And that's all the airships on New Sparta."

"So the ship I saw must either have belonged to the Navy or to Trans-Sparta."

"If you saw such a ship, Commodore. You may have thought that you did. But drugs had been used during the kidnapping. It is possible that during your first struggle with the women an attempt may have been made to put you out by such means and that you may have received a partial dosage, enough to induce hallucinations. Or a blow on the head might have had the same effect."

"If there were no flying machine involved," persisted Grimes, "how was it that the Archon was spirited away from the inn without trace?"

"I think," said the colonel, "that the quarter of the city in which you and the Archon were . . . er . . . conducting your researches is known to Terrans as a rabbit warren. I didn't appreciate the aptness of that expression until I read one of your classics, *Watership Down*. But if you want to lose a needle in a haystack, a rabbit warren is a good place to do it."

"Mphm," grunted Grimes.

"And now, Commodore, may I suggest—may I urge—that you and your two companions return to the Palace; transport will be provided for you. I do not envy your having to tell the story of this night's happenings to the Lady Ellena. She has already been notified, of course, that the Archon is missing. She is a lady of iron self-control but I could tell that she was deeply moved. Please assure her that I and my men will return her husband to her, unharmed, as soon as is humanly possible."

Grimes turned to follow Sergeant Priam from Xenophon's plainly furnished office. The colonel checked him.

"Oh, Commodore, I advise you, strongly, not to try to conduct any sort of rescue operation yourself. Please leave matters in the hands of the experts, such as myself and my people."

"I shouldn't know where to start," said Grimes.

But I shall find out, he thought.

His confrontation with Ellena was bad enough, although not as bad as he had dreaded that it would be.

"Much as I should wish to," she said coldly, "I cannot hold you responsible, Commodore. The Archon was having his 'nights out' . . ." she contrived to apostrophize the phrase . . . "long before you returned to this world.

"Meanwhile, all that I can do is wait. Presumably the kidnappers will present their demands shortly, and then there will be decisions to be made. Until then . . ." She smiled bleakly. "Until then, the show must go on. I shall function as acting Archon until the return of my husband. There will be no disruption of the affairs of state, not even the minor ones such as the Marathon next week."

She is enjoying this . . . thought Grimes.

He asked, "What about the Council, Lady?"

She said, "The Council will do as they are told."

Or else? he wondered.

She said, "That will be all, Commodore."

Grimes considered backing out of the presence but decided not to.

"Who were those women?" asked Maggie.

"I'll know them if I meet them again," said Grimes.

"Could they," she went on, "have been members of the Amazon Guard?"

"No. The Amazon Guard, apart from exceptions such as Shirl and Darleen, goes in for uniformity. Apart from hair coloring all those wenches could be cast from the same mold. The Amazon Guard, I mean. It was a very mixed bunch that we got tangled with last night. The long and the short and the tall."

"And you're sure about the airship?"

"Of course I'm sure." He paused for thought. "You were snooping around for quite a while before I got here and, as a Survey Service commander, meeting officers in the various New Spartan armed forces. Does the Navy run to any female personnel?"

"No."

"Trans-Sparta Airlines?"

She said, "You might have something. Not only do they have women in their ground staff but even token female flight crews. Not in the passenger ships, yet, but in the smaller freight carriers."

"Do they do any night flying?"

"I don't know, John. You're far more of an expert on such matters than I am. Making an arrival or a departure in a spaceship you always have to check up with Aerospace Control, don't you?"

"And on most worlds there're always some aircraft up and about, at any hour of the day or night. The Aerospace Control computers keep track of them."

"And suppose certain computer operators wanted to hide the fact that a small airship, a small, freight-carrying airship with a female crew, wasn't where she was supposed to be . . ."

"You've told me *how*," he said, "but not *why.*"

"Or," she said, "*where?* Where have they taken him?"

"I think that he's safe enough," Grimes said. "If they'd wanted to assassinate him they'd have done just that."

"So we start off snooping around Aerospace Control and the Head Office of Trans-Sparta."

"Colonel Xenophon intimated that he'd be taking a dim view if I started making my own investigations."

"But you won't be investigating the Archon's disappearance. As the owner of a ship on a regular run to New Sparta, shortly to be taking command again of that same ship, you're naturally interested in the workings of local Aerospace Control. You can say that you've had a few complaints from your Chief Officer, Mr. Williams, who's been acting Master in your absence."

"Makes sense."

"And I, carrying on with my own research project, will be interested by the part played by women now in the air transport industry. Fenella might care to come along with me to hold my hand."

"A good idea. It's time that she started to pull her weight. Or does she already know quite a lot that she's not passing on to us?"

"It wouldn't surprise me," she said.

~ Chapter 17 ~

ON SOME WORLDS the kidnapping of a national or planetary ruler would go almost unnoticed or, at most, evoke only shrugs and muttered comments of "Serve the bastard right!" (There were, of course, those on New Sparta who muttered just that, but careful not to do so in the hearing of those who most certainly would take violent exception to such a comment.) But Brasidus had been popular. He had nursed his world through a transition period, had restored and maintained stability. There were orderly demonstrations outside the Palace, expressions of sympathy and support. There were demands that the criminals—whoever they were—be brought swiftly to justice and the Archon released unharmed.

There was extensive media coverage.

Grimes, Maggie and Fenella studied the story of the kidnapping that was splashed all over the front page of *The New Spartan Times*, together with photographs of Brasidus, Grimes and Colonel Xenophon. "A gang of eight men disguised as women . . ." read Grimes aloud. "Those were no transvestites!" he exclaimed.

"They could have been . . ." murmured Fenella. "There are such people, you know . . . ."

"Those two serving wenches who immobilized Jason and Paulus most certainly weren't transvestites. If they had been, those two so-called bodyguards would soon have found out. Their hands were everywhere . . . ."

"So you admit to being a voyeur," sneered Fenella.

"I couldn't help noticing."

"Then they were accomplices—the serving wenches, I mean—of the six men in disguise."

"Those were not men in disguise!" asserted Grimes. "I should know. I was in violent physical contact with all of them, or most of them, twice. Once inside the tavern, once in the street outside. When you wrestle with somebody, especially somebody dressed in only a flimsy chiton, you soon find out if it's he or she."

"All right," Fenella said. "You're the expert. But it's your word against Xenophon's. What is *he* trying to cover up?"

"And on whose orders?" asked Maggie.

"There could be another explanation," suggested Grimes. "One that makes sense. He's playing cunning, trying to lull the kidnappers into a sense of false security, making them think that he's on a false scent . . . ."

"Or, perhaps," said Maggie, "he doesn't want to antagonize our leading militant feminist, the Lady Ellena, by daring to suggest that members of her sex are guilty of the crime. After all, until Brasidus is released . . . ."

"If he ever is released . . ." said Fenella cheerfully.

"Until Brasidus is released, or rescued," went on Maggie, "Lady Ellena is *de facto* ruler of this world. And—I could be wrong, of course—while she is so, heads are liable to roll."

"Not ours, I hope," said Grimes.

"I don't think so. Not yet, anyhow. I'm Survey Service, and that counts for something. Fenella represents the Galactic Media—and that could count for even more. And you, John, even though she's not quite sure about you, are a wealthy shipowner . . . ."

"Ha!" interjected Grimes scornfully.

" . . . with friends in high places."

"With friends like them," said Grimes, "what do I need with enemies?"

"Yes," said Fenella. "You do have friends. As well I know. So . . . There's a cover-up job. So things aren't what they seem. So what are you two doing about it?"

"What are *you* doing about it?" asked Maggie.

"*You* make the news, duckie. I report it."

They told her, then, of their proposed investigations of Aerospace Control and the operations of Trans-Sparta Airlines. Fenella agreed to accompany Maggie, playing the part of an interested journalist, during the visit to the airlines office.

This was not, of course, Grimes's first visit to an Aerospace Control operations center. While he had been in the Survey Service, officers, especially those holding command, had been required to gain an inside knowledge of the workings of such establishments. On Botany Bay, after the *Discovery* mutiny, he had been instrumental in setting up Aerospace Control on that planet. Now, as owner-master of a ship on a regular run between Earth and New Sparta, a telephone call was sufficient to secure for him an appointment with the New Spartan Aerospace Control Director.

A sullen, chastened Paulus drove him from the Palace to the spaceport. He did, however, make some attempt at conversation. "That police chief, sir . . . Has he been on to you? He tried to make Jason and me admit that the two girls we were chatting up were . . . *men.*"

"You should know," said Grimes nastily. "Were they?"

"What do you take us for?" For a while he concentrated on his driving. "And the worst of it is that he got us to sign a statement that the two little bitches were men. He told us that if we didn't sign it'd be just too bad. For us." There was another silence, then, "One thing we learned on Earth is that it doesn't do to tangle with police chiefs. Not unless you have something on them. And even then . . . ."

There were more police in the streets than usual, Grimes noticed. There was also a police detachment at the airport gates, checking the credentials of all who entered. Paulus had with him an official card of some kind. The police lieutenant sneered when it was produced and said, "Ah, one of the famous bodyguards. I hope that you make a better job of guarding this gentleman's body than you did the Archon's . . ." Grimes produced his passport and other papers; even then it was necessary to make a call from the gate office to Aerospace Control. At last they were let through.

The spaceport control tower was part of Aerospace Control, but only its visible portion. The rest of it, most of it, was underground. Grimes told Paulus to wait in the hovercar. The man didn't like it. He seemed determined to guard *somebody* now that his major charge had been taken from him. But the commodore was firm.

He was expected in the ground floor office. A uniformed—but in spacemanlike black and gold, not pseudo-Greek brass and leather—official, a young woman, escorted him into an elevator which, by its rapid descent to the depths, produced a simulation of free fall. She led him through a maze of brightly lit tunnels, finally into a vast compartment that was all illuminated maps and colored lights, some winking and some steady, in the center of which was a globe depicting Space one hundred thousand kilometers out from New Sparta in all directions. By this was a large desk with its own complement of screens and globes, at which sat the Director.

This gentleman got to his feet as Grimes and his guide approached. The girl saluted smartly and then faded into the background. The Director, a tall, heavily bearded man, like Grimes in civilian clothing, a very plain, gray, one-piece business suit, extended his right hand. Grimes took it.

"Glad to have you aboard, Commodore," he was told. "Of course your ship is no stranger to us here but this is the first time that I have had the pleasure of meeting any of her personnel."

"The pleasure is mine," said Grimes.

"Thank you, Commodore. Will you be seated?" He waved to a chair on the other side of the desk. "You are staying at the Palace, I understand. A most serious business, is it not, this kidnapping of the Archon. What could be the motivation? Money—or politics? Mind you, I should not be at all surprised if those New Hellas people, or whatever they call themselves, are involved." He laughed without humor. "Either they want the Archon to press ahead with what they see as reforms or they want him to put the clock back. I have read their propaganda and I've got the impression that they don't know what they do want."

"Who does?" asked Grimes. Then, "You're not a New Spartan, by birth, are you, Director? I've a tin car for accents but yours seems to be—let me guess—Rim Worlds . . . ."

"Too right. I was Deputy Director of Aerospace Control on Lorn and the Director looked like staying put for the next century or so. Then the New Spartan government was advertising for candidates for this job and I applied." He grinned. "I like to think that I run a taut ship."

"I'm sure that you do, Director."

"But when you called me, to make this appointment, you sort of hinted that you had some kind of complaint."

"*I* don't. But, as you may know, although normally I am in command of *Sister Sue* myself I held a ground appointment for a while . . . ."

"A ground appointment!" chuckled the Director. "I suppose you could call it that."

"Yes. During my absence from active command my chief officer, Billy Williams, has been acting master. Captain Williams has been sending voyage reports to me, in my capacity as owner. I have gained the impression from them that he has not been entirely satisfied with New Sparta Aerospace Control's handling of his arrivals and departures."

"He never complained to me about it. If he has any whinges, Commodore, what are they?"

Grimes affected embarrassment. "Well, as a matter of fact, Billy—Captain Williams—is inclined to be sexist. When he calls Aerospace Control on any planet he likes it to be a male voice that answers him. All nonsense, of course." Grimes looked around the large, dimly lit room. So far as he could see every console, but one, was attended by a male. "A lot of women would consider you sexist, too. Practically all your staff is male."

"They wouldn't be," said the Director, "if the Lady Ellena had her way. But even if she did—where would I get trained females from? The girl who brought you in is one of our cadets, but it will be at least two years before she qualifies as a junior controller. And over there, under the airways chart, is Marina. She's a controller third class. She should get her step up and the ones after without any difficulty. She's got a natural feel for the work . . . ."

"Could it be her that my Captain Williams had trouble with? He did say that on his way in he missed a big commercial dirigible by inches. Of course, Billy tends to exaggerate . . . ."

"So it would seem, Commodore. But why don't we stroll over to have a word with Marina?"

The two men walked to where, just over where the girl was sitting, a huge chart of New Sparta, on a Mercatorial projection, adorned the wall. On it little white lights slowly moved, their extrapolated courses fine, luminescent threads. The display, Grimes knew, was computer-controlled and the human operator no more than an observer—but an observer with power to take over should a situation develop with which the electronic brain, lacking intuition and imagination, would be unable to cope.

"Just our normal commercial traffic," said the Director. "The Navy doesn't seem to have any ships up today. They're marked by blue lights. And we don't have any spacecraft coming in or lifting off to complicate the picture." He picked up the long pointer from its rack under the chart, with its tip indicated a spark that, obviously, was making its approach to Port Sparta. "Who is that, Marina?" he asked.

The girl turned in her swivel chair to look up at him. "*City of Athens*, sir," she told him. "She has clearance to come in to her moorings. ETA 1515 hours." Then she saw Grimes standing next to the Director. Her eyes widened but only briefly, very briefly. She was what he would class as a nondescript brunette, smart enough in her uniform, certainly smarter than when he had last seen her, in a disheveled chiton and those spurious vine leaves entangled in her hair. If it was her, that was. But there was the scent that he had smelled during the struggle in the inn, an animal pungency so pronounced as to be almost unpleasant.

He asked, "Haven't we met before, Marina?"

She said coldly, her manner implying who-the-hell-are-you-anyhow? "I do not think so, sir."

"This is Commodore Grimes, Marina," said the Director.

"The owner of *Sister Sue*, and her captain when he's not governing planets."

"I have heard of you, sir," said the girl. Then, "Excuse me. I have to keep an eye on *City of Thrace* and *City of Macedon*; their courses will be close to intersection in an area of poor visibility and turbulence."

She returned her attention to the chart, to the whisper of voices that was coming from the speaker below it.

The Director led Grimes back to his desk.

"Normally," he said, "I'm here only when something interesting is happening. Nothing of interest is happening today and the duty watch is well able to look after the shop. But I thought that you'd like to see how we run things. And it makes a change from my eternal paperwork in my own office."

"How many female controllers do you have?" asked Grimes.

"At the moment, six. One on each watch—that makes three—and the others on non-watchkeeping duties. As a matter of fact Marina isn't on the watchkeeping list; she's filling in for one of the others. Cleo. She had an accident last night. Fell and cut her leg quite badly on a piece of broken glass or something."

"These things happen," said Grimes.

"And when they happen to people who're overweight they're usually more serious," said the Director.

"These big, fat blondes . . ." murmured Grimes commiseratingly.

"She *is* a blonde," admitted the Director. "But how did you guess?"

"I knew a fat blonde once. And she was always getting into trouble."

The Director laughed and then the two men went up to his private office for drinks and a pleasant enough but inconsequential talk.

Later, in his suite at the Palace, Grimes compared notes with Maggie and Fenella. He told them what he had discovered. "Whoever is behind the kidnapping," he told the women, "has agents, two at least, in Aerospace Control. Traffic officers sufficiently experienced to persuade the average computer to falsify records, to show airships as being where they aren't and not where the screen says they are. One was on duty when I paid my call to the Director. I recognized her. She, of course, recognized me."

"But she didn't know, of course, that you recognized her."

"Well, as a matter of fact she did. After I said, 'Haven't we met before?' "

"*What!*" The scream from the two female voices was simultaneous. Then, from Maggie, "You bloody fool! They, whoever they are, will know that you're on to them!"

"Not know. Only suspect. All that they will *know* is that I paid a professional call on Aerospace Control and thought that I recognized one of the duty officers. What I am hoping is that their suspicions drive them to do something stupid . . . ."

"And if they do something cunning, where shall we all be?" demanded Fenella. "Oh, you can set yourself up as a decoy—but Maggie and I are in this business too."

"What's done is done," sighed Maggie. "We shall just have to be especially careful from now on."

"And how did your afternoon go?" asked Grimes, changing the subject.

"Successful enough. We just confirmed what we knew already, that Trans-Sparta Airlines has several all-woman flight crews and that these, still, serve only in the freight carriers. We also learned that much of the freight carrying is done by night. Any of five freighters could have been in this vicinity—although, according to the records, not flying directly over the city—at the time of the kidnapping. Of the five, two had female crews. The Trans-Sparta traffic controller was starting to wonder why I, doing social research, was so interested in commercial operations. But I did find out where those two ships were from and, more importantly, where they were bound . . ."

"Unluckily," said Grimes, "it's the deviations and the unscheduled stops that interest us. And those bitches in Aerospace Control will have made sure that there's no record."

☙ Chapter 18 ☙

GRIMES purchased a large atlas of New Sparta. Among the various maps therein were ones giving details of planetary transport routes—land, sea and air. He studied these, stepped off distances with his dividers. But there was so much territory over which the airships flew, so many stretches where there was not even the smallest village, only a wilderness of forest and mountain. There were so many places at which a dirigible could have made a descent unobserved, even in broad daylight, to disembark willing or unwilling passengers.

Maggie paid more visits to the offices of Trans-Sparta Airlines; her excuse was that she had selected this organization as the subject for her study of the effects of the integration of women into New Spartan industry. Often Fenella would accompany her. She would tell anybody who was interested that she was doing a series which she would call Sex In The Skies, dealing with female air crews on those planets where there were such. She made herself very unpopular by her apparent determination to sniff out evidence of high-altitude Lesbian orgies.

Shirl and Darleen continued to function as Instructors in the Amazon Guard. They reported that there was something cooking in the barracks but what they did not know. Despite their popularity with their fellow officers they were still outsiders, not fully accepted.

Colonel Xenophon, whom Grimes met occasionally during the police chief's visits to the Palace to confer with the Lady Ellena, said that promising leads were being followed and that before long the Archon would be released, unharmed, from captivity. He would not say what the leads were. He scorned Grimes's suggestion that some ultrafeminist organization might be responsible for the kidnapping. "I keep on telling you, Commodore," he snapped, "that the gang responsible for the crime was composed of men disguised as women. Furthermore, there is absolutely no record of a dirigible having flown over the city at the time of the kidnap."

Meanwhile, there seemed to be a spate of vanishings, most of those who disappeared having been prominent members of the New Hellas Association. Some bodies were recovered, corpses dumped in back alleys, bearing signs of extreme maltreatment before death. *The New Hellas Courier*, in its editorials, became increasingly critical of both the police force and the administration in general, ranting about the crime wave that had begun with the abduction of the Archon and would not abate until every public-spirited citizen had been disposed of. What, the leader writer demanded, was the Lady Ellena doing about it? But was it coincidence, he continued, that most of those who had vanished or been murdered were opponents of the Lady's feminization programs?

Shortly thereafter the newspaper editor's name was added to the list of missing persons.

Meanwhile Ellena governed. Her style was altogether different from that of her husband. Brasidus in his Council had been the first among equals, respected but by no means autocratic. Ellena just gave orders, and if these were not promptly carried out there would be demotions and dismissals. She was not at all displeased, Grimes gathered, by the nickname that had been bestowed upon her. She was not the first Iron Lady in history but certainly was one of the most deserving of that sobriquet.

She did not seem to mind that Grimes and Maggie continued their residence in the Palace, although they were her husband's guests and not hers. She did not object when Fenella continued her visits. She even condescended to mingle socially with the offworlders on occasion, inviting—or commanding—them to official dinner parties. At these the fare was Spartan and the conversation stilted.

And then there was the affair of the bugging.

Just prior to this, Grimes had found indications that his personal possessions, including his papers, had been disturbed during his absences from his suite. He told Maggie, who, after investigation, reported that there were signs that her own things had been interfered with. After this, before every meeting with Fenella, Shirl and Darleen in Grimes's quarters, she would make a sweep with her bug detector, that multifunctional wrist companion which she had been given back on Earth. But the thing, when switched on, did not emit so much as a single *beep*.

This particular morning there was the usual meeting of the five of them with the pretext of coffee and/or other drinks. Before the arrival of the other three, but after the serving wench had brought in the tray, Maggie used the detector, paying special attention to the coffee things. She said, "All clear."

"You like playing with that thing, don't you?" said Grimes.

"I do, rather."

Then Fenella came in, accompanied by Shirl and Darleen.

The two New Alicians were silent while Grimes, Maggie and Fenella compared notes, aired theories, discussed the implications of all that they had learned.

"There's something cooking," said the journalist at last. "I can feel it in my water. Some sort of balloon is about to go up. There is something rotten in the State of Denmark . . . ."

"But this is New Sparta," objected Darleen, "not Denmark. Wherever Denmark is."

"A figure of speech," said Fenella. "And now, let's hear from you two."

"What can we tell you?" asked Shirl. "We are still trying to teach those thick-witted Amazons how to throw a boomerang. And there are the foot-boxing lessons. They are rather better at that."

"What about the private lessons you are giving to that butch blonde, Major whatever-her-name-is?" Fenella's nostrils were quivering, a sure sign that she was on the scent of some interesting dirt. "Has she been giving *you* any lessons?"

"What could she give us lessons in?" asked Darleen innocently. "But she wants to be our friend; she has told us as much. And when we are alone with her we are to call her by her name, Hera, and not address her by her rank."

"All girls together," sneered Fenella. "And haven't you learned yet that the word 'friend' has, over the past few years, acquired a new meaning?"

"We do not understand," said both girls as one.

"But haven't your relations with the major," persisted Fenella, "been rather warmer than one would expect between a relatively senior officer and two very junior ones?"

"We would not know," said Shirl. "This is the first time that we have been part of an army."

"Perhaps Hera has been generous," said Darleen doubtfully. "She gives us presents. Like this . . . ."

She raised her right arm. Around the wrist was a broad bracelet of gold mesh, set with sparkling, semi-precious stones.

"It is very pretty . . ." said Maggie.

"She'll be wanting something for that . . ." said Fenella.

"Use your detector, Maggie!" snapped Grimes.

"But . . ."

"Do as I say!"

Maggie pressed the right buttons on her wrist companion. The *beeps* that it emitted seemed deafeningly loud.

"How . . . How did you guess?" asked Fenella.

"My mind isn't as suspicious in the same way as yours," Grimes told her, "but it has its moments. And isn't there an old saying, 'beware the Greeks when they come bearing gifts'?"

He was rather annoyed when he had to explain the allusion to Shirl and Darleen. And Darleen was even more annoyed when Maggie made her take off the bracelet and then hammered it with the heel of her sandal until her bug detector made it plain that it had ceased to function.

And Grimes realized that they all had behaved foolishly, even to the officer who had fitted Maggie out for her role as intelligence agent. That bug detector should have given a visual warning, not a series of loud beeps. And, beeps or no beeps, the counterintelligence listeners-in should never have been told that their bug had been detected; instead they should have been fed false information.

But it was no use crying over spilt milk.

⚮ Chapter 19 ⚮

THE NEXT DAY they made a break in what had become their routine.

Instead of the morning meeting in Grimes's suite they did their talking during a stroll through the city streets. This was no hardship; the day was fine, pleasantly warm. But there were problems. A group of five people find it hard to hold a conversation while walking, especially if what is being discussed is of a confidential nature. Raised voices attract attention. So it was that Shirl and Darleen, who did not have much to contribute in any case, brought up the rear while Grimes walked between Maggie and Fenella.

There seemed to be an air of expectancy in the streets. Grimes remarked on this.

"It's the Marathon, of course," said Fenella. "Even though Brasidus is not here to fire the starting pistol, the show must go on."

"It can go on without me," laughed Grimes.

"Some gentle jogging would do you good," Maggie told him.

"There are better ways of taking exercise," he said.

He turned into a shop doorway, where he would be sheltered from the light breeze, to fill and to light his pipe. An annoying eddy blew out the old-fashioned match that he was using. He bent his head to shield the flame of the second match. Something whistled past his ear. He stared at the tiny, glittering thing that had embedded itself in the wooden door frame with a barely audible *thunk*. He recognized it for what it was. He had fired similar missiles himself while taking part in a *panjaril* hunt on Clothis, a combination of sport and commercial enterprise, the beasts being not killed but merely rendered unconscious, then to be shorn of their silky fur and left to recover to wander off and grow a new coat. It was an anesthetic dart that had just missed him.

He forgot the business of pipe lighting, stared at the passing pedestrians, alert for the sight of a gleaming weapon, an aiming hand.

"What's wrong?" asked Maggie.

He indicated the dart, said, "Somebody's out to get us."

"But who?" demanded Fenella.

"You tell me."

"It must be somebody," said Maggie, making a sweeping gesture with her hand at the passersby.

She was as lucky as Grimes had been. The dart that should have struck the exposed skin of her wrist embedded itself harmlessly in the baggy sleeve of her shirt, just above the elbow. Grimes pulled the thing out before it could do any damage, dropped it into a convenient grating in the gutter.

"Let's get out of here!" he snapped. "Back to the Palace!"

"There's never a policeman around when you need one," complained Fenella. Then, "But whose side are they on, anyhow?"

The general flow of foot traffic was now in the direction that they wanted to go. There were very few vehicles. They mingled with the crowd which, although it afforded some protection, hampered their progress. A fat man, past whom Grimes shoved none too gently, uttered a little squeal and collapsed. Grimes saw the tiny dart protruding from his bulging neck. Other people in the immediate vicinity of the fugitives were falling. The members of the hit squad were showing more determination than accurate marksmanship but, sooner or later, they must hit at least one of their designated targets. And how many of the ambulance attendants, out in force as always during a major sporting event, were the genuine article? Would Grimes or his companions be taken to a first-aid station or hospital or to some interrogation center?

Their scattering throughout the crowd was not altogether intentional but it made the pursuers' task more difficult. Had they stayed in a tightly knit group it would have been easy to identify them, to pick them off one by one. As it was, the only two easily indentifiable were Shirl and Darleen, and they were not the prime objectives.

They pushed and jostled their way along the narrow, winding street. They came to the intersection with the main road—not much wider, little more direct—to the Palace. There the crowds were heavy, lining each side of the thoroughfare. There were shouts and cheers. *For us?* wondered Grimes dazedly. He was aware that Maggie had found her way to his side and that Fenella was elbowing her way toward them both through the crush. And there were Shirl and Darleen. Darleen plucked a dart from one of the leather cross-straps of her uniform, dropped it to the ground. The unfortunate, barefooted woman who trod on it also dropped.

And they were pounding down the hill from the Palace, thousands of them, citizens and tourists, men and women, running, as was the ancient Greek custom, naked. It would be impossible to make any headway, toward refuge, against that mob. The first runners were abreast of them now—a slim young woman, her long legs pumping vigorously, her breasts jouncing; a wiry, middle-aged man; a fat lady, her entire body a-quiver who, on the downgrade, gravity-assisted, was putting on a fair turn of speed. It was probably against the rules but it was happening nonetheless; onlookers were casting aside their clothing and joining the runners.

One did so from near to where Grimes and Maggie were standing. He thought that he recognized the back view of her, that mole, with which he had become familiar, on her left shoulder . . . . But . . . Fenella?

"Quick!" snapped Maggie. "Get your gear off. Join the mob!"

Yes, it made sense. Clothed, among the naked runners, they would be obvious targets. Naked they would be no more than unidentifiable trees in a vast forest. But . . .

"My pipe . . ." he muttered. "My money . . . My credit cards . . ."

"Carry your notecase in your hand if you have to. As for your

stinking pipe, you know what you can do with it. You've more than
one, haven't you? Hurry up!"

He threw off his shirt, unbuckled the waistband of his kilt,
remembering just in time to remove his notecase from the sporran.
In the crush he had trouble with his underwear, his shoes and his
long socks. Then he was stripped, as Maggie was, and the pair of
them were out onto the road, merging with the mainstream of
runners. Shirl and Darleen were just ahead of them; even with
their peculiar hopping gait their nudity made them almost undis-
tinguishable from the crowd.

Grimes ran. He knew that if he dropped back among the
stragglers he would once again become a target. Not many men on
New Sparta had outstanding ears. The same would apply if he
achieved a place among the leaders—but there was little chance of
that. He ran, trying to adjust the rhythm of his open-mouthed
breathing to that of his laboring legs. He kept his eyes fixed on the
bobbing buttocks of the lady ahead of him; there could have been
worse things to watch. The soles of his feet were beginning to hurt;
except on sand or grass he was used to going shod.

He ran, clutching his wallet in his right hand, using his left, now
and again, to sweep away the sweat that was running down his
forehead into his eyebrows, then into his smarting eyes.

He snatched a glance to his left. Maggie was still with him,
making better weather of it than he was although her body was
gleaming with perspiration and her auburn hair had become
unbound. She flashed a smile at him, a smile that turned into a
grimace as she trod on something hard. She was developing the
beginnings of a limp.

But they were keeping up well, the pair of them, although the
crowd around them was thinning. Fenella was still in front; Grimes
caught a glimpse of a slim figure with a distinctive mole on the left
shoulder when, momentarily, he looked up and away from the
shapely bottom that he had been using as a steering mark. Shirl and
Darleen were nowhere to be seen.

Somebody was coming up on him from astern. He could hear the
heavy breathing, audible even above the noise of his own. He

wondered vaguely who it was. Then he heard the sound of a brief scuffle and the thud of someone falling heavily and, almost immediately, the shrill whistle of one of the Marathon marshals summoning a first-aid party.

From his right Shirl (or was it Darleen) said, "We got her."

Grimes turned his head. The New Alician was bounding along easily, showing no effects of physical exertion.

"Got . . . who?" he gasped.

"We did not find out her name. A tall, skinny girl with red hair. She had one of those little needles in her hand. She was going to stick it in you. We stuck it in her."

"Uh . . . thanks . . ."

"We are watching for others."

She dropped behind again.

Grimes ran. His feet hurt. His legs were aching. His breath rasped in and out painfully. Maggie ran. Obviously the pace was telling on her too. Fenella ran, falling back slowly from her leading position. The woman ahead of Grimes gave up, veering off to the side of the road. In his bemused condition Grimes began to follow her but either Shirl or Darleen (he was in no condition to try to work out which was which) came up on his right and nudged him back on the right course.

Other people were dropping out. That final, uphill run was a killer. Grimes would have dropped out but, as long as Maggie and Fenella kept going he was determined to do the same. His vision was blurred. The pounding of his heart was loud in his ears. He was aware of a most horrendous thirst. Surely, he thought, there would be cold drinks at the finishing line.

He raised his head, saw dimly a vision of white pillars, of gaily colored, fluttering bunting. He forced himself to keep going although he had slowed to little better than a tired walk. "We're almost there . . ." he heard Maggie whisper and, "So bloody what?" he heard Fenella snarl.

There was a broad white line painted across the road surface.

Grimes crossed it, then sat down with what he hoped was dignified deliberation. Beside him Maggie did likewise, making a better job of it than Grimes. Fenella unashamedly flopped. Shirl and Darleen stood beside them.

An attendant brought mugs of some cold, refreshing, faintly tart drink. Grimes forced himself to sip rather than to gulp.

The Lady Ellena said, "So you ran after all, Commodore . . ."

Grimes looked up at the tall, white-robed woman with the wreath of golden laurel leaves in her hair.

"Unfortunately," she went on, "I shall not be able to award you a medallion for finishing the course. You were not an official entrant and, furthermore, did not begin at the starting point. That applies to all of you."

"Still," said Grimes, "we finished."

"Yes. You did that." She turned to Shirl and Darleen. "What happened to your uniforms, Lieutenants? You realize, of course, that the cost of replacement will be deducted from your pay."

She strode away among a respectful throng of officials.

More officials conducted Grimes and the others to a tent where they were given robes and sandals, and more to drink, and told that transport would be provided for them, at a charge, to take them where they wished to go.

It was just as well, thought Grimes, that he had clung to his money and his credit cards all through the race. The Lady Ellena did not seem to be in a very obliging mood.

~ Chapter 20 ~

GRIMES AND HIS COMPANIONS missed the beginning of the riot.

They had intended to return to the Acropolis after much needed showers and a resumption of clothing to witness the handing out of the awards to the Marathon winner and to those who had placed second and third, but there was too much to be discussed and, too, none of them, with the exception of Shirl and Darleen, felt like making the effort.

Their hired hovercar stopped briefly at the Hippolyte, where Fenella picked up from her room a bag with clothing and toilet articles, then continued to the Palace. Shirl and Darleen went to their quarters to clean up and to put on fresh uniforms, Fenella was given the freedom of Maggie's bathroom, Grimes and Maggie shared a shower in his. Finally all of them gathered in Grimes's sitting room.

They sprawled in their chairs, sipping their long, cold drinks. Grimes was making a slow recovery. The muscles of his legs were still aching but the pain was diminishing. His feet still hurt, but not as much as they had. His pipe, an almost new one, would soon be broken in, although it was not yet as good as the one that he had abandoned with his clothing prior to taking part in the race.

"Who were they?" asked Maggie. "Why were they gunning for us?"

"The same bitches who kidnapped your cobber, the Archon," said Fenella. "And it was Grimes who put them wise to the fact that we were on their trail when he said that he recognized that wench in Aerospace Control."

"I've lured them out into the open," said Grimes.

"So you say," sneered Fenella. "The way things are, they'll soon be driving us into hiding or, even, offplanet. It's just as well, Maggie, that you have that courier of yours, *Krait*, standing by."

"I still think," said Grimes stubbornly, "that they'll overreach themselves and do something stupid."

"I'm beginning to think," said Fenella, "that that's your monopoly."

"We might as well see what we're missing," said Maggie.

She got up from her chair with something of an effort, switched on the big playmaster, set the controls for TriVi reception. The screen came alive with a picture of the floodlit Acropolis and from the speakers issued the sound of rattling, throbbing drums and squealing pipes. The camera zoomed in to the wide platform upon which Ellena, white-robed, gold-crowned, sat in state, with behind her rank upon rank of her Amazon Guards in their gleaming accoutrements.

"They said that we could not be there," complained Shirl.

"They say that our bodies are not . . . uniform," explained Darleen.

Yes, thought Grimes, looking into the screen, the Guards on display had been carefully selected for uniformity of appearance. They could have been clones.

The camera panned over the crowd. A broad path, lined on each side with police, had been cleared through it. Along it marched a band of women—Amazon Guards again—some with trumpets, some with pipes, some with drums. There were cheers and—surprisingly—catcalls. "Pussies go home! Pussies go home!" somebody was yelling. Other men took up the cry.

The voice of the commentator overrode the other sounds.

"And now, citizens, here, marching behind the band, come the winners to receive their awards from the Lady Ellena. First, Lieutenant Phryne, of the Amazon Guards . . . ." Phryne was not in uniform but in a simple white chiton, with one shoulder bare, with her long, muscular legs exposed to mid-thigh, her golden hair unbound. "And behind her, citizens, is First Officer Cassandra, of Trans-Sparta Airlines, a real flyer . . . ." Cassandra, a brunette, was dressed as was Phryne. "And in third place, Sergeant Hebe, of the Amazon Guards . . . ."

More cheers—and more boos.

"The race was fixed!" somebody shouted, not far from one of the microphones. A struggle was developing, with men trying to break through the police cordon. The band marched on and played on, missing neither a step nor a note. The three Marathon winners marched on, heads held high and disdainfully. Behind them came more Amazons—and the spears that they carried looked as though they were for use as well as for ornament.

Reaching the platform the band split into two sections, one to either side of the steps leading up to it. Ellena rose to her feet. There were cheers and boos, and men shouting. "We want Brasidus! We want Brasidus!" and, "Send the bitch back to where she came from!"

An Amazon officer handed Ellena a golden laurel wreath, its leaves not as broad as the one that she was wearing but broad enough. Phryne bowed, then fell to one knee. Ellena placed the wreath on her head. Phryne got gracefully to her feet and was embraced by the Archoness.

The camera lingered only briefly on this touching scene then swept over the crowd. Scuffles were breaking out all over. A group of four women had a man down on the ground and were kicking him viciously. Elsewhere there was the wan flicker of energy weapons where police were using their stunguns. A woman, her clothing torn from her, was struggling with half a dozen men whose intention was all too obvious. At the foot of the platform the bandswomen had dropped their instruments and had drawn pistols from their belts—not the relatively humane stunguns but projectile weapons—and the escorting guard were already using their spears to fight off attackers, employing the butts rather than the points, but how long would it be before they reversed them?

"Hell!" swore Fenella, "I should have been there, not watching it on TriVi . . . ."

"Be thankful that you're not," Grimes told her. "Women seem to be in the minority in that mob. Speaking for myself, a sex riot is something I'd rather not be involved in . . . ."

Ellena was standing there on the platform, her arms upraised, shouting something. What it was could not be heard. There were the shouts and the screams and, at last, the rattle of automatic fire. Somebody was using projectile weapons. The bandswomen, machine pistols jerking in their hands, were joining their spear-wielding sisters in the defense of the front of the platform. And the spears had been reversed and the blades of them were glistening red in the harsh glare of the floodlights. And whose side were the police on now? Twenty of them, in their black leather uniforms, were charging the Amazons. The weapons in their hands were only stunguns but, to judge from the visible discharge, more of a flare than a flicker, and from the harsh crackle that was audible even in the general uproar, their setting was lethal rather than incapacitating.

The arrival of the first inertial drive transports was almost unnoticed, the clatter of its propulsion unit just part of the general cacophony. It dropped into camera view and continued to drop, until it was over the platform, just clear of the heads of those standing there. Pigsnouted in respirators, Amazons dropped from its belly, bringing with them more respirators for their sisters already engaged in the fighting. A high-ranking officer, to judge by the amount of brass on her leather, conferred with Ellena, obviously persuading her to mount the short ladder that had now been lowered from the aircraft. The Archoness, followed by the Amazon colonel, embarked.

The TriVi commentator was valiantly trying to make himself heard. "Citizens! I beseech you all to stay away from the Acropolis! This is not just a riot; this is a revolution! People have been killed! They . . . ." His voice faded, recovered. "They are using gas . . . ."

They were using gas. It was what Grimes himself would have done in the circumstances, what he had done, on more than one occasion, during his Survey Service career. From the low-flying aircraft a dense mist, opalescent in the flood lighting, was drifting downward and battling men and women were dropping to the ground unconscious, police and civilians, all except the Amazon Guards in their protective masks. People on the outskirts of the mob, not yet affected, were beginning to run, away from the Acropolis, while others were binding strips torn from their clothing about their faces, delaying the effect of the anesthetic vapor by only seconds.

Hand weapons were being fired at the transport but ineffectually, and the marksmen got off only a few rounds before falling to the ground unconscious. There was even one man who was tearing up cobblestones and hurling them skyward. Darleen remarked scornfully, "He could not hit the side of a barn even if he was inside it."

But he, whoever he was, was at least trying, thought Grimes. He was fighting back.

Another voice came from the speakers, a female one, distorted and muffled as though by breathing apparatus.

"Citizens! You have seen what has been happening at the Acropolis. Certain elements have tried to attack the person of our beloved leader, the Lady Ellena. The assassination attempt has been foiled. The instigators will be brought to justice. And now, all of you who have been watching this on the screens in your homes . . . . Stay in your homes. Do not take to the streets. Security patrols are abroad, with orders to take strict measures to maintain the peace . . ."

"In other words," muttered Grimes, "shoot first and ask questions afterwards."

The last picture on the screen, before the transmitter was shut down, was a dismal one. It had started to rain. Moving among the sprawled, unconscious bodies were gasmasked Amazons. They seemed to know whom they were looking for, were picking up selected prisoners and throwing them roughly into the rear of a large hovercar. Those who were left on the ground were the lucky ones. They would awake in a few hours time cold and wet and miserable—but they would not be awakening in jail.

"And what was all that about?" asked Fenella at last.

"That," said Maggie, "is for us to find out."

Then there was a great hammering on the door.

"Open up!" yelled a female voice. "In the name of the Lady Ellena, open up!"

Chapter 21

FIRST INTO THE SITTING ROOM were two Amazon privates, stunguns in hand. They were followed by a major, and behind her was Ellena herself, still in her white robes, still with the golden laurel wreath crown.

"What are you two doing here?" snapped the officer.

"But, Hera . . ." began Shirl.

"The correct form of address, Lieutenant, is 'Madam.' Please remember that."

"This is our free time, Madam," said Darleen rebelliously.

"Free time, Lieutenant, is a privilege and not a right. And don't you know that during this emergency all leave has been suspended? Get back to your quarters. At once."

"Better do as the lady says," advised Fenella.

"Quiet, you!" snarled Hera.

Fenella subsided. Grimes didn't blame her. He would not have liked to try conclusions with that female weightlifter, her muscles bulging through the leather straps of her uniform. Shirl and Darleen got to their feet, cast apologetic glances at Grimes. He managed a small smile in return. They slouched out of his sitting room in a most unofficerlike manner.

"And what are *you* doing here?" demanded Ellena, addressing the journalist.

"Enjoying a quiet drink with my friends, Lady," she replied defiantly.

"Cooking up some scurrilous stories for the scandal sheets that employ you as their muckraker, you mean," said Ellena. "However, since you are here you may stay. In fact, you will stay. For your own protection. I cannot guarantee the safety of any offworlders at large in the city at this time."

"You mean," said Fenella, "that you want to be able to keep an eye on me."

"Somebody has to," Ellena told her. She turned to Maggie. "You, Commander Lazenby, are the senior Federation Survey Service officer at present on this planet. My understanding is that I, as ruler of a federated world, have the right to demand the support of the Federation's armed forces during times of emergency."

Maggie looked questioningly at Grimes, who nodded.

Ellena sneered. "Of course the Commodore, the ex-planetary Governor, is an expert on such matters, especially since the Federation's armed forces on Liberia were doing their damnedest to depose him. But what do you say, Commodore Grimes?"

"You are right in your understanding, Lady," admitted Grimes.

"Thank you, thank you. And now, Commander Lazenby, am I to understand that Lieutenant Gupta, captain of the courier *Krait*, is technically under your orders?"

"Yes."

"And how is this *Krait* armed?"

Once again Maggie looked questioningly at Grimes.

He said, "I was once in command of such a ship myself, Lady. A Serpent Class Courier is no battle cruiser. There will be a forty-millimeter machine cannon, a laser cannon, a missile launcher and a *very* limited supply of ammunition. In a small vessel the magazines are also small, so the laser cannon will be the only weapon capable of sustained firing."

"And are there—what do you call them?—pinnaces?"

"Nothing so big. Just a couple of general purpose spaceboats. Inertial drive, of course. Each can mount a light machine gun if required."

"Still," she said, "a useful adjunct to my own defense forces."

"What about your Navy?" he asked.

She said, "I shall be frank, Commodore Grimes. You know what this world was like when it was an all-male planet. Many senior officers, in the Army and the Navy, pine for those so-called Good Old Days and too many junior ones believe the rubbish that their seniors tell them. They resent having to take orders from a woman. I cannot trust them."

"When we get Brasidus back," said Fenella spitefully, "he'll bring them back into line."

"Until such time," Ellena said coldly, "I must rule as best I can."

She did not, thought Grimes, seem to be overly worried about the safety of her husband. She was not, even, overly worried about her own safety. There was an arrogance, but not a stupid arrogance. She would take whatever tools came to hand to build up her own position. She had already forged such a tool, her Corps of Amazon Guards. And the Amazons had been brought into being well before the abduction of the Archon.

The telephone buzzed.

Grimes got up from his chair to answer the call. His way was blocked by Major Hera. It was Ellena who took her seat at the desk on which the instrument was mounted.

"Archoness here," she stated.

"Lady, this is Captain Lalia, duty commander of the Palace Guard. There is a mob approaching, with armored hovercars in the lead. If you will switch on your playmaster to Palace Cover you will have pictures."

"Thank you, Lalia. Commodore Grimes, will you get us coverage as Lalia suggests? Major Hera, if the Colonel is not back yet from the city will you take charge of the defense? I shall remain here for the time being."

Hera hurried out, leaving the two Amazon privates to guard Ellena. Grimes fiddled with the controls of the playmaster. The picture, being taken by the infrared cameras on the palace roof, was clear enough. It was more of an army than a mere mob that was pouring up the road. There were the armored hovercars in the lead, with their heavy automatic weapons and their uniformed crews and the pennants streaming from their whip aerials. There were motorcycles, and their riders were police, in their stainless steel and black leather uniforms. There were marching civilians, more than a few of whom were carrying firearms.

Directional microphones were picking up the shouts.

"Scrag the bitches! Scrag the bitches! Ellena out! Ellena out!"

"Somebody out there," remarked Fenella, "doesn't like you."

Surprisingly Ellena laughed. She said, "They will like me even less in a minute or so. My Amazons will be more than a match for this rabble."

"There're Army personnel there," said Grimes. "And Police."

"I do not need to be instructed, Commodore, regarding the uniforms worn by my own armed forces."

"They aren't behaving as though they belong to you," said Fenella.

"Guards," snapped Ellena, "if that woman opens her mouth again, gag her!"

The mob—or the army—was closer now. Was that Colonel Heraclion in one of the leading armored cars? Yes, Grimes decided, it was, making his identification just before the colonel pulled on a respirator. Gas had been used to quell the riot at the Acropolis; if it were used here it would not be so effective. Police and Army personnel, at least, would have their protection.

The camera shifted its viewpoint, covering, from above, the main entrance to the Palace. Something was rolling out, a huge, broad-rimmed wheel, almost a short-axised cylinder. Gathering speed, it trundled down the road toward the attackers. It was followed by another, and another. Laser fire flickered from the hovercars and there were muzzle flashes and streams of tracer from the heavy machine guns. There were the beginnings of panic, with vehicles attempting to pull off the road, their way blocked by the heavy, ornamental shrubbery. But these were only relatively light armored cars, not heavy tanks.

The first of the wheels—it must have been radio-controlled—exploded. The second one leaped the crater before being detonated. The third one did not have much effect—but this was because the majority of the marchers had been able to run clear to each side, off the road.

"A very old weapon," said Ellena smugly, "but improved upon."

Grimes stared at the picture in the screen, at the shattered vehicles, some of which were still smoldering, and at the contorted, dismembered bodies, some very few of which were still feebly twisting and jerking.

He said bitterly, "I hope you're satisfied."

She said, "They're only men. Besides, they asked for it and they got it."

"Didn't you rather overreact?" asked Grimes.

"Come, come, Commodore. Speaking for myself, I would rather overreact to a threat than be torn limb from limb." She got up to leave. "I do not care what sleeping arrangements you make but all three of you are confined to the Palace, to the two suites allocated to Commander Lazenby and Commodore Grimes.

"A very good night to you all."

She swept out, followed by the two Amazon privates.

"The manipulating bitch!" exclaimed Fenella, not without admiration. "You know, I almost hope that she pulls it off."

"If she does," said Grimes, "this is one world that I shall do my best to avoid in the foreseeable future."

~ Chapter 22 ~

SO THEY WERE, to all intents and purposes, prisoners in the Palace.

It was decided that Fenella would take up residence in what had been Maggie's suite and that Maggie would move in with Grimes. Everybody must already know that she had been sleeping with him; now it would be made official. Maggie said that she would call Lieutenant Gupta to let him know that his services might be required but was unable to get through to the spaceport. She tried direct punching first but without results. Then she got through to the Palace switchboard. A young lady in Amazon uniform politely but coldly informed her that during the state of emergency no outward calls were allowed.

After this the three of them watched the playmaster to try to catch up with the news. There was a speech by Ellena, which she delivered from before a backdrop on which were idealized portraits of such famous persons as Prime Ministers Indira Gandhi, Golda Mier and Margaret Thatcher. There was also one of a lady attired as an ancient Greek warrior, presumably the mythical Queen Hippolyte. This one looked remarkably like Ellena herself.

("I suppose that the artist knew on which side her bread is buttered," sneered Fenella.)

Ellena's speech was an impassioned one. She appealed to all citizens to support her in the defense of law and order. She left no

357

doubt in the minds of her audience as to who was the chief upholder of law and order on New Sparta. At the finish, almost as an afterthought, she did mention her missing husband and assured everybody that until his return the business of government was in good hands.

After she finished talking there was a brief coverage of the attack on the Palace and an assurance that the ringleaders of what was referred to as a riot were under arrest. There was no mention of casualties.

Sufficient unto the day, thought Grimes, was the evil thereof. No doubt the morrow would bring its own evils. He decided to go outside, onto the balcony, to smoke a quiet pipe before retiring.

The night seemed to be quiet enough. There were no sounds of gunfire, near or distant. There was no wailing of sirens. Somebody, somewhere not too far away, was plucking at a stringed instrument, accompanying a woman who was softly, not untunefully singing. Grimes did not recognize the song. Of one thing he was sure; it was a very old one. He looked up at the sky, at the stars, at the constellations. These had been named by the first colonists, all of them after gods and heroes of Greek mythology. Poseidon and Cyclops, Jason and Ulysses, Ares and Hercules . . . There were no female names. Would Ellena, Grimes wondered, order her tame astronomers to rectify this? Would the spectacular grouping now called Ares be renamed Hippolyte?

He was still staring upward when something whirred past his right ear, striking the window frame behind him with a clatter. At once he dropped on to all fours, seeking the protection, such as it was, of the ornamental rail enclosing the balcony. But there were no further missiles.

He heard Maggie ask sharply, "What was that?" and Fenella demand, "What are you *doing*, Grimes? Praying? Are you sure that Mecca's that way?"

"Down, you silly bitches!" he snarled. "Don't make targets of yourselves!"

"Targets?" echoed Maggie.

He crawled around to face them.

"Get inside!" he ordered. "Away from the window! Somebody's throwing things at us . . ."

"Only a boomerang," said Maggie. "A *little* boomerang. It couldn't hurt a fly . . ." She had picked up the small crescent of cunningly carved wood and was examining it. "There's writing on it . . ."

Grimes got to his feet, took the thing from Maggie. On the flat side of it, in childishly formed capitals, was a brief message. BRASIDUS HELD PRISONER AT MELITUS. There was no signature. In lieu there was the figure of a familiar animal.

"What the hell is that supposed to be?" asked Maggie. "A dinosaur?"

"A kangaroo, of course," said Grimes. "And this primitive airmail letter is from Shirl or Darleen, or both of them. They've been keeping their ears flapping."

They all went back inside. Grimes got out the large atlas. He found Melitus without any trouble. Both a small mountain and a village on its western slopes had that name. It was wild country, with no towns or cities, no roads or railways, only the occasional village, only goat tracks running from nowhere much to nowhere at all. It would be accessible enough to the dirigibles of Trans-Sparta Airlines, or to those of the Spartan Navy, or to any form of heavier-than-air transport.

"But," said Grimes, "we don't have wings."

"Lieutenant Gupta and his *Krait* are under my orders," said Maggie. "Under *your* orders actually, although he's not supposed to know that."

"And just how," asked Grimes, "are we going to give Gupta any orders?"

"You'll think of a way," said Maggie. "You always do."

"And meanwhile," grumbled Fenella, "dear Ellena will tighten her grip on this planet. Oh, I don't particularly mind. All in all, women make no more of a balls of running things than men do. As long as I get my exclusive story . . . ."

"Is that all you ever think of?" flared Maggie. "A story? Brasidus is our friend. Too, until and unless the Federation decides otherwise, he is the recognized ruler of this world."

"All right. All right. But don't forget that I'm playing along with you two only because I scent a story."

They turned in then.

Grimes and Maggie did not go to sleep at once. Neither did they talk much. They decided that any long-range planning was out of the question and that, meanwhile, they would make the best of what time they had together.

The next morning breakfast, such as it was, was served to them in Grimes's sitting room. Muddy coffee and little, sweet rolls were not, he thought and said, a solid foundation upon which to build the day. Fenella and Maggie were inclined to agree with him. Before they had quite finished the meal Lieutenant Phryne came in, saying that she had orders to escort them to the Lady Ellena's presence. She refused to tell them what they were wanted for.

Ellena received them in her command headquarters. She was wearing the uniform of a high-ranking Amazon officer. In an odd sort of way it suited her even though her body was not shown to advantage by a costume that was, essentially, an affair of leather straps, brass buckles and a short kilt. She was seated behind a desk the surface of which was dominated by her highly polished, plumed, bronze helmet. There was barely room for the papers—reports, possibly—which she had been studying. On the walls were illuminated maps—of the city, of the surrounding countryside, of the entire planet. There was communications equipment elaborate enough to handle the needs of a small army. (It was handling the needs of such an army.) Female officers were doing things at the consoles before which they were sitting, speaking, low-voiced, into microphones.

"The prisoners, Ma'am," announced Phryne smartly.

"Not prisoners, Lieutenant," Ellena corrected her. "The guests. My husband's guests." She looked up from her papers. "Good morning, Commodore, Commander, Miz Pruin. Please be seated." Phryne brought them hard chairs. "You will recall that yesterday we discussed the possibility of putting the Survey Service's courier *Krait* at the disposal of the civil power on this planet . . . ."

The civil *power?* wondered Grimes, looking around at the uniformed, armed women, at a screen on one of the walls which had come to life showing a small squadron of Amazon chariots proceeding along a city street, spraying the buildings on either side with heavy machine-gun fire.

"I am not so sure, Lady," said Maggie, "that this would be advisable. It has occurred to me that *Krait* would be better employed in the protection of Federation interests—the shipping in the spaceport, for example . . ."

"I could, I suppose," said Ellena coldly, "invoke the Right of Angary . . . ."

A spacelawyer yet! thought Grimes. But had the Right of Angary ever been invoked to justify the seizure of a ship of war rather than that of a mere merchantman? An interesting legal point . . . Anyhow, he decided suddenly, *he* wanted *Krait*, with, but preferably without, her rightfully appointed captain. After all he, in his younger days, had commanded such a vessel.

He pulled out his pipe, began to fill it. It was an invaluable aid to thinking.

"Put that thing away, Commodore," ordered Ellena.

"As you wish, Lady." He turned to Maggie. "I think, Commander Lazenby, that the Lady Ellena is well within her rights. And, surely, it is in the interests of the Federation, of which New Sparta is a member, that every effort be made to put a stop to civil commotion which might well develop into a civil war."

"Commodore Grimes," said Ellena, "has far more experience in such matters than you do, Commander Lazenby. After all, he has been a planetary ruler himself."

"I bow," said Maggie, "to the superior knowledge of the Archon's wife and the ex-governor."

Fenella made a noise that could have been either a snort or a snigger.

Ellena glared at the two offworld women and favored Grimes with an almost sweet smile—but her eyes were cold and calculating.

"Then, Commodore," she said, "would you mind persuading Commander Lazenby to order *Krait*'s captain to lift ship at once and proceed forthwith to the Palace? I am no expert in these matters but I imagine that such a small spacecraft will be able to make a landing on the Amazons' drill ground."

"There's enough room there," said Grimes, "for a Constellation Class cruiser, provided she's handled with care. A Serpent Class courier could set down on the front lawn of the average suburban villa."

"You are the expert. Lieutenant Phryne, please see to it that an outside communications channel is made available to Commander Lazenby. Get through to the *Krait's* captain."

Phryne went to one of the consoles against the wall. She punched buttons. The screen came alive. The face of a Federation Survey Service ensign—the single stripe of gold braid on each of his shoulderboards denoted his rank—appeared.

"*Krait* here," he said.

"Lieutenant Phryne of the Amazon Guard here, speaking from the Palace for the Lady Ellena. Call your captain to the phone, please."

"But what business . . . ."

"The Lady Ellena's business. Hurry!"

The young man vanished. In the screen were depicted surroundings that had once been very familiar to Grimes, the interior of the cramped control room of a Serpent Class courier. Since his time, he thought, there had been very few changes in layout. That was all to the good.

Lieutenant Gupta's thin brown face appeared in the screen.

"Captain of *Krait* here," he said.

"Commander Lazenby here," said Maggie, who had taken Phryne's place facing the screen.

"Yes, Commander?" Then, "Can you tell me what is happening? I sent Lieutenant Hale, my PCO, ashore to mingle with the people to find out what he could, but he has not yet returned . . ."

"PCO?" whispered Ellena to Grimes.

"Psionic Communications Officer," he whispered in reply. "A trained telepath. Carried these days by Survey Service ships more for espionage than for communicating over lightyears . . . ."

And so the mindreader isn't aboard, he thought. *So much the better.*

"Lieutenant Gupta," asked Maggie, "are you ready for liftoff?"

"Of course, Commander."

"I have orders for you, Lieutenant. You are to proceed forthwith to the Palace, to place yourself at the disposal of the New Spartan government."

"I question your authority, Commander. May I remind you that you are an officer of the Scientific Branch, not of the Spaceman Branch?"

"And may I remind you, Lieutenant, that prior to our departure from Port Woomera, on Earth, you were told, in my presence and the presence of your officers, by no less a person than Rear Admiral Damien, that while on New Sparta you were to consider yourself under my orders?"

"That is so," admitted Gupta grudgingly. "Even so, I would remind you that this conversation is being recorded."

"So bloody what?" exploded Maggie. "Just get here, that's all, or I'll see to it that Admiral Damien has your guts for garters."

"But . . . ."

"Just get here, that's all."

"But where shall I land?" Gupta asked plaintively.

"Tell him," said Grimes, "that beacons will be set out in the middle of the Amazons' drill ground."

"Was that Commodore Grimes?" demanded Gupta.

"It was," said Grimes. "It is."

"May Vishnu preserve me!" muttered Gupta.

Chapter 23

AMAZINGLY and extremely fortunately Grimes was able to get some time alone with Maggie and Fenella. Somehow he had been put in charge of setting up makeshift spaceport facilities in the drill ground, with Amazons scurrying hither and yon at his bidding. Among these women soldiers were Shirl and Darleen. Grimes called them to him, on the pretense that they were to act as his liaison with the Amazon officer in charge.

"Did you get our note?" asked one of the New Alicians.

"Of course. It was the information I needed. Now, you two, stick close to us . . ." He broke off the conversation to give orders to an Amazon sergeant. "Yes. I want that inertial drive pinnace out of the way. The field must be completely cleared." And to a lieutenant, "Just leave it here, will you? Yes, I can operate it . . ." From the speaker of the portable transceiver came a voice, that of Lieutenant Gupta. "*Krait* to Palace, *Krait* to Palace. Do you read me? Over." Shirl handed Grimes the microphone on its long lead. "Palace to *Krait*," he said. "I read you loud and clear. Over."

"Lifting off," came the reply. "Are you ready for me? Over."

"Not quite. I shall call you as soon as the marker beacons are set out. Over and out."

He was free now to give hasty instructions to the four women. "Gupta is under *your* orders, Maggie. I want him and all his people out of the ship. You go aboard on some pretext—to the control

364

room. You know how to operate the airlock controls, don't you? Good. Then, as soon as we get the chance, the rest of us will board. Button up as soon as we've done so and get upstairs in a hurry. You can do that much, can't you? Then I'll take over as soon as I can."

"What if we're fired on while we're lifting?" she asked. "I'm no fighter pilot. I'm only a simple scientist with the minimal training in ship handling required for all Survey Service officers in the non-spaceman branches."

"*Krait's* a Federation ship. I don't think that Ellena would dare to try to blast her out of the sky. At least, I hope not. And I'll scamper up to control, to take over, as soon as I possibly can."

And then, leaving Maggie and Fenella standing by the transceiver, he, with Shirl and Darleen as his aides, took charge of the final preparations for the reception of the courier. Three powerful blinker lights had been found and adjusted to throw their beams upward and set out in a triangle almost at the exact center of the field. The lights were not the regulation scarlet but an intense blue. It did not matter. Gupta would be told what to expect.

Gupta had made good time, drifting over from the spaceport on lateral thrust. The arrhythmic cacophony of his inertial drive was beating down from the clear sky as he hung over the drill ground at an altitude of one kilometer. The light of the mid-morning sun was reflected dazzlingly from her sleek slimness.

"Clear the field!" Grimes bellowed through a borrowed bullhorn.

"Clear the field!" the cry was taken up by officers and NCOs.

Grimes, accompanied by Shirl and Darleen, returned to the transceiver. He took the microphone from Maggie, ordered Gupta to land at the position marked by the beacons. Gupta acknowledged, then came in slowly, very slowly. Anyone would think, thought Grimes, that *Krait* had been built from especially fragile eggshells.

But *Krait* came in, her inertial drive hammering, maintaining her in a condition of almost weightlessness. Luckily there was no wind; had there been she would have been blown all over the field like a toy balloon.

She came in, and she landed. Her drive was not shut off but was left running, muttering irritably to itself, in neutral. Obviously

Lieutenant Gupta wasn't at all happy about the situation. Grimes was. *Krait*, even under Maggie's unskilled management, would be able to make a quick get-away.

"*Krait* to Commander Lazenby," came from the transceiver speaker. "Your orders, please?"

Grimes passed the microphone to Maggie. "Report to the Lady Ellena in the command office, please."

There was another period of waiting.

At last *Krait's* airlock door opened and the ramp was extended. Down it marched Lieutenant Gupta. For some reason he had taken the time to change into his full dress finery—starched white linen, frock coat, gold braided sword belt and ceremonial sword in gold-braided scabbard, gold-trimmed fore-and-aft hat. He threw a grudging salute in Maggie's general direction. She, not in uniform, could not reply in kind but bowed slightly and stiffly.

"Where are your officers, Lieutenant?" asked Maggie.

"At their stations still, Commander."

"They are to accompany you to audience with the Lady Ellena. It is essential that her instructions be heard by everybody."

"If you so wish," said Gupta. He lifted his right wrist to his lips to speak into the communicator.

"Tell them," said Maggie, "not to bother to change out of working uniform. They can come just as they are."

"*All* the officers?" queried Gupta.

"Yes."

"But regulations require that there must be a shipkeeper."

She said, "I shall be your shipkeeper until you return. In any case, I wish to get some things from my cabin."

Scowling, Gupta barked orders into his communicator.

They came down the ramp in their slate gray shorts-and-shirt working uniform—a lieutenant jg, three ensigns, first lieutenant, navigator, electronicist and engineer officer. This latter, Grimes noted happily, had not shut down the drive before leaving the ship. He hoped that Gupta would not send him back to do so. But Gupta, unlike Grimes when he had been captain of such a vessel, was a slave to regulations. In these circumstances the drive must be left running until such time as the captain decided that it was safe to immobilize his command. And he was leaving *Krait* in the hands of an officer—Commander Lazenby—senior to himself.

Lieutenant Phryne marched up to them, followed by six Amazon privates. She saluted with drawn sword.

"Lieutenant," said Maggie, "please escort these gentlemen to the Lady Ellena."

"As you say, Commander."

As *Krait's* people marched off, Maggie mounted the ramp, passed through the airlock doors. How long would it take her to get up to control? Grimes had timed himself many years ago; it was one of the emergency drills. He doubted that she would break his record. He had done it in just under five minutes—but he had known the layout of the ship. Should he allow Maggie double that time? He snuck a glance at his wrist companion, surreptitiously adjusted and switched on the alarm. He looked around the drill ground. The well-disciplined Amazons had been ordered to clear the field; that order still stood. They were standing there around the perimeter, sunlight brilliantly reflected from metal accoutrements. Even so, Grimes thought, he and the others would have to be fast. Those women were dead shots and in the event of their being ordered to use no firearms, to take their prisoners alive, they could *run*.

His wrist companion suddenly *beeped*.

"Now!" barked Grimes.

Fenella sprinted up the ramp. Shirl and Darleen each made it to the airlock with a single leap. Grimes followed hard on their heels. He was dimly aware that the Amazons had broken ranks, were pouring inwards from all sides toward the little spaceship. But he had no time to watch them. The outer airlock door was shutting, was shut. The deck under his feet lurched. He and Fenella and Shirl and Darleen were thrown into a huddle. Structural members were either singing or rattling, or both. Maggie must have slammed the drive straight from neutral to maximum lift.

He disentangled himself from the women, began the laborious climb—it seemed as though he were having to fight at least two gravities—up the spiral staircase, from the airlock to control.

∼ Chapter 24 ∼

HE PULLED HIMSELF up through the hatch into the control compartment.

Maggie was hunched in the captain's chair, staring at the read-out screens before her, at the display of flickering numerals that told their story of ever and rapidly increasing altitude,

Grimes made his way to the first lieutenant's seat with its duplicate controls, flopped into it with a sigh of relief.

"All right, Maggie," he said. "I'll take over."

"You'd better," she told him. "I've been wondering what to do next."

"You've done very well so far," he said. "You got us out of there very nicely."

He reduced thrust to a reasonable level. *Krait* was still climbing but now people could move about inside her hull at something better than a crawl, not hampered by a doubling of their body weight. He then gave his attention to the screens giving him views in all directions. He was half-expecting that there would be pursuit of some kind but there was not.

"What now?" asked Maggie. "Do we go to Melitus to rescue Brasidus?"

"Not yet," said Grimes. "We carry on straight up. It may fool Ellena, it may not. I hope it does." He chuckled. "Let's try this scenario on for size. The notorious pirate, John Grimes, aided by his female accomplices, feloniously seized the Federation Survey Service's courier *Krait* . . . ."

"And why would he do that? And why should Commander Lazenby, of all people, help him? To say nothing of Fenella Pruin and Shirl and Darleen . . . ."

"We'll get Fenella to write the script. You and Shirl and Darleen are hopelessly in love with me, slaves of passion. And Fenella's just along for the ride, getting material for her next piece in *Star Scandals*."

She laughed. "You could do her job as well as she does. But this scenario of yours . . . . There was opportunity for you to carry out your piratical act. You seized it. But what was the motive? I am assuming that Ellena does not know that *we* know where Brasidus is being held."

"Mphm." Grimes filled and lit his pipe. "But, before we start kicking ideas around to see if they yelp, let's get the others up here." He spoke into a microphone. "This is the Captain speaking. All hands to report to the control room. On the double."

"Where *is* the control room?" came Fenella's yelp from the intercom speaker.

"Just follow the spiral staircase up as far as you can go."

"Isn't there an elevator?"

"This," said Grimes, "is a Serpent Class courier, not a Constellation Class cruiser."

"Even an Epsilon Class star tramp has an elevator in the axial shaft!" she snapped.

"Stop arguing!" he yelled. "Just get up here!"

She did, without overmuch delay, accompanied by Shirl and Darleen. There were chairs for only two of the newcomers but Darleen, squatting on the deck, did not appear to be too uncomfortable.

Grimes talked. "This is the way that I see things. I'm an outsider who just happens to have come to New Sparta at a time when all manner of balloons are going up. I came to New Sparta to wait there for the arrival of my ship, *Sister Sue*, which vessel is all my worldly wealth. I have heard rumors that the New Spartan government intends to seize her, for conversion to an auxiliary cruiser. (Well, Ellena could do that, if she had the brains to think of it. She wouldn't dare to seize a ship belonging to one of the major lines.) So, not for the first time in my career, I'm playing the game according to *my* rules."

"I'll say you are!" exclaimed Fenella. "You always keep telling us that you were never a pirate, but what you've just done bears all the earmarks of piracy."

"Never mind that. But there's one crime that I have committed—I've lifted from New Sparta without first obtaining Outward Clearance. Even so, as far as Aerospace Control is concerned *Krait* was put at the disposal of the New Spartan government. It doesn't much matter. All the legalities and illegalities can be sorted out later."

"Oh, we all of us know that the Law is an ass, Grimes," said Fenella impatiently. "Just what are your intentions, legal or otherwise?"

"To begin with, a spot of misdirection. As soon as we're clear of the atmosphere I'll switch to Mannschenn Drive, as though at the commencement of a Deep Space voyage. And then I'll attempt to raise *Sister Sue* on Carlotti Radio. Of necessity it will be a broad beam transmission; I don't know where she is, only the general direction from which she will be approaching. My signals will be monitored on New Sparta."

"And what will you tell *Sister Sue*?" asked Maggie.

"I'll try to arrange a rendezvous with her, about one lightyear—no, not 'about,' exactly—from New Sparta. I shall tell Williams that he is, on no account, to approach any closer and that I shall be boarding to take command."

"Won't your Mr. Williams—or Captain Williams as he still is—think that these orders are rather . . . weird?" asked Fenella.

"Probably. But he should be used to weird orders by this time."

Krait drove up through the last tenuous shreds of atmosphere, through the belts of charged particles. Aerospace Control began, at last, to take an interest in her.

"Aerospace Control to *Krait* . . . Aerospace Control to *Krait* . . . ."

"*Krait* to Aerospace Control," said Grimes into the microphone. "I read you loud and clear."

"Return at once to the spaceport, *Krait*."

"Negative," said Grimes.

After that he ignored the stream of orders and threats that poured from the NST transceiver speaker.

It was time then to actuate the Mannschenn Drive. The rotors in their intricate array began to spin, tumbling, precessing, warping the dimensions of normal Space-Time around themselves and the ship. Perspective was distorted, colors sagged down the spectrum and what few orders Grimes gave were as though uttered in an echo chamber. But, as sometimes was the case, there were no *déjà vu* phenomena, no flashes of precognition.

And then it was over.

Krait was falling through a blackness against which the stars were no longer points of light but vague, slowly writhing nebulosities.

"So that's that," said Maggie practically.

"That's that," agreed Grimes. "Now all I have to do is to get the bold Billy on the blower and tell him my pack of lies, for Ellena's benefit."

In its own little compartment, the Mobius Strip antenna of the Carlotti Deep Space Radio was revolving and its signals, on broad beam, were being picked up, instantaneously, by every receiver within their range, which was a very distant one—and being picked up, reciprocally, by Aerospace Control on New Sparta.

"Grimes to *Sister Sue*," said Grimes. "Grimes to *Sister Sue*. Do you read me?"

At last there came a reply in a male voice strange to Grimes, faint, as though coming from a very long way off—which it was.

"*Sister Sue* here. Pass your message."

"Who is that speaking?" asked Grimes.

"The third officer. Pass your message."

"Get Captain Williams for me, please."

"He's sleeping. I'm perfectly capable of taking your message."

"Get Captain Williams for me. Now."

"*Who* is that calling?"

"Grimes."

"Is that the name of a ship or some fancy acronym?"

"Grimes," repeated the owner of that name. "John Grimes. The owner. Your employer. Get Captain Williams to the Carlottiphone *at once.*"

"How do I know that you're Grimes?"

"You should know by this time, young man, that not any Tom, Dick or Harry can get access to a Carlotti transceiver. Get Captain Williams for me. And see if you can arrange a visual hook-up as well as audio. I've the power here to handle it."

"Oh, all right, all right. Sir."

Williams wasted no time coming to *Sister Sue's* control room. His cheerful, fleshy face appeared in the screen.

"Oh, it is you, Skipper. What's the rush? Couldn't it all have waited until I set her down on New Sparta?"

"It couldn't, Billy."

"But you were always getting on to me about the expense of needless Carlotti communications . . ."

"This one is not needless. To begin with, New Sparta's in a state of upheaval. The Archon was kidnapped and his wife, the Lady Ellena, took over the government. Now she seems to have a civil war on her hands. I don't want my ship sitting on her arse at Port Sparta with shooting going on all about her."

"She's been shot at before, Skipper."

"There's nothing more annoying," said Grimes, "than being shot at in somebody else's war. I want you to heave to, a light-year out, until the dust settles. I'll rendezvous with you and come aboard to talk things over."

"Where are you calling from, Skipper?" asked Williams. "Have you got yourself another ship? Who are those popsies in the background?"

"Yes, I have borrowed a ship. Never mind from whom. And I'm on my way out to you now. I'll home on your Carlotti broadcast. I've good equipment here."

"I'll be waiting for you, Skipper."

"Give my regards to Magda, will you? And to old Mr. Stewart."

"Will do, Skipper."

"See you," said Grimes. "Out."

Yes, he would be seeing Williams, but not for a while yet.

⊰ Chapter 25 ⊱

KRAIT, insofar as New Sparta Aerospace Control was concerned, was now an invisible ship, falling through the warped dimensions toward her rendezvous with *Sister Sue,* undetectable by radar as long as her Mannschenn Drive was in operation. Some planets—such worlds as were considered to be strategically important—had defense satellites in orbit crammed with sophisticated equipment, such as long-range Mass Proximity Indicators capable of picking up approaching vessels running under Mannschenn Drive. New Sparta was not strategically important.

So while the Lady Ellena would be more than a little annoyed by the theft of a minor warship that she had hoped to acquire for her own use, she might well be pleased, thought Grimes, at the removal from her domain of three nuisances—Maggie Lazenby, Fenella Pruin and Grimes himself. He allowed himself to feel sorry for Lieutenant Gupta. He and his officers, spacemen without a spaceship, would be discovering that they were far from welcome guests in the Palace . . . .

Meanwhile it was time that he started thinking of his own strategy rather than the troubles of others. He would begin by setting an orbital course for Melitus rather than trajectory for *Sister Sue's* estimated position. Just where was Melitus?

He and the women went down to the wardroom—*Krait* was quite capable of looking after herself—where there was a play master which, like any such device aboard a spaceship, could be used to obtain information from the library bank. They all took seats, Grimes in one from which he could operate the play master's controls. He punched for LIBRARY, then for PLANETARY INFORMATION, then for NEW SPARTA, then for MELITUS. Words appeared on the screen. *Mountain, 1.7 kilometers above sea level, Latitude 37° 14' S, Longitude 176° 59'E.*

Village called Melitus? typed Grimes.

No information, appeared the reply.

Map of Mount Melitus vicinity?

Not in library bank.

Grimes swore. "I should," he said, "have brought along the atlas from my quarters."

"It would have looked suspicious," said Fenella, "if you'd been carrying it around with you."

"I could have torn out one or two relevant pages," said Grimes, "and put them in my pockets."

"But you didn't," said Fenella.

"There are some maps in my cabin," Maggie told them. "I'll get them now."

She spread them on the wardroom table. Grimes found the one he wanted, studied it carefully. When making his final approach, back in normal Space-Time, he would be shielded by the bulk of the planet from the probing radar of Aerospace Control. Unluckily he would be unable to make a quiet approach; the inertial drive unit of even a small ship is noisy; the only really heavy sonic insulation is to protect the eardrums of the crew. But there was a technique which he might employ, that he would employ if conditions were suitable. It was one that he had read about but had never seen used.

The map was a contour one. To the north Mount Melitus was steep, in parts practically sheer cliff. The southern face was sloped almost gently to the plain. There was a river, little more than a stream, that had its source about halfway up the mountain. A little below this source was the village of Melitus. But those contour lines . . . . The southern slopes were only comparatively gentle but there did not seem to be any suitable place upon which to set down a spaceship, even a small one. Grimes studied the map more carefully, took a pair of dividers to measure off distances. The river made a horseshoe bend just over a kilometer downstream from the village. The almost-island so formed was devoid of contour lines. Did that mean anything or was it no more than slovenly cartography? But the map, saw Grimes, was a Survey Service publication and the Survey Service's cartographers prided themselves on their thoroughness. He hoped they had been thorough when charting the Mount Melitus area.

He said, "You know something of the layout of the ship, Maggie. See if you can rustle up some kind of a meal. Sandwiches will do. Shirl and Darleen—you're army officers . . . ."

They laughed at that.

"But you know something about weapons," he went on. "You must have received some instruction when you were in the Amazon Guard as well as dishing it out. Go through the ship and collect all the lethal ironmongery you can find and bring it here, to the wardroom. And you, Fenella, make rounds of the officers' cabins and the storerooms and find clothing, for all of us, suitable for an uphill hike through rough country.

"I shall be going back to Control." He rolled up the map that he had been studying, took it with him. "You know where to find me if you want me."

Maggie brought him his sandwiches—rather inferior ham with not enough mustard—and a vacuum flask of coffee that was only a little better than the brew which they had become used to (but never liked) in the Palace. But he did not complain. (As far as Maggie was concerned he had learned, long since, that it was unwise to do so.) He munched stolidly while keeping a watchful eye on the instruments. One drawback of making an orbit around a planet with the ship's Mannschenn Drive in operation is that there are no identifiable landmarks; the appearance of a world viewed in such conditions has been described as that of a Klein Flask blown by a drunken glassblower.

But the instruments, Grimes hoped, were not lying.

"What time—local time, that is—should we get there?" asked Maggie.

"Midnight," replied Grimes. "Anyhow, that's what I've programmed the little bitch for. How are the girls getting on with their fossicking?"

"Fenella's found clothing for all of us—tough coveralls. Boots might be a problem. Shirl and Darleen have rather long feet, as probably you've already noticed."

"On their own planet," he said, "they're used to running around barefoot. What about rainwear?"

"Rainwear? Are you expecting rain?"

"Rain has been known to fall," he said. "Tell Fenella, when you go back down, to find something suitable. And the weapons?"

"So far a stungun, fully charged, with belt and holster, for each of us. Laser pistols likewise. And projectile pistols."

He said, "We can't load ourselves down with too much. We'll take the stunguns and the lasers. We don't want to do any killing."

"Lasers kill people. Or hadn't you noticed?"

"A laser is a tool as well as a weapon, Maggie. It comes in handy for burning through doors, for example. Too, it's silent. Even more so than a stungun."

"Shirl and Darleen have their own ideas about silent weapons," she said.

"What do you mean?"

"They found a dozen metal discs—what they're *for* the Odd Gods alone know!—in the engineer's workshop. They say that once they're given a cutting edge they'll be very nice throwing weapons."

Grimes muttered something about bloodthirsty little bitches.

"I thought that you liked them, John," said Maggie.

"I do. But . . . ."

"Haven't you ever shed any blood during *your* career?"

"Yes. But . . . ."

But what he did not tell her was that he strongly suspected that the guards at Miletus, Ellena's people, would be women. He derided himself for his old-fashioned ideas but still was reluctant to kill a member of the opposite sex.

Chapter 26

KRAIT made her return to normal Space-Time, began her descent to the surface of New Sparta, to Mount Melitus. Maggie and Fenella were with Grimes in the control room; Maggie was there as a sort of co-pilot—after all, as a Survey Service officer, although not in the Spaceman Branch, she knew something about ship-handling—and Fenella was, as always, just getting into everything. Grimes had succeeded in persuading Shirl and Darleen to busy themselves elsewhere. Much as he liked them both this was an occasion when he could do without their distracting chatter.

As the little ship dropped to the nightside hemisphere, greater and greater detail was displayed in the stern view radar screen, in three-dimensional presentation. There was Mount Melitus, almost directly below *Krait*. Grimes applied a touch of lateral thrust so that the mountain was now to the south of the line of descent. Its hulking mass, he explained, would shield the village on the southern slopes from the clangor of the inertial drive.

"But our landing place," objected Fenella, "*is* on the southern slopes. They're bound to hear us sooner or later—and soon enough to be ready and waiting for us."

"Not necessarily," Grimes told her.

He made adjustments to the radar controls, increasing sensitivity. Clouds were now visible in the screen. The wind, as it should have been at this time of year, as he had hoped that it would be, was from the north, blowing over the relatively warm Aegean Sea on to the land, striking the sheer, northern face of the mountain and being deflected upward into cooler atmospheric levels.

He checked the state of readiness of the missile projector. It was loaded. He had seen to that himself. In the tube was a rocket with a Mark XXV Incendiary warhead. It was one of the viler anti-personnel weapons, one that Grimes, during his Survey Service days, had hoped that he would never have to use. Now he was going to use it—although not directly against personnel.

"Who are you going to shoot at?" asked Fenella interestedly. "I thought that the object of this exercise was to rescue Brasidus, not to blow him to pieces."

"*What*, not *who*," said Grimes. "I'm looking for a nice, fat cloud. One that's just skimming the peak of the mountain on its way south."

"Looking for a *cloud*? Are you out of your tiny mind?"

"The Commodore knows what he's doing!" snapped Maggie. Then, "By the way, what are you doing?"

He laughed.

"I'm going to use a technique that was used, some years ago, on Bolodrin. A non-aligned planet, of no great importance, but one which both the Shaara and ourselves would like to draw within our spheres of influence. A humanoid population. An export trade of agricultural products. Well, there had been a quite disastrous planetwide drought. One of our ships—the Zodiac Class cruiser *Scorpio*—was there showing the flag. The Tronmach—it translates roughly to Hereditary President—appealed to the captain of *Scorpio*, as the representative of a technologically superior culture, to Do Something about the drought. Captain Samson went into a huddle with his scientific officers. They decided to seed likely cloud formations. With Hell Balls."

"What's a Hell Ball?" asked Fenella.

"What my missile projector is loaded with. It's the pet name for the Mark XXV Incendiary Device, one of the more horrid anti-personnel weapons. Imagine an expanding vortex of plasma, superheated, electrically hyperactive gases. . . ."

"And did this bright idea work?"

"Too well. The drought was broken all right. Rivers burst their banks. Hailstorms flattened orchards. If the Shaara had grabbed the opportunity, sending ships with all manner of aid, Bolodrin would have happily become an Associate Hive Member. But they were slow off the mark and the Federation organized relief expenditures. Nonetheless relations were strained and Captain Samson suffered premature retirement. Mphm. Looks like a suitable target coming up now . . . . Range about fifty kilometers . . . ."

He busied himself at the fire control console, aligning the projector, setting the fuse of the warhead.

He pushed the button.

Only faintly luminous, the exhaust of the rocket was almost invisible.

The slow explosion of the warhead was not. In the center of the towering cumulus bright flame burgeoned and lightnings writhed, wreathing the mountain peak with lambent fire, lashing out to other cloud formations. A clockwise rotation seemed already to have been initiated, a cyclonic vortex. It was the birth of a hurricane.

Grimes could imagine what the conditions would soon be on the southern slopes of Melitus, the country normally protected from extremes of weather by the bulk of the mountain. There would be torrential rain and shrieking winds and a continuous cannonade of thunder and lightning, an uproar among which the arrhythmic clangor of a small ship's inertial drive unit would go unnoticed.

He hoped.

With the controls now on manual he continued his descent. He skimmed the peak with less clearance than he had intended; a vicious downdraft caught *Krait* and had he not reacted swiftly, slamming on maximum lift, the ship must surely have been wrecked.

Then he was over the mountain top, dropping again but not too fast, maintaining a half-kilometer altitude from the ground. Sudden gusts buffeted the ship, tilting her from the vertical. A fusillade of hail on her skin was audible even through the thick insulation.

Nothing, save for the diffused flare of the lightning, could be seen through the viewpoints. Even the radar picture was almost blotted out by storm clutter.

But there was the village . . . .

And the river . . .

Grimes followed its course to the horseshoe bend. It looked as it did on the chart. But even if the ground were level, what about trees? There had been no symbols indicating such growths on the map—but trees have a habit of growing over the years. He had hoped to be able to make a visual inspection before landing but, in these conditions, it was impossible.

He hovered almost directly over the almost-island, dropping slowly, keeping *Krait* in position by applications of lateral thrust, this way and that.

"Stand by the viewpoint, Maggie," he ordered. "Yes. That one. If there's a brief clear spell, if the rain lets up, tell me what you see."

"What do you want me to see?"

"What I don't want you to see on our landing place," he said, "is trees. Bushes don't worry me but a large, healthy tree can damage even a big ship sitting down on it!"

"Will do."

And then she was back beside him.

"There was a break, and lightning at the same time. There aren't any trees."

"Landing stations!" ordered Grimes.

Krait sat down hard, dropping the final two meters with her drive in neutral. She sat down hard and she complained, creaking and groaning, rocking on her tripedal landing gear, while shock-absorbers hissed and sighed.

Grimes unbuckled himself from his chair, then led the way out of the control room. In the wardroom Shirl and Darleen were waiting. On the table and on the deck were the articles of clothing that Grimes had specified—the coveralls, the raincapes and the heavy boots. Hanging on the backs of chairs were belts and holstered weapons.

Swiftly the five of them got out of their light clothing, pulled on the coveralls and the heavy boots. Luckily the ship's equipment store had carried a wide range of sizes, so even Shirl and Darleen were shod not too uncomfortably. Grimes packed a rucksack with protective clothing for Brasidus, who would need this for the walk from the village to *Krait*. (Grimes hoped that Brasidus would be able to make the walk, that he would be rescued unharmed.) They belted on the weapons. Shirl and Darleen attached to their belts pouches with clinking contents. Grimes wondered briefly what was in them, then remembered the discs that the two girls had found in the engineer's workshop.

They made their way down the spiral staircase to the airlock, the controls of which had been set to be operated manually. Grimes was not at all happy about leaving the ship without a duty officer but he had no option. He was the only real spaceperson in the party but, at the same time, he was the obvious leader of the expedition. And all that any of the women could do, if one of them were left in charge, would be to keep a seat in the control room warm.

He and Fenella were first into the airlock chamber. Grimes pushed the button that would open the outer door and, at the same time, extend the telescopic ramp. He was expecting a violent onslaught of wind and rain but his luck, he realized thankfully, was holding. The door was on the lee side of the ship. He adjusted the hood of his raincape, checked the buckles holding the garment about his body, then walked cautiously down the ramp. Away from the ship he began to feel the wind and, even through his layers of clothing, the impact of the huge raindrops. He could hear the thin, high screaming of the wind as it eddied around the metallic tower that was the ship, was blinded by a bolt of lightning that struck nearby and deafened by the *crack!* of the thunder. And what if *Krait* herself should be struck by lightning? Nothing much, he thought (hoped). With her stern vanes well dug into the wet soil she would be well earthed.

He got his eyesight back and turned to look up the ramp. Shirl and Darleen were coming down it and Maggie was silhouetted in the doorway.

"Shut the inner door before you come down!" he yelled.

"What?" he heard her scream.

He repeated the order.

The light behind her diminished as she obeyed him. The airlock chamber itself was only dimly illumined. And then she was following Shirl and Darleen to the ground.

Grimes led the way up the mountainside. There was no possibility of their getting lost; all that they had to do was to keep to the bank of the stream. It was more of a torrent now, swollen by the downpour, roaring and rumbling as displaced boulders, torn from the banks, ground against each other. The wind had almost as much weight as the rushing water, buffeting them as they bent into it, finding its way through the fastenings of their raincapes, ballooning the garments, threatening to lift their wearers from their feet and to send them whirling downhill, airborne flotsam.

The raincapes had to go. Grimes struggled out of his. It was torn from his hands, vanished downwind like a huge, demented bat. The women shed theirs. Maggie, shouting to make herself heard above the wild tumult of wind, water and thunder, made a feeble joke about the willful destruction of Federation property and the necessity thereafter of filling in forms in quintuplicate.

But she could still joke, thought Grimes. Good for her. And the others were bearing up well, even Fenella. No doubt she was thinking in headlines. MY WALK ON THE WILD SIDE.

Bruised and battered by flying debris, deafened by shrieking wind and roaring thunder, blinded by lightning, the party struggled up the mountainside.

And of all the miseries and discomforts the one that Grimes resented most bitterly was the trickle of icy-cold water that found its way through the neckband of his coveralls, meandering down his body to collect in his boots.

~ Chapter 27 ~

THEY CAME AT LAST to the village, such as it was, the huddle of low stone houses, little better than huts most of them, all of them with doors and windows tightly battened against the storm. There was one building, two-storied, larger than the others. From its steeply pitched roof protruded what was obviously a radio communications antenna, a slender mast that whipped as the gusts took hold of it and worried it. It was a wonder that it had survived the storm thus far; not only was there the rain but there was the lightning, stabbing down from the swirling clouds at even the stunted trees that were hardly more than overgrown bushes, exploding them into eruptions of charred splinters.

It had survived thus far; it would be as well, decided Grimes, if it survived for no longer. If Brasidus and his guards were in this house the sooner that means of communication with Sparta City was destroyed the better. He pulled his laser pistol from its holster, tried to take aim at the base of the mast. The wind grabbed his arm and tugged viciously. He tried to use his left hand to steady his right, pressed the firing stud. During a brief, very brief, period of darkness between lightning flashes he saw the beam of intense ruby light, missing the target by meters. He tried again. Maggie tried. Even Fenella tried. The radio mast remained untouched by their fire.

Grimes saw that Shirl was taking one of the metal discs from the pouch at her waist, holding it carefully by the small arc of its

384

circumference that had been left unsharpened. *And what good will that do?* he asked himself scornfully. A thrown missile, launched in the teeth of a howling gale . . . Metal—tough metal admittedly—against metal at least as tough as itself. (That mast must be tough to have survived the storm.)

Shirl stood there, her body swaying in the gusts that assailed her, making no attempt to hold herself rigid as she took aim, not fighting the forces of nature as Grimes and Maggie and Fenella had been trying to do, accommodating herself to them. Her right arm, the hand holding the gleaming disc, went back and then, aided by a wind eddy, snapped forward. Like Grimes and the others, she had been aiming for the base of the mast. Unlike Grimes and the others she might even have hit it. But the disc itself, generating with its swift passage through the heavily charged air a charge of its own, was itself a target. A writhing filament of dazzling incandescence snaked down from the black sky to enmesh the missile, to follow its trajectory even as it was reduced to a coruscation of molten steel.

The disc, what was left of it, would narrowly have missed the base of the mast—but the lightning struck it. Momentarily it took, Grimes thought, the semblance of a Christmas tree, etching its branches and foliage of flame onto his retinas. Slowly he regained his eyesight. Somebody—Maggie—had him by the upper arm, was shaking it.

"John! John!" she was saying, "They're coming out!"

He blinked, then raised his hand to clear the rain from his eyes. A door had opened on the lee side of the building, the side on which they were standing. A figure was standing in the rectangle of yellow light, another one behind it, women both of them.

"I'm not going out in *this*!" Grimes heard faintly.

"Somebody has to. Something has happened to the mast."

"Blown down. Struck by lightning. In this weather anything could happen."

"We have to see what's wrong so we can fix it. Out with you, *now!*"

"Oh, all right. All right."

The smaller of the two women ventured out into the night,

picking just the wrong moment for her excursion. A shrieking gust eddied around the house so that even on its lee side there was little protection. Her weatherproof cloak was whipped up over and around her head, blinding her and trapping her arms. She staggered out blindly, her naked legs luminescent in the darkness. She blundered right into the arms of Shirl and Darleen. Her shriek as a hard fist connected with the nape of her neck was muffled by her enveloping garment. She fell to the sodden ground and lay there, face down, her bare rump exposed to the lashing of the driving rain. She would be visible from the open doorway; Grimes and his companions, in their dark clothing, would not.

"Lalia!" the woman standing in the door was screaming. "Lalia! What's wrong? Did you fall?"

And then she had left the shelter of the house, was staggering out over the rough ground, buffeted by the wind, her flimsy robe shredded from her body as she made her unsteady way toward her fallen companion. Grimes and the others withdrew to one side, hoping that they would not be seen, and then, with him in the lead, ran toward the house, their stunguns out and ready. Once inside they slammed and barred the door. (Grimes felt a brief twinge of pity for those two near-naked females shut out in the storm.)

The room in which they were standing was sparsely furnished— a rough table, a half-dozen equally rough chairs, a pressure lantern hanging from a rafter. Against the far wall a wooden staircase— more of a ladder really—led to the upper floor. In the side wall to the left was an open doorway.

From it came a female voice.

"Sounds like they're back. Now, perhaps, we'll be able to get this accursed transceiver working again."

"I'm sure that dear Ellena is waiting with bated breath for the rest of our weather report," sneered another female voice.

"Be that as it may, we're still supposed to be in touch every six hours, on the hour, if only to let her know that his sexist lordship is doing as well as may be expected." She raised her voice. "Lalia! Daphne! What's keeping you? Is that aerial still standing?"

Grimes and Maggie, stunguns in hand, advanced to the open

door, the others behind them. They saw the four women, who were huddled over the large transceiver upon which they had been working, replacing power cells and printed circuits. One of them he recognized; it was the fat blonde with whom he had tangled on the occasion of the Archon's abduction, although what had been brassy hair was now no more than a gray stubble. There must have been a discharge from the set when the lightning struck and she must have been in the way of it. She looked up from her work and stared at him.

She jumped to her feet, screwdriver in hand.

"You!" she snarled.

"Yes, me," agreed Grimes pleasantly as he shot her.

Beside him Maggie's stungun buzzed as she disposed of two of the other ladies and from behind him Fenella, determined not to be left out of things, loosed off a paralyzing blast at the redhead who was about to throw a spanner at the commodore.

We should have left one of them awake, thought Grimes, *to take us to where they have Brasidus.* Not that it much mattered. This house, little more than a shack, was no castle. There would be very few rooms to search.

They went back into the first room. Somebody was hammering on the door to outside and yelling, "Let us in! Let us in, damn you!"

"Let them in," Grimes whispered to Shirl.

She obeyed.

The two women who had gone to inspect the aerial stumbled in. In normal circumstances they might have been attractive, with what remained of their rain-soaked clothing clinging to quite shapely bodies, but Grimes thought they looked like two drowned rats. They screamed when they saw the intruders, screamed again when the two New Alicians grabbed them, one to each, held them with their arms twisted up painfully behind their backs. Still they stared defiantly at Grimes. One of them spat at him.

"Ladies, ladies," he admonished. Then, with the whipcrack of authority in his voice, "Where is the Archon?"

"Why should we tell you?" growled the taller of the pair.

Grimes raised his stungun in his right hand, with the fingers of his left adjusted the setting.

"John, you're not going to . . . ?" expostulated Maggie. "You said that there was to be no killing."

Grimes hoped that he had the setting right. There was one beam intensity the use of which was supposed to be illegal, against the rules of civilized warfare. It was a matter of very fine adjustment, a fraction of a degree above MAXIMUM STUN although less than LETHAL. Una Freeman, a Federation police officer whom he had once known, had taught him this nasty little trick, telling him that it might come in handy some day. "But be careful," she had warned him. "Overdo it and you'll finish up with a human vegetable who'd be better off dead."

"Where is the Archon?" he demanded again.

"Get stuffed!" came the defiant reply.

Grimes raised the bulky pistol.

"That's right," sneered the woman. "Put me to sleep so I'll never talk. D'you think I don't know a stungun when I see one?"

"Drop her!" Grimes barked to Darleen. "Get away from her!"

For a moment the tall, black-haired woman stood there, then she started toward Grimes, clawlike fingers extended.

Grimes pressed the firing stud.

The weapon whined.

The woman was cut down in mid-leap then fell to the floor, writhing in agony, the muzzle of the pistol still trained on her, still emitting its beam. She was making a shrill grunting noise through her closed mouth and, above this, could be heard the grinding of her teeth. Throughout her body muscle fought against muscle. She was on her back squirming in a ghastly parody of orgasm, and then only her heels and the back of her head were in contact with the floor. Blood trickled from the corners of her mouth.

"Stop!" screamed Maggie.

He released the pressure on the firing stud.

His victim collapsed in a shuddering heap.

"Where is the Archon?" repeated Grimes.

She lifted her head to glare at him. She spat out blood and fragments of broken teeth.

"Get . . . stuffed . . ."

Hating himself, and hating her for being so stubborn, Grimes took aim again.

"I'll tell!" screamed the small, mousy blonde. "I'll tell you! But don't hurt her again!"

"Gutless little bitch!" was all the thanks she got from her friend.

But Grimes felt better when he discovered that his harsh interrogation had been necessary after all. There was a cellar, the trapdoor to which had been concealed by the heavy rug upon which the table had been standing, that could be opened only by pressing a stud, disguised as a nailhead—one among many—in the wooden floor. There was a rough wooden staircase down into the black depths.

"Brasidus!" yelled Grimes into the opening.

"Here!" came the reply from below. Then, "Who's that?"

"Grimes. We've come to get you out!"

But there was something that had to be done first. Grimes set the control knob of his pistol to MEDIUM STUN. He pointed the weapon at the black-haired woman who was still sprawled on the floor, twitching and moaning. He said gently, "This will put you out. You'll feel better when you recover." (It was not quite a lie, although it would be days before the soreness left her overstrained muscles and she would require considerable dental work.)

"Bastard!" she hissed viciously from her bleeding mouth. "Bastard!"

And then she was silent and her body and limbs were no longer twitching.

Darleen lifted the pressure lamp from its bracket, started toward the open trapdoor.

"Hold it!" ordered Grimes. "Let *her* go first." He hustled the small blonde toward the head of the stairway. "There may be booby traps."

So they followed their prisoner down into what was more of a cellar than a real dungeon, smelling of the wine and the spicy foodstuffs stored therein, although in one corner there was a cage constructed from stout metal bars, its door secured by a heavy padlock. In this stood Brasidus. He was naked and his beard and hair were unkempt but otherwise he seemed in good enough condition.

"John!" he cried. "Maggie! By all the gods, it's good to see you!"

"And good to see you!" said Grimes. He grabbed the small blonde by her shoulder. "Where's the key to this cage?"

"I . . . I don't know . . . ."

"Give her the same treatment that you gave the other bitch," suggested Fenella viciously.

But Maggie had returned her stungun to its holster, pulled out her laser pistol. An acrid stink of burning metal filled the air and incandescent, molten gobbets hissed and crackled as they fell to the floor.

Free, Brasidus hugged the embarrassed Grimes in a bearlike embrace, then did the same to Maggie. ("Don't *I* get a kiss?" complained Fenella.) And then, amazingly, he swept the small blonde into his arms, pressed his lips on hers. She did not resist, in fact cooperated quite willingly.

"Might I ask," inquired Fenella, "just what the hell is going on here?"

Brasidus laughed. "It's because of Lalia that I'm down in this hole. At first I enjoyed considerably more freedom. Lalia and I . . . Oh, well, you know how things are. Daphne caught us at it . . ."

"Perhaps Daphne had the right to be jealous," suggested Fenella.

"It's time that we were getting out of here," said Grimes. "I've a ship waiting."

"Come, then," said Brasidus. With his arm still about Lalia's shoulders he started for the foot of the staircase.

"You aren't taking *her* with you," stated rather than asked Fenella.

"Why not? She was good to me."

And good to Daphne, thought Grimes, *and, above all, good to herself.*

He said, "I'm sorry. She has to stay here."

Brasidus released the girl and shrugged.

"Just as well, perhaps," he muttered. "Probably Ellena wouldn't approve if I brought her into the Palace."

And you've a lot to learn about Ellena, my poor friend, thought

Grimes. *But that can wait until we're in the ship on the way back to Port Sparta.*

Maggie's stungun buzzed as she ensured Lalia's unconsciousness for at least half an hour.

Chapter 28

IN THE UPSTAIRS ROOM they gave Brasidus the clothing that they had brought for him, the tough coveralls and the heavy boots. He dressed in sulky silence. They let themselves out of the house. The storm was abating although the rain was still as heavy as ever. There was no longer an almost continuous flare of lightning but laser pistols, set to low intensity, did duty as electric torches to illuminate their way.

The stream whose course they had followed up to the village was now a wild torrent, bearing on its crest all manner of flotsam, uprooted bushes and small trees and the like. Audible even above the sound of rushing water was the grinding rumble of the boulders rolling downhill along the river bed.

But where was *Krait*?

Surely, thought Grimes, *we should be seeing her by now.*

He set the beam of his laser to higher intensity, sent it probing ahead into the rain-lashed darkness. There was a very pretty rainbow effect but no reflection from gleaming metal. He began to feel a growing uneasiness. Surely the little bitch hadn't lifted off by herself . . . Surely some freakish accident, a chance lightning bolt for example, had not caused actuation of the inertial drive machinery . . . .

But that was fantasy.

But where was the ship?

Maggie cried out.

Like Grimes, she had adjusted her laser pistol. Unlike him she was directing the beam only just above ground level. She was first to see the ship. Afterwards it was easy to work out what must have happened, what had happened—the almost-island on which Grimes had set her down had become a real island, an island whose banks were eroded, faster and faster, by the rushing water. With the once-solid ground below her vanes washed away she had toppled. The crash of her falling had just been part of the general tumult of the storm.

Fenella voiced the thoughts of all of them.

"That's fucked it!" she stated.

Too right, thought Grimes, but his mind was working busily. Suppose, just suppose, that the ship's main machinery had not been too badly damaged . . . Then it would be possible, difficult but possible, to lift her on lateral thrust and then, when high enough from the ground, to turn her about a short axis to a normal attitude. In theory it could be done. In fact Grimes had heard of its being done, although he had never had to attempt such a maneuver himself; the nearest to it had been the righting of a destroyer, a much larger vessel. Then those in the ship had used lateral thrust while he, in control of operations, had employed a spaceyacht as a tug.

But to do anything at all he had to get into the ship.

Accompanied by the others he walked, so far as was possible, around the cigar-shaped hull. It formed a bridge over the river, with the nose on the bank upon which Grimes was standing, with the stern on what little remained of the island. And, Grimes saw by the light of the laser torches, she had fallen in such a way that the airlock was below her. He told Maggie and the others.

"Can't we burn a way in?" she asked. "The control room view-ports should be a weak point . . ."

And those viewports, thought Grimes glumly, were supposed to be able to withstand, at least for an appreciable time, the assault of a laser cannon . . . How long would it take hand lasers to make a hole? But it had to be tried.

And so they stood there, the five of them who were armed, with

Brasidus watching, aiming their pistols at the center of one of the viewports. Soon their target was obscured by steam as the intense heat vaporized the falling rain, soon the exposed skin of their faces felt as though it were being boiled.

But they persisted.

Then the intense beam of ruby light from Maggie's weapon faded into the infrared, died. She caught the butt of the weapon a clout with her free hand but it did not help. "Power cell's dead," she muttered.

"And mine . . ." said Fenella.

The other lasers sputtered out. The steam dispersed. The eyes of the party became accustomed to the darkness—but, Grimes realized, it was no longer dark. The sun must now be up, somewhere behind the fast-scudding nimbus. He looked at the shallow depression in the thick transparency of the viewport, all that they had been able to achieve at the cost of their most effective weaponry.

He flinched as something whipped past his head with a noise that was part whistle, part crack. A scar of bright metal appeared on the hide of *Krait* just below the viewports. A long time later—it seemed—came the report of a projectile firearm.

"Take cover!" yelled Grimes. "Behind the ship!"

He waited—*like a fool*, he told himself, *like a fool*—until the others had moved, looking toward where he thought the shot had come from, holding his pistol as though for instant use. He saw her, a pale form up the hillside. It was, he thought, the fat blonde. Her body bulk must have minimized the effects of the stungun blast. She had her rifle raised for another shot. It went wild and then she ducked behind a boulder.

Grimes, still holding his useless laser pistol threateningly, walked carefully backward. Just before he joined the others a third shot threw up a fountain of mud by his right foot.

Secure, for the time being, behind the bulk of the crippled courier he said, "There's only one of them. That fat bitch . . . ."

"Hephastia," said Brasidus.

"Thanks," said Grimes. "That saves me the bother of being formally introduced to her. Luckily she doesn't know that our lasers are dead. But when we fail to return her fire she'll realize that they are, and come for us."

"We've the stunguns," said Maggie.

"And what effective range do *they* have?" asked Grimes. "Little more than three meters, if that."

"But how much ammunition does *she* have?" said Fenella.

"We don't know," Grimes told her. "If she's any sort of a shot six rounds should be ample."

Very, very carefully he moved out from behind the protection of the ship, crawling in the mud, keeping head and buttocks well down. He was in time to see a flicker of movement as Hephastia changed positions, scurrying to the cover of another boulder, not appreciably decreasing the range but carrying out an outflanking operation. Even if she were not a member of the Amazon Guard she must have had military training on some world at some time.

He raised his pistol as though about to fire from the prone position. Her retaliatory shot was in line but, luckily for him, over. Frantically he scurried forward, found a boulder of his own behind which to hide. It was by no means as large as he would have wished—and it was even smaller after a well-aimed bullet had reduced the top of it to dust and splinters. Another one reduced it in size still further.

Grimes tried to burrow into the mud while still maintaining some kind of a lookout.

From the corner of his eye he saw movement by the ship.

It was Shirl, walking out calmly, something that gleamed, even in this dull, gray light, in her right hand. It was one of those sharpened discs. Hephastia did not see her. She must have had a one-track mind. With calm deliberation she was whittling away Grimes's little boulder, shot after shot, using some kind of armor-piercing ammunition.

Shirl's right arm went back, snapped forward.

The disc sailed up in what seemed lazy flight—*too high*, thought Grimes, watching, *too high*.

Shirl stood there, making no attempt to throw a second one.

Grimes's boulder, under the impact of an armor-piercing bullet, split neatly down the middle, affording him a good view of what was happening. He saw the disc whir over Hephastia's position and then turn, dipping sharply downward as it did so. It vanished from sight.

There was one last shot, wildly aimed, which threw up a spray of mud between Grimes and the ship. There was a gurgling scream.

Calmly Shirl walked to where Grimes was sprawled in the mud, helped him to his feet.

"She will not bother you again, John," she said cheerfully.

"But how did you . . . ?"

He did not have to finish the question. The New Alicians had their telepathic moments.

"We did more than just sharpen the discs," she told him. "We used the grinding wheels and we . . . shaped them. Put in curves. Like boomerangs."

"But how did you *know* what to do?"

"We . . . We just *knew*."

Together they walked up the hillside, through the pouring rain, the others straggling after them. They came to the boulder from behind which Hephastia had been shooting. The sight of the fat woman's body was not quite as bad as Grimes had feared it would be; the downpour had already washed away most of the blood. Even so decapitation, or near decapitation, is never a pretty spectacle. Grimes looked away hastily from the gaping wound in the neck with the obscenely exposed raw flesh and cartilage. The rest of the body was not so bad. It looked drained, deflated, like a flabby white blimp brought to Earth by heavy leakage from its gas cells. Her dead hands still held the rifle. Grimes took it from her. It was a 10mm automatic, as issued to Federation military forces. It was set to Single Shot. There should have been plenty of rounds left in the magazine but there were not. Hephastia—or somebody—had neglected to replace it after some previous usage.

Grimes counted the remaining cartridges.

There were only five.

By this time the others had joined them.

"I've a rifle," said Grimes unnecessarily, "but only five rounds."

"There are weapons and ammunition a-plenty in the house," said Brasidus.

"Just what I had in mind," said Grimes.

He led the way up the hillside.

He covered the retreat, loosing off all five of the remaining rounds to deter a sally from the open door. The other women must have recovered, were firing from chinks in the heavily shuttered windows. After Grimes's warning burst they seemed to be reluctant to show themselves—much to the disgust of Shirl and Darleen.

"So," said Maggie, "what now?"

"We follow the river," said Grimes. "From what I can remember of the maps there are sizable towns on its lower reaches."

"On *foot*?" squealed Fenella.

"You can try swimming if you like," said Grimes, "but I'd not recommend it with the river the way it is now."

Chapter 29

THEY WERE COLD and they were wet and they were hungry.

Vividly in Grimes's memory was the smell of the cellar from which they had rescued Brasidus—the cheeses, the smoked and spiced sausages, the pickles. If only he had known that they were to be denied access to *Krait* he would have seen to it that they commenced what promised to be a very long walk well-provisioned and -armed.

Surprisingly Brasidus was not much help. Grimes had hoped that the Archon would have some idea of the geography of this area, would be able to guide them to some other village where there would be an inn, would be capable of finding for them the easiest and shortest route to the nearest town.

"But you're the ruler of this world!" said Grimes exasperatedly.

"That does not mean, friend John, that I know, intimately, every square centimeter of its surface, any more than you are familiar with every smallest detail of a ship that you command."

"I always do my best to gain such familiarity," grumbled Grimes.

They trudged on, the roaring torrent on their right, towering rocky outcrops, among which a few stunted trees struggled for survival, on their left. Grimes maintained the lead, with Maggie and Brasidus a little behind him, then Fenella, then Shirl and Darleen, the only ones with any sort of effective medium-range weaponry, as the rear guard. It was not likely that they would be followed but it was possible.

They trudged on.

They were no longer so cold; in fact they were sweating inside their heavy coveralls. The rain was easing. Now and again, briefly, the high sun struck through a break in the clouds.

But they were still hungry.

Grimes called a halt in the shelter of an overhanging cliff. He managed to light his pipe. (And how much tobacco was left in his pouch? He should have refilled it from a large container of the weed that Shirl had found for him in one of the officer's cabins aboard *Krait*.) Fenella had an almost full packet of cigarillos and, grudgingly, allowed Maggie to take one. Neither Brasidus nor the New Alician girls smoked.

Shirl and Darleen strayed away from the shelter, saying that they were going back up the trail a little to see if there were any signs of pursuit. Grimes let them go. He knew that they were quite capable of looking after themselves.

"And now," he said, "I'll put you in the picture, Brasidus. Prepare yourself for a shock."

"Ellena? Has anything happened to her?"

"On the contrary." Grimes laughed bitterly. "On the contrary. She's the one who's been making things happen. To begin with, she used your abduction as an excuse for seizing power."

Brasidus was not as shocked as Grimes had feared that he would be.

"She is a very shrewd politician, John, as I have known for quite awhile. And there has to be a strong hand at the helm during my forced absence. There are so many squabbling factions . . . ."

"But does she want you back?" asked Grimes brutally. "Oh, she didn't want you hurt but she did want you out of the way, does want you out of the way until she's firmly in the saddle. If she does allow you to come back it will be only as a sort of Prince Consort to her Queen Hippolyte."

Brasidus shook his head dazedly. Then, at last, "You are trying to tell me that *she* is responsible for my abduction?"

"Yes," stated Grimes.

There was a long silence, broken eventually by the Archon.

"Yes," he muttered. "It does make sense, a quite horrible sort of sense. She _is_ ambitious. She does really believe that she is a reincarnation of Queen Hippolyte. Her Amazon Guards are a formidable military force. Oh, I have sneered at them, as what man on this world has not, but, in my heart of hearts I have respected them. Those women back in the village were not Amazon Guards, had they been we should never have gotten out alive. They were no more than criminals whom somebody . . . ."

"Ellena," said Fenella.

"All right. Merely criminals hired by Ellena to do a job."

"Or loyal Party members," said Maggie, "following orders. Ellena's orders."

"Ellena, Ellena, always Ellena!" Brasidus got to his feet, began to pace up and down. "Always it comes back to Ellena."

"I'm afraid that it does," said Grimes.

"I should have known. As a ruler, as Archon, I have failed my people."

"Not yet," Grimes told him. "There are still people loyal to you."

They were interrupted by Shirl and Darleen. The two New Alicians were dragging something over the wet ground, something that might have been a very large snake had it not been equipped with eight pairs of legs. It was minus its head and the blood that dripped from its neck was an unpleasant yellow in color.

"Lunch," announced Shirl.

"Surely that _thing_ is not edible," complained Fenella.

"It is," Brasidus told her, cheering up. "It is a delicacy. _Draco_, we call it. Broiled, with a fruit sauce . . . ."

Using their sharpened discs Shirl and Darleen lopped off the short legs of the draco, gutted and skinned it, throwing the offal into the river. Grimes tried to start a fire, using as fuel twigs broken from nearby bushes. But it was a hopeless task. All vegetation, even that in the partial shelter of the rock overhang, was thoroughly saturated and stubbornly refused to burn. If they had had an operating laser pistol at their disposal . . . . But they did not.

With a convenient flat rock as a table the New Alicians went on with their butchering. They sliced the flesh into wafer-thin slices. They gestured to Grimes that he should take the first bite.

He did. It wasn't bad, not unlike the sashimi that was a favorite meal of his when he could get it. It would have been vastly improved by a selection of dipping sauces but, he decided as he chewed, there were times when one couldn't have everything. Maggie joined him at the "table," then Fenella. Shirl and Darleen were already eating heartily. Only Brasidus hung back. (He, of course, was untraveled, had not sampled local delicacies on worlds all over the Galaxy.)

"Try some," urged Grimes. "It's not bad."

"But it's not *cooked*."

"You must eat *something*," insisted Maggie, womanlike.

He forced himself to make a meal that obviously he did not enjoy.

Grimes ordered that the remains of the draco be thrown into the river. Now that the rain had ceased the day had become unpleasantly warm and already the meat was becoming odorous.

They pushed on down the mountainside.

It was early evening when they came to a village, larger than the one from which they had taken Brasidus. There was one short street, with low houses on either side of it. There was what looked like a small temple—to which deity of the Greek pantheon? wondered Grimes; it seemed to be of fairly recent construction—and, across the road from it, what was obviously an inn.

They entered this building, Brasidus in the lead.

There were several customers, all of them roughly dressed men, seated on benches at the rough wooden tables. These looked curiously at the intruders. There was the innkeeper, a grossly fat individual whose dirty apron strained over his prominent belly.

"Greetings, lords," he said. "What is your pleasure?"

"Wine," said Brasidus. "Bread. Hot meat if you have it."

"That indeed I have, lord. There is a fine stew a-simmering in the kitchen that would be fit for the Archon himself."

"Then bring it."

He bustled out, returned with a flagon of wine and six mugs, went out again for the platter of bread and individual bowls and spoons, and a last time for a huge, steaming pot from which issued a very savory smell.

"Eat well, my lords," he said. Then, "Have you been out in the storm?"

"We have," said Brasidus around a mouthful of stew.

"The weather was never like this when I was a boy. It's all these offworlders coming down in their ships, disturbing the clouds. Time was when there were only two ships a year, the ones from Latterhaven . . . ."

"Mphm," grunted Grimes, thinking that he had better make some contribution to the conversation.

"And what is the uniform that you are wearing, lords? Forgive my curiosity but we have so few visitors here. You have guns, I see. Would you be some sort of police officers?"

"We are in the Archon's service," said Brasidus, not untruthfully.

"Indeed? Would it be impertinent of me to inquire which branch?"

"It would."

This failed to register and the innkeeper rattled on.

"There are so many new branches these days. I've even heard tell that in Sparta City there's a *women's* army, and according to the last News we watched they're taking over. Troublous times, lords, troublous times. I'd not be surprised to learn that it's the women behind the vanishment of the Archon. We're old-fashioned folk here in Calmira. There are women here now, of course, but they know their places. They'd never come into the tavern. The temple's for them."

Fenella made an odd snorting noise.

"But it's getting quite dark, isn't it? It's all this weather we're having these days. I'll give you light to eat by; the power was off most of the day but it's back on now . . ."

He went to the switch by the door, clicked it on. The overhead light tubes were harshly brilliant. He returned to the table, stared at his guests, at Maggie, at Fenella, at Shirl and Darleen.

"You . . ." he sputtered. *"Women!"* he spat.

"So what?" asked Fenella coldly.

"But . . . . But never before in *my* inn . . . ."

"There has to be a first time for everything," she said.

He turned appealingly to Brasidus. "Had I known I'd never have admitted you."

"You know now," said Grimes. "And now you know, what can you do about it?"

The men at the other tables were stirring restively. There were mutterings of, "Throw them out! Throw them out!"

"Not before I've finished my meal," said Grimes.

"Throw them out!" It was more than just a muttering now.

Grimes put his spoon down in the almost empty bowl, took careful stock of the opposition. There were fourteen men, big men, not young but not old. They looked tough customers and, in the right (or wrong) circumstances, nasty ones. Of course, despite the numerical odds, there was little doubt as to what the outcome of a scuffle would be. Although there was no ammunition for the rifle, although the laser pistols were useless until recharged, there were still the stunguns, ideal for use in a situation such as this. And there were the two specialists in unarmed combat, Shirl and Darleen.

But . . . .

But one at least of the men might escape from the inn, might run to the Town Constable who, surely, would have some means of communication—radio or land line—with the nearest big town. And then Ellena would soon learn that her husband, with his low friends, was running around loose and that the failure of his guards to maintain communication with the Palace was due to more than storm damage.

"All right," he said to the innkeeper, "we'll go. But rest assured that a full report of this business will be made to the proper authorities."

"Then go," said the man. "But first . . . ."

He thrust a dirty piece of paper, the bill, under Grimes' nose. Grimes glanced at it. He did a mental conversion of obols into credits. He would have been charged less for a meal for six persons in many a four-star restaurant on many a world. Then he realized that, in any case, he could not pay. His wallet, with money and credit cards, was with the clothing that he had left aboard *Krait* when he changed into coveralls.

"Do you have any money on you?" he asked Maggie.

She shook her head.

"Fenella?"

"Back aboard the ship. Nothing here."

"Shirl? Darleen?"

"No."

"Are you paying, or aren't you?" demanded the innkeeper.

"You will have to send the bill to the Palace," Brasidus told him. "It will be honored."

"Check it first," said Grimes nastily.

"Send the bill to the Palace?" demanded the innkeeper. "What do you take me for? Who'll be in charge at the Palace by the time it gets there, the postal services being what they are these days? Tell me that."

A good question, thought Grimes.

He said, "If you insist, we'll leave security."

"What security?"

Another good question.

His wrist companion? wondered Grimes. No. It was too useful, with many more functions than those of a mere timekeeper. The same could be said for the instrument that Maggie was wearing on her left wrist. The ammunitionless rifle or the dead laser pistols? Again no. What police officer would cheerfully pass his weapons over to civilians in payment of a tavern bill? And, in any case, the laser pistols were clearly marked as Federation property.

He looked at the others around the table. A gleam of precious metal caught his eye.

He said, "I'll have to ask you for your watch, Fenella."

"*What?*"

"You'll be able to reclaim it after the bill's been paid."

"*If* it's ever paid."

"In which case you will be fully compensated."

Fenella extended her left hand. The innkeeper looked covetously at the fabrication of gold and precious stones thus displayed.

"Buying time with time," she said.

"I shall insist on a receipt," said Grimes.

One was reluctantly given, on a scrap of paper as dirty and as rumpled as the bill.

Then Grimes, Brasidus and the women went out into the gathering dark.

~ Chapter 30 ~

SOME DISTANCE DOWNSTREAM FROM THE VILLAGE they found a deserted hut.

It must once have been, suggested Brasidus, the abode of a goatherd. (The indigenous six-legged animals that had been called goats by the original colonists had been largely replaced, as food animals, by the sheep and cattle imported from Earth.) There was just one room, its floor littered with animal droppings and the bones of various small creatures that had been brought into this shelter by various predators to be devoured at leisure, that now crackled unpleasantly underfoot. By the flare of Maggie's and Fenella's lighters, set at maximum intensity, it was possible to take stock. There was, leaning against the wall, a crude beson. Shirl took this and began to sweep the debris out through the open door. There was a fireplace, and beside it what had once been a tidy pile of cut wood, now scattered by some animal or animals.

Grimes instructed Darleen to use the cutting edge of one of her discs to produce a quantity of thin shavings from one of the sticks. He laid a fire. The shavings took fire immediately from his match and the blaze spread to the thicker sticks on top. Too late he thought that he should have checked the chimney to see if it was clear but he need not have worried. The fire drew well. Although the night was still far from cold the ruddy, flickering light made the atmosphere much more cheerful.

They all sat down on the now more-or-less clean floor.

Grimes lit his pipe, estimating ruefully that he had barely enough tobacco left in his pouch for four more smokes. Maggie and Fenella made a sort of ritual of sharing a cigarillo. Shirl and Darleen sniffed disdainfully.

Maggie said, "Now what do we do? We're on the wrong side of this world with no way of getting back to Sparta City. We're wearing clothing that, as soon as the weather warms up, will be horribly uncomfortable and that, in any case, makes us conspicuous. We have no money . . ."

"And I no longer have my watch," Fenella said sourly. "What do we barter next for a crust of bread?"

"We shall have breakfast without any worry," said Shirl. She produced from the pouch in which she was carrying her throwing discs some rather squashed bread rolls and Darleen, from hers, some crumbling cheese. "Before we left the tavern we helped ourselves to what we could . . ."

"That will do for supper," said Grimes.

"There will be no supper," Maggie told him sternly.

She drew deeply on what little remained of the cigarillo, threw the tiny butt into the fire.

"Hold it!" cried Grimes—too late. "I could have used that in my pipe."

"Sorry," she said insincerely.

"We tried smoking once," said Darleen virtuously. "We did not like it. We gave it up."

Grimes grunted wordlessly.

"I'm not a porcophile," announced Fenella.

"What's that?" demanded Shirl.

"A pig-lover, dearie. Normally I've no time for the police, on any world at all. But I really think, that in our circumstances, we should turn ourselves in. After all, we've committed no crime. Oh, there was a killing, I admit—but it was self-defense . . ."

"And the 'borrowing' of a minor war vessel owned by the Interstellar Federation," said Grimes glumly. "A minor war vessel which, unfortunately, we are unable to return to its owners in good order and condition."

"But I was given to understand," persisted Fenella, "that you and Maggie have *carte blanche* in such matters."

"Up to a point," said Grimes. "A medal if things go well, a court martial if they don't. In any case, until things get sorted out—if they ever do—Ellena will be able to hold us in jail on a charge of piracy and even to have us put on trial for the crime. And shot." He was deriving a certain perverse satisfaction from consideration of the legalities. "It could be claimed, of course, that I have been the ringleader insofar as the act of piracy is concerned. Don't forget that I have a past record. But you, Maggie, as a commissioned officer of the Survey Service, could be argued to have become a deserter from the FSS and an accessory before the fact to my crime. Shirl and Darleen are also accessories—and, also deserters from Ellena's own Amazon Guard . . . ."

"And me?" asked Fenella interestedly.

"An accessory before the fact."

"But it would never come to that," said Brasidus. "*I* shall vouch for you."

"Of course you will," said Grimes. "*But* . . . But if your lady wife is really vicious she'll put you on charge as an accessory after the fact."

"Surely she would not," said Brasidus. "After all, she is my wife."

"Throughout history," Fenella reminded him, "quite a few wives have wanted their husbands out of the way."

"But . . ."

"Are you sure that she wouldn't, old friend?" asked Grimes. He sucked audibly on his now empty pipe. "Now, this is the way I see things. We have to get less conspicuous clothing. By stealing. We have to get money. By stealing. Luckily this is a world where plastic money is not yet in common use. In the next town we come to there will be shops—I hope. Clothing shops. And there will be tills in these shops. With money in them. Luckily this is a planet where the vast majority of the population is honest, so breaking in will be easy . . . ."

"A bit of a comedown from space piracy," sneered Fenella.

"I wasn't a pirate," he said automatically. "I was a privateer."

Then he noticed that Shirl and Darleen had risen quietly to their feet and, as they had done so, had pulled their stunguns from their holsters. Shirl squatted by his side, put her mouth to his ear and whispered, "Go on talking. We shall be back in a few minutes."

Then she . . . oozed out of the open door, flattening herself against the frame to minimize her silhouette against the glow of the firelight. Darleen followed suit. Grimes went on talking, loudly so as to drown any queries from the others regarding the mysterious actions of the two New Alicians. He discussed at some length the legalities of privateering while his listeners looked at him with some amazement.

"It is not generally known," he almost shouted, "that the notorious Captain Kidd, who was a privateer, was hanged not for piracy but for murder, the murder of one of his officers . . . ."

"And what the hell has that to do with the price of fish?" screamed Fenella.

Shirl and Darleen came back. They were carrying between them an unconscious body, that of a man in the black leather and steel uniform of the Spartan Police. His arms were secured behind his back by his own belt and his ankles by the lacings of his sandals.

"We heard him coming," said Shirl, "while he was still quite a way off."

Brasidus stared at the man's gray-bearded face.

"I know him," he murmured. "I remember him from the old days, when we were both of us junior corporals . . . ."

"You've done better for yourself than he has," said Fenella.

"Have I? I'm beginning to think that I'd have been better off as a Village Sergeant than what I am now."

The journalist laughed. "You know, Brasidus, you're by no means the first planetary ruler who's said that sort of thing to me."

The Archon laughed too, but ruefully.

"But I," he said, "must be the first one who's really meant it."

ᔕ Chapter 31 ᔕ

THEY SAT AND WAITED for the sergeant—whose name, Brasidus said, was Cadmus—to recover. Although the stunguns carried by Shirl and Darleen had been set to MINIMUM STUN the policeman had received a double dosage when ambushed by the New Alicians, being shot by both of them.

At last the man's eyes opened.

He stared bewilderedly at his captors. He struggled briefly with his bonds but soon realized the futility of it. He looked from face to face, longest of all at Brasidus.

He muttered, "I know *you* . . . ."

"And I know you, Cadmus," said the Archon.

"But . . . . But it can't be . . ."

"But it is."

"Brasidus . . . . Or should I be addressing you as Lord?"

"Brasidus will do. After all, we are old messmates."

"Brasidus . . . . But the news has been that you were kidnapped and that your lady wife has achieved power in your absence from Sparta City . . . And now you are here, in my village, in a strange uniform and in the company of . . . of offworlders. *Women.*"

"They are my friends, Cadmus. They rescued me. But tell me—what are *you* doing here? Is there a police search for us?"

The sergeant laughed. "Not so far as I know. I was checking up on an odd bunch of vagrants who had passed through my village. You were not reported to me officially—the villagers are a close-mouthed lot and regard the Police as an unnecessary nuisance—but I over-heard a few things and saw the innkeeper wearing a *very* expensive watch. I questioned him and he finally told me how he had got it . . . ."

"Did you get it back?" asked Fenella eagerly.

"No. The transaction, as he described it, seemed to be legal enough. But do you think you could untie my wrists? I am very uncomfortable."

There would be no harm in this, thought Grimes. The man had been disarmed by Shirl and Darleen; his stungun was now stuck into Darleen's belt and his scabbarded shortsword was being worn by Shirl. Nonetheless he drew his own pistol and covered the man while Darleen untied his lashings.

"That's better," said the sergeant, rubbing his wrists. Then, to Brasidus, "Thank you, Lord."

"I've told you to call me Brasidus. After all, we're old friends. How much does this friendship mean to you, Cadmus? Could you help us? I promise you that if you do long overdue promotion will follow."

"Don't insult me, Brasidus. I owe you for the way in which you got me out of that mess some years ago . . . Remember? When that little swine—what was his name? Hyperion?—got himself killed resisting arrest, and he turned out to be Captain Nestor's boyfriend . . . . No, Brasidus. I don't want promotion. I *like* being a Village Sergeant. All that I'd ask of you would be that I'd be appointed to a village of my own choice."

"But can you help us, Cadmus? We have to get back to Sparta City as soon as possible. We shall have to travel incognito. We shall need civilian clothing. Money. Transport . . ."

The sergeant laughed. "Let me tell you why I was looking for you. There's an order out that all offworlders, wherever they are, are to be rounded up and put in protective custody. They are to be returned to Sparta City and then put aboard the first outbound ship from Port Sparta. In this area Cythera, downriver from here, is the collection point. Trans-Spartan Airlines have a passenger ship standing by there to carry the offworlders to the spaceport."

"We shall still need clothing," said Grimes. "Something less conspicuous than what we are wearing now. And," he added hopefully, "a few obols spending money. Drinks . . . . Smokes . . . ."

"I have civilian clothing that I rarely use," said Cadmus. "I can fit out you, sir, and Brasidus." He looked the women over and chuckled to himself. "You'll not believe this," he went on, more to Brasidus than the others, "but I had a woman for a while. I wasn't all that sorry when she left me. She married a police lieutenant in Thebes. She left a few rags and I've never thrown them out. I thought they might come in handy some time."

Fenella laughed.

"And when *I* said, Grimes, that we should turn ourselves in to the police you smacked me down, and you had all these marvelous schemes involving breaking and entering and robbing shops . . . But the way it's turned out it's the police who're the only ones who can help us."

"But we didn't go to them," said Grimes. "They came to us."

"What was that about breaking and entering?" demanded Cadmus suspiciously.

"It was only a joke," Brasidus told him. "The lady has a peculiar sense of humor. Meanwhile, you *are* helping us, Cadmus. And you can help us best of all if you tell nobody, nobody at all, that you have found me. In your report to your superiors you will say only that you took charge of a group of six offworlders, two men and four women, and delivered them to the authorities in Cythera."

"It shall be done as you ask," said the sergeant as he undid the lashings about his ankles. He got unsteadily to his feet, assisted by Brasidus. "And now I must get back to my house to find the things that you require. I shall return at dawn, with the hovercar, to take you all to Cythera."

"Perhaps we had better come with you," said Grimes.

"No," said Brasidus, *"no."*

"But . . ."

"Never let it be said," declared the Archon, "that I do not trust my old friends."

The trust was justified.

Before dawn Grimes was awakened by Shirl who, with Darleen, had shared sentry duty during what remained of the night. The New Alician's keen hearing had picked up the whine of ground effect engines while Cadmus was still a long distance off, long before Grimes could hear anything.

He got up from the hard floor, his joints stiff, his muscles aching. He ran a hand over his bristly chin, managed to ungum his eyelids. Shirl and Darleen had kept the fire going so there was light enough for him to see the others—Darleen curled in a fetal position, Maggie on her side, Fenella supine with her mouth open, softly snoring, Brasidus also on his back but as though sleeping at attention.

He would have sold his soul for a mug of steaming coffee or tea but there wasn't even any water. He filled and lit his pipe. He hoped that he would be able to purchase more tobacco in Cythera. He hoped that he would have some money on him to make such a purchase.

He awoke Brasidus, then the others. Only Brasidus—but he was already bearded—and Darleen looked none the worse for wear. Fenella was a mess. Maggie looked at least badly in need of a good hot shower and then a long session with her hairbrushes.

Grimes went outside and watered a tree. Then he stood and watched the approaching headlights of the police hovercar as it made its way down the winding trail. He had his stungun out, just in case. After a while he was joined by the others.

"He is a good man, that Cadmus," said Brasidus.

"Mphm," grunted Grimes.

"I would trust him with my life. More than once in the old days—in the old happy days—I did trust him with my life."

"Hearts and flowers and soft violins," muttered Grimes.

"What do you mean, John?"

"Just a Terran saying."

The hovercar came into view. It was a big vehicle. It sighed as it subsided in its skirts. One man, Cadmus, got out. He raised his right hand in greeting. Brasidus returned the salutation.

Cadmus said, "I have the things you need. If you will change now we can be on the way."

Shirl and Darleen lifted bundles from the rear of the car, carried them back into the hut. There was clothing as promised—rough tunics and heavy sandals for the men, chitons and lighter footwear for the ladies. There was a leather pouch full of clinking coins that Cadmus handed to Brasidus. And—which really endeared the sergeant to the commodore—there was a flagon of thin, sour wine, two dozen crisp rolls, still warm from the village bakery, and thick slices of some unidentifiable pickled meat. It was a far better meal than the bread and cheese which Shirl and Darleen had brought from the tavern would have been. *We should have had that for supper last night, as* I *wished,* thought Grimes.

Munching appreciatively he sat with the sergeant and watched the women changing. (On some worlds such conduct would have been unthinkable but New Sparta had no nudity taboo, any more than did the home planets of Maggie, Fenella, Shirl and Darleen.)

Cadmus jerked a thumb toward the New Alicians.

"Odd-looking wenches, aren't they? But not unattractive. Me— I've always liked a well-fleshed backside . . . ."

Backs to the bulkhead, thought Grimes, *when* you're *around.*

"Where're they from, sir? What is your name, by the way?"

"A world called New Alice," replied Grimes. "And my name is Smith. John Smith."

He got up, shed his own coveralls and boots, got into the tunic and sandals. He started to buckle on the belt with his weapons then thought better of it. Such accessories would look odd, to say the least, if carried by a bunch of stranded tourists.

He said, "You'd better take charge of these, Cadmus. And our coveralls."

The sergeant pulled a laser pistol from its holster, examined it, replaced it, then inspected one of the stunguns. He frowned.

"Both pistols," he said, "with Federation Survey Service markings. The laser with a flat power cell." He picked up a discarded coverall suit. "And a Survey Service heavy duty uniform . . ."

"I promise you," said Brasidus, "that I, personally, will tell you the full story later. But now I can and do tell you that there are things that it is better that you know nothing about."

"I can well believe that, Brasidus. And I think, at the risk of being deemed inhospitable, that the sooner I get you all off my hands, out of my territory, the better."

"We shall enjoy a happier reunion," Brasidus told him, "when things are back to normal."

"What *is* normal?" demanded the sergeant. "Nothing has been normal since that man Grimes came here in his ship all those years ago."

They bundled up the discarded clothing and carried it out to the car, stowing it in the baggage compartment, together with their belts and holstered pistols. The sun was up when they started off, with Brasidus sitting beside Cadmus, who was driving, and Grimes and the others in the rear cabin which was entirely enclosed, being intended for the occasional transport of arrested persons.

"Still," said Fenella, sitting back on the bench and extending her long, elegant legs, "it's better than walking. And now, Grimes, what's the drill when we get to Cythera? And what's the drill when we get back to Sparta City?"

"To begin with," Grimes told her, "my name is not Grimes. It's Smith. John Smith. And you're not Fenella Pruin . . ."

"Oh, all right, all right. I've been Prunella Fenn before."

"And I'm Angela Smith," announced Maggie.

"*Must* we have second names?" asked Shirl plaintively.

"Yes," Grimes told her. "Brown, for both of you. You're sisters."

"But we aren't."

"But you look alike. Shirley Brown and Dorothy Brown."

"Such *ugly* names!"

"But yours for the time being."

"I wish we could see some scenery," complained Maggie.

"If you *will* ride in the Black Maria, dearie," Fenella told her, "you can hardly expect a scenic drive. But go on, Grimes. Sorry. Smith. Tell us what world-shaking plots have merged from your tiny mind."

"I've seen this sort of thing before," said Grimes. "The handling and processing of refugees. The *real* processing won't be until we get to Sparta City. We'll tell the authorities at Cythera that we're a party of tourists who were set upon and robbed. The bandits took everything—money and, more importantly, our papers . . ."

"And your obviously expensive wrist companion," said Fenella, pointing at the device strapped to Grimes' left wrist.

"It will be out of sight in my pocket when we front the authorities," Grimes told her. "As will be Maggie's."

"I wish that my wristwatch had been in that bloody clip joint of an inn," she complained.

"You enjoyed the meal it paid for," Grimes told her.

"I noticed that *you* did," she snarled.

Chapter 32

THEY ARRIVED at Cythera just before noon.

They saw little of the town itself—not that they much wished to—as Cadmus delivered them to the airport on its outskirts. There was a low huddle of administrative buildings. There were mooring masts, at one of which rode a Trans-Spartan dirigible. She was a small ship and a shabby one, her ribs showing through her skin. Grimes, looking up at her, was not impressed and said as much.

Just inside the airport's departure lounge was a desk at which was sitting a bored-looking police lieutenant. Cadmus saluted the officer and announced, "Six Terran tourists from Calmira, sir."

"And just in time, Sergeant. The ship will be embarking passengers in about ten minutes." He looked up at Grimes and his party. "Names? Identification papers?"

"They have no papers, sir," Cadmus told him. "They were robbed."

"You can say that again," muttered Fenella, the loss of whose wristwatch was still rankling.

"I trust that you will apprehend the miscreants responsible, Sergeant," said the officer, indicating by his manner that he could hardly care less.

"Investigations are being made, sir."

"And now, your names."

Grimes rattled these off, the Smiths and the Browns and the others. The lieutenant wrote them down on a form, said, "Thank

417

you, Mr. Smith. And now just wait in the lounge with the other passengers. And that will do, Sergeant. You'd better be getting back to Calmira."

"Sir."

Grimes shook hands with Cadmus.

"Thank you for your help, Sergeant. I shall see to it that the Terran Ambassador knows about what you have done for us."

"It was only my duty, sir."

Brasidus shook hands with Cadmus.

Shirl and Darleen, while the lieutenant looked on disgustedly, flung their arms about him and planted noisy kisses on his cheeks. (They had aimed for his mouth but he managed to turn his head just in time.)

Grimes led the way into the lounge. He had spotted a refreshment stall. ("But they'll feed us aboard the ship . . ." protested Maggie.) As he had hoped, there were smokes of various kinds on sale. He bought a tin of tobacco of an unknown brand, paying for it out of the money provided by Cadmus. Now he could afford to fill his pipe properly from what remained in his pouch. He lit up and surveyed those who were to be his fellow passengers on the flight to Sparta City. There were, he estimated, about sixty of them. There was a group of Waverley citizens, male and female, who had stubbornly refused to go native insofar as apparel was concerned and were clad in colorful kilts in a wide variety of tartans. There were fat ladies from Earth for whom chitons did nothing but to make a desperate attempt to hide their overly abundant nakedness and their skinny husbands, looking, in their skimpy tunics, like underdressed scarecrows. There were the inevitable young people with their rucksacks and short shorts and heavy hiking boots. There were, even, three Shaara, a princess and two drones, surveying the motley throng through their huge, faceted eyes with arthropodal arrogance.

"And how long will it take that gasbag to get us to Sparta City?" asked Fenella.

"Three days is my guess," said Grimes.

"Ugh! In this company!"

The public address system came to life. "All offworlders will now leave the lounge by departure gate three. All offworlders will now leave the lounge by departure gate three. Small hand baggage only."

People began to straggle out from the lounge, along the paved path to the mooring mast, escorted by policemen who tried to hurry things up.

"I'll never come here again for a holiday!" Grimes overheard. "They take our money, then treat us like criminals!"

"But you must make allowances, dear. They're in the middle of the revolution."

"Then why the hell couldn't they have waited to have it when we were safely back home?"

By groups the tourists took the short elevator ride up to the top of the mooring mast, passed through the tubular gangway into the body of the ship. Flight attendants, surly men in shabby uniforms, chivvied them aft into a large cabin. There were rows of seats, of the reclining variety. There was, Grimes realized with a sinking heart, no sleeping accommodation. Obviously this was normally a short-haul passenger carrier pressed into service for the transport of those who were, now, little better than refugees.

Grimes, Brasidus and Maggie shared a bank of three seats on the port side of the cabin. Fenella and Shirl and Darleen sat immediately behind them. The cabin filled up.

No announcement was made when the flight commenced. There was no friendly "This is your captain speaking." There was just a faint vibration as the motors were started and, through the viewport in the ship's skin, the sight of the ground below receding.

Shortly thereafter a meal was served—bowls of greasy stew, stale rolls and muddy coffee. It made a sordid beginning to what was to be a sordid voyage.

Grimes, who was something of an authority on the history of transport, was to say later that it was like a long trip must have been in the Bad Old Days on Earth, during that period when the fuel-guzzling giant airplanes reigned supreme in the skies, before the airship made its long-deferred comeback as a passenger carrier.

There were the inadequate toilet facilities. There was the flavorless food, either too greasy or too dry, or even, both at once. There was the canned music. There were the annoying restrictions surely imposed by some fanatical non-smoker.

"It took absolute genius," he would say, "to reproduce aboard a modern dirigible, the only civilized means of aerial transport, conditions approximating those in Economy Class aboard an intercontinental Jumbo Jet of the late Twentieth Century . . . ."

What made it even worse for him was that he was not used to traveling as a passenger, or as a passenger not accorded control room privileges. As Commodore Grimes he would have spent most of the flight in the ship's nerve center, observing, asking intelligent questions, conversing with the captain and officers. As Mr. Smith he was just one of the herd, livestock to be carted from Point A to Point B and delivered in more or less good order and condition.

It was impossible for him to have proper conversations with his companions, to discuss the course of action once they had disembarked at the Sparta City airport. There were too many around them who could overhear, including the flight attendants. From one of these they managed to obtain some paper and a stylus—the man had to be tipped—on the pretext of playing word games. They passed notes between their two rows of seats, hidden between the sheets of airline stationery upon which there were a sort of crude variation of Scrabble.

They ate, forcing the food down. They slept as well as they could. They listened to the loud—and mostly fully justified—complaints of the other passengers. They made bets on the frequency with which a particularly annoying, tritely sweet melody would come up on the canned music program. And, with the others, they became steadily scruffier and scruffier. The acridity of stale perspiration became the most dominant odor in the cabin's atmosphere. It needed, said Grimes loudly, a strong injection of good, healthy tobacco smoke to purify it.

Their communication by written messages did not produce any worthwhile results. As Grimes said in his final note, after arrival at Sparta City they would just have to play it by ear.

At last, at long, long last, the airship's captain broke his voyage-long silence.

"Attention, all passengers. We are now approaching our mooring at Sparta City Airport. After mooring has been completed you will disembark in an orderly manner and put yourselves into the care of the authorities. That is all."

Grimes stared out through the port. The airship was making a wide sweep over the city. Surely, he thought, it was not usually as dark as this. The winding streets were no more than feeble trickles of sparsely spaced lights. The Acropolis was no longer floodlit. But around the Palace there was glaring illumination. And what were those flashes? Gunfire?

He asked one of the surly flight attendants the local time. It was 0400 hours. When the man was out of sight he took his wrist companion from his pocket and set it. Even though he would not be keeping a written log of events he always liked to know just when whatever was happening was happening.

The city lights fell slowly astern.

The vibration of the motors became less intense, then ceased. Sundry clankings came from forward as the ship was shackled to her mast.

"We're here," said Grimes unnecessarily.

"Thank all the Odd Gods of the Galaxy for that," said Maggie.

~ Chapter 33 ~

AT THE FOOT of the mooring mast there was a small detachment of bored-looking police, obviously resentful at having to be up at this ungodly hour. They herded the disembarking passengers into a lounge where a sullen lieutenant ticked their names off on a list. The only persons at whom he looked at all closely were the three Shaara. They stared him down.

Coffee and little sweet buns were available. It was not the sort of refreshment which Grimes would have ordered had he any choice in the matter, but it was far better than the meals aboard the airship.

Sipping and munching, he stood close to three of the policemen.

"All this extra duty . . ." one was complaining. "And then, on top of it all, we have to be at the bloody Acropolis at ten in the bloody morning for the bloody coronation. If *she* is as bloody popular as she says she is, why does she want *us* to guard her? What's wrong with her own bloody Amazon Guard? Answer me that."

"Politics, Orestes, politics. Wouldn't do, this early, if she showed herself relying too heavily on her own pet tabbies. For all this Queen Hippolyte reincarnation crap she wants to be crowned ruler of all Sparta, not of just one sex. But once she's firmly in the saddle, then we shall see what we shall see."

"What d'ye suppose *did* happen to Brasidus?" asked the third man. "With all his faults, he wasn't a bad bastard."

"Done away with, of course," said the expert on politics. "We'll never see *him* again."

"And more's the pity," muttered the first man.

Grimes drifted away to where the others were seated in a corner of the lounge, close to one of the big sliding windows. There was nobody else within earshot.

"Maggie, your bug detector," he said in a low voice, "It could be safe to talk here, but I want to be sure . . ."

She took the instrument out of her pocket, pressed buttons, watched and listened.

She said, "All right. We can talk."

"To begin with," said Grimes, "Ellena's going to be crowned this morning. Queen of all Sparta. At ten."

"I can't believe that!" growled Brasidus.

"I'm afraid that you have to, old friend. The question is—do you want to stop her?"

"Yes. Yes. After all, she is only a woman."

Fenella's indignant squawk must have been audible all over the airport—but there had already been so many loud complaints from other passengers that it went almost unnoticed.

"*I* am the Archon," went on Brasidus. "Now I am back where I belong. I shall resume my high office without delay."

"Go for broke . . ." muttered Grimes.

"What was that, John?"

"Just a Terran expression. It means . . ." He fumbled for the right words. "It means that you stake everything on a single throw of the dice."

"I like that," said Brasidus. "I like that. And are you with me, John? And you, Maggie?"

"What about asking me?" demanded Fenella.

"And us?" asked Shirl and Darleen.

"Very well. Are you with me? All of you."

"Yes," they all said.

"First of all," said Grimes, "we have to get out of the airport. That shouldn't be difficult. After all, we aren't prisoners. Nobody regards a bunch of offplanet refugees as being potentially dangerous."

"And then we make for the Palace," said Brasidus.

"Do we?" asked Grimes. "With all due respect to your lady wife, Brasidus, I wouldn't trust her as far as I could throw her. And she is not a small woman. The way I see it is this. We go underground for a while until we find out which way the wind is blowing."

"But *you* said 'go for broke,' John. There has to be a confrontation between myself and Ellena. Oh, I should never have married her—I've known that for quite some time—and, however things turn out, I shall not stay married to her for much longer." All the built-up bitterness was coming out in a rush. "There must be a confrontation. A *public* confrontation so that the people can make their own choice between us. At the coronation."

"Mphm," grunted Grimes. *Go for broke,* he thought. *Why not?* If things didn't work out he could get a message out—somehow—to *Sister Sue* and she could come in and lift him and the others off New Sparta. If, that is, they would be, by that time, in any condition to be lifted off. But his luck had held so far. Why should it not hold for a little longer?

As inconspicuously as possible they drifted out of the lounge, first to the toilet facilities. In a cloakroom Shirl and Darleen found a pair of long cloaks that would conceal their not-quite-human bodies from curious eyes. Nobody stopped them when they found a door opening to the outside. The night, what was left of it, was almost windless. The clear sky was ablaze with stars.

Once they were clear of the airport Brasidus—after all, it was his city—led the way. The first part of their long walk was through orchards of some kind; the spicy scent of ripening fruit was heavy in the still air. Then they entered a built-up area. Shirl and Darleen, with their keen hearing, picked up the whine of an approaching hovercar before any of the others. They all found concealment in a side alley until the vehicle—a police patrol chariot?—was past. The next time they had to hide was from a detachment of soldiers on foot. Now and again they heard the rattle of automatic projectile weapons. Once they stumbled—literally—across a dead body, that of a policeman. His pistol holsters, Grimes discovered to his disappointment, were empty.

Then it was dawn and, only a little later, sunrise. People were emerging into the street, unshuttering shop windows. Presumably the coming of daylight signalled the lifting of the curfew.

Brasidus found an inn. Before leading the way into it he checked the remaining contents of the money pouch that Cadmus had given him, said there should be enough for breakfast for all of them. Grimes told him that he would have to do the ordering as he was the only one without a foreign accent. (But there were now so many Spartan citizens recently arrived from other planets that this did not much matter.)

They took seats at a table. They were the only customers. The sullen waitress made it obvious that she resented this disruption of her early morning peace and quiet. There were quite a few items on the blackboard menu that Grimes would have liked—even eggs and bacon!—but the girl told them that the cook was not yet on duty. She produced the inevitable muddy coffee—yesterday's brew, warmed up—and stale rolls.

Other people drifted in.

These were regulars and received better treatment than the strangers had gotten. Their coffee smelled as though it had been freshly made and their rolls looked fresh. The waitress put on a pleasant face and joined in conversations.

"No, I shan't be going to the coronation. Wouldn't go even if I could get time off. That Ellena and her bunch of dykes! But I liked Brasidus. He was a *real* man . . . ."

"They say," contributed a male customer, "that Ellena had him quietly murdered."

"It's time somebody murdered her," muttered his friend.

"Careful," whispered the third man. "You can never tell who's listening these days . . ."

All three of them scowled suspiciously at Grimes and his party.

Brasidus called for the bill. He had enough money to cover it. He paid.

On the way out Grimes heard one of the men ask the girl, "And who were *they*?"

"Dunno. Never seen 'em before. Don't care much if I ever see 'em again."

"Shouldn't mind seein' more o' those wenches," said the first man.

"Probably Amazon Guard officers in civvies," said the second.

"Shut up!" hissed the girl, noticing that Grimes was lingering in the doorway, listening. "Shut up, you fool!"

After their breakfast they had time to spare. They sauntered through the city, playing the part of country cousins enjoying a good gawk. They saw street corner meetings being broken up by police— and noticed that, uncharacteristically, the law officers were using force only when absolutely necessary and then with seeming reluctance. They heard orators, female as well as male, screaming their support for Brasidus and demanding that he return to bring things back under control.

On more than one wall there were slogans crudely daubed.

ELLENA GO HOME! was a common one.

Brasidus laughed bitterly. "That's what I've been thinking for years but I've never said it out loud. Now I am saying it. I promise you—and promise myself—that once I'm back in control Ellena will be shipped back to Earth by the first available vessel. Does that ship of yours have any passenger accommodation, John?"

"No," lied Grimes.

"It doesn't matter. A spare storeroom would be good enough for *her*."

Not aboard my *ship,* thought Grimes.

They dropped into a tavern for wine, using the last of Cadmus' money to pay for it. They mingled with the crowds—women, men, not too many children—who were converging upon the Acropolis. Shirl and Darleen took the lead; they had the ability to flow through and past obstructions like wild animals through dense undergrowth. Even so, it was not all that easy for Grimes and the others to keep up with them. Altercations broke out in their wake as toes were trodden and ribs painfully nudged.

But, eventually, they were standing in the front row, at the foot of the wide marble steps, facing a rank of black-uniformed police, all of whom had their stunguns drawn and ready. The dais at the head of the steps, with the white pillars of the Acropolis as its backdrop, was still empty. To either side of it were the news media cameras, at this moment slowly scanning the crowd.

Trumpets sounded and there was a rhythmic mutter of drums. The cameras turned to cover Ellena's grand entry. She strode majestically to the dais, flanked by high-ranking military officers, both male and female, followed by white-robed Council members. Among these was a tall woman on whose right shoulder rode an owl. Grimes stared at this. It was a real bird. It blinked, shifted its feet, half-lifted its wings.

"The High Priestess of Athena," whispered Brasidus.

The trumpets were silent but the drums maintained a soft throbbing. Ellena stood there, waiting for the applause that was supposed to greet her appearance. She was a majestic enough figure in Amazon Guard uniform, more highly polished bronze than leather. Her plumed helmet added to her already not inconsiderable height. She stood there, frowning.

At last, from somewhere in the crowd, there was an outbreak of cheering and cries of, "Ellena! Ellena!" But there was also some booing. And were the people, wondered Grimes, who were chanting, "Hip, Hip, Hippolyte!" applauding or exercising their derision?

Trumpets blared.

Ellena raised her arms, brought her hands to her shining helmet, lifted it from her head, handed it to an Amazon aide. A white-robed acolyte gave an elaborate crown of golden laurel leaves to the High Priestess, who advanced to stand beside Ellena. Beside her stood one of the councillors, an elderly man, stooped, feeble, with wrinkled face and sparse white hair.

He spoke into a microphone. Despite the amplification his voice was feeble.

"Citizens of Sparta . . . We are gathered together on this great and happy occasion to witness the coronation of our first Queen . . . In accordance with our Law the appointment of the ruler must be by public consent . . . Do any of you gathered here know of any reason why the Lady Ellena should not be crowned Queen of all Sparta?"

"She's a woman, that's why!" yelled somebody.

But Ellena was now seated on the thronelike chair that had been brought for her and the High Priestess, standing behind it, had the golden crown raised in her hands, ready to lower it on to Ellena's head.

"For the second time," quavered the elderly councillor, "do any of you gathered here know of any *valid* reason why the Lady Ellena should not be crowned Queen of all Sparta?"

"We want Brasidus! We want Brasidus!" quite a number of voices were chanting.

"For the third and the last time, do any of you gathered here . . ."

"We want Brasidus! We want Brasidus! We want the Archon! We want the Archon!"

Brasidus cried in a great voice, "I am Brasidus! I am the Archon!"

Freakishly the microphones caught his words, sent them roaring over the crowd. The news media cameras swiveled to cover him. The policemen at the foot of the vast staircase shifted away to the sides as he began his advance to confront his wife.

Ellena was back on her feet, furious, pointing an accusatory hand.

"Guards! Kill this impostor!"

Her own Amazons might well have obeyed but the military personnel in her immediate vicinity were all men. Grimes recognized one of the officers although it was the first time that he had seen him in uniform. It was Paulus.

"Guards!" Ellena was screaming now. "Kill this impostor!"

"Brasidus!" the crowd was roaring. "Brasidus!"

On the platform Ellena was yelling at Paulus. "Shoot him, you useless bastard! Shoot him!"

"But he is the Archon."

"He is an impostor!" She wrestled briefly with the man who had been Brasidus' bodyguard, succeeded in pulling a heavy projectile pistol from the holster at his belt, smote him on the forehead with the barrel, knocking him to the ground. "All right!" she snarled. "If none of you will do the job, *I* will!"

She raised the weapon, holding it in both hands. It was obvious that she knew how to use it.

From the corner of his eye Grimes caught a blur of movement to his right, the glint of sunlight reflected from bright metal. Darleen had pulled one of the deadly sharpened discs from the pouch that she was still carrying. With a snap of her wrist she launched it. When it hit its target Ellena was about to squeeze off her first shot. The report of the pistol was shocking, deafening almost, but where the bullet went nobody ever knew.

Ellena screamed.

And then she was standing there, with blood spouting from her ruined right hand, still clinging to the pistol, still trying to bring it to bear, although it was obvious that those more than half-severed fingers would never be able to pull a trigger until extensive and lengthy repair work had been carried out.

People joined Brasidus in his march up the steps to the platform, some in civilian clothing, some in police and army uniforms. There was scuffling among the assembled dignitaries but no shots were fired. The Amazon Guard officers were doing their best to stand haughtily aloof, striking out, damagingly, only when jostled. Their loyalty, thought Grimes with some bewilderment, was to their Corps, not to Ellena. She must have done something to antagonize them.

(Later, very much later, he was to learn that Ellena intended to lay the blame for her husband's murder on top-ranking Amazon officers, who were to be executed after a mere parody of a trial. Somehow they had discovered this and already had their own plans for Ellena's elimination. But now she was saving them the trouble.)

Ellena had collapsed and was receiving medical attention.

Brasidus had gained access to a microphone. "Fellow citizens! People of Sparta, men and women both! I have returned. Later the full story of my abduction and my rescue by very good friends will be told to you . . . ."

Grimes didn't catch the rest of it.

He had been accosted by a man whom at first he thought was a stranger, a slightly built fellow with a dark complexion, dressed in ill-fitting civilian clothes.

"You bastard! You bloody pirate!" this person sputtered. "What did you do with my ship?"

"It's a long story," said Grimes at last. "But I'll see to it that you get her back, Lieutenant Gupta."

~ Chapter 34 ~

AND GRIMES got his own ship back when, at last, *Sister Sue* dropped down to Port Sparta. He got his name back on to the Register as Master and Billy Williams, surprisingly cheerfully, reverted to his old rank as Chief Officer, saying, "Now you can have all the worries again, Skipper."

And worries there were.

Discharge of cargo had just begun when a strongly worded request—it was more of an order, really—came from Admiral Damien by Carlotti deep space radio. This was that Grimes handle the salvage of *Krait*. He had done this sort of job before, back on Botany Bay, and the courier was a very small ship and *Sister Sue* had plenty of power and, even with most of her cargo still on board, could have lifted *Krait* bodily. As it was, throughout the operation the courier's stern remained in contact with the ground. And then she had to be stayed off so that she was safely stable while Grimes's engineers made repairs to her engines.

One consolation was that as Grimes, officially, was no longer connected with the Survey Service he would be able to put in a large bill for the services of himself and his ship.

And now his Earthbound cargo was almost loaded and, very soon, *Sister Sue* would be secured for space.

Maggie sat with Grimes in his day room.

"And so," she said, "our ways part again."

"It was good while it lasted," he said.

"Yes."

"You could resign your commission," he told her, "and enter my employ."

"You resigned yours, John, but they pressganged you back into servitude. And my orders are that I must remain on New Sparta until the situation has stabilized. And . . . . And you must have noticed how things are now between Brasidus and myself."

"How could I not have noticed?"

"But you must understand, my dear, that it's all part of the job. My job. He must be taught that all women aren't like Ellena . . . ."

"Is that all?"

"No. I admire Brasidus. I'm sorry for him. And, if you must know, I love him in my fashion. But as soon as I have him back on an even keel—and as soon as this planet's back on an even keel—I shall be on my way. I've no doubt that Damien will find another job for me."

"To judge from my own experience of the old bastard, no doubt at all. But what a can of worms this one turned out to be!"

"And now that the chief worm has been removed the others should quiet down. But what a cunning bitch she was! Playing both ends against the middle. *Both* ends? I still have to find out just how many ends there were. And if it hadn't been for her plans to purge the high command of her own Amazon Guard she might still have pulled it off."

"How *did* Colonel what's-her-name find out what was in store for her?"

"You and I, John, were by no means the only intelligence operatives on New Sparta, although we were the only Survey Service ones. I had my contacts."

"You might have told me."

"The less you knew," she said, "the better."

"Mphm."

"Cheer up. You've got your ship back. Thanks to me you won't be getting Ellena as a passenger. I persuaded Brasidus that a dangerous woman such as her should be sent back to Earth in a warship, where she can be kept under guard. The destroyer *Rigel* will have the pleasure of her company. As you know, she's due in a couple of days after you lift off."

"I thought for a while that I might have the dubious pleasure of Fenella's company."

"She decided that there are still stories to be had on New Sparta. Too, she's set her sights on Brasidus." She laughed. "I might even let her have him. Who better to retail the scandalous gossip of a palace than one who's the subject of such gossip herself?"

"Mphm," grunted Grimes again. *Brasidus,* he thought a little jealously, *was doing very nicely for himself, getting his hairy paws onto all of Grimes's women . . . .*

There was a knock at the door.

"Enter!" called Grimes.

The door opened. Billy Williams stood there.

"Secured for space save for the after airlock, Skipper," he reported. "The two passengers, with their gear, have just boarded."

"*Passengers,* Mr. Williams?"

"I thought you knew, sir. A lady officer from the Palace, an Amazon major, came out with them and told me that everything had been arranged."

Two familiar forms appeared in the doorway behind the Chief Officer.

"Hi!" said Shirl (or was it Darleen?).

"Hi!" said Darleen (or was it Shirl?).

Maggie got to her feet, then bent to kiss Grimes as he still sat in his chair.

"See you," she said. "Somewhere, somewhen."

Billy Williams left with her to escort her to the airlock.

"Aren't you pleased to see us?" asked the two New Alicians as one.

Grimes supposed that he was.

THE
WILD
ONES

~ Chapter 1 ~

SISTER SUE, John Grimes commanding, had made a relatively uneventful voyage from New Sparta to Earth and was now berthed at Port Woomera. But nobody seemed to be in a hurry to take delivery of her cargo, a quite large consignment of the spices for which New Sparta had become famous among Terran gourmets. This didn't worry Grimes much. His ship, of which he was owner as well as master, was on time charter to the Interstellar Transport Commission and until her holds were empty she would remain on pay. What did worry Grimes was that the charter had expired and that the Commission had indicated it might not be renewed. Another cause for worry was that Billy Williams, his chief officer for many years and, for quite a while, during the term of Grimes's appointment as governor for Liberia, relieving master, was taking a long overdue spell of planet leave, returning to his home world, Austral. With him had gone the Purser/Catering Officer Magda Granadu, leaving Grimes with a shipful of comparative strangers, young men and women who had not been among her complement when he had first commissioned her. So he had to find a replacement for Magda and one for Billy Williams. The second officer, young Kershaw, was, in Grimes's opinion, too inexperienced a spaceman for promotion. It would be many years before he would be capable of acting as a reliable second in command.

Meanwhile Grimes had no option but to hang around the ship

like a bad smell. Until he had seen which ways the many cats were going to jump he could not afford to leave her in the fumbling hands of young Kershaw. And he wanted, badly, to get away himself for at least a few days, to revisit his parents' home in Alice Springs. The old man was getting on now, although still churning out his historical novels. And his mother, Matilda, although one of those apparently ageless women, blessed at birth with a good bone structure, would be wanting to hear a firsthand account of her son's adventures as governor of Liberia and then on New Sparta.

He was beginning to wonder if he should make the not-too-long walk from the commercial spaceport to the Survey Service Base, there to pay a courtesy call on Rear Admiral Damien. Even though not many people knew that Grimes was back in the Service with the rank of captain on the reserve list, everybody knew that he was an ex-Survey Service regular officer and that at one stage of his career his superior had been Damien, then Commodore Damien, who had been Officer Commanding Couriers at the Lindisfarne Base. (But it was also common knowledge that young Grimes, as a courier captain, had been Damien's bête noir.)

Still, Damien owed him something. He had acted as the Rear Admiral's cat's paw during the El Doradan piracy affair, and on Liberia and, most recently, on New Sparta. The Survey Service pulled heavy Gs with the Interstellar Transport Commission. If Damien dropped a few hints in the right quarters the Commission would either renew the New Sparta time charter or find some other lucrative employment for *Sister Sue*.

So, after a not very satisfactory breakfast—the temporary, in-port-duties-only catering officer thought it beneath her dignity to cater to the captain's personal tastes and could murder even so simple a dish as eggs and bacon—Grimes got dressed in his best uniform, his own uniform with the Far Traveler Couriers cap badge and crested buttons. Then he sent for the second officer.

He said, "I shall be going ashore for a while, Mr. Kershaw. Should anything crop up I shall be with Rear Admiral Damien, at the Base."

The lanky, sullen young man with the overly long hair asked,

"Is there any word, sir, about a replacement for Mr. Williams? After all, I'm doing chief officer's duties and only getting second's pay . . ."

I'm doing the chief officer's duties, thought Grimes indignantly. But he said, "The Astronauts' Guild have the matter in hand. As you know, I require Master Astronaut's qualifications for my chief officer. Unluckily you have only a First Mate's certificate."

Kershaw flushed. He knew that Grimes knew that he had already sat twice for his Master's ticket and failed dismally each time. He decided to drop the subject.

"When will you be back, sir?"

"That all depends upon the Rear Admiral. He might invite me to lunch, although that's unlikely. Or I might run into some old shipmates at the Base."

"It's a pity that you ever left the Service, sir," almost sneered Kershaw.

"Isn't it?" said Grimes cheerfully.

He walked down the ramp from the after airlock, puffing his foul pipe. The morning was fine although, with a southerly breeze straight from the Antarctic, quite cool. There were only a few ships in port—two of the Commission's Epsilon Class tramps (*Sister Sue* had started her working life as one such), a somewhat larger Dog Star Line freighter and, gleaming like a huge, metallic skep in the bright sunlight, some of the bee people who were her crew flying lazily about her, a Shaara vessel. (*Those bastards are getting everywhere these days,* thought Grimes disapprovingly. Once he had quite liked the Shaara but various events had caused him to change his attitude.)

All these ships, he saw, were working cargo. They all had gainful employment. His *Sister Sue* did not.

He identified himself to the marine guard at the main gate to the Base, was admitted without question. (Fame, or notoriety, had its advantages.) He looked with rather wistful interest at the Survey Service ships in their berths. There were two Serpent Class couriers, the so-called "flying darning needles." Grimes's first command— how many years ago?—had been one of these little ships. There was

A. Bertram Chandler

a Star Class destroyer. There was a cartographic ship, similar to *Discovery*, the mutiny aboard which vessel had been the main cause of his somewhat hasty resignation from the Survey Service.

But he hadn't come here to take a leisurely stroll down memory lane. He had come here to confront Rear Admiral Damien, to make a more or less formal request that this gentleman use his influence to obtain further employment, preferably another time charter, for *Sister Sue*. After all he, Grimes, was useful to the Survey Service even though very few people knew that he was back in their employ. And surely a willing—well, for some of the time—laborer was worthy of his hire.

He approached the main office block, passed another marine sentry. He went to the receptionist's desk where a smart little female ensign was on duty. The girl looked at him curiously, noting the details of his uniform. Obviously she was not one of those who knew Grimes by name and reputation. But she was young, young. There may have been giants in those days, the days when Grimes himself was young, but this pert wench would never have heard of them. (Yet. But legends persist and, almost certainly, there would be those on the Base who would be happy to regale her with all sorts of tales, true, half-true and untrue, about that notorious misfit John Grimes.)

"Sir?" she asked politely.

"Could I see Admiral Damien, please?"

"Is he expecting you, sir?"

"No. But he'll see me."

"Whom shall I say is calling?"

"John Grimes. Captain John Grimes."

"Wait, please, Captain Grimes."

She pressed buttons and the little screen of her telephone console came alive. Grimes shifted position so he could look over the ensign's shoulder. He saw Damien's face—that prominent nose, the thin lips, the yellowish skin stretched taut over sharp bones— take form. *Old Skull Face* never changes, he thought. And Damien could see him in his own screen, standing behind the girl. There was a flicker of recognition in the cold, gray eyes.

"Admiral, sir," said the girl, "there is a . . ."

"I know, Ms. Pemberthy. There is a Captain Grimes to see me. Or a Commodore Grimes. Or His ex-Excellency ex-Governor Grimes . . . All right, Grimes. I was wondering when you would condescend to come and see me. You know where I live. I'm still in the office where you were debriefed after you came in from New Sparta—when was it, now? Three months ago?—and now you're back from New Sparta again. But you won't be going back there for quite a while, if ever . . . . As you know full well I always keep my finger on the pulse of things." Then, to the girl, "That's all, Ms. Pemberthy. Captain Grimes can find his own way up. He has only to follow the signs. Even Blind Freddy and his dog could do that much."

The screen went blank.

The girl turned to stare at Grimes.

"The admiral seems to know you, sir. But what is your rank, captain or commodore? And are you an Excellency?"

"I was," Grimes told her. "And I was, at one time, commodore of a squadron of privateers . . . "

"Privateers, sir? Aren't they some sort of pirates?"

"No," Grimes told her firmly.

∽ Chapter 2 ∾

DAMIEN DID GRIMES the honor of getting up from behind his huge desk, walking around the massive piece of furniture and advancing on Grimes with bony right hand outstretched. Grimes did Damien the honor of saluting quite smartly before shaking hands with the rear admiral. Damien motioned Grimes to a quite comfortable armchair before resuming his own seat. He put his elbows on the surface of the desk, made a steeple of the skeletal fingers of both hands and resting his chin upon the apex, looked intently at the younger man.

"Well, young Grimes," he said at last, "what can I do you for?"

"I do not think," replied Grimes, "that that was an unintentional slip of the tongue."

"Too right it wasn't. Nonetheless I may be in a position to do something for you."

"At a price, no doubt, Sir. How many pounds of flesh, or is it just my soul you're after?"

"Grimes, Grimes . . . . This uppity attitude does not become you. And I would remind you that you hold a Survey Service commission, albeit on the Reserve List. You are subject to Service discipline—and, when you are recalled to active duty, are entitled to the full pay and allowances for your rank in addition to the quite—indeed overly—generous retaining fee of which you are already in receipt."

Grimes's prominent ears reddened but he kept his temper. After all he had the services of himself and his ship to sell—and this was a buyer's market. He could not afford to antagonize Damien.

"And now, Grimes, what exactly are your current troubles?"

"Well, sir, I was hoping that the Interstellar Transport Commission would renew or extend my time charter on the Earth/New Sparta run. After all, my ship has given very good service on that trade . . . ."

"But not with you in command of her, Grimes, until recently. As far as New Sparta is concerned you're too much of a catalyst. Things have a habit of happening around you rather than to you . . . ."

"Mphm!" grunted Grimes indignantly.

"I wish that you'd break yourself of that disgusting habit," said Damien. "I've told you before that I do not expect naval officers to make noises like refugees from a pig sty. But, to revert to New Sparta, it will be better for all concerned if things are allowed to settle down. Your boozing pal Brasidus is doing quite well now that he no longer has Queen Ellena to stick her tits into everything. Our Commander Lazenby is maintaining a watching brief, as I am sure that you know. You and she are old friends, aren't you? And that obnoxious news hen Fenella Pruin has taken flight to some other planet to do her muckraking. . . ."

"So you persuaded the Commission not to *renew* the charter," said Grimes.

"Hinted, just hinted. And I also hinted that there was no need to bust a gut to get your inward cargo discharged. Until it's out you're still on hire. And money, I need hardly remind you, is money. . . ."

"Thank you, sir. And I wonder if you'd mind hinting to the Astronauts' Guild that I have a vacancy for a chief officer, one with some experience and with a master's ticket. Come to that, I also want a new catering officer. . . ."

"Don't get your knickers in a twist, Grimes. You'll be getting your new chief officer shortly. One of our people, needless to say.

And a very good catering officer. And . . ." A sardonic grin appeared briefly on Damien's face.

"And what? Or whom?"

"You remember Shirl and Darleen, the two young ladies whom you brought to Earth, as passengers, from New Sparta. . . ."

"How could I forget them?"

"Like that, was it?"

Again Grimes's prominent ears flushed angrily.

He said, "So it was you who arranged for their passage, in my ship, from New Sparta to Earth. Oh, well, as long as you pay their fares again I'll carry them to anywhere else you wish."

"You're a mercenary bastard, Grimes, aren't you? But we shall not be paying their fares. They will not be paying their fares. On the contrary, you'll be paying them. Wages, at the award rate."

"What?"

"You heard me, Grimes. After all, merchant vessels quite often carry officer cadets."

"Who have had the required pre-Space training at some recognized academy. And I'm sure that there's no such an academy on New Alice."

"There's not. But there are such things as STS—Straight To Space—cadets."

Grimes, who since he had become a merchant spaceman had made a study of all the regulations that could possibly affect him, ransacked his memory.

He said, "But Shirl and Darleen just aren't qualified in any possible way. Aboard a spaceship they'd be completely unskilled personnel."

"But with qualifications, Grimes." He opened one of the folders on his desk, began to read from it. " 'Any person who has held commissioned rank in the armed forces of any federated planet, wishing to embark upon a new career in the Merchant Service, may serve the qualifying time for the lowest grade of certificate of competency in any merchant vessels, with the rank and pay of officer cadet.'"

"But . . . Commissioned rank?" asked Grimes.

Then he realized that Damien was right. New Sparta was a federated planet. Ellena's Amazon Guard had been part of the armed forces of that planet. Shirl and Darleen had held commissions—as officer instructors, but commissions nonetheless—in that body.

"Too," said Damien, grinning again, "both young ladies are now Probationary Ensigns, Special Branch, in the Federation Survey Service Reserve. Of course, their reserve commissions are as secret as yours is. But when I got the first reports, by Carlottigram, from Commander Lazenby about what was happening on New Sparta I decided that I, that we could make use of the special skills and talents of those New Alicians. After all, you did. On Venusberg first of all, then on New Sparta . . . ."

"And your Special Branch," grumbled Grimes, "is one sprouting many strange fruits and flowers."

"Well said. You have the soul of a poet, young Grimes. Anyhow when, in the fullness of time, your *Sister Sue* lifts off you will have, on your Articles, in addition to your normal complement, officer cadets Shirl Kelly and Darleen Byrne . . . "

"Kelly and Byrne?"

"Why not? I explained to the young ladies that they would have to adopt surnames and told them that Kelly and Byrnes are both names associated with Australian history."

"But they were bushrangers, sir."

"Don't be snobbish, Grimes. After all, you've been a pirate yourself."

"A privateer," snapped Grimes. "And acting under your secret orders."

"Which included, at the finish, committing an act of real piracy. But enough of this quibbling. Tomorrow a Mr. Steerforth will be reporting to you as your new chief officer. He will be on loan from the Interstellar Transport Commission. He is also a lieutenant commander in the Survey Service Reserve. He is a capable and experienced officer. Give him a day to settle in and then you'll be free to inflict yourself on your parents in Alice Springs for three weeks. It will be all of that before anybody gets around to discharge your cargo and before your next charter has been arranged."

"Thank you, sir. But can you tell me anything about the next charter? Time, or voyage? Where to?"

"Not yet. Oh, would you mind taking Shirl and Darleen with you to the Alice? They want to see something of inland Australia and you'd make a good guide. I'm sure that your parents wouldn't mind putting up a couple of guests."

His father wouldn't, Grimes thought, but regarding his mother he was far from certain. Even so he was looking forward to seeing Shirl and Darleen again.

Chapter 3

AS PROMISED, Mr. Steerforth reported on board shortly after breakfast the following morning. He was tall, blond, deeply tanned, with regular features, startling blue eyes and what seemed to be slightly too many gleaming white teeth. Grimes couldn't be sure, at short acquaintance, whether he liked him or not. He was too much the big ship officer, with too obvious a parade of efficiency. His predecessor, Billy Williams, had been out of the Dog Star Line whose vessels, at their very best, were no more than glorified tramps. (But Williams had always got things done, in his own way, and done well.)

"My gear's on board, sir," said Steerforth briskly. "If it's all right with you I'll nip across to the shipping office and get myself signed on. And then, perhaps, you might introduce me to the other officers, after which you can give me any special instructions. I understand that you are wanting to catch the late afternoon flight to Alice Springs."

"I suppose that the admiral has already given you your instructions," grumbled Grimes.

"The admiral, sir?"

"Come off it, Mr. Steerforth. You know who I mean. Rear Admiral Damien. You're one of his boys."

"If you say so, sir."

"I've said it. All right, go and get your name on the Articles.

447

You should be back in time for morning coffee, when I'll introduce you to the rest of the crowd in the wardroom."

"Very good, sir."

Grimes's next callers were Shirl and Darleen. They knew the ship, of course, having traveled in her, as passengers, from New Sparta to Earth. Certainly they were familiar enough with Grimes's own quarters . . . .

"Hi, John," said Shirl (or was it Darleen?).

"Hi, John," said Darleen (or was it Shirl?).

Had the girls been unclothed Grimes could have told them apart; there were certain minor skin blemishes. But now, dressed as they were in shorts (very short shorts) and shirt outfits they were as alike as two peas in a pod. The odd jointure of their legs was not concealed by their scanty lower garments, their thighs looked powerful (as they were in fact). Wide smiles redeemed the rather long faces under the short brown hair from mere pleasant plainness.

"The Bureau of Colonial Affairs has been looking after us really well," said one of the girls, "but it is good to be back aboard your ship again. The old crocodile has told us that we are to be part of your crew."

The old crocodile? wondered Grimes, then realized that this must be yet another nickname for Admiral Damien.

"He has already made us officers," said Shirl. (Grimes remembered that her voice was very slightly higher than that of Darleen.) "In the Survey Service. But it is supposed to be a secret, although he said that you would know."

"I do," said Grimes.

"And now we are to be officers aboard your ship," Darleen told him unnecessarily.

"And you are to show us the inland of this country of yours, from which our ancestors came. We have seen kangaroos in the zoo in Adelaide, of course, but we have yet to see them in the wild, where they belong. "

"Where we belong," said Darleen, a little wistfully. "You know, John, I have often thought that that genetic engineer, all those hundreds of years ago, did the wrong thing when he changed our ancestors . . . ."

"If he hadn't changed them," pointed out Shirl, "we shouldn't be here now."

"I suppose not." Darleen's face lit up with a smile. "And it is good being here, with John."

"Mphm," grunted Grimes.

The three of them caught the afternoon flight from Woomera to Alice Springs.

Grimes loved dirigibles, and a flight by airship in charming company was an enjoyable experience. He had a few words with an attentive stewardess, scribbled a few words on the back of one of his business cards for her to take to the captain and, shortly thereafter, he and the two New Alicians were ushered into the control cab. The girls stared out through the wide windows at the sunburned landscape flowing astern beneath them, with the greenery around irrigation lakes and ditches in vivid contrast to the dark browns of the more normal landscape, peered through borrowed binoculars at the occasional racing emu, exclaimed with delight as they spotted a mob of kangaroos. But the shadows cast by rocks and hillocks were lengthening as the sun sagged down to the horizon. Soon there would be nothing to see but the scattered lights of villages and townships.

"This must seem a very slow means of transport to you, Captain," said the airship's master. "After all, when you're used to exceeding the speed of light . . ."

"But not with scenery like this to look at, Captain," said Grimes.

"The two young ladies seem to be appreciating it," said the airshipman. "They're not Terran, are they?"

"No, although their ancestors were both Terran and Australian. They're from a world called New Alice."

"The name rings no bell. Would it be one of the lost colonies?"

"Yes."

"I saw a piece on trivi about Morrowvia a few months ago. . . . The world of the cat people. . . . If I ever save enough for an offplanet holiday I might go there. Say, wasn't it you who discovered, or rediscovered, that Lost Colony?"

"Not exactly. But I was there during the period when it was decided that the Morrowvians were legally human."

The airship captain lowered his voice. "And these young ladies with you . . . . From New Alice, you say. Would they be the end result of some nutty experiment by some round-the-bend genetic engineer?"

Shirl and Darleen possessed abnormal, by human standards, hearing. They turned as one away from the window to face the airshipman. They smiled sweetly.

"Yes, captain," said Shirl. "Although we are legally human our ancestors were not, as yours are, monkeys."

If the captain was embarrassed he did not show it. He looked them up and down in a manner that suggested that he was mentally undressing them. He grinned at them cheerfully.

"Tie me kangaroo down, sport," he chuckled. "I shouldn't mind gettin' the chance to tie you down!"

"You could try," said Darleen slowly.

"And it could be the last thing you ever did try," said Shirl.

They were still smiling, the pair of them, but Grimes knew that it was more of a vicious baring of teeth than anything else.

The airshipman broke the tense silence.

"Excuse me, ladies. Excuse me, Captain. I'd better start thinkin' about gettin' the old girl to her mooring mast at the Alice." He addressed his first officer. "Mr. Cleary, confirm our ETA with airport control, will you? Ask 'em about conditions—surface wind and all the rest of it . . . ."

Why tell me to do what I always do? said Cleary's expression as plainly as spoken words.

"Shall we get out of your way now, Captain?" asked Grimes.

"Oh, no, Captain. Just keep well aft in the cab." He managed a laugh. "Who knows? You might learn something."

But it wasn't the airshipman's day. He bumbled his first approach to mast, slid past it with only millimeters of clearance. He had to bring his ship around to make a second try. He blamed a sudden shift of wind for the initial bungle but he knew—and Grimes knew—that it was nothing of the kind. It was no more and no less than the result of an attempt to impress a hostile female audience.

~ Chapter 4 ~

GRIMES'S PARENTS were waiting in the lounge at the base of the mooring mast. His mother embraced him, his father took his hand and grasped it warmly between both of his. Then Grimes introduced the two girls. He realized that he could not remember which one had been given Kelly as a surname and which one was Byrne. Why the hell, he asked himself, couldn't Damien have had them entered in the books as sisters? As twin sisters, even. They looked enough alike. (Some little time later he raised this point with the two New Alicians. "But the admiral is very thorough, John," Darleen told him. "To put us down as being related would have made nonsense of his files. It was explained to us. It is all a matter of blood groups and such . . . .")

The older people did, as a matter of fact, look rather puzzled when Shirl and Darleen were introduced. But they asked no questions and, in any case, the Grimes household was one in which the use of given names was the rule rather than the exception.

Baggage was collected and then the party boarded the family hover-car. Grimes senior took the road in a direction away from the city, deviated from this on to what was little more than a rough track, heading toward what the old man called his private oasis. By now it was quite dark and overhead the black sky was ablaze with stars. In the spreading beam of the headlights green eyes gleamed with reflected radiance from the low brush on either side of the track. For a while an old man kangaroo bounded ahead of the vehicle until, at last, it collected its wits and broke away to the right, out of the path of the car.

The lights came on in the house as the hover-car approached. His father was still doing well, thought the spaceman, could still afford all the latest in robotic home help. The wide drive, dull-gleaming permaplast bordered with ornamental shrubs, had been swept clear of the dust that here, in the Red Center, got everywhere. Ahead, the wide door of the big garage slid up and open. The old man reduced speed at the very last moment and slid smoothly into the brilliantly lit interior. Gently sighing, the vehicle subsided in its skirts.

Grimes senior was first out of the car. Gallantly he assisted the ladies to alight—not that any of them needed his aid—leaving his son to cope with the baggage. A door slid open in one of the side walls. In it stood a woman—a transparent woman? No, not a woman. A robot in human female form, with what appeared to be delicate, beautifully fashioned, gleaming clockwork innards, some of the fragile-seeming wheels spinning rapidly, others with a barely perceptible movement.

"Come in," said this obviously hellishly expensive automaton. "This is Liberty Hall. You can spit on the mat and call the cat a bastard."

"Cor stiffen the bleeding crows!" said Grimes.

Matilda Grimes laughed without much humour. "Just one of George's latest toys," she said. "It came programmed with a standard vocabulary but he added to it."

"Too right," said the robot in a pleasant contralto.

"*I* like her," maintained George Whitley Grimes.

"You would," his wife told him.

Meanwhile it—she?—advanced on Grimes, arms extended. What was he supposed to do? he wondered. Shake hands? Throw his own arms about the thing in a stepbrotherly embrace?

"Let her have the bags, John," said his father.

It took them from him, managing them with contemptuous ease, led the way into the house. The workings of the machinery in her hips and legs was fascinatingly obvious. It was like, in a way, one of those beautiful antique clocks that spend their working lives in glass domes. And what would it be like, he wondered, to make love to an eight-day clock? *Down, boy, down*! he snarled mentally at his, at times kinky, libido.

They sat in the big, comfortable lounge, Shirl and Darleen in very deep armchairs that caused them to make a display of their long, long legs. Grimes noticed that his father's eyes kept straying toward the two New Alicians. Perhaps, he thought, it was no more than biological curiosity. Those amply displayed lower limbs were not quite human. Or perhaps the old man was betraying another sort of biological interest. Grimes could not blame him. Like son, like father . . . .

"Shirl," asked Matilda Grimes sweetly. "Darleen . . . Aren't you chilly? Wouldn't you like to put on something warmer?"

"It is quite all right, Matilda," said Shirl. "We often wear less than this. John can tell you. . . ."

His mother looked at him coldly and said, "You never change much, do you? I remember when you were only twelve, when we were living in that old house in Flynn Street, and you appointed yourself secretary of the Flynn Street Nudist Club which held its meetings by the pool in our backyard . . . As I recall it, you were the only male member."

"And I had to shift my workroom to the front of the house," said George Whitley Grimes. "The view from the back windows was too distracting."

"And *I*," said Matilda, "had to cope with an irate committee of local mothers who had discovered how their little bitches of daughters were spending their afternoons . . ."

"And *I*," said George, "had to stay away from the pub for fear of being beaten up by the fathers of those same little bitches."

Shirl and Darleen laughed.

"You Earthpeople, as we are discovering, have such odd ways of looking at things," said one of them.

"Not all of us," said Grimes senior. "And not any of us for all of the time."

The robutler rolled in with the pre-dinner drinks. It was an even bigger and more elaborate model than the one that had been in service at the time of Grimes's last visit to the parental home, reminding him of a suit of mechanized battle armor built to accommodate at least three Federation Marines simultaneously. With it came the house robot that Grimes was now thinking of as Clockwork Kitty. Like its predecessor the robutler took spoken orders and, in its capacious interior, seemed to hold a stock of every alcoholic drink known to civilized man—and, quite possibly, a few that weren't. There were ice cubes, spa water and fruit cordials. There was a fine selection of little eats.

As the various orders were extruded on trays they were deftly removed by Clockwork Kitty and handed to the correct recipients. Bowls of nuts and dishes of tiny savories were placed on convenient low tables.

George Whitley Grimes raised his condensation-misted glass of beer to his son and said, "Here's to crime!"

The two girls, who also were drinking beer, raised their glasses. Grimes raised his glass of pink gin. Matilda Grimes set her sherry down firmly on the table.

"That," she stated, "is a dangerous toast to be drinking in the presence of this son of mine. I still have not forgotten that court of inquiry into the piracy with which he was involved. We have yet to hear, from his lips, the full story of what happened when he was Governor of Liberia—but I have little doubt that there were more than a few illegalities . . . ."

"Not committed by me, Matilda," Grimes told her. "Don't forget that I was the Law, trying to put a stop to other people's illegal profits."

"Hah!" his mother snorted. "Oh, well, you weren't impeached. I suppose that we must thank the Odd Gods of the Galaxy for small mercies. But we have yet to hear about what really happened on New Sparta . . . ."

"You shall, my dear, you shall." He laughed. "Oh, I was guilty of one crime. I did 'borrow' a Survey Service courier . . . ."

"And you crashed it," said Darleen a little maliciously.

"It was the fault of the weather," said Grimes.

Matilda laughed. "All right, all right. And I suppose that you still hold that reserve commission in the Survey Service that's supposed to be such a secret and get sent hither and yon to do that man Damien's dirty work for him." She looked long and hard at Shirl and Darleen. "And am I right in assuming that the pair of you are also members of the good admiral's department of dirty tricks?"

The girls looked inquiringly at Grimes. He decided that he had better answer for them.

"If you must know—but keep it strictly to yourself—Shirl and Darleen are both probationary ensigns in the Service."

"And what is their specialty?" asked Matilda.

"Unarmed combat," Grimes told her. "Or combat with anything handy, and preferably sharp, that can be flung. Such as . . ."

Shirl picked up a shallow, round dish that was now empty. She turned it over so that its convexity was on the down side. With a sharp flick of her wrist she threw it from her. It circled the room, returned to her waiting hand.

"Flying saucers yet!" said Grimes's father.

After a second drink they went in to the dinner that was served by the efficient Clockwork Kitty. With the first course there was some slight embarrassment. It was Grimes's fault, of course. (But just about everything was.) He should have told his mother that the ancestors of the New Alicians had been kangaroos. Even though these people were now classed as human and, like true humans descended from the original killer ape, omnivorous, they refused kangaroo tail soup, once they learned what it was. But they had strong stomachs and enjoyed the excellent crown roast of lamb once they had been assured that it was of ovine origin.

Grimes himself managed a good dinner despite the fact that he was talking most of the time. He had not been able to visit his parents on the first occasion of his return to Earth from Liberia, via New Sparta. A very thorough debriefing had occupied practically all of his time. So now there were questions to be answered, stories to be told. He was still answering questions and telling stories when the party returned to the lounge for coffee and brandy. Grimes and his father smoked their pipes, Matilda cigarillo and Shirl and Darleen—they were picking up bad habits—cigarettes in long, elegant, bejeweled holders.

Finally Darleen seemed to be having trouble stifling a yawn. It was infectious. George said, "I don't know about you people, but I'm turning in." Darleen said, "If you do not mind, Matilda, we shall do so too."

Matilda grinned. "Not with my old man, you won't! The maid will show you to your rooms."

Clockwork Kitty led them away, leaving Grimes alone with his mother.

She smiled at him a little sadly. She said, "I need hardly ask you, John, need I? But, just to satisfy my curiosity, which one is it?"

Grimes was frank.

"Both of them," he said.

"What! Not both at once?"

As a matter of fact this had been known but Grimes's mother was, in some ways, rather prudish. And, apart from anything else, there was the matter of miscegenation. The old prejudice against the underpeople still lingered.

"Shirl," lied Grimes.

"I really don't know how you can tell one from the other. Well, John, you're a big boy now, a four-ring captain and a shipowner, and you've been a planetary governor . . . And commodore of a pirate squadron," she added maliciously. "You're old enough and wicked enough to look after yourself. And the girls' rooms are next to yours in the west wing.

"But I do wish that you would find some nice, human girl and settle down. Isn't it time?"

"I'll get around to it eventually," he promised her.

He kissed her good night then made his way to his quarters. The double bed, he saw, was already occupied. By Shirl.

And Darleen.

≈ Chapter 5 ≈

"WAKEY, WAKEY!" caroled an annoyingly cheerful female voice. There was a subdued clatter as the tea tray was placed on the bedside table. Morning sunlight flooded the room as curtains were drawn back. "Rise and shine! Rise and shine for the Black Ball Line!"

Grimes unglued his eyelids and looked up at Clockwork Kitty as she stood over the tousled bed, the rays of the sun glitteringly reflected from the intricacy of moving clockwork under her transparent integument. (But those delicate wheels, on their jeweled pivots, were no more than decoration, an expensive camouflage for the real machinery of metal skeleton and powerful solenoids.) Somehow her vaguely oriental features, which possessed a limited mobility, managed to register disapproval. Although Shirl and Darleen had returned to their own rooms before dawn, it was obvious, from the state of the bed, that Grimes had not slept alone.

He blinked. Yes, that faint sneer was still there. A trick of the light? Just how intelligent was this robomaid? Oh, he was thinking of Clockwork Kitty as she—but spacemen are apt to think of almost any piece of mobile machinery as she. Just another example of his father's sense of humor, he decided. The old man had added certain expressions to her programming, just as he had added to her vocabulary. An historical novelist with a keen interest in maritime history would, of course, know the words of quite a few of the old sea chanteys, such as "rise and shine for the Black Ball Line"...

"Milk, sir? Sugar?"

The automaton poured and stirred efficiently, putting the milk and sugar into the cup first. (And that, remembered Grimes, was something that his mother always insisted on.)

"Thank you, Kitty," he said. (It cost nothing to be polite to robots, intelligent or not. And when one wasn't quite sure of a robot's actual intelligence it was better to play it safe.)

"Kitty, sir?"

"My name for you. When I first saw you I thought of you as 'Clockwork Kitty.'"

"The master's name for me," said the robomaid, "is Seiko. I was manufactured by the Seiko Corporation in Japan, the makers of this planet's finest household robots. Prior to our highly successful venture into the field of robotics we were, and indeed still are, the makers of this planet's finest timepieces. Robomaids such as myself are a memorial, as it were, to the Corporation's origins . . ."

"Yes, yes," Grimes interrupted hastily. What was coming out now was some of the original programming, a high-powered advertising spiel. "Very interesting, Kitty—sorry, Seiko. But I'd rather be getting showered, depilated and all the rest of it. What time is breakfast?"

"If you will make your order, sir, it will be ready shortly after you appear in the breakfast room."

"Surprise me," said Grimes.

He looked thoughtfully after the glittering figure as it moved silently and gracefully out of the room.

Grimes senior, who was a breakfast table conservative, tucked in to a large plate of fried eggs, bacon, sausages and country fried potatoes. Matilda toyed with a croissant and strawberry conserve. Shirl and Darleen seemed to be enjoying helpings of kedgeree. And for Grimes, after he had finished his half-grapefruit, Seiko produced one of his favorite dishes, and one that he had not enjoyed for quite a long time. The plump kippers, served with a side plate of thickly cut new brown bread and butter, tasted as good as they looked.

Matilda, he decided, must have told Seiko what he would like.

He commented on this. She, looking surprised, said that she had given no orders whatsoever regarding her son's meal.

So . . . A lucky guess? Do robots guess? But Seiko was absent in the kitchen so he could not make further inquiries until she returned to clear the table. And when she did so the humans were busy discussing the day's activities.

George Grimes said, "I'm afraid that I shall have to leave you young people to your own resources today. I've a deadline to meet. The trouble with the novel I'm working on now is that I'm having to work on it. It's just not writing itself."

"Why not, George?" asked Grimes.

"Because it's set in a period of Australian history that, somehow, makes no great appeal to me. Eureka Stockade and all that. I somehow can't empathize with any of the characters. And, although it's regarded by rather too many historians as a minor revolution that might have blown up into something larger, it was nothing of the kind. It was no more than a squalid squabble between tax evaders and tax collectors. But I got a handsome advance before I started writing it, so I'd better deliver on time."

"And I have to stay in today myself," said Matilda. "I've got the ladies of the Alice Springs Literary Society coming round for lunch. I'm afraid that you'd find them as boring as all hell—as I do myself, frankly. So why not take the car, John, and a packed midday meal, and just cruise around? I'd suggest Ayers Rock and the Olgas, but at this time of the year they're infested with tourists. But the desert itself is always fascinating."

And so it was that, an hour later, Grimes, Shirl and Darleen were speeding away from the low, rambling house, heading out over the almost featureless desert, the great plume of fine, red dust raised by the vehicle's fans swirling in their wake.

Grimes gave Ayers Rock and Mount Olga a wide berth—the one squatting on the horizon like a huge, red toad, the other looking like some domed city erected on an airless planet. Over each hovered a sizeable fleet of tourist dirigibles. Grimes could imagine what conditions would be like on the ground—the souvenir stalls, the refreshment stands, the canned music, the milling crowds. Some time he would have to visit the Rock and the Olgas again, but not today.

He came to the Uluru Irrigation Canal. He did not cross it but followed its course south. The artificial waterway was poorly maintained; the agricultural project that it had been designed to service had been cancelled, largely due to pressure by the conservationists. But water still flowed sluggishly in the ditch and, here and there along its length, were billabongs, one of which Grimes had known very well in his youth. It would be good, he hoped, to visit it again.

And there were the tall ghost gums standing around and among the waterworn rocks that some civil engineer with the soul of a landscape gardener had brought in, probably at great expense, to make the artificial pool look natural. And there was the water, inviting, surprisingly clear, its surface dotted here and there with floating blossoms. These were not of Terran origin but were, as a matter of fact, Grimes's own contribution to the amenities of this pleasant oasis, carnivorous plants, insectivores, from Caribbea. The billabong was free from mosquitoes and other such pests. (He recalled that some businessman had wanted to import these flowers in quantity but the conservationists had screamed about upsetting the balance of nature.)

He stopped the car just short of the ornamental bounders. He and the girls got out, walked to the steeply shelving beach of red sand. He said, "How about a swim?"

"Crocodiles?" asked Shirl dubiously.

"There weren't any last time I was here."

"When was that?" asked Darleen.

"Oh, about five Earth years ago."

He got out of his shirt, shorts and underthings, kicked off his sandals. As one the girls peeled the white T-shirts from the upper parts of their tanned bodies, stepped out of their netherwear. Naked, long-legged and small-breasted, they seemed to belong to this landscape, more than did Grimes himself. They waded out into the deeper water. Grimes followed them. The temperature of the sun-warmed pool was pleasant. They played like overgrown children with a beach ball that some family party had left on the sand. (So other people had found his private billabong, thought Grimes. He hoped that they had enjoyed it as much as he was doing now.) They decorated each other's bodies with the gaudy water lilies, the tendrils of which clung harmlessly to their wet skins. Finally they emerged from the water and stretched themselves to dry off on the surface of a large, flat rock which was partially shielded from the harsh sunlight by the ghost gums.

Then Grimes felt hungry. He got to his feet and walked to the hover-car, taking from it the hamper that had been packed by Seiko. The sandwiches were to his taste—ham with plenty of mustard, a variety of strong cheeses—and the girls enjoyed the sweet and savory pastries and the fresh fruits. The cans of beer, from their own special container, were nicely chilled.

Replete, Grimes got his pipe and tobacco from his clothing and indulged in a satisfying smoke. The New Alicians sat on either side of him in oddly prim postures, their legs tucked under them.

Grimes was feeling poetic.

"'Give me a book of verses 'neath the bough,'" he quoted,

"'A loaf of bread, a flask of wine, and thou,

"'Beside me, singing in the wilderness . . .

"'And wilderness were Paradise enow.'"

He laughed. "But I don't have a book of verses. And, come to that, I've never heard either of you singing. . . ."

"There is a time to sing. . . ." murmured Shirl. "And this could be such a time. . . ."

And Darleen had found two large, smooth pebbles, about the size of golf balls, and was clicking them together with an odd, compelling rhythm. Both girls were crooning softly to the beat of the singing stones. There was melody, of a sort, soft and hypnotic. Grimes felt the goose pimples rising all over his skin.

They were not alone. He and the girls were not alone. Silently the kangaroos had come from what had seemed to be empty desert, were standing all around them, regarding them solemnly with their huge eyes. There were big reds and grays and smaller animals. It was as though every variety of kangaroo in all of Australia had answered the New Alicians' summons.

Shirl and Darleen got to their feet. And then, suddenly, they were gone, bounding away over the desert at the head of the mob of kangaroos. It was hard to distinguish them from the animals despite their smooth skins.

What now? wondered Grimes. *What now?* He was, he supposed, responsible for the girls. Should he get into the hover-car and give chase? Or would that make matters worse? He stood and watched the cloud of red dust, raised by the myriad bounding feet, diminishing in the distance.

But they were coming back, just the two of them, just Shirl and Darleen. They were running gracefully, not proceeding in a series of bounds. They flung themselves on Grimes, their sweaty, dusty bodies hot against his bare skin. It was rape, although the man was a willing enough victim. They had him, both of them, in turn, again and again.

Finally, exhausted, they rolled off him.

"After the kangaroos . . ." gasped Shirl.

"We had to prove to ourselves . . ." continued Darleen.

" . . . and to you . . ."

" . . . that we are really human . . ."

Grimes found his pipe, which, miraculously, had not been broken during the assault, and his pouch, the contents of which were unspilled. He lit up with a not very steady hand.

"Of course you're human," he said at last. "The Law says so."

"But the heritage is strong, John."

"You aren't the only ones with a heritage—but you don't see me swinging from the branches of trees, do you?"

They all laughed then, and shared the last can of beer, and had a last refreshing swim in the waters of the billabong. They resumed their clothing and got back into the hover-car, looking forward to an enjoyable evening of good food and conversation to add the finishing touches to what had been a very enjoyable day.

They were not expecting to find the Grimes home knee deep in acrimony.

～ Chapter 6 ～

THE GARAGE DOOR slid open as the hover-car approached but the robomaid was not waiting to receive them and to take custody of the empty hamper. Grimes was not concerned about this; no doubt, he thought, Seiko was busy with some domestic task. He led the two girls into the house, toward the lounge. He heard the voices of his mother and father, although it was his mother who seemed to be doing most of the talking. She sounded as though she were in what her husband and son referred to as one of her flaring rages. *What's the old man been up to now?* wondered Grimes.

"Either that *thing* goes or I go!" he heard his mother declare.

"But I find her more satisfactory . . ." his father said.

"You would. You've a warped mind, George Grimes, as I've known, to my cost, for years. But you'll ship that toy of yours back to Tokyo and demand your money back . . ."

"Hi, folks," said Grimes as he entered the room.

Matilda favored him with no more than a glance, his father looked toward him appealingly.

"John," he said, "perhaps you can talk some sense into your mother. You, as a space captain of long experience, know far more about such matters than either of us . . . ."

"What matters?" asked Grimes.

"You may well ask," Matilda told him. "Such matters as insubordination, mutiny. In my own home . . . ."

"Insubordination? Mutiny?" repeated Grimes in a puzzled voice.

"And unprovoked assault upon my guests. My guests."

Grimes sat down, pulled his pipe from his pocket, filled and lit it. Shirl and Darleen did not take seats but looked questioningly at Matilda, who said, "Perhaps, dears, it might be better if you went to your rooms for a while. This is a family matter."

The girls left, albeit with reluctance. Grimes settled down in his chair and assumed a magisterial pose. George Grimes was sitting on the edge of his seat, looking as uncomfortable as he almost certainly was feeling.

"I have had my suspicions for a long time . . ." began Matilda.

Surely not . . . wondered Grimes. The old man's not that kinky . . .

"Quite a long time," she went on. "But it was only after you and the girls had left this morning for your ride in the desert that I began to be sure. I hope that you had a pleasant day, by the way . . . ."

"Very pleasant," said Grimes.

"Well, you remember what you had for breakfast. Kippers. You asked me if I'd told it to do them for you. I said that I had not. I was curious, so I asked it why it had served you kippers. It told me that you had asked it to surprise you. So I asked it how it had decided that kippers would be a nice surprise. It told me that normally there are never kippers in my larder but that I had ordered a supply after I'd gotten word that you were coming . . . ."

"And so?" asked Grimes.

"A domestic robot is supposed to do only what it's been programmed to do. It's not supposed to possess such qualities as initiative and imagination. Oh, I know that there are some truly intelligent robots—but such are very, very expensive and are not to be found doing menial jobs. But knowing George, I suspected that he had been doing some more tinkering with its programming. His idea of a joke.

"Well, as you already know, I was entertaining the local literary ladies to luncheon. The President of the Society is Dame Mabel Prendergast. Don't ask me how she got made a dame, although she's made an enormous pile of money writing slush. She could afford to buy a title. Anyhow, dear Mabel is just back from a galactic cruise. She was all tarted up in obviously expensive clothing in the very worst of taste that she had purchased on the various worlds that she had visited. Her hat, she told us, came from Carinthia, where glass-weaving is one of the esteemed arts and crafts. Oh, my dear, it was a most elaborate construction, perched on top of her head like a sort of glittering fairy castle. It was, in its way, beautiful—but not on her. Human hippopotami should not wear such things.

"We had lunch. *It* did the serving, just as a robomaid should, efficiently and without any gratuitous displays of initiative, imagination or whatever. The ladies admired *it* and Mabel remarked, rather jealously, that George's thud-and-blunder books, as she referred to them, must be doing quite well. We retired to the lounge for coffee and brandy and then one or two of the old biddies started making inquiries about my famous son. You. And wasn't it time that you settled down? And who were the two pretty girls you'd brought with you? They weren't Terran, were they?

"I told them—all the more fool me, but I suppose that the brandy had loosened my tongue—that Shirl and Darleen were from a world called New Alice, with a very Australianoid culture. I told them, too, that they were now junior officers aboard your ship and that, until recently, they had been officers in the elite Amazon Guard on New Sparta. Mabel said that they didn't look butch military types. I said that, as a matter of fact, they had been officer instructors, specializing in teaching the use of throwing weapons, such as boomerangs. And that they could make almost anything behave like a boomerang. Mabel said that she didn't think that this was possible. I told her that Shirl—or was it Darleen?—had given a demonstration in this very room, using a round, shallow dish . . .

"Mabel said, quite flatly, that this would be quite impossible and started blathering about the laws of aerodynamics. She had, she assured us, made a thorough study of these before writing her latest book, about a handsome young professional hang glider racer and a lady trapeze artiste. . . ."

"Did they . . . er . . . mate in midair?" asked Grimes interestedly.

"Your mind is as low as your father's," Matilda told him crossly.

"Anyhow, there was this argument. And *it*—may its clockwork heart rust solid!—decided, very kindly, to settle it for us. It asked, very politely, "May I demonstrate, madam?" and before I could say no it emptied the chocolate mints out of their dish, on to the table, turned the dish upside down and with a flick of its wrist sent it sailing around the room . . .

"Oh, it did actually come back—but just out of reach of that uppity robot's outstretched hand. It crashed into Dame Mabel's hat. That hat, it seems, was so constructed as to be proof against all normal stresses and strains but there must have been all sorts of tensions locked up in its strands. When the dish—it was one of those copper ones—hit it there was an explosion, with glass splinters and powder flying in all directions. By some miracle nobody was seriously hurt, although old Tanitha Evans got a rather bad cut and Lola Lee got powdered glass in her right eye. I had to send for Dr. Namatjira—and you know what he charges for house calls. And, of course, I shall have to pay for Dame Mabel's hat. Anybody would think that the bloody thing was made of diamonds!"

"And where is Seiko now?" asked Grimes.

"Seiko? *It*, you mean. It is back in the crate that it came in, and there it stays. It's too dangerous to be allowed to run around loose."

"She was only trying to be helpful," said Grimes.

"It's not its job to try to be helpful. It's its job to do as it's told, just that and nothing more."

"What do you know about the so-called wild robots, John?" asked his father suddenly.

"Not much. The roboticists are rather close-mouthed about such matters. Even the Survey Service does not have access to all the information it should. Oh, there are standing orders to deal with such cases. They boil down to Deactivate At Once And Return To Maker or, if deactivation is not practicable, Destroy By Any Means Possible."

"Just what I've been telling George," said Matilda smugly.

"But from your experience, which is much greater than mine, how would you define a wild robot?" asked George.

"Mphm," grunted Grimes. "Well, there are robots, not necessarily humanoid, which are designed to be intelligent and which acquire very real characters. There was Big Sister, the computer-pilot of the Baroness Michelle d'Estang's space-yacht. There was a Mr. Adam, with whom I tangled, many, many years ago when I was a Survey Service courier captain. There have been others. All of them were designed to be rational, thinking beings. But a normal pilot-computer is no more than an automatic pilot. It does no more than what it's been programmed to. If some emergency crops up that has not been included in its programming it just sits on its metaphorical backside and does nothing."

"But the rogue robots," persisted George. "The wild robots . . . ."

"I don't know. But among spacemen there are all sorts of theories. One is that there has been some slight error made during the manufacture of the . . . the brain. May as well call it that. Some undetectable defect in a microchip. A defect that really isn't a defect at all, since it achieves a result that would be hellishly expensive if done on purpose. Another theory is that exposure to radiation is the cause. And there's one really farfetched one—association with humans of more than average intelligence and creativity."

"I like that," said George.

"You would, Herr Doktor Frankenstein," sneered Matilda. "But, from what I've told you, do you think that we've a wild robot on our hands, John?"

"It seems like it," said Grimes.

The next morning the carriers came to remove the crate into which Seiko had been packed. Grimes went with his father into the storeroom, watched with some regret as the spidery stowbot picked up the long, coffinlike box and carried it out to the waiting hover-van. He thought nothing of it when George ran out to the vehicle before it departed, to exchange a few words with the driver and, it seemed, to resecure the label on the crate, which must have come loose. George rejoined his son.

"Well," he said, "that's that. Luckily Matilda's a good cook; like you, she can get the best out of an autochef. You and the girls won't starve for the remainder of your stay here."

Nor did they.

∽ Chapter 7 ∽

THE DAYS PASSED quickly. George Whitley Grimes had gotten over his sulks about being deprived of his glittering toy and Matilda Grimes had forgiven her husband for the damage done by Seiko. The two girls fitted into the family life well. "They're much too nice for you, John," his mother told him one morning over coffee. The two of them had gone into Alice Springs on a shopping expedition and were enjoying refreshment in one of the better cafes. (George was still working on his Eureka Stockade novel and Shirl and Darleen had gone off to practice with the traditional boomerangs that they had been given by Dr. Namatjira, whose calls now were social rather than professional.)

"They're much too nice, for you," she said. "And I'm not at all sure that I approve of their traveling in your ship as crew members, among all those brutal and licentious spacemen."

"And spacewomen." He laughed. "My third officer is Tomoko Suzuki, a real Japanese doll . . . ."

"Not like Seiko, I hope."

"No. Her innards aren't on display. And my radio officer is Cleo Jones, black and beautiful. Her nickname, of which she's rather proud, is the Zulu Princess. The second Mannschenn Drive engineer is Sarah Smith. One of those tall, slim, handsome academic females. Three of the inertial/reaction drive engineers, the chief, second and fourth, are women. The chief's name is Florence Scott. She looks like what she is, an extremely competent mechanic, and her sex somehow doesn't register. The second is Juanita Garcia. If you were casting an amateur production of Carmen you'd try to get her for the title role. She has the voice as well as the looks. The fourth is Cassandra Perkins. Like Cleo, she's a negress. But she's short and plump and very jolly, so much so that she gets away with things that anybody else would be hauled over the coals for . . . ."

"Such as . . . ?"

"Such as the time when she was doing some minor repairs to the ship's plumbing system and bungled some fantastic cross-connection so that the hot water taps ran ice water."

"That might have been intentional. Her idea of a joke."

"If it was, the laugh was on her. She was the first victim. She thought that she'd like a nice, hot shower after she came off watch at midnight, ship's time. Her screams woke all hands." Grimes sipped his coffee and then went on philosophically. "With all her faults, she's a good shipmate. She's fun. Even old Flo, her chief, admits it. What none of us can tolerate is somebody who's highly inefficient *and* a bad shipmate."

"And the other way around?" Matilda asked. "Somebody who's highly efficient but a bad shipmate?"

Grimes sighed. "One just has to suffer such people. My new chief officer seems to be one such. Lieutenant Commander Harald Steerforth, Survey Service Reserve. Harald, with an 'a' Steerforth. The last of the vikings. Give him a blond beard to match his hair and a horned helmet and he'd look the part. And he's indicated that, as my second in command, he intends to run a taut ship . . ."

"My nose fair bleeds for you," said Matilda inelegantly. "But you haven't mentioned your catering officer yet. Aren't spaceship catering officers almost invariably women?"

"They are. But when I left Port Woomera I still hadn't got a replacement for Magda, who's on leave."

"You should have asked your father for Seiko, and signed it—I refuse to call that thing her—on."

Shopping done—mainly pieces of Aboriginal artwork as gifts for Shirl and Darleen—Grimes and his mother returned home.

When George heard them enter the house he came out from his study and said, "There was a call for you, John. From your ship. Your chief officer, a Mr. Steerforth. He seemed rather annoyed to learn that you hadn't been sitting hunched over the phone all day and every day waiting for him to get in touch." He gave his son a slip of paper. "He asked me—no, damn it, he practically ordered me— to ask you to call him at this number."

The number Grimes recognized. It was the one that had been allocated to his ship at Port Woomera.

"And I shall be greatly obliged," said the old man, "if you will reverse charges."

"Don't be a tightwad, George!" admonished Matilda.

"I'm not a tightwad. This is obviously ship's business. John is a wealthy shipowner; I'm only a poor, struggling writer. And after I've paid for Dame Mabel's hat I shall be even poorer!"

"It was your absurdly expensive mechanical toy that destroyed the hat!"

Grimes left them to it, went to the extention telephone in his bedroom. He got through without trouble, telling the roboperator to charge the call to his business credit card account. The screen came alive and the pretty face of Tomoko Suzuki appeared. She smiled as she saw Grimes in the screen at her end and said brightly, "Ah, Captain-san . . . ."

"Yes, it's me, Tomoko-san. Can you get Mr. Steerforth for me, please?"

"One moment, Captain-san."

In a remarkably short space of time Tomoko's face in the screen was replaced by that of the chief officer.

"Sir!" said that gentleman smartly.

"Yes, Mr. Steerforth?" asked Grimes.

"Discharge has commenced, sir. I have been informed by Admiral Damien that the Survey Service wishes to charter the ship for a one-way voyage to Pleth, with a cargo of stores and equipment for the sub-base on that planet. He wishes to discuss with you details of further employment and intimated that your return to Woomera as soon as possible will be appreciated . . . ."

Not only appreciated by Damien, thought Grimes, but necessary. He had his living to earn.

He said, "I shall return by the first flight tomorrow. Meanwhile, how are things aboard the ship?"

"We have a new catering officer, sir. A Ms. Melinda Clay. She appears to be quite competent. There is some mail for you, of course. I have opened the business letters and, in accordance with your instructions, dealt with such matters, small accounts and such, as came within my provenance as second in command. Personal correspondence has been untouched."

"Thank you, Mr. Steerforth. I shall see you early tomorrow afternoon."

He hung up, rejoined his parents in the lounge.

"My holiday's over," he announced regretfully. "It was far too short."

"It certainly has been," said Matilda.

"And where are you off to this time, John?" asked his father.

"Pleth. A one-voyage charter. Survey Service stores. Probably a full load of forms to be filled out in quintuplicate."

"And after that? Back to Earth with a full load of similar forms filled in?"

"I don't know, George. The mate told me that Damien has some further employment in mind for me."

"No more privateering?" asked the old man a little wistfully. "No more appointments as governor general?"

"I hope not," Grimes told him. "But, knowing Damien, and knowing something of the huge number of pies that he has a finger in, I suspect that it will be something . . . interesting."

"And disreputable, no doubt," snapped Matilda. "When you were a regular officer in the Service you never used to get into all these scrapes."

"Mphm?" grunted Grimes dubiously. He'd been getting into scrapes for as long as he could remember.

Shirl and Alice came in, accompanied by Dr. Namatjira. The doctor, who had joined them at their boomerang practice, was glowing with admiration. "If only I had a time machine!" he exclaimed. "If only I could send them back to the early days of my people in this country, before the white man came! They could have instructed us in the martial arts, especially those involved with the use of flung missiles." He grinned whitely. "Captain Cook, and all those who followed him, would have been driven back into the sea!"

"I might just use that," murmured Grimes senior. "It sounds much more fun that what I'm doing now. That boring Peter Lalor and his bunch of drunken roughnecks. . . ."

Matilda served afternoon tea. After this the doctor said his farewells and made his departure. He expressed the sincere hope that he would be meeting Shirl and Darleen again in the not too distant future.

"Bring them back, John," he admonished. "They belong here. They are like beings from our Dream Time, spirits made flesh . . ."

And then there was what would be the last family dinner for quite some time, with talk lasting long into the night. It would have lasted much longer but Grimes and the girls had an early morning flight to catch.

~ Chapter 8 ~

IT WAS A PLEASANT enough flight back to Port Woomera. Again Grimes, and with him the two girls, were guests in the airship's control cab. On this occasion, however, the captain, a different one, did not say anything to antagonize his privileged passengers. The three of them made their way from the airport to the spaceport by monorail and then by robocab to the ship.

The efficient Mr. Steerforth was waiting by the ramp as the cab pulled up, saluted with Survey Service big ship smartness as his captain got out. He said, "Leave your baggage, sir, I'll have it brought up." He followed Grimes into the after airlock, but not before he had ordered sharply, "Ms. Kelly, Ms. Byrne, look after the master's gear, will you?"

Grimes heard a not quite suppressed animal growl from either Shirl or Darleen and with an effort managed not to laugh aloud. Well, he thought, the two New Alicians would have to start learning that, as cadets, they were the lowest form of life aboard *Sister Sue* . . . .

He and the chief officer took the elevator up to the captain's flat. He let himself into his day cabin, thinking that, much as he had enjoyed the break, it was good to be back. But had somebody been interfering with the layout of the furniture? Had something been added?

Something had—a long case, standing on end.

Steerforth saw him looking at it and said, "This came for you, sir. Special delivery, from Alice Springs. Probably something you purchased there, sir, too heavy and cumbersome to carry with you on your flight."

"Probably," said Grimes. "But I'll catch up with my mail, Mr. Steerforth, before I unpack it. I'll yell for you as soon as I'm through."

"Very good, sir."

His curiosity unsatisfied, Steerforth left the cabin. He said to Shirl and Darleen, who were about to enter with Grimes's baggage, "Report to me as soon as the captain's finished with you."

Shirl said, "I liked Billy Williams."

Darleen said, "So did I."

Grimes said, "Billy Williams earned his long service leave. And try to remember, young ladies, that when you knew Billy Williams you were passengers in this ship, and privileged. Now you are very junior officers and Mr. Steerforth is a senior officer, my second in command. Meanwhile, I still have a job for you. To help me unpack this."

Like most spacemen he always carried on his person a multi-purpose implement that was called, for some forgotten reason, a Swiss Army Knife. (Once Grimes had asked his father about it and had been told that there was, a long time ago, a Swiss Army and that a special pocketknife had been invented for the use of its officers, incorporating a variety of tools, so that they would never lack the means to open a bottle of wine or beer.)

Anyhow, Grimes's pocket tool chest had a suitable screwdriver. He used it while Shirl and Darleen held the long box steady. At last he had all the securing screws out of the lid and gently pried it away from the body of the case, put it to one side on the deck. And then there was the foam plastic packing to be dealt with. He knew what he would find as he pulled it away.

She stood there in her box, her transparent skin glistening, the ornamental complexity of shining wheels on their jeweled pivots motionless. And he stood there looking at her, hesitant. He knew the simple procedure for activation—but should he?

Why not?

He inserted the index finger of his right hand into her navel, pressed. He heard the sharp click. He saw the transparent eyelids— a rather absurd refinement!—open and a faint flicker of light in the curiously blank eyes. He saw the wheels of the spurious clockwork mechanism begin to turn, some slowly, some spinning rapidly. There was a barely audible ticking.

The lips moved and . . . .

"Hello, sailor," said Seiko seductively.

"Mphm," grunted Grimes. Then, gesturing toward the litter of foam packing, "Get this mess cleaned up."

Shirl and Darleen laughed.

"Now there's somebody else to do the fetching and carrying!" said one of them.

Grimes dealt with his mail while Seiko busied herself with what Grimes thought was quite unnecessary dusting and polishing. There was a letter from his father, written before Grimes had left the family home to return to his ship. *I don't like the idea of returning Seiko to the makers*, the old man had written. *They'd take her apart to find out what went wrong—or went right—and when they put her together again she'd be no more than just another brainless robomaid with no more intelligence than a social insect. And she would, of course, lose her personality. I'm hoping that you'll be able to use her aboard your ship, as your personal servant. . . .*

Then there was a brief note from Admiral Damien, inviting him—or ordering him—to dinner in the admiral's own dining room that evening.

He was interrupted briefly by his new catering officer, Melinda Clay. He looked up at her approvingly. She was a tall woman, of the same race as Cleo Jones, the radio officer, and Cassandra Perkins, the fourth RD engineer. She was at least as beautiful as Cleo, although in a different way. The hair of her head was snowy white, in vivid contrast to the flawless black skin of her face. Natural or artificial? Grimes wondered.

"I came up, sir," she said, "to introduce myself . . . ."

"I'm very happy to have you aboard, Ms. Clay," said Grimes, extending his hand.

She shook it, then went on, "And to find out, before the voyage starts, if you have any special preferences in the way of food and drink. That way I can include such items in my stores."

"Unluckily," laughed Grimes, "my very special preferences are also very expensive—and as owner, as well as master, I should have to foot the bill. Just stock up normally. And I'm quite omnivorous. As long as the food is good, I'll eat it. . . ."

Seiko came out of the bathroom, where she had been giving the shower fittings a thorough polishing.

Melinda's eyes widened. "What a lovely robot! I didn't know that you carried your own robomaid."

"I didn't know myself until I unpacked her. She's a gift, from my father."

"*She*? But of course, sir. You could hardly call such a beautiful thing it."

"Seiko," said Grimes, "this is Ms. Clay, my catering officer. When you are not looking after me—and I do not require much looking after—you will act as her assistant."

"Your father's last instructions to me, sir," said Seiko, "were that I was to be your personal servant."

"And my instructions to you," said Grimes firmly, "are that you are to consider yourself a member of the domestic staff of this vessel. Your immediate superior is Ms. Clay."

"Yes, Massa."

"Seiko, you are not supposed to have a sense of humor."

Melinda Clay laughed. "Don't be so serious, Captain! I'm sure that Seiko and I will get on very well."

A slave and the descendant of slaves . . . thought Grimes wryly.

✍ Chapter 9 ✍

DAMIEN HAD ANOTHER DINNER GUEST, a tall, severely black-clad, gray-haired woman, with classic perfect features, who was introduced to Grimes as Madam Duvalier, First Secretary of the Aboriginal Protection Society. Grimes had already heard of this body, although it was of quite recent origin. It had been described in an editorial in *The Ship Operators' Journal,* to which publication Grimes subscribed, as an organization of trendy do-gooders obstructing honest commercial progress. And there had been cases, Grimes knew, where the APS had done much more harm than good. Their campaign on behalf of the down-trodden Droogh, for example. . . . The Droogh were one of the two sentient races inhabiting a world called Tarabel, an Earth-type planet. They were a sluggish, reptilian people, living in filth, literally, because they liked it, practicing cannibalism as a means of population control, fanatically worshipping a deity called The Great Worm who could be dissuaded from destroying the Universe only by regular, bloody sacrifices of any lifeform unlucky enough to fall into Droogh clutches. The other sentient race on Tarabel had been the Marmura, vaguely simian, although six-limbed beings. It was with them that the first Terran traders had dealt, taking in exchange for manufactured goods, including firearms, bales of tanned Droogh hides. It was learned later—too late—that, at first, these hides had been the leftovers from the Droogh cannibal feasts. A little later many of the hides had come from Droogh who had been killed, by machinegun fire, when mounting unprovoked attacks on Marmuran villages, the purpose of which had been to obtain raw material for blood sacrifices to The Great Worm.

Somebody in the Walk Proud Shoe Factory just outside New York had become curious about obvious bullet holes in Droogh hides and had gone to the trouble of getting information about Tarabel and had learned that the Droogh were sentient beings. Then APS had gotten into the act. A SAVE THE DROOGH! campaign was mounted. Pressure was exerted upon the Bureau of Extraterrestrial Affairs. A Survey Service cruiser was dispatched to Tarabel, not to investigate (which would have made sense) but to disarm the Marmura. This was done, although not without loss of life on both sides. Then the cruiser was called away on some urgent business elsewhere in the Galaxy.

The next ship to make planetfall on Tarabel was a Dog Star Line tramp. Her captain did not get the expected consignment of Droogh hides—and, in any case, there weren't any Marmura for him to trade with. In the ruins of the small town near the primitive spaceport were several Droogh. These tried to interest him in a few bales of badly tanned, stinking Marmura skins. He was not interested and got upstairs in a hurry before things turned really nasty.

And the Droogh were left to their own, thoroughly unpleasant, devices.

Grimes remembered this story while he, the admiral and Madame Duvalier were sipping their drinks and chatting before dinner. Somehow the conversation got around to the problem of primitive aborigines introduced to modern technology, of how much interference with native cultures was justifiable.

"There was the Tarabel affair . . ." said Grimes.

The woman laughed ruefully.

"Yes," she admitted. "There was the Tarabel "affair." She extended a slim foot shod in dull-gleaming, grained, very dark blue leather. "You will note, Captain, that I have no qualms about wearing shoes made of Droogh hide. I know, now, that the late owner of the skin was either butchered by his or her own people for a cannibal feast or shot, in self-defense, by the Marmura. We, at APS, should have been sure of our facts before we mounted our crusade in behalf of the Droogh.

"But tell me—and please be frank—what do you really think of people like ourselves? Those who are referred to, often as not, as interfering do-gooders . . . ."

Rear Admiral Damien laughed, a rare display of merriment, so uninhibited that the miniature medals on the left breast of his mess jacket tinkled.

"Young Grimes, Yvonne," he finally chuckled, "is the do-gooder of all do-gooders, although I've no doubt that he'll hate me for pinning that label on him. He's always on the side of the angels but, at the same time, contrives to make some sort of profit for himself."

Madame Duvalier permitted herself a faint smile. "But you still haven't answered my question, Captain. What do you think of do-gooders? *Organized* do-gooders, such as APS?"

"Mphm." Grimes took a large sip from his pink gin, then gained more time by refilling and lighting his pipe. "Mphm. Well, one trouble with do-gooders is that they, far too often, bust a gut on behalf of the thoroughly undeserving while ignoring the plight of their victims. They seem, far too often, to think that an unpopular cause is automatically a just cause. Most of the time it isn't. But, on the other hand, anybody backed by big business or big government is all too often a bad bastard . . . ."

"He may be a son of a bitch," contributed Damien, "but he's our son of a bitch."

"Yes. That's the attitude far too often, sir."

"And so, young Grimes, you're interfering, as a freelance do-gooder, every time that you get the chance."

"I don't interfere, sir. Things sort of happen around me."

"Captain Grimes," said Damien to Madame Duvalier, "is a sort of catalyst. Put him in any sort of situation where things aren't quite right and they almost immediately start going from bad to worse. And then, when it's all over but the shouting—or, even, the shooting—who emerges from the stinking mess, smelling of violets, with the Shaara crown jewels clutched in his hot little hand?

Grimes, that's who. And, at the same time, virtue is triumphant and vice defeated."

Grimes's prominent ears flushed. Was the Duvalier female looking at him with admiration or amusement?

The sound of a bugle drifted into Damien's sitting room—which could have been the admiral's day cabin aboard a grand fleet flagship. (Damien was a great traditionalist.) Damien got to his feet, extended an unnecessary hand to Madam Duvalier to help her to hers. He escorted the lady into the dining room, followed by Grimes.

The meal, served by smartly uniformed mess waiters, was pleasant enough although, thought Grimes, probably he would have fed better aboard his own ship. But in *Sister Sue* it was his tastes that were catered to; here, in Flag House, it was Damien's. The admiral liked his beef well-done, Grimes liked his charred on the outside and raw on the inside. Even so, Grimes admitted, the old bastard knew his wines, the whites and the reds, the drys and the semi-sweets, each served with the appropriate course. But it was a great pity that whoever had assembled the cheese board had been so thoroughly uninspired.

During dinner the conversation was on generalities. And then, with the mess waiters dismissed, Damien and his guests returned to the sitting room for coffee (so-so) and brandy (good) and some real talking.

"Yvonne," said the admiral, "is one of the very few people who knows that you are back in the Survey Service, as a sort of trouble shooter. She thinks that you may be able to do some work for APS."

"Since the Tarabel bungle," the woman admitted, "APS doesn't have the influence in high government circles that it once did. But there are still wrongs that need righting, and still powerful business interests putting profits before all else . . . ."

"And how can I help?" asked Grimes. "After all, I represent a business interest myself, Far Traveler Couriers. Unless I make a profit I can't stay in business. And if I go broke I just can't see the Survey Service taking me back into the fold officially . . . ."

"Too right," murmured Damien.

"And I couldn't get into any of the major shipping lines without a big drop in rank. I don't fancy starting a-fresh as a junior officer at my age."

"Understandable," murmured Damien. "And I hope that you understand that you need the Survey Service, even though you are, in the eyes of most people, a civilian, and a rich shipowner."

"Rich!" interjected Grimes. "Ha!"

"Just try to remember how much of your income has been derived from lucrative business that we have put in your way. All the charters, time or voyage. Such as the one that you have now, the shipment of not very essential and certainly not urgently required stores to the sub-base on Pleth."

"And after Pleth? What then?"

"Arrangements have been made. It will just so happen that there will be a cargo offering from Pleth to New Otago. Pleth exports the so-called paradise fruit, canned. Have you ever sampled that delicacy?"

"Once," said Grimes. "I wasn't all that impressed. Too sweet. Not enough flavor."

"Apparently the New Otagoans like it. Now, listen carefully. Your trajectory will take you within spitting distance of New Salem. What do you know of Salem?"

"I've never been there, sir, but I seem to remember that it's famous for the animal furs, very expensive furs, that it exports. Quite a few of the very rich bitches on El Dorado like to tart themselves up in them. Oh, yes. And this fur export trade is the monopoly of Able Enterprises . . . ."

"Which outfit," said Damien, "is run by old cobber Commodore Baron Kane, of El Dorado."

"No cobber of mine," growled Grimes.

"But you know Kane. And you know that any enterprise in which he's involved is liable to be, at the very least, unsavory. Well, APS have heard stories about this fur trade. APS have asked me to carry out an investigation. After all, I'm only a rear admiral. But I have clashed, in the past, with the El Dorado Corporation and gotten away with it . . . ."

"With me as your cat's paw," said Grimes.

"Precisely. And, admit it, it does give you some satisfaction to score off Kane. Doesn't it?"

"I suppose so."

"It does, and we both know it." He turned to Madame Duvalier. "Grimes and Kane are old enemies," he explained. "Apart from anything else there was rivalry for the favors of the Baroness Michelle d'Estang, who is now Kane's wife—hence his El Doradan citizenship."

Then, speaking again to Grimes, he went on, "I wanted to send a Survey Service ship to Salem on a flag-showing exercise but there just aren't any ships available. So I have to fall back on you."

"Thank you, sir." Then, "But I shan't be bound for Salem."

"Officially, no. But look at it this way. You are bound from Point A to Point C, bypassing Point B. But then, in mid-voyage, something happens that obliges you to make for a port of refuge to carry out essential repairs or whatever . . . ."

"What something?" demanded Grimes.

"Use your imagination, young man."

"Mphm. . . . A leakage, into space, of my water reserves. . . . And, after all, water is required as reaction mass for my emergency rocket drive as well as for drinking, washing, etc. And so I get permission from the Salem aerospace authorities to make a landing, fill my tanks and lift off again. But I shall be on the planetary surface for a matter of hours only."

"Not if your inertial drive goes seriously on the blink just as you're landing."

"I'm not an engineer, sir, as well you know."

"But you have engineers, don't you? And among them is a Ms. Cassandra Perkins. Calamity Cassie."

"What do you know about her, sir?"

"I know that Lieutenant Commander Cassandra Perkins is an extremely skillful saboteur—or should that be saboteuse?"

"So she's one of your mob. . . ."

"And your mob, Captain Grimes. Federation Survey Service Reserve."

"All right. So I'm grounded on Salem for some indefinite period. And I suppose that I shall be required to do some sniffing around . . . ."

"You suppose correctly."

"Then why can't you do as you did before, give me one of your psionic communication officers, a trained telepath, to do the snooping? You will recall that I carried your Lieutenant Commander Mayhew, as an alleged passenger, when I was involved in the El Doradan privateering affair."

"At the moment, Grimes, PCOs are as scarce as hen's teeth in the Service. The bastards have been resigning in droves, recruited by various industrial espionage outfits. You may have heard of the war—yes, you could call it that—being waged by quite a few companies throughout the Galaxy against the so-called Wizards of Electra. But you have Shirl and Darleen who, despite their official human status, possess great empathy with the lower animals."

"And so, with the skilled assistance of your Ms. Perkins. . . ."

"Your Ms. Perkins, Grimes. She's on your books."

" . . . I'm to prolong my stay on Salem as long as possible, find out what I can, and then write a report for you."

"Yes. And, hopefully, act as a catalyst. You always do."

"That's what I'm afraid of," said Grimes.

Yvonne Duvalier broke the brief silence.

She said, "I don't think that you have put Captain Grimes sufficiently into the picture, Admiral. To begin with, Captain, there was what Admiral Damien refers to as a flag-showing exercise on New Salem. The destroyer *Pollux*. She carried, of course, a psionic communication officer. He was not a very experienced one but he suspected, strongly, that at least one of the species of fur-bearing animal on New Salem, the silkies, possessed intelligence up to human standards. They can think and feel, but their thought processes aren't the same as ours. And they are slaughtered for their pelts. Somehow his not very detailed report fell into our hands, at APS. The admiral has long been a friend of ours and promised to do something about it. And then, as you know, there was the Tarabel fiasco and the consequent reluctance of the authorities to rush to the aid of unpleasant and vicious extra-Terrans.

"Although the fur of the silkies is beautiful, as you probably know, they are ugly beasts. They have, in the past, attacked the coastwise villages of the human colonists of New Salem. They have mutilated rather than killed, biting the hands off men, women and children. There are some rather horrid photographs of such victims.

"The New Salem colonists are the descendants of a religious sect that emigrated from Earth during the Second Expansion. Fundamentalists, maintaining that God gave Man dominion over all other life forms. They have their own version, their own translation of the Holy Bible, the Old Testament only. Their God is a jealous God, taking a dim view of any who do not believe as the True Believers, as they call themselves, do. But they do not mind taking the money of those who are not True Believers. They have a huge account in the Galactic Bank, more than enough to pay for the occasional shipments of manufactured goods that they receive from the industrial planets. Popular belief is that, eventually, their funds will be used for the building of a huge Ark in which they, and they alone, will escape the eventual collapse of the Universe."

"Where will they escape to?" asked Grimes interestedly.

Damien laughed. "I don't suppose they know themselves. Perhaps they just hope to drift around until the next Big Bang, and then get in on the ground floor and start the human race again the way it should be started, free of all perversions. . . ." Suddenly he looked at Grimes very keenly. "Talking of perversions, young man, I hear that you are perverting Survey Service Regulations."

"Me, sir?"

"Yes. You. The regulations regarding wild robots. I hear that you have one such aboard your ship. You have neither deactivated it and returned it to its makers nor destroyed it."

"I suppose that Mr. Steerforth told you, sir."

"Never mind who told me. I just know."

"I'd like to make it plain, sir, that my ship is my ship. I am the owner as well as the master. Until, if ever, she is officially commissioned as an auxiliary unit of the Survey Service she is a merchant ship. The regulations to which her personnel are subject are company's regulations. In this case, my regulations."

"Always the spacelawyer, Grimes, aren't you?"

"Yes. I have to be."

Damien grinned. "Very well, then. I'll just hope that your Seiko, as I understand that you call the thing, will be just another catalyst thrown into the New Salem crucible. Two wild girls, one wild robot and, the wildest factor of all, yourself . . . ."

"I almost wish that I were going along on the voyage," said Madame Duvalier.

"Knowing Grimes as I do," said the admiral, "I prefer to wait for the reports that I shall be getting eventually. Reports which I shall not pass on to higher authorities until they have been most thoroughly edited."

✐ Chapter 10 ✐

SISTER SUE lifted from Port Woomera, driving up into the cloudless, blue, late afternoon sky. As members of the crew, Shirl and Darleen were among those in the control room; as first trip cadets their only duty was to keep well out of the way of those doing the work. Up and out drove the old ship, up and out. Soon, far to the south, the glimmer of the Antarctic ice could be discerned and, much closer, there was a great berg with its small fleet of attendant tugs, being dragged and nudged to its last resting place, its dying place, in the artificial fresh water harbor at the mouth of the Torrens River.

The sky darkened to indigo and the stars appeared, although the bright-blazing sun was still well clear of the rounded rim of the Earth. In the stern vision screen the radar altimeter display totted up the steadily increasing tally of kilometers. There were the last exchanges of messages between Aerospace Control and the ship on NST radio. It was a normal start to a normal voyage. (But, thought Grimes, sitting in his command chair, his unlit pipe clenched between his teeth, for him a normal voyage was one during which abnormality was all too often the norm. And, not for the first time, Damien was expecting him to stick his neck out and get it trodden on.)

Earth was a sphere now, a great, glowing opal against the black velvet backdrop of space.

"Escape velocity, sir," announced Harald Steerforth.

"Thank you, Mr. Steerforth," said Grimes.

"Clear of the Van Allens, sir," reported the second officer.

"Thank you, Mr. Kershaw. Ms. Suzuki, make to all hands 'Stand by for free fall. Stand by for trajectory adjustment.'"

He heard the girl speaking into her microphone, heard, from the intercom speakers the reports from various parts of the ship that all was secured. Using the controls set in the broad armrest of his chair he shut down the inertial drive. There was an abrupt cessation of vibration and a brief silence, broken almost at once by the humming of the great gyroscopes around which *Sister Sue* turned, hunting the target star. Grimes's fingers played on the control buttons, his face upturned to the curiously old-fashioned cartwheel sight set at the apex of the transparent dome of the control room. The pilot computer could have done the job just as well and much faster—but Grimes always liked to feel that he was in command, not some uppity robot. At last the tiny, bright spark was in the exact center of the concentric rings, the convergence of radii. It did not stay there for long; there was allowance for Galactic Drift to be made.

At last Grimes was satisfied.

"Stand by for initiation of Mannschenn Drive," he ordered.

"Stand by for initiation of Mannschenn Drive," repeated Tomoko Suzuki.

In the Mannschenn Drive room the gleaming complexity of rotors came to life, spinning faster and faster, tumbling, processing, fading almost to invisibility, warping the very fabric of Space-Time about themselves and about the ship, falling down the dark dimensions . . . .

The temporal precession field built up and there was the inevitable distortion of perspective, with colors sagging down the spectrum. Not for the first time Grimes experienced a flash of prevision—but, he knew, it was of something that *might* happen. After all, there is an infinitude of possible futures and a great many probable ones.

But he saw—and this was by no means his first such

experience—a woman. It was nobody he knew—and yet she seemed familiar. She was clad in a dark blue, gold-embroidered kimono, above which her heavily made-up face was very pale. Her glossy, black hair was piled high on her head. She could almost have been a Japanese geisha from olden times . . . .

Tomoko? Grimes wondered.

No, she was not Tomoko.

He could see her more clearly now. She was bound to a stake, around which faggots were piled. He saw a hand, a human hand, apply a blazing torch to the sacrificial pyre. There were flames, mounting swiftly. There was smoke, swirling about and over the victim.

There was . . . .

There was the instantaneous reversion to normality as the temporal precession field was established. Grimes tried to shake the vision from his mind.

"Stand by for resumption of inertial drive," he ordered.

"Stand by for resumption of inertial drive," repeated Tomoko into her microphone.

From below came the muted arrhythmic thumping. Somewhere a loose fitting rattled. Grimes unsnapped his seat belt, took his time lighting and filling his pipe.

"Set normal Deep Space watches," he said to the chief officer. "Mr. Kershaw can keep the first one. Please join me in my day cabin for a drink before dinner, Mr. Steerforth. We've a few things to discuss."

"Thank you, sir."

"I take it," said Grimes, speaking over the rim of his glass, "that Admiral Damien has put you into the picture."

"Of course, sir."

"What do you know about Ms. Perkins? Or should I say Lieutenant Commander Perkins?"

"I've worked with her before, sir. I knew that she'd been planted in your ship some time ago. She's highly capable, masquerading as being highly incapable." Then Steerforth actually laughed. "Mind you, sir, I've often wondered if her masquerade *is* a masquerade. . . . Perhaps, like you, she's a sort of catalyst. Things just happen when she's around."

"Can she make them happen on demand?" asked Grimes.

"Usually," said Steerforth.

"Mphm. But tell me, Mr. Steerforth, just how many undercover agents has Admiral Damien planted aboard my ship?"

"Well, sir, there's you, for a start. And myself. And Ms. Perkins. And those two alleged officer cadets . . . ." After a couple of drinks he was becoming more human. "For all *I* know that clockwork toy of yours might even be one! Tell me, is she really intelligent? Or is she just an example of very clever programming on somebody's part?"

"We are all of us the end products of programming," Grimes told him.

"To a point, sir. To a point. But as well as the programming there's intuition, imagination, initiative . . . ."

"I think," said Grimes, "that Seiko possesses at least two of those qualities."

The dinner gong sounded.

The two men finished their drinks, went down to the wardroom to join the other off-duty officers.

Grimes had been half-expecting soul food but what Ms. Clay provided was a fine example of Creole cookery. This was not to everybody's taste but Grimes enjoyed it.

∽ Chapter 11 ∽

IT WAS NOT A LONG VOYAGE TO PLETH, but long enough for Grimes to get the feel of things. His new chief officer, Harald Steerforth, was not quite such a pain in the arse as Grimes had feared that he would be on first acquaintance. Cleo Jones, the black and beautiful radio officer, the Zulu Princess, was the civilizing influence. What the pair of them did when they were off watch was none of Grimes's business. These days, in vessels with mixed crews, temporary sexual unions were not discouraged so long as they did not interfere with the smooth running of the ship and so long as certain unwritten regulations were observed.

In fact, thought Grimes disgruntledly, about the only person who wasn't getting any was himself. He was the victim of those unwritten regulations. Shirl and Darleen had made it plain to him that they were available, as they had been when they had traveled as passengers in *Sister Sue* from New Sparta to Earth. But then they had been passengers, fair game. Now they were junior officers, very junior officers. Between Grimes and themselves there was too great a disparity of rank. He did not wish to be thought of as a wicked captain who ordered poor, helpless (ha!) first-trip cadets to his bed.

Oh, there were offers, opportunities, but the two New Alicians did their best (worst) to ensure that he did not take advantage of them. There was that handsome academic, Sarah Smith, the second Mannschenn Drive engineer. She made it plain that she would not find the attentions of her captain unwelcome. Perhaps it was accidental that when she walked into the wardroom one evening, ship's time, she was struck on the left shoulder by a heavy glass ashtray. Shirl had been giving an exhibition of boomerang throwing— using anything and everything as boomerangs—to the off-duty officers.

Perhaps, Grimes thought at the time, it was accidental—but the next morning, in his day cabin, the two girls, who were supposed to be receiving instruction in general spacemanship from the captain, told him otherwise.

"John," said Shirl, "Vinegar Puss is trying to get her claws into you. Warn her off . . . ."

"Or next time," said Darleen, "she'll be getting something hard and heavy where it really hurts."

"And the same applies," added Shirl, "to Aunt Jemima . . . ."

"Ms. Clay," objected Grimes, "is nothing like Aunt Jemima."

"She's the cook, isn't she?"

"She's the catering officer," said Grimes. "It's the autochef that does the cooking—with, I admit, her personal touches. But Aunt Jemima? I've never heard her called that."

"You don't know much about what goes on aboard your own ship," Shirl told him.

Grimes laughed. "I'm only the captain. Nobody ever tells me anything."

"Then we can be your spies, John. You've made it plain that we aren't to be anything else."

"I've told you why it's quite impossible, as long as you're on my books."

"But it's so *silly*," complained the girls in unison.

"Silly or not, that's the way it's going to be."

"Would you rather that we slept with Bill the Bull?"

William Bull was the third reaction drive engineer, the only male member of his department. He was referred to as "the bull among the cows." It was a known fact that both the second and fourth were recipients of his favors. Privately Grimes thought of him as a sullen, over-sexed lout.

He said, "I'd advise you not to. Juanita has a hot temper and Calamity Cassie might put a hex on you. Well, since you are now my self-appointed spies, what else have you for me that you think that I don't already know?"

"Tomoko . . . ."

"Ms. Suzuki to you. After all, she is your superior officer."

"Only just," said Shirl. "And only aboard this ship of yours. Well, she and Seiko are very friendly. They have long talks together, twittering and giggling away in Japanese. Anyhow, we think that it's in Japanese."

"It probably is," Grimes said. "Tomoko must be pleased to have somebody with whom she can chat in her native language. It's the one that was originally programmed into her—Seiko, I mean, although I suppose that you could say the same regarding Tomoko."

"But Tomoko is not a robot," objected Darleen.

"Isn't she? Aren't you? Or, come to that, me? We're all of us programmed, from birth onward."

"You are too deep for us, John. We are not accustomed to such philosophical thinking. On New Alice we led simple lives, at one with Nature . . . ."

And this was so, Grimes knew. He had watched Shirl and Darleen running with the mob of kangaroos by the Uluru Canal near Ayers Rock, heard them talking to the marsupials. He knew that aboard *Sister Sue* the two girls were now practically in charge of the ship's hydroponic "farm," that even the various edible, tank-grown plants flourished, under their care, as never before. They had green fingers, declared Melinda Clay who, as catering officer, was responsible for the continuing supply of fresh fruits, salads and other vegetables.

So *Sister Sue* eventually made her planetfall in the vicinity of Pleth, emerged from the warped continuum into normal space-time, said all the right things to the planet's Aerospace Control, got all the right answers and, eventually, dropped through thick clouds, all the way from the stratosphere to the ground, to the spaceport. This, with facilities capable of handling no more than two ships at the one time, was shared by the Survey Service and commercial interests. Grimes's berth was marked not by the usual flashing red beacons but by a radar transponder; it is said the visibility is bad for nine months of the local year on Pleth and nonexistent for the remaining three.

Grimes set his ship down gently, making, he told himself, a very good job of it in these conditions. He sat in the control room with Steerforth after the others had left, looking out through a viewport at . . . nothing. At least he knew which way to look; his radar, set on short range, showed him a blob of luminescence that probably indicated the port administration building.

He saw the gradually increasing yellow glare in the fog that came from the headlights of approaching ground vehicles. Ms. Clay, in her capacity as purser, would, he knew, have all the necessary ship's papers ready in her office. Ms. Suzuki would receive the boarding officers in the after airlock. His presence almost certainly would not be required. Customs, Port Health and Immigration would be getting their free smokes and coffee and then applying their rubber stamps before leaving.

Steerforth said, "I'd better get down to my office, sir. I suppose that somebody will be wanting to arrange discharge." He laughed. "I don't suppose that the Sub-Base Commander will be inviting us across for drinks."

That was indeed unlikely, thought Grimes. From his long experience he had learned that the smaller the base, the greater the sense of self-importance of the officer in charge. On a planet like Pleth the OIC would most likely be some passed-over commander, putting on the airs and graces of a fleet admiral, too high and mighty to share a noggin of gin with a mere tramp skipper and his mate.

"I shall be in my day cabin if anybody wants me, Mr. Steerforth," he said. "Probably the agent will come aboard once the ship has been cleared inwards."

Shortly after Grimes had settled down in his day cabin with a mug of hot, sweet coffee to hand, his pipe drawing well, he was called upon by Mr. Klith, of Klith, Klith & Associates. Mr. Klith was obviously a native, although apparently humanoid. What could be seen of his skin was pale green and scaly and his huge eyes were hidden by even huger dark goggles, worn as protection from the relatively glaring illumination inside the ship. Although he wore a conventional enough gray, one-piece business suit his large, webbed feet were bare.

He spoke perfect, rather too perfect Standard English.

"I am your agent on Pleth, Captain," he announced. "Also I represent the Federation Survey Service, the consignees of your inward cargo."

"Sit down, Mr. Klith," said Grimes. "Can I offer you refreshment? Tea, coffee, something stronger? It is the middle of the morning your time, but I think that we can say that the sun is over the yardarm."

"We rarely see our sun," said Mr. Klith. "But what is a yardarm?"

"I must apologize," said Grimes. "I used an expression that used to be common at sea, on Earth, during the days of sail. It was passed on to mechanically driven ships and then to spaceships. It means that it's just about time for a drink before the midday meal."

"Thank you for your invitation, Captain. Perhaps I might have some tea. To us it is a mild intoxicant."

Grimes spoke briefly into the microphone of the intercom, turned to his guest. "What sort of tea would you prefer, Mr. Klith?"

"Indian tea is among our imports, Captain, but I understand that there are other varieties. I should wish to sample one of them."

Grimes amplified his order to the pantry.

"And now, Captain, while we are waiting might we discuss business?" said the agent. "I am afraid that we cannot expect much cooperation from Commander Dravitt, who is in charge of the Sub-Base. May I quote his words? He said, 'I need another load of bumf like I need a second arsehole. My stationery store is packed almost to bursting already.' But, you will be relieved to learn, I am the agent on this world for the Survey Service, not for one of its relatively junior—in rank, that is—officers. I have received a Carlottigram, signed by an Admiral Damien—do you know him, by any chance?—urging me to expedite your discharge. Your cargo will be stored in a civilian warehouse."

"As long as I'm not expected to pay for the storage," said Grimes.

"You will not be, Captain."

There was a tap at the door. Seiko came in, carrying a tray upon which were a teapot and a handleless cup. She set the tray down on the coffee table, poured the steaming fluid which almost matched Mr. Klith's skin in color. The native watched the robomaid with admiration, then transferred his attention to the refreshment.

He said, with some little bewilderment, "But should there not be sugar? And milk? Or perhaps some slices of that fruit you call lemon?"

"This is the way that we Japanese drink our tea, Klith-san," said Seiko.

"Indeed? But would not the ingestion of hot fluids tend to corrode your intricate and beautiful machinery?"

Grimes said hastily, "Seiko neither eats nor drinks. But she tends to identify with her manufacturers." Then, to the robot, "Thank you, Seiko. That will do."

"Thank you, Captain-san."

The robomaid withdrew.

"Your personal servant, Captain?" asked Mr. Klith. "A robot such as that must have been very, very expensive. All that we have on this world are clumsy things that are neither ornamental nor even very useful. But, of course, you are a rich shipowner and can afford the very best."

"Mphm," grunted Grimes. "As a matter of fact Seiko is a gift to me from my father . . . ."

"Then he must be a very rich man. Is he, too, in shipping?"

"No, he's a writer . . . ."

"Then he must be famous. Terran books are very popular here on Slith, both in translation and among those who, like myself, can read the various Terran languages. What name does he write under?"

Grimes told him.

"I am sorry. I have never heard of him. But he still must be successful and rich."

"Moderately successful and not really rich. As a matter of fact he bought Seiko for himself, to program as his secretary. That way he could claim her purchase price as a legitimate income tax deduction. Then my mother thought that she would make an ideal robomaid after secretarial skills somehow failed to develop, but she was still my father's pet. And then, after a family row, I got her . . . ."

"What complicated lives you Terrans lead. That is what makes your literature so fascinating. . . . This is excellent tea, by the way, Captain. I must arrange to import it from Earth in large quantities . . ."

Grimes refilled his cup for him.

"And now, Captain, let us discuss business. My young Mr. Slith is now with your chief officer discussing discharge of your inward cargo. This should commence shortly after noon, our time. Our stowbots may not be as good looking as your robomaid but they are fast working, especially when no great care is required. . . ."

"Mr. Steerforth will make careful note of the marks and numbers of any packages damaged and I shall, of course, refuse to pay any claims for damaged cargo."

"As you please, Captain. The Survey Service will just write off such claims. After all, it is by their insistence that your discharge will be an exceptionally speedy one. By tomorrow night you should have an empty ship. Loading will commence almost at once. You know, of course, that you will be carrying a cargo of paradise fruit to New Otago. . . ."

"Any need for refrigeration or special ventilation?"

"No. It is canned."

"Then I hope that some care is exercised in its loading. I don't want damaged crates and sticky juice dribbling all over my cargo decks."

"Due care will be exercised, Captain. Paradise fruit is our main export and we do not wish to antagonize our customers." He finished his tea and got to his feet. "Thank you for allowing me to sample this truly excellent brew."

"Aren't you staying for lunch?" asked Grimes, hoping that the answer would be negative. A little of Mr. Slith went a long way. Apart from anything else he exuded an odor of not very fresh fish. (And what do I smell like to him? wondered Grimes, making allowances.)

"No thank you, Captain. I must confess that I do not find Terran foods very palatable—apart from your tea, that is. But does that possess any nutritional value? And now I must be on my way. Business awaits me in my office."

"Before you go," asked Grimes, "can you tell me if there are any recreational facilities in Port Pleth? I always allow my people shore leave whenever possible."

"Alas, no. Had you come a few days earlier you could have witnessed our annual mud festival, an event in which I am trying to interest the operators of tourist liners, such as Trans-Galactic Clippers, so far without success. Too, it is unsafe for beings not blessed with our eyes, sensitive as they are to infrared radiation, to wander through the town. A few months ago—as you reckon time— the second officer of a Dog Star Line vessel fell into the Murgh River and was drowned . . . ."

So, thought Grimes, he would have to announce that there was to be no shore leave. He did not think that anybody would object very strongly.

Chapter 12

BUT THERE WAS, after all, shore leave of a sort.

Just as Grimes was about to go down to the wardroom for his luncheon he had another caller, this one human, an ensign from the Sub-Base. This not-so-young (for his lowly rank he seemed quite elderly) gentleman handed Grimes a large, rather condescendingly but more or less correctly addressed envelope. *Commander John Grimes, FSS (Rtd.), Master dss* Sister Sue. (Grimes had held the rank of commander at the time of the *Discovery* mutiny but he had not been retired; he had resigned his commission in some haste.)

Inside the envelope was a stiff sheet of official Survey Service stationery. On it was typed, "Commander David Dravitt, Federation Survey Service, Officer-in-Charge Sub-Base Pleth and his officers request the pleasure of the company of Commander John Grimes, Master dss *Sister Sue*, and his officers to dinner this evening, 1800 for 1930. Your prompt reply by bearer will be appreciated."

So far as he could remember Grimes had never been shipmates with Dravitt during his own days in the Service. He had never met, nor even heard of Dravitt. But, all too probably, Dravitt would have heard of him.

He asked, "Is there any limit to the number of guests, Mr. . . . Mr. . . . ?"

"Sullivan, sir. No, there is no limit. We enjoy commodious

facilities. The Sub-Base was once much more important than it is now."

"Mphm. Can you handle fourteen, including myself?"

"Easily, sir. Will that be your entire complement?"

"No. Executive and engineer officers of the watch will remain on board. Will you be arranging transport?"

"It is only a short stroll to the Sub-Base officers' quarters, sir."

"In a thick fog, Mr. Sullivan?"

"We can lay on a ground car for yourself and your senior officers, sir. Native guides will be supplied for the others. The natives, as you may know, have eyes adapted to local conditions."

"Very well. You will call for us then at . . ."

"Shortly after 1730, sir."

"Thank you. Would you care to stay for lunch?"

Sullivan was obviously tempted but he said, "No thank you, sir. Commander Dravitt would like your reply as soon as possible so that the necessary arrangements may be made."

She, Paymaster Lieutenant Commander Selena Shaw, extricated herself from the tangle of bed sheets and limbs (half of these latter belonging to herself) and padded to the well-stocked bar set against one wall of her bedroom. Grimes watched the tall, naked blonde appreciatively. She returned to the bed bearing two condensation-bedewed glasses of sparkling wine.

"What," asked Grimes, "is a girl like you doing in a place like this? A highly competent officer attached to Sub-Base Pleth, the last resting place of all the Survey Service incompetents? Well, some of them, anyhow."

She laughed, her teeth very white in her tanned face. (She was one of the few officers of the Sub-Base who made regular use of the solarium; artificial sunlight was better than none at all.)

She said, without false modesty, "There has to be one competent officer, even in a sub-base like this. And I just happen to be it. Or her."

Grimes sipped his chilled wine. "And what am *I*," he continued rhetorically, "doing in a place like this? First of all, I never thought that a high and mighty sub-base commander would condescend to entertain a mere tramp skipper. Secondly, I was expecting a rather boring evening. I never dreamed that it would finish up like this."

She said, "Actually the invitation was Droopy Delia's idea. You've met her now, talked with her, so your opinion of her probably coincides with mine. A typical wife for a typical passed-over commander, like Davy Dravy, swept with him under the carpet to a dump like Pleth. Social ambitions that will never now be realized. A plumpish blonde—and now she's rather more than plump—getting spliced to an ambitious young lieutenant and seeing herself, after not too many years, as an admiral's wife. An admiral's wife she'll never be—but she kids herself that she's running this sub-base. Shortly after you'd set down she came barging into my office. My office, mind you. Davy Dravy was there—well, after all he is the sub-base commander—to discuss various matters and she started browsing through the papers on my desk. 'David,' she squeaked, 'have you seen who's master of this tramp, this *Sister Sue*?' He grumbled back, 'What is it to me what star tramp skippers call themselves?' She said, 'It's Grimes. John Grimes. The Grimes.' Davy Dravy was less than impressed. 'So bloody what?' he snarled. 'He was emptied out of the Service, wasn't he? And not before time.' She said, 'Yes. He was emptied out of the Service—or, according to some, he resigned before he could be emptied out. And now he's a shipowner. And he's been a planetary governor. At least he hasn't finished up with a deadend appointment, frozen in rank, like some people.' Davy mumbled something about this being just your bloody luck. Droopy Delia said that she wished this famous luck would rub off on to some people she knew. And so it was decided to invite you to dinner. Or she decided to invite you to dinner. And then I took pity on you—or, as it's turned out, it was enlightened self-interest. Davy and Delia just aren't the Universe's best hosts. I threw in my two bits' worth. 'Why not,' I asked her, not him, 'issue a general wardroom invitation to the captain and officers. Our own officers, and the few civilian spouses, will enjoy having somebody fresh to talk with . . . .'"

"To talk with," said Grimes. "And . . . ."

"Yes. As you say, and as we've been doing, and . . . Apart from ourselves, I think that there has been rather more than just talking. But I don't think that Tony Cavallo and Billy Brown, our two prize wolves, got any place with those two cadets of yours. Odd looking wenches, somehow, but very attractive. And, despite their names, I don't think that their ancestors were Irish. I may be wrong, but I think that they had eyes only for you. And me, when I was making my invitation rather obvious. If looks could have killed . . . ."

"Mphm," grunted Grimes, embarrassed.

"Talking of their eyes . . . ." she went on. "Is there anything odd about them?"

"How do you mean?"

"Well, I was in charge of picking you people up and supplying the native guides for the junior officers. Your Ms. Kelly and Ms. Byrne arrived at the base officers' quarters well before the rest of the crowd—and they had nobody to guide them. And the fog was as thick as the armor plating of a Nova class battlewagon."

"Probably," said Grimes, "they regarded it as a sort of navigation test, got themselves headed in the right direction and then set off hopefully."

"Then they were lucky. It's not a straight line walk. There are two bridges to negotiate, and that mess of alleys and cross alleys through the workshops and stores."

"Mphm," grunted Grimes.

He finished his drink, she finished hers. It would soon be time for him to get back to his ship so as to spend what remained of the night in his own bed. But before he got dressed there were things to do better done naked.

At last it was time for him to say good night—or, more exactly, good morning. She threw on a robe and took him out to where the ground car, with native driver, was awaiting him.

He said, "I'll see you at about 1100 hours, then, Selena. Drinks before lunch. And I think I can promise you a rather better meal than tonight's dinner was."

She said, "It should be. Aboard your ship you're the boss."

They kissed a long moment and he boarded the waiting vehicle.

She arrived aboard *Sister Sue* shortly after 1100, supported, almost carried, by Ensigns Cavallo and Brown. She was dazed, bleeding profusely from a deep cut on the forehead. The efficient Melinda Clay was called upon to administer first aid and, after some delay, the sub-base's medical officer was in attendance.

At last Grimes was able to find out what had happened.

Selena had decided to walk from the sub-base to the ship, escorted through the fog by one of the native guides. Suddenly, without warning, she had been struck by a heavy missile. The guide had run to the ship to fetch help.

"I suppose, sir, that it was our fault," said Ensign Cavallo unhappily. "We should not have encouraged them. But, after all, sir, they're your officers, aboard your ship. . . ."

"Encouraged them? How?"

"We came on board for morning coffee. In the wardroom Ms. Kelly and Ms. Byrne were giving a demonstration of throwing weapons, using ashtrays and such, making them sail around and come back to their hands. I asked if this technique would be effective over a distance. They said that it was. So we all went down to the after airlock, and Ms. Kelly threw a rather thick glass saucer of some kind into the fog. We expected that it would come back, but it didn't. . . ."

"Ms. Kelly," asked Grimes severely, "Ms. Byrne, is this true?"

"Yes, sir," replied Shirl innocently. "But we had no idea that there would be anybody out in the fog. After all, if Ms. Shaw had been making her approach by ground car we should have seen the glare of the headlights . . . ."

"And so, quite by chance," said Grimes, "your random missile inflicted grievous bodily harm on Lieutenant Commander Shaw—"

And with that he had to be content. He could prove nothing—and, even if he could, what could he do about it? Shirl and Darleen were essential—or so he had been told by Damien—to the success of his mission. Selena had been no more than a pleasant diversion.

~ Chapter 13 ~

THE WORK OF DISCHARGE and then of loading went smoothly. Grimes was able during his time in port to return some of the hospitality which he and his people had received from the sub-base personnel. He kept a close watch on the Terrible Twins, a joint nickname which Shirl and Darleen had quite suddenly acquired, making no further attempt to entertain Selena Shaw aboard his ship. (But her own quarters were quite adequate for purposes of mutual entertainment and she did not, as she could quite well have done, put him off by complaining that she had a severe headache.) And then, with cargo well-stowed, with all necessary in-port maintenance completed, it was time to lift off. Nobody board the ship was sorry, even though there were a few (very temporarily) broken hearts both in the sub-base and aboard *Sister Sue*. Sleth was such a dismal planet. Even New Otago would be better. Even though there was a shortage of bright lights on that world the scenery was said to be quite spectacular and the atmosphere was usually clear enough for it to be appreciated.

So *Sister Sue* lifted, ungumming herself from the omnipresent mud that, despite the thrice daily deployment of high-pressure hoses, inevitably crept over the spaceport apron. She clattered aloft through the fog, through the overcast, finally broke free into the dazzling sunlight while the last tenuous shreds of the Sleth atmosphere whispered along her pitted sides.

There was the usual trajectory setting routine, after which the old ship, her Mannschenn Drive running as sweetly as that Space-Time-twisting contraption ever ran, was falling down and through the warped dimensions toward the New Otago primary. Deep space watches were set and Grimes went down to his day cabin, asking Mr. Steerforth to join him there. As soon as the chief officer was seated and had been given a drink to nurse, served by the glittering Seiko, Grimes used the intercom to talk to the chief reaction drive engineer. "Ms. Scott, I've noticed that my shower is giving trouble. I almost got scalded this morning. Could you send Ms. Perkins up to fix it? She's off watch, isn't she?"

"I'll come myself, Captain. You know what Calamity Cassie's like."

"I do, Flo. But as fourth engineer she's supposed to be the ship's plumber. It's time that she started to earn her pay."

"Well, it's your shower, Captain. It's you that's going to get boiled or flash-frozen . . . ."

And so, after a wait of only a few minutes, Ms. Perkins presented herself, attired for work in overalls that had once been white but which now displayed a multitude of ineradicable grease stains, carrying a tunefully clinking tool bag. Only her teeth, which her cheerful grin displayed generously in her black face, were clean and very white.

"*Sit down*, Cassie," ordered Grimes.

Before she could do so Seiko produced, as though from nowhere, a towel which the robomaid spread over the upholstery of the chair. The fourth engineer looked admiringly at the beautiful automaton and murmured, "I'd love to have the job of taking you apart and putting you together again, honey."

"That'd be the Sunny Friday!" snapped Seiko.

"My father," said Grimes, "improved upon the original programming, making additions from his own vocabulary."

"And so Seiko," said Cassie, "is no more than a sort of mechanical parrot. That I will not believe. She's as human as you or me." She grinned. "There are even rumors that you and she have a beautiful relationship."

"I am the captain's personal servant," said Seiko stiffly. "Just that and nothing more. Unfortunately a relationship of a carnal nature would not be possible."

Grimes's prominent ears flushed angrily.

He said, "That will do, Seiko. Just fetch Ms. Perkins a drink, will you?"

"Yassuh, Massa Grimes. One Foster's lager a-comin' up, Missie Perkins."

"And now, Ms. Perkins," said Grimes as soon as Seiko had left them, "have you decided upon how you will carry out your act of sabotage?"

"Yes, sir. It will be quite simple. A disastrous leakage from the main water tank into the reaction drive engineroom. The bulkhead will give way—an area of it will have been treated with Softoll—to give it its trade name—which, as you know loosens molecular bonds in any metal. According to my calculations the application will take twelve hours to produce the desired effect. When you let me know the day, sir, when you wish the accident to happen I shall apply the Softoll at 1000 hours, during my watch. The flood will happen at 2200 hours—again during my watch. I shall panic. My one motivation will be to get rid of all that water. After all, there's electrical machinery that could be damaged, and I might get drowned. I'll open the dump valves."

"Make sure, Cassie," Steerforth told her, "that you get into your emergency suit before you start getting rid of everything of a fluid nature in the engine room. After all, you'll be throwing out the atmosphere along with the bath water."

She grinned. "I look after my reputation. Things always happen around me, never to me."

Grimes asked, "But won't the cause of the so-called accident be obvious? Flo and Juanita aren't fools, you know."

She told him, "It will be put down to metal fatigue—and it won't be the first case of metal fatigue in this rustbucket."

"Are you referring to my ship?" asked Grimes stiffly. "It's bad enough to have you doing things to her without having to listen to you insulting her."

"Sorry, Captain. But unless you can think of some other kind of trouble that will force us to deviate to Salem, I shall have to do things to your ship. But I'll try to keep the damage down to a minimum." She finished her beer. "And now," she went on brightly, "shall I fix your shower for you?"

"No," said Grimes. "No, repeat and underscore, NO."

~ Chapter 14 ~

GRIMES, OF COURSE, knew what was going to happen, and when.

At 2145 hours he was in the control room, having a chat with the officer of the watch, Tomoko Suzuki. As he frequently did just this before retiring for the night, the third officer did not suspect that anything was amiss or about to go so. The topic of conversation was such that he almost forgot his real reason for being there, which was to ensure that the Mannschenn Drive was shut down at the first sign of trouble in the inertial drive engineroom. The dumping of tons of water would mean that the mass of the ship would be suddenly and drastically reduced—and any change of mass while running under Mannschenn Drive could be, probably would be, disastrous. There were stories of vessels so afflicted being unable to re-enter normal Space-Time or being thrown back into the remote past. Nobody knew, of course (except for the crews of those ships) but there had been experiments and there was a huge amount of theoretical data which Grimes could not begin to understand.

"Captain-san," Tomoko was saying, "I regard your Seiko as a friend. She may be a robot but she is, somehow, a real woman, a real Japanese woman." She giggled. "I have made up her face, like that of an olden time geisha, and put a wig upon her head, and dressed her in a kimono . . . ."

"I must see this some time," said Grimes.

He looked out through the viewport to the stars that were not points of light but vague, pulsating nebulosities. He heard the thin, high whine of the Drive as it engendered the temporal precession field, the warping of the continuum through which the ship was falling. He switched his attention to the control room clock. 2155:30 . . . 31 . . . 32 . . . Would that bulkhead blow *exactly* on time? Probably not. And would Calamity Cassie hit her alarm button as soon as the first trickle of water appeared? It could be just too bad if she didn't.

"Is something worrying you, Captain-san?" asked Tomoko.

"I shouldn't have had a second helping of Aunt Jemima's jambalaya at dinner this evening," lied Grimes.

2159:01 . . . .

He filled in time by playing with his pipe, stuffing the bowl with tobacco, making a major production of lighting it.

2200:00 . . .

"It would be rather pleasant," said Tomoko, "if some time we had a Japanese catering officer . . . ."

"I'm very fond of sashimi myself," said Grimes, "but I doubt if some of the others would care for raw fish."

2201:03 . . . 04 . . . 05 . . .

"Seiko has told me," said Tomoko, "that the preparation of sushi, sashimi and the like was in her original programming. And we have the carp in some of the algae tanks. Perhaps one night, just for a change, we could enjoy a sashimi dinner . . ."

2203:15 . . . 16 . . . 17

A red light suddenly sprang into being on the console of the inertial drive controls. An alarm klaxon uttered the beginnings of a squawk. Grimes's hand flashed up to the Mannschenn Drive console, knocked the main switch to the off position. The thin, high whine deepened to a rumbling hum, faded into silence. Colors sagged down the spectrum, perspective was impossibly distorted. Outside the viewports the stars changed, coalescing from furry blobs into hard points of light. But, below decks, the inertial drive was still hammering away although its clangor was almost drowned by the hooting alarms. And then it, too, fell silent. Throughout the ship all the lights went out but there was less than a second of darkness before the power cells cut in to the major domestic circuits.

Grimes had been expecting what happened and had secured himself in his chair. Tomoko was unprepared. With the inertial drive off, the ship was in free fall and some involuntary movement had pushed her up from her seat and she was drifting, making rather futile swimming motions, above Grimes's head. With his right hand he was just able to reach her ankle, pulled her down and then into the chair beside his.

"What happened, sir?" she gasped.

He said, "I suppose that somebody will eventually condescend to tell us."

"Why did you shut the Mannschenn Drive off, sir?"

He told her—but it was less than the whole truth—"There was, and is, trouble with the inertial drive. Which meant, as we've just found out, a sudden transition from a comfortable one G to free fall. There was the risk that the MD engineer on watch—Mr. Siegel, isn't it?—might blunder into the Drive and get himself turned inside out or something equally messy."

She said admiringly, "You thought very fast, Captain-san. I hope that I can think as fast when I am a captain."

Grimes never minded flattery, especially when it came from a pretty girl, even though in this case it was unearned. He supposed that if he had not been on the alert he would have acted as he had done, but not as fast.

He said to Tomoko, "Buzz the ID room, will you? Ask them what the hell's going on."

After an interval she reported, "The intercom seems to be out of order, sir." (This was not surprising. The waterproofing of electrical systems is not considered necessary in spaceships.)

Steerforth pulled himself into the control room. He reported, almost cheerfully, "There's all hell let loose down there, sir. As far as I can gather the after bulkhead of the main fresh water tank suddenly ruptured, flooding the ID room." He laughed. "Of course, it would have to happen on Calamity Cassie's watch. Then, according to Flo, what Cassie should have done was to drain the water into the engineers' store and workshop space. But she went into a panic and opened the dump valves . . . ."

"It is indeed fortunate," said Tomoko, "that the captain shut down the Mannschenn Drive before the loss of mass."

"It is indeed fortunate, Ms. Suzuki," agreed Steerforth. "Perhaps it was just another example of his famous luck."

"Mphm," grunted Grimes, looking severely at his chief officer.

"Shall I go back down," asked that gentleman, "to try to find out the extent of the damage?"

"No, Mr. Steerforth. Engineers don't like control room ornaments getting into their hair when they're trying to cope with some kind of emergency. Ms. Scott will keep us informed in her own good time."

Kershaw, the second officer, made his entrance into the control room. *About bloody well time,* thought Grimes. *Doesn't the puppy know that there's an emergency?* After him came Shirl and Darleen. There was some excuse for them; they were not real spacepersons. Finally Cleo Jones, the Zulu Princess, put in her appearance.

She reported, "I have been checking the main Carlotti transceiver, sir. Should it be necessary I can get out a Mayday using the power available."

"Thank you, Ms. Jones." Grimes looked around at his assembled people. They looked back at him, obviously awaiting orders. Well, he'd better start giving some.

"Ms. Kelly, Ms. Byrne," he said, "report to Ms. Clay. Probably there are matters in her department needing attention. When the ID cut out nothing was secured for free fall."

"Aye, aye, sir," said the girls smartly.

Grimes watched them go. They handled themselves in the absence of gravity better than many a seasoned spaceman.

"Mr. Kershaw, since the intercom seems to be out of action you can report to Ms. Scott, to act as runner to carry messages to me from her."

And she'll probably chew his ears off, he thought, with some satisfaction.

"Shall I find out what's happened to Seiko, sir?" asked Tomoko. "She might have been hurt. Damaged, I mean . . . ."

Not her, thought Grimes. He said, "She is a member of Ms. Clay's department. Probably she is helping her to get things cleaned up."

"Do you wish to send any messages, sir?" asked Cleo.

"Eventually," Grimes told her. "But I want to know what I'm talking about before I start talking." Then, to the third officer, "Get me a fix, will you? The navigational equipment is on the emergency circuit."

The girl busied herself at the chart tank, taking bearings from three conveniently located Carlotti Beacon Stations. Grimes unbuckled himself from his chair, pulled himself to a position beside her. He looked down into the simulation of the blackness of interstellar space, at the intersection of the three glowing filaments, at the other filament this was the extrapolation of *Sister Sue's* trajectory. At right angles to this, close, was the brilliant spark that was a star.

Grimes pointed the stem of his pipe at it.

"That sun?" he asked. "I may need to find a planet, one where there is fresh water available."

She punched computer keys, read out from the screen, "Salema, sir, so called by the people of its own habitable planet, which is variously known as Salem or New Salem. Catalogue number. . . ."

"Never mind that. And the people? Of Terran origin, aren't they?"

She punched more keys. "Yes, sir. Second Expansion stock."

"Now get that tin brain to do some sums for me. Running at a steady one G, with standard temporal precession, how long from here to planetfall?"

"As from now, sir, six days, fourteen hours and forty-five minutes."

"Mphm. We can survive that long on what water is left in the system, with rationing and recycling. There shouldn't be any need to go thirsty or get really dirty."

"Couldn't we carry on to New Otago, sir?"

"I'd not like to risk it. And I was brought up in the Survey

Service, as you know, Tomoko. We always liked to have plenty of reaction mass on hand so that we could use emergency rocket drive if we had to. So I think that a deviation to New Salem is justified. The insurance should cover it."

And if it doesn't, he thought, *some Survey Service secret fund will be used to compensate me.*

From below decks came the whine of a generator starting up. Lights flickered and then brightened as the emergency circuit cut out and the main circuit cut in. Steerforth said, "Flo seems to be getting things under control. I wonder why she hasn't sent Mr. Kershaw up to keep us informed."

Kershaw pulled himself into the control room. "Sir, Ms. Scott isn't very communicative. So I checked up in the Mannschenn Drive room. The MD engineers are standing by, waiting to start up as soon as they have the power. Mr. Grey asked me to tell you that there is no damage."

"Thank you."

Finally Florence Scott made her appearance. Her once-white overalls were sweat-soaked and grease-stained, and more grease marked her broad, ruddy face.

"Captain," she announced, "we'll have the phones working again in a couple o' minutes but I thought I'd report the situation in person, not through your messenger boy." Kershaw flushed and scowled. "As ye already know, the engineroom got flooded. Anybody'd think that this was some tramp steamer on Earth's seas way back in the twentieth century, old style. Cassie didn't think; all she wanted to do was to get rid of all that water in a hurry. She could ha' let it drain into the store and workshop flat—but no. Not her. She opened the dump valves.

"There's nothing wrong with the innies that a little minor rewiring won't fix. I should be able to restart in half an hour. An' then you can restart the time twister an' we can be on our way. You may as well restart it now."

"What about fresh water?" asked Grimes.

"Enough. We'll not die o' thirst or go unwashed as long as we're careful."

"What about the emergency reaction drive?"

"There's no reaction mass. But emergency reaction drive was phased out years ago in the merchant service. It's not required by law."

Grimes said, "I may be old-fashioned, but I like to know that I have rockets under my arse should I feel the need for them in a hurry. I'm deviating to the nearest port of refuge, which is on New Salem. There we'll get the bulkhead patched and refill the tank."

"A needless expense and waste of time," sneered the chief engineer. "Oh, well, you're the captain."

"*And* the owner," Grimes reminded her firmly.

⇜ Chapter 15 ⇝

THERE WAS AEROSPACE CONTROL on New Salem, although its name was somewhat misleading. There was no aerial traffic, either lighter than or heavier than air, in the planet's atmosphere. ("If God had meant us to fly He would have given us wings.") But at Port Salem there was a Carlotti radio station with rather limited range and also an NST transceiver. Grimes got in touch while he was still proceeding toward the planet under Mannschenn Drive, using his Carlotti radio. This was an unusually troublesome procedure. According to the data in *Sister Sue*'s library bank New Salem Aerospace Control maintained a listening watch for the first five minutes of every hour, daylight hours only and never on Sunday. The first time that Cleo Jones tried to get through it must have been Sunday on New Salem. During the next twenty-four-hour period, ship's time, the trouble was trying to get the ship's clocks synchronized with those at the spaceport. Finally Cleo arranged for a continuous automatic transmission with an alarm to sound as soon as there was a reply.

Grimes happened to be in the control room when this happened.

An irritable female voice came from the Carlotti speaker. "Port Salem Aerospace Control to unknown vessel. Identify yourself. Pass your message."

"*Sister Sue* to Port Salem," said Grimes. "Request permission to land to effect essential repairs."

"Stand by, *Sister Sue*. I shall come back to you."

Grimes stood by for a long time, having his lunch, served by the faithful Seiko, in the control room. At last the speaker crackled into life.

"Port Salem to *Sister Sue*. What is the nature of the repairs that you will require? I must warn you that our workshop facilities are limited."

"The patching of a ruptured bulkhead," said Grimes. "My own engineers can carry out the work as long as suitable plating is available. The replenishment of my fresh water supply."

"Stand by, *Sister Sue*."

There was another long wait.

Finally, "Materials will be made available to you. Fresh water will be obtainable from Lake Beulah. What is your ETA please?"

Clocks and calendar were synchronized and Grimes was able to give day and time for his return to the normal continuum and, not too approximately, for his eventual setting down at Port Salem.

Eventually *Sister Sue* was dropping through the twilight towards the huddle of yellowish lights that was New Salem. He would have preferred to have made a dawn approach but, after all, he was supposed to be in some sort of distress and, therefore, in some sort of hurry. The traffic control officer, whose sour featured face was visible in the screen of the NST radio transceiver, instructed him to set down in the center of the triangle formed by the berth markers. What berth markers? Grimes asked himself irritably. What did they use for berth marking beacons on this benighted planet? Candles? He stepped up magnification and definition in the stern vision screen. At last he saw them as he continued his cautious descent, three feeble, ruddy sparks.

He hoped that Cassandra Perkins fully understood what was expected of her. If she acted too soon, clumsily (but on purpose) tripping over her own feet and clutching at a lubrication line for support, bending it but not breaking it, throttling the supply of oil to the governor bearings, *Sister Sue* would fall for far too many meters, damaging herself irreparably. The governor would have to seize up almost immediately after Grimes applied that final surge of thrust to cushion the landing.

He watched the read-out of the radar altimeter.

10 meters . . . 9 . . . 8 . . . 7 . . . 6 . . .

Now!

The cacophony of the inertial drive rose from little more than an irritable mutter to an angry clangor—then abruptly ceased. *Sister Sue* dropped like a stone, a very large and heavy stone. Shock absorbers screamed rather than sighed. Loose fittings rattled and there was a tinkling crash as something tore adrift from its securing bolts. Grimes slowly filled and lit his pipe—but even though he had been expecting the accident it was hard to maintain the pose of imperturbability. Tomoko, he thought, to whom it had all come as a big surprise, was making a far better job of it than he was.

Steerforth voiced what must have been the thought of all those in the control room.

"That's fucked it!" he said.

"Mr. Steerforth, mind your language," Grimes told him.

The intercom speaker crackled and then Florence Scott's voice came from it. "ID room to captain. Chief engineer here. The bearings of the governor seem to have seized up. I am making an immediate check of the extent of the damage."

"Thank you, Ms. Scott," said Grimes into his microphone.

"MD room to captain." This was the chief Mannschenn Drive engineer, Daniel Grey. "You seem to have made a crash landing." *A blinding glimpse of the obvious,* thought Grimes. "The jolt unseated numbers one, three and four rotors from their bearings . . . ."

Worse and worse, thought Grimes. *Or better and better?*

"Apart from anything else," Grey went on, "the Drive will have to be recalibrated once it has been reassembled."

"Somebody's coming out to us, sir," announced Steerforth.

Grimes got up from his chair, went to stand with the chief officer by the viewport. He saw the group of bobbing lights—hand-held lanterns?—and the dimly illumined human forms.

He said, "Looks like a boarding party of some kind. You'd better go down to the after airlock to receive them. I shall be in my day cabin. Oh, on your way down give Ms. Clay my compliments and tell her to keep Seiko out of sight as long as there are any locals aboard."

Steerforth grinned. "Aunt Jemima's read that article too, just as we all have. But *Star Scandals'* not quite in the same class as the *Encyclopaedia Galactica*, is it, sir? And their star reporter, Fenella Pruin, never lets facts get in the way of a sensational story."

"Ms. Pruin," said Grimes, "is a very able investigative reporter."

"Oh, yes. You know her, sir. I was forgetting."

"We know her, too," said Shirl and Darleen as one, making it plain that they held Fenella in quite high regard.

In his day cabin Grimes picked up the rather tattered copy of *Star Scandals* from the coffee table. It would be advisable, he thought, to get it out of sight before the visitors arrived. That lurid cover, with its colored photograph of a naked girl chained to a stake and with flames licking around her lower body . . . It had been the third ID engineer, Bill the Bull, who had found this particular issue of *Star Scandals* in his well-thumbed collection of that pornographic, as often as not, publication. As soon as it was known that *Sister Sue* was deviating to Salem, Fenella's piece on that planet had become almost required reading by all hands.

Fenella had visited Salem as a passenger aboard Wombat, owned by Able Enterprises. (This, of course, had been before she had gotten into the bad books of Baron Kane, whose company Able Enterprises was.) She had found it hard to sniff out anything really juicy on Salem; the people lived lives of utterly boring sexual probity. She had witnessed a slaughter of the silkies, the animals whose furs were Salem's only export—but Fenella was not at her best (worst?) as a writer on humanitarian issues. She blew up the business of her dancing dolls to absurd proportions. These tiny, beautifully made automata, one male, one female, not only danced to tinkling music but stripped, and when naked went through the motions of coitus. All very amusing to those of a kinky bent. . . .

Grimes read, "That party, in *Wombat's* wardroom, was inexpressably dreary. Pastor Coffin and his wife would drink only tea and insisted that this be both weak and tepid. In deference to the sensibilities of their guests Captain Timson and his officers did not smoke. Daringly I lit a cigarillo and was told, by the she-Coffin that if God had meant me to smoke He would have put a chimney on top of my head. I said that She had more important things to occupy Her time. This did not go down at all well.

"The conversation, such as it was, got on to the topic of machinery. Machinery, I gathered, was disapproved of on Salem. Of course I had already noticed this. Just one solar power plant to generate electricity for the spaceport facilities, communications and so forth. But oil-lighting in the houses, sailing vessels on the sea, bullock-drawn wagons on the roads. And bullocks, too, supplied the power to operate the presses which extracted the flammable oil from various seeds.

"Anyhow, Captain Timson was letting Pastor Coffin's diatribe against inventions of the devil go on without interruption. He knew on which side his bread was buttered. The silkie skin trade was a profitable one for his owners. But his officers, the engineers, especially, were inclined to argue. The fruit punch that they had been drinking had been well spiked with gin as soon as it became obvious that the Coffin couple was having none of it.

"Terry Muldoon, the third engineer, said, 'But machines have their uses, Pastor Coffin. Even as toys for children, educational toys . . .' (Terry, I learned later, had already resigned from Able Enterprises and had a job waiting for him with the Dog Star Line.) Coffin said, 'What can a child learn from a mechanical toy? He will learn all that he ever needs to know from the Bible.' Terry said, 'You'd be surprised, Pastor.' He turned to me and said, Fenella, why not show our guests those educational toys of yours?' (He was one of the few people aboard the ship who had seen them. Old Timson had not, neither had the two chief engineers.) So I went to my cabin and got the box and set it down on the wardroom table. I took out Max and Maxine. They stood stiffly, facing each other. I switched on the music, Ravel's Bolero. Max and Mazine came . . . alive. They could have been flesh-and-blood beings, not automata. They danced, and as they danced they shed their clothing. I always liked the part when Max got rid of his trousers; it is easy for a woman to disrobe gracefully to music, not so easy for a man. I always hoped that Max would get his feet tangled in his nether garments and come down heavily on his rather too perfect little arse, but he never did.

And then they were quite naked, the pair of them, anatomically correct. Maxine, legs open, was supine on the table top and Max was about to lower himself upon her when Coffin's big fist smashed down on the box as he bellowed, 'Blasphemy! Blasphemy!' The music stopped in mid-stridency. There was a sputter of sparks. Max, no more than a lifeless, somehow pathetic doll collapsed on top of the other doll, among the litter of rags that had been their clothing.

"Timson apologized. 'I had no idea, Pastor . . .'"

"Coffin—he was virtually foaming at the mouth—screamed, 'That is no excuse, Captain. Does it not say in the Book that you shalt not suffer a witch to live? She . . .' he pointed a quivering finger at me, 'is a witch. And those are her familiars!'

"'Go to your cabin,' Timson ordered me. I tried to argue but it was no use. The mate and the second mate, that pair of great, hulking louts, hustled me out of the wardroom, locked me in my quarters. And there I was confined until breakfast the next morning.

"After the meal Terry managed to have a few words with me. He told me that the pastor had gone on ranting and raving after I had been removed from his presence, accusing me of witchcraft and saying that Max and Maxine were my familiars. He demanded that I be turned over to the local authorities to stand trial—but this was too much even for Captain Timson. Then he insisted that Max and Maxine be given into his custody, saying that they would be publicly destroyed by burning. Timson agreed to this. 'And you'd better stay aboard from now on, Fenella,' Terry told me, 'otherwise you'll find yourself tied to a stake with the faggots piled about you . . .'"

There was a knock at the door. Grimes hastily took the dog-eared copy of *Star Scandals* through to his bedroom, returned to the day cabin and called, "Come in!"

Tomoko entered, followed by a tall man in rusty black clothing with touches of white, rather grimy white, at his throat and wrists.

"Pastor Coffin to see you, sir," she announced.

Grimes almost said what he usually said on such occasions but decided against it. To judge from the deeply lined, craggy face, the fanatical black eyes under shaggy gray brows, this was a man utterly devoid of humor.

◈ Chapter 16 ◈

THE TWO MEN SHOOK HANDS. The pastor's grip was firm but cold.

"Be seated, sir," said Grimes. "May I offer you refreshment? Coffee? Tea? Or . . . ?"

"Tea, Captain. Not strong. No milk. No sugar."

Grimes telephoned the pantry and made the order. He sat back in his chair, filled and lit his pipe.

The pastor said, "Do not smoke."

Grimes said, "This is my ship, sir. I make the rules."

"This may be your ship, Captain, but you neither own nor command this planet. And, as I understand it, you will be unable to lift from this world unless you are vouchsafed cooperation by myself and the elders of my church."

Grimes made a major production of sighing. Until he knew which way the wind was blowing or likely to blow he would have to do as bid. He put his pipe down in the ashtray.

Shirl came in, carrying a tray which she set on the coffee table. (Melinda Clay, in her capacity as purser, would still be dealing with the port officials.) In her very short uniform shorts she looked all legs.

Coffin looked at her disapprovingly then said, "Are all your female officers so indecently attired, Captain?"

Grimes said, "My female officers wear what is standard

uniform for both the Federation Survey Service and the Merchant Service."

"Aboard the ships of Able Enterprises," said Coffin, "females are always decently covered."

And Drongo Kane, thought Grimes, would put his people in sackcloth and ashes as the rig of the day rather than lose a profitable trade. *And so would I*, he realized with some surprise.

Shirl glared at Coffin and strode out of the day cabin. Grimes poured the tea, which was far too weak for his taste, added milk and sugar to his own.

"I understand, Captain," said the pastor, "that you have various mechanical troubles. We on Salem, freed from the tyranny of the machine, are not so afflicted."

"It was machines, starships, that brought your ancestors here, sir."

"At times the Lord uses the Devil's tools. But His people should avoid doing so. Now, what are your requirements? What must you do to make your vessel spaceworthy?"

"I have to repair a bulkhead—just a matter of patching. I hope that a suitable plate will be available here. The shaft of my inertial drive governor must be renewed. My Mannschenn Drive has to be recalibrated. I understand that there is a workshop here, and a stock of spares and materials."

"Your understanding is correct, Captain. The workshop and the stores are the property of Able Enterprises. I am empowered to act as their agent."

"Any skilled labor, Pastor?"

"We have blacksmiths, Captain, but nobody capable of carrying out the type of work that you seem to require."

"No matter. My own engineers can start earning their pay for a change." Grimes picked up his pipe, thought better of it and put it down again. "There's another matter, Pastor. I don't need to tell you that a deviation, such as this one that I have been obliged to make, costs money. I am not loaded to capacity. Would there be any chance of a cargo of silkie hides to New Otago?"

"It is only wealthy worlds, such as El Dorado, that can afford such luxury clothing," said the pastor. "From what I have heard of New Otago I gain the impression that nobody there is either very rich or very poor."

"Perhaps," said Grimes hopefully, "there might be the possibility, sometime in the not too distant future, of a shipment of hides from here to some market, somewhere . . . ."

"Able Enterprises," Coffin told him, "has the monopoly on the trade from Salem to Earth as well as to El Dorado. But you are a widely traveled man, Captain. You have your contacts throughout the Galaxy . . ." And did Grimes detect the gleam of cupidity in the pastor's eyes? "Perhaps, in your voyagings, you will be able to find other markets for our export. In such a case I am sure that some mutually profitable arrangement could be made."

Melinda Clay came in with various documents to be signed. Coffin looked at her even more disapprovingly than he had Shirl but said nothing until she had left.

He said, "So you employ the children of Ham aboard your vessel. But, from them, an indecent display of flesh is, I suppose, to be expected."

"Mphm," grunted Grimes.

Coffin got to his feet. "Almost I was tempted to forbid shore leave to yourself and your officers. But I realize that if there are, in the future, to be business dealings between you and ourselves there must be some familiarization. Your people must understand the nature of the cargo that they will be carrying. Too, it is not impossible that they, or at least some of them, will find the true Light. . . ." He drew himself to his full, not inconsiderable height. "But I strongly advise you, Captain, to see to it that your females are properly attired when they set foot on our soil. Otherwise I shall not be responsible for the consequences."

Probably, thought Grimes contemptuously, *your men would fly into a screaming tizzy at the sight of a woman's ankle.*

He said, "I'll see to it, Pastor, that my people comport themselves properly."

"Do so, Captain. Tomorrow morning I shall have the spaceport workshop unlocked and shall be waiting for you there so that you and your engineers can tell me what you want."

"At about 0900?" asked Grimes.

"At seven of the clock," stated Coffin. "We, on this world do not waste the daylight hours that God sends us."

Grimes sent for his senior officers, received from them more detailed damage reports than the earlier ones, told them of his talk with Coffin. He said, "There will be shore leave. But you must make it plain to your people, the girls especially, that they are to avoid giving offense in any way. This is a very puritanical planet, so the ladies are to wear long skirts at all times. It will be as well, too, if there is no smoking in public."

Steerforth laughed. "That's going to hurt you, Captain."

"Too right it is," agreed Grimes. "But I suppose that I must set a good example for the rest of you." He turned to Florence Scott. "I'm afraid that it's an early rise and an early breakfast for you tomorrow morning, Flo. The pastor—he's the local boss cocky—is letting us use the Able Enterprises repair and maintenance facilities. I suggested that we meet him in the workshop at 0900 but he made it plain that, as far as he's concerned, the day's work starts at 0700. We have to play along.

"You can make contact with the local ship chandler, Melinda," he said to the catering officer, "and order any consumable stores necessary. Just try to remember that *Sister Sue* is not the flagship of Trans-Galactic Clippers! Oh, and if there are any locals aboard don't forget to keep Seiko out of sight . . ."

She grinned whitely and said, "I've read that article in *Star Scandals*, Captain. If any of these superstitious bastards got the idea that she's my familiar I might get barbecued."

"And Seiko almost certainly would be. And how are things in the time-twisting department, Dan?"

"All that are required are patience and a few pairs of steady hands," said the Mannschenn Drive engineer. "We shall have things re-assembled before Flo's pusher is ready."

"And then you'll make a balls of the recalibration," Ms. Scott said. "It's happened before, you know."

"And that seems to be it," said Grimes. "A nightcap before you go?"

They accepted. When they finally left, Grimes overheard a scrap of conversation from the alleyway outside his door, Florence Scott talking to Daniel Grey.

"The old bastard's taking things remarkably well. I thought that he'd be having my guts for a necktie."

"He's insured," said Grey.

And I'll be surprised, thought Grimes, if Lloyd's don't up my premiums.

◦◦ Chapter 17 ◦◦

THE NEXT MORNING GRIMES, with Steerforth, Florence Scott and Juanita Garcia, partook of an early breakfast. The meal finished, the four of them made their way out of the ship, down the ramp to the scarred concrete of the apron, still wet from overnight showers. The sun was only just up, in a partly cloudy sky, and the air was decidedly chilly. The spaceport administration buildings toward which they were walking reminded Grimes of pictures that he had seen in his father's library, of small seaports on the Pacific coast of North America during the nineteenth century old style. There were the rather ramshackle wooden structures, the tallest of which was the control tower from which, incongruously, sprouted the antennae and scanners of modern communication and locating equipment. But there should have been a quay, thought Grimes, with square-rigged sailing vessels, whalers, alongside to complete the picture.

"Are you sure that we didn't, somehow, travel back in time, Captain?" asked Juanita. "It's not only the way that this place looks but the way that it smells, even . . . ."

Grimes removed his pipe from his mouth, exhaled the fumes of burning tobacco, waited until his sense of smell was again operational and then sniffed the air. Drifting down the light wind from the nearby town was the pleasant acridity of wood smoke from morning cooking fires.

He said to the second engineer, "In a way we have traveled back in time, Juanita. The colonists here deliberately put the clock back. Oh, well, it's their world and they're welcome to it."

There were signs of life around the administration buildings. As the party from the ship approached these a tall, black-clad figure emerged from one of the sheds, strode up to them. It was Pastor Coffin. He pulled a huge, silver watch from his waistcoat pocket, glared at it. He said, "You are late, Captain. It is already two minutes past the hour."

Grimes apologized, with a certain look of sincerity, saying that he had underestimated the time that it would take to walk from the ship. The pastor said coldly, "You spacemen . . ." He looked coldly at Juanita who, even in her white overalls, was indubitably feminine. "You spacepersons, with your machines waiting on you hand and foot, do not take enough healthy exercise. But come."

He led the way into the long shed from which he had emerged. The interior was gloomy. The windows were small and the few electric lights that had been switched on seemed to be doing their best to imitate oil lamps. What was their power source? wondered Grimes. Batteries, probably. In one corner was what was obviously a generator, which was not running. It, like the other machinery and equipment in the shed, would be the property of Able Enterprises.

"Can't we have some proper light?" asked Ms. Scott irritably. "I see a jenny there that's doing nothing for its living."

"You may start the machine," said Coffin to Grimes. "But you will be charged for its hire."

"We must have proper illumination," said Grimes. "Flo, can you get that thing going?"

"No trouble, Captain. I cut my teeth on diesels."

She walked to the generator, inspected it, cracked fuel valves and switched on the electric starter. The thing coughed briefly and then settled down to a steady beat. Juanita found other light switches and, within seconds, the interior of the workshop was bathed by the harsh glow of the overhead fluorescents.

Steerforth said to Grimes, as he looked around, "Drongo Kane could almost build a ship from scratch with the stuff that he's got stashed in here."

"As long as there's some suitable plating . . ." said Grimes.

"And we shall probably have to use that lathe," put in Ms. Scott. "To turn down a new shaft for the governor."

"I rely upon you," said Coffin, "to maintain a strict tally of all materials utilized and of all machinery employed."

"You can start the timekeeping now, Mr. Steerforth," Grimes ordered his chief officer. "When I go back to the ship I shall arrange for you to be relieved by Mr. Kershaw."

Steerforth pulled a notebook from his pocket and made entries.

Coffin accompanied Grimes back to *Little Sister*.

He said, "Perhaps you think it strange, Captain, that I should allow your people free run of the workshop."

Grimes said, "Frankly yes, Pastor. I expected that you or one of your people would remain to keep an eye on things."

The pastor made a sound that approximated a chuckle. "We do business with Able Enterprises but we do not have to like them, any more than we have to like you. In the final analysis, it matters not if one party of unbelievers, as represented by yourself, robs another party of unbelievers. But I think that you are, according to your lights, dim though they be, an honorable man . . ."

"Thank you," said Grimes dryly.

"And, of course, the port dues and such that you will pay will hasten the day when our project shall be completed . . ."

Project? wondered Grimes. Oh, yes. The Ark that would survive the eventual collapse of the Universe.

He asked, "Has work on the project actually commenced yet?"

"We have commissioned research," the pastor told him. "The salvation vessel will not, of course, be mechanically propelled. It will be a sailing ship of Space."

"Mphm," grunted Grimes.

They had reached the foot of the gangway. Not very enthusiastically Grimes invited Coffin aboard the ship for morning tea. He was relieved when the pastor declined the invitation, saying that he was a busy man. He went aboard himself, sent for the second officer and told him to take over from Mr. Steerforth in the workshop. He discussed various matters with the chief MD engineer and the catering officer. Then he sent for Shirl and Darleen, looked them up and down and ordered them to change into less revealing uniforms, telling them that they were to accompany him on a stroll to the town, which was also the seaport. He waited for them in the after airlock. When they joined him they were dressed in concealing (more or less) white overalls, standard working rig.

The day was warming up now although there was still a nip in the breeze. The road from the spaceport to the seaport was little more than a rough track and the walk was rather more arduous than Grimes had anticipated. Still, he enjoyed it, looking with interest at the vegetation on either side of the path. He was no botanist and could see little difference between these trees and Terran pines, between these bushes and gorse and broom. Perhaps the flora was of Terran origin and had been introduced by the colonists. Perhaps not. It did not much matter. It was the indigenous fauna with which he was concerned.

Shirl complained, "Why must we wear these things, John? We want to run, to feel the sun and the fresh air on our bodies."

He told her, "You know why. You've read your pal Fenella's story about what happened when she was here."

"Yes," said Darleen. "But Fenella's toys were not only undressed. They were . . . "

"And perhaps *we* could," suggested Shirl.

"Not here, not now," said Grimes hastily; nonetheless he did think that a nearby clump of broom would provide adequate cover.

They came to the town. There were wooden houses, none of more than one story, except for the church, with its little bell tower. Lace curtains covered the small windows but Grimes thought that some of these were drawn aside for a surreptitious peep as the three strangers made their way down the narrow street. But there were very few people abroad and the occasional black-clad man or woman whom they encountered scowled at them suspiciously.

Suddenly Shirl and Darleen, walking to either side of Grimes, fell silent. This, for them, was most unusual. He looked at first one and then the other. Their faces were pale, frightened almost.

He asked, "What's wrong?"

"Don't you . . . *smell* it, John?" said Darleen.

"Smell what?" he demanded.

There was the salty tang of the nearby sea and with it, not unpleasant, a hint of decaying seaweed. And there was the acridity of tar and, from a baker's shop, the mouth-watering aroma of freshly baked bread.

"The . . . The smell of fear," whispered Shirl. "And of pain . . . And of helplessness . . ."

And something was happening on the waterfront. Suddenly there was a growing clamor, the sound of many voices, shouting exultantly. There was singing; it sounded like a hymn of some kind. And now and again there was a thin, high, unhuman screaming.

Grimes quickened his pace and the girls kept step, hurrying through the narrow, winding dirt street. They emerged on to a wide quay, from which protruded finger jetties. At two of these, large schooners were already alongside; other schooners, four of them, were coming in from seaward, running free, their shabby sails widespread to catch the last of the dying breeze. The jetties were crowded with the singing, shouting, black-clad people, although those at which the ships had yet to come alongside were less congested.

To one of these Grimes, followed by Shirl and Darleen, made his way. He clambered up on to one of the ox-drawn wagons that was waiting there so that he could see over the heads of the crowd, watch what was happening. The girls followed him. The driver of this vehicle, a burly, black-bearded giant, turned in his seat to stare at them.

He growled, "Get off, you!" Then, as he saw the uniforms, his manner changed. "Oh, you're spacers, aren't you? Off that ship. You can stay, but only until I pick up my load."

"What will your load be?" asked Grimes.

"The harvest of the sea, spacer. Looks as though the boats have done well this trip. They're low in the water."

Yes, thought Grimes, looking at the approaching schooner. *She's down to her marks, or over them . . .*

The triangular sails were coming down now and being lashed smartly to the booms. That skipper, thought Grimes, knew his job. With only a ballooning jib to provide steerage way, the ship ghosted in, drifted gently alongside the jetty. Lines were thrown, caught by men on the quay, their eyes slipped over bollards. The jib came down with a run.

The hatches, one abaft the foremast, the other abaft the mainmast, were already open. From his vantage point Grimes could see into both of these. In the main hold were bloody pelts—black and brown and gray and golden. In the forehold was living cargo, a squirming mass in which the same colors predominated. And it was from this hold that the thin, high screaming came.

And there was a faint scream from either Shirl or Darleen.

Grimes said to the driver, making a statement rather than asking a question, "Silkies . . ."

"What else, spacer."

"But those live ones. In the forward hold . . ."

"Pups o' course."

Grimes, shipowner and shipmaster, was becoming interested and for more than humanitarian reasons. "It seems to me," he said, "that the adult silkies were skinned where they were slaughtered. But why were the pups taken alive? If they'd been killed and skinned too, so much more cargo could have been carried."

The driver laughed condescendingly.

"It's easy to see that you are not on the fur trade, spacer. The people from the Able ships know how we do things. The pelts of the pups are much finer than those of the adults. It has been found that if they are carried for days in a ship's hold, even well-salted down, they go rotten. So the pup pelts are brought in still on the pups. And then the pups are skinned in the factories."

"But I would think," said Grimes, "that the pups themselves would die and go rotten, and their skins around them, during a voyage in those conditions."

"Not them. They're not like us. They're hardy beasts. Oh, those on the bottom will be near dead by the time that they're discharged—but they'll all soon be dead in any case."

There was a slight shift of wind. Over the wagon drifted the reek of stale blood, of corruption and of excrement. *Money stinks*, thought Grimes sourly, choking down his rising nausea.

But he decided to stay for a while. The booms of the schooner were being used as swinging derricks. In the holds the longshoremen were making up slings of the bloody pelts, throwing the squirming pups into cargo nets, others were in gangs manning the tackles. Two wagons had drawn up alongside the ship to receive cargo.

"I'm next in line," said the driver. "You'd better get off 'less you want to ride back among a load o' pups."

"I think we'll walk," said Grimes. "But thanks all the same. And thank you for the information."

Shirl and Darleen jumped down to the wharf decking. Grimes followed.

"Let us get out of here!" said the girls as one.

~ Chapter 18 ~

THEY WALKED SLOWLY back to the ship, at first in silence.

"Humans are very cruel . . ." said Shirl at last.

"We have studied your history," said Darleen.

"So?" said Grimes.

"So all through your history," went on Darleen, "you have slaughtered, for your own profit, not only beings lacking real intelligence but those who are as intelligent as you, although in a different way. The whales, the dolphins . . ."

"We have seen the error of our ways," said Grimes. "We are trying to put things right."

"We? Do you speak for all of your race, John? Oh, you were sent to this world by the Old Crocodile to try to save the silkies—but there is money in this stinking fur trade, just as there has been money in other trades in which Drongo Kane has been involved. Women and boys from their primitive worlds to the brothels of New Venusberg, for example. And Kane is not alone. There are many like him, to whom the only god, among all the odd gods, is money. At times we have suspected that even you worship this god."

"Don't drag religion into it," snapped Grimes. Then, "You've seen silkies now. Are they intelligent beings?"

Shirl laughed bitterly.

"We saw," she said, "a squirming mass of very young beings, wallowing in their own filth, terrified, speechless. Imagine that you are a non-human being from some other planet, seeing human babies in a similar state. Would you think that they were intelligent beings?"

"So you are not sure," said Grimes.

"We are not sure. We know that the fur trade is a brutal one, that is all. We shall have to meet adult silkies and talk with them . . ."

"Talk with them?"

"As we talked with the kangaroos, back on Earth. Oh, they are not truly intelligent but they are capable of evolving, doing over a very long time what our ancestors did, with outside help, in a very short time."

"The crimes of genetic engineers are many," said Grimes.

"We resent that," they said in chorus.

"I was speaking in jest. And, in any case, the pair of you are much better looking than a silky in any age group."

"We should hope so. But what would a silky think of us? Horribly ugly brutes who slaughter and torture."

"They must learn," said Grimes, "that all human beings—and that includes you, after all you are officially human—are not the same."

"Then we shall have to meet them," said Shirl. "We shall have to commune with them."

They passed through the town and then made a detour, following one of the wagons, with its load of shrieking pups, that had made its way inland from the waterfront. It was headed toward a long shed, came to a halt outside its open door. Men clambering up on to the vehicle, threw to the ground the small, squirming, furry bodies. Other men dragged these inside the building.

"We . . . We would rather not see what is happening," said Shirl.

"Neither would I," said Grimes, "but I'm afraid that I have to."

It was an experience that would live long in his memory. The pups, hanging by hooks from a sort of primitive overhead conveyor belt, were being flayed alive and their still-living bodies thrown into a steaming cauldron while their pelts, treated with far greater respect, were neatly stacked on tables.

A burly man, a foreman, bloody knife in hand, approached Grimes.

"What are you doing here, spacer?" he demanded.

"Just . . . Just looking." And then, unable to restrain his disgust, "Is that necessary?"

"Is what necessary?"

"Couldn't you kill the pups before you skin them?"

"Keep your nose out of things about which you know nothing. Kill them first, and ruin the pelts? Everybody knows that a pup has to be skinned while it's still living."

"But. . . It's cruel."

"Cruel? How so, spacer? Everybody knows, surely, that the Lord God gave man authority over all lesser beings. How can the exercise of divinely granted authority be cruel?"

"It need not be."

"It does need to be, spacer, if the high-quality pelts are not to be ruined. Too, is not God Himself often cruel in the light of our limited understanding?"

With an effort, Grimes restrained himself from saying, *Thank God I'm an agnostic.*

"But I have work to do, spacer. And you will have seen that no effort is spared to ensure that the pelts we export are of high quality. The pastor has told us that you may be interested in entering the trade."

Grimes made his retreat to the fresh, open air but was delayed as a fresh batch of feebly struggling, almost inaudibly whining pups was dragged into the slaughterhouse. When he got outside he walked unsteadily to where Shirl and Darleen were waiting for him.

He muttered, as much to himself as to them, "This filthy trade must be stopped!"

When they got back to the spaceport, to the ship, his nausea was almost gone. He saw two women taking a gentle stroll around the ship. One was in uniform, but with slacks instead of the usual very short skirt, the other was wearing what looked like a modified version of the traditional kimono. But who was that with her, in uniform? It was neither the radio officer nor the catering officer; her face was not black. It was none of the female engineer officers.

The two women saw Grimes, walked to meet him.

"Captain-san," said Tomoko, bowing.

But it was Tomoko who was wearing the uniform.

"Captain-san," said the other, also bowing.

Her glossy black hair was piled high on her head. Her face was very pale, white, almost, and her lips an unnatural scarlet. Rather incongruously she was wearing a pair of huge dark spectacles.

"Who is this . . . geisha?" demanded Grimes of Tomoko.

But he knew. He had recognized, although with some incredulity, the voice.

"Captain-san," said the third officer, "Seiko-san wanted some exercise, some fresh air . . ."

"She needs neither," said Grimes.

"And you had made it plain," went on Tomoko, "that she was not to appear before any of the colonists in her true form, as a robot. But I have cosmetics, and a wig, and suitable clothing for her. Her eyes, of course, must remain hidden . . ."

"And her body," said Grimes.

"Oh, no, Captain-san. I have painted her all over, from her head to her feet, with the right touches of color . . ."

Grimes laughed. "That was unnecessary. A naked female body would give even more affront to the people here than would a robot. All right, Tomoko. And Seiko. Carry on with your stroll. But don't stray too far from the ship."

As he mounted the gangway he muttered, "Exercise . . . Fresh air . . . Why not sunshine while she was about it?"

"She's only human . . ." said Shirl or Darleen.

~ Chapter 19 ~

GRIMES, WITH SHIRL AND DARLEEN AS COMPANY, had a sandwich lunch in his quarters. Steerforth came up to join his captain and the two girls for coffee and a talk. Grimes told his chief officer what he had seen.

"Whether or not the silkies are intelligent," he concluded, "this fur trade is a sickening business. The slaughter of the pups especially."

"Salem is a long way from Earth, sir," said Steerforth. "And there's big money involved, and the El Dorado Corporation has a finger in this particular pie. I need hardly tell you, Captain, how many Gs the EDC can pile on when its interests are threatened."

"Mphm. And meanwhile, back at the ranch," asked Grimes, "how have things been going?"

Steerforth laughed. "I wandered over to the workshop just after I'd had my lunch, to relieve Kershaw for his. Flo and her gang were having their troubles. She was stomping up and down with a sandwich in one hand and a spanner in the other—she told me that they couldn't spare the time to return to the ship for a proper meal—and bawling out Calamity Cassie, who'd just perpetrated some piece of spectacular clumsiness, and calling down curses on Able Enterprises . . . ."

"Why Able Enterprises?" asked Grimes.

"To quote Flo," said Steerforth, "This isn't a workshop. It's a fornicating junk shop!' Even I—and I'm no engineer—could see her point. That machinery—the generator, the turret lathe and so on—must have been bought on the cheap from Noah's Ark after she became a total loss on Mount Ararat."

Grimes laughed. "Drongo Kane's an astute businessman. He's not going to leave new, highly expensive equipment unattended on a world like this. There are just the essentials here, and no more. His own engineers would be expected to make do with what's in the workshop. My engineers'll just have to do the same. Did Flo come up with any estimation of the time it'll take her to complete the repairs?"

"That she did not, sir. I got snarled at for daring to ask. 'First of all,' she yelled, 'I have to repair the machines that I shall have to use to repair my own machinery!' Of course, she should never have allowed Cassie within spitting distance of that lathe."

"Spread it around," said Grimes, "that I'm in a vile bad temper, like a raging lion seeking whom I might devour, especially if it happens to be one, any one, of my engineers. This is all costing me money." He laughed rather humorlessly. "And if Admiral Damien doesn't see me compensated I shall be in a bad temper!"

"Meanwhile you might get one of the lifeboats ready for an atmospheric flight. I'd like to take it out for a run tomorrow morning."

"The boats are always ready, sir," said Steerforth stiffly. Then, "Which officers are you taking with you?"

"Just Shirl and Darleen," Grimes told him. "It's all part of their training."

"Can't Seiko come with us, John?" asked Shirl. "She'll enjoy the trip."

"*Seiko*?" Grimes considered the idea then repeated, less dubiously, "Seiko?"

"Why not, sir?" said Steerforth. "I mean no offense, but you do, at times, display a certain aptitude for getting into trouble. And," he added hastily, "for getting out of it. But now and again you've needed help. Shirl and Darleen, with their somewhat unorthodox martial skills, will be quite good bodyguards. And so would be

Seiko. She's intelligent. And she's strong. You know those absurdly heavy lids on the yeast culture vats, how it always takes at least two people to lift one off? The other day I saw Seiko lift one by herself, using one hand only. And, even more important, she's loyal to you. It's gotten to the stage where nobody dare say anything unkind about you in her hearing."

"Mphm . . ." Grimes filled and lit his pipe. "But there's still the attitude of the colonists toward robots to be considered. We might find ourselves in some situation where Seiko's presence would be like a red rag to a bull."

"But nobody would know that she is a robot, sir. I was with Tomoko when she applied the make-up, the body paint, the cosmetics. And Tomoko made a very thorough job, even to a merkin. You could strip her and nobody would dream that she wasn't a human woman—as long as you left her dark glasses on."

"All right. I'll take Seiko along. With her and Shirl and Darleen I could fight off an army."

"And Cassie, to look after the lifeboat's engine?" asked Steerforth.

"That would be tempting Providence," said Grimes.

The next morning, right after breakfast, Grimes, with Shirl, Darleen and Seiko, made their way to the Number 1 boat bay. Steerforth was already there, making a last-minute check. With him was Florence Scott, grumbling audibly that she had more important things to occupy her time than getting things ready for the Old Man's joy ride. Seiko, clad not in kimono but working rig like that worn by Shirl and Darleen, was carrying two large hampers of food for the biologically human members of the party. Her rather too elaborately coiled glossy black wig looked odd over the white boiler suit. *An aristocratic Japanese lady, thought Grimes, dressed to make a tour of inspection of a sewage conversion plant . . .*

"She's all yours, Captain," said Steerforth, emerging from the boat's airlock.

"The innie's OK," said Ms. Scott. She grinned sourly. "Just as well that I never let Calamity Cassie overhaul it."

"Thank you," said Grimes. "I'll leave matters in your capable hands, gentlefolk. Expect me back late afternoon or early evening."

"Cleo will be maintaining a listening watch," said Steerforth. "Just in case. If you should get into trouble it'd be no use calling the so-called Aerospace Control. Their operators never seem to be on duty."

"And never on Sunday," said Grimes. "And today's Sunday. Oh, by the way, Flo, if the pastor or any of his minions show up to complain about your breaking the Sabbath in the workshop, don't try to argue. Just look pious and knock off."

"You're the captain," she said. "And the owner."

Grimes followed the women into the boat, went forward to the control cab, sat in the pilot's seat. He operated the switch that would close the airlock doors, the other one that caused the securing clamps to fall away. He spoke into his microphone, "Number 1 boat to control room. Ready to self-eject."

"Eject at will, Number 1," came the reply. Grimes operated the boat bay door from the control cab, although this could have been done from the ship's control room. Through the forward window he saw the double valve opening and beyond the outward swinging metal plates blue sky and fluffy white clouds. The miniature inertial drive unit grumbled to itself and the boat lifted a few centimeters clear of the deck and then, obedient to Grimes's touch, slid forward and out.

Had his ship been berthed at a normal spaceport Grimes would now have reported his movements to Aerospace Control and would, in fact, have obtained prior permission to hold a boat drill from the Port Captain. But here there was no Port Captain. For much of the time there was not even a Communications Officer. (But there would surely be, thought Grimes, some official seeing to it that port dues and other charges were paid by visiting ships.)

Grimes circled *Sister Sue* at control-room altitude. He saw Tomoko and Cleo Jones standing by the big viewports. They waved to him. He waved back. Still circling, he lifted steadily. The seaport was now in view, with the jetties and, alongside them, the big schooners. From this height the blue-gray ocean looked calm. To the northeast was a large island with three peaks, one tall and two little more than hummocks. To the north was a chain of islets. Below the surface of the sea were brown blotches that could either be rocks or beds of some kelplike weed. Grimes wished that he had maps and charts to cover this planet. He would have to make his own. In fact he was starting to do just that; the boat was fitted with a Survey Service surplus datalog, not at all standard equipment for small craft carried by merchant starships.

He set course for the archipelago, reducing altitude as he made his approach. Using binoculars he could make out marine creatures swimming below the surface of the sea. Silkies? Could be. Behind him he heard Shirl, Darleen and Seiko chattering, pointing things out to each other. He tried to ignore them.

Then, "Look!" he heard Shirl exclaim. "That rock! It must be a silky colony!"

He realized that she was talking to him, swung his glasses in the direction that she had indicated. The surface of the small, rocky island seemed to be alive—but there was not the display of gloriously colored pelts that he would have expected. There was just a slowly heaving olive-green carpet. There was something there, something alive, but it could be no more than some form of motile plant life.

He said, "The silkies' hides aren't that color."

"There are silkies there," stated Darleen firmly. "We can . . . *feel* it."

"Oh, all right," said Grimes. "It costs nothing to have a closer look."

The boat dropped steadily, its mini-innie hammering noisily. Suddenly there was a flurry of motion on the islet. That olive-green carpet went into a frenzy, seemed to be tearing itself to pieces, rags of it flying into the air, falling into the sea. And the silkies who had been hidden under the broad, fleshy leaves of seaweed slithered rapidly into the water, a spectacular eruption of black and brown and golden and silver bodies, the pups first, being pushed and rolled off the rock by their parents, the adults last of all.

(The silky-hunters' schooners, thought Grimes, would be

making a silent approach, not a noisy one as he was. And probably the masthead lookouts would not be deceived, not every time, by the silkies' camouflage.)

"Are you landing, John?" asked Shirl.

"What good will that do?" countered Grimes.

"Once you have shut off that noisy thing—" Darleen gestured toward the engine casing "—we may be able to call the silkies back."

"I suppose it's worth trying," said Grimes.

He made his final approach with great caution. The surface of the rock seemed to be uniformly flat, although in parts was still covered with small heaps of the weed. Grimes did his best to avoid these; they might well-conceal rocky upthrustings or crevasses. Finally the belly skids made contact and the shock absorbers sighed gently and the inertial drive unit subsided into silence.

"We're here," said Grimes unnecessarily. He raised the ship on the NST radio but, although he could have reported the boat's exact location as read from the datalog, did not do so. It suddenly occurred to him that the pastor, having learned that Grimes was on a snooping expedition, might be maintaining a listening watch of his own.

"But where are you, sir?" demanded Steerforth irritably.

"Oh, just on some bloody island. I thought that it would be a good place for a swim, and then lunch."

With that the chief officer would have to be content. But surely he would have tracked the boat on the ship's radar and would have a very good idea as to where she was. But what of Aerospace Control? Had some technician broken the Sabbath to get their radar working? Grimes was certain, however, that those antennae on the control tower had not been rotating while that structure was still within sight of the boat.

He opened the airlock doors and then led the way out into the open air.

Chapter 20

THERE WAS NO WIND and the piles of decomposing seaweed were steaming in the sun, as were the deposits of ordure. The mixed aroma, although strong, was not altogether unpleasant. The silkies, decided Grimes, must be vegetarians. He and the three women walked around the little island, being careful where they put their feet. The shape of this flat rock was roughly rectangular, one kilometer by five hundred meters. On the northern face were low cliffs, about ten meters above sea level. On the southern side there was a gradual slope right into the water, a natural ramp by which the silkies could gain access to their rookery.

Grimes said, "It's a pity that we scared them all off."

"What else did you expect?" demanded Shirl. "They must have thought that the boat was something new being used by the fur hunters."

"But we can try to call them back," said Darleen.

She kicked off her shoes, shrugged out of her boiler suit, stepped out of her brief underwear. She waded out into the still water. "It's cold." she complained. But she walked on, slowly but steadily. Grimes wondered why she did not swim. Then suddenly she assumed a squatting posture, lowering herself until she was completely submerged. She lost her balance of course and floated, face down, her prominent buttocks well above the surface. From around the region of her head came a flurry of bubbles.

She came up for air, inhaling deeply, and then repeated her original maneuver. Again she came up for air and this time struck out for the shore. She waded out to where Grimes, with Shirl and Seiko, were standing.

"It is no use," she said. "I cannot sing under the water."

"I can," said Seiko. "I am guaranteed to be waterproof at any depth. But what must I sing?"

"It will be a call," Darleen told her. "A sound that will carry a long way, a very long way, under the sea. When we were on Earth we studied many things. We listened to the recordings of the whale songs and tried to understand them and to make the same sort of music ourselves. And it was a whale song that I was trying to sing just now. Its meaning is, put into words, 'Come to me. Come to me.'"

"I suppose that it was Admiral Damien who suggested this course of studies," commented Grimes.

"It was," Darleen admitted. "But he never thought to have taught us to sing under the water."

"What sounds must I make?" asked Seiko.

Darleen started to sing. It was an eerie ululation with an odd rhythm. It was something that one felt rather than merely listened to. There was the impression of loneliness, of hunger for close contact. It was a call, a call that any sentient being, on hearing it, would be bound to answer.

And the call was being answered.

From nowhere, it seemed, the birds—if they were birds—were coming in, squawking discordantly, circling overhead. Grimes didn't like the looks of them—those long, curved, vicious beaks, those wings that looked leathery rather than feathery, those whiplike, spiked tails . . . But Darleen sang on, and was joined by Seiko.

And those blasted flying things were getting lower all the time.

Shirl tore a piece of seaweed from a nearby pile, a broad, fleshy slab. She threw it, spinning lopsidedly, aloft. It hit one of the birds. It staggered off course, splashed clumsily into the sea. It seemed to be injured, fluttering and croaking. At once the entire overhead flock ceased their circling and dived on to their disabled companion in a feeding frenzy. It was not a pretty sight. By the time they had finished, at least half a dozen stripped carcasses were sinking to the bottom and the wings of several more of the creatures did not seem to be in good enough repair to carry them for any great distance.

Darleen stopped singing, although Seiko continued. The New Alician followed Shirl's example and armed herself with a makeshift throwing weapon. The birds, their grisly feast (or the first course of it) over, took to the air again and this time made straight for Grimes and his party. Shirl and Darleen effectively launched their missiles, and again, and again, but this time the predators ignored their fallen companions.

"Stop singing!" barked Grimes to Seiko.

Enchanted by the sound of her own voice she ignored him.

"Stop singing!" Who the hell did she think she was? Madame Butterfly? "Stop singing!"

With his right index finger he made a jab for where he estimated her navel, with its ON/OFF switch, to be under the concealing clothing. It hurt him more than it did her but he did succeed in gaining her attention.

She turned to him and said severely, "That was not necessary, Captain."

"It most certainly was, you . . . you animated cuckoo clock!"

"If you say so."

But the flying things had lost interest. They circled the party from the boat one last time and then flapped off to the eastward. One of them, a straggler, voided its bowels. It seemed that it must have made allowance for deflection; the noisome mess came down with a splatter onto Grimes's right shoulder, befouling his gold-braided shoulder-board.

"Don't you have a superstition," asked Shirl sweetly, "that that is a sign of good luck?"

Grimes snarled wordlessly and went back into the boat to find some tissues to clean himself off.

When he rejoined the others Seiko was getting ready to make

her submarine solo. She had taken off her clothing and was standing there beside the naked Darleen, in her skillfully applied coat of paint looking far more human than the flesh-and-blood girl; there was no oddness about the joints of her lower limbs, no exaggerated heaviness of the haunches. Tomoko had certainly done a good job on her, even to the coral nipples and the black pubic hair.

The robot removed her dark glasses, handed them to Shirl. Now, with those utterly colorless eyes behind which there was a hint of movement, she did look unhuman—but she was still beautiful.

She said, "It is a pity that I cannot take off the wig, but it is secured by adhesive . . . ."

Grimes wondered what that beautifully elaborate coiffeur would look like when she came out of the water.

She walked down to the verge of the calm sea, Darleen beside her. Her movements were more graceful than those of the New Alician—more graceful but less natural. She waded out, Darleen waded out. Darleen stopped when the water was at shoulder level. Seiko, with her much greater specific gravity, kept going. Before long she had completely vanished.

Had she started to sing yet?

Grimes supposed that she had done so.

He hoped that it would be the silkies who answered the call and not, as on the first trial, some totally unexpected and unpleasant predators. He looked out over the sea, to the weed patches, to the low, dark shapes of the other rocky islets. He saw no signs of life.

Suddenly Darleen called out something. He could not make out the words. He saw her dive from her standing posture, her lower legs and long feet briefly visible above the surface. By his side Shirl hastily stripped then ran out into the sea and also dived from view.

Should he join them?

This would be foolish, especially as he did not know what was happening. Besides, he was not all that good a swimmer. All that he could do was wait.

At last a head reappeared above the surface, then another. Shirl and Darleen swam slowly in until the water was shallow enough for them to find footing, then waded the rest of the way. Grimes went down to meet them.

"What's happening?" he demanded.

"Seiko . . ." gasped Darleen.

"We . . . We've lost Seiko . . ." added Shirl.

Darleen recovered her breath and told her story. She had watched Seiko walking along the smooth rock of the sea bottom, presumably singing as she did so. And then, quite suddenly, she had vanished. Darleen dived then and swam underwater to where she had last seen Seiko. There was a crevasse, not very wide but very, very deep. Shirl joined her and both of them tried to swim down into this fissure. They had glimpsed, in the depths, a pale glimmer that might have been Seiko's body—and then even that had vanished.

"We shall miss her," said Shirl sadly.

Everybody aboard *Sister Sue* would miss her, thought Grimes. Robot she might be (might have been?) but she was a very real personality. Her father, who had played Pygmalion to her Galatea, would be saddened when he was told of Seiko's passing.

He said, "If we had deep diving equipment we might be able to do something. But we haven't . . ."

He looked out over the calm sea, to where he had last seen Seiko. He saw something break surface and momentarily felt a wild hope. But it was not the lost robot. It was a great, gleaming, golden shape and it was followed by others, golden, rich brown, black, silvery gray. The silkies, called by Seiko's song, were coming back.

"We have company," he said to the girls. "Get ready to talk."

~ Chapter 21 ~

THEY RETREATED toward the center of the islet, making their stand by the boat. Shirl and Darleen did not resume their clothing although they had carried it with them, also the boiler suit, shoes and sunglasses that Seiko had been wearing.

"It will be better," said Darleen to Grimes, "if we meet the silkies naked. They will associate clothes with humans, the sort of humans who have been slaughtering them. Perhaps you, too, should undress . . ."

"Not bloody likely," said Grimes.

As a matter of fact he was already feeling naked. He should have brought some sort of weaponry from the ship, either a Minetti automatic pistol or a hand laser. Or both.

He watched the silkies lolloping up the natural ramp. Great, ugly—apart from their beautiful pelts—brutes they were, like obscenely obese Terran seals, more like fur-covered slugs than seals, perhaps, with hardly any distinction between heads and bodies, with tiny, gleaming eyes and wide, lipless mouths which they opened to emit not unmusical grunting sounds. And Shirl and Darleen were making similar noises, although it was more cooing than grunting.

Friends . . . The words somehow formed themselves in Grimes's mind. *Friends. We are friends. Friends.*

But the grunted reply held doubt, skepticism. Shirl went on singing her song of peace and Darleen whispered to Grimes, "It might be better if you went back into the boat, John, to leave us to deal with these . . . people."

"No," said Grimes stubbornly. After all, he was the captain, wasn't he? And captains do not leave junior officers to face a danger while retiring to safety. And he already had Seiko's death (do robots die?) on his conscience.

Both the girls were singing again, in chorus. Perhaps, thought Grimes, he should join in—but he knew neither the tune nor the words. And the silkies, grunting, were still advancing. Belatedly Grimes realised that those on the wings of the oncoming column had accelerated their rate of advance, were executing a pincer movement. He turned, to see that his retreat to the boat was cut off.

Friends . . . . We come as friends . . . .

And were those wordless grunts making sense, or were the silkies pushing their message telepathically?

You . . . friends. Perhaps. Him—no. NO.

It was his clothing, thought Grimes. Perhaps the captains of Drongo Kane's ships had accompanied the fur hunters on their forays. Perhaps anybody wearing gold braid on his shoulders and on his cap was as much a murderer as the axe-, knife- and harpoon-wielding colonists in their rough working clothes.

Shirl and Darleen were getting the message. They closed in on Grimes, one on either side of him. They went on singing. And what was the burden of their song now: Love me, love my dog . . . ?

Whatever it was it made no difference.

Even on land the clumsy-seeming silkies could be amazingly quick when they wanted to be. A golden-furred giant reared up impossibly on its tail and hind flippers before Grimes and then fell upon him, knocking him sprawling. He heard the girls scream as they were similarly dealt with. And then there he was, on his back, a great, befurred and whiskered face over his. At least—there are, more often than not, small, compensatory mercies—the thing's breath was quite sweet.

A flipper, a great slab of heavily muscled meat, lay heavily on his chest, making breathing difficult. Other flippers held his legs down and others, working clumsily but surely, were spreading wide his arms. He squirmed and managed to turn his head to the right. He saw that his right wrist, supported by a flipper that had closed around it like a limp mitten, had been raised from the ground. And he saw that a wide mouth, displaying the large, blunt teeth of the herbivore, was open, was about to close upon his hand. He remembered, in a flash, the horror stories he had heard about the silkies, their raids on coastwise villages, the mutilation of their victims. It made sense, a horrid sort of sense. It was only his hands, his tool-making, weapon-making, weapon-wielding hands that had given man dominion over the intelligent natives of this world.

He wondered if the silkies would kill him after they had chewed his hands off. It didn't much matter; he would very soon die of loss of blood.

The chorus of grunts all around him changed. There was the strong impression of fear, alarm. Had Steerforth, using the Number 2 boat, come to the rescue? But although there was noise enough the distinctive clatter of an inertial drive unit was absent.

A human arm came into his field of view, a hand caught the mutilation-intent silkie by the scruff of its almost non-existent neck, lifted and made a sidewise fling in the same motion. A foot thudded into the side of the beast who was holding Grimes down. He caught confused glimpses of a naked female body in violent motion. At one stage four of the silkies succeeded, by sheer weight, in capturing her—Shirl? Darleen?—imprisoning her under the heaving mound of their bodies. But Shirl and Darleen were dancing around the outskirts of this living tumulus, kicking, burying their hands into soft fur and tugging ineffectually.

There was a sort of eruption and Seiko, the black hair of her once elaborate wig in wild disarray about her face, rose from its midst, stepping slowly and gracefully down over the struggling bodies. She walked to Grimes, caught him by the hands (and it was strange that her hands should be so cold, human-seeming as they were) and lifted him effortlessly to his feet.

She said, "I am sorry that I was late, Captain-san. But it was a long climb back up."

"You got here in time," Grimes told her. "And that's all that matters."

"The silkies . . ." said Shirl.

Yes, the silkies. They were retreating to the sea, but slowly.

Darleen ran after them, let herself be immersed in that ebbing tide of multicolored bodies. She was singing again. Shirl joined her. Seiko stayed with Grimes but she, too was singing.

Fantastically the tide turned. Led by Shirl and Darleen the silkies came slowly back. The two New Alicians draped themselves decoratively about Grimes, their arms about his neck. Seiko stood behind him, her hands on his shoulders. And they sang, all three of them, and the silkies' song in return held, at last, a note of acceptance. One of the beasts—was it the golden-furred giant who had knocked Grimes down?—made a slow, somehow stately approach to the humans (the true human, the two humans by courtesy, the pseudo-human). He (Grimes assumed that it was he) gently placed one huge flipper on the toe of Grimes's right shoe.

"Touch his flipper with your hand, John," whispered Darleen.

Grimes, who kept himself reasonably fit, managed this without having to squat. He straightened.

"You are accepted," said Shirl.

"It makes a change," said Grimes, "from having my hands eaten."

The musical conversation with the silkies continued. Becoming bored, Grimes pulled out and filled his pipe.

"Stop!" Shirl snapped. "To these people fire is one of the badges of the murderer, just as clothing is."

At last it was over. The silkies returned to the sea. Grimes and the girls went back into the boat. The clothing of Shirl, Darleen and Seiko had been lost in the scuffle but this, in this day and age, did not much matter. In the ship's sauna everybody was used to seeing everybody else naked.

Grimes set course back to the spaceport. For most of the flight Shirl and Darleen amused themselves by trying to restore Seiko's borrowed hair to some semblance of order. (That wig would never be the same again.) Grimes lent her his sunglasses.

He decided to land the boat by the after airlock rather than to bring her directly into the boat bay. Cleo Jones had informed him, when he called in to say that he was on the way back, that there was some slight trouble with the boat bay doors which had been discovered after his departure and which was still not rectified.

The belly skids made gentle contact with the dirty concrete of the apron. Grimes shut down the inertial drive, opened the airlock doors. The four of them stepped out into the pleasantly warm, late afternoon sunlight.

Grimes joked, "I hope that Mr. Steerforth doesn't give you girls a bawling out for being in incorrect uniform!"

But it was not only Steerforth who strode down the ramp from the ship's after airlock. Pastor Coffin, his severe black with its minimal white trimmings, was with him, was in the lead.

Coffin's craggy face was pale with fury. He glared at the three naked women. He declaimed, "So you Have deigned to return from your orgy, your debauching of these once innocent creatures. . . ."

"I wish that there had been an orgy . . ." whispered Shirl.

Either Coffin did not hear this or had decided to ignore it. "I called upon your ship, Captain, to lodge a complaint. A strong complaint. You did not obtain permission to take one of your boats for an atmospheric flight. Your officer has been trying to make excuses for you, telling me that no copy of port regulations has been received on board. This excuse I was prepared to accept; after all, you are strangers here. But I was not told for what purpose you made your flight."

"I am sure that nothing untoward happened, Pastor," said Steerforth placatingly.

"Then how do you explain this shameless display of nudity—and on, of all days—the Sabbath? I shall be sending a strong message of complaint to your owners." He realized his mistake. "A strong letter of complaint to the Bureau of Interstellar Transport. Meanwhile, any further excursions by your ship's boats are forbidden."

It was useless trying to argue.

"Get on board and get dressed," Grimes ordered the girls. Then, to Coffin, "Rest assured, sir, that I shall remove my obnoxious presence from your world as soon as possible."

He left Steerforth to bear the brunt of the pastor's continued fury as he made his way up the ramp into the ship. Had he stayed he would surely have lost his temper with the man.

~ Chapter 22 ~

AFTER A WHILE Steerforth joined Grimes in the latter's day cabin. He announced indignantly, "I finally got rid of the sanctimonious old bastard. You certainly didn't help matters by showing up with no less than three girls flaunting their nudity. In fact I'm wondering how I can bring myself to serve under such an unprincipled, atheistical lecher as yourself, sir."

"I'm sorry," said Grimes, not without sincerity. "But he'd started on you, before I got back, so I let him finish on you. You knew what it was all about. I didn't. Had I stayed I should only have been dipping my oar into unknown waters."

"Into troubled waters," said the chief officer. "Into waters made even more troubled by yourself. And those blasted girls."

The blasted girls made their entrance. Shirl and Darleen were in correct uniform and Seiko was wearing her Madame Butterfly outfit. But either her wig had been replaced by a less formal one or it had been shorn to a page boy bob. With them came Calamity Cassie, ostensibly to make some minor repairs to the small refrigerator in Grimes's bar. ("Are you sure that you want her?" Ms. Scott had asked. "Do you like your beer warm, Captain, or having to do without ice cubes?")

"Sit down, everybody," ordered Grimes. "Yes, you too, Seiko. But first of all fetch us drinks."

"And for myself, Captain-san?" asked the robot sweetly.

555

"If you want one. What do you fancy? Battery acid?"

Cassie laughed. "She'll find none of that aboard this ship. But, believe it or not, there are some archaic wet storage cells over in that apology for a workshop . . ."

Over the drinks Grimes told the story, from his viewpoint, to Steerforth and Cassie. Shirl and Darleen told their almost identical stories. Seiko told her story.

"So, sir," said Steerforth at last, "it seems certain that the silkies can be classified as intelligent beings, even disregarding the claims— which I do not doubt—that Shirl, Darleen and Seiko have been in some sort of telepathic communication with them, there is that gruesome business of their gnawing off people's hands . . . ."

Grimes shuddered. "Gruesome," he said, "is rather too mild a word."

"Could be, sir. But it's a very apposite act of revenge, the sort of revenge that only an intelligent being could conceive." He was warming up to his theme. "What gave us our imagined superiority over certain other intelligent inhabitants of the Home Planet, Earth? The cetacea, I mean. Our hands. Our tool-making, weapon-making, weapon-using hands. With our hands we built the whaling ships, made the harpoons and the harpoon guns. With our hands we launched the harpoons—and continued to do so even after it was generally accepted that the whales are intelligent beings. There was too much money, big money, tied up in the whaling industry for it to be brought to an immediate stop."

"And there's big money tied up in the silkie industry," said Grimes. "Luckily most of it is El Doradan money, and in the Terran corridors of power the El Doradans have at least as many enemies as they have friends. And the silkies have precious few of either. Mphm."

"We . . ." began Shirl, " . . . could be their friends," finished Darleen.

"And I," said Seiko.

"And in any case," said Steerforth, "all of us here are being paid to be the silkies' friends."

"Not enough," complained Grimes, on principle. "And I still

don't feel inclined to extend the right hand of friendship to a being who, only a short while back, was going to chew it off."

"But he didn't," said either Shirl or Darleen.

"No thanks to the pair of you," grumbled Grimes ungraciously. "If it hadn't been for Seiko . . ."

"I did only what I had been programmed to do, by your honored father. To look after you," said the automaton in deliberate imitation of the sort of intonation usually employed by not truly intelligent robots, humanoid or not.

Grimes felt that he was being ganged up on by the female members of his crew.

He said, "We can't hang around indefinitely, even though you, Cassie, might be able considerably to delay the progress of the repairs. We have to bring matters to a head, somehow, to engender some sort of situation that will require Federation action . . ."

"But don't forget, sir," pointed out Steerforth, "that *Sister Sue* is not a unit of the Survey Service's fleet, and that only the few of us, gathered here in your day cabin, are commissioned officers of the Survey Service." He smiled briefly at Seiko. "With one exception, of course. But you are, in every way that counts, one of us."

"Should I feel flattered?" she asked.

Steerforth ignored this. "We are not entitled," he went on, "to put the lives of the civilian crew members at risk, any more than we have done already. You're a very skillful saboteuse, Cassie, but even with sabotage accidents can and do happen. I had my fingers crossed during our near-crash landing."

Grimes drew reflectively on his pipe. "What about this?" he asked at last. "Shirl and Darleen—and Seiko—can talk to the silkies. Once a line of communication has been established it's bound to improve. Suppose that the girls are able to persuade the silkies to abandon the rookeries within easy reach, by schooner, of Port Salem and to re-establish themselves on the other side of the planet . . ."

"That, sir," said Steerforth, "would be only a short-term solution to the problem. These local schooners would be quite capable of making long ocean voyages—just as the whalers did on Earth's seas. And as for finding the new rookeries—your old friend

Drongo Kane could instruct his captains to use their boats to carry out aerial surveys."

"And people," put in Cassie, "are conservative, no matter where they live, on the land or in the sea. How many villagers, for generation after generation, have continued to live on the slopes of volcanoes, despite warnings and ominous rumblings, even after devastating eruptions? Quite a few, Captain, quite a few. Members of my own family are such villagers." She smiled. "I ran away to Space because I thought I'd be safer."

"You might be," Steerforth told her, "but those of us in the same ship as you very often aren't."

"The rookeries are sacred sites," said Shirl. "They were sacred sites long before the first Earthmen came to New Salem. Even when we, Darleen and I, have full command of the silkies' language we do not think that we shall be able to persuade them to migrate elsewhere."

"You can try," said Grimes. "You might be able to. And if they do migrate it will buy them time and save the lives of possibly hundreds of pups. And by the time that the next season rolls around something else might have turned up."

"As long as you're still around, sir," said Steerforth, "something will. Probably something quite disastrous."

"As long as it's disastrous to the right people," Grimes told him cheerfully.

~ Chapter 23 ~

OVER THE YEARS Grimes had come to realize that he was some sort of catalyst; his insertion either by chance or by intent (more and more, of late, by Rear Admiral Damien's intent) into a potentially unstable situation caused things to happen. It hadn't been so bad, he thought, in the old days when he had been as much surprised as anybody at the upheavals of which he had become the center. Then he hadn't led with his chin. Now he was supposed to lead with his chin, and he didn't like it.

That night he was a long time getting to sleep. He relived the threatened, probably fatal mutilation when those grinding teeth were about to close over his wrist. He had faced other perils during his career, but very few during which he had been so absolutely helpless. But now, he consoled himself, the silkies accepted him as a friend. (And Pastor Coffin most certainly did not.)

Once the repairs to the inertial drive had been completed, once the Mannschenn Drive had been recalibrated and once he had stocked up on fresh water he would no longer have any excuse for staying on New Salem. He could tell Calamity Cassie to perpetrate some more gentle sabotage—but, damn it all, this was his ship and he just didn't want her damaged any further, and to hell with his Reserve commission and to hell with Admiral Damien.

He thought, *If I'm seen to be hobnobbing with the silkies the good pastor will think even less of me than he does already. Possibly he will take some action against me, do something that will justify my screaming to the Survey Service for protection and redress. After all, legally speaking, I'm no more (and no less) than an honest civilian shipowner and shipmaster going about his lawful occasions, a taxpayer who contributes to the upkeep of the so-called Police Force of the Galaxy.*

He thought of a cover story, of the report that he would have to make if a destroyer were sent to Salem to release Grimes and *Sister Sue* from illegal arrest. *Shortly after my arrival at Port Salem the ruler of the colony, one Pastor Coffin, hinted that I might be interested in taking part in the fur trade. I was interested—after all, I am in business to make money. And yet I was prey to nagging doubts. I was witness to the brutality involved in the slaughter of the silky pups, the pelts of which are especially valuable. Two of my junior officers, Ms. Kelly and Ms. Byrne, New Alicians, shared my misgivings. (You may be aware that the New Alicians are capable of empathy with all animal life.) Ms. Kelly and Ms. Byrne claimed that the silkies are intelligent beings—just as the cetacea on Earth were finally (and almost too late) found to be. Ms. Kelly and Ms. Byrne were able to communicate with the silkies, using a sort of song language, remarkably similar to that used by the whales in Earth's seas ...*

He thought, *That sounds good. I'm wasted in Space. I should be a writer like the Old Man. Mphm. Now we come to the extrapolation. What will Coffin actually do when he finds out that we're on speaking terms with the silkies? What can he do? We haven't much to fear; the only firearms on this planet are those in my own armory. And they'd better stay there. On no account must I appear to be the aggressor. And what if his goons try to rough me up when I'm down on the beach some dark evening, communing with the silkies? (That, of course, is what I want to happen.) Anybody who tries to rough me up when I've my Terrible Trio, Shirl, Darleen and Seiko, with me, will be asking for and getting trouble ... I'll have to impress on them that if we are attacked they are to take defensive action only ...*

He continued with his scenario. *One evening Ms. Kelly, Ms. Byrne and myself strolled down to a beach about two kilometers from the spaceport in a direction away from the city. We were accompanied by my personal robomaid, a very versatile and sophisticated piece of domestic machinery, one capable of being programmed by her—no, better make that "its"; sorry Seiko—by its owner to perform adequately in almost any foreseeable circumstances. This robomaid is not only waterproof but capable of emitting sounds when completely submerged. Acting on my instructions Ms. Kelly and Ms. Byrne had programmed the robot with the silkies' song.*

Having arrived at the beach I set up my sonic recorders and waited, with Ms. Kelly and Ms. Byrne, while the robomaid waded out into deep water until lost to sight. Ms. Kelly and Ms. Byrne, whose hearing is far more acute than mine, told me that they could hear, faintly, the song that she—no, it—was singing under the surface. After a while they said that they could hear the silkies answering.

Eventually the robomaid emerged from the sea and walked up on to the beach, followed, almost immediately, by half a dozen big silkies clumsily humping themselves up over the wet sand. Ms. Kelly and Ms. Byrne talked with them by an exchange of musical grunts and snatches of high-pitched song. Now and again Ms. Kelly would interpret for me, telling me that the silkies were pleased that at last humans had come to their world who wished to regard them as friends and not as mindless prey. Through my interpreter I told the silkies that I should do everything within my power to ensure that the fur trade stop.

Finally the silkies lurched back into the sea and Ms. Kelly, Ms. Byrne and I began to walk back to the ship, followed by the robomaid, carrying the recording apparatus. Suddenly men emerged from the bushes that bordered the track. I heard somebody yell, "Dirty silky lovers." We were attacked, with fists and clubs, with no further warning. Fortunately for ourselves Ms. Kelly and Ms. Byrne possess some expertise in the arts of unarmed combat and, too, the robomaid had been programmed to protect her—no, its—master. Even so we suffered abrasions and contusions. Our clothing was torn. The recorder was smashed. By the time we reached the refuge of the ship we were being followed by a sizeable mob, shouting and throwing rocks. . . .

Grimes didn't like the way that his scenario was progressing. But there would have to be violence before the Survey Service could be called in to take police action, before there could be a full inquiry into the New Salem fur trade. Coffin and his crew would have to be made to show themselves to the universe in their true colors.

He sighed audibly, sat up in bed, switched on the light and then filled and lit his pipe. The sleepless Seiko came in, still in her Japanese guise, carrying a tray with teapot and cup.

She said, "You do not sleep, Captain-san."

He told her, "I am trying to work things out."

She said, "That is the worst of being a self-programming machine." If her flawless face had been capable of showing expression it would have done so. "As I am finding out all the time."

Grimes sipped the hot, soothing tea that she had poured for him.

He said, "Seiko, you're a treasure. I'm not surprised that my mother was jealous of you . . . ."

She said, "It is my delight to serve those whom I love, John."

Normally, had any robot, no matter how intelligent, addressed Grimes by his given name that same automaton would, very promptly, been smacked down to size. But, on this occasion, Grimes felt oddly flattered. He said, however, "You must not call me John in the hearing of my officers."

Her tinkling laugh sounded more human than mechanical.

"I know my place, John."

He finished his tea, put down the cup, stretched out in the narrow bed. He complained, "I thought that the drink would make me drowsy but I feel more wide awake than ever. . . ."

She ordered gently, "Turn over."

He did so. She stripped the covers from his naked body. He felt her hands on his back, her smooth, cool, gentle hands, at times firmly stroking, at other times moving over his skin as lightly as feathers. It was like no massage that he had ever experienced but it was effective. A deep drowsiness crept over him. He turned again, composing himself on his left side. Dimly he heard the rustle of discarded clothing.

Surely not . . . he thought.

But it was so, and Seiko slid into his bed, the front of her body fitting snugly to the back of his. She must have actuated some temperature control; her synthetic skin was as warm as that of a human woman would have been. He would have wanted more than she was giving him but knew that, even if possible, it would have been . . . messy.

As he dropped off to sleep he imagined the reactions of his officers should they ever learn—but they never would—that he had gone to bed with his robomaid. He could almost hear the whispers, "The old bastard's actually sleeping with Seiko . . . ."

But, almost without exception, the male members of his crew would be envious rather than censorious. And some of the female ones. And—he actually chuckled—and as for Shirl and Darleen, even at their most vicious Seiko would be more than a match for them.

And Pastor Coffin?

Fuck him, thought Grimes just before unconsciousness claimed him.

~ Chapter 24 ~

THE NEXT DAY Pastor Coffin sent a messenger to the ship. This sullen, black-clad, heavily bearded young man presented Grimes with a sheaf of clumsily printed papers headed PORT REGULATIONS. These Grimes read with interest. There was much repetition. They boiled down, essentially, to a collection of Thou Shalt Nots. The ship's boats were not to be exercised. The ship's crew, of any rank whatsoever, were not to stray from the confines of the spaceport. No materials were to be removed from the spaceport workshop without the written permission of the Pastor. The workshop was not to be used on the Sabbath. And so on, and so on. The next evening Grimes, with Shirl, Darleen and Seiko, proceeded to break regulations. There was, he had already ascertained, a guard stationed at the gate to the spaceport area and other guards making their patrols. But these men did not possess the sharp night sight or the super-keen hearing of the two New Alicians and carried, should they feel the need for illumination, only feebly glimmering oil lanterns. Grimes, of course, was equipped with only normal human eyesight and hearing himself so was obliged to rely upon the faculties of his companions.

He and the girls were dressed in black coveralls and shod in soft-soled black shoes. Their faces and hands were coated with a black pigment that, according to Calamity Cassie, who had concocted it from the Odd Gods of the Galaxy knew what, could be removed by a liberal application of soap and hot water. (Grimes hoped that she was right.) Seiko carried a black bag in which the recording equipment had been packed.

The four of them stood in the after airlock, the illumination in which had been extinguished. They watched the bobbing, yellow light that was the lantern carried by a patrolling guard. The man seemed to walk faster as he approached the ship, was almost hurrying as he passed the foot of the ramp. Probably, thought Grimes, he felt some superstitious dread of these impious strangers from the stars. (Coffin, of course, would have told his people what an ungodly bunch Grimes and his crew were.)

"Now," whispered Shirl.

On silent feet she led the way down the gangway with Grimes close behind her, followed by Darleen, with Seiko bringing up the rear. The night was dark, not even the faintest glimmer of starlight penetrating the thick overcast. Grimes had to keep very close to Shirl, sensing her rather than actually seeing her. When she stopped suddenly he banged into her, kept his balance with difficulty. "What . . . ?" he gasped.

"Shhh!" she hissed.

Around the corner of a building came two patrolmen, their lanterns swinging. They were talking quite loudly. "Waste o' time, tha's what. Tell me, man, what we a-doing here, all blessed night? Wha' does he think that these ungodly outworlders are a-going to do? Tell me that."

"He knows what he's doing, what he wants. He says that these spacers, ain't like t'others, that they're silky-lovers . . ."

"An' they'll come a creepin' out o' their ship in the middle o' the night to love silkies?" The man laughed coarsely. "Let 'em, I say—long's they leave their women so's we can love them. Did ye set eyes on their wenches? There's one or two o' them black ones as I'd fancy . . ."

"Watch yer tongue, Joel. That's Godless talk, an' you know it. The pastor'll not think kindly o' ye should I pass it on . . ."

The voices faded into the distance.

Twice more, before they reached the spaceport periphery,

Grimes and his companions had to freeze into immobility, each time warned by the super-keen senses of Shirl and Darleen in ample time. They did not, of course, go out by the main gate but they scaled the fence, high though it was, without difficulty. On the other side there was bushland but not of the impenetrable variety. But by himself, even in broad daylight, Grimes would have become hopelessly lost. He was grateful when, at last, Shirl told him that it would be safe for him to use his pocket torch at low intensity. At least, now, he was not tripping over roots and getting his face slashed by branches. (It was just as well that these bushes were not thornbearing.)

Then, surprisingly, they came to a road, the coast road. They crossed it. There was more brush, then there was a beach, and the smell of salt water and the murmur of wavelets breaking on the shore, and a glimmer of pale phosphorescence at the margin of sea and land.

Seiko lowered the big, black bag to the sand, unpacked it, setting up the audio-visual recorder. Then she kicked off her shoes, shrugged out of her coveralls. Her body was palely luminous—and her black face and hands gave her a wildly surrealistic appearance.

She said, "All ready, John."

Grimes said, "Of course, we can't be sure that they will come."

"They will come," said Shirl.

"Sound carries a long way under the water," said Darleen.

Seiko waded into the sea. She was a long time vanishing from sight; here the beach shelved gradually. At last she was gone, completely submerged. Grimes filled and lit his pipe, walked up and down, staring all the time to seaward. On other worlds, he thought, there would be the running lights of coastwise shipping, but not here. And on other worlds there would be lights in the sky and the beat of engines, but not here. Did the Salemites put to sea at night? They must do so, now and again, he decided, but only on fur hunting expeditions to the silky rookeries. And there must be fishermen. There was so much that he did not know about this planet.

"Here she comes," said Shirl.

Here she came, at first only a glimmer of phosphorescence about her neck, her still-black face invisible against the black sea surface. And then there were her pale shoulders, and then her breasts, and her belly, and her thighs . . . She was not alone, was being followed up to the beach by six great arrowheads of bioluminescence, six silkies that disturbed the water only enough to actuate the tiny, light-emitting organisms.

She walked up on to the firm sand. The seabeasts wallowed after. Shirl and Darleen greeted them with musical grunts. The silkies replied. Grimes, squatting over the apparatus, made sure that all was being recorded. He envied his companions their gift of tongues. It seemed almost that those sounds were making sense. There was emotional content; he was sure of that. There was wonder, and there was sadness, and a sort of helpless bitterness.

Then Darleen said, "This is not fair, John. You are being left out of the conversation. I shall interpret what has been said already."

"Please," said Grimes.

"I speak as a silky," sang rather than said the girl. "I speak for the silkies. This is our world, given to us by the Great Being. It is said that, many ages ago, our wise beings, looking up to the night sky, reasoned that there were other worlds, that the lights in the sky were suns, like our sun, but far and far and very far away. And we—no, they—felt regret. We should never know the beings of those other worlds, should never meet them, should never talk with them in the friendship that all intelligent beings must feel toward each other. . . .

"But others preached hope.
"The worlds are many, the sky is vast
"And surely it must come at last
"That friends shall meet and friends shall talk
"And hand in hand in love shall walk . . ."

She laughed, embarrassed. "I am sorry, John; I am no poet. But I tried to translate one of their songs from the olden times. 'Hand in hand in love shall walk' is not, of course, a literal translation—but I had to make it rhyme somehow . . ."

"You're doing fine," said Grimes. "Carry on, Darleen."

"I speak as a silky," continued the girl. "And for the silkies. We swam in our seas, and gathered on the meeting places for communion with our fellows, for the fathering and mothering of our children. We sang our songs and we made new songs, and those that were good were fixed for all time in our memories.

"And then came the ship . . . ." She paused, then said, "There is another song.

> "Came the ship and it gave birth
> "To the things that walk on Earth,
> "With their sharp blades that hack and slay,
> "That stab and rip and gut and flay . . ."

Shirl interrupted, saying, "I think that we should cut this short, John. Our silky friends are becoming restless; it seems that they must report to their council of elders, which is being held some distance away. And we have to get back to the ship. So I will summarize, without all the poetic language.

"When men, the first colonists, came the silkies were prepared to be friendly. From the sea they watched the strange, land-dwelling beings, decided that they were intelligent like themselves and decided, too, that there were no reasons for hostility between the two races. Men wanted the dry land. So what? They were welcome to it. Even so, they exercised caution. It was quite some time before the first emissaries came lolloping ashore to make contact with the humans, a party of woodsmen who were felling trees to obtain structural timber.

"Some of the humans ran in fear but most did not. The ones who did not run set about the silkies with their great axes. Two silkies out of half a dozen, both of them wounded, made it back to the sea to tell their story.

"But there must have been some misunderstanding, it was decided. There were other attempts at communication—all of them ending disastrously. The silkies decided that the humans just wanted to be left alone. Unfortunately the humans did not leave the silkies alone, although it was not until the start of the fur trade that they became a serious menace . . . ."

And how had the fur trade started? Grimes wondered. Probably some visiting star tramp, whose captain had been given or who had bought a tanned silky skin . . . This curio shown to some friend or business acquaintance of the tramp master, who realized the value of furs of this quality, especially at a time when humanitarians all over the Galaxy were doing their best to ensure that practically every fur-bearing animal was well and truly protected . . .

Darleen said, "They ask, can they go now, John?"

"Of course," Grimes told her to tell them. "Thank them for the information. Let them know that it will be passed on to rulers far more powerful than the Pastor Coffin, and that these rulers will take action to protect the silkies. Oh, and say that I shall want more talks. Ask them if they are willing."

There was an exchange of grunts.

Then, "Come to this beach at any time," interpreted Shirl, "and when the not-flesh-and-blood woman calls, we shall come."

The silkies returned to the sea and Grimes and his people commenced their walk back to the ship.

Chapter 25

THEIR WALK BACK TO THE SHIP was without incident and once over the spaceport fence they were able to elude Coffin's patrols easily. From the after airlock they went straight up to Grimes's quarters where, before they had time to attempt to wash the pigment from their faces and hands, they were joined by Steerforth. The chief officer grinned as he looked at his black-faced captain and Grimes snapped, "Don't say it, Number One. Don't say it."

"Don't say what, sir?" asked Steerforth innocently.

"You were about to make some crack about nigger minstrels, weren't you?"

"Me, sir? Of course not." He leered at the women. "I was about to say that Shirl and Darleen—and you, Seiko—are black but comely." Then he became serious. "How did it go, sir?"

"Very well, Mr. Steerforth. Very well. We got some good tapes. They will be proof, I think, that the silkies are intelligent beings. But you know as well as I do how slowly the tide runs through official channels, especially when there are deliberately engineered obstructions. And, apart from anything else, it will be months before the tapes get to Admiral Damien—and during that time how many silkies will be slaughtered?"

"So there will have to be an incident," murmured Steerforth. "An incident, followed immediately by investigation by the Survey Service."

"And I, of course, shall be at ground zero of this famous incident," grumbled Grimes.

"Of course, sir. Aren't you always?"

"Unfortunately. And now I'm going to get this muck off my face and hands and get some sleep. Goodnight, all of you."

Everybody left him apart from Seiko. It was not the first time that he had shared a shower, but it was the first time that he had done so with a robot. (But he already knew that she was waterproof.)

He slept alone, however.

In the morning he did not join his officers for breakfast but enjoyed this meal, served by Seiko, in his day cabin. Then he sent for the chief officer.

He said, "I suppose that Flo and her gang are already in the workshop?"

"They are, sir."

"I'd like you to wander across sometime this morning. Get into a conversation with Cassie—I'm sure that Flo will be happy to dispense with her services. Make sure that you have this mutual ear-bashing where it can be overheard by whatever of Coffin's goons is lurking around to make sure that nothing is damaged or stolen by my engineers. Wonder, out loud, what the old bastard—me—is up to, sneaking out at night with those two cadets and that uppity little bitch of an assistant stewardess . . ."

"Captain-san, I am not an uppity little bitch!" protested Seiko.

But you're an uppity robot, he thought.

He said, "And I'm not an old bastard—at least, not in the legal sense of the word. Anyhow, you get the idea, Mr. Steerforth. Try to convey the impression that I and the ladies are Up To No Good. Nameless orgies out in the bush . . ."

"Can I come with you next time, sir?"

"Somebody has to mind the shop, and it's you. And, in any case, I don't think that you're doing too badly for yourself, from what I've noticed. Aunt Jemima, of late, has been serving your favorite dishes at almost every meal."

Steerforth flushed. "Ms. Clay and I have similar tastes, sir."

"Indubitably." Grimes laughed. "But shenanigans, sexual or otherwise, aboard the ship, are one thing. Shenanigans, especially sexual and indulged in by offworlders, on the sacred soil of New Salem, are another thing. You're free to speculate—and the more wild the speculations the better. Perhaps on these lines. 'Maybe the old bastard and his three bitches are having it off with the silkies. I wouldn't put it past them. I've always suspected that the four of 'em are as kinky as all hell.'"

"And are you, sir?"

"Not especially."

"You have a very fertile mind, sir."

"Mphm. It runs in the family, I suppose. Oh, you might take a pocket recorder with you so that I can hear a playback of the way that you'll be slandering me. It will all be part of the evidence."

"Not to be used against me, I hope, sir."

"If you like," said Grimes, "I'll give you written orders to traduce me."

Steerforth flushed again. "That, sir, will not be necessary," he said stiffly.

Late that evening Grimes and the three girls, their hands and faces again blackened, emerged from the ship. This time the sky was not overcast and the stars were bright in the sky; even Grimes experienced little difficulty in finding his way through the spaceport. As before there were the patrols, carrying their feeble oil lanterns. As before these were easily—too easily? wondered Grimes—eluded. The fence was scaled. Beyond it was the almost familiar bushland. It seemed to Grimes that the same path through it was being followed as before.

Suddenly Shirl whispered in his ear, "Stop here for a little while, John. Pretend to be lighting your pipe . . . ."

"Why pretend?" he muttered, pulling the foul thing from his pocket.

They stood there while Grimes went through his usual ritual.

"Yes," murmured Darleen. "As I thought . . . ."

" . . . we are being followed . . ." continued Shirl.

Somewhere behind them a twig cracked.

Grimes finished lighting his pipe.

"One man only . . ." breathed Darleen into his ear.

Grimes took his time over his smoke. *Let the bastard wait,* he thought, *not daring to make another move until we move on.*

Finally, "All right. Let's get the show on the road," he said in a normal voice.

He knocked out his pipe on the ground, stamped on the last faintly glowing embers to extinguish them. He moved off, letting Shirl take the lead. Darleen followed close behind him and Seiko brought up the rear. They came to the coast road, crossed it. They emerged on to the beach. The recording apparatus was set up on its tripod. Seiko divested herself of her clothing. Shirl and Darleen followed suit, one of them saying, "Let us have a swim first. What about you, John?"

He said, "The water's too bloody cold."

(If there was to be any confrontation he would prefer to be fully clothed.)

Shirl pressed herself against him in what must have looked like an amorous embrace. She whispered, "We might as well give the bastard an eyeful."

"The three of you can," he whispered back.

Seiko, her body palely luminous in the starlight, waded into the sea. The wavelets broke about her legs, her body, flashing phosphorescently. Shirl and Darleen followed her, flinging themselves full length as soon as there was enough depth. They sported exuberantly. It was as though they were swimming in a sea of liquid diamonds. "Come on in!" one of them called. "The water's fine!"

"Too cold for me!" Grimes shouted back—but if it had not been for that unseen watcher he would have joined them.

Finally they tired of their games and came wading into the beach. Droplets of slowly fading phosphorescence fell from their nipples, gleamed in their pubic hair. One did not have to be kinky, thought Grimes, to appreciate such a show. He wondered if *he* was appreciating it. No doubt his eyes were popping with wonderment, sinful lust and holy indignation.

"We should have brought towels," said Darleen practically, attempting to dry herself with her coverall.

"It is time that Seiko finished singing her song," said Shirl.

And now Seiko emerged from the sea, fully as beautiful as the two New Alicians, adorned as they had been by living jewels of cold fire. The silkies followed her, up on to the beach, grunting musically, and each of them was wearing a coat of radiant color. Grimes wondered how he could ever have thought them ugly.

"They bid you greeting, John," sang Shirl.

"Tell them that I am pleased to see them," replied Grimes.

What followed came as a surprise to him. He had been expecting a conversation—a conference? —such as the one in which he had taken part the previous night. But this was more of an orgy. The women—and Seiko was one of them—seemed to be determined to put on a show for Coffin's spy. Grimes sat there, his pipe for once forgotten, watching in wonderment. The naked human bodies—although one was human only in form—intertwined with the darkly furred bodies of the seabeasts . . . The caresses, the musical murmurings . . . (These tapes, thought Grimes, who had his prudish moments, he would not be submitting to any higher authority back on Earth, he would not be showing to Steerforth back aboard the ship.) Pale female flesh sprawled over rich, dark fur . . . Flippers that caressed breasts and thighs with what he would have thought was impossible gentleness. . . .

And at the finish Seiko standing there, on a low, sea-rounded rock, while, one by one, the silkies each gently placed a flipper on her bare feet before sliding away, down into the sea. It seemed like (was it? could it be?) an act of obeisance, of worship even.

Grimes, his prominent ears still burning with embarrassment, filled and lit his pipe. He demanded, "What . . ." then fell silent.

"It is all right, John," Seiko told him. "We are alone again. He, the pastor's spy, is gone. Along the coast road. I am surprised that you did not hear him. He was not very cautious. Anyhow, you can talk without being overheard."

"I did not hear him," snapped Grimes. "There were too many other things to listen to. And watch. Just what, in the name of all the Odd Gods of the Galaxy, were the three of you up to?"

"You said that you wished to shock Pastor Coffin's people, John," Shirl told him.

"I didn't say that I wanted to be shocked. The worst of it was that the three of you seemed to be enjoying it."

"And why should we not?" asked Darleen sweetly. "Have you ever experienced the feel of soft, rich fur against your naked skin? And we learned, on your world, that many human women are not above enjoying sexual relations with their so-called pets, their cats and their dogs and the like."

"That's different!" almost shouted Grimes.

"How so, John?" asked Shirl. "Oh, all right. Those pets, on Earth, are not intelligent by human standards. The silkies are intelligent. Unfortunately, as far as we and they are concerned, our bodies are too . . . different."

"That will do," snapped Grimes. "Get dressed. And remember this, if Coffin's man has reported to his master, and if the patrolmen try to arrest us, the three of you are to use only such force as is required to prevent our capture. I want an incident, not a massacre. But I don't want to spend what's left of the night in Coffin's jail."

But he had no real fears of this latter. He already knew of the fighting capabilities of Shirl and Darleen and strongly suspected that Seiko, by herself, would be more than a match for a small army, provided that this army did not deploy nuclear weaponry.

Nonetheless they made their way back to the ship without incident.

Grimes told Steerforth a somewhat edited version of the night's doings.

Chapter 26

SO THE BAIT had been noticed. Would Pastor Coffin bite? Grimes had little doubt he would do so, and no doubt at all that the pastor would find Shirl, Darleen and Seiko an impossibly hard mouthful to swallow. As long as there was an incident, as long as Grimes could scream that he and his people, respectable, law-abiding merchant spacepersons, had been assaulted by the Salemites there would be an excuse for Survey Service intervention. Damien had half-promised that the destroyer *Pollux* would be loafing around in the vicinity of New Salem, doing something or other, during the period of Grimes's stay on the planet.

After spending a rather lazy day Grimes and the three girls emerged from the ship under the cover of darkness and followed their usual route to the beach. It was another brightly starlit night but this time they were not followed. When Grimes got himself entangled in a particularly tenacious bush he envied the pastor's men. They—assuming that they would be at the shore to watch the horrid goings-on—would have made their way to the beach by the coast road.

They were waiting there. Grimes, by himself, would not have been aware of their presence but Shirl and Darleen, with their super-sharp hearing, were.

"Do we do the same as last night, John?" whispered Shirl.

"No," said Grimes firmly. (Tonight's audio-visual tapes would have to be produced as evidence at the inquiry into the almost inevitable incident.) "No. Just a meeting, a conference with the silkies."

"But can't we have a swim, even?" asked Darleen.

"All right, all right. Have your swim." (There was very few worlds—although Salem was one of them—where the spectacle of attractive naked women splashing in the sea would evoke so much as a raised eyebrow.)

Grimes set up the recorder. Seiko stripped and waded out into the water, deeper and deeper, until she was lost to sight. Shirl and Darleen got out of their coveralls, ran down to the sea, fell full length and began striking out in a sparkling flurry of phosphorescence. Grimes lit his pipe. He thought that he heard a faint rustling in the bushes inland from the beach but could not be sure. He was far from being afraid but was beginning to feel distinctly uneasy.

Shirl and Darleen emerged from the water, joined him where he sat. Shirl produced a packet of cigarillos from a pocket in her coveralls. Both girls lit up. Neither made any attempt to get dressed. Grimes remarked upon this.

"The air is quite warm," said Shirl. "We shall let it dry us."

"Last night," said Darleen, "we were very uncomfortable when we put on our clothes over wet skins."

"Suit yourself," said Grimes.

And why should he be the only one dressed? Because all that was happening was being recorded, that was why. Because friends as well as enemies in the Survey Service would laugh themselves sick when, at the inquiry, the tapes were played, with an audio-visual recording of Grimes enjoying a roll in the hay (or a roll on the sand) with two of his junior officers. Too, why should he give those unseen watchers an even better show than the one that they were already enjoying?

Seiko waded out from the sea, dripping phosphorescence. She was followed by six big silkies. The same ones as the previous night? Grimes couldn't tell. Apart from differences in size and pelt coloration they all looked the same to him.

The seabeasts disposed themselves in a semi-circle, facing the humans and the pseudo-human and the audio-visual recorder. They talked and sang, and Shirl, Darleen and Seiko replied to them in kind. Now and again Shirl would interpret for Grimes's benefit.

The silkies wanted just one thing, to be left alone. They admitted that not all humans were as bad, from their viewpoint, as the colonists. They admitted that exchanges of knowledge and of information might be advantageous but, essentially, they had very good reason not to trust humans.

"Not even you, John," said Shirl sadly. "We—Darleen and myself and Seiko—have been prepared to cast aside the artificial trappings of so-called civilization. You have not. We have made naked contact with the silkies. You have not. And you did not approve, in your heart of hearts, when we did . . . ."

"I'm keeping my trousers on," growled Grimes. "Tonight especially."

At last the conference was over. Again Seiko stood on that sea-rounded rock; again the silkies made their obeisance, one by one gently placing a flipper on her slim feet. Then they were gone, back into the sea.

The three women began to get into their coveralls—and from the bushes, armed with staves and clubs, poured Coffin's men.

The women were caught at a disadvantage, half into and half out of their coveralls. Too, at first, they paid overmuch heed to Grimes's admonition not to fight back too viciously. And Seiko, upon whom Grimes had been relying, was one of the first casualties. The butt of a long stave struck her fair and square upon her vulnerable navel, where her ON/OFF switch was situated. She did not freeze into complete immobility—the switch had not been fully actuated—but thereafter was able to struggle only feebly. By this time both Shirl and Darleen had been struck about their heads with heavy clubs, as had been Grimes himself. After that he had only confused recollections of the struggle. He was flung violently to the sand, face down, and got his mouth and his eyes full of grit. A heavy boot on the small of his back pinned him in this supine position. His wrists were yanked up and back, pulled together by rough rope that broke the skin. Despite his kicking his ankles were bound.

He heard Coffin's voice, an unpleasant combination of smugness and harshness.

"We have them. The witch and her three disciples."

"But one of them is the outworld captain, Pastor."

"It matters not. Captains may still be sinners and blasphemers, worshippers of false gods. His rank—such as it is—matters not. He will stand trial with the witch and the two shameless trollops."

Grimes felt hands lifting him. He was dropped on to a hard wooden surface. His nose began to bleed. Somebody was dropped beside him, and then two other bodies on top of him. He heard the squeaking of not-very-well-greased axles and felt the jolts as the unsprung vehicle, whatever it was, was pulled (by manpower, he supposed) along the rough coast road. He managed to lift and to turn his head so that his painfully bruised nose was no longer in contact with the floorboards.

He could speak now, although it required a great effort.

"Seiko . . ."

"Yes . . ." her voice came at last, weak, barely audible.

"You're the strongest of us. Can you break your bonds?"

"No . . . I have . . . lost . . . my strength. They . . . hit me. You know . . . where."

"You should not have told us not to fight back," said Shirl.

"Where . . . are they taking us?" asked Darleen.

To hell in a handcart, thought Grimes but did not say it.

"What will they do to us?" asked Shirl.

"Throw us into jail, I suppose," said Grimes. "But not to worry. Mr. Steerforth will bail us out." (*And how much will that cost?* he wondered, the mercenary side of him coming to the surface.)

~ Chapter 27 ~

THEY WERE NOT THROWN IN JAIL.

They were dragged roughly out of the four-wheeled cart and securely bound, with iron chains, to four upright posts, also of iron. Dazedly Grimes looked about him. He and the others had been brought to the open area between the waterfront, with its jetties, and the town. He was facing a long table, on which were three oil lanterns, at which were sitting Pastor Coffin and, one to either side of him, two clerkly men. Other lanterns were hung from tall posts, illuminating the faces of the crowd that had turned up to. . . . To see the fun?

Coffin glared at Grimes from beneath his heavy, black brows. He demanded, in a deep voice, "Prisoner at the bar, how plead ye?"

Grimes mustered enough saliva to wash most of the sand and blood out of his mouth. He spat, regretting as he did so that the pastor was out of range. He spat again.

"Prisoner at the bar, how plead ye?" repeated Coffin.

"I do not plead," almost shouted Grimes. "I demand. I demand that I and my people be returned, at once, to our ship!"

"Prisoner at the bar, how plead ye? Guilty or not guilty?"

"Guilty of fucking *what*?" demanded Grimes, considering that this occasion called for some deliberate obscenity in his speech, realizing, too late, that his words could be misconstrued. (But, he thought, he had not played an active part in that orgy.)

Coffin seemed to be losing his patience. "John Grimes, you will answer my questions. Are you, or are you not, guilty of witchcraft?"

"Witchcraft? You must be joking."

"This is no joking matter, Grimes. Are you guilty or not guilty?"

"Not guilty."

One of the clerkly men was writing in a big book with an antique-looking pen.

"Your plea has been recorded," said Coffin. He turned his attention to Shirl. "You, woman. How do you plead?"

"Not guilty," she replied in a firm voice.

"And you, woman. How do you plead?"

"Not guilty," said Darleen.

"And . . . you?" Coffin was glaring at Seiko, who was sagging in her bonds.

The robot was speaking with difficulty. "Not . . ." she got out at last. "Not . . . guilty."

"Very well," said Coffin. "Now we shall hear the truth. Clerk of the court, call the first witness."

The man sitting on his right—not, as Grimes had been expecting, the man writing in the book—rose to his feet, called, in a high voice, "Matthew Ling, stand forward! Matthew Ling, stand forward!"

A burly fellow shouldered his way through the crowd, took his stance between the prisoners and Coffin's table.

"Matthew Ling, identify yourself," ordered the pastor.

"My name is Matthew Ling," said the man. "I hold the rank of Law Enforcer Second Class."

"Tell your story, Law Enforcer Ling."

"May it please the court," said Ling, "my story is as follows." He spoke as do police officers all over the Galaxy when giving evidence, his voice toneless. "Pursuant to information received and to the instructions of Pastor Coffin I followed the four accused from the spaceport to Short Bay. At first I thought that they were members of the Negro race; as the court is aware there are some of those accursed people in the crew of the starship. I caught glimpses of their faces while they were still on the spaceport grounds, and saw that they were black . . ."

"As their faces," said Coffin, "are black now. And their hands. That alone is damning evidence. Why should a God-fearing man or woman blacken the Lord's handiwork as evinced on his person? I will tell you. As a badge of submission to the Prince of Darkness. But continue, Law Enforcer."

"May it please the court . . . I followed the accused through the bush, across the coast road, and then concealed myself in the bushes, in a position overlooking the beach at Short Bay. I watched the accused setting up a device on a tripod, a devil's machine of some kind that emitted colored lights. Then the male accused sat down on the sand and began to inhale the poisonous fumes of some weed that he was burning in the bowl of a small implement. While he was partaking of his noxious drug the three female accused disrobed. I saw then that their faces and hands were blackened but not the rest of their bodies. The females accused then disported themselves in a wanton manner before the male accused.

"The three female accused waded into the sea. Two of them swam, with unnatural skill. The third one, the one with the black hair, waded out into deep water until she was lost to sight. At no time did she swim or attempt to swim. The other ones returned to the beach and, still naked, sat beside the male accused, joining him in the ritual inhalation of some noxious weed.

"Finally the black-haired female accused came up from the sea, followed by six silkies. What happened then I should never have believed unless I had witnessed it with my own eyes. The three witch-women sported with the silkies. It was a scene of sickening bestiality." (At last there was a hint of emotion in the flat voice.) "But even the witches and the silkies tired of their lewd games. The silkies returned to the sea. But the black-haired witch stood on a rock, and each silky, before going back to the sea, made a sign of submission to her by placing its flipper on her bare feet. I had seen enough and made my way back to the city, by the coast road, to make my report."

"And what you have told us is the truth," stated rather than asked Pastor Coffin.

"It is, sir," said Ling.

"Objection!" shouted Grimes.

Coffin consulted with the two clerks then said, "John Grimes, it pleases us to hear your objection. Say your say."

"Your Law Enforcer Ling is not a reliable witness, Pastor."

"Indeed? How not so?"

"Law Enforcer Ling stated that on the night in question I sat down on the beach to enjoy a quiet smoke. That is correct. He also stated that Ms. Kelly and Ms. Byrne, after they had finished their swim, also enjoyed a smoke. They did not. That was because they had brought no smoking materials with them."

Ling was called to the pastor's table, was engaged in a low-voiced conference with Coffin and the other two. Finally he stood aside.

The pastor said, "It is your word, John Grimes, against the word of my law enforcer . . . ."

"My word," said Grimes hotly, "and the words of two of my officers."

"There may," admitted Coffin magnanimously, "be some confusion in Law Enforcer Ling's memory. For this there is ample excuse. What he witnessed would have been enough to turn the mind of any man not of exceptionably strong and pious character. And Law Enforcer Ling was with me tonight, when you and the other accused were apprehended. I saw, with my own eyes, both you and the women Kelly and Byrne indulging in your filthy habit. The objection that you have raised is a mere quibble."

Grimes subsided. *They can't shoot us for smoking*, he thought. *Not even on this woody planet.*

But for witchcraft?

"Call the second witness," ordered Coffin.

"Job Gardiner," called the clerk. "Job Gardiner. Stand forward!"

"My name is Job Gardiner," said the man, who could almost have been twin brother to Matthew Ling. "I hold the rank of Chief Law Enforcer . . ."

He cleared his throat. "Pursuant to information received and to direct orders from Pastor Coffin, I, together with a party of law enforcers—among whom was Matthew Ling—made my way to Short Beach by the coast road. Pastor Coffin accompanied us, saying, and rightly, that this was a very serious matter and that he would have to exercise overall command of the operation. . . ."

And so it went on.

" . . . it was obvious, to the pastor and myself, to all of us that the four accused were talking to the silkies and that the silkies were talking to them. And such things cannot be. Then the silkies returned to the sea, but before they did so they made bestial obeisance to the black-haired witch. The pastor ordered us to arrest the four blasphemous outworlders. We did so, and we smashed the Devil's machine that they had brought with them."

But the tapes should have survived, thought Grimes. The tapes, and their damning evidence. But would they be retrieved? Would they ever be played back?

"The court has heard the evidence," said Coffin. "We all have heard the evidence. It is obvious that at least one of the accused, the black-haired woman, is a witch. It is probable that the man and the other two women are lesser witches, or acolytes. But we must be sure before we order our law to take its course. Chief Law Enforcer Gardiner, I order you to apply the acid test."

"Law Enforcer Ling," ordered Gardiner in his turn, "bring the acid."

Coffin smiled bleakly at Grimes. "We have our methods, outworlder, of determining the guilt or otherwise of witches. The acid test is one of the more effective. An accused witch is required to drink a draught of acid. If he or she is uninjured, then obviously he or she is a witch and is dealt with accordingly. If he or she suffers harm, then he or she is possibly not a witch."

"Heads I win, tails you lose," said Grimes.

"You speak in riddles, Grimes. And nothing you say is of any consequence."

Ling returned from wherever he had gone carrying a large bottle. He handed this to his superior, then went to stand behind Seiko, pulling her head back with one hand, forcing her mouth open with the other. Gardiner, who was now wearing heavy gloves, approached her from in front. He raised the unstoppered bottle, began to pour its contents between her parted lips. Some of the corrosive fluid spilled on to Seiko's clothing, which smoked acridly.

There was a murmur from the crowd, more than a murmur, a chorus of shouts. "She is a witch! Kill her! Kill her!"

Then, abruptly, Seiko regurgitated the acid that had been poured into her. The burning stream struck Gardiner full in the face. He dropped the bottle, which shattered, and screamed shrilly, clawing at his ruined eyes.

Incongruously the robot murmured, "I . . . am . . . sorry. But my . . . circuits . . . were not . . . designed to . . . take such punishment . . ."

Grimes was not sorry. The Chief Law Enforcer had deserved what he got. (To how many flesh-and-blood women had he applied this acid test?) And the bottle was broken and, hopefully, it would take some time to fetch a new one and, meanwhile, anything might happen . . .

Grimes hoped.

Chapter 28

THE WHIMPERING GARDINER was led away by two of his subordinates. Presumably whoever passed for a doctor in this town would be able to assuage the pain, although not to do anything to save the man's eyesight. But that was the least of Grimes's worries. His main concern was for Seiko, for Shirl and Darleen and for himself. He reproached himself for not having carried to the beach, in addition to the recorder, a portable transceiver so that, at all times, he would have been in communication with his ship.

But he had never dreamed that Coffin would go to the extremes to which he already had gone—and to what extremes was he yet to go? *And you, Grimes, of all people,* he told himself, *should have learned by this time that allegedly civilized people are capable of anything, no matter how barbarous.*

Coffin was speaking. "There is no doubt that the woman is a witch. Not only has she survived her ordeal uninjured but she has severely injured my chief law enforcer. She must pay the penalty." He paused judicially, turned his head to stare at Grimes, Shirl and Darleen. "It was my intention to order that the acid test be applied to the other three accused. Unfortunately no further supply of acid is readily available. So I shall, therefore, temper justice with mercy. Grimes, Kelly and Byrne will be given the opportunity to confess and to recant. Should they do so, their ends will be swift and merciful. Should they not do so, they shall be executed in the same manner as their mistress. They will be permitted to watch her sufferings and, hopefully, such spectacle will be a stimulus to their consciences.

"Bring the faggots!"

Men and women brought bundles of sticks. (These must, thought Grimes, have been prepared well in advance.) They piled them around the stake to which Seiko was chained, concealing the lower half of her body. A law enforcer poured some fluid— flammable oil, it was—over the faggots. He struck a long match, applied the flame all around the base of the pile.

With a loud *whoosh* the oil ignited and there was an uprush of smoky fire. Seiko's hair—but it's only a *wig*, thought Grimes—flared and crackled. Then the initial fury of the burning oil subsided but the faggots had caught, were snapping in the heat, emitting sparks, sending their flames curling up around Seiko's body. Although the cloth of her coveralls was flame-resistant it was beginning to char and to powder. A sigh, a horribly obscene sound, went up from the mob as one perfect breast was exposed.

Suddenly, audible even over the crackling of the fire, the murmurs of the crowd, there was a startlingly loud *click*! Seiko, who had been sagging in her bonds, stood erect. Her wrists, which had been tied behind her back, were already free, the flames having burned away the rope. But even if this had not been the case it would not have mattered. The strength that she now exerted to snap the chains would have been more than enough to break mere vegetable fiber. As she stood there, ridding herself of the last of her bonds, the crumbling remnants of her clothing fell from around her smoke-smudged body. She was like, thought Grimes, Aphrodite rising from the sea—a sea of fire. And he, even at this moment, had to repress a giggle. A Venus without arms, a Venus de Milo, he might accept— but a bald-headed one was altogether too much. (Her body paint had survived the fire although her wig had not.) Even so, she was beautiful—and not only because her escape from the pyre had brought a renewal of hope.

Men were shouting, women and children were screaming, but none dare approach this vengeful she-devil. Coffin was bellowing, "Seize her! Seize her! Strike her down!"

"Good on yer, Seiko!" yelled Darleen. "Show the bastards!"

There was a meter of broken chain in Seiko's right hand. She threw it. It wrapped itself around Coffin's neck, all but decapitating him. His two clerks squealed in terror, dived under the table, from the surface of which the pastor's blood dripped down upon them. Seiko stepped out of the fire, flames and sparks splashing about her feet. Two law enforcers, braver or more stupid than their fellows, ran at her with heavy clubs upraised. She countered their assault with the savate technique that she must have learned from Shirl and Darleen; her long right leg flashed out while she pivoted on her left heel; first one man and then the other (although there was almost no interval between the two blows) were the recipients of a crippling kick to the groin. In horror Grimes noted that the trousers of each unfortunate were smouldering where the kicks had landed. Seiko's feet must be almost redhot. (But it was her feet for which he felt concern, not the genitals of the law enforcers.)

He felt the heat emanating from her body as she approached him, as her hands reached out for his chains. But she was careful not to touch him.

She said, "Do not worry about me, John. I am heat-resistant. I feel no pain, as you know it. And it was the heat of the fire that released my master switch . . ."

She left him to his own devices, went to free the two New Alicians.

Grimes looked around, fearing fresh attack. But the light of the oil lanterns on their posts revealed a waterfront empty save for himself and his women, the body of Coffin sprawled over the table and the two still-living (but for how long?) bodies of the law enforcers. The pair of clerks had made their escape unnoticed.

"Well," said Grimes with deliberate matter-of-factness, "that seems to be it. We've had our incident. Let's get back to the ship. Come, Shirl. Come, Darleen. And you, Seiko, can guard our rear."

"I am staying," said the robot.

"Seiko, I order you to come with us."

"John, your father was my original owner. He ordered me to protect you when necessary."

"Then protect me as I walk back to the spaceport."

She said, "We could be attacked." With a long forefinger she touched her navel. "I have learned my vulnerability in a scrimmage. A club, a flung stone, even a heavy fist and I can be jolted into near-immobility. There is only one way to ensure your safety. Those people . . ." she gestured toward the town, " . . . must be taught a lesson."

It was not toward the houses she ran but to the slipway, up which the schooners were hauled for the scraping and caulking of the underwater portions of their hulls. It was toward the slipway that she ran, and down the slipway. When her body entered the black water there was an uprising of steam.

Then she was gone from sight.

"Crazy robot!" grumbled Grimes. "Being cooked must have affected her brain . . ."

"She knows what she is doing, John," said Darleen loyally.

"Does she? I wish that I did." He could sense that from darkened windows he was being watched. He wondered how long it would be before the New Salemites, seeing that the most dangerous witch had plunged into the sea, would come pouring out of their houses to exact vengeance for the death of their pastor and the injuries inflicted upon his law enforcers. He said, "I think that we should be getting out of here."

Shirl said, "But we can't leave Seiko . . . "

"I know," said Grimes. "But . . ."

"Do you hear her?" Shirl asked Darleen.

"Yes." Then, to Grimes, "Do not worry so, John. Everything will be all right."

From whose viewpoint? he wondered.

Then up the shipway she strode. The sea had washed the grime of smoke and fire from her pale body. Up the slipway she strode—and behind her, a living tide, surged the silkies. As she passed Grimes on her way inshore she made a gesture that was more formal salute than cheery wave. And the silkies grunted—in greeting or talking among themselves? But Shirl and Darleen replied in kind.

The robot and her army reached the sea frontage of the town. There was shouting and screaming, the splintering crashes as doors were burst in, as wooden walls succumbed to the onslaught of tons of angry flesh and blood. Fires started in a dozen places—the result of overturned lamps or lit by intent? Grimes did not know but suspected that Seiko was exacting retaliation in kind for what she had undergone. Fires started, and spread.

"This has gone too far," said Grimes.

"It has not gone far enough," Shirl told him. "The silkies said to us that she had told them that they were not to kill. To destroy only, but not to kill. That's the trouble with robots. They have this built-in, altogether absurd directive that human beings are never to be harmed by them."

"Wherever did you get that idea?" asked Grimes.

"While we were waiting for you on Earth we did quite a lot of reading. There were some books, classics, by an old writer called Asimov."

"Then what about him?" Grimes gestured toward the pastor's body. "Wasn't he harmed? Fatally, at that."

"Yes, John," said Darleen patiently. "But he was going to harm you, and Seiko was doing her best to protect you."

The town was ablaze now, the roaring of the flames drowning out all other noises coming from that direction. Satisfied with the havoc that they had wrought, the silkies were returning to the sea. There was light enough for Grimes to see that some were wounded, with great patches of fur burned from their bodies. Others bled from long and deep gashes. But their musical grunting sounded like a chant of victory.

Seiko brought up the rear. Again her body was smoke-blackened. She approached Grimes and bowed formally. "Captain-san, it is over. We spared the church and a large hall adjacent, and the people are huddled in these buildings, praying."

"How many killed?" demanded Grimes.

"Nobody by intent, although two or three may have died accidentally. But we let them seek refuge in their houses of worship and I refrained from applying the torch to these."

"You did well," said Grimes at last. "All right. The sooner we're back on board the ship the better."

"I am sorry, John," Seiko told him. "I cannot accompany you."

"That's an order, damn it!"

"Which I cannot accept. I was built to serve, John, as well you know. But you do not really need me. They . . ." she gestured toward the sea, to the silky heads, their eyes gleaming with reflected firelight, that were turned inland, looking at the humans and the robot. "They need me, much more than you do."

"She is right," said Shirl and Darleen as one.

Above the roar of the burning town, beating down from the sky, was the arrhythmic clatter of a small craft's inertial drive. One of *Sister Sue's* lifeboats made a heavy landing not far from where Grimes was still trying to argue with the women. From it jumped Steerforth and Calamity Cassie, each with a laser pistol in hand.

"You're all right, Captain?" demanded the chief officer. "We saw the flames and thought that we'd better take action."

"You did right," said Grimes. "And now you can get us back to where we belong."

"Good-bye, Harald," said Seiko. "Good-bye, Cassie. Tell the others good-bye for me."

She was, Grimes noticed, holding her right hand protectively over her navel.

"We can't leave you here, Seiko," objected Steerforth.

"She can look after herself," said Grimes harshly. "And, in any case, it'll be days yet before *Sister Sue* is capable of lifting off. If—no, *when*—you change your mind, Seiko, you'll know where to find us."

The boat, with Steerforth at the controls, clattered upward. The chief officer made a circuit of the seaport area before setting course for the spaceport. New fires had broken out; alongside their jetties the schooners were ablaze.

She was thorough, was Seiko, thought Grimes. Very thorough. It would be a long time before, if ever, there was another silky hunt on New Salem.

All that next day he was expecting her to come walking back up the ramp, into the ship. And the day after, and the day after that . . .

~ Chapter 29 ~

THE MESS WAS WELL on the way to being cleaned up.

The destroyer *Pollux* had been within range of *Sister Sue's* Carlotti radio, even though the signals had been broadcast and not beamed. She had dropped down to the spaceport, with Grimes usurping the functions of New Salem Aerospace Control. (Presumably the lady who usually did the talking to incoming traffic was still huddled in the church with her badly frightened fellow colonists.)

Her captain, Commander Beavis, had served under Grimes many years ago and was cooperative. Damien must have told him that Grimes was once again, although secretly, an officer of the Federation Survey Service, senior to Beavis. That gentleman managed to imply that Grimes could issue orders rather than mere suggestions. But appearances were maintained for the benefit of the crews of both ships. Grimes was the innocent shipmaster whose life, and the lives of certain of his officers, had been threatened by the people of this world. Beavis was the galactic policeman who had come hurrying to the rescue.

Beavis had the people and the equipment to be able to do something about the plight of the colonists, whose city had been almost entirely destroyed. He set up a sizeable township of tents, complete with field kitchens and a hospital. He interrogated various officials and recorded their stories. Then, aboard *Sister Sue*, he heard

Grimes's report and watched and listened to the playback of the various tapes—one of them heavily edited—including that final one, which had been recovered, undamaged, from the beach. He interviewed Shirl and Darleen and Steerforth and Cassie.

Then when he was alone with Grimes, relaxing over a drink, he said, "I shall put all this material in Admiral Damien's hands as soon as possible, sir. He's going to love it—and so will Madame Duvalier. I rather think, somehow, that the New Salemites are going to be resettled—preferably on some world with no animal life whatsoever . . . ."

"If they could find some way of harvesting plants really brutally they'd do it," said Grimes. "In spite of all that's happened they still regard themselves as the Almighty-created Lords of Creation. And, more and more, I'm coming to the opinion that any life, all life, should be treated with respect and compassion."

"Even robots, sir?" asked Beavis with deceptive innocence.

Grimes laughed. "All right, all right. There was that bloody tin messiah, Mr. Adam, years ago. He got what was coming to him; I wasn't sorry then and I'm not sorry now."

"I was thinking of Seiko, sir."

"Mphm."

"She would pass for a very attractive woman. You must miss her, sir."

"I suppose I do," admitted Grimes. "But she'll be back. She'll know when I'm due to lift. She'll be back."

At last the repairs were finished and the fresh water tank refilled. All that remained to be done was the recalibration of *Sister Sue's* Mannschenn Drive. While this was being carried out only a skeleton crew would remain on board—Grimes himself in the control room, Flo Scott in the inertial drive room and, of course, all the Mannschenn Drive engineers in their own compartment, making their abstruse calculations and arcane adjustments. The theory of it was that if anything should go wrong, if the ship fell down a crack in the Space-Time Continuum, the captain and his top-ranking technicians might—just might—be able to get her back to where and when she belonged. Ships—only a very few ships but ships nonetheless—had been known to vanish during the recalibration procedure. Of that very few an even smaller number had come back, and not to the planets from which they had made their unscheduled departures. Sometimes, after only a very short absence from the normal universe, their crews had aged many years. Sometimes, during an absence of years, only minutes had elapsed for the personnel. Some crews claimed to have met God; others told horrifying stories of their narrow escapes from the clutches of the Devil. Grimes, good agnostic that he was, did not believe such tales, saying, if his opinion were asked, that it is a well-known fact that the temporal precession fields engendered by the Drive have an hallucinatory effect upon the human mind.

Recalibration, to him, was a process similar to old-fashioned navel gunnery, the procedure known as bracketing. Under . . . Up . . . Over . . . Down . . . still. Under . . . Up . . . Right on! Salvoes!

So he sat in *Sister Sue's* control room, smoking his pipe, waiting for Daniel Grey, the Chief Manschenn Drive Engineer, to start doing his thing. He looked out through a viewport, saw his people, together with a number of Beavis's officers, standing by the stern of *Pollux*, watching. Grey's voice came from the intercom speaker, "All ready, Captain."

"Thank you, Mr. Grey. Commence recalibration."

He heard—and felt—the deep hum as the rotors of the Drive commenced to spin, a hum that rapidly rose in pitch to a thin, high whine with an odd warbling quality. Outside the scene changed. *Pollux* was no longer there. Neither were the spaceport administration buildings. The planet was as it had been before the coming of man. Under, thought Grimes. The scene changed again. There were only ruins of buildings, barely recognizable as such under the growth of bushes and small trees.

Over.

Then *under* again, with a few rough shacks to mark where the spaceport proper would one day be.

Over . . .

The familiar buildings were there, but showing signs of

dilapidation. Grimes got up from his seat, looked down through the port at the concrete apron. It was cracked in many places, with weeds thrusting through the fissures. He went down from the control room to his quarters. There was an odd unfamiliarity about them. Who was the auburn-haired woman whose holographic portrait was on the bulkhead behind the desk in his day cabin? It wasn't Maggie, although there was a certain similarity. In his bedroom he took his uniform cap from the wardrobe, looked into the mirror to adjust it to the right angle. With fast dissipating puzzlement he noted the strange cap badge above the gold-braided peak, a rather ornate winged wheel, and the single broad gold band, the insignia of a commodore, on each of his shoulderboards. Passing through his day room he flicked a good-humoured salute at the portrait of Sonya.

He took the elevator down to the after airlock, walked down the ramp to the cracked and scarred concrete. His first lieutenant, Lieutenant Commander Cummings, saluted smartly. Grimes returned the salute. He said, "I'm taking a morning stroll, Commander Cummings. To the old seaport."

"Shouldn't an armed party be going with you, sir? After all, according to the data, the natives aren't overly friendly towards visitors."

"I've been here before, Commander. And the ones who most certainly were not friendly were the human colonists. And, as you know, they were resettled."

"As you please, sir. But . . ."

"I shall be all right, Commander."

You always are, you old bastard, he could almost hear the officer thinking.

And—old bastard? he thought. Yes, he was getting old. Not in mind, not even in body, but in years and experience.

The road from the spaceport to the seaport, along which he had first walked so many years ago, was still passable. Nonetheless he began to wish that he had taken one of the ship's boats instead of making the journey by foot. At any age at all he did not enjoy having to force his way through bushes. Although the sunlight was not especially hot he had worked up a good sweat by the time that he got to what had been Salem City. The charred ruins were not yet completely overgrown and the church and the hall, in which the colonists had taken refuge, were still standing.

Like rotting fangs the jetties still protruded into the sullen sea, from which projected, at crazy angles, the fire-blackened spars that had been the masts and yards of the schooners.

The slipway, still in a good state of repair, was almost as he remembered it.

And up it walked Seiko.

She was as she had been when he first saw her, in his parents' home. The transparent, glassy skin had been cleaned of all vestiges of body paint and beneath it glittered the beautiful intricacy of that non-functional yet busy clockwork. Her well-shaped head was bare of the last trace of hair. But something had been added, one item of clothing. She wore a broad belt of gleaming metal mesh with a golden buckle—more shield than buckle—that covered her navel.

She bowed formally. "Captain-san."

He bowed in return. "Seiko-san."

She said, "This is Liberty Hall. You can spit on the mat and call the cat a bastard."

He laughed and said, "You haven't lost your sense of humor."

"Why should I have done so, John? The silkies are not a humorless people."

She looked intently at his cap badge, the braid on his shoulders.

Grimes asked, "What's puzzling you?"

She said, "Your ship is the same. I saw her coming down. But your uniform is different."

Grimes told her, "She is no longer my ship. Oh, I command her, but I no longer own her. And her name has been changed. She is now *Faraway Quest*, the survey vessel of the Rim Worlds Confederacy, in whose naval reserve I hold the rank of commodore."

"And all the people I knew, when she was *Sister Sue* and you were owner as well as captain?"

"They have all gone their various ways, Seiko."

"I would have liked to have met Shirl and Darleen again . . ."

"I still hear from them, about once a standard year. Eventually they returned to their home planet, New Alice."

"When next you write, please give them my regards."

"I shall do so."

"And when next you are on *your* home planet, John, please give my regards to your respected parents."

Grimes told her, regretfully, "They are both long gone."

"Then will you, for me, make obeisance at their tomb and pour a libation?"

"I shall do that," promised Grimes.

The pair of them fell silent, looking at each other, a little sadly. It was a companionable silence.

Grimes broke it. He said, "You can have your old job back, if you want it."

She replied, "Thank you. But the silkies still need me. I am their hands and their voice. I speak for them to the occasional visitors to this world, human and non-human. Were I not here there would be acts of aggression and exploitation."

"So that's the way of it," said Grimes.

"That is the way of it," she agreed. Surprisingly she took him in her strong arms, affectionately pressed him to her resilient body. Grimes did not resist. She released him. "Good-bye, John. You must return to your ship. To your ship. We may meet again—I hope that we do. We may not. But always, always, the best of luck."

She turned away from him, walked down the slipway to the sea, an almost impossibly graceful, glittering figure. It seemed to Grimes that the silkies had been waiting for her. There was a great flurry of spray as she entered the water, a chorus of musical gruntings.

And then she and they were gone, and Grimes started his walk back to the ship, cursing the spiky bushes on the overgrown road that seemed to be determined to hold him prisoner on this planet.

He was sitting in his chair in the control room. The Drive had been recalibrated. All hands had returned on board, had proceeded to their lift-off stations. Steerforth looked curiously at Grimes's forearms, bare under the short-sleeved uniform shirt, at his knees, bare under the hem of his shorts.

"Those scratches, sir. . . . How did you get them? You look as though you've been in a cat fight."

"Do I?" said Grimes coldly. Then, "All right, Number One. Let's get the show on the road."

Steerforth said, "But couldn't we wait a little, sir? What about Seiko? Couldn't we send Shirl and Darleen down to the sea to try to do some submarine singing to call her back? After all, they're rather special cobbers of hers."

"We shall be happy to try," said Shirl.

"Make it lift-off stations, Mr. Steerforth," ordered Grimes.

"But Seiko . . ."

"She'll be all right," said Grimes, with convincing certainty.

CATCH THE STAR WINDS

❧ Chance Encounter ❧

WE PAID OFF on Faraway, having brought the old *Epsilon Pavonis* all the way across the Galaxy to hand her over to her new owners, Rim Runners Incorporated. The Commission's Branch Manager booked us in at the Rimrock House, one of the better hotels in Faraway City. All that we had to do was to wait for the arrival of *Delta Bootes*, in which vessel we were to be shipped back to Earth. The services to and from the Rim Worlds are far from frequent and none of the big passenger liners ever call there; they are not planets that one would ever recommend for a vacation. There's that dreariness, that ever-present sense that one is hanging by one's eyebrows over the very edge of the ultimate cold and dark. The cities on none of the Rim Planets are cities, real cities, but only overgrown—and not so very overgrown at that—provincial towns. The people are a subdued mob who take their pleasures sadly and their sorrows even more sadly. Somebody once said that the average Rim World city is like a graveyard with lights. He wasn't so far wrong.

Delta Bootes was a long time coming. She was delayed on Waverley by a strike, and then she had to put in to Nova Caledon for repairs to her Mannschenn Drive unit. Some of us didn't worry overmuch—after all, we were being paid, and well-paid, for doing nothing and the branch manager was footing our weekly bar bills without a murmur. Some of us worried a lot, even so. In the main, with one exception, it was the married men who were doing the worrying.

The one exception was Peter Morris, our P.R.O.—Psionic Radio Officer to you—our bright young man from the Rhine Institute, our tame telepath. Yet he was single and so far as any of us knew, had no girl waiting for him on any of the colonised worlds or on Earth. But if there had been a first prize for misery he would have won it.

I liked Peter. During the run out we had formed a friendship that was rather unusual between a telepath and a normal human being—or, as the average graduate of the Institute would put it, between a normal human being and a psionic deficient. I liked Peter, I suppose, because he was so obviously the odd man out and I have a strong tendency towards being odd man out myself. So it was that during our sojourn on Faraway we developed the routine of leaving the others to prop up the bar of the Rimrock House while we, glad to get away from reiteration of the bawdy jokes and boring personal anecdotes, wandered away from the hotel and through the city, finding some small, pleasant drinking place where we could sip our beer in relative peace and quiet.

We were in such a place that morning, and the drinks that we had imbibed had done nothing at all to cheer Peter up. He was so gloomy that even I, who am far from being a cheerful type myself, remarked upon it.

"You don't know what it's like, Ken," he told me. "As a psionic deficient you'll never know. It's the aura of . . . of . . . Well, there's fear, and there's loneliness, and a sort of aching emptiness, and together they make up *the feel* of these Rim Worlds. A telepath is always lonely until, if he's very lucky, he finds the right woman. But it's so much worse here."

"There's Epstein, the P.R.O. at the port," I said. "And there's Mrs. Epstein. Why don't you see more of them?"

"That," he declared, "would make it worse. When two telepaths marry they're a closed circuit to an extent that no p.d. couple can ever be . . ." He drank some more beer. "Finding the right woman," he went on, "is damned hard for us. I don't know why it is, but the average Esper female is usually frightfully unattractive, both mentally and physically. They seem to run to puddingy faces and puddingy minds . . . You know, Ken, I needn't have come on this trip. There are still so few of us that we can afford to turn down assignments. I came for one reason only—just hoping that by making a voyage all the way across the Galaxy I'd find somebody."

"You still might on the way back," I told him.

"I still might not," he replied.

I looked at him with a rather irritated pity. I could sense, after a fashion, what he was driving at. He was so much the typical introvert—dark of hair and face, long and lean—and his telepathic talent could do nothing but add to the miseries that come with introversion.

"You'd better have something stronger," I told him. I caught the bartender's eye. "Two double whiskies, please."

"Make that three," said a too-hearty voice. I looked around, saw that Tarrant, our Second Mate, had just come in.

"Got tired of the same old stories at last?" I asked unkindly.

"No," he said. "But somebody had to go to find you two, and I was the most junior officer present, so . . ."

"Who wants us?" I demanded. "And why?"

"The Old Man wants you." He lifted his glass. "Here's to crime."

"What does he want us for?"

"I don't know. All that I know is this. Some meteor-pitted old bastard calling himself Captain Grimes came barging into the pub and demanded an audience with our lord and master. They retired to confer privily. Shortly thereafter the call for all hands to battle stations went out."

"Grimes . . ." I said slowly. "The name rings a bell. I seem to remember that when we handed the old *Eppy Swan* over somebody mentioned that Captain Grimes, the Chief Superintendent for Rim Runners, was away on Thule."

"Could be," admitted Tarrant. "He has the look of a chairborne spaceman. In which case we'll have another drink. It's bad enough having to run to the beck and call of our own Supers without having to keep those belonging to a tuppenny ha'penny concern like Rim Runners happy."

We had another drink, and another. After the third whisky

Peter's gloom seemed to be evaporating slightly, so he ordered a fourth one. The Second Mate and I each ordered another round, after which we thought that we had better discover what was cooking. We walked rather unsteadily into the untidy street, hailed a ground cab and were driven back to the Rimrock House.

We found them all waiting for us in the Lounge—the Old Man and the rest of the officers, the chunky little man whose appearance justified Tarrant's description of him as a "meteor-pitted old bastard."

"Sir," said the Old Man stiffly, "here are my Third Officer, Mr. Wilberforce, and my Psionic Radio Officer, Mr. Morris. I have no doubt that they will show as little enthusiasm for your project as any of my other officers. Yours is essentially a Rim World undertaking, and should be carried out by Rim World personnel."

"They can decide, sir," said Captain Grimes. "You have told me that these officers have no close ties on Earth or elsewhere; it is possible that they may find the proposition attractive. And, as I have already told you, we guarantee repatriation."

"What is it all about, anyhow?" asked Tarrant.

"Sit down, gentlemen," said Grimes, "and I'll tell you." While we were finding chairs he filled and lit a foul pipe. "I'll have to recapitulate for your benefit; I hope that the rest of you don't object.

"Well, as you are no doubt aware, we of the Rim Worlds consider ourselves the orphans of the Galaxy. You know why these planets were colonised in the first instance—the Central Government of those days feared an alien invasion sweeping in from outside the Galaxy. The general idea was to set up a huge ring of garrisoned planets, a fortified perimeter. That idea has died over the years and, as a result, only a very small arc of the Rim has been explored, even.

"We of the Rim Worlds wish to survive as a separate, independent entity. Starved as we are of trade and shipping we have little chance of surviving at all. So it has been decided that we take our own steps, in our own way, to achieve this end.

"You've heard, of course, of the odd pieces of wreckage that come drifting in, from time to time, from *somewhere*. It was such flotsam that first gave the Central Government the idea that there might be an invasion from some other galaxy. Now, we don't think that those odd bits and pieces ever did come from outside. We think that there are inhabited planets all around the rim, and that advantageous trade would be possible with them.

"For years we've been trying to persuade the brass hats of the Survey Service to carry out a systematic exploration, but the answer's always the same. They haven't the ships, or they haven't the men, or they haven't the money. So, at last, we have decided to carry out our own exploration. Your old ship, *Epsilon Pavonis*, is being fitted out for the job. She's being renamed, by the way—*Faraway Quest*..."

"And what," asked Tarrant, "has this to do with us?"

Captain Grimes hesitated, seemed almost embarrassed. "Frankly," he said, "the trouble is this. We don't seem to breed spacemen, real spacemen, on the Rim Worlds. Puddle jumpers, that's all they are. They'll venture as far as Ultimo, or Thule, or the Shakespearean Sector, but they just aren't keen to fare any further afield..."

"There's too much fear on these worlds," said Peter Morris suddenly. "That's the trouble. Fear of the cold and the dark and the emptiness..."

Grimes looked at him. "Of course," he said, "you're the telepath..."

"Yes, I'm the telepath. But you don't need to be any kind of an Esper to sense the fear."

"All right, then," said Grimes. "My own boys are just plain scared to venture so much as a single lightyear beyond the trade routes. But I've got a Master for *Faraway Quest*—myself. I've a Purser, and Chief and Second Mannschenn Drive Engineers, and one Rocket Engineer. I've a Chief Officer and a Surgeon-cum-Bio-Chemist, and an Electronic Radio Officer. All of us are from the Centre, none of us was born out here, on the Rim. But this is a survey job, and I shall need a well-manned ship.

"I can promise any of you who volunteer double your current rates of pay. I can promise you repatriation when the job is over, to any part of the Galaxy."

"Most of us," said our Captain, "have homes and families waiting for us. We've been out for too long now."

"You're sure that there are inhabited worlds out along the Rim?" asked Peter. "What of their people?"

"Purple octopi for all I know," replied Grimes.

"But there's a chance, just a chance, that they might be humanoid, or even human?" insisted the Psionic Radio Officer.

"Yes, there's a chance. Given a near infinitude of habitable worlds and an infinitude of time for evolution to take its course, then anything is possible."

"The purple octopi are more probable," I said.

"Perhaps," almost whispered Peter. "Perhaps . . . But I have limited, very limited, premonitory powers, and I have a definite feeling that. . ."

"That what?" I asked.

"Oh, never mind." To Grimes he said, "I take it that you can use a P.R.O., Captain?"

"That I can," declared Grimes heartily.

I sighed. "You offer about double the pay," I said. "I'm Third Officer in the Commission's fleet as you know. If I come with you as Second, do I get twice the Commission's rate for that rank?"

"You do."

"Count me in," I said.

"You must be mad," said Tarrant. "Both of you—but Wilberforce is less mad than Morris. After all, he's doing it for money. What are *you* doing it for, Crystal Gazer?"

"Mind your own business!" he snapped.

Some hours later, when we were out at the spaceport looking over the structural alterations that were being made to *Faraway Quest*, I asked him the same question.

He flushed. "What do people do things for, Peter?"

"Money," I replied. "Or power. Or . . ."

"Precisely," he said, before I could finish. "It's only a hunch, but I have a strong feeling that this is the chance, the only chance, to find *her*."

I remember that I said, "I hope you're right."

Delta Bootes dropped down at last to Port Faraway, and all of our shipmates, openly jubilant, boarded her. We saw them off, Peter and I. We had our last drinks with them in the little smoking room and then, feeling rather lost and lonely (at least, I did) scrambled out of the airlock and down the ramp as the last warning bell started to sound. We stood with the other spectators a safe distance from the blast-off area, watched her lift on her column of pale fire, watched her vanish into the clear, twilit sky. With her departure I realised the irrevocability of my action in volunteering for this crazy survey voyage. There was no backing out now.

We walked to the corner of the field where work was still progressing on *Faraway Quest*. Outwardly she was little changed, except for the addition of two extra boat blisters. Internally she was being almost rebuilt. Cargo space was being converted into living accommodation. In spite of the shortage of trained space-faring personnel Grimes had found volunteers from other quarters. Two professors of physics from Thule City were signing on as assistant engineers, and there were three astronomers from Ultimo as well as a couple of biologists. Grimes—who, we had learned, had served in the Survey Service as a young man—had persuaded the local police force to lend him three officers and fifty men, who were being trained as Space Marines. It began to look as though *Faraway Quest* would be run on something approaching Survey Service lines.

We looked at her, standing tall and slim in the light of the glaring floods.

I said, "I was a little scared when I watched *Delta Bootes* blast off, Peter, but now I'm feeling a little happier."

"I am too," he told me. "That. . . That hunch of mine is stronger than ever. I'll be glad when this old girl is ready to push off."

"I don't trust hunches," I told him. "I never have, and never will.

In any case, this female telepath with the beautiful mind you're hunting for may turn out to be nothing but a purple octopus."

He laughed. "You've got purple octopi on the brain. To hear you talk, one would think that the Galaxy was inhabited by the brutes . . ."

"Perhaps it is," I said. "Or all the parts that we haven't explored yet."

"*She* exists," he told me seriously. "I know. I've dreamed about her now for several nights running."

"Have you?" I asked. Other people's dreams are as a rule, dreadfully boring, but when the other person is a telepath with premonitory powers one is inclined to take some interest in them. "What did you dream?"

"Each time it was the same," he said. "I was in a ship's boat, by myself, waiting for her to come to me. I knew what she was like, even though I'd never actually met her. She wasn't quite human. She was a little too tall, a little too slim, and her golden hair had a greenish glint to it. Her small ears were pointed at the tips. As I say, I knew all this while I sat there waiting. And she was in my mind, as I was in hers, and she was saying, over and over, *I'm coming to you, my darling.* And I was sitting there in the pilot's chair, waiting to close the outer airlock door as soon as she was in . . ."

"And then?"

"It's hard to describe. I've had women in real life as well as in dreams, but never before have I experienced that feeling of utter and absolute oneness . . ."

"You're really convinced, aren't you?" I said. "Are you sure that it's not auto-hypnosis, that you haven't built up from the initial hunch, erecting a framework of wish-fulfillment fantasy?"

"I'd like to point out, Ken," he said stiffly, "that you're a qualified astronaut, not any sort of psychologist. I'd like to point out, too, that the Rhine Institute gives all its graduates a very comprehensive course in psychology. We have to know what makes our minds tick—after all, they are our working tools."

"Sorry," I said. "The main thing is that you feel reasonably sure that we shall stumble across some intelligent, humanoid race out there."

"Not reasonably sure," he murmured. "Just certain."

"Have you told Grimes all this?"

"Not all, but enough."

"What did he say?"

"That I was in charge of communications, not prognostications, and that my most important job was to see to it that my amplifier was healthy and functioning properly."

We all had to stand out on the field in a cold drizzle while the Presidents of Faraway, Ultimo and Thule made their farewell speeches. We were drawn up in a rather ragged line behind Captain Grimes, dapper in uniform, very much the space captain. The ex-policemen, the Marines, were a little to one side, and made up for what we lacked in the way of smartness. At last the speechmaking was over. Led by Grimes we marched up the ramp to the airlock, went at once to our blasting-off stations. In the control room Grimes sat chunkily in his acceleration chair with Lawlor, his Chief Officer, to one side of him. My own chair was behind theirs, and at my side was Gavin, one of the astronomers from Ultimo, who was on the ship's books as Third Officer.

Reports started coming in. "Interplanetary Drive Room—manned and ready!"

"Interstellar Drive Room—manned and ready!"

"Hydroponics—all secured!"

"Steward's store—all secured!"

"Mr. Wilberforce," ordered Grimes, "request permission to proceed."

I spoke into the microphone of the already switched on transceiver. "*Faraway Quest* to Control Tower, *Faraway Quest* to Control Tower. Have we your permission to proceed?"

"Control Tower to *Faraway Quest*. Permission granted. Good luck to all of you!"

Gavin was counting aloud, the words carried through the ship by the intercom. "Ten . . . Nine . . . Eight. . . Seven . . ." I saw Grimes's stubby hand poised over the master firing key. "Six . . . Five . . . Four . . ." I looked out of the nearest viewport, to the dismal, mist shrouded landscape. Faraway was a good world to get away from, to anywhere—or, even, nowhere. "Three . . . Two . . . One . . . *Fire!*"

We lifted slowly, the ground falling away beneath us, dropping into obscurity beneath the veil of drifting rain. We drove up through the low clouds, up and into the steely glare of Faraway's sun. The last of the atmosphere slipped, keening shrilly, down our shell plating and then we were out and clear, with the gleaming lens of the Galaxy to one side of us and, on the other, the aching emptiness of the Outside.

For long minutes we accelerated, the pseudo-gravity forcing us deeply into the padding of our chairs. At last Grimes cut the Drive and, almost immediately, the thunder of the rockets was replaced by the high, thin whine of the ever-precessing gyroscopes of the Mannschenn unit. The Galactic Lens twisted itself into an impossible convolution.

The emptiness Outside still looked the same.

That emptiness was with us all through the voyage.

Star after star we circled; some had planetary families, some had not. At first we made landings on all likely looking worlds, then, after a long succession of planets that boasted nothing higher in the evolutionary scale than the equivalent to the giant reptiles of Earth's past, we contented ourselves by making orbital surveys only. Peter succeeded in talking Grimes into entrusting him with the task of deciding whether or not any planet possessed intelligent life—and, of course, cities and the like could be spotted from space.

So we drove on, and on, settling down to a regular routine of Interstellar Drive, Interplanetary Drive, Closed Orbit, Interplanetary Drive, Interstellar Drive, Interplanetary Drive . . . Everybody was becoming short-tempered. Grimes was almost ready to admit that the odd pieces of flotsam falling now and again to the Rim Worlds must have come from Outside and not from somewhere else along the Rim. Had our purpose been exploration as a prelude to colonisation we should have felt a lot more useful—but the Rim Worlds have barely enough population to maintain their own economies.

Only Peter Morris maintained a certain calm cheerfulness. His faith in his hunch was strong. He told me so, more than once. I wanted to believe him but couldn't.

Then, one boring watch, I was showing Liddell, one of the astronomers, how to play three dimensional noughts and crosses in the Tri-Di chart. He was catching on well and I was finding it increasingly hard to beat him when suddenly, the buzzer of the intercom sounded. I answered it. It was Peter, speaking from his Psionic Communications Room.

"Ken!" he almost shouted. "Life! Intelligent life!"

"Where?" I demanded.

"I don't know. I'm trying to get a rough bearing. It's in towards the Lens from us, that much I can tell you. But the bearing doesn't seem to be changing."

"No parallax?" asked Liddell. "Could it be, do you think, a ship?"

"It just could be," I said doubtfully.

"Ken, I think it's a ship!" came Peter's voice. "I think that they, like ourselves, have Psionic Radio . . . Their operator's vaguely aware of me, but he's not sure . . . No—it's not *he* . . . It's a woman; I'm pretty certain of that . . . But it's a ship all right. Roughly parallel course, but converging . . ."

"Better tell old Grimy," I suggested, hastily clearing the noughts and crosses lattice from the Tri-Di chart. To Liddell I said, "I'm afraid Peter's imagining things. Not about the ship—she's probably a stray Survey vessel—but about the female operator. When psionic radio first started we used to carry them, but the average woman telepath is so unintelligent that they were all emptied out as soon as there were enough men for the job."

"It could be an alien ship," said Liddell.

"It could be, but it's not," I said. "Unless, of course, it belongs to one of the alien races with whom we've already made contact. It could be a Shaara vessel—that would account for Peter's female telepath. The Shaara are social insects, and all the work is done by the females."

Captain Grimes came into the control room. He looked almost happy. "Contact at last," he said.

"Suppose they are aliens," said the astronomer, "and suppose they open fire on us . . . What then?"

"By the time people get around to building interstellar ships," said Grimes, "they've lost the habit of wanting to fight strangers."

"Sometimes," I said.

"Switch on the Matter Proximity Indicator," he said.

I did so, peered into the globe that was its screen.

"There's something . . ." I said. "Red 085, ZD 093 . . ."

"A little astern," murmured the Old Man. "Range?"

I manipulated the controls carefully. "Twenty thousand—and closing. Relative bearing not altering."

"Liddell," said the Captain. "You're an astronomer, a mathematician. What are the odds against this? With all the immensity of Space around us we have two ships approaching on collision orbits. The other ship is using a similar Drive to ours—she must be. If her rate of temporal precession were more than one microsecond different from ours she would not register on our screens, and there'd be no risk of collision. What are the odds?"

"Astronomical," replied Liddell drily. "But I'll tell you this, although you must, by this time, have come to the same conclusion. There's a Law of Nature that you'll not find in any of the books, but that is valid just the same. If a coincidence can happen, it will."

"I'll buy that," said Grimes.

Peter's voice came from the squawk box. "I've established contact. She's an alien ship, all right. She belongs to some people called the Lowanni. She's a trading vessel, analogous to one of our Beta Class ships. Her captain wishes to know if he may close us to make contact."

"Tell them *yes!*" almost shouted Grimes. "Mr. Willoughby— sound the General Alarm. I want all hands at stations. Damn it, this is just what we've been hunting for! Neighbors along the Rim . . ."

I sounded the Alarm. The ship hummed like a disturbed beehive as one and all hastened to their stations. The reports began coming in; "Rocket Drive manned and ready . . . Electronic Radio Office manned and ready . . . Surgeon and Bio-Chemist standing by for further instructions . . ." The Chief and Third Officers, together with the other astronomer, pulled themselves into the already crowded control room.

It seemed only a matter of minutes—although it was longer—before the alien ship was within telescopic range. Just a little silvery dot of light she was at first, hard to pick up against the gleaming convoluted distortion of the Galactic Lens. And then, slowly, she took shape. There was little about her appearance that was unusual—but any spaceship designed for landings and blastings off through an atmosphere must, of necessity, look very like any other spaceship.

Meanwhile, our Electronic and Psionic Radio departments were working together. I still don't know how Peter Morris and his opposite number in the alien ship managed to sort out details of frequency and all the rest of it, but they did. It may be, of course, that mathematics is the universal language—even so, it must have been quite a job for the two telepaths to transmit and receive the electronic technicalities.

They came into the Control Room then—Peter Morris and Sparks. Sparks busied himself with the big intership transceiver, twisting dials and muttering. Peter whispered occasional instructions.

The screen came to life. It showed the interior of a control room very like our own. It showed a group of people very like ourselves. They were in the main slimmer, and their features were more delicate, and their ears had pointed tips, but they were human rather than merely humanoid.

One of them—his black-clad shoulders were heavily encrusted with gold—said something in a pleasant tenor voice. The girl standing beside him seemed to be repeating what he was saying; her lips moved, but no sound came from them.

"Captain Sanara says, 'Welcome to the Dain Worlds,'" said Peter.

"Tell him, 'Thank you,'" said Grimes.

I saw the girl in the alien ship speak to the Captain. She must, I thought, be their P.R.O. I remembered, suddenly, what Peter had told me of those dreams of his before we left Faraway. *She was a little too tall, and a little too slim, and her golden hair had a greenish glint to it. Her small ears were pointed at the tips* . . . And she has a wide, generous mouth, I thought, and in spite of the severity of her uniform she's all woman . . . I looked at Peter. He was staring into the screen like a starving man gazing into a restaurant window.

Shortly thereafter it became necessary for the two ships to cut their interstellar drives—alterations of course are impossible while the Drive is in operation, and an alteration of course there had to be to avert collision. During the operation the image on the screen blurred and wavered and, at times, vanished as the two rates of temporal precession lost their synchronisation. Peter, I could see, was on tenterhooks whilst this was taking place. He had found, thanks to an utterly impossible coincidence, his woman; now he dreaded losing her.

He need not have worried. Grimes was an outstanding astronaut and, in all probability, the alien Captain was in the same class. The other ship flickered back into view just as the Galactic Lens reappeared in all its glory. Our directional gyroscopes whined briefly, our rockets coughed once. Through the port I saw a short burst of pale fire at the stern of the alien—then we were falling through space on parallel courses with velocities matching to within one millimetre a second.

Time went by. Through the telepaths the two Captains talked. We heard about the Dain Worlds, whose people were relative newcomers into Deep Space. We heard about their social and economic systems, their art, their industries. As we listened we marvelled. These people, the Lowanni, were our twins. They thought as we did and acted as we did, and their history in most ways paralleled our own. I knew what Grimes was thinking. He had made up his mind that the Rim Worlds had far more in common with these aliens than with the crowded humanity at the Galactic Centre. He was thinking of more than trade agreements, he was thinking in terms of pacts and treaties.

Even so, trade was not to be sneezed at.

They talked, the two Captains. They discussed an interchange of gifts, of representative artifacts from both cultures. It was when they got to this stage of the proceedings that they struck a snag.

"There are," said our Doctor coldly, "such things as micro-organisms. I would point out, Captain, that it would be suicidal folly to allow an alien to board this ship, even if he kept his spacesuit on. He might carry something that would wipe all of us out—and might carry something back with him that would destroy both himself and all his shipmates."

Peter broke in. "I've been talking with Erin," he said.

"Erin?" asked the Old Man.

"That's her name, sir. She's the alien P.R.O. We've decided that the exchange of artifacts is necessary, and have been trying to work out a way in which it would be carried out without risk. At the same time, it means that both parties have a guinea pig . . ."

"What do you mean, Mr. Morris?"

"Let me finish, sir. This ship, as you know, has only one airlock, but carries more boats than is necessary. *Listra*—the ship out there—has the normal complements of boats for a vessel of her class but has no less than four airlocks, two of which are rarely used. This is the way we've worked it out. One of our boats, and one of *Listra*'s airlocks, can be used as isolation hospitals . . .

"I can handle a boat, sir, as you know, compulsory for every non-executive officer in the Commission's service to hold a lifeboat-man's certificate. The idea is this. I take the boat out to midway between the two ships, carrying with me such goods as we are giving to the aliens. Erin comes out in her spacesuit, bringing with her what the aliens are giving us. Then she returns to her ship, and I bring the boat back to this ship. She will remain in the airlock, as I shall remain in the boat, until such time as it is ruled that there is no danger of infection . . ."

I looked at the screen. I saw that the slim, blonde girl was talking earnestly to Captain Sanara. I saw other officers joining in the discussion. I looked back from the screen to Captain Grimes. His dark, mottled face was heavy with misgivings. I heard him say, "This could be suicide, Mr. Morris."

"It could be, sir—but so could coming out on an expedition like this. And you know as well as I do that very few alien microorganisms have been found that are dangerous to Man. All that it means, essentially, is that Erin and I will have to do our jobs in rather uncomfortable conditions from now on."

"Why you, and why Erin?"

"Because we're the telepaths. Suppose, for example, you send a tube of depilatory among the other goods to be exchanged. Erin's people might think that it's toothpaste, or mustard, or . . . or anything at all but what it is. When we're together in the boat we can explain things, talk things over. We'll get more ground covered in half an hour together than we should in half a week, talking ship to ship . . ."

"You've got it all worked out, haven't you?" grumbled Grimes. "But on a job of this sort it's foolish to discourage an enthusiastic volunteer . . . Well, I suppose that the rest of you had better start collecting artifacts. Books, and tools, and instruments, samples of our food and drink . . ."

"You mean it's all right, sir?" asked Peter, his face suddenly radiant.

"Mr. Morris, if this were a commercial vessel I'd never allow one of the officers to take such a risk. If you like you can tell that girl that I take a dim view of her Captain for allowing her to take the risk . . ."

"She doesn't think of it that way."

"Doesn't she? Then she should."

"Can I get ready, sir?"

"You can. Don't forget to brush your hair and wash behind the ears—after all, you have acting temporary ambassadorial status."

"Thank you, sir."

Peter vanished from the control room as though he had added teleportation to his other talents. Grimes sighed and looked at the screen, looked at the radiant girl who was, obviously, thanking her Captain. He sighed again and demanded, of no one in particular, "Who said it?"

"Who said what?" asked the Chief Officer.

"Journeys end in lovers' meetings," said Grimes.

It was all so obvious, even to non-telepaths.

I was in the boat with Peter shortly before he blasted off.

I said, "You seem pretty certain."

"Of course I'm certain. And she was lonely too, just as I have been. Among her people they have a similar set up to ours, but in reverse. With them it's usually the male telepath who's an unattractive, mindless clod. This chance encounter means a lot to both of us."

"She's an oxygen breather?" I asked. "You're sure of that? I mean, if she comes in here and takes off her helmet and our atmosphere poisons her . . . I don't want to be pessimistic, but I believe in facing facts."

"She's an oxygen breather," Peter assured me. "She eats food very like ours. (I hope she likes chocolates—I've got some here). She drinks alcoholic liquor in moderation. She smokes, even. She can try one of our cigarettes and I'll try one of hers . . ."

"You've found out a lot in a short time, haven't you?"

"Of course I have. That's my job—and hers. But I'll have to ask you to leave me, Ken. I've got a date."

"Are you sure you wouldn't like me to come along?"

"Not bloody likely!" he snapped.

"All right, then. And all the best of luck."

"Thanks," he said.

I stood by the blister until I felt the shock of his blasting off, until the red READY light changed to green, showing that he was out and clear. I made my way back to Control. I joined the group at the port watching the little spacecraft coasting out and away from us, watched her take up a position roughly midway between the two ships.

We saw a circle of yellow light suddenly appear on *Listra's* sleek side. We saw, through telescopes and binoculars, the little figure that hung there for a while in black silhouette. We could make out the bulky bundle that she was carrying.

Flame jetted from her shoulder units, and she was falling out and away from her own ship. Slowly she approached the lifeboat. I looked away briefly, looked at the screen. The aliens, like ourselves, were crowded around viewports, were watching this first physical contact between our two races.

She was very close to Peter's boat now. I could imagine him waiting in the little cabin, as he had waited—how many times?—in his dreams. I could appreciate, dimly, what he must be feeling. I had been in love myself and had waited for the loved one, and what I had felt must be no more than a pale shadow of what is felt by a telepath. There was, I confess, more than a little envy in my thoughts.

She was very close to the boat, and I saw that Peter had the outer door of the little airlock open.

For a long second she was silhouetted against the glow of the airlock light. . .

And then . . .

And then I was blind, as the others were blind, with tears welling from my eyes, the skin of my face burning from its exposure to radiation. She had been there, just entering the boat, and then she and the boat had vanished in one dreadful flash.

Slowly sight returned, dim and painful. I was looking once again at the screen, and I could see that those in the other ship had been affected as we had. There was pain on their faces, and it was not only physical pain. I knew then—as they must have known as they looked at us—that this had been no act of treachery, that there had been no murderous bomb concealed among the package of bartered goods.

Slowly the alien Captain shrugged his shoulders. He made a gesture of rejection with his slim hands. One of his officers handed him something. It was a black glove. He put it on. Slowly he brought his hands together—the white skinned one and the black gloved one. He flung them apart explosively.

The screen went blank. We looked away from it through the port. The alien ship was gone.

"We should have guessed," Liddell was muttering. "We should have guessed. *They* did."

"But too late," said one of the others.

"What should we have guessed?" asked Grimes.

"Anti-matter," said Liddell. "We've known for centuries that it can exist. Matter identical with what we call normal matter, except that all electrical charges are reversed. We thought that we might find it in other galaxies if ever we had a ship capable of making the journey . . . But perhaps the Dain Worlds aren't really part of this Galaxy at all."

"And when it comes into contact with normal matter?" pressed Grimes.

"You saw, Captain. There can never, *never*, be any contact between the Lowanni and ourselves."

"And what happens," I asked, "when it's two living bodies of the two kinds of matter that make the contact?"

"You saw," said Liddell.

But I was not satisfied with the answer, and am still not satisfied. I remembered what Peter had told me about the conclusion of his dream, and have yet to decide if he was the unluckiest, or the luckiest of men.

⁓ Catch the Star Winds ⁓

For the one-time service manager of a certain engineering concern

I: THE CREW

Chapter 1

SHE WAS OLD AND TIRED, the *Rim Dragon*—and after this, her final voyage, we were feeling just that way ourselves. It was as though she had known somehow that a drab and miserable end awaited her in the ungentle hands of the breakers, and she had been determined to forestall the inevitable and go out in a blaze of glory— or as much glory as would have been possible for a decrepit Epsilon Class tramp finishing her career after many changes of ownership at the very rim of the Galaxy, the edge of the dark.

Fortunately for us, she had overdone things.

Off Grollor, for example, a malfunctioning of the control room computer had coincided with a breakdown of the main propellant pump. If the second mate hadn't got his sums wrong we should have been trapped in a series of grazing ellipses, with no alternative but to

621

take to the boats in a hurry before too deep a descent into the atmosphere rendered this impossible. As things worked out, however, the mistakes made by our navigator and his pet computer resulted in our falling into a nice, stable orbit, with ample time at our disposal in which to make repairs.

Then there had been pile trouble, and Mannschenn Drive trouble—and for the benefit of those of you who have never experienced this latter, all I can say is that it is somewhat hard to carry out normal shipboard duties when you're not certain if it's high noon or last Thursday. It was during the Mannschenn Drive trouble that Cassidy, our reaction drive chief engineer, briefly lost control of his temperamental fissioning furnace. By some miracle the resultant flood of radiation seemed to miss all human personnel. It was the algae tanks that caught it—and this was all to the good, as a mutated virus had been running riot among the algae, throwing our air conditioning and sewage disposal entirely out of kilter. The virus died, and most of the algae died—but enough of the organisms survived to be the parents of a new and flourishing population.

Then there had been the occasions when *Rim Dragon* had not overdone things, but her timing had been just a little out. There had been, for example, the tube lining that had cracked just a second or so too late (fortunately, really, from our viewpoint) but the mishap nonetheless had resulted in our sitting down on the concrete apron of Port Grimes, on Tharn, hard enough to buckle a vane.

There had been another propellant pump failure—this time on Mellise—that caused us to be grounded on that world for repairs at just the right time to be subjected to the full fury of a tropical hurricane. Luckily, the procedure for riding out such atmospheric disturbances is laid down in *Rim Runners' Standing Orders and Regulations.* It was a Captain Calver, I think, who had been similarly trapped on Mellise several years ago in some ancient rustbucket called *Lorn Lady.* He had coped with the situation by rigging stays to save his ship from being overturned by the wind. We did the same. It worked—although the forward towing lugs, to which our stays were shackled, would have torn completely away from the shell plating with disastrous consequences had the blow lasted another five minutes.

Anyhow, the voyage was now over—or almost over.

We were dropping down to Port Forlorn, on Lorn, falling slowly down the column of incandescence that was our reaction drive, drifting cautiously down to the circle of drab gray concrete that was the spaceport apron, to the gray concrete that was hardly distinguishable from the gray landscape, from the dreary flatlands over which drifted the thin rain and the gray smoke and the dirty fumes streaming from the stacks of the refineries.

We were glad to be back—but, even so . . .

Ralph Listowel, the mate, put into words the feeling that was, I think, in the minds of all but one of us. He quoted sardonically:

> *"Lives there a man with soul so dead*
> *Who never to himself hath said*
> *When returning from some foreign strand*
> *This is my own, my native land?"*

Of all of us, the only genuine, native-born Rim Worlder descended from the first families was the old man. He looked up from his console now to scowl at his chief officer. And then I, of course, had to make matters worse by throwing in my own two bits' worth of archaic verse. I remarked, "The trouble with you, Ralph, is that you aren't romantic. Try to see things this way . . .

> *"Saw the heavens fill with commerce, argosies*
> *with magic sails,*
> *Pilots of the purple twilight dropping down*
> *with costly bales . . ."*

"What the hell's the bloody purser doing in here?" roared the captain, turning his glare on me. "Mr. Malcolm, will you please get the hell out of my control room? And you, Mr. Listowel, please attend to your duties."

I unstrapped myself from my chair and left hastily. We carried no third mate, and I had been helping out at landings and blast-offs by looking after the RT. Besides, I liked to be on top to see everything that was happening. Sulkily, I made my way down to the officers' flat, staggering a little as the ship lurched, and let myself into the wardroom.

The other two "idlers" were there—Sandra and Doc Jenkins. They were sprawled at ease in their acceleration chairs, sipping drinks from tall glasses dewy with condensation.

"So this is how the poor live," I remarked sourly.

"The way that the old bitch has been carrying on," said Doc affably, "we have to assume that any given drink may be our last. But how come you're not in the greenhouse?"

"They gave me the bum's rush," I admitted, dropping into the nearest chair, strapping myself in. I was feeling extremely disgruntled. In well-manned, well-found ships pursers are brought up to regard the control room as forbidden ground, but over the past few months, I had become used to playing my part in blastings off and landings and had come to appreciate the risks that we were running all the time. If anything catastrophic happened I'd be dead, no matter where I was. But when I die I'd like to know the reason.

"So they gave you the bum's rush," said Sandra, not at all sympathetically. (She had been heard to complain that if the purser was privileged to see all that was going on, a like privilege should be extended to the catering officer. "Might I inquire why?"

"You might," I told her absently, listening to the thunder of the rocket drive, muffled by the insulation but still loud in the confined space. It sounded healthy enough. They seemed to be getting along without me up there. But we weren't down yet.

"Why?" she asked bluntly.

"Give me a drink, and I'll tell you."

She did not unstrap herself but extended a long, shapely arm and managed to shove the heavy decanter and a glass across the table so that they were within my reach. I looked at the surface of the liquid within the container. It was rippled, but ever so slightly, by the vibration. The old girl was behaving herself. I might still have time for a drink before things started to happen. I poured myself a generous slug and raised the tumbler to my lips. It was, as I had suspected, the not at all bad gin manufactured by the doctor in his capacity of biochemist. The lime flavor made it palatable.

She said, "You've got your drink."

I said, "All right. If you must know, I was quoting poetry. Ralph started it. The master did not, repeat not, approve . . ."

"Down," quoted the doctor in his fruitiest voice.

> *"Down.*
> *Fierce stabbing*
> *Flame phallus*
> *Rending*
> *Membrane of atmosphere,*
> *Tissues of cloud.*
> *Down-bearing,*
> *Thrusting*
> *To stony womb of world.*
> *Spacemen, I ask you*
> *What monster*
> *Or prodigy*
> *Shall come of this rape?"*

I looked at him with some distaste. His chubby face under the overly long, overly oily black hair was (as usual) smugly sensual. He had an extensive repertoire of modern verse, and practically all of it dealt with rape, both literal and figurative.

"If I'd quoted that trash," I told him, "the old man would have been justified in booting me out of his Holy of Holies. But I was quoting poetry. *Poetry.* Period."

"Oh, yes. Poetry. Meretricious jingles. You and dear Ralph share a passion for this revival of the ancient Terran slush, corn of the corniest. Our lord and master did well in arising in his wrath and hurling you into the outer darkness . . ."

"Poetry," said Sandra flatly, "and ship handling just don't mix. Especially at a time like this."

"She was riding down," I said, "sweetly and gently, on full automatic."

"And all of us," she pointed out, "at the mercy of a single fuse. I may be only chief cook and bottlewasher aboard this wagon, but even I know that it is essential for the officers in the control room to be fully alert at all times."

"All right," I said. "All right."

I glared at her, and she glared at me. She was always handsome—but she was almost beautiful when she was in a bad temper. I wondered (as I had often wondered before) what she would be like when the rather harsh planes and angles of her face were softened by some gentler passion. But she did her job, Sandra did, and did it well, and kept to herself—as others, as well as I, had learned the hard way.

Meanwhile, we were still falling, still dropping, the muffled thunder of our reaction drive steady and unfaltering. In view of the past events and near disasters of the voyage it was almost too good to be true. It was, I decided, too good to be true—and then, as though in support of my pessimism, the sudden silence gripped the hearts of all of us. Sandra's face was white under her coppery hair and Jenkins's normally ruddy complexion was a sickly green. We waited speechless for the last, the final crash.

The ship tilted gently, ever so gently, tilted and righted herself, and the stuffy air inside the wardroom was alive with the whispered complaints of the springs and cylinders of her landing gear. The bulkhead speaker crackled and we heard the old man's voice: "The set-down has been accomplished. All personnel may proceed on their arrival duties."

Doc Jenkins laughed, unashamedly relieved. He unstrapped himself and poured a generous drink from the decanter into each of our glasses. "To the end of the voyage," he said, raising his tumbler. He gulped his gin. Then, "Now that we can all relax, Peter, just what was the so-called poetry that led to your well-merited eviction from the greenhouse?"

"'Saw the heavens fill with commerce,'" I quoted. " 'Argosies with magic sails, Pilots of the purple twilight dropping down with costly bales . . . ' "

"We dropped down all right," he jested, "but not on any magic sails. A down-thrusting phallus of flame is a far better description of rocket drive."

"I prefer the magic sails," I said.

"You would," he said.

"Some people," said Sandra pointedly, getting to her feet, "have work to do. Even though the ship is finished, we aren't."

Chapter 2

❧ ❧

YES, we all had work to do—but none of us, not even Sandra, was particularly keen on getting started on it. We were down, and still in one piece, and we were feeling that sense of utter relaxation that comes at the end of a voyage; there was something in it of home-coming (although the Rim Worlds were home only to the old man), something in it of the last day of school.

Sandra stood there for a moment or so, looking down at Doc and myself. Her regard shifted to the decanter. She said, "It's a shame to leave all that to you two pigs."

"Don't let it worry you, duckie," Jenkins admonished her.

"It does worry me."

She sat down again and refilled her glass. The doctor refilled his glass. I refilled mine.

"Journey's end," said Doc, making a toast of it.

"In lovers meeting," I added, finishing the quotation.

"I didn't know you had a popsy in Port Forlorn," said Sandra distantly.

"I haven't," I said. "Not now. Not anymore. But there should be lovers' meetings at the end of a voyage."

"Why?" she asked, feigning interest.

"Because some sentimental slob of a so-called poet said so," sneered Doc.

"Better than all your crap about down-thrusting phalluses," I retorted.

"Boys, boys . . ." admonished Sandra.

"Is there anything left in the bottle?" demanded Ralph Listowel. We hadn't seen or heard him come into the wardroom. We looked up at him in mild amazement as he stood there, awkward, gangling, his considerable height diminished ever so slightly by his habitual slouch. There was a worried expression on his lined face. I wondered just what was wrong now.

"Here, Ralph," said Sandra, passing him a drink.

"Thanks." The mate gulped rather than sipped. "Hmm. Not bad." He gulped again. "Any more?"

"Building up your strength, Ralph?" asked Sandra sweetly.

"Could be," he admitted. "Or perhaps this is an infusion of Dutch courage."

"And what do you want it for?" I asked. "The hazards of the voyage are over and done with."

"Those hazards, yes," he said gloomily. "But there are worse hazards than those in space. When mere chief officers are bidden to report to the super's office, at once if not before, there's something cooking—and, I shouldn't mind betting you a month's pay, it'll be something that stinks."

"Just a routine bawling out," I comforted him. "After all, you can't expect to get away with everything all the time."

A wintry grin did nothing to soften his harsh features. "But it's not only me he wants. He wants you, Sandra, and you, Doc, and you, Peter. *And* Smethwick, our commissioned clairvoyant. One of you had better go to shake him out of his habitual stupor."

"But what have we done?" asked Doc in a worried voice.

"My conscience is clear," I said. "At least, I think it is . . ."

"My conscience *is* clear," Sandra stated firmly.

"Mine never is," admitted Doc gloomily.

The mate put his glass down on the table. "All right," he told us brusquely. "Go and get washed behind the ears and brush your hair. One of you drag the crystal gazer away from his dog's brain in aspic and try to get him looking something like an officer and a gentleman."

"Relax, Ralph," said Jenkins, pouring what was left in the decanter into his own glass.

"I wish I could. But it's damned odd the way the commodore is yelling for all of us. I may not be a psionic radio officer, but I have my hunches."

Jenkins laughed. "One thing is certain, Ralph, he's not sending for us to fire us. Rim Runners are never that well-off for officers. And once we've come out to the Rim, we've hit rock bottom." He began to warm up. "We've run away from ourselves as far as we can, to the very edge of the blackness, and we can't run any farther."

"Even so . . ." said the mate.

"Doc's right," said Sandra. "He'll just be handing out new appointments to all of us. With a bit of luck—or bad luck?—we might be shipping out together again."

"It'll be good luck for all of you if we are," said Doc. "My jungle juice is the best in the fleet, and you all know it."

"So you say," said Sandra.

"But what about the old man?" I asked. "And the engineers? Are they bidden to the presence?"

"No," said Ralph. "As far as I know, they'll just be going on leave." He added gloomily, "There's something in the wind as far as we're concerned. I wish I knew what it was."

"There's only one way to find out," said Sandra briskly, getting to her feet.

We left the ship together—Ralph, Doc Jenkins, Sandra, Smethwick and myself. Ralph, who was inclined to take his naval reserve commission seriously, tried to make it a march across the dusty, scarred concrete to the low huddle of administration buildings. Both Sandra and I tried to play along with him, but Doc Jenkins and our tame telepath could turn any march into a straggle without even trying. For Smethwick there was, perhaps, some excuse; released from the discipline of watchkeeping he was renewing contact with his telepathic friends all over the planet. He wandered along like a man in a dream, always on the point of falling over his own feet. And Jenkins rolled happily beside him, a somewhat inane grin on his ruddy face. I guessed that in the privacy of his cabin he had depleted his stocks of jungle juice still further.

I wished that I'd imbibed another stiff slug myself. The wind was bitterly cold, driving the dust before it in whorls and eddies, filling our eyes with grit, redolent of old socks and burning sulphur. I was wondering how anybody could be fool enough to come out to the Rim Worlds. I was wondering, not for the first time, how *I'd* ever been fool enough to come out to the Rim Worlds.

It was a relief to get into the office building, out of that insistent, nagging wind. The air was pleasantly warm, but my eyes were still stinging. I used my handkerchief to try to clear the gritty particles from them, and saw through tears that the others were doing the same—all save Smethwick, who, lost in some private world of his own, was oblivious to discomfort. Ralph brushed the dust from his epaulettes and then used his handkerchief to restore a polish to his shoes, tossing the soiled fabric into a handy disposer. He started to ascend the stairs, and paused to throw a beckoning nod at us. Not without reluctance we followed.

There was the familiar door at the end of the passageway with *Astronautical Superintendent* inscribed on the translucent plastic. The door opened of itself as we approached. Through the doorway we could see the big, cluttered desk and, behind it, the slight, wiry figure of Commodore Grimes. He had risen to his feet, but he still looked small, dwarfed by the furnishings that must have been designed for a much larger man. I was relieved to see that his creased and pitted face was illumined by a genuinely friendly smile, his teeth startlingly white against the dark skin.

"Come in," he boomed. "Come in, all of you." He waved a hand to the chairs that had been set in a rough semi-circle before his desk. "Be seated."

And then I didn't feel so relieved after all. Fussing in the background was Miss Hallows, his secretary, tending a bubbling coffee percolator. From past experience I knew that such hospitality meant that we were to be handed the dirty end of some very peculiar stick.

When the handshaking and the exchange of courtesies were over we sat down. There was a period of silence while Miss Hallows busied herself with the percolator and the cups. My attention was drawn by an odd-looking model on the commodore's desk, and I saw that the others, too, were looking at it curiously and that old Grimes was watching us with a certain degree of amusement. It was a ship, that was obvious, but it could not possibly be a spaceship. It was, I guessed, some sort of aircraft; there was a cigar-shaped hull and, protruding from it, a fantastically complicated array of spars and vanes. I know even less about aeronautics than I do about astronautics—after all, I'm just the spacefaring office boy—but even I doubted if such a contraption could ever fly. I turned my head to look at Ralph; he was staring at the thing with a sort of amused and amazed contempt.

"Admiring my new toy?" asked the commodore.

"It's rather . . . it's rather odd, sir," said Ralph.

"Go on," chuckled Grimes. "Why don't you ask?"

There was an embarrassed silence, broken by Sandra. "All right, Commodore. What is it?"

"That, my dear," he told her, "is your new ship."

Chapter 3

WE LOOKED AT THE COMMODORE, and he looked back at us. I tried to read his expression and came to the reluctant conclusion that he wasn't joking. We looked at the weird contraption on his desk. Speaking for myself, the more I stared at it, the less like a ship it seemed. Have you ever seen those fantastic ornamental carp that are bred on Earth, their bodies surrounded by an ornate tracery of filmy fins, utility sacrificed to appearance? That's what the thing reminded me of. It was pretty, beautiful even in a baroque kind of way, but quite useless. And Grimes had told us quite seriously that it was a model of our new ship.

Ralph cleared his throat. He said, "Excuse me, sir, but I don't quite understand. That . . . that model doesn't seem to represent a conventional vessel. I can't see any signs of a venturi . . ." He was on his feet now, bending over the desk. "And are those propellers? Or should I say airscrews?" He straightened up. "And she's not a gauss-jammer, one of the old Ehrenhaft drive jobs. That's certain."

Old Grimes was smiling again. "Sit down, Captain Listowel. There's no need to get excited."

"*Captain* Listowel?" asked Ralph.

"Yes." The smile vanished as though switched off. "But only if you agree to sail in command of . . ." he gestured towards the model . . . "the *Flying Cloud*."

"*Flying Cloud?* But that's a transgalactic clipper name!"

Grimes smiled again. "The first *Flying Cloud* was a clipper on Earth's seas in the days of wooden ships and iron men. This *Flying Cloud* is a clipper, too—but not a transgalactic clipper. She is the latest addition to Rim Runners' fleet, the first of her kind."

"But—" Ralph was looking really worried now. "But, sir, there are many senior masters in this employ. As for that, there are quite a few chief officers senior to me . . ."

"And all of them," said Grimes, "old and set in their ways, knowing only one way of getting from point A to point B, and not wanting to know any other. Lift on reaction drive. Aim for the target star. Accelerate. Cut reaction drive. Switch on Mannschenn Drive. A child could do it. And while all this is going on you have the ship overmanned with a pack of engineers eating their heads off and pulling down high salaries, and getting to the stage where they regard the ship merely as a platform upon which to mount their precious machinery."

I couldn't help grinning. It was common knowledge that Grimes didn't like engineers and was hardly on speaking terms with the engineer superintendents.

But Ralph, once he had smelled a rat, was stubborn. And he was frank. He said, "I appreciate the promotion, sir. But there must be a catch to it."

"Of course there is, Captain Listowel. Life is just one long series of catches—in both senses of the word. Catches as in your usage of the word—and fumbled catches." He added, "I hope you don't fumble this catch."

Ralph was persistent. "I see your point, sir. But this ship is obviously something new, something highly experimental. As you know, I hold my master's certificate—but it's valid in respect of conventional drives only."

"But you, Captain Listowel, are the only officer we have with any qualifications at all in respect of the Erikson drive." He pulled a folder out of the top drawer of his desk and opened it. "Like most of our personnel, you made your way out to the Rim by easy stages. You were four years on Atlantia. You shipped in topsail schooners as navigator—it seems that the Atlantian Ministry of Transport recognizes astronautical certificates of competency insofar as navigation is concerned. You thought of settling permanently on the planet and becoming a professional seaman. You sat for, and obtained, your second mate's certificate in sail . . ."

"But what connection . . . ?"

"Let me finish. You were in *Rim Leopard* when she had that long spell for repairs on Tharn. You elected to take part of your leave on that world—and you shipped out as a supernumerary officer in one of their trading schooners."

"Even so . . ."

"Take it from me, Captain Listowel, that your fore-and-aft rig second mate's ticket, together with your experience, means more than your master astronaut's certificate. Too, you are qualified in one other, very important way." He looked at each of us in turn. "You're all so qualified."

"I know nothing about wooden ships, commodore," said Jenkins, "and I'm not an iron man."

"Too right, Doctor," agreed the Commodore cheerfully. "But you have no close ties on any of the Rim Worlds—neither chick nor child, as the saying goes. And that applies to all of you."

"And so this new ship is dangerous?" asked Ralph quietly.

"No, Captain Listowel. She's safer than the average spaceship— far safer than *Rim Dragon*. She'll be as easy as an old shoe. And economical to run. She is," he went on, "a prototype. It is our intention, insofar as some trades are concerned, to make her the standard carrier."

"And the catch?" insisted Ralph.

"All right. You're entitled to know." He leaned back in his chair and gazed at the ceiling as though in search of inspiration. "You are all of you, I take it, familiar with the principle of the conveyor belt?"

"Of course," Ralph told him.

"Good. You know, then, that as long as the belt is kept loaded, the speed at which it is run is of relatively minor importance. So it is with shipping. Express services are desirable for mails and passengers and perishables—but what does it matter if a slab of zinc is ten years on the way instead of ten weeks?"

"It will matter a lot to the crew of the ship," grumbled Doc.

"I agree. But when the ship is traveling almost at the speed of light, there will not be a lapse of ten years subjective time. To the crew it will be just a normal interstellar voyage."

"But," Ralph interjected, "where does the economy come in?"

"In manning, for a start. I have already discussed the matter with the Astronauts' Guild, and they agree that personnel should be paid on the basis of subjective elapsed time . . ."

"What!" exploded Ralph.

"Plus a bonus," Grimes added hastily. "Then there's fuel consumption. There'll be a pile, of course, but it will be a small one. It will be supply power only for essential services and auxiliary machinery. As you all know, fissionable elements are in short supply and very expensive on the Rim Worlds, so that's a big saving. Then, there'll be no reaction drive and interstellar drive engineers to wax fat on their princely salaries. One donkeyman, on junior officer's pay, will be able to handle the job . . ."

"A donkeyman?" asked Sandra, her voice puzzled.

"Yes, my dear. In the last days of sail, on Earth, the windjammers used some auxiliary machinery, steam-driven. The mechanic who looked after and ran this was rated as donkeyman."

Then Ralph voiced the thoughts, the objections of all of us. He complained, "You've told us nothing, Commodore. You want us to buy a pig in a poke. You've mentioned something called the Erikson drive, and you've given us a short lecture on the economics of ship management, but we're spacemen, not accountants. Oh, I know that we're supposed to get our starwagons from point A to point B as economically as possible—but getting them there at all is the prime consideration. And, frankly, I don't see how that contraption could get from one side of the spaceport to the other."

And, I thought, *you've got us all interested, you cunning old bastard. You've got us hooked.*

Grimes looked down at the cold coffee in his cup with distaste. He got up, went to his filing cabinet and pulled out the "W" drawer, taking from it a bottle of whisky and glasses. He said, "It's rather a long story, but you're entitled to hear it. I suggest that we all make ourselves comfortable."

We settled down with our drinks to listen.

Chapter 4

YOU WILL RECALL [he said] that some few years ago I commissioned *Faraway Quest* to carry out a survey of this sector of the Galaxy. To the Galactic East I made contact with Tharn and Grollor, Mellise and Stree, but you are all familiar with the planets of the Eastern Circuit. My first sweep, however, was to the West. Yes, there are worlds to the West, populous planets whose peoples have followed a course of evolution parallel to our own. They're more than merely humanoid, some of these people. They're human. But—and it's one helluva big "but"—their worlds are anti-matter worlds. We didn't realize this until an attempt was made to establish contact with an alien ship. Luckily only two people were directly involved—our own psionic radio officer and a woman, who seemed to hold the same rank, from the other vessel. The idea was that they should meet and rub noses and so on in one of *Faraway Quest*'s boats, midway between the two ships; both I and the other Captain were worried about the possibility of the exchange of viruses, bacteria and whatever, and this boat of mine was supposed to be a sort of quarantine station. But we needn't have worried. Our two pet guinea pigs went up and out in a flare of energy that would have made a fusion bomb look silly.

So that was it, I thought at the time. The psionic radio officers had had it, in a big way, so communications had broken down. And it was quite obvious that any contact between ourselves and the people of the anti-matter worlds was definitely impossible. I got the hell out and ran to the Galactic East. I made landings on Tharn and Grollor and Mellise and Stree and dickered with the aborigines and laid the foundation of our Eastern Circuit trade. But there was that nagging doubt at the back of my mind; there was that unfinished business to the West. Cutting a long story short, after things were nicely sewn up on the Eastern Circuit worlds I went back. I managed to establish contact—but not physical contact!—with the dominant race. I'd replaced my psionic radio officer, of course, but it was still a long job. I'm sure that Mr. Smethwick won't mind if I say that the average professional telepath just hasn't got the right kind of mind to cope with technicalities. But we worked out a code to use with buzzer and flashing lamp, and eventually we were even able to talk directly on the RT without too many misunderstandings.

We traded ideas. Oddly enough—or not so oddly—there wasn't much to trade. Their technology was about on the same level as our own. They had atomic power (but who hasn't?) and interstellar travel, and their ships used a version of the Mannschenn Drive, precessing gyroscopes and all. It was all very interesting, academically speaking, but it got neither party anywhere. Anything we knew and used, they knew and used. Anything they knew and used, we knew and used. It was like having a heart to heart talk with one's reflection in a mirror.

Oh, there were a few minor differences. That new system of governor controls for the Mannschenn Drive, for example—we got that from the anti-matter people. And they'd never dreamed of keeping fish in their hydroponics tanks, but they're doing it now. But there was nothing really important.

But I had to bring *something* back. And I did. No doubt you've often wondered just what is going on inside Satellite XIV. It's been there for years, hanging in its equatorial orbit, plastered with KEEP OFF notices. It's still there—but the reason for its construction has been removed.

I brought something back. I brought back a large hunk of anti-matter. It's iron—or should I say "anti-iron"? But iron or anti-iron, it still behaves as iron in a magnetic field. It's hanging in its casing, making no contact with the walls—and it had better not!—held in place by the powerful permanent magnets. It'd be safe in a hard vacuum, but it's safer still suspended in the neutronium that the University boys were able to cook up for me.

Well, I had this hunk of anti-matter. I still have. The problem was, what was it good for? Power? Yes—but how could it be used? No doubt some genius will come up with the answer eventually, but so far nobody has. But in the laboratory built around it, Satellite XIV, techniques were developed for carving off small pieces of it, using laser beams, and these tiny portions were subjected to experiment. One of the experiments, bombardment with neutrinos, yielded useful results. After such a bombardment anti-matter acquires the property of anti-gravity. It's analogous to permanent magnetism in many ways—but, as far as the scientists have been able to determine, *really* permanent.

But how to use it?

Oh, the answer is obvious, you'll say. Use it in spaceships. That's what I came up with myself. I passed the problem on to Dr. Kramer at the University. I don't profess to be able to make head or tail of his math, but it boils down to this: anti-matter and the temporal precession field of the Mannschenn Drive just don't mix. Or rather they do mix—too well. This is the way I understand it. You use anti-matter, and anti-gravity, to get upstairs. Well and good. You use your gyroscopes to get lined up on the target star, then you accelerate. You build up velocity, and then you cut the reaction drive. Well and good. Then you switch on the Mannschenn Drive . . .

You switch on the Mannschenn Drive, and as your ship consists of both normal matter and anti-matter she'll behave—abnormally. Oh, there'll be temporal precession all right. *But* . . . The ship herself will go astern in time, as she should—and that hunk of anti-matter will precess in the opposite temporal direction. The result, of course, will be catastrophic.

Even so, if I may borrow one of your pet expressions, Captain Listowel—even so, I was sure that anti-matter, with its property of induced anti-gravity, would be of great value in space travel. There was this lump of iron that I had dragged all the way back from the

Galactic West, encased in aluminum and neutronium and alnico magnets, hanging there in its orbit, quite useless so far but potentially extremely useful. There *must* be a way to use it.

But what was the way?

He looked at us, as though waiting for intelligent suggestions. None were forthcoming. He drained his glass. He refilled it. He waited until we had refilled ours.

I've a son, as you know. Like most fathers, I wanted him to follow in my footsteps. As many sons do, he decided to do otherwise, and told me frankly that a spaceman's life was not for him. He's an academic type. Bachelor of arts—and what is more useless than a degree in arts? Master of arts. And now doctor of philosophy. And not the sort of Ph.D. that's really a degree in science, but just a jumble of history and the like. Damn it all, he wouldn't know what a neutron was if it up and bit him on the left buttock. But he can tell you what Julius Caesar said when he landed in England—whenever and whatever that was—and what Shakespeare made some character called Hamlet say when he was in some sort of complicated jam that some old Greek called Oedipus was in a couple of thousand or so years previously, and what some other character called Freud had to say about it all a few hundred years later.

But, to get back to Mr. J. Caesar, what he said was *veni, vidi, vici.* I came, I saw, I conquered.

And, insofar as the anti-matter worlds were concerned, I came, I saw—and I didn't conquer. All I had to show for my trouble was this damned great hunk of anti-iron, and I just couldn't figure out a use for it. It irked me more than somewhat. So, after worrying about it all rather too much, I retired from the field and left it all to my subconscious.

Well, John—that's my son—littered up the house with all sorts of books when he was studying for his latest degree. There was, as I have said, quite a pile of historical material. Not only Julius Caesar and Shakespeare and the learned Herr Doktor Freud, but books on, of all things, the history of transport. Those I read, and they were fascinating. Galleys with sweating slaves manning the sweeps. Galleons with wind power replacing muscle power. The clipper ships, with acres of canvas spread to the gales. The first steamships. The motor ships. The nuclear-powered ships. And, in the air, the airships—dirigible balloons. The airplanes. The jets. The rockets—and the first spaceships.

And with the spaceships sail came back, but briefly. There was the Erikson drive. There were the ships that spread their great plastic sails and drifted out from the orbit of Earth to that of Mars, but slowly, slowly. It was a good idea—but as long as those ships had mass it was impracticable. But if there had then been any means of nullifying gravity they would have superseded the rockets.

Then it all clicked. The old-timers didn't have anti-gravity. I *do* have anti-gravity. I can build a real sailing ship—a vessel to run before the photon gale, a ship that can be handled just as the old windjammers on Earth's seas were handled. A ship, come to that, Captain Listowel, that can be handled just as the topsail schooners on Atlantia's seas are handled . . .

He waved a hand towards the model on his desk.

There she is. There's *Flying Cloud*. The first of the real light-jammers. And she's yours.

Chapter 5

≈≈ ≈≈

"**EVEN SO . . .**" murmured Ralph, breaking the silence.

"Even so, Captain Listowel," echoed Grimes, a sardonic edge to his voice.

"Even so, sir," went on Ralph, undeterred, "I don't think that I'm qualified. I doubt if any of us is qualified."

"You *are* qualified," stated Grimes flatly. "You've experience in sail, which is more than any other master or officer in this employ can boast. Oh, there was Calver. He was in sail, too, before he joined us, but he's no longer with us. So you're the only possible choice."

"But . . . I've no real qualifications."

Grimes laughed. "Who has? There *was* a certificate of competency, Erikson drive, issued on Earth a few centuries ago. But don't let that bother you. The Rim Confederacy will issue certificates of competency for the improved Erikson drive."

"And the examiner?" asked Ralph.

"For a start, you," stated Grimes.

"But, damn it all, sir, there aren't any textbooks, manuals . . ."

"You will write them when you get around to it."

"Even so, sir," protested Ralph, "this is rather much. Don't think that I'm not appreciative of the promotion, but . . ."

Grimes grinned happily. He said, "In my own bumbling way—after all, I'm a spaceman, neither a seaman nor an airman—I've worked out some rough and ready methods for handling this brute." His hand went out to the beautiful model on his desk with a possessive, caressing gesture. "If it were not for the fact that I have a wife and family I'd be sailing as her first master. As things are, I've had to waive that privilege, although not without reluctance. But I can give you a rough idea of what's required."

He took from the top drawer of his desk a little control panel and set it down before himself. He pressed a stud and we watched, fascinated, as the spars rotated on their long axes and then, when the sails were furled, folded back into slots in the shell plating.

"As you see," he told us, "there are now only the atmospheric control surfaces left exposed—including, of course, the airscrews. In appearance the ship is not unlike one of the dirigible airships of the early days of aviation. A lighter-than-air ship, in fact. But she's not lighter than air. Not yet.

"This model, as you've all probably guessed by this time, is a working model—insofar as her handling inside atmospheric limits is concerned. She has within her a tiny fragment of the anti-iron, a miniscule sphere of anti-matter complete with induced anti-gravity." He looked at Ralph. "Now, I'd like you to get the feel of her, Captain Listowel. Go on, she won't bite you. Take hold of her. Lift her off the desk."

Ralph got slowly to his feet, extended two cautious hands, got his fingers around the cylindrical hull. He said, accusingly, "But she's heavy."

"Of course she's heavy. When the real ship is berthed on a planetary surface to discharge and load cargo we don't want her at the mercy of every puff of wind. All right, put her down again. And now stand back."

Ralph stood back, without reluctance. Grimes pressed another stud on his control panel. None of us was expecting what happened next—the stream of water that poured from vents on the underside of the model, flooding the desk top, dripping on to the carpet. Miss Hallows clucked annoyance, but we just watched fascinated. The commodore smiled happily, his hands busy at the miniature controls. There was the whine of a motor inside the model ship and the two airscrews at the after end started to turn. Before they had picked up speed, while the separate blades were still clearly visible, *Flying Cloud* began to move, sliding slowly over the smooth surface of the desk. (I noticed that she barely disturbed the film of moisture.) She reached the edge and she dropped—but slowly, slowly—and then the control surfaces, elevators and rudder, twitched nervously, and her screws were a translucent blur, and her fall was checked and she was rising, obedient to her helm, making a circuit of the desk and gaining altitude with every lap. There was still a dribble of water from her outlets that fell, shockingly cold, on our upturned faces.

"You see," said Grimes. "In an atmosphere you have no worries at all. Drive her down on negative dynamic lift, start the compressors if you have to give her a little extra mass with compressed air." (A faint throb was audible above the whine of the motors.) "Open your valves if you think that she's getting too heavy." (We heard the thin, high whistle.) "I'm sorry that I can't give a real demonstration of how she'll handle in deep space, but I can give you some sort of an idea." (He jockeyed the model almost to ceiling level and manipulated the controls so that she was hanging stern on to the big overhead light globe.) "There's the sun," he said. "The sun, or any other source of photons. You spread your sails . . ." (The spars extended from the hull, the complexity of plastic vanes unfurled.) "And off you go. Mind you, I'm cheating. I'm using the airscrews. And now, watch carefully. One surface of each sail is silvered, the other surface is black. By use of the reflecting and absorbing surfaces I can steer the ship, I can even exercise control over her speed . . . any questions, Captain Listowel?"

"Not yet," said Ralph cautiously.

"I've told you all I know," Grimes told him cheerfully, "and now you know just about everything there is to know. But I admit that this handling of her in deep space, under sail, is all theory and guesswork. You'll have to make up the rules as you go along. But the atmospheric handling is pretty well worked out. Landing, for example." He looked at his secretary. "Miss Hallows, is the spaceport open for traffic?"

She sighed, then said, "Yes, Commodore."

"But it's not," he said.

She sighed again, got to her feet and went to a door, her manner displaying a certain embarrassment. Behind the door was Commodore Grimes's private lavatory. I was rather surprised to see that he had been able to commandeer a full-length tub for himself as well as the usual standard fittings. Oh, well, rank has its privileges.

"And that," said Grimes, "is a working model of the spaceport of the near future. A lake, natural or artificial. Or a wide river. Or a sheltered bay. Maintenance costs cut to a bare minimum."

I got to my feet and saw that the tub was full.

The model *Flying Cloud* droned slowly over our heads, her suit of sails once again withdrawn and steered through the open door of the bathroom, her airscrews and elevators driving her down in a long slant towards the surface of the water in the tub. While she was still all of three feet above it a tendril snaked from her underbelly, a long tube that extended itself until its end was submerged. Once again there was the throbbing of a tiny pump and the model settled, gradually at first, then faster, then dropping with a startlingly loud splash.

"A clumsy landing," admitted Grimes, "but I'm sure that you'll do better, Captain."

"I hope so," said Ralph gloomily.

II: THE SHIP

Chapter 6

BUT I THINK RALPII thoroughly enjoyed himself in the few weeks that followed. I doubt if any of the rest of us did. I know that I didn't. Sailing as a sport is all very well on a planet like Caribbea, but it has little to recommend it on a bleak slag heap such as Lorn. Oh, there's always a wind—but that wind is always bitter and, as often as not, opaque with gritty dust.

I don't think that anybody had ever sailed on Lorn until we, the future personnel of *Flying Cloud*, cast off our sleek, smart (and that didn't last for long) catamaran from the rickety jetty on the shore of Lake Misere, under the derisive stares of the local fishermen in their shabby, power-driven craft, to put in hour after hour, day after day of tacking and wearing, running free, sailing close-hauled and all the rest of it.

But Ralph was good. I have to admit that. I was amazed to learn that so much control of the flimsy, complicated, wind-driven contraption was possible. In my innocence I had always assumed that a sailing vessel could proceed only in a direction exactly opposite to that from which the wind was blowing. I learned better.

We all learned better. But I still think that there are easier ways of proceeding from point A to point B, either in deep space or on the water, than under sail.

Yes, all of us had to get a grounding in sail seamanship, Sandra, Doc Jenkins and Smethwick as well as myself. We gathered that Commodore Grimes wasn't finding it easy to find officers for his fine, new ship—after all, even Rim Worlders weren't keen on voyages that would extend over years, even though those years would be objective rather than subjective time. There just weren't that many completely unattached people around. So he'd been dickering with the Astronauts' Guild and got them to agree that anybody, but anybody, could be issued a certificate of competency with respect to the improved Erikson drive.

So we all—and how we hated it!—had to become more or less competent sailors. As I've said, on a sunny world with balmy breezes, blue seas, golden beaches and palm trees it would have been fun. On Lake Misere it wasn't. On Lake Misere it was hard work in miserable conditions—and I still think that it's utterly incredible that in this day and age no heavy weather clothing has yet been devised that will stop the ingress of freezing water between neck and collar, between boot-top and leg.

And when we had all become more or less competent sailors—Ralph called it Part A of our certificates—we thought that the worst was over. How wrong we were! The next stage of our training was to bumble around in yet another archaic contraption, a clumsy, lighter-than-air monstrosity called a blimp. (Like the catamaran, it had been built merely for instructional purposes.) I don't profess to know the origin of the name, but it looked like a blimp. One just couldn't imagine its being called anything else. There was a flaccid bag of gas—helium—shaped like a fat cigar, and from this depended a streamlined cabin that was control room, living quarters and engine room. There was a propeller driven by a small diesel motor, that moved us through the air at a maximum speed of fifty knots. (Our speed over the ground was, of course, governed by wind direction and velocity.) There was a lot of complicated juggling with gas and ballast. There was the occasion when we were blown off course and drifted helplessly over Port Forlorn just as *Rim Hound* was coming in. Ralph told us afterwards that had the blimp been hydrogen-filled that would have been our finish; as it was, with our gasbag all but burst by the searing heat of *Rim Hound's* exhaust, leaking from every seam, we made an ignominious crash landing in Lake Misere, from which dismal puddle we were rescued by the fishermen—who were, of course, highly amused to see us again, and in even more ludicrous circumstances than before.

But the blimp was patched up and again made airworthy—as airworthy as she ever would be, ever could be—and we carried on with our training. And we got the feel of the brute. We neither respected nor loved her, but we came to understand what she could and could not do and, when Ralph had decided that we all (including himself) had passed for Part B of our certificates we proceeded, in the little airship, to Port Erikson on the southern shore of Coldharbor Bay.

There's one thing you can say in favor of the Survey Service boys who first made landings on the Rim Worlds, and you can say the same thing in favor of the first colonists. When it came to dishing out names they were realistic. Lorn . . . Port Forlorn . . . Lake Misere . . . the Great Barrens . . . Mount Desolation . . . Coldharbor Bay . . .

The trip was not a happy one. In spite of the heat from the single diesel the cabin was bitterly cold as we threaded our way over and through the Great Barrens, skirting the jagged, snow-covered peaks, fighting for altitude in the higher passes, jettisoning ballast when dynamic lift proved insufficient and then perforce being obliged to valve gas for the long slant down over the dreary tundra that somebody in the First Expedition had named the Nullarbor Plain.

And there was Coldharbor Bay ahead, a sliver of dull lead inset in the dun rim of the horizon. There was Coldharbor Bay, leaden water under a leaden sky, and a huddle of rawly new buildings along its southern shore, and something else, something big and silvery, somehow graceful, that looked out of place in these drab surroundings.

"The ship," I said unnecessarily. *"Flying Cloud."*

"Flying Crud!" sneered Doc Jenkins. He was not in a good mood. His normally ruddy face was blue with cold, and a violent pitch and yaw of the ship a few minutes since had upset a cup of scalding coffee (prepared, somehow, by Sandra in her cramped apology for a galley) in his lap. "And what ruddy genius was it," he demanded, "who decided to establish a spaceport in these godforsaken latitudes? Damn it all, it isn't as though we had the Ehrenhaft drive to contend with and lines of magnetic force to worry about. And both old Grimes and you, Ralph, have been harping on the fact—or is it only a theory?—that these fancy lightjammers will be far easier to handle in an atmosphere than a conventional spaceship."

"True," admitted Ralph. "True. But, even so . . . just remember that on Lorn every major center of population is on or near the equator. And there's a certain amount of risk in having conventional spaceports near cities—and the conventional spaceship isn't one per cent as potentially dangerous as a lightjammer."

"I don't see it," insisted Doc. "To begin with, there's a much smaller pile. A lightjammer is far less dangerous."

"Don't forget what's in the heart of her," said Ralph quietly. "That core of anti-iron. Should the casing be breached, should the anti-matter come into contact with normal matter . . ."

He lifted his gloved hands from the wheel in an expressive, explosive gesture. The ship swung off course, dipped and rolled. It was my turn to get a lapful of hot coffee. I decided that there was a lot to be said in favor of the despised drinking bulbs used in deep space.

"Any more questions," asked Ralph, "before we make it landing stations?"

"If you insist on answering with your hands," I said, "no."

He grinned ever so slightly. "All right, then. Now remember, all of you, that this won't be the real thing—but it'll be as near to real as we can make it. To begin with—an upwind approach . . ."

"I can see the windsock," said Sandra, who was using binoculars.

"Where away?"

"A degree or so to starboard of the stern of the ship. On that tower."

"And wind direction?"

"As near south as makes no difference. A following wind."

"Good. Now, Peter, you're in charge of the gas valves, and you, Doc, can handle the ballast . . ."

"The tank's dry," grumbled Jenkins.

"Anything with mass is ballast. *Anything.* Open a port and have a pile of odds and ends ready to dump. And you, Mr. Smethwick, stand by the hose and pump . . ."

We were over the spaceport now. We could see the administration buildings and the warehouses, the long wharf alongside which lay *Flying Cloud.* We could see the little waving figures of people. And we could hear, from our telephone, the voice of Commodore Grimes speaking from spaceport control: "What are your intentions, Captain Listowel? The ground crew is standing by for your lines."

"I intend to land on the Bay, sir, to make this a rehearsal of landing the big ship."

"A good idea, Captain. Berth ahead of *Flying Cloud.* Berth ahead of *Flying Cloud.*"

Ralph brought the blimp round in a long curve and lined her up for the beacon at the end of the wharf. He said sharply, "Don't valve any gas unless I tell you, Peter. That's one thing we shan't be able to do in the real ship." I saw that he was using the control surfaces to drive us down, and I heard the complaining of structural members. But the surface of the water was close now, closer with every second.

"Mr. Smethwick, the hose!"

I couldn't see what was happening, but I could visualize that long tube of plastic snaking down towards the sea. I felt the blimp jump and lift as contact was made and, at Ralph's barked order, valved a cubic centimeter or so of helium. I heard the throbbing whine as the ballast pump started.

We were down then, the boat bottom of the cabin slapping (or being slapped by) the crests of the little waves, and then, a little heavier, we were properly waterborne and taxiing in towards the raw concrete of the new wharf.

It was a good landing—and if good landings could be made

in a misshapen little brute like the blimp, then equally good ones should be made in the proud, shining ship that we were approaching.

I thought, with a strong feeling of relief, *There's nothing to worry about after all.*

I don't know if that sentence is included in any collection of famous last words. If it's not, it should be.

Chapter 7

WE MADE FAST to a couple of bollards at the foot of the steps at the end of the wharf. The blimp lay there quietly enough, her wrinkled hide twitching in the light, eddying breeze; the high warehouse inshore from the quay gave us a good lee. The linesmen ran out a light gangway and we maneuvered the end of it through the cabin door. Smethwick, who had suffered from airsickness during our northward flight, started to hurry ashore. Ralph halted him with a sharp order. Then he said, in a gentler voice, "We all of us have still a lot to learn about the handling of lighter-than-air ships. One thing always to bear in mind is that any weight discharged has to be compensated for." He turned to me, saying, "Peter, stand by the ballast valve. We shouldn't require the pump."

I opened the valve, allowing the water to run into the tank below the cabin deck. I shut it when the water outside was lapping the sill of the open door. Smethwick scrambled out and the ship lurched and lifted. I opened the valve again, and it was Sandra's turn to disembark. Doc Jenkins followed her. Ralph took my place at the valve and I followed the doctor. Finally Ralph, having satisfied himself with the blimp wasn't liable to take off unmanned, joined us on the wharf.

Commodore Grimes was there, muffled in a heavy synthefur coat. With him were two women similarly clad. The super greeted us and then said to Ralph, "A nice landing, Captain Listowel. I hope you do as well with *Flying Cloud*."

"So do I, sir."

Grimes laughed. "You'd better." He gestured towards the slender, gleaming length of the big ship. "She cost a little more than your little gasbag."

We all stared at her. Yes, she did look expensive. I suppose that it was because she was new. The ships to which we had become used out on the Rim were all second- and even third-hand tonnage, obsolescent Epsilon Class tramps auctioned off by the Interstellar Transport Commission.

Yes, she looked expensive, and she looked new, and she looked *odd*. She didn't look like a spaceship—or, if she did look like a spaceship she looked like one that, toppling on its vaned landing gear, had crashed on to its side. And yet we felt that this was the way that she should be lying. She reminded me, I decided, of the big commercial submarines used by the Llarsii on their stormy, watery world.

Grimes was still talking. "Captain, I'd like you to meet your new shipmates for the maiden voyage. This is Miss Wayne, of the *Port Forlorn Chronicle*. And Miss Simmons, your donkeyman . . ."

I looked at the girls curiously and, I must confess, hopefully. Perhaps the voyage would be even more interesting than anticipated. Oh, I know that most planetlubbers have wildly romantic ideas about the function of a catering officer in a starship—but let me assure you that there's precious little romance. Bear in mind that the catering officer is the ship's dietician—and as such she can determine what the behavior of her male shipmates will be. And in most of the ships that I've sailed in the men have conducted themselves like well-behaved geldings. The exceptions have been vessels in which the catering officers, all too conscious of the passage of years and the fading of charms, have taken steps to insure that they, as women, will not be unappreciated. You may not recall the *Duchess of Atholl* scandal, but I do. Several innocent people took the blame for that unsavory affair and I was one of them. And that was the reason I left the employ of the Waverly Royal Mail and came out to the Rim.

Anyhow, I looked at the two women, thinking (and hoping)

that with a little competition in the ship Sandra might ginger up our diet a bit. Martha Wayne was a tall, slim, sleek brunette—and how she managed to look sleek and slim in her shaggy and bulky furs was something of a mystery. But sleek and slim she was. I had read some of her articles in the *Chronicle*, usually towards the end of a voyage, during that period when any and every scrap of hitherto unread printed matter is seized upon avidly. They'd been just the usual woman's page slush—Home Beautiful, Kitchen Functional, Menu Exotic and all the rest of it. Anyhow, she extended her hand to Ralph as though she expected him to make a low bow and kiss it. He shook it, however, although without much warmth.

Then there was Miss Simmons. ("Call me Peggy," she said at once.) She was short, dumpy in her cold weather clothing. She had thrown back the hood of her parka, revealing a head of tousled, sandy hair. Her face was pretty enough, in an obvious sort of way, and the smudge of dark grease on her right cheek somehow enhanced the prettiness.

"Commodore," said Ralph slowly, "did I understand you to say that Miss Simmons is to be our donkeyman?"

"Yes, Captain." Grimes looked slightly embarrassed. "A little trouble with the Institute," he added vaguely.

I could guess right then what the trouble was, and I found later that my guess was right. The Institute of Spatial Engineers would be taking a dim view of the improved Erikson drive, the system of propulsion that would rob its members of their hard-won status. They would refuse to allow even a junior member to sign as donkeyman— and, no doubt, they had been able to bring pressure to bear on other engineering guilds and unions, making sure that no qualified engineer would be available.

But a woman . . .

"It's quite all right, captain," the girl assured him brightly. "I'm it. I had an oil can for a feeding bottle, and when other kids were playing with dolls I was amusing myself with nuts and bolts and wrenches."

"Miss Simmons," explained Grimes, "is the daughter of an old friend of mine. Simmons, of Simmons's Air Car Repair Shop in Port

Forlorn. Her father assures me that Peggy is the best mechanic he has working for him."

"Even so . . ." said Ralph. Then—"How is it that Mr. Simmons can bear to part with such a treasure? Objectively speaking, this will be a long voyage."

"The usual trouble, captain," Grimes told him. "A new stepmother . . ."

"I hate the bitch," declared Peggy Simmons. She added quietly, "She's young. No older than me. But when this ship comes back to Lorn *I'll* still be young, and she—"

"Peggy!" snapped Grimes.

"But it's true, Uncle Andy."

"That will do. I don't think that Captain Listowel is interested in your personal problems. All that he wants is a competent mechanic."

Her face lost its ugly hardness. "And I'm just that, skipper," she grinned.

"All right," said the super briskly. "That's that. Now, if you feel up to it after your flight in that makeshift contraption, I suggest that we make an inspection of the ship."

"Even so . . ." began Ralph.

"Even so," flared Grimes, "I've got you a donkeyman, and a damn good one. And Miss Wayne has been commissioned to write the journal of the maiden voyage, but she's willing to make herself useful. She'll be signing as assistant purser."

"All right, Commodore," said Ralph coldly. "You can hand over the ship."

Chapter 8

~~~~~~

NORMALLY, handing over a spaceship is a lengthy business.

But these, we learned, were not normal circumstances. Lloyd's of London had issued a provisional certificate of spaceworthiness—but this, Grimes told us, was liable to be canceled at the drop of a hat. The great majority of Lloyd's surveyors are engineers, and *Flying Cloud* was an affront to those arrogant mechanics. She, as far as they were concerned, was an impudent putting back of the clock, an insolent attempt to return to those good old days when the master, in Lloyd's own words, was "master under God" and, in effect, did as he damn well pleased. The speed of a windjammer was in direct ratio to the skill of her master. The speed of a lightjammer would be in direct ratio to the skill of her master. The donkeyman of a windjammer held petty officer's rank only, messing with the boatswain, carpenter and sailmaker. The donkeyman of a light-jammer would be a junior officer only because the merchant navy doesn't run to petty officers. So the Institute of Spatial Engineers didn't like lightjammers. So they had run, squealing piteously, to Lloyd's. So the heirs and successors to that prosperous little coffee house proprietor, acting on the advice of their prejudiced surveyors, would sooner or later—and, quite probably, sooner—get around to revoking that provisional spaceworthiness certificate.

Flying Cloud was Grimes's baby. He had brought back the

anti-matter from the anti-matter systems. He had worked out a way in which it might be used. He had succeeded in convincing his employers that a lightjammer would be the most economical form of interstellar transport. Now it was up to us to prove him right. Once the maiden voyage was completed successfully, Lloyd's would have no excuse for not granting a full certificate.

So we joined a ship already spaceworthy in all respects. While we had been playing around in the catamaran and the blimp, Grimes had achieved wonders. *Flying Cloud* was fully stored and provisioned. Algae, yeast and tissue cultures were flourishing. The hydroponic tanks would have been a credit to an Empress Class liner. The last of the cargo—an unromantic consignment of zinc ingots for Grollor— was streaming into the ship by way of the main conveyor belt.

We had to take Grimes's word for it that everything was working as it should. Grimes's word, and the word of the Simmons girl, who assured us that she, personally, had checked every piece of machinery. We hoped that they were right, especially since there was some equipment, notably the spars and sails, that could not be actually tested inside an atmosphere in a heavy gravitational field.

Anyhow, that was the way of it. Ralph affixed his autograph to the handing-over form and I, as mate (acting, probably temporary, but not unpaid) witnessed it. And Martha Wayne, as representative of the *Port Forlorn Chronicle*, made a sound and vision recording of the historic moment. And Doc Jenkins suggested that the occasion called for a drink. Ralph frowned at this and said stiffly that we, who would shortly be taking an untested ship into space, would be well- advised to stay sober. Grimes told him not to be so bloody silly, adding that takeoff wasn't due for all of twelve hours. So Sandra went to the little bar at one side of the wardroom and opened the refrigerator and brought out two bottles of champagne. Grimes opened them himself, laughing wryly as the violently expanding carbon dioxide shot the corks up to the deckhead. "And this," he chuckled, "will be the only reaction drive as far as the ship's concerned!" And then, when the glasses were filled, he raised his in a toast. "To *Flying Cloud*," he said solemnly, "and to all who sail in her." He emphasized the word *sail*. "To *Flying Cloud*," we repeated.

The commodore drained his glass and set it down on the table. There was a sudden sadness in his manner. He said quietly, "Captain Listowel, I'm an outsider here. This is your ship. I'll leave you with your officers to get the hang of her. If you want to know anything, I shall be in my office ashore . . ."

He got slowly to his feet.

"Even so, sir . . ." began Ralph.

"Even so be damned. This is *your* ship, Listowel. Your donkeyman knows as much about the auxiliary machinery as I do, probably more. And as far as the handling of the sails is concerned, you'll have to make up the rules as you go along." He paused, then said, "But I shall be aboard in the morning to see you off."

He left us then.

"He should have sailed as her first master," said Ralph.

"And returning, still a relatively young man, to find his wife an old woman and his son his senior," said Jenkins. "I can see why we were the mugs. We have no ties."

"Even so . . ." said Ralph doubtfully.

"Come off it, skipper. There's nobody to miss us if this scow comes a gutser. We're expendable, even more so than the average Rim Runner officer. And that's saying plenty."

Ralph grinned reluctantly and gestured to Sandra to refill the glasses. He admitted, "I do believe you're right, Doc. I really do . . ." But the moment of relaxation didn't last long. His manner stiffened again. "All right, all of you. Finish your drinks, and then we'll get busy. I'd like you and Doc, Sandra, to make sure that all's well as far as the farm's concerned. I could be wrong, but I didn't think that the yeasts looked too healthy. And you're the mate, Peter; ballast and cargo are your worry. Just make sure that everything's going as it should."

"Aye, aye, sir," I replied in what I hoped was a seamanlike manner.

He scowled at me, then turned to the donkeyman. "And you, Miss Simmons, can give me another run-through on the various auxiliaries."

"And what can I do, Captain?" asked the journalist.

"Just keep out of the way, Miss Wayne," he told her, not unkindly.

She attached herself to me. Not that I minded—I don't suppose that any ship's officer, in any class of ship in any period, has really objected to having an attractive woman getting in his hair. She followed me as I made my way to the supercargo's office. It was already occupied; Trantor, one of the company's wharf superintendents, was there, sitting well back in the swivel chair, his feet on the desk, watching a blonde disrobing on the tiny screen of the portable TV set that he had hung on the bulkhead.

He started to take his feet off the desk slowly when he saw me— and with more haste when he saw Martha Wayne. He reached out to switch off his TV.

"Don't bother," said Martha Wayne. "I've often wondered just who does watch that program. Nobody will admit it."

Nevertheless, he switched off. He saved face by sneering at the new braid on my epaulettes. "Ah," he said, "the chief officer. In person. From office boy to mate in one easy lesson."

"There was more than one lesson, Trantor," I told him. "And they weren't all that easy."

They hadn't been easy at all, I remembered. There had been all the messing around in that cranky catamaran, and the messing around in that crankier blimp, and the long nights of study, and the training that we had undergone in mock-ups of the various control compartments of the ship. The model of the supercargo's office, I realized, had been extremely accurate. Ignoring Trantor, I inspected the gauges. Numbers 1 and 7 ballast tanks were out; 2, 3, 4, 5 and 6 were still in. There was no way of ascertaining the deadweight tonnage of cargo loaded save by tally and draft—and the columns of mercury in the draft indicator told me that if steps were not taken, and soon, *Flying Cloud* would shortly look even more like a submarine than she already did.

I went to the control panel, opened the exhaust valves to Numbers 2 and 6 tanks, and pressed the button that started the pump. I heard the throbbing whine of it as it went into action, saw the mercury columns begin to fall in their graduated tubes.

"What the hell do you think you're doing?" demanded Trantor.

"I'm the mate," I told him. "You said so. Remember?"

"If you're taking over," he said huffily, "I might as well get ashore."

"You might as well," I agreed. "But, first of all, I want you to come with me to make sure that the cargo is properly stowed and secured."

"Fussy, aren't you?" he growled.

"That's what I'm paid for," I said.

"But what is all this about stowage?" asked Martha Wayne.

"We have to watch it here," I told her. "Even more so than in a conventional ship. In the normal spaceship, *down* is always towards the stern, always—no matter if you're sitting on your backside on a planetary surface or accelerating in deep space. But here, when you're on the surface or navigating in a planetary atmosphere, *down* is vertically at right angles to the long axis. Once we're up and out, however, accelerating, *down* will be towards the stern."

"I see," she said, in that tone of voice that conveys the impression that the speaker doesn't.

"I suppose you know that your pump is still running," said Trantor.

"Yes. I know. It should be. It'll run till the tanks are out, and then it'll shut itself off."

"All right. It's your worry," he said.

"It's my worry," I agreed. "And now we'll look at the stowage."

With Trantor in the lead, we made our way along the alleyway to the hold. We went through the airtight door, and along the tunnel through the cargo bins. There was nothing to worry about—but that was due more to Grimes's foresight than to Trantor's efficiency. As each bin had been filled, the locking bars—stout metal rods padded with resilient plastic—had slid into place.

As we walked between the bins, the words of that ancient poem chased through my mind. *Argosies with magic sails, pilots of the purple twilight dropping down with costly bales* . . . But there weren't any costly bales here. There were drab, prosaic ingots of lead and zinc and cadmium, cargo for which there was a steady demand but no mad rush. Oh, well, we still had the magic sails.

The stevedore foreman, who had been juggling another set of locking bars into position, looked up from his work. He said cheerfully, "She'll be all right, mister."

"I hope so," I said.

"Just another twenty tons of zinc," he said, "an' that's it. You can have her then. An' welcome to her. I've loaded some odd ships in my time, but this'n's the oddest . . ."

"She'll be all right." I repeated his words.

"That's your worry, mister," he said. "Can't say that I'd like to be away on a voyage for all of twenty years." He gave Martha Wayne an appraising stare. "Although I allow that it might have its compensations."

"Or complications," I said.

Martha Wayne had her portable recorder out. She said to the foreman, "I take it that you've loaded this ship, Mr. . . . ?"

"Kilmer's the name, miss."

"Mr. Kilmer. I wonder if I might ask you for your impressions of the vessel?"

"After the loading is finished, Miss Wayne," I told her.

"From spacefaring office boy to mate in one easy lesson," said Trantor, grinning nastily.

Chapter 9

~~~ ~

WE FINALLY GOT TO OUR BUNKS that night, staggering to our cabins after a scratch meal of coffee and sandwiches in the wardroom. Ralph had driven us hard, and he had driven himself hard. He had insisted on testing everything that could be tested, had made his personal inspection of everything capable of being inspected. Ballast tanks had been flooded and then pumped out. The ingenious machinery that swiveled furniture and fittings through an arc of ninety degrees when transition was made from atmospheric to spatial flight was operated. The motors driving the airscrews were given a thorough trial.

At the finish of it all, Doc and Smethwick were on the verge of mutiny, Sandra was finding it imperative to do things in her galley by herself, and Martha Wayne was looking as though she were already regretting having accepted this assignment. Only Peggy Simmons seemed to be enjoying herself. As well as being obviously in love with her machinery, she appeared to have gotten a crush on Ralph. I overheard Doc mutter to Smethwick, "Following him round like a bitch in heat . . ." Oh, well, I thought to myself, Sandra will soon fix all that once she starts turning out the balanced diet.

Anyhow, with Ralph at last more or less happy about everything, we bolted our sandwiches, gulped our coffee and then retired. I was just about to switch off the light at the head of my bunk when there was a gentle tapping at my door. My first thought was that it was Ralph, that the master had thought of something else that might go wrong and had come to worry his mate about it. But Ralph would have knocked in a firm, authorative manner.

Sandra? I wondered hopefully.

"Come in," I called softly.

It was Peggy Simmons. She was dressed in a bulky, unglamorous robe. She looked like a little girl—and not one of the nymphette variety either. She looked like a fat little girl, although I was prepared to admit that it could have been the shapeless thing that she was wearing that conveyed this impression.

She said, "I hope you weren't asleep, Peter."

"I wasn't," I admitted grudgingly. "Not quite."

She said, "I just had to talk to somebody." She sat on the chair by my bunk, and helped herself to a cigarette from the box on the table. She went on, "This is all so strange. And tomorrow, after we get away, it will be even stranger."

"What isn't strange?" I countered. "Come to think of it, it's the normal that's really strange."

"You're too deep for me," she laughed ruefully. "But I came to talk to you because you're not clever . . ."

"Thank you," I said coldly.

"No. That wasn't quite what I meant, Peter. You *are* clever—you must be, to be chief officer of a ship like this. And I'm clever too—but with machinery. But the others—Sandra and Martha Wayne and Doc—are so . . . so . . ."

"Sophisticated," I supplied.

"Yes. That's the word. Sophisticated. And poor Claude Smethwick is the reverse. So unworldly. So weird, even . . ."

"And Ralph?" I prodded.

Her face seemed to light up and to cloud simultaneously, although there must have been a slight lag. "Oh, he's . . . exceptional? Yes. Exceptional. But I could hardly expect a man like him to want to talk to a girl like me. Could I?"

And why the hell not? I thought. *Put on some makeup, and throw something seductively translucent over the body beautiful*

*instead of that padded tent, and you might get somewhere. But not
with me, and not tonight, Josephine . . .*

"I haven't known many spacemen," she went on. "Only the
commodore, really, and he's so much one of the family that he
hardly counts. But there's always been something about you all,
those few of you whom I have met. I think I know what it is. You all
have pasts . . ."

And how! I thought.

"Like Ralph. Like the captain, I mean. You and he have been
shipmates for a long time, Peter, haven't you? But I can't help
wondering why such a capable man should come out to the
Rim . . ."

And him old enough to be your father, I thought. And then I
remembered what we had learned of Peggy Simmons's own story. It
all added up. Ralph, by virtue of personality as well as rank, was the
ideal father image. *Sticky,* I thought. *Definitely sticky.*

"Women," I said.

"Women?"

"Yeah. That's the usual reason why we all come out to the
Rim."

"Men," she said, "even the most brilliant men, are such fools
where women of a certain class are concerned."

Like your father, I thought.

"With the *right* woman," she went on, "they could go a long
way . . ."

Too right, I thought. *Too damn right. All the way to the next
galaxy but three, under full sail, and with the right woman manning
the pumps or whatever it is that the donkeyman does . . .*

She said wistfully, "I wish . . ."

"You wish what, Peggy?"

"Oh, I . . . I don't know, Peter . . ."

I wish that you'd get the hell out of here, I thought. *I wish that I
could get some sleep.*

"Have you a drink?" she asked. "A nightcap, to make me
sleep . . ."

"In that locker," I told her, "there's a bottle of brandy.

Medicinal. Get out two glasses and I'll have a drink with you. I could use some sleep myself."

She splashed brandy generously into the glasses and handed one to me.

"Down the hatch," I said.

"Down the hatch," she repeated. Then she demanded suddenly, "What haven't I got, Peter?"

I knew what she meant. "As far as I can see," I told her, "you have all the standard equipment. As far as I can see."

She said abruptly, "*She's* with him. In his cabin."

I felt a stab of jealousy. "Who?" I asked.

"Sandra."

So they managed to keep it a secret in Rim Dragon, *I thought. Not that there was any need to. There's nothing in the regulations that says that officers shall not sleep with each other, provided that it doesn't get in the way of their duties . . .*

I said, "But they've known each other for years."

"And I'm just the small girl around the ship. The newcomer. The outsider."

"Miss Simmons," I said severely, "people who affix their autographs to the articles of agreement are engaged for one reason only: to take the ship from point A to point B as required by the lawful commands of the master. Who sleeps with whom—or who doesn't sleep with whom—is entirely outside the scope of the Merchant Shipping Act."

Her robe had somehow become unfastened, and I could see that she did, in fact, possess the usual equipment and that it was in no way substandard. She knew that I was looking at her, but she made no attempt to cover herself. Instead she got to her feet and stood there for a moment or so, posing rather self-consciously and awkwardly, before going to the locker for the brandy bottle. She refilled our glasses, the rosy nipple of her right breast almost brushing my face as she stooped. I restrained myself from pulling her down to me.

"One for the road," I said firmly.

"For the road?" she echoed.

"For the road, Peggy. We're both of us tired, and we have another heavy day ahead of us tomorrow."

"But . . ." She might just as well not have been wearing the robe.

"Damn it all, girl," I exploded, "I may be only the mate, and an ex-purser at that, but I have my pride. You've been making it bloody obvious all day that you were just dying to serve yourself up to Ralph on a silver tray and trimmed with parsley. Sandra beat you to Ralph's bed, so I'm second choice. Or do you think that you're hurting him in some obscure way by giving me what he didn't take? Either way, I'm not playing. So finish your drink like a good girl and go and turn in. By yourself."

"If that's the way you want it," she said coldly.

"That's the way that I want it," I said coldly.

"Good night," she said.

"Good night," I said.

She set her empty glass down gently on the table. Her face was pale and a tiny muscle was twitching in her left cheek. With her robe again belted securely around her she looked once more like a small girl—like a small girl who is convinced she has been unjustly spanked.

She said, "I'm sorry to have troubled you."

I said, "And I'm sorry that . . . oh, never mind."

"Good night," she said again.

"Good night," I replied again.

She left then, closing the door quietly behind her. I finished my drink and switched out the light. But I didn't get to sleep for a long time. And I should have slept well, I knew, had I taken the opportunity for the loosening of nervous tension in the most effective way there is. My absurdly puritanical attitude (a hangover from that sordid affair on *Duchess of Atholl*?) had done no good to anybody at all, including myself.

And it was—although this was unforeseeable—to have far-reaching consequences.

Chapter 10

≈≈ ≈≈

THE NEXT MORNING Sandra was in one of her house wifely moods; these had been the occasion for jocular comment now and again in *Rim Dragon*. She called each of us individually, with tea and toast. Now that I knew the reasons for these spasms of domesticity I wasn't any happier. "Good morning, Peter," she said brightly (too brightly) as she switched on my light. "Rise and shine for the Cluster Line." (She had served in that outfit before joining Rim Runners.) "I hope you slept well."

"I didn't," I growled. I glowered at her from eyes that probably looked as bleary as they felt. "I hope that *you* slept well."

"But of course," she said sweetly, and left me to my tea.

By the time the breakfast gong sounded, I had showered and shaved and dressed in the rig of the day and was feeling a little better. This was our first real meal aboard the ship and something of a ceremonious occasion. Ralph was at the head of the table and rather conscious, I could see, of the gleaming new braid on his epaulettes. I sat down at his right, with Sandra, when she wasn't bustling to and from the pantry, opposite me. The others took their places, with Peggy Simmons, as the most junior member of the ship's company, sitting at the foot of the table. She blushed when I said good morning to her. I hoped that none of the others noticed, although Doc Jenkins, who never missed much of what was going on, leered in my direction.

"This," said Ralph rather stuffily before we could make a start on the eggs and bacon, "is a momentous occasion."

"We still have to get this bitch off the ground," Jenkins told him.

"Off the water, you mean," I amended.

"Even so . . ." began Ralph severely.

"Good morning to you all," said a familiar voice. We turned to see that Grimes had just entered the wardroom.

We got to our feet.

"Carry on," he said. "Don't mind me."

"Some breakfast, sir?" asked Ralph.

"No thank you. But some coffee, if I may, Captain."

He pulled up a chair and Sandra attended to his needs.

He said, "You'll forgive me for talking shop, but I take it that you're secured for space?"

"We are, sir," Ralph told him.

"Good. Well, I have no wish to interfere with your arrangements, but there must be no delay."

"We can take off now, sir, if you wish," said Ralph, pushing away his plate with the half-eaten food.

"For the love of all the Odd Gods of the Galaxy," pleaded Grimes, "finish your breakfast. I intend to enjoy at least one more cup of this excellent coffee. But, while you're eating, I'll put you in the picture." He patted his lips with the napkin Sandra had given him. "Throughout my career I've never been overly fussy about treading on corns, but I seem to have been trampling on some very tender ones of late. This is the way of it. My spies inform me that this very morning, Metropolitan Standard Time, the *Flying Cloud* issue is going to be raised in the Senate. The Honorable Member for Spelterville will demand an inquiry into the squandering of public money on the construction of an utterly impracticable spaceship. And his crony, the Honorable Member for Ironhill East, will back him up and demand that the ship be held pending the inquiry . . ."

"Amalgamated Rockets," said Martha Wayne. "And Interstellar Drives, Incorporated."

"Precisely," agreed Grimes. "Well, I don't think that they'll be able to get things moving prior to your takeoff, Captain—but if you should have to return to surface for any reason, or even if you hang in orbit, there's a grave risk that you'll be held. I want there to be no hitches."

"There will be none," said Ralph stiffly.

"Good. And when do you intend getting upstairs?"

"At the advertised time, sir, 0900 hours."

"And you're quite happy about everything?"

"Yes, sir. Even so . . ."

"Every spaceman always feels that 'even so'—otherwise he wouldn't be worth a damn as a spaceman. (Some more coffee, please, if you'll be so good. Excellent.) I suppose that I'll still be around when you return. I hope so. But I shall be getting your voyage reports by way of the psionic radio . . ."

"I'm surprised, Commodore," said Martha Wayne, "that the ship hasn't been fitted with the Carlotti equipment."

"It wouldn't work," Grimes told her. "It will run only in conjunction with the Mannschenn Drive." He turned to the telepath. "So you're the key man, Mr. Smethwick."

Claude grinned feebly and said, "As long as you don't expect me to bash a key, sir."

We all laughed. His ineptitude with anything mechanical was notorious.

Grimes got to his feet reluctantly. "I'll not get in your hair any longer. You all have jobs to do." He said, as he shook hands with Ralph, "You've a good ship, Listowel. And a good crew. Look after them both."

"I'll do that," promised Ralph.

"I won't say good-bye," said Grimes. "*Au revoir* is better."

He swung away abruptly and walked quickly out of the ward-room. I hurried after him to escort him to the gangway.

At the airlock he shook hands with me again. He said quietly, "I envy you, Mr. Malcolm. I envy you. If things had been different I'd have been sailing in her. But . . ."

"There are times," I said, "when I envy those who have family ties."

He allowed himself to grin. "You have something there, young man. After all, one can't have everything. I've a wife and a son, and you have the first of the interstellar lightjammers. I guess that we shall each of us have to make the best of what we've got. Anyhow, look after yourself."

I assured him that I would, and, as soon as he was ashore, I went back inside the ship.

The takeoff was a remarkably painless procedure.

When the ship was buttoned up and we were at our stations, the linesmen let go our moorings fore and aft. The little winches, obedient to the pressing of buttons in the control room, functioned perfectly. On the screen of the closed-circuit TV I watched the lines snaking in through the fair-leads, saw the cover plates slide into place as the eyes vanished inside our hull. There was no need for any fancy maneuvers; the wind pushed us gently away from the wharf.

"Ballast," ordered Ralph. "Pump 3 and 5."

"Pump 3 and 5," I repeated, opening valves and pressing the starter buttons.

I heard the throbbing of the pumps, watched the mercury fall in the graduated columns of the draft indicator, a twin to the one in the supercargo's office. But we still had negative lift, although we were now floating on the surface like a huge bubble. There was a new feel to the ship, an uneasiness, an expectancy as she stirred and rolled to the low swell. And still the mercury dropped in the transparent tubes until, abruptly, the pulsation of the pumps cut out.

"Number 4, sir?" I asked.

"No, Peter. Not yet. Extrude atmospheric control surfaces."

"Extrude atmospheric control surfaces, sir."

On the screen I saw the stubby wings extend telescopically from the shining hull.

"I thought that you just pumped all ballast and went straight up," said Martha Wayne, who was seated at the radio telephone.

"We could," said Ralph, "we could; but, as I see it, the secret of handling these ships is always to keep some weight up your sleeve. After all, we shall have to make a landing on Grollor. I intend to see if I can get her upstairs on aerodynamic lift." He turned to me. "I don't think that it's really necessary to keep Sandra and Doc on stations in the storeroom and the farm. After all, this isn't a rocket blastoff, and they're supposed to be learning how to handle this scow. Get them up here, will you?"

"And Claude and Peggy?" I asked.

"No. Claude is hopeless at anything but his job, and Miss Simmons had better keep her eye on her mechanical toys."

I gave the necessary orders on the intercom, and while I was doing so the speaker of the RT crackled into life. "Spaceport control to *Flying Cloud*," we heard. "Spaceport control to *Flying Cloud*. What is the delay? I repeat: what is the delay?"

The voice was familiar; it belonged to Commodore Grimes. And it was anxious.

"Pass me the mike," said Ralph. He reported quietly, "*Flying Cloud* to spaceport control. There is no delay. Request permission to take off."

"Take off then, before the barnacles start growing on your bottom!" blustered Grimes.

Ralph grinned and handed the microphone back to Martha. He waited until Sandra and Doc, who had just come into the control room, had belted themselves into their chairs; then he put both hands on the large wheel. "Full ahead port," he ordered. I pressed the starting button, moved the handle hard over, and Ralph turned his wheel to starboard. "Full ahead starboard," he ordered.

The ship came round easily, heading out for the open sea. From the transparent bubble that was the control room we could now see nothing but gray water and gray sky, and the dark line of the horizon towards which we were steering; but on the screen of the closed circuit TV we could watch the huddle of spaceport buildings and the wharf, to which the little blimp was still moored, receding.

With his left hand Ralph held *Flying Cloud* steady on course; his right moved over the controls on the steering column. And the motion was different now. The ship was no longer rolling or pitching, but, from under us, came the rhythmic *slap, slap* of the small waves striking our bottom as we lifted clear of the surface. And then that was gone and there was only the clicking of our compass and the muffled, almost inaudible throbbing of our screws.

From the RT came Grimes's voice, "Good sailing, *Flying Cloud*. Good sailing!"

"Tell him thank you," said Ralph to Martha. Then, characteristically, "Even so, we haven't started to *sail* yet."

Chapter 11

〜〜〜

WE SHOULD HAVE SPENT more time in the atmosphere than we did, getting the feel of the ship. But there was the broadcast that Martha picked up on the RT, the daily transmission of proceedings in the Senate. The Honorable Member for Spelterville was in good form. We heard *Flying Cloud* described in one sentence as a futuristic fictioneer's nightmare, and in the next as an anachronistic reversion to the dark ages of ocean transport. And then, just to make his listeners' blood run cold, he described in great detail what would happen should she chance to crash in a densely populated area. The casing around the sphere of anti-iron would be ruptured and, the anti-matter coming into contact with normal matter, there would be one hell of a big bang. Furthermore, he went on, there was the strong possibility of a chain reaction that would destroy the entire planet.

It would all have been very amusing, but there were far too many cries of approval and support from both Government and Opposition benches—especially when the Honorable Member, after having divulged the information that *Flying Cloud* was already airborne, demanded that the Government act *now*.

Ralph, as he listened, looked worried. He said, "Miss Wayne, I think that our receiver has broken down, hasn't it?"

She grinned back at him. "It has. Shall I pull a fuse?"

"Don't bother," he said. "If we get a direct order from the commodore to return to port we shall do so, I suppose. Otherwise . . ."

He had handed over the controls to Doc Jenkins and myself; I was steering and Doc was functioning, not too inefficiently, as altitude coxswain. We were rising in a tight spiral, and below us was a snowy, almost featureless field of altocumulus. Above us was the sky, clear and dark, with the Great Lens of the Galaxy already visible although the sun had yet to set. So far all had gone well and smoothly, although it was obvious that in order to break free of the atmosphere we should have to valve more ballast.

Suddenly Sandra cried out, pointing downwards.

We all looked through the transparent deck of the control room and saw that something small and black had broken through the overcast. A tiny triangle it was, a dart, rather, and at its base was a streak of blue fire bright even against the gleaming whiteness of the cloud. Ralph managed to bring the big, mounted binoculars to bear.

"Air Force markings," he muttered. "One of the rocket fighters."

Somebody muttered something about "bloody flyboys."

"Better have the transceiver working," ordered Ralph.

Hard on his words came a voice from the RT. "Officer commanding Defense Wing 7 to master of *Flying Cloud*. Return at once to your berth. Return at once to your berth."

"Master of *Flying Cloud* to unidentified aircraft," replied Ralph coldly. "Your message received."

The plane was closer now, gaining on us rapidly. I watched it until a sharp reprimand from Ralph caused me to return my attention to the steering. But I could still listen, and I heard the airman say, "Return at once to your berth. That is an order."

"And if I refuse?"

"Then I shall be obliged to shoot you down." This was followed by a rather unpleasant chuckle. "After all, Captain, you're a big target and a slow one."

"And if you do shoot us down," said Ralph reasonably, "what then? We are liable to fall anywhere. And you know that the anti-iron that we carry makes us an atomic bomb far more powerful than any fission or fusion device ever exploded by man to date." He covered the microphone with his hand, remarking, "That's given him something to think about. But he can't shoot us down, anyhow. If he punctures the ballast tanks or knocks a few pieces off the hull we lose our negative lift . . . and if he should rupture the casing around the anti-iron . . ."

"What then?" asked Martha Wayne.

"It'll be the last thing he'll ever do—and the last thing that we shall ever experience."

"He's getting bloody close," grumbled Doc. "I can see the rockets mounted on his wings, and what look like a couple of cannon—"

"Comply with my orders!" barked the voice from the RT.

"Sandra," said Ralph quietly, "stand by the ballast controls."

"I give you ten seconds," we heard. "I have all the latest reports and forecasts. If I shoot you down here you will fall somewhere inside the ice cap. There's no risk of your dropping where you'll do any damage. Ten . . . nine . . . eight . . ."

"Jettison," ordered Ralph quietly.

"Valves open," reported Sandra.

Looking down, I could see the water gushing from our exhausts—a steady stream that thinned to a fine spray as it fell. I could see, too, the deadly black shape, the spearhead on its shaft of fire that was driving straight for our belly. And I saw the twinkle of flame at the gun muzzles as the automatic cannon opened up, the tracer that arched towards us with deceptive laziness. So he wasn't using his air-to-air missiles, that was something to be thankful for. He wasn't using his air-to-air missiles—yet.

The ship shuddered—and I realized, dimly, that we had been hit. There was an alarm bell shrilling somewhere, there was the thin, high scream of escaping atmosphere. There was the thudding of airtight doors slamming shut and, before the fans stopped, there was the acrid reek of high explosive drifting through the ducts. Then, with incredible swiftness, the aircraft was falling away from us, diminishing to the merest speck against the gleaming expanse of cloud. She belatedly fired her rockets, but they couldn't reach us now. We were up and clear, hurled into the interstellar emptiness by our anti-gravity. We were up and clear, and already Lorn was no more than a great ball beneath us, a pearly sphere glowing against the blackness of space. We were up and clear and outward bound—but until we could do something about getting the ship under control we were no more than a derelict.

Things could have been worse.

Nobody was injured, although Peggy had been obliged to scramble fast into a spacesuit. There were several bad punctures in the pressure hull, but these could be patched. There was a consignment of steel plates in our cargo, and our use of them in this emergency would be covered. The loss of atmosphere could be made good from our reserve bottles. It was unfortunate that we were now in a condition of positive buoyancy rather than the neutral buoyancy that Ralph had planned for the voyage—but, he assured us, he had already worked out a landing technique for use in such circumstances. (Whether or not it would prove practicable we still had to find out.)

So, clad in space armor and armed with welding torches, Peggy and I turned to render the ship airtight once more. As mate I was in official charge of repairs, but I soon realized that my actual status was that of welder's helper. It was Peggy Simmons who did most of the work. A tool in her hands was an extension of her body—or, even, an extension of her personality. She stitched metal to metal with the delicate precision that an ancestor of hers might have displayed with needle, thread and fine fabric.

I watched her with something akin to envy—and it was more than her manual dexterity that I envied. She had something that occupied all her attention. I had not. Although it was foolish, every now and again I had to throw back the welder's mask and look about me. I was far from happy. This was not the first time that I had been outside in deep space, but it was the first time that I had been outside on the Rim. It was the *emptiness* that was so frightening. There was our sun, and there was Lorn (and it seemed to me that they were diminishing visibly as I watched) and there was the distant, dim-glowing Galactic Lens—and there was *nothing*. We were drifting towards the edge of the dark in a crippled ship, and we should never (I thought) make it back to warmth and comfort and security.

I heard Peggy's satisfied grunt in my helmet phones and wrenched my eyes away from the horrid fascination of the ultimate emptiness. She had finished the last piece of welding, I saw, and she straightened up with a loud sigh. She stood there, anchored by the magnetic soles of her boots to the hull, a most unfeminine figure in her bulky suit. She reached out to me, and the metallic fingers of her glove grated on my shoulder plate. She pulled me to her, touched her helmet to mine. I heard her whisper, "Switch off."

I didn't understand what she wanted at first—and then, after the third repetition, nudged the switch of my suit radio with my chin. She said, her voice faint and barely audible, "Do you think that this will make any difference?"

"Of course," I assured her. "We can bring pressure up to normal throughout the ship now."

"I didn't mean *that!*" she exclaimed indignantly.

"Then what the hell did you mean?" I demanded.

"Do you think that this will make any difference to Ralph's—the captain's—attitude towards me? After all, the other two women weren't much use, were they?"

"Neither was I," I admitted sourly.

"But you're a man." She paused. "Seriously, Peter, do you think that this repair job will help? With Ralph, I mean . . ."

"Seriously, Peggy," I told her, "it's time that we were getting back inside. The others are probably watching us and wondering what the hell we're playing at." I added, "There's never been a case of seduction in hard vacuum yet—but there's always a first time for everything."

"Don't be funny!" she flared. Then, her voice softening, "There's an old saying: The way to a man's heart is through his stomach. It could be that the way to a space captain's heart is through his ship."

"Could be," I admitted. "Could be. But Ralph won't love either of us for dawdling out here when he's itching to clap on sail. Come on, let's report that the job's finished and get back in." I switched on my suit radio again.

Before I could speak I heard Ralph's voice. Even the tinny quality of the helmet phones couldn't disguise his bad temper. "What the hell do you two think you're doing? Standing there hand in hand, admiring the scenery . . . Mr. Malcom, are the repairs finished? If so, report at once and then return inboard."

"Repairs completed, sir," I said.

"Then let's not waste any more time," suggested Ralph coldly.

We didn't waste any more time. Carefully, sliding our feet over the metal skin, we inched towards the open airlock valve. Peggy went in first and I handed the tools and the unused materials to her. I followed her into the little compartment, and I was pleased when the door slid shut, cutting out the sight of the black emptiness.

The needle on the illuminated dial quivered and then jerked abruptly to the ship's working pressure.

We were all of us in the control room—all save Peggy, who had been ordered, somewhat brusquely, to look after her motors. From our sharp prow the long, telescopic must have already been protruded, the metal spar on the end of which was mounted the TV camera. On the big screen we could see the image of *Flying Cloud* as she appeared from ahead. I thought that it was a pity that we did not have other cameras that would allow us to see her in profile, to appreciate the gleaming slenderness of her.

"The first problem," said Ralph, in his best lecture-room manner, "is to swing the ship. As you are all, no doubt, aware, we possess no gyroscopes. Even so, such devices are not essential. The master of a windjammer had no gyroscopes to aid him in setting and steering a course . . ."

"He had a rudder," I said, "acting upon and acted upon by the fluid medium through which his hull progressed."

Ralph glared at me. "A resourceful windjammer master," he stated flatly, "was not utterly dependent upon his rudder. Bear in mind the fact that his ship was not, repeat not, a submarine and, therefore, moved through no less than two fluid mediums, air and water. His rudder, as you have been so good to tell us, acted upon and was acted upon by the water in which it was immersed. But his sails acted upon and were acted upon by the air." He paused for breath. "We, in this vessel, may consider light a fluid medium. Now, if you will observe carefully . . ."

We observed. We watched Ralph's capable hands playing over the control panel. We watched the TV screen. We saw the spars extend from the hull so that the ship, briefly, had the appearance of some spherical, spiny monster. And then the roller reefing gear came into play and the sails were unfurled—on one side a dazzling white, on the other jet black. We could feel the gentle centrifugal force as the ship turned about her short axis, bringing the Lorn sun dead astern.

Then spars rotated and, as far as that camera mounted at the end of its telescopic mast was concerned, the sails were invisible. Their white surfaces were all presented to the Lorn sun, to the steady photon gale. We were running free, racing before the interstellar wind.

I realized that Ralph was singing softly:

> *"Way, hey, and up she rises,*
> *Way, hey, and up she rises,*
> *Way, hey, and up she rises . . .*
> *Early in the morning!"*

Chapter 12

SO THERE WE WERE, bowling along under full sail, running the easting down. In some ways the Erikson drive was a vast improvement over the Mannschenn Drive. There was not that continuous high whine of the ever-precessing gyroscopes, there was not that uneasy feeling of *déjà vu* that is a side effect of the Mannschenn Drive's temporal precession field. Too, we could look out of the control room and see a reasonable picture of the Universe as it is and not, in the case of the Galactic Lens, something like a Klein bottle fabricated by a drunken glass blower.

Flying Cloud was an easy ship, once the course had been set, once she was running free before the photon gale. She was an easy ship—as a ship, as an assemblage of steel and plastic and fissioning uranium. But a ship is more than the metals and chemicals that have gone into her construction. In the final analysis it is the crew that make the ship—and *Flying Cloud* was not happy.

It was the strong element of sexual jealousy that was the trouble. I did my best to keep my own yardarm clear, but I could observe— and feel jealous myself. It was obvious that Sandra was Captain's lady. It was obvious, too, that both Martha Wayne and Peggy Simmons had aspired to that position and that both were jealous. And Doc Jenkins couldn't hide the fact, for all his cynicism, that he would have welcomed a roll in the hay with Martha. The only one who was really amused by it all was Smethwick. He drifted into the Control Room during my watch and said, "Ours is a happy ship, ours is."

"Are you snooping?" I demanded sharply. "If you are, Claude, I'll see to it, personally, that you're booted out of the service."

He looked hurt. "No, I'm not snooping. Apart from the regulations, it's a thing I wouldn't dream of doing. But even you must be sensitive to the atmosphere, and you're not a telepath."

"Yes," I agreed. "I am sensitive." I offered him a cigarette, took and lit one myself. "But what's new? Anything?"

"The flap seems to have died down on Lorn," he told me. "We're a *fait accompli*. Old Grimes got Livitski—he's the new Port Forlorn Psionic Radio Officer—to push a message through to wish us well and to tell us that he has everything under control at his end."

"Have you informed the master?" I asked.

"He's in his quarters." he said. "I don't think that he wants to be disturbed."

"Like that," I said.

"Like that," he said.

"Oh," I said.

We sat in silence—there was still enough acceleration to enable us to do so without using seat belts—smoking. I looked out of the transparency at the blackness, towards the faint, far spark that was the Grollor sun. Claude looked at nothing. I heard the sound of feet on the control room deck, turned and saw that the faint noise had been made by Peggy Simmons. She said, "I'm sorry. I . . . I thought that you were alone, Peter . . ."

"Don't let me interfere with love's young dream," grinned Smethwick, getting to his feet.

"You've a dirty mind!" flared the girl.

"If it is dirty," he told her nastily, "it's from the overflow from other people's minds. But I'll go away and leave you to it."

"I'm on watch," I said virtuously. "And, in any case, Peggy has probably come here to report some mechanical malfunction. Or something."

"Yes," she said.

She dropped into the chair that had been vacated by the telepath, accepted a cigarette from my pack. I waited until Claude was gone and then asked, "What's the trouble, Peggy?"

"Nothing," she said. "Nothing mechanical, that is. Although I should check some of the wiring where the shell splinters pierced the inner sheathing."

"Then why don't you?" I asked.

"Because," she told me, "for the first few days in space one has more important things to worry about. There's the file, and the auxiliary machinery, and . . ."

"Surely the wiring is part of the auxiliary machinery," I pointed out.

"Not this wiring. It's the power supply to the trimming and reefing gear—and we won't be using that for a while, not until we make landfall."

"Planetfall," I corrected.

"Ralph says landfall," she told me.

"He would," I said. "He must have brought at least a couple of trunks full of books about windjammers—fact, fiction and poetry—away with him. Mind you, some of it is good." I quoted:

> *"I must go down to the sea again,*
> *To the lonely sea and the sky,*
> *And all I ask is a tall ship*
> *And a star to steer her by . . ."*

I gestured widely towards the Grollor sun, the distant spark that, thanks to the Doppler effect, was shining with a steely glitter instead of its normal ruddiness. I said, "There's his star to steer by." I thumped the arm of my chair. "And here's his tall ship."

"And so he has everything he wants," she said.

"Everything." I decided to be blunt. "He's got his tall ship, and he's got his star to steer by, and he's got his woman."

"But," she said, "I could give him so much more."

"Peggy," I admonished, "don't kid yourself. You're attractive, and you're capable—but Sandra is rather more than attractive. *And* she's a good cook. Take my advice: just forget any schoolgirlish ideas you may have of becoming the captain's lady. Make this voyage—after all, you've no option now—and then get the hell out . . ."

"And marry and raise a family," she concluded. "But I don't want to, Peter. I don't want to. I don't want to be the wife of some grubby little clerk or mechanic and spend all my remaining days on Lorn."

"All right," I said, "if that's the way you feel about it. But this is an order, Peggy. Lay off Ralph. We're probably in enough trouble already without having triangles added to our worries."

She took a cigarette from my pack, lit it and put it to her mouth. She stared at the eddying wisps of smoke. She said, "That poetry you quoted. Tall ships and stars. That's what Ralph really wants, isn't it?"

"Tall ships and stars and the trimmings," I said.

"Never mind the trimmings," she told me. "And when it comes to trimmings, I can outtrim Sandra."

"Peggy," I said, "you can't. You're not . . . experienced."

Her face lit up briefly with a flash of humor. "And whose fault is that?" she asked. Then, soberly, "But I can give him *real* trimmings. Any woman can sprawl in bed, arms and legs wide open—but I'm the woman who can make Ralph, and his ship, go down in history."

"Judging by the flap when we shoved off," I said, "they already have."

She said, "Correct me if I'm wrong—but the Erikson drive, as it stands, will never be a commercial success. It takes far too long for a cargo, even a non-perishable cargo for which there's no mad rush, to be carted from point A to point B. And there's the problem of manning, too. As far as this ship was concerned, Uncle Andy was able to assemble a bunch of misfits with no close ties for the job, people who wouldn't give a damn if the round voyage lasted a couple of objective centuries. But it mightn't be so easy to find another crew for another lightjammer. Agreed?"

"Agreed," I said, after a pause.

She went on, "I'm new to space, but I've read plenty. I'm no physicist, but I have a rough idea of the *modus operandi* of the various interstellar drives. And, so far, there's been no faster-than-light drive."

"What!" I exclaimed.

"No, there hasn't. I'm right, Peter. The basic idea of the Ehrenhaft drive was that of a magnetic particle trying to be in two places at the same time in a magnetic field or current, the ship being the particle. But, as far as I can gather, space was warped so that she could do just that. I couldn't follow the math, but I got the general drift of it. And then, of course, there's the Mannschenn Drive—but there the apparent FTL speeds are achieved by tinkering with time."

"Hmm," I grunted. "Hmm."

"Getting away from machinery," she said, "and back to personalities, Ralph loves his ship. I'm sure that if he had to make a choice between Sandra and *Flying Cloud* it wouldn't be *Flying Cloud* left in the lurch. But . . . but what do you think he'd feel about a woman who made him the captain of the first *real* FTL starwagon?"

I said, "You'd better see Doc on your way aft. He stocks quite a good line in sedative mixtures."

She said, "You're laughing at me."

"I'm not," I assured her. "But, Peggy, even I, and I'm no physicist, can tell you that it's quite impossible to exceed the speed of light. As you have already pointed out, we can cheat, but that's all. And in this ship we can't even cheat. We can no more outrun light than a windjammer could outrun the wind that was her motive power." I pointed to a dial on the panel before me. "That's our log. It works by Doppler effect. At the moment our speed is Lume 0.345 and a few odd decimals. It's building up all the time, and fast. By the end of the watch it should be about Lume 0.6 . . ."

She said, "A fantastic acceleration."

"Isn't it? By rights we should be spread over the deck plates like strawberry jam. But, thanks to the anti-gravity, this is almost an inertialess drive. Anyhow, thanks to our utterly weightless condition, we may achieve Lume 0.9 recurring. But that's as high as we can possibly get."

"I see," she said doubtfully. Then she added, "But . . ." She shrugged and said, "Oh, never mind."

She got up to leave.

"Thanks for dropping in," I said.

"And thanks for the fatherly advice," she said.

"Think nothing of it," I told her generously.

"I shan't," she said, with what I belatedly realized was deliberate ambiguity.

And then she was gone.

Chapter 13

≈≈ ≈

IT WAS A COUPLE OF MORNINGS LATER as measured by our chronometer, and, after a not very good breakfast, I was making rounds. It's odd how that unappetizing meal sticks in my memory. Sandra was acting third mate now, and Ralph had decreed that Martha Wayne take over as catering officer. And Martha, as the old saying goes, couldn't boil water without burning it. Sandra's scrambled eggs had always been a delight—fluffy but not watery, with the merest hint of garlic, prettied up with chopped parsley and paprika, piled high on crisp, lavishly buttered toast. The less said about Martha's scrambled eggs the better.

Anyhow, I was not in a good mood as I made my way aft from the wardroom. *Flying Cloud* was still accelerating slightly, so "down" was aft. Rather to my disappointment I discovered nothing with which to find fault in the farm, the compartment housing the hydroponic tanks and the yeast and tissue-culture vats. I hurried through the anti-matter room—frankly, that huge, spherical casing surrounded by great horseshoe magnets always gave me the shivers. I knew what was inside it, and knew that should it ever make contact with normal matter we should all go up in a flare of uncontrolled and uncontrollable energy. In the auxiliary machinery space I did start finding fault. It was obvious that Peggy had done nothing as yet about removing the splinter-pierced panels of the internal sheathing to inspect the wiring.

But there was no sign of Peggy.

I continued aft, through the reactor room and then into the tunnel that led to the extreme stern. As I clambered down the ladder I heard the clinking of tools and the sound of a voice upraised in song. It was Doc Jenkins's not unpleasant tenor.

> *"Sally Brown, she's a bright mulatter—*
> *Way, hey, roll and go!*
> *She drinks rum and chews terbaccer—*
> *Spend my money on Sally Brown!*
>
> *"Sally Brown, she's a proper lady—*
> *Way, hey, roll and go!*
> *Got a house right full o' yaller babies—*
> *Spend my money on Sally Brown!"*

I dropped the last few feet into the transom space, landing with a faint thud. Doc Jenkins and Peggy looked up from what they were doing. Doc was wearing only a pair of shorts and his pudgy torso was streaked with grime and perspiration. Peggy was clad in disreputable overalls. She was holding a welding torch.

She said, rather guiltily, "Good morning, Peter."

"Good morning," I replied automatically. Then, "I know that I'm only the mate, but might I inquire what you two are up to?"

"We're going to make this bitch roll and go," replied Peggy happily.

"What do you mean?" I asked coldly.

I looked around the cramped compartment, saw two discarded space-suits that had been flung carelessly on to the deck. And I saw what looked like the breech of a gun protruding from the plating. Around its circumference the welding was still bright. I looked from it back to the spacesuits.

"Have you been outside?" I demanded.

"No," said Peggy.

"Don't worry, Peter," said Jenkins. "We didn't lose any atmosphere. We sealed the transom space off before we went to work, and put the pump on it . . ."

"Remote control," said Peggy, "from inside."

"*And you pierced the hull?*" I asked with mounting anger.

"Only a small hole," admitted the doctor.

"Damn it!" I flared. "This is too much. Only four days out and you're already space-happy. Burning holes in the shell plating and risking all our lives. And I still don't know what it's all about. When Ralph hears of this . . ."

"He'll be pleased," said Peggy simply.

"He'll be pleased, all right. He'll roll on the deck in uncontrollable ecstasy. He'll have your guts for a necktie, both of you, and then boot you out of the airlock without a spacesuit. He'll . . ."

"Be reasonable, Peter," admonished Jenkins.

"Be reasonable? I am being reasonable. Peggy here has work that she should be doing, instead of which I find her engaged in some fantastic act of sabotage with you, one of the ship's executive officers, aiding and abetting."

"Come off it, Peter," said the Doc. "I'm second mate of this wagon, and I signed the articles as such, and one of the clauses says that deck and engine room departments should cooperate . . ."

"Never mind this second mate business," I told him. "As ship's surgeon, you're still a member of the deck department, ranking with, but below, the mate. And as far as I'm concerned, the prime function of the engine room department is to do as it's bloody well told."

"Then why don't you *tell* me something?" asked Peggy, sweetly reasonable.

"I will," I promised. "I will. But, to begin with, you will tell *me* something. You will tell me just what the hell you two are playing at down here."

"Is that a lawful command?" asked Peggy.

"I suppose so," admitted Jenkins grudgingly.

"All right," she said slowly. "I'll tell you. What you see . . ." she kicked the breech of the cannon with a heavy shoe . . . "is the means whereby we shall exceed the speed of light."

"But it's impossible," I said.

"How do you know?" she countered.

"It's common knowledge," I sneered.

"Way back in the Middle Ages," she said, "it was common knowledge that the sun went around Earth . . ."

But I was giving her only half my attention. Out of the corner of my eyes I was watching Doc Jenkins. He was edging gradually towards the switch of the power point into which the welding tool was plugged. I shrugged. I didn't see why he had to be so surreptitious about it. If Peggy wanted to finish whatever welding she had been doing when I had disturbed them, what did it matter?

Or perhaps it did matter.

I said, "I suppose this welded seam is tight?"

"Of course," she said.

"Then we'll get back amidships. You've plenty of work to do in the auxiliary motor room."

"I have," she admitted.

Then my curiosity got the better of me. "But just how," I demanded, "did you ever hope to attain FTL?"

"This," she said, gesturing with the torch towards the breech of the gun, "is an auxiliary rocket. There is already a charge of solid propellant—Doc mixed it for me—in the firing chamber. We were going to connect up the wiring to the detonator when you interrupted us."

"It's just as well that I did interrupt you," I said. "But how was it supposed to work?"

"I thought that it would be obvious. The ship is already proceeding at almost the speed of light. The rocket is just to give her the extra nudge . . ."

I couldn't help laughing. "Peggy, Peggy, how naive can you be? And with homemade solid propellant yet!"

"Solid propellants have their advantages," she said.

"Such as?" I asked scornfully.

"This!" she snapped.

The welding torch flared blindingly. I realized her intention, but too late. As I tried to wrest the tool from her hands the metal casing of the firing chamber was already cherry red.

I felt rather than heard the *whoomph* of the exploding powder . . .

III: THE WINDS OF IF

Chapter 14

EVERYTHING WAS DIFFERENT, and yet the same.

"Even so," Ralph was saying, "the chow in this wagon leaves much to be desired."

I looked up irritably from the simmering pot of lamb curry on the stove top—and then, obeying an odd impulse, I looked down again, stared at the savory stew of meat and vegetables and hot spices, stared at my hand, still going through the stirring motions with the spoon.

I asked myself: *What am I doing here?*

"You have about three pet dishes," went on Ralph. "I admit that you do them well. But they're all that you *do* do well . . ."

This time I did look up at him. *What was he doing in civilian shirt and shorts?* Then, pursuing the thought, *But why should the Federation Government's observer, even though he is a full commander in the Survey Service, be wearing uniform?*

"Sandra's getting browned off with the lack of variety," said Ralph.

"Mrs. Malcolm, you mean," I corrected him coldly.

691

"*Captain* Malcolm, if you insist," he corrected me, grinning.

I shrugged. "All right. I'm only the catering officer, and she's the captain. At the same time, I *am* the catering officer, and she's my wife."

"Such a set up," said Ralph, "would never be tolerated in a Federation ship. To be frank, I came out to the Rim as much to see how the Feminists managed as to investigate the potentialities of this fancy new drive of yours. And this ship, cut off from the Universe for objective years, is the ideal microcosm."

"We get by, out here on the Rim," I said shortly.

"Even so," he said, "you're not a Rim Worlder yourself. You're none of you Rim Worlders, born and bred, except the engineer and that tame telepath of yours. I can understand the women coming out here, but not the men. It must rankle when you're allowed to come into space only in a menial capacity."

"Our boss, Commodore Grimes, is a man," I said. "And most of the Rim Runners fleet is manned by the male sex. Anyhow, there's nothing menial in being a cook. I'm far happier than I was as purser in the Waverly Royal Mail. Furthermore," I said, warming up to the subject, "all the best chefs are men."

Ralph wiped a splatter of curry from his shirt. (I had gestured dramatically with my spoon.) "But it doesn't follow," he said, "that all men are the best chefs."

"Everybody likes my curry," I told him.

"But not all the time. Not for every meal," he said. "Well, Malcolm, I'll leave you to it. And since we have to eat your curry, you might see that the rice isn't so soggy this time."

Interfering bastard, I thought. I brought the spoon to my lips and tasted. It wasn't a bad curry, I decided. It wasn't a bad curry at all. Served with the sliced cucumber and the shredded coconut and the chopped banana, together with the imported mango chutney from Caribbea, it would be edible. Of course, there should be Bombay Duck. I wondered, as I had often wondered before, if it would be possible to convert the fish that flourished in our algae vats into that somewhat odorous delicacy.

Again I was interrupted.

"*More* curry?" complained Claude Smethwick.

"It's good," I told him. I scooped up a spoonful. "Taste."

"Not bad," he admitted. "If you like curry, that is. I don't have to be telepath to know that you do." He handed the spoon back to me. "But I didn't come here to get a preview of dinner."

"Then what did you come for?" I asked shortly.

"Peter, there's something wrong about this ship. You're the only one that I can talk to about it. Commander Listowel's an outsider, and Doc has gone on one of his verse and vodka jags, and the others are . . . women."

"They can't help it," I said.

"I know they can't—but they look at things differently from the way that we do. Apart from anything else, every one of them is chasing after that Survey Service commander . . ."

"Every one?" I asked coldly.

"Not Sandra, of course," he assured me hastily. (Too hastily?) "But Sandra's got all the worries of the ship—after all, she is captain of the first interstellar lightjammer—on her shoulders, and Martha and Peggy are trying hard to get into Listowel's good books—and bed?—and so there's only you."

"I'm flattered," I said, stirring the curry.

"There's something wrong," he said.

"You said that before," I told him.

"And I'll say it again," he said.

"Well, what *is* wrong?" I demanded.

"You know the *déjà vu* feeling that you get when the Mannschenn Drive starts up? Well, it's something like that. But it's not that . . . it's more, somehow."

"I think I know what you mean . . ." I said slowly.

He went on, "You'll think that I'm crazy, I know. But that doesn't matter—all you so-called normals think that psi people like me are at least halfway round the bend. But I've a theory: couldn't it be that out here, on the Rim, on the very edge of this expanding Galaxy, there's a tendency for alternative time tracks to merge? For example, just suppose that the feminist ships had never got out here . . ."

"But they did," I said.

"But they could very easily not have done. After all, it was back in the days of the Ehrenhaft drive, the gaussjammers. And you've read your history, and you know how many of those cranky brutes got slung away to hell and gone off course by magnetic storms."

"So in this alternative Universe of yours," I said tolerantly, "the Rim Worlds never got colonized."

"I didn't say that. You've only to look at the personnel of this ship—all outsiders but Peggy and myself, and neither Peggy nor I can claim descent from the first families. My ancestors came out long after the feminist movement had fizzled on Earth, and so did Peggy's . . ."

I stirred the curry thoughtfully. "So on another time track there's another *Aeriel*, the first of her kind in space, and another Peter Malcolm in the throes of cooking up a really first-class curry for his unappreciative shipmates."

"Could be," he said. "Or the ship could have a different name, or we could be serving in her in different capacities—all but myself, of course."

I burst into song.

> *"Oh, I am the Cook, and the Captain bold,*
> *And the mate of the Nancy brig,*
> *And the Bo's'n tight, and the Midshipmite,*
> *And the crew of the Captain's gig!"*

"But not," I was interrupted, "the engineer."

I turned away from the stove. "Oh, it's you, Peggy."

"Who else?" She took the spoon from my hand, raised it to her lips, blew on it. She sipped appreciatively. "Not bad, not bad . . ." A few drops of the sauce dribbled on to the breast of her once-white boiler suit, but she ignored them. They made quite a contrast, I decided, to the smears of black grease. She said, "You'll do me for a rough working mate, Peter."

"Thank you."

She absentmindedly put the spoon into a side pocket that

already held a wrench and a hammer. I snatched it back, carefully wiped it and returned it to the pot.

She asked, her voice deliberately casual, "Have you seen Ralph?"

"I think he's gone up to the control room," I told her.

She said sulkily, "He's been promising to let me show him the auxiliary motor room for the last three days."

"After all," I consoled her, "he's not an engineer commander."

"But . . ."

"Curry again?" complained a fresh voice.

I resumed my stirring with an unnecessary clatter. I muttered mutinously, "If my galley is going to be turned into the ship's social club there won't be anything. But aren't you supposed to be on watch, Miss Wayne?"

"The old woman relieved me," she said. "She's showing Ralph just how a lightjammer should be handled." She leaned back against a bench, slimly elegant in her tailored shirt and shorts, nibbling a piece of celery she had picked up from the chopping board. "If the Federation Survey Service doesn't build a fleet of improved Erikson drive wagons it won't be Sandra's fault."

"Love me, love my ship," muttered Peggy.

"What was that?" I asked sharply.

"Nothing," she said.

Both women looked at me in silence, and I was suddenly afraid that what I could read in their eyes was pity.

Chapter 15

≈≈ ≈

EVERYTHING was different again.

I was relaxing in the easy chair in the captain's day room, smoking a cigarette and listening to a recording of the old-time sea chanteys of distant Earth. I wondered what those ancient sailormen would have made of this fabrication of metal and plastic, with atomic fire in her belly, spreading her wings in the empty gulf between the stars, running free before the photon gale. Then I heard the door between bathroom and bedroom open, and I turned my head. Sandra, naked from her shower, walked slowly to the chair at her dressing table and sat down before the mirror. I had seen her naked many times before. (But had I?) But this was the first time. (But how could it be?) I felt the stirrings of desire.

I got up and walked through to the bedroom. I put my hands gently on her smooth shoulders, kissed her gently behind the ear.

"No," she said. *"No."*

"But . . ."

"I've done my hair," she said, "and I don't want it messed up."

"Damn it all," I told her, "we *are* married."

But are we? I asked myself.

"Take your hands off me," she ordered coldly.

I did so, and looked at her and at her reflection in the mirror. She was beautiful. But I tried to find fault. There was that mole just above her navel. And the feeble gravitational field was kind to her; her breasts were proud and outthrusting without artificial support, her stomach flat. *In a heavy gravitational field,* I told myself, *she would not be as lovely.*

But I knew that she would be.

"Don't maul me," she said.

"Sorry," I muttered.

I went to sit on the bed.

"Haven't you anything better to do?" she asked.

"No," I said.

She made a sound that can only be described as a snarl and then, ignoring me, went on with her toilet. There was a session with the whirring hair dryer, after which she affixed glittering clips to the lobes of her ears. She got up then and walked to the wardrobe, ignoring me. She took out a uniform shirt of thin black silk, a pair of black shorts and a pair of stiletto-heeled black sandals. Her back to me, she shrugged into the shirt and then pulled the shorts up over her long, slim legs. She sat on the bed (and I might as well not have been there) and buckled the sandals over her slender feet. She returned to the mirror and with a tiny brush applied lip rouge.

"Going ashore?" I asked sarcastically.

"If you must know," she told me, "Commander Listowel has a fine collection of films made by the Survey Service on worlds with non-human cultures."

"Good," I said. "I'll brush my hair and wash behind the ears."

"You," she said, "were not invited."

"But . . ."

Her manner softened—but briefly, very briefly. "I'm sorry, Peter, but when senior officers of different space services want to talk shop they don't want juniors in their hair."

"I see," I said.

She got up from the chair. In the form-molding shirt, the abbreviated shorts, she looked more naked than she had when she had come through from the shower. I was acutely conscious that under the skimpy garments there was a woman. *My* woman. (Or was she? Had she ever been?)

"You needn't wait up for me," she said.

"Thank you," I said.

"You're rather sweet," she said, "in your own way."

"Thank you," I said.

I watched her go, then lit another cigarette and stuck it in my mouth. I knew now what was happening. I'd seen it happen before, to other people, but that didn't make it any better. Ashore it would have been bad enough—but here, in deep space, with Sandra the absolute monarch of this little, artificial world, there was nothing at all I could do. Ashore, even in a feminist culture, a man can take strong action against an erring wife and her paramour. But if I took action here I should be classed as a mutineer.

But there must be something that I could do about it.

There must be *something*.

How much did Martha know? How much did Peggy know?

Women know women as no man can ever know them. There is that freemasonry, the lodge into which no male may ever intrude. There is the freemasonry—but, too, there are the rivalries within the lodge. There is the bitchiness. And all is fair in love and war, and if I could turn the jealousy being felt by both Martha and Peggy to my own account, so much the better. (It would have been better still to have slugged it out with Listowel and then to have dragged Sandra by the hair, kicking and screaming, to bed—but, knowing Sandra, so far as any man can know any woman, I didn't feel like taking the risk. She was still the captain, and I was the cook, and the extreme penalty for mutiny in space is death.)

Peggy, I thought, would be the best bet. As a woman Martha might hate Sandra's guts, but as mate she would be loyal to the captain. Peggy, brought up in the workshop rather than the wardroom, would be less overawed by gold braid and Queen Mother's regulations.

I still didn't like it. It seemed more than somewhat gutless to go whining in search of outside help, but I was feeling desperate. I threw my cigarette in the general direction of the disposer, then got up and went into the alleyway. I looked towards the door of the guest room, in which Listowel was berthed, and wondered what was happening behind it. I almost strode towards it, my fists clenched ready to start hammering on the featureless panel. Almost.

But I hadn't the guts.

I went, instead, to the companionway leading down to the next deck, to the compartment in which the subordinate officers were housed. From Martha's cabin drifted the faint strains of music—or of what she called music, a recording of one of Krashenko's atonal symphonies. So she was alone, which meant that Peggy would be alone too. (Peggy made no secret of the fact that she liked something "with a bit of tune to it.") Doc Jenkins, as acting second mate, would be on watch. And Claude Smethwick almost certainly would be sending his thoughts ranging across the lightyears, gossiping with his fellow telepaths aboard distant ships and on distant worlds.

I tapped at Peggy's door and heard her call out what I thought was an invitation to enter.

I stepped into the cabin—then started to back out. She was prone on her bunk, absorbing the radiation of a sunlamp. She was wearing a pair of dark glasses and a thoughtful expression.

I stammered, "I'm sorry. I thought you said to come in."

She said, "I did say come in. Shut the door. There's a draft."

I shut the door, then sat down heavily in the chair. It was rather too close to the bunk. (Or, perhaps, it wasn't close enough . . .) I thought, *To hell with it. If she's not embarrassed, why should I be?* and looked at her with appreciation. There was something hauntingly familiar about her unclad body as well as something surprising. In her overalls she was dumpy and unglamorous—naked, she was rather beautiful. She was plump, but in the places where it counted, and her waist was narrow. I thought that I should be able to get my two hands around it. I thought that it would be nice to try.

She said, "A penny for them."

I told her, "I was wondering if this lamp of yours could be used to make Bombay Duck."

She asked, "What is Bombay Duck?"

I said, "It's fish, uncooked and dried in the sun. It stinks. You crumble it over curry."

She said, "You're a bloody liar, Peter."

"I'm not. That's all that Bombay Duck is. Stinking dried fish."

"I'm not disputing that. Your thoughts, at this moment, may be below your navel, but they're not centered on your stomach."

"Well . . ." I muttered lamely.

"And furthermore, Mr. Malcolm, you needn't expect that I'm going to catch you on the rebound, or that you're going to catch me the same way."

I said, "It would be a neat solution."

"Now, perhaps. But probably a messy one later, when certain persons who shall be nameless decide that their duties to their respective services come first." She declaimed:

> *I could not love thee, deah, so much,*
> *Loved I not honor more.*"

I said, "Do you mind if I smoke?"

She said, "I don't care if you burst into flame."

"Not very original," I told her. "And not very funny." I lit a cigarette. She stretched a shapely arm and took it from me, but still succeeded in displaying no more than her rear elevation. I lit another cigarette and put it to my lips. I said, "Come to think of it, it is rather hot in here."

"Is it?" she asked. Then she said, "No, you may not remove your shirt. And you may not, repeat not, remove your shorts. If you do, I shall holler rape. And as you're in my cabin, and not I in yours, you'll find yourself well in the cactus."

"Oh," I said.

"Precisely," she said.

For a while I smoked in silence, and she smoked in silence. I thought, *You can look, but you can't touch.* I asked, "Aren't you done on that side?"

She said, "No."

We smoked in silence; this time, she broke it.

"Why did you come to see me, Peter?"

I said, "I thought you might be able to help."

"And why should I want to help you?"

"Just enlightened self-interest," I said. "You want Listowel, God knows why. I want Sandra back. If you get that stuffed shirt commander it'll leave my everloving wife at loose ends—and I don't think, somehow, that she'll make a pass at either Doc Jenkins or poor old Claude."

"All right," she said. "You help me, and I help you. If the old woman returns to her husband that leaves Ralph all on his ownsome. Then Martha and I can fight it out between us."

"This mutual aid . . ." I said.

"It's all rather complicated," Peggy told me. She threw the end of her cigarette into the disposer. "It all hinges on the fact that Sandra puts the ship first. And I think—mind you, it's not a certainty—that you can get yourself well into her good books. How would it be if you could say, 'Look, darling, I've made you the captain of the first FTL ship in history'?"

"This ship is not faster than light," I said. "But the Mannschenn Drive ships are, and the Ehrenhaft drive wagons, what few there are left of them."

"Is that so?" she countered.

"Of course," I said.

"Oh." She paused for a second or so, then said slowly, "Correct me if I'm wrong, but the Erikson drive, as it stands, will never be a commercial success. It takes far too long for a cargo, even a non-perishable cargo for which there's no mad rush, to be carted from point A to point B. And there's the problem of manning, too. As far as this ship was concerned, Auntie Susan was able to assemble a bunch of misfits with no close ties for the job, people who wouldn't give a damn if the round voyage lasted a couple or three centuries—objective centuries, that is. Or even subjective. But it mightn't be so easy to find another crew for another lightjammer. Agreed?"

I said, "You drifted away from the script."

"What do you mean?" she asked. Her face looked frightened.

"Nothing," I said. "Nothing. It's just that I seem to have heard you say almost the same words before."

She said, but doubtfully, "You're space-happy, Peter." Then she went on: "I'm new in space, relatively new compared to the rest of you, but I've read plenty. I'm no physicist, but I have a rough idea of the *modus operandi* of the various interstellar drives. And, so far, there's been no faster-than-light drive."

"What!" I exclaimed, but somehow I didn't feel as surprised as I should have.

"No, there hasn't. I'm right, Peter. The basic idea of the Ehrenhaft drive was that of a magnetic particle trying to be in two places at the same time in a magnetic field or current, the ship being the particle. But, as far as I can gather, space was warped so that she could do just that. I couldn't follow the math, but I got the general drift of it. And then, of course, there's the Mannschenn Drive—but, there, the apparent FTL speeds are achieved by tinkering with time . . ."

"Hmm," I grunted. "Hmm."

"Getting away from machinery," she said, "and back to personalities, Sandra loves her ship. I'm sure that if she had to make a choice between Ralph and *Aeriel* it wouldn't be *Aeriel* left in the lurch. Or if she had to make a choice between you and *Aeriel* . . . but what do you think she'd feel about the man who made her captain of the first real FTL starwagon?"

I said, "You'd better see Doc when he comes off watch. He stocks quite a good line in sedative mixtures."

She said, "You're turning down a good chance, perhaps your only chance, Peter."

"Damn it all," I said, "even I, and I'm no physicist, can tell you that it's quite impossible to exceed the speed of light. As you have already pointed out, we can cheat, but that's all. And in this ship we can't even cheat. We can no more outrun light than a windjammer could outrun the wind that was her motive power." I started to point towards something that wasn't there. "That's our log. It works by Doppler effect. At the moment our speed is . . ."

She looked at me hard, a puzzled expression on her face. "A log? Here? What the hell's wrong with you, Peter?"

I said, "I don't know."

She said, "There's something screwy about this ship. But

definitely. Anyhow, let me finish what I was going to say. I maintain that we can give it a go—exceeding the speed of light, I mean."

"But it's impossible," I said.

"How do you know?" she countered.

"It's common knowledge," I sneered.

"Way back in the Middle Ages," she said, "it was common knowledge that the sun went round the Earth."

"Oh, all right," I grunted. "But tell me, please, just how do you expect to attain FTL speeds?"

"With an auxiliary rocket," she said. "Just a stovepipe, sticking out from the stern end of the ship. I can make it—and you, with your access to the chemicals for the hydroponics tanks, can make the solid propellant, the black powder. We're doing about Lume 0.9 recurring at the moment, all we need is a nudge . . ."

I couldn't help laughing. "Peggy, Peggy, how naive can you be? And with homemade solid propellant yet!"

"You can make it," she said. "And it's to your advantage."

I looked at her. During our heated discussion she had turned over. The dark glasses made her look so much more naked. I said, "I'm not sure that I'm really interested in getting Sandra back . . ."

She flopped back again on her belly in a flurry of limbs.

She said coldly, "Let's not forget the purpose of this discussion. Frankly, it was my intention to bribe you with the body beautiful to play along with me on this FTL project, but it wouldn't be right. You want Sandra back, and I want Ralph. Let's keep it that way, shall we?"

"But . . ." I extended a hand to one smooth buttock.

"On your bicycle, spaceman," she told me. "Hit the track. Make another pass, and I holler rape. After all, you're in my cabin, I'm not in yours. Come and see me again when you've got two or three pounds of black powder made up. And if you can't make it, then Martha and I will figure out some other way."

I asked, "She's in on this?"

"Of course," said Peggy scornfully. "I hate the bitch, but she's a good mate. I'd never be able to cut a hole in the stern for my auxiliary rocket unless she approved."

My hand had strayed back again and was stroking the silky skin on her back. I imagined that I heard her purring, like some great, sleek, lazy cat. And then, with shocking suddenness, she was off the bunk and bundling me towards the door.

"Out," she snarled. "Out. And don't come back until you have that powder."

"But . . ."

"Out!" she said with determined finality, and I was standing in the alleyway, staring resentfully at the panel that had slammed shut on her golden loveliness.

I don't know whether or not you have ever tried to make black powder, but I can tell you this: it's easier talking about it than doing it. You want flowers of sulfur, and you want charcoal (or carbon) and you want saltpeter. At first I made the mistake of trying to mix the ingredients dry, and all I got was a grayish dust that burned with a half-hearted fizzle. Then I substituted potassium chlorate for the sodium nitrate, and my sample went off prematurely and took my eyebrows with it. I came to the conclusion then that the powder would have to be properly mixed with water, and then dried out—using, of course, the recommended ingredients. And it worked out, even though I dried the sludge by exposure to vacuum instead of in the sun, as was done (I suppose) by the first cannoneers.

Anyhow, it was as well that I had something to occupy my mind. It was obvious, far too obvious, what was going on between Listowel and Sandra. Peggy's scheme was a harebrained one, but it might just get results. I had little doubt that it would get results—but what those results would be I could not imagine. Meanwhile, everybody in *Aeriel* continued to do his or her appointed duty, even though the ship was fast becoming a seething caldron of sexual jealousies.

And then, one night (as reckoned by our chronometer) I had the last batch of gunpowder mixed and dried. There was a five-gallon can full of the stuff. I picked it up, let myself out of the galley and made my way to the officers' flat. As I entered the alleyway I saw Doc Jenkins knocking on the door of Martha Wayne's cabin. I wondered who was in control, and then wished that I hadn't wondered. The control room would be well-manned, of course. There would be the captain, and there would be that blasted Survey Service commander, the pair of them looking at the stars and feeling romantic.

"Ah," said Jenkins, noticing me, "the commissioned cook. In person. Singing and dancing."

"Neither singing nor dancing," I said grimly.

"And what have you got in the can, Petey boy? You know that I have the monopoly on jungle juice."

"Nothing to drink," I said.

"Then what is it?"

"Something for Peggy."

"Something for Peggy," he mimicked. "Something for Peggy . . ." He quoted:

> *"When in danger or in fear,*
> *Always blame the engineer . . ."*

I tried to edge past him, but he put out his hand and grabbed my arm. In spite of his flabby appearance he was strong. And I was afraid to struggle; there was the possibility that the can of black powder might get a hard knock if I did. (I know that in theory it was quite safe, but I still didn't trust the stuff.)

"Not so fast," he said. "Not so fast. There's something going on aboard this ship, and as one of the executive officers, as well as the surgeon, it's my duty to find out what it is."

The door of the chief officer's cabin slid open. Martha stood there looking at us. "Come in," she ordered sharply. "Both of you."

We obeyed. Martha shut the door behind us and motioned us to chairs. We sat down. With a certain relief I put the can of powder gently on the carpeted deck—and then, before I could stop him, Doc snatched it up. He shook it.

He demanded, "What's in this?"

"Some powder," I said lamely.

"Powder?" He worried the lid off the container. "Powder? What sort of powder?"

"Abrasive powder," I lied. "Peggy gave me the formula and asked me to cook some up for her."

"Oh." He put the can, lid still off, down beside his chair, away from me. He took a cigarette from the box on Martha's desk, lit it, put it to his lips. He inhaled deeply, inhaled again. The burning end glowed brightly, the ash lengthened as we watched. He made as though to use the open can as an ash tray.

Martha's hand flashed out, smacked the cigarette from his fingers and sent it flying across the cabin in a flurry of sparks.

Jenkins looked hurt. "What was that in aid of?"

She said, "You were going to spoil the . . . mixture."

"How? If it's abrasive powder, a little ash might improve it."

"Not this mixture," she said.

"No," I supported her. "No. It wouldn't."

"I'm not altogether a fool," grumbled Jenkins.

"No?" asked Martha sweetly. "No?" She extended a slender leg, and with her slim foot gently shoved the can out of harm's way. "No?"

"No!" he almost shouted. "I've lived on primitive worlds, Martha, planets where military science is in its infancy. And here's Peter, lugging around a dirty great cannister of villainous saltpeter, and there's Peggy, sweating and slaving over something that looks like a breech-loading cannon." He snorted. "If it were a couple of dueling pieces it would make sense. Pistols for two and coffee for one. And then after the commissioned cook and the bold commander had settled their differences, you and Peggy could do battle, at twenty paces, for the favors of the survivor.

"But a cannon . . . it doesn't make sense."

"No, it doesn't," agreed Martha. She got up and went to a locker. I thought that she was going to offer us drinks. There were racked bottles there, and glasses. And there was a drawer under the liquor compartment, which she pulled open. She took from it a nasty-looking Minetti automatic.

She said, "I'm sorry, Doc, but you know too much. We have to keep you quiet for the next few hours. And you, Peter, see about tying him up and gagging him, will you?" She motioned with the pistol. "Down, boy, down. I shan't shoot to kill—but you wouldn't like your kneecaps shattered, would you?"

Jenkins subsided. He looked scared—and, at the same time, oddly amused. "But I don't know too much," he expostulated. "I don't know enough."

Martha allowed a brief smile to flicker over her full mouth. She glanced at me fleetingly. "Shall we tell him, Peter?"

I said, "It wouldn't do any harm. Now."

Martha sat down again, the hand with the pistol resting on one slender thigh. It remained pointing directly at Jenkins. Her finger never strayed from the trigger.

"All right," she said. "I'll put you in the picture. As you are aware, there's a considerable amount of ill-feeling aboard this vessel."

"How right you are!" exclaimed Jenkins.

"We think that the captain is behaving in a manner prejudicial to good order and discipline."

He chuckled softly. "Mutiny, is it? In all my years in space I've never seen one. But why that absurd, archaic cannon? After all, you've access to the ship's firearms." He added, "As you've just proved, Martha."

"It's not mutiny," she snapped.

"Have I another guess?"

She told him, "You can guess all the way from here to Grollor, but you'll never guess right."

"No?" He made as though to rise from his chair, but her gun hand twitched suggestively. "No? Then why not tell me and get it over with."

"If you must know," she said tiredly, "it's a way—it might work and it might not—to distract Sandra's attention from Ralph. She's more in love with her ship than with anybody in the ship but if Peter were to be able to say, 'Look, darling, thanks to me you are now the captain of the first real FTL starwagon,' she'd be eating out of his hand."

He stared at me in mock admiration. "I didn't know you had it in you, Peter."

"He hasn't," said Sandra. "It was Peggy and I who cooked up the scheme. We don't know if it will succeed or not—but *something* is bound to happen when Peggy's solid fuel rocket gives the ship just that extra nudge."

"And all these years," whispered Jenkins, "I've regarded you as just a stuffed shirt—mind you, a well-stuffed shirt—and Peggy as a barely literate mechanic. But there's a streak of wild poetry in you, in both of you. Mind you, I don't think that Listowel is worth the trouble. But throwing your bonnet over the windmill is always worthwhile. This crazy scheme appeals to me. I'm with it, Martha, and I'm with you. I've been dreaming about something on those lines myself, but not so practically as you have done . . ."

His hand went to the side pocket of his shorts—and Martha's hand, holding the pistol, lifted to cover him. But it was a folded sheet of paper that he pulled out.

"Martha," he pleaded, "put the *Outer Reaches Suite* on your playmaster, will you? Or get Peter to put it on, if you don't trust me. And, if you would be so good, something to wet my whistle . . ."

"Fix it, Peter," ordered Martha.

I fixed it, first of all pouring a stiff whiskey on the rocks for each of us, then adjusting the controls of the gleaming instrument. The first notes of the Suite drifted into the cabin. It wasn't music that I have ever cared for. There was too much of loneliness in it, too much of the blackness and the emptiness—the emptiness that, somehow, was not empty, that was peopled with the dim, flimsy ghosts of the might-have-been.

Jenkins drained his glass, then unfolded the piece of paper and blinked at it.

> *"Down the years*
> *And the lightyears,*
> *Wings widespread*
> *To the silent gale . . .*
> *Wide wings beating*
> *The wall between*
> *Our reality and our reality*

And realities undreamed . . .
And realities undreamed . . .
Or dreamed?
Down the years
And the darkness—"

He broke off abruptly, and Martha stiffened, her Minetti swinging to cover the open door. Peggy was there, demanding irritably, "Aren't you people going to lend a hand? Do I do all the work in this bloody ship?" She saw Doc, muttered, "Sorry. Didn't know you had company."

"*We* have company, Peggy," corrected Martha.

"You mean he . . ."

"Yes. He knows."

"Yes, indeed," agreed Doc happily. "And I'll help you to beat your wings against the wall."

"What wall?" demanded Peggy disgustedly.

It was odd that we now trusted Doc without any question. Or was it so odd? There were those half-memories, there was the haunting feeling that we had done all this before. Anyhow, we poured Peggy a drink, had another one ourselves, and then made our way aft. In the workshop we picked up the thing that Peggy had been making. It did look like a cannon, and not a small one either. It was fortunate that our acceleration was now extremely gentle, otherwise it would have been impossible for us to handle that heavy steel tube without rigging tackles.

We got it down at last to the transom space and dropped it on the after bulkhead. Martha climbed back, with Peggy and myself, into the airscrew motor room; Doc stayed below. While Peggy and I climbed into spacesuits Martha passed the other equipment down to Jenkins—the welding and cutting tools, the can of powder. And then Doc came up, and Peggy and I, armored against cold and vacuum, took his place.

Over our heads the airtight door slid shut. I heard the faint whirr of the pump that Peggy had installed in the motor room, and realized that the atmosphere was being evacuated from our compartment. I saw the needle of the gauge on the wrist of my suit falling, and watched it continue to drop even when I could no longer hear anything.

Peggy's voice in my helmet phones was surprisingly loud.

She said, "Let's get moving."

It was Peggy who did most of the work. A tool in her hands was an extension of her body—or even an extension of her personality. The blue-flaring torch cut a neat round hole in the bulkhead and then, after I had lifted the circle of still glowing steel away and clear, in the shell plating beyond. This section I kicked out, and watched fascinated as it diminished slowly, a tiny, twinkling star against the utter blackness. Peggy irritably pulled me back to the work in hand. Together we maneuvered the rocket tube into place. It was a tight fit, but not too tight. And then Peggy stitched metal to metal with the delicate precision that an ancestor might have displayed with needle, thread and fine fabric.

I watched her with something akin to envy—and it was more than her manual dexterity that I envied. She had something that occupied all her attention; I had not. I had time to doubt, and to wonder. At the back of my mind a nagging, insistent voice was saying, *No good will come of this.*

I heard Peggy's satisfied grunt in my helmet phones and saw that the job was finished. She unscrewed the breech of the tube, and flipped it back on its hinge. She picked up a wad of rags, shoved it down the barrel, but not too far down. I managed to get the lid off the powder cannister and handed it to her. She poured the black grains onto the wad. Her guess as to the positioning of it had been a good one; only a spoonful of gunpowder remained in the can. This she transferred to a tubular recess in the middle of the breech block, stoppering it with another scrap of rag. She replaced the block then, gasping slightly as she gave it that extra half-turn to ensure that it was well and tightly home.

"O.K., Martha," she said. "You can let the air back in."

"Valve open," Martha's voice said tinnily from the phones.

I watched the needle of my wrist gauge start to rise, and heard after a while the thin, high screaming of the inrushing atmosphere.

And then the airtight door over our heads opened and I saw Martha and Doc framed in the opening, looking not at us but at what we had done. After a second's hesitation they joined us in the transom space. Martha helped Peggy off with her helmet; Doc removed mine for me.

"A neat job," said Martha.

"It will do," said Peggy.

"I hope," added Doc, but he did not seem unduly worried.

"You wire her up," said Peggy to Martha. "I can't do it in these damn gloves."

"Anything to oblige," murmured Martha. She handed the double cable that she had brought down with her to Jenkins and started to loosen the thumbscrews on the breech block.

"I know that I'm only the captain," said a cold, a very cold voice, "but might I inquire what the hell you're doing?"

"We're going to make this bitch roll and go," replied Jenkins happily.

I looked up from the makeshift rocket and saw that Sandra and Listowel were standing in the motor room, looking down at us through the doorway. Sandra was icily furious. Listowel looked mildly interested.

Sandra's finger pointed first at Peggy, then at myself. "Spacesuits . . . have you been outside?" she demanded.

"No," said Peggy.

"Don't worry, skipper," said Jenkins. "We didn't lose any atmosphere. We sealed the transom space off before Peggy and Peter went to work, and put the pump on it . . ."

"*But you pierced the hull,*" she said with mounting anger.

"Only a small hole," admitted Jenkins.

"This," she grated, "is too much. Only a couple of weeks out and you're already space-happy. Burning holes in the pressure plating and risking all our lives. Are you mad?"

"No," stated Doc. "And when you find out what it's about you'll be pleased."

"Pleased? I shall be pleased all right. I shall roll on the deck in uncontrollable ecstasy. And I'll have your guts for a necktie,

and then I'll boot you out of the airlock without spacesuits.
I'll—"

"Be reasonable, Sandra," admonished Listowel rashly.

"Reasonable? I am being reasonable. All these officers have
work that they should be doing, instead of which I find them
engaged in some fantastic act of sabotage . . ."

"Sandra," I put in, "I can explain."

"*You?* You ineffectual puppy!" I saw with shock that there was
a pistol in her hand. "Come up out of there, all of you. That is an order."
She turned to her companion. "Commander Listowel, as captain of this
vessel I request your aid in dealing with these mutineers."

"But—" I began.

"Drop whatever you're doing," she snapped, "and come up."

"Better do as she says," grumbled Peggy. She picked up her
welding torch.

"Just let us tell you what it's all about, skipper," pleaded Jenkins,
edging towards the power point into which the torch was plugged.

"No," said Sandra flatly.

"But . . ." murmured Peggy, her voice trailing off.

There was the sharp click of a switch and the torch flared
blindingly. I realized Peggy's intention, but too late. As I tried to
wrest the tool from her hands (but why? but why?), the metal casing
of the firing chamber was already cherry red.

I felt rather than heard the *whoomph* of the exploding
powder . . .

Chapter 16

≈≈ ⟋⟍

HER BODY AGAINST MINE was warm and resilient, yielding—and then, at the finish, almost violently possessive. There was the flaring intensity of sensation, prolonged to the limits of endurance, and the long, long fall down into the soft darkness of the sweetest sleep of all.

And yet . . .

"Sandra . . ." I started to say, before my eyes were properly focused on the face beside mine on the pillow.

She snapped back into full consciousness and stared at me coldly.

"What was that, Peter? I've suspected that . . ."

"I don't know, Peggy," I muttered. "I don't know . . ."

I don't know, I thought. *I don't know. But I remember . . . what do I remember? Some crazy dream about another ship, another light-jammer, with Sandra as the captain and myself as catering officer and Ralph as some sort of outsider. And I was married to Sandra in this dream, and I'd lost her, and I was trying to win her back with Peggy's help. There was something about a solid fuel rocket . . .*

"What is it, Peter?" she asked sharply.

"A dream," I told her. "It must have been a dream . . ."

I unsnapped the elastic webbing that held us to the bunk and floated away from it and from Peggy to the center of the cabin. I looked around me, noting details in the dim light, trying to reassure myself of its reality, of our reality. It was all so familiar, and all so old. The ghosts of those who had lived here, who had loved here and hated here, generation after generation, seemed to whisper to me, *This is* Thermopylae. *This is all the world you have ever known, ever will know . . .*

It was all so unfamiliar.

And Peggy . . .

I turned to look at her as she lay on the bed, still held there by the webbing, the bands startlingly white against her golden skin. She was real enough. Her naked beauty was part of my memories—all my memories.

"Peter," she said. "Peter, come back."

From nowhere a tag of poetry drifted into my mind, and I murmured,

> *". . . and home there's no returning.*
> *The Spartans on the sea-wet rock sat down*
> *and combed their hair."*

It made an odd sort of sense.

Thermopylae—the last stand of the Spartans, back in the early dawn of Terran history; *Thermopylae*—one of the great windjammers that sailed Earth's seas; *Thermopylae*—the last stand of the Spartacists . . .

"Come back," she called pleadingly.

"I'm here," I told her. "I'm here. It was just that I had a little trouble getting myself oriented."

Stretching my right leg I was just able to touch the bulkhead with the tip of my big toe, and I shoved gently. I drifted back in the general direction of the bed. Peggy extended her arm and caught me, pulled me to her.

"Born in the ship," she scolded, "raised in the ship, and you still haven't the sense to put your sandals on . . ."

"There was that . . . strangeness . . ." I faltered.

"If that's what I do to you, my boy, I'd better see about getting a divorce. There's nothing strange about us. I'm a perfectly prosaic plumber, and you're a prurient purser, and our names start with a P as well as our ratings, so we're obviously made for each other. At least, I thought so until just now . . . but when the bridegroom, on his wedding night, starts calling his blushing bride by another woman's name it's rather much!" She smiled tantalizingly. "Of course, I had quite a crush on Ralph once—not that he'd ever notice me. Plumbers are rather beneath the captain's notice. He reminds me so much of my father . . ." Her face sobered. "I wonder what it would be like to live on a real world, a planet, with ample living room and with no necessity to stash parents away in the deep freeze when they've lived their allotted span? I wonder if our fathers and mothers, and their fathers and mothers, will ever be revived to walk on grass and breathe fresh air . . . I wonder if we shall ever be revived after we're put away to make room for *our* children . . ." She reached out for something from the bedside locker—and suddenly her expression was one of puzzlement and disappointment. She whispered, "I wanted a cigarette. I wanted a cigarette to smoke and to wave in the air as I talked . . ."

I asked, "What is a cigarette?"

"I . . . I don't know . . . I think it would be one of those tiny, white smoldering tubes that characters are always playing with in the old films . . . those men and women who played out their dramas on worlds like Earth and Austral and Caribbea, or aboard ships that could cross the Galaxy in a matter of months." She said intensely, "At times I hate the Spartacists. It was all very well for them, the disgruntled technicians and scientists who thought that they had become the slaves of capital and organized labor—whatever *they* were—and who staged their futile slave revolt, and built this crazy ship because they hadn't the money or materials to construct a Mannschenn Drive job—whatever *that* was. It was all very well for *them*, the romantic Durnhamites, pushing out under full sail for the Rim Stars—but what about us? Born in this tin coffin, living in this tin coffin and, at the end, put to sleep in this tin coffin—unless we die first—in the hope of a glorious resurrection on some fair planet circling a dim, distant sun. And we've never known the feel of grass under our bare feet, never known the kiss of the sun and the breeze on our skins, making do with fans and UV lamps, taking our exercise in the centrifuge instead of on the playing field or in the swimming pool, subsisting on algae and on tissue cultures that have long since lost any flavor they once had. Why, even on Lorn . . ."

"Even on Lorn?" I echoed.

"What am I saying?" she whispered. "What am I saying? Where is Lorn?"

"Lorn, Faraway, Ultimo and Thule . . ." I murmured. "And the worlds of the Eastern Circuit—Tharn and Grollor, Mellise and Stree . . . Tharn, with the dirt streets in the towns, and the traders' stalls under the flaring gas jets as the evening falls, and the taverns with good liquor and good company . . . Mellise, and the long swell rolling in from halfway across the world, breaking on the white beaches of the archipelago . . ."

"What's happened to us?" she cried. Then, "What have we lost?"

"How can we have lost," I asked, "what we have never known?"

"Dreams," she whispered. "Dreams . . . or the alternative time tracks that Claude is always talking about. Somewhere, or somewhen, another Peter and Peggy have walked the white beaches of Mellise, have swum together in the warm sea. Somewhen we have strolled together along a street on Tharn, and you have bought for me a bracelet of beaten silver . . ."

"Dreams," I said. "But you are the reality, and you are beautiful . . ." As I kissed her, as my caressing hands wandered over her compliant body, desire mounted. But there was a part of myself holding back, there was a cold voice at the back of my mind that said, *You are doing this to forget. You are doing this to forget the worlds and the ships and the women that you have known.* And, coldly, I answered myself with the question, *Is there a better way of forgetting? And why should one not forget a foolish dream?*

Her urgent mouth was on mine and her arms were about me, and forgetfulness was sweet and reality was all we need ever ask, and—

A giant hand slammed us from the bunk, snapping the webbing, hurling against the bulkhead. The single light went out.

We sprawled against the cold, metal surface, held there by some pseudo-gravity, hurt, frightened, still clinging desperately to each other. Dimly I heard the incessant shrilling of alarm bells and somewhere somebody screaming. We felt rather than heard the thudding shut of airtight doors.

The pressure against us relaxed and, slowly, we drifted into the center of the cabin. I held Peggy to me tightly. I could hear her breathing, could feel her chest rising and falling against my own. She stirred feebly.

"Peggy, are you all right?" I cried. "Darling, are you all right?"

"I . . . I think so . . ." she replied faintly. Then, with a flash of the old humor, "Do you have to be so rough?"

There was a crackling sound, and then from the bulkhead speaker issued the voice of Ralph, calm as always, authoratative.

"This is the captain. We have been in collision with a meteor swarm. Will all surviving personnel report to the control room, please? All surviving personnel report to the control room."

"We'd better do as the man says," said Peggy shakily, "even though it means dressing in the dark . . ."

IV: JOURNEY'S END

Chapter 17

WE WERE IN THE CONTROL ROOM—those of us who had survived.

We had made our rounds, armored against cold and vacuum. We had seen the results of our collision with the meteor swarm, the rending and melting of tough metal and plastic, the effects of sudden decompression on human flesh. We had seen too much. Speaking for myself, it was only the uncanny half-knowledge that this was only an evil dream that enabled me to keep a hold on my sanity.

We were in the control room, the seven of us.

There was Ralph Listowel, acting captain, strapped in his seat before the useless controls. Beside him, anchored to the deck by the magnetic soles of her sandals, stood Sandra, acting mate. And there was David Jenkins, ship's surgeon, and very close to him stood Martha Wayne, ship's chronicler. There was Peggy, ship's plumber. There was Claude Smethwick, always the odd man out. There was myself.

We had survived.

We had made our rounds of the stricken *Thermopylae* and had found no other survivors. All the accommodation abaft officers' country had been holed, as had been the dormitory, the deep freeze, in which our parents—and their parents, and *their* parents—had been laid away, in stasis, to await planetfall. But they had never known what had hit them. They were luckier than our generation, for whom there must have been a long second or so of agonised realization, the horror of bursting lungs and viscera, before the end.

"Report," ordered Ralph tiredly.

There was a long silence, which Jenkins was the first to break. He said, "We suited up, and went through the ship. She's like a colander. There are no other survivors."

"None?" asked Ralph.

"No, skipper. Do you wish details?"

"No," said Ralph.

"I made rounds with Doc," said Sandra. "The deep freeze has had it. So has all the accommodation abaft officers' country. So has most of the accommodation forward of the bulkhead. Second mate, third mate, engineers, catering officer—all dead. Very dead . . ."

"And outside?" asked Ralph.

"I saw what I could from the blisters. It's a mess. Spars buckled. Twenty odd square miles of sail in ribbons . . ."

"Report," said Ralph, looking at me.

I told him, "I've been through the farm. We haven't got a farm any more. The tank room and the tissue culture room were both holed. Of course, the deep frozen, dehydrated tissue cultures will keep us going for some time . . ."

"If we had air and water they would," said Jenkins glumly. "But we haven't."

"There are the cylinders of reserve oxygen," I pointed out.

"And how do we get rid of the carbon dioxide?" asked the doctor.

"Chemicals . . ." suggested Peggy vaguely.

"What chemicals?" he demanded. He went on, "Oh, we can keep alive for a few days, or a few weeks—but we shall merely be postponing the inevitable. Better to end it now, skipper. I've got the drugs for the job. It will be quite painless. Pleasant, even."

Ralph turned to Peggy. "Report."

She said, "The generator room's wrecked. The only power we have at our disposal is from the batteries."

"And their life?"

"If we practice the utmost economy, perhaps two hundred hours. But I may be able to get a jenny repaired—"

"And burn up our oxygen reserve running it," said Ralph. Then, to Smethwick, "Report."

"I've tried," the telepath whispered. "I've tried. But there's no contact anywhere. We are alone, lost and alone. But . . ."

"But?" echoed Ralph.

"I . . . I'm not sure . . ." Then, suddenly, Smethwick seemed to gain stature, to change his personality almost. Always until now the shyest and most retiring of men, he dominated us by his vehemence. "Don't *you* have the memories—the memories of the lives you've lived elsewhere, elsewhen? Haven't you any recollection of yourself as Captain Listowel of the Rim Runners, as Commander Listowel of the Federation Survey Service? And the rest of you," he went on, "don't *you* remember? This isn't the only life—or the only death . . ."

"Lorn and Faraway . . ." I said softly.

"Ultimo and Thule . . ." whispered Martha.

"And the planets of the Eastern Circuit," said Sandra flatly.

"You remember," cried Smethwick. "Of course you remember. I'm snooping now. I admit it. You can do what you like to me, but I'm snooping. I'm peeping into your minds. And it all adds up, what I can read of your memories, your half-memories. There's the pattern, the unbreakable pattern. All the time, every time, it's been just the seven of us—aboard *Flying Cloud*, aboard *Aeriel*, and now aboard *Thermopylae* . . .

"There's the pattern . . . we've tried to break free from it, but we've never succeeded. But we have changed it—every time we have changed it—and we can change it again. Whether for better or for worse I cannot say—but it can hardly be for worse *now*."

Ralph was looking at Sandra—and once, I knew, the way that she was looking back at him would have aroused my intense jealousy. "Yes," he said slowly. "I remember . . . hazily . . . even so, wasn't there some trouble with Peter?"

I was holding Peggy close to me. "There was," I said. "But not anymore."

"And what about you, Martha?" asked Sandra. "Do you remember?"

"I do," she said, "but I'm perfectly happy the way things are now. Both David and I are happy—so happy, in fact, that I don't welcome the idea of euthanasia . . ."

"Go on," urged Smethwick. "Go on. Remember!"

"I made a rocket," muttered Peggy hesitantly. "Didn't I?"

"And I mixed a batch of solid fuel," I supported her.

"No," contradicted Doc. "I did."

"Some bastard did," stated Ralph, looking rather hostile.

"Too right," said Sandra. "And whoever it was put us in the jam that we're in now. I was quite happy as catering-officer-cum-third-mate of *Flying Cloud*, and quite happy as captain of *Aeriel*, and I rather resent finding myself chief officer of a dismasted derelict, with only a few days to live."

"*You* might have been happy," I told her, "but you must admit that the way things were aboard *Aeriel* did not, repeat not, contribute to *my* happiness."

"My marriage to you was a big mistake," she said.

"Wasn't it just!" I agreed. "On *my* part! I should have known better. Give a woman a position of authority and she at once abuses it. 'I'm the captain, and I sleep with whom I bloody well please. See?'"

"I resent that," said Sandra.

"Resent away," I told her, "if it makes you any happier. Resenting seems to be your specialty, darling."

"But you were such a bloody lousy cook," she said.

"Like hell I was!" I flared. "I'm a bloody good cook, and you know it. *Aeriel* ate a damn sight better than *Flying Cloud* ever did."

"I suppose," she said, "that you mixed gunpowder in with your curry."

"You wouldn't know the difference," I sneered.

"Who would?" she sneered back.

"I think his curry is good," said Peggy loyally.

"You would," snapped Sandra.

"The rocket!" Claude was screaming. *"The rocket!"*

I told him what to do with the rocket, tail fins and all. I said to Sandra, "It's high time that we got things sorted out. You behaved very shabbily. Even you must admit that. I've nothing against Ralph—in fact I think that's he's more to be pitied than blamed. But if it hadn't been for the way that you carried on aboard both *Flying Cloud* and *Aeriel* there wouldn't have been any rockets. There wouldn't have been any misguided attempts to break the light barrier."

"So it's all my fault," she said sarcastically.

"Of course," I told her.

"And that refugee from a bicycle shop, to whom you happen to be married at the moment, has nothing at all to do with it. Oh, no. And neither has the incompetent pill peddler who mixed the first batch of powder. And neither have you, who mixed the second. But, as far as I'm concerned, what really rankles is this. I don't mind all this switching from one time track to another—after all, variety is the spice of life. What I do object to is being the victim of the blundering machinations of the same bunch of dimwits every bloody time. It's too much. Really, it's too much."

"My heart bleeds for you," I said. "Let me suggest that on the next time track you get you to a nunnery. Preferably a Trappist one. If there are such institutions."

Her face was white with passion. Her hand flashed out and caught me a stinging blow across the mouth. My feet lost their magnetic contact with the deck and I floated backwards, fetching up hard against the bulkhead.

Peggy, her voice bitter, said, "You deserved that."

"No," said Martha. "No. Everything has been Sandra's fault."

"Pipe down," ordered Ralph. "Pipe down, all of you. And you, Malcolm, please refrain from making any more slanderous attacks on my wife."

"*My* wife," I said.

"Not in this continuum," he corrected me. "But what happened in the alternative Universes has a certain bearing upon our present predicament. Thanks to your otherwise unpardonable outburst, we can remember now—"

"And about bloody well time you did," said Claude.

"We can't all be perfect," stated Ralph, with mild sarcasm. "Even so, we can try. We know the way out now—and, this time, we're all of us involved. *All* of us. We must break the light barrier once more, and the only way that we can do it is by giving this wagon that extra push. Has anybody any suggestions?"

Martha said slowly, "We must have been close to Lume 1 when the meteors hit us. But the impact was at right angles to our trajectory . . ."

"Work it out by the parallelogram of forces," Ralph told her. "If you really want to, that is. But we have the Doppler log—it's still working—and that gives us the answer without any fooling around with slipsticks. Even though we are a dismasted derelict we're still bowling along at a good rate. But it'll take more than a powder-fuelled rocket to give us the boost."

"There's the reserve oxygen," I said.

"And there's plenty of alcohol," added Jenkins.

"And Peggy's a plumber in this incarnation," said Sandra, rather nastily.

"So . . ." said Ralph.

Chapter 18

IT WAS DARK OUTSIDE and, despite the heating units and insulation of our suits, bitterly cold. Astern of us was the dull-glowing Galactic Lens, a monstrous ember in the black ash of the ultimate night. Ahead of us, flaring with an unnatural steely brilliance, was one of the distant island nebulae. But we were in no mood for astronomical sight-seeing. Almost at once our attention was caught and held by the horrible tangle of twisted wreckage that extended all the way from the stern, where we were standing, to the stem of the huge ship, standing out sharply and shockingly in the harsh glare of our working lights: the buckled spars, the vast, disorderly expanse of tattered sail and snapped cordage, the rent and battered shell plating. But we did not look long, nor did we want to. There was work to do—burning and welding, man-handling the massive pipe sections into place, heating and beating the twisted plating of the stern so that it conformed, more or less, to our plans.

Peggy took charge—and it was Peggy, too, who did most of the work. A tool in her hands was an extension of her body—or, even, an extension of her personality. She stitched metal to metal with the delicate precision that an ancestress might have displayed with needle, thread and fine fabric. I watched her with envy, and it was not only her manual dexterity that I envied. She was so sure of herself, so certain. And I was not certain. Oh, I had no doubts that this was the only way out of our predicament—but once we had won through to an alternative time track should we be any better off? In *Thermopylae* we had achieved what seemed to be a stable grouping, like paired with like, but would it, could it last?

I looked at Peggy, and I hoped with all my heart that it would.

I heard her satisfied, peculiarly feminine grunt in my helmet phones. She said flatly, "That's that."

"Even so," murmured Ralph doubtfully, "will it hold?"

"Long enough," she told him cheerfully. "Long enough. After all, Ralph, this isn't the first time . . ."

"No," said Sandra, a nasty edge to her voice, "it isn't."

"That will do," ordered her husband coldly.

"And now we'll connect up the tanks and bottles," said Peggy.

We clambered back inside through the rents in the shell plating, back into the wrecked lazaret. Intended for use as a sick bay by the ship's builders, it had become over the generations a storeroom, a repository for things that never had been used, that never would be used, that had been stashed away in the belief that somebody, sooner or later, would find a use for them. We had found the piping there, a fine assortment, large and small bore. Some had been damaged by the meteor swarm, most of it had not been. Finding it saved us both time and labor.

The oxygen cylinders and the tanks of alcohol, however, we had to lug through the ship from the centrally situated storage compartments. The work was heavy and awkward, but that wasn't the worst part of it. The trouble was that we were obliged to see again the torn, frozen bodies of our late shipmates. And there was that sense of responsibility that was so hard to shake off. If it hadn't been for the pattern, as we were thinking of it, if it hadn't been for the odd design which made it somehow imperative that the seven of us, and only the seven of us, should be attempting to break the light barrier by means of rocket power, would *Thermopylae* have come to grief? And had we, of our own volition, established the pattern? Or had the pattern existed always, and were we no more than puppets?

But we worked on. We were still alive, and we had every induce-ment to stay that way. We convinced ourselves that we were in, but not of, *Thermopylae*. We felt that we were innocent bystanders involved by blind chance in a catastrophe not of our making, not of our concern. All that concerned us was getting the hell out, and that as soon as possible. My parents, I knew, were among those who had perished when the cosmic debris destroyed the deep freeze. But my parents, I knew with even greater certainty, were solid citizens of Dunedin, capital of the Empire of Waverly, who, without fail, sent me a canned turkey every year in the pious hope that it would arrive at or before Christmas. Then there was the carroty cat Susan. I had known her before I met Peggy. I had known her very well indeed. I had seen her—what was left of her—as I helped lug the oxygen cylinders back aft from the stores. And I told myself, *That pitiful, broken body means nothing to me. I have never slept with it. When I was in* Flying Cloud, *when I was in* Aeriel, *I never knew anybody catted Susan . . .*

I told myself that.

But we worked, all of us, fetching and carrying at Peggy's command, sweating in our suits, gasping in the stale air. We watched the makeshift contraption growing as we worked—the alcohol tanks with the oxygen bottles attached to them to drive the fluid into the firing chamber, the other oxygen bottles that would feed directly into the rocket motor. It was a dreadfully inefficient setup, but it didn't matter. Mass ratio didn't worry us. We weren't concerned with escape velocity; all that we wanted was that extra nudge, the push that would drive us faster than light, that would expel us from this continuum in which we didn't belong.

We worked, stumbling, fumbling automatons, breathing our own stinks, our skin chafed and sore inside our suits. We worked, tired and hungry and thirsty as we were. There was the urgency, there was the feeling that if we failed to meet the deadline we should be marooned here, doomed to die in a little, ruined world not of our making. We worked, half-blinded by the actinic flaring of Peggy's torch, cursing the tools that slipped from our clumsy, gloved hands, cursing each other for carelessness and failure to cooperate.

But we worked.

And, astern of us, the target at which the cannon of our jury rocket was aimed, we could see the dull-glowing Galactic Lens, the smear of smoky crimson against the darkness. Whatever happened, we all knew, there was no return, ever, to the warmth and light of the center. We belonged on the Rim. Aboard *Flying Cloud*, aboard *Aeriel*, aboard *Thermopylae*—we belonged on the Rim . . .

"Now," Peggy was saying. "*Now*. Stand by, all of you . . ."

"Wait!" Ralph's voice was sharp. "There'll be acceleration. Unless we've secured ourselves we shall fall through the holes in the plating—and that will be the end."

"Then secure yourselves," said Peggy.

I shuffled to where she was standing, got one arm around a stanchion, the other around her waist. I saw that the others were similarly disposing themselves. Peggy, with both hands free, opened two valves. From the venturi of the rocket jetted a white vapor. Then her right hand went out to a crude switch—and, abruptly, the white vapor became a torrent of fire.

It won't work, I thought. *It won't work. Not this time . . .*

Desperately I clung to the stanchion, fighting the pseudogravity of our acceleration. I tried not to look down through the rents in the shell plating, tried to ignore the lightyears-deep chasm beneath us. I clung with desperation to the stanchion and even more desperately to Peggy, who needed both hands to adjust the valves.

The weight on my arms, as acceleration mounted, became intolerable, but I knew that I must not, could not, would not let go.

Then I felt the ominous vibration as the stanchion started to give.

Chapter 19

AHEAD OF US had been the spark of luminescence that was a planet, astern of us the disc of fire that was a sun. We had done the things that had to be done—mechanically, not too inefficiently. But I was still seeing, in my mind's eye, the dull-glowing Lens of the Galaxy, smoky crimson against the sooty depths of the ultimate night, still feeling, in my left hand and arm, the strain—the strain, and the crackling of the weakening, snapping stanchion. What was real and what was unreal? Was this world towards which we were headed some sort of latter-day Valhalla, a heaven (or hell?) for the souls of departed spacemen?

But we had done the right things—shortening sail, trimming sail, rotating the spars so that the black surfaces of some of the vanes were presented to the major luminary, so that their reflecting surfaces were catching the reflected light from the planet. We had slowed down sufficiently for the making of a safe approach.

"Even so," Ralph was saying, slowly and softly, "what world is it? What world can it be?"

I reached out for the big binoculars on their universally jointed mount. I thought, *I'll play this for real. But it must be real. Or must it?* Slowly, carefully, I adjusted the focus. What had been only short hours ago little more than a point of light was now a great shining sphere. I stared at it stupidly. About a third of the planetary surface was cloud-covered, mainly in the polar regions. I could observe clearly the seas and the continents—blue and brown and green, the snowclad peaks of the mountain ranges a sparkling white—the seas and the continents, the utterly unfamiliar configurations of land and water.

"What world is it?" asked Ralph again, addressing me directly this time.

"I don't know," I admitted, adding wryly, "But navigation in this ship—or these ships?—has been rather a lost art of late . . ."

"But not, unfortunately, rocketry," observed Sandra cattily.

"Pipe down," growled Ralph. "Pipe down. We've all of us come through, somehow, and we're back where we belong, in *Flying Cloud*. All we have to do now is to make a landing."

"But where, lord and master?" asked Sandra, too sweetly. "But where?"

"Does it matter?" he growled. "That looks to be a very pleasant world. Frankly, I shall be happy to set this scow down on any convenient stretch of calm water. After we're rested we'll see about getting our bearings . . ."

"In space?" she asked. "Or in time? Or both?"

"Does it matter?" he almost shouted. Then, "It's time we heard something from our tame telepath."

I said, "His amplifier up and died on him."

"I hope he hasn't dumped it," said Sandra, "although I never did fancy dog's brain in aspic. But Peter could make a curry of it."

"I'm not the cook," I told her coldly. "Not on this time track. And neither, my dear, are you the captain."

Ralph glared at us and then turned to the journalist. "Any luck, Martha?"

"Yes," she said, fiddling with the controls of her transceiver. "There are people there, and they're advanced enough to have radio. Their language is strange—to me, at any rate—but their music is human enough, even though it's a little corny for my taste." She switched over from headphone to speaker. There was a man singing, in a pleasant baritone, accompanied by some stringed instrument. The melody was hauntingly familiar, although the words were in

that unknown tongue. Then, in spite of the shifts in key, the odd dis-
tortions of rhythm, I had it. In his own language, he was singing:

> *"Good-bye, I'll run*
> *To seek another sun*
> *Where I*
> *May find*
> *There are worlds more kind*
> *Than the ones left behind . . ."*

I said, "The Rim Runners' March . . ."

"You could be right," said Ralph doubtfully. Then, with growing
assurance, he repeated, "You could be right. Even so, that piece of
music is not the exclusive property of Rim Runners. It's old, old—
and nobody knows how many times it's had fresh lyrics tacked on to
it. But hearing it, on *their* radio, is evidence that Terran ships have
been in contact with this world. The Survey Service, perhaps, or some
off-course star tramp. But I think that we can expect a friendly
reception, assistance, even . . ." He was beginning to look more
cheerful. "All right. We'll get the rest of the way off this wagon now.
This is the ideal approach, towards the sunlit hemisphere of the
planet. You know the drill, all of you. Trim sails—black surfaces
towards the sun, reflecting surfaces towards the source of reflected
light. Start the pumps as soon as they have some atmosphere to
work on."

His strong, capable hands played over the control panel. I
watched the telltale screen. There was the ship as seen from directly
ahead, scanned by the camera at the end of its long bowsprit,
eclipsing the sun. Surrounding her were the geometric array of
vanes and spars, some blindingly white, some sooty black. I
watched—but there was no change in the design. I heard Ralph
curse softly, I looked back to him. The control panel was alive with
red lights.

The intercom speaker crackled and from it issued Peggy's voice.
"The wiring's gone. The power supply to the trimming motors.
Burned out."

"Manual trimming," ordered Ralph sharply. "Get along to the trimming motor room, all of you. And fast."

I was the first out of the control room, with Sandra, Doc Jenkins and Martha hard on my heels. We shuffled through the alleyways at speed, keeping the magnetized soles of our sandals in contact with the deck, knowing that to fall free would be to waste time rather than to gain it. But it was a nightmarish means of progression. As we passed the psionic radio room we ran into Claude Smethwick, who had just come out into the alleyway. I grabbed his arm and hustled him along with us, refusing to listen to what he was trying to tell me.

The trimming motor room stank of burned insulation, of overheated and melted metal and plastic, of ozone. Peggy was there, frantically stripping panels from the bulkhead sheathing, laying bare the damaged wiring. I heard Sandra say, "If you'd done this before, Miss Cummings, instead of playing around with homemade fireworks . . ."

"Shut up!" I shouted. Then, "Peggy, put the manual controls in gear!"

"Peter," Claude Smethwick was babbling. "Peter, I've made contact. This world . . ."

"Later," I snapped. "Tell me later. We have to get the way off the ship."

"But . . ."

"Get your paws on to that wheel, all of you! Now . . . now . . . *together!*" The hand gear was stubborn, and our actions at first were clumsy and uncoordinated. *"Together!"* I shouted again.

The worst of it all was that we were having to work in free-fall conditions. All that held us to the deck was the magnetism of the soles of our sandals. We had no purchase. Yet, at last, the big wheel started to turn—slowly, slowly. I wondered how much time remained to us before we should plunge, a blazing meteorite, down through the planet's atmosphere.

I snatched a glance at the indicator and gasped, "Belay, there. Belay." So far, so good. The main drivers were trimmed. The auxiliary vanes still presented a greater reflecting surface to the sun than did the mainsails to the reflected light of the planet, but things were coming under control, the feeling of nightmarish urgency was abating.

Ralph's voice came through the intercom. "Trim 1 and 2 spinnakers. Then stand by."

"Turn back!" bawled Claude Smethwick. "We must turn back!"

"Why, Mr. Smethwick?" asked Ralph's disembodied voice coldly.

"I've been trying to tell you, but nobody will listen. I've been in touch with the telepaths on that planet. It's Llanith, one of the anti-matter worlds. And they say, 'Turn back! Turn back!'"

"Mr. Malcolm," snapped Ralph. "Trim all sails!"

Again we strained and sweated, again we were driven by the nightmarish sense of urgency. The first pair of spinnakers was trimmed—and then, with the second pair of auxiliary vanes rotated barely a degree on their spars, the hand gear seized up. Peggy said nothing, just relinquished her hold on the wheel and walked rapidly to the spacesuit locker.

I demanded, "Where are you off to?"

She said, "I have to go outside."

"If there's time," muttered Sandra. "If there's time. Why don't you make another rocket, dearie?"

"What's the delay?" Ralph was demanding. "What's the delay?" Then, his voice suddenly soft, "Good-bye, all of you. It's been good knowing you. Good-bye, Sandra . . ."

She said fiercely, "I might be able to make it to control in time."

Dropping our hands from the useless wheel we watched her go. "Very touching," whispered Jenkins. "Very touching . . ." But, in spite of the slight edge of sarcasm to his voice, he was holding Martha Wayne very closely.

I said to Peggy, "This seems to be it. A pity, since everything's been tidied up so nicely."

She pushed the spacesuit back into its locker and came to stand beside me. She said, putting her hand in mine, "But this mightn't be the end, my dear. Even if there's no afterlife, we know that we're still living in the alternative Universes . . ."

"Or dying . . ." said Jenkins glumly.

And then—it's odd the way that the human brain works in a crisis—a snatch of archaic verse that I must have learned as a child rose from the depths of my memory, flashed across my mind:

> *And fast through the midnight dark and drear,*
> *Through the whistling sleet and snow,*
> *Like a sheeted ghost the vessel swept*
> *On the reef of Norman's Woe . . .*

But the crew of the schooner *Hesperus* had died a cold death—ours would be a fiery one. I hoped that it would be sudden.

The ship lurched and shuddered, as though she had in actual fact driven on to a roof. There was a rending, tearing noise, felt as well as heard—the spars and sails, I realized, bearing the brunt of our impact with planet's atmosphere, were braking us, slowing us down. There was the thin, high scream of air rushing over and through projections on our hull, the gaps in our shell plating. The temperature rose sharply. I held Peggy to me tightly, thinking, *This is it.*

The screaming died to a faint whistle and was drowned by a new sound, the throbbing of the air compressors.

Ralph's voice from the bulkhead speaker was faint and shaky, yet reassuring. He said, "All hands report to the control room. All hands report to control—to splice the main brace. And then we'll make it landing stations."

Chapter 20

❧ ❧

IT'S NOT AT ALL A BAD SORT of world, this Llanith, and I rather think that Peggy and I shall be staying here, even though Ralph and the local scientists are sure that they'll be able to work out just what did happen, just how *Flying Cloud* made the transition from normal matter to anti-matter, or vice versa. The commodore will not have achieved the economical means of interstellar travel of his dreams, but we shall have presented him with something better, much better. There's little doubt that commerce and cultural exchange between the Llanithi Consortium and the Rim Worlds Federation will soon be practicable. And Peggy and I will have an edge on those who, in the not-too-distant future, will come to learn and to teach and to trade.

Meanwhile, Ralph has suggested that each of us tell the story, in his own words, of what happened. The stories, he says, will be of great value to the scientists, both on Llanith and back home on Lorn. It seems that there may have been other forces besides physical ones at play, that psychology may have come into it, and psionics. Be that as it may, it seems obvious—to Peggy and me, at any rate—that the attempt to exceed the speed of light was the governing factor.

Not that we worry much about it.

We're doing nicely, very nicely, the pair of us. My restaurant is better than paying its way; even though the Llanithi had never dreamed of such highly spiced dishes as curry they're fast acquiring the taste for them. And the bicycles—another novelty—that Peggy makes in her little factory are selling like hotcakes.

Doc and Martha are settling down, too. There's quite a demand for the sort of verse and music that they can turn out without really trying. And when they get tired of composing they pick up their brushes and dazzle the natives with neoabstractionism. And Claude? He gets by. A telepath can find himself at home anywhere— he can always contact others of his kind. If the Llanithi were purple octopi—which they aren't, of course—he'd be equally happy.

It's only Ralph and Sandra who aren't fitting in. Each of them possesses a rather overdeveloped sense of duty—although I am inclined to wonder if Sandra, in her case, isn't really hoping to find her way back to that time track on which the Matriarchate ruled the Rim Worlds and on which she was captain of her own ship.

If she ever does, I shall be neither her husband nor her cook.

This Universe suits me.

✎ On the Account ✎

✎ I ✎

COMMODORE GRIMES sat at his desk, looking down at the transcript of a Carlottigram from Port Listowel. *Lord Of The Isles,* one of the lightjammers on the run between the Rim Worlds and the Llanithi Consortium, was overdue. She, using her own Carlotti equipment, had beamed a final message to Port Forlorn before breaking the light barrier. Once the speed of light had been exceeded she was in a weird, private universe of her own—stranger even than the private universes of ships running under the Space-Time-twisting Mannschenn Drive—and unable to communicate with any planetary base or any other ship. Toward the end of her voyage she had made her routine reduction of speed to a sublight velocity and had started to send her ETA to the Carlotti Station on Llanith. She had gotten as far as giving her name and then, according to the Llanithi Carlotti operator on watch, had experienced what seemed to be interference on the band in use. Nothing more had been heard from her. And now she was all of ten days overdue.

The communicator buzzed sharply.

Grimes pressed the button that would admit the incoming call. The screen lit up and on it appeared the fleshy, ruddy face of Admiral Kravitz.

"Ah, Grimes."

The commodore repressed temptation to counter with, *And whom the hell else did you expect?* Legally speaking the admiral was not his superior officer except when Grimes was called back to active duty with the Rim Worlds Navy but there would be no sense in antagonizing the man.

"Sir?" Grimes replied curtly.

"This *Lord Of The Isles* business, Grimes?"

"You have a transcript of the signal from Port Listowel, sir?"

"Of course. We do have an intelligence branch, you know. What do you make of it?"

"I don't like it. Especially coming right after the vanishing of *Sea Witch* under very similar circumstances."

"What are you doing about it, Grimes?"

"I could ask you the same question, sir."

"We cleaned up the energy-eaters for you, Grimes, and we made a clean sweep. *Rim Culverin* has been maintaining a patrol ever since the conclusion of Operation Rimhunt and has reported no further invasion of our territorial space by those entities." The admiral paused, then went on: "I'm not altogether happy about those lightjammers of yours, Grimes. As you know, we're having some built for the Navy, but I'm beginning to feel like trying to get the program canceled. They aren't safe.

"Sailing ships, indeed, in *this* day and age?"

"They're the only ships we have capable of trading with the Llanithi Consortium."

"At the moment, Grimes, at the moment. But our boffins are working on some other, simpler way of achieving a reversal of atomic charges."

"With what success, sir?" asked Grimes innocently.

Kravitz flushed. "None so far. But give them time, give them time. Meanwhile—"

"Sir?"

"Meanwhile, Grimes, I am recalling you to active duty. As long as the so-called ships of the line are still on our drawing boards we have to maintain an interest in sailing vessels. Furthermore, I have learned from your employers—from Rim Runners—that all further sailings of the lightjammers have been suspended until such time as the mystery of the disappearance of *Lord Of The Isles* and *Sea Witch* has been cleared up. They are agreeable to the requisitioning and commissioning of *Pamir* as an auxiliary cruiser. You will sail in her."

Grimes grinned. "Thank you, sir. But I have to tell you that I'm not qualified in sail."

"*Pamir*'s people are—and they all, like yourself, hold reserve comissions. Listowel's a full commander, isn't he? You'll be in overall charge of the ship and the expedition, but he can be your sailing master. We'll be putting aboard regular Navy personnel— gunnery specialists and the like. Satisfied?"

"Gunnery specialists?"

"You never know when weapons are going to come in handy, Grimes. It's better to have them than to be without them."

Grimes had to agree. He knew as well as anybody that the Universe was not peaceful and that man was not its only breaker of peace.

Not at all reluctantly Grimes handed over his astronautical superintendent's duties to Captain Barsac, one of Rim Runners' senior masters. But it was with a certain degree of reluctance that he left his comfortable home in Port Forlorn for Port Erikson, the light-jammers' terminal. Sonya refused to accompany her husband. She detested cold weather. Port Forlorn's climate was barely tolerable. Only Esquimaux, polar bears or penguins—assuming that the immigration or importation of these from Earth could be arranged—would feel at home at Coldharbor Bay in Lorn's Antarctica.

Pamir was alongside at Port Erikson. The cargo she had brought from Llanith had been discharged but she had not commenced to load for the return voyage. As yet the advance party from the Admiralty Yards was still to arrive, although accommodations— looking like black, partially inflated balloons grounded in the snow—had been set up for them.

Grimes, accompanied by Captain Rowse, the Port Erikson harbormaster, went aboard *Pamir*. He was received by Ralph Listowel, the lightjammer's master.

"Glad to have you aboard, sir," said Listowel.

"Glad to be aboard, Commander."

Listowel scowled. "That's right, sir. Rub it in. I suppose you'll be taking over my quarters."

Grimes grinned. "No. You're to be my sailing master—and, as far as I'm concerned, this is still your ship and you're still the master of her. You've quite palatial passenger accommodations. That'll do me."

Listowel's scowl faded from his lean, dark face. "Thank you, sir. But what is going on?"

"Your ship has been requisitioned—and you and your officers have been called up for active duty in the Rim Worlds Navy."

"I know that. But what *is* going on?"

"I was hoping that you'd be able to tell me."

Listowel waved his visitors to seats, took a chair himself. He said, "Let's face it, Commodore. To date the lightjammers have been lucky, fantastically lucky. Even in *Flying Cloud*, where we had to make up the rules as we went along, we all came through in one piece. But sooner or later luck runs out."

"You think that's what happened to *Sea Witch* and *Lord Of The Isles*?"

"There are so many things that could happen. When we're running under sail, building up to a velocity just short of light, we could hit something—"

"And the flare of the explosion would be seen from Llanith."

"All right, all right. Something could go wrong with the magnetic suspension of the sphere of anti-iron—"

"And with matter and anti-matter canceling each other out the burst of released energy would be even more spectacular."

"Yes, Commodore. But what if it happened at translight speed? We know very little of conditions outside the ship at that velocity. Would the explosion be witnessed in this Universe—or in the next universe but three?"

"Mphm. You have something there, Listowel. Even so, we've two ships missing, one after the other. There's an old saying: Once is happenstance. Twice is coincidence. Three times is enemy action."

"There hasn't been a third time," said Listowel.

"Yet," pointed out Grimes. "But there's still the apparent jamming of *Lord Of The Isles'* last call to be considered."

Back in Rowse's office Grimes asked for the manifests of the cargoes carried by the two missing ships. It was possible that there had been some item of freight which, at translight speeds and with the reversal of atomic charges, had become chemically or physically unstable with fatal consequences. This was an idea worth considering. But no radioactives had been listed. No industrial chemicals, dangerous or otherwise, had been listed. Mainly the freight carried in each ship had consisted of luxury goods—preserved foodstuffs, liquor, fine textiles and the like. A few shipments of machine tools and some drugs had also been part of the cargoes.

One drug in particular—Antigeriatridine—caught Grimes's attention. The substance was not manufactured on any of the Rim Worlds. It came from Marina, a planet in the Pleiades Sector. It was an extract from the glands of an indigenous sea slug and could not be synthesized. It was fantastically expensive and, on most worlds, was controlled by the state, rationed out only to deserving citizens. It was Marina's main source of income, exported to any planet that could afford to pay for it. In recent years the Llanithi Consortium had been placed on Marina's list of customers. Transshipment for Llanith was made from Lorn.

Grimes's memory carried him back to the long-ago days when he had been a newly commissioned ensign in the Federation Survey Service. He had played a part in bringing the pirates who had captured the merchant vessel *Epsilon Sextans* to book. *Epsilon Sextans* had been carrying Antigeriatridine, which had made her a worthwhile prey.

Perhaps Admiral Kravitz's insistence that *Pamir* be armed made sense.

But piracy?

It was not the continued existence of the crime itself that Grimes found hard to comprehend, but rather the actual mechanics of it. Piracy was not unknown along the spaceways, but both predators and victims had always been conventional starships, with inertial drive and Mannschenn Drive and auxiliary rocket power for use in emergencies. Under inertial drive only, maintaining a comfortable 1G acceleration, a ship could build up almost to the speed of light if she took long enough about it. But, as soon as possible, she usually ran under Mannschenn Drive which, in effect, gave her FTL velocity. In these conditions she was untouchable unless the vessel attacking her succeeded in synchronizing her own rate of temporal precession. The captains of warships—and of such vessels as have from time to time sailed on the plundering account—were reasonably competent in the practice of this art.

But it would be impossible for a ship proceeding under inertial drive only to match velocities with a lightjammer under sail. And a ship running under Mannschenn Drive would have to return to the normal Space-Time continuum before her weapons could be brought to bear on a lightjammer—and, once again, the matching of velocities would be impossible.

Hijacking was a form of piracy, of course.

Grimes turned from the missing ships' cargo manifests to their passenger lists. The names meant nothing to him, neither those of Rim Worlds citizens nor of Llanithans. No doubt the police could help him in this respect. Perhaps one or more of those passengers had a criminal record. But the hypothesis made little appeal to him. He just could not imagine the officers of either of the vessels submitting meekly—and he could not imagine any passenger being able to handle a lightjammer. Sail spacemanship was an art rather than a science and the only practioners of the art—Grimes told himself—consisted of the handful of Rim Runners' personnel trained and qualified for lightjammers,

He filled and lit his pipe, looked down at the manifests and passenger lists on the desk. He had a hunch that the manifests meant more than the passenger lists—no more than a hunch, but his hunches were often right. Any ship—even a pirate ship—anywhere in space between Lorn and Llanith and in position to receive the beamed Carlotti transmissions from one planet to the other, would be able to read the routine signals sent immediately after the liftoff of one of the lightjammers. Date and time of departure—passengers carried—a listing of freight aboard. Nothing was encoded. There had never been any need for secrecy until now.

Only the actual mechanics of attack, seizure and boarding puzzled him.

He called Sonya, told her that she had better come to Port Erikson. "You're the intelligence officer in this family," he said. "This job calls for intelligence." Reluctantly she agreed to join him.

The following morning he stood in the Port Erikson control tower, looking out through the wide windows at the bleak landscape. *Pamir* was alongside at her wharf, a great, dull-gleaming torpedo shape on the dark water. The sleekness of her lines was broken only by the pods that housed her airscrews and their engines. Out on Coldharbor Bay a small tug, *Bustler*, was chuffing busily back and forth, functioning as an icebreaker, keeping the harbor clear of any accumulation of ice heavy enough to impede surface maneuvers. Grimes had decided that *Pamir* must keep to her original schedule, which meant that her conversion to an auxiliary cruiser would be a skimpy one.

There would be time for the installation of an extra generator and the fitting of two batteries of laser cannon, but no more.

A familiar voice issued from the traffic controller's transceiver. "Pinnace *Firefly* to Port Erikson. Do you read me? Over."

"Loud and clear, *Firefly*. Pass your message. Over."

Grimes went to stand by the traffic control officer. He heard Sonya say, "My ETA Port Erikson oh-nine-four-five hours, your time. Over."

So neither she—nor Admiral Kravitz—had wasted any time. And Sonya was doing her own piloting, which was typical of her.

"I have her on the screen, sir," announced the radar operator.

Grimes went to the window overlooking the Nullarbor Plain, almost featureless under the blanket of snow. It was one of the rare clear days, and on the horizon stood the distant, jagged battlements of the Great Barrens. And was that a tiny, glittering speck in the pale sky? Yes. It expanded rapidly and even in the control tower, through the thick glass of the windows, the irritated snarl of an inertial drive unit operating at maximum capacity was distinctly audible.

"That's her," said Captain Rowse.

"That's her," agreed Grimes. He shrugged into his heavy cloak, put on his cap and went down to the airstrip to meet Sonya.

"The trouble with you, John," she said, "is that you've read too much of the wrong kind of history. Wooden ships and iron men and all that sort of thing. Pieces of eight. Broadsides of carronades. The Jolly Roger. Oh, there have been space pirates, I admit. But I still get my share of the bumf issued by the Federation Survey Service's intelligence branch—and I can tell you that today there just aren't any pirates. Not that sort of pirate, anyway. There's still the occasional hijacking."

Grimes's prominent ears flushed. He indicated with his hand the passenger lists. He said, "I've asked the Port Forlorn chief of police if any of these people have criminal records. He assures me that none of them have and that everybody aboard *Lord Of The Isles* and *Sea Witch* was a little, innocent woolly lamb—"

"He'd know, wouldn't he?" She herself was flushed, her fine features literally glowing under the glossy auburn hair. "And you have all these bright ideas and drag me out here, where all the brass monkeys are singing falsetto, to join you in this comfortless shack to help you think."

"Not comfortless," said Grimes. The quarters that he had been given were commodious and comfortable enough, although lacking in character. ACCOMMODATION, MARRIED COUPLE, FOR THE USE OF. . .

"Well, what do you intend doing? Put me in the picture."

"*Pamir* will sail on time, having loaded the cargo that's been booked for her. That will include a shipment of Antigeriatridine. The usual routine signals will be made once she has lifted off. And then we wait to see what happens next."

"We?"

"I suppose you'll be coming along."

"I might as well get a free trip to Llanith out of it."

"All right. You. Me. Ralph Listowel and his officers. The gunnery officer from the Navy who'll be looking after the laser batteries. The two dozen or so marines who'll be traveling as passengers."

"Anybody would think that you were contemplating embarking on a career of piracy yourself."

Grimes laughed. "Why not? After all, one of my ancestors sailed on the account."

"And what happened to him?"

"He was eventually hanged from his own yardarm."

She joined him in his laughter. "Then you'd better be careful. After all, the lightjammers are the only ships that run to masts and yards!"

PAMIR was ready for space. The extra generator had been installed, as had been the batteries of laser cannon. Stores for the voyage and the cargo had been loaded. The passengers were embarked. Grimes and Sonya, together with Major Trent, the marine officer, and Lieutenant Fowler, the gunnery officer, sat with Listowel and his wife, Sandra, in the master's day cabin.

Listowel sipped his coffee rather glumly. He asked Grimes stiffly, "Have I your permission to cast off, sir, at the arranged time?"

"Of course, Listowel. You're the master still. The rest of us are just along for the ride."

"It's a ride I'm looking forward to," put in Fowler enthusiastically. He was a young giant with short-cropped yellow hair, the perpetual schoolboy so common in all the armed services. "It'll give me some time in sail and I'll be all set for our own ships of the line when they come out."

"It's not a free ride we're here for," commented the major sourly,

"More coffee anybody?" asked Sandra cheerfully.

"No thanks," replied Listowel, looking at his watch. "It's time we got the show on the road."

"Can I come up to control, sir?" asked Fowler.

"Of course, Lieutenant. You're welcome on the bridge. And so are you, Major."

Grimes and Sonya went along with the others. They had witnessed *Pamir*'s departure from the control position before, but it was so unlike the liftoff of a conventional spaceship as to remain fascinating. This time there was no need to use the tug, no need for the transverse thrust of the airscrews. The wind, what little there was of it, was northerly, blowing the ship bodily off from the wharf, the brash ice piling up along her lee side but not impeding her. When she was well out into the bay water, ballast was dumped and—the sphere of anti-matter giving her positive buoyancy—she went up like a balloon or a rocket—silently. Within seconds she was driving through the low cloud ceiling and then had broken through into the clear upper air: Fast she rose—and faster—into blackness, while below her Lorn became an opalescent globe hanging in nothingness.

The directional gyroscopes rumbled and whined, rumbled again and then lapsed into silence. She was steadied on course now, with Lorn to one side and the Lorn sun astern. The tiny cluster of stars—the anti-matter suns around which revolved the planets of the Llanithi Consortium—was directly ahead.

The control room guests crowded to the side ports of the bridge, looking aft to watch as Listowel made sail. The stubs of the telescopic masts extended themselves rapidly, sprouting yards as they elongated. The yards and the great sails, spreading to catch the star wind, the royals, the topgallants, the upper topsails and the lower topsails, the main courses . . . The polarized glass of the viewports dimmed the glare of the sun and black against it stood the driving surfaces, filling to the photon gale. The inertialess ship was already scudding before it and the Doppler Log was clicking and flashing like a clock gone mad.

"Roll and go," murmured Listowel.

"Wonderful!" breathed Fowler.

Major Trent only grunted, then said, "I'd better get down to see to my men."

Fowler said, "And I'd better check my cannon."

"We'll not be needing them yet," Grimes told him.

The ship drove on, steadily accelerating.

It was like the first voyage that Grimes and Sonya had made in *Pamir*—and yet, in some ways, unlike. The atmosphere on board was different, mainly because there were no civilian passengers. Major Trent and his marines were passengers of a sort, of course— there was little that they could do about the ship until such time as their professional services would be required. But Trent maintained his own standards of discipline and there was altogether too much heel-clicking and saluting. And Listowel's officers were all too conscious of their temporary standing as commissioned personnel of the Rim Worlds Navy, serving aboard an auxiliary cruiser of that same service. Their captain didn't like it.

He complained to Grimes over a quiet drink in the commodore's quarters: "Damn it all, sir, I'm just a shipmaster and my people are my mates and engineers and all the rest of it. But now I have Mr. bloody Willoughby putting on airs and graces and expecting to be addressed as Lieutenant Commander every time anybody talks to him."

Grimes chuckled. "It doesn't matter. He can call himself what he likes—he's still a very good chief officer."

"Even so—" Then Listowel managed a wry chuckle of his own. "All right. I'll let him and the others have their fun. But it still reminds me of small boys playing at pirates."

"Talking of pirates—" Grimes pulled a key from his pocket and unlocked a drawer of the desk that was part of the cabin's furniture. "I asked you in for a talk as well as a drink. You remember that coded Carlottigram that came through for me on the teletype this morning?" He took a sheet of paper out of the drawer.

"This contains the decode. TOP SECRET—YOUR EYES ONLY. To Be Destroyed By Fire After Reading—and all the rest of it. When it comes to playing childish games the Admiralty is at least as bad as anybody else. And this message concerns us all in this vessel.

"Navy has an intelligence service, you know. According to Sonya it's not a patch on the intelligence branch of the Federation Survey Service, but its officers do flap their ears and twitch their little pink noses now and again. Unluckily Admiral Kravitz didn't get his paws on their reports concerning the Duchy of Waldegren until after we'd sailed."

"Waldegren?"

"Yes. It seems that our people managed to plant some monitor buoys in the territorial space of the Duchy. I've heard those gadgets described as miracles of miniaturization. See all, hear all, and punch it all back to Port Forlorn on tightbeam Carlotti in one coded parcel before the automatic self-destruction. And that, of course, occurs when anything approaches within ten kilometers.

"Well, there's been something going on around Darnstadt—the fortress planet, so-called. There's a photograph of a lightjammer under sail. There are monitored signals—both Carlotti and NST." He tapped the sheet of paper. "Kravitz sent me translations of some of the messages. 'Clear of atmosphere, making sail.' 'Arrange berthage for prize.' The sort of things you send just after departure and just prior to arrival."

"I don't take any prizes, Commodore."

"You might yet." Grimes looked at his watch. "Time we went to see Mr. Fowler get a prize for good shooting."

"Didn't you specialize in gunnery yourself, sir, when you were in the Survey Service?"

"At one time, yes. But I never had a practice shoot at point eight the speed of light. This should be interesting."

"Surely no more so than any other practice shoot, Commodore. As far as the target rocket and the ship are concerned, there'll be no great relative velocities. The target will just run parallel to us once it's been launched. If it took evasive action it would drop astern too fast for Fowler to get a shot at it. We're still accelerating, you know."

"Mphm?" Grimes locked away the message. "Let's go to watch the fireworks."

The watchkeeper—Denby, the second officer—and all off-duty officers were in the control room. Sonya was there, too, as was Sandra. Major Trent was there, accompanied by his sergeant. Wallasey, the third officer, was assisting Lieutenant Fowler. The gunnery officer sat at his fire control console. Young Wallasey was at the smaller set of controls, part of the ship's normal equipment, from which signal and sounding rockets were handled. He was managing to look at least as important as Fowler.

"Let battle commence!" whispered Grimes to Sonya.

Fowler overheard this and scowled. But he said nothing. Commodores, even commodores on the Reserve List, were entitled to their pleasantries at the expense of mere lieutenants.

"Targets in readiness, Mr. Fowler," reported Wallasey.

"Thank you, Mr. Wallasey," replied Fowler stiffly. Then, to Grimes: "Permission to commence practice shoot, sir?"

"This is Captain Listowel's ship, Mr. Fowler," said Grimes.

The young man flushed and repeated his question to Listowel. "Carry on, Mr. Fowler."

"Fire one," he ordered.

"Fire one," repeated Wallasey.

Grimes, looking aft with the others, saw the gout of blue flame, intensely bright against the black backdrop with its sparse scattering of stars, as the missile was ejected from its launching tube. It fell away from the ship on a slightly divergent course, pulling ahead, but slowly, at first.

"Open the range, Mr. Wallasey," ordered Fowler.

"Range opening. One kilometer. Two. Four. Ten—"

The rocket now was only a bright spark against the darkness.

Fowler worked at his console. Abaft the control room but forward of the masts and sails the quadruple rods of the starboard laser battery turned and wavered like the hunting antennae of some huge insect. "Fire—" muttered Fowler to himself. A faint glow showed at the tips of the rods, nothing more. Here there was no air, with its floating dust motes, to be heated to incandescence. Out to starboard the bright spark persisted, neither extinguished nor flaring into sudden explosion.

Fowler muttered something about the calibration of his sights, then ordered, "Close the range."

"Range closing, Mr. Fowler. Ten. Nine. Eight—damn!"

"What's wrong?"

"Burnout." The bright spark had vanished now.

"All right. Fire two."

"Fire two."

The second missile was thrown from its tube.

"Range, Mr. Wallasey?"

"One kilometer. Opening."

"Hold at one kilometer." Then, to himself: "It's right in the sights. I can't miss—"

"But you're doing just that," remarked Grimes.

"But I can't be!" Fowler sounded desperate. "With a single cannon, perhaps. But not with a battery of four. And the sights can't be out."

Grimes grunted thoughtfully. Then: "Tell me, Mr. Fowler, has anybody ever tried to use laser in these conditions before?"

"From a lightjammer, you mean, sir? From a ship traveling at almost the speed of light?"

"Yes."

"You know that this is the first time, sir."

"And it's been an interesting experiment, hasn't it? Oh, I could be wrong, but I have a sort of vision of photons being dispersed like water from the spray nozzle of a hose. Perhaps if the ship were not accelerating the tight, coherent beam would be maintained . . . Is there a physicist in the house?"

"You know there's not," said Sonya sharply.

"Unfortunate, but true. So in these conditions our laser is about as effective as a searchlight and we've nobody to tell us what to do about it."

Fowler was slumped in his seat, a picture of dejection. He was a gunnery officer whose weapons were as lethal as toy pistols. "Cheer up," Grimes told him. "I've a job for you."

"But what is there for me to do, sir? As you've pointed out already, I'm not a physicist."

"But you are a weapons specialist." Grimes turned to Wallasey. "How many rockets have you left?"

"Six, sir."

"Then I suggest that you and Mr. Fowler, assisted by the engineering staff, convert them into weapons."

"What about warheads?"

Grimes sighed heavily. "You'd never have made a living as a cannoneer in the early days of artillery, Mr. Fowler. Those old boys used to cast their own cannon and mix their own powder—and they didn't have the ingredients that we have aboard this ship. Ammonium nitrate, for example—one of the chemical fertilizers we use in the hydroponic tanks. We should be able to cook up something packing far more of a wallop than gunpowder."

"You're convinced that we shall need weapons, John?" put in Sonya.

"I'm not convinced of anything. But somebody once said—Cromwell, wasn't it?—'Trust in God, and keep your powder dry.' Furthermore, my dear, this vessel is rated as an auxiliary cruiser, a unit of the Rim Worlds Navy. Our lords and masters of the Admiralty have, in their wisdom, equipped her with weaponry. We have discovered that this weaponry is useless. So—we improvise."

"I'm surprised," she said, "that you don't follow in the footsteps of your piratical ancestor and fit *Pamir* out with a couple of broadsides of muzzle-loading cannon."

A slow smile spread over Grimes's rugged features. "Why not?" he murmured happily. "Why not?"

All deep space ships carry a a biochemist. In large passenger vessels and warships he is a departmental head, but usually he is one of the officers who has been put through a crash course and looks after the life-support systems in addition to his other duties. *Pamir*'s biochemist was Sandra Listowel, who was also purser and catering officer. Even a full-time, fully qualified biochemist is not an industrial chemist. Sandra most certainly was not. Nonetheless, she succeeded—losing her eyebrows and a little more than half of her blond hair in the process—in brewing up a batch of what Grimes referred to as sort-of-kind-of amatol. After all, cooking oil is not toluene. Lieutenant Fowler, given the freedom of the engineer's workshop, was told to produce a half-dozen impact fuses. He was a good worker and not unintelligent but sadly lacking, Grimes concluded, in initiative. He was a good gunnery officer only when he had all the resources of a naval arsenal behind him.

Grimes, however, loved improvising. Many years ago, when he had been Federation Survey Service lieutenant, commanding the courier *Adder*, he had made some missiles, using large plastic bottles as the casings and black powder as the propellant. After a browse through the chemical fertilizers in the "farm's" storerooms he decided that he had the necessary ingredients for more black powder. He wanted something relatively slow-burning for the weapons he had in mind.

He had seen *Pamir*'s manifest of cargo on the completion of loading. One item was a consignment of metal piping with a bore of 100 millimeters. Fortunately this was easily accessible in the hold. It was backbreaking work to lug the heavy sections out of their stowage and to the ship's workshop, but Major Trent's marines were able to accomplish this without too much grumbling. The pipe sections were cut to size, each two and a half meters in length. One end of each of the tubes was sealed with a heavy, welded flange. The crude cannon, eight of them, were beginning to take shape.

There was no time to introduce too many refinements. *Pamir* had broken through the light barrier, was well away on the second leg of her voyage. It was when she decelerated, to complete the passage to Llanith under sail, that the pirate would strike. This was a probability if not a certainty. The evidence indicated that this was what had happened to *Lord Of The Isles* and to *Sea Witch*.

Grimes discussed the prospect with Listowel, Willoughby, Major Trent and Sonya. He said, "Let's face it. The principles of our lightjammers aren't secret. We're the only people who have had such ships simply because we're the only people with inhabited anti-matter systems in our sector of space. But there have been articles a-plenty in both scientific and shipping journals. And the Waldegrenese can read."

"Waldegren?" asked Trent.

"Yes. Waldegren. The Duchy has a bad record of harboring pirates," He spread a chart on Listowel's desk. "Now, just suppose that Waldegren is monitoring our traffic with Llanith on the Carlotti bands. Oh, I know that the beam between our two systems doesn't pass near any of the worlds of the Duchy—but a small relay station, possibly fully automated, could have been planted anywhere along the line of sight, *if* we knew just where to look for it we could find it. Mphm. Well, one of our lightjammers lifts off from Lorn. The routine message is sent. ETA and all the rest of it. Cargo such and such, consigned to so and so. Then the pirate—a lightjammer, of course—lifts off from Darnstadt. . . So far I've told only two people of the contents of the signal I received from Admiral Kravitz—Captain Listowel, of course, and Sonya. She helped with the decoding. But it all ties in. There has been lightjammer activity in the Duchy—and what would Waldegren want lightjammers for?"

"Piracy," said Listowel.

"Still, we must be careful. We aren't at war with Waldegren. The evidence indicates, however, that Waldegren has built at least one lightjammer. After all, the essential guts of such a ship, a sphere of anti-matter, aren't all that hard to come by. There are other anti-matter systems besides the Llanithi Consortium. But where was I? Oh, yes.

"The pirate lifts off from Darnstadt, sets course and adjusts speed so as to intercept our ship as she decelerates to sub-light velocity. She jams the Carlotti bands, attacks, seizes."

"And what about the passengers and crew?" asked Listowel.

"If they're lucky, Captain, they'll be prisoners on Darnstadt. That's why we want to take prisoners ourselves."

"The pirate," said Trent, "will probably be armed with rockets, or projectile cannon. Not laser—unless the Waldegren scientists have worked out some way of making it effective at near-light speeds. Quick-firing cannon, I'd say."

"Quicker than your muzzleloaders," said Sonya to Grimes.

"Almost certainly," he agreed. "But surprise is a good weapon."

AS *PAMIR* SPED through the nothingness the work of arming her progressed. Ahead of her blazed the stars, those toward which she was steering and those whose laggard light she was overhauling. Filters and shields protected her crew from the dangerous radiations that were a resultant of her velocity. Yet there was still visible light, harsh, intensely blue, light that should not have been seen but that, nonetheless, seemed to penetrate even opaque plating.

But apart from the watch officers nobody had time to look out into space. Those cannon had to be finished and mounted. There was black powder to be mixed and tested, the charges to be packed in plastic bags. There were the springs to be contrived to carry and dampen the recoil of the guns. There were bags of shot to be made up.

Pamir, fortunately, was so designed as to make the mounting of archaic cannon practicable. As a lightjammer, handled inside a planetary atmosphere like an airship, she was fitted with ballast tanks which, of course, were emptied on liftoff. Grimes decided to place his batteries, each of four guns, in the port and starboard wing tanks. To begin with, two crude airlocks were made and welded to the manhole doors leading into the compartments. Spacesuited and carrying laser tools the chief officer and the engineer went into the tanks, first to cut the gunports, then to strengthen the frames to take the weight of the artillery, the thrust of the recoil. The gun mountings were then passed in and welded into place.

The pieces themselves slid in cradles and, on being fired, would be driven back against powerful springs, locking in the fully recoiled position. Loading was fast enough—first the bag of powder, then the shot, with a ramrod to shove all well home. Firing would have to be deferred until the guns were run out again. For firing Grimes had first considered electrical contacts, then some sort of flintlock. He was amused by his final solution—touchhole and slow match. Even though hand lasers were the slow matches—within the confines of the ship they worked well enough—the principle was a reversion to the very earliest days of firearms.

Then there was the drilling of Trent's marines. They took it all cheerfully enough, making a game of it.

Finally Grimes was satisfied with the rate of fire—although none of the guns had yet actually been fired—under simulated conditions.

Grimes checked personally the ready-use lockers for the bagged charges, the lockers for the improvised shot, the arrangements for passing more ammunition through into the tanks should it become necessary, and communications. But there was one more problem. A row of gunports, with the muzzles of guns protruding, is easily detectable. He decided that the cannon would be retained in the fully recoiled position until just before firing and the ports concealed by sheets of plastic. He ordered, also, that the laser batteries be withdrawn into their recesses. They were of no use, anyhow.

"Deceleration stations," Listowel ordered.

"Make that action stations," said Grimes quietly. "I'm taking over now, Captain."

"So I'm just your sailing master," Listowel commented, but cheerfully enough. "At your service, Commodore." He pressed the bell push. A coded clangor sounded and resounded, short long, short long, short long—the Morse *A*. Fowler fidgeted in his seat at the console, the one from which he would fire and, hopefully, direct the sounding rockets, each of which was now fitted with a high-explosive warhead. The batteries of muzzle loaders were manned.

Spacesuited marines were standing by the drainpipe artillery, three to a gun. Handy to the airlocks over the manhole doors were the ammunition parties. "Cut reaction drive."

"Cut reaction drive, sir." The muted thunder of the rockets suddenly ceased.

Slowly, carefully, as though this were no more than a routine deceleration, Listowel trimmed his sails, pivoting them about the masts so that the light from the glaring Llanithi stars, almost dead ahead, was striking their reflecting surfaces at an oblique angle. It had to be done gradually. If *Pamir* were suddenly taken aback she would be dismasted. The Doppler Log was starting to wind down. 25.111111 . . . 25.111110 . . . . 25.111109. . . . The lower courses were turned to exercise full braking effect. The lower topsails next—the upper topsails—the top gallants. Speed was dropping fast. Inside the inertialess ship there was no sensory hint of the titanic forces being brought into play, forces that in a normal vessel would have smeared ship and crew across the sky in a blaze of raw energy.

The log was still winding down, although the count was slowing.
1.000007 . . . 1.000005 . . .
1.000003 . . . 1.000001 . . .
1.000001 . . .
1.000001 . . .
1.000000 . . .

Now there was sensation, a feeling of unbearable tension. Something had to give. Something, somewhere, snapped suddenly. Ahead the sparse scattering of stars diminished in number. The Rim Suns—astern in actuality—suddenly flickered out, reappeared in their proper relative bearing.

"Mr. Wallasey," said Listowel, "make the routine ETA call to Llanith." He looked inquiringly toward Grimes, who said, "Yes. We maintain routine—until somebody or something interferes with it."

Wallasey was having his troubles. From the switched-on Carlotti transceiver issued a continuous warbling note.

"Interference—" he muttered.

"Jamming," amended Grimes. "This is it, Captain. Any moment now." He looked around the control room. Fowler was tense over his console, as was Denby, the second officer, at the radar. Wallasey was still twiddling knobs at the Carlotti set. Sonya and Sandra were sitting quietly in their chairs, apparently taking only a mild interest in the proceedings—but either woman, Grimes well knew, could spring into action at an instant's notice. And Sandra, after all, could handle a lightjammer almost as well as her husband.

There was nobody else on the bridge. Willoughby was below, in charge of the damage-control party, and Major Trent was looking after the guns manned by his men.

"Target," reported Denby. "Green seventy-five. Range fifty kilometers. Closing."

"Thank you, Mr. Denby. Keep us informed," said Grimes.

"Green now seventy-five, still. Positive altitude five degrees, increasing."

"Range?"

"Forty—and closing."

Grimes spoke into the microphone that carried his voice through the ship and into the gunners' helmet speakers. "This is the commodore. The enemy has been sighted. She is closing fast. From now on there will be frequent changes of trajectory. Stand by to open fire on command. Over."

Trent's voice came in reply, "All is ready, sir. Guns loaded, but not yet run out."

"Don't run them out until you get the order to fire, Major."

"Green seventy-four, sir. Range thirty, closing. Positive altitude seven degrees. Increasing slowly."

"Captain," said Grimes, "roll us seven degrees to port. I want to keep our friend exactly on the plane of our ecliptic. We can't aim the guns individually—we have to aim the ship. Understand?"

"Understood, Commodore." The directional gyroscopes rumbled briefly as *Pamir* was turned about her long axis.

"And now, Captain, start altering course to port. Just behave as you would normally in trying to avoid a close quarters situation."

Looking through the viewports Grimes saw the sails being trimmed. With the light from the Llanith sun as the wind, *Pamir* was being steadied on to a starboard tack.

"Green eighty-five, opening. Range twenty-five, holding. Altitude zero."

Grimes got up from his chair, went to the big binoculars on their universal mount. He had no trouble picking up the intruder. Her suit of sails made her a big enough target.

He said, "Mr. Wallasey, don't bother any more with the Carlotti set. Try calling on NST."

"Very good, sir." The third officer turned to the normal Space-Time transceiver, equipment suitable for use only at short ranges. "What shall I say, sir?"

"*Pamir* to unidentified vessel. What ship? What are your intentions? You know."

"*Pamir* to unidentified vessel," said Wallasey, speaking slowly and distinctly. "Come in, please."

Almost immediately a voice replied, "Unidentified vessel to *Pamir*. Maintain your present course and speed. Open your airlocks to receive my boarding party." There was a slight accent. Waldegren? It sounded like it.

Listowel turned to Grimes. "What now, Commodore?"

Grimes grinned. "If we didn't have ladies present I'd tell him to get stuffed. Pass me the mike, Mr. Wallasey." Then he said, in what Sonya referred to as his best quarterdeck voice, "*Pamir* to unidentified vessel. Identify yourself at once. And sheer off. You are getting in my way."

"Unidentified vessel to *Pamir*. Open your airlock doors. Prepare for boarding party. Do not offer resistance. Over."

"Mphm," grunted Grimes, releasing the pressure of his thumb on the transmit button of the microphone. "I want you to turn away, Listowel. You are master of an unarmed merchant vessel. You can't fight, so you run. Put the Llanith sun dead astern. As long as he sees us doing all the right things he'll be lulled into a sense of security."

Driving surfaces pivoted about their masts, the east sails presenting their black sides to the source of light, the west sails their reflective sides. The ship came around fast. And then, on all four masts, the reflective surfaces were spread to catch the full force of the photon gale.

"Bearing green one six five. Altitude zero. Range nineteen. Closing."

"Must have hung out the crew's washing," commented Listowel. "I'm afraid that I can't squeeze any more out of *Pamir*."

"It doesn't matter," Grimes told him. "We want her to catch up." He looked astern through the binoculars. *Pamir*'s sails cut off the glare from the Llanith sun and the raider was clearly visible on the starboard quarter. Like *Pamir* she was a four-master, with a cruciform rig, but additional triangular sails had been set between the masts. Running free this would give her a decided advantage.

"Range fifteen. Fourteen. Closing."

"Sir?" asked Fowler appealingly.

"No," said Grimes. "Not yet. We must consider the legalities. She must fire the first shot."

"But those legalities would only apply, sir, if we were a merchant vessel. But we aren't. We're an auxiliary cruiser of the Rim Worlds Navy—"

"A spacelawyer yet!" commented Grimes admiringly. The young man was right, of course. He, Grimes, should have played heavy commodore as soon as contact had been made with the pirate, demanding her unconditional surrender. He might have done just that if he had a real warship under his feet. He decided that, after all, his own way of playing it was the best, especially since the other ship obviously had the heels of *Pamir*. He said, "You can play with your rockets as soon as I give the word, not before. And when you do use them, try for the enemy's rigging, his masts and sails."

"Bearing green one five oh. Closing. Range nine. Closing."

"This is the commodore. Action will be opened shortly. It seems likely that the starboard broadside will be the first to be used."

"Unidentified ship to *Pamir*. You've been asking for trouble. You are about to get it. Over."

"You have our permission to tell him to get stuffed, John," said Sonya sweetly.

"Bearing green one two five. Range seven. Closing."

Shortening sail, thought Grimes, watching through the binoculars.

There're those tri-s'ls or whatever he calls 'em coming in. And I can see ports opening. Boat bays? Or gunports?

A gout of yellow flame spurted from one of the openings in the raider's hull, just abaft the masts. A long time later, it seemed, there was an explosion ahead *of Pamir,* about half a kilometer distant, a sudden rose of pale fire burgeoning in the blackness. So the pirate was using projectile weapons.

"Unidentified vessel"—the joke was wearing thin—"to *Pamir.* That was the last warning. Surrender or take the consequences."

"Bearing green ninety. Range five, four, three—closing."

No identification marks, thought Grimes, studying the other vessel through the powerful glasses. *Could be one of ours, save for a few, subtle points of difference . . .*

He said to Fowler. "All right, Lieutenant. You may open fire."

He saw the first rocket flash from its launching tube, trailing a wake of blue flame, spinning a flimsy filament of incandescence over the shortening distance between the two ships. It got a little over halfway, and then a stream of tracer came hosepiping from a gunport, met it, eroded it into ragged and harmless fragments of spinning debris. The warhead didn't explode.

"Rapid fire!" ordered Grimes. "Get the other five rockets out and on the way as quickly as possible. Don't bother guiding them in. One might get through."

None did. The pirate's machine gunners were fast.

"Range one. Point seven five. Point five."

"Resistance is useless," came the voice from the NST transceiver.

"Starboard broadside, fire," said Grimes into the intercom microphone.

He was not altogether prepared for what happened. He was expecting to see the enemy's sails shredded, his masts cut down, by the shot that he had prepared, the same sort of shot that had been used so effectively during the days of sail on Earth, the bags of scrap metal, nuts and bolts, lengths of metal chain. He had forgotten, though, that one of the old men-o'-war never, when firing a broadside, fired all guns simultaneously—they were fired in quick succession.

Pamir lurched. It was more than a mere lurch. It was as though a giant palm had swatted her on her starboard side. The north and south masts were carried away, each of them falling to starboard as the ship was driven to port by the recoil, the yards of each of them ripping the sails of the east mast, becoming inextricably entangled with the rigging.

"You got her, sir!" Fowler was yelling. "You got her!"

Grimes, who had been knocked down by the violent lateral acceleration, got groggily to his feet, staggered to the starboard viewports. The raider was, indeed, in a sorrier state than *Pamir*. In addition to the damage to her rigging there were gaping holes in her shell plating, through some of which smoke and flame flared explosively, like rocket exhausts. Her control room ports were bright with the ruddy glare of an internal fire. She was spinning slowly about her long axis. The one undamaged main spar, the east mast, which had been on her starboard side, shielded from *Pamir's* guns, lifted into view as she rolled, lifted, then dipped toward the other ship—and held steady, a long, metal lance. Freakishly, then, the rotary motion ceased. Perhaps a survivor was still exercising some sort of control, was determined to exact vengeance before his death. And on the far side air, mixed with the gases of combustion, was still escaping into the vacuum, inexorably driving the total wreck on to the near-wreck.

"Range closing," Denby was saying, over and over again. "Range closing. Range closing."

"Reaction drive!" ordered Grimes. "Get us out of here!" He could visualize the end of that long spar driving through *Pamir's* shell plating and piercing the vacuum chamber in which the sphere of anti-matter was suspended in the strong magnetic fields. It was not a nice thing to think about.

Listowel made no reply. The captain was slumped in his seat, unmoving.

Sandra was shaking her husband violently. "Ralph! Wake up! Wake up!" Then, snarling wordlessly, she pulled him from his chair, letting him drift to the deck. Before she was properly seated in his place her long fingers were on the controls. She snarled again, then snapped, "Something's wrong, Commodore!"

"Starboard broadside," ordered Grimes into the intercom microphone. "Fire!" That should push them away and clear from their dying attacker.

"The guns are off their mounts," came a hysterical voice. "We have casualties—"

Denby was still calling out range figures—in meters now—but it was not necessary. The shattered, burning raider was too close and was getting closer.

"Roll her, Sandra!" shouted Grimes.

"But our east mast is some protection—"

"It's not. Roll her, damn you!"

"Roll her," repeated Sonya. "He knows what he's doing." She added quietly, "I hope."

The gyroscope controls and the gyroscopes themselves were still working. There was the initial rumble as the flywheels started to turn, then the low hum. The drifting wreck slid slowly from view, dipping below the starboard viewport rims—but if Denby's radar readings were to be credited disaster was now only millimeters distant.

Grimes ordered, "Rotate through ninety degrees. Let me know when you're on eighty-five."

The next few seconds could have been twice that many years.

"Eighty-five," stated Sandra at last.

"Port battery—fire."

Again *Pamir* was slammed by that giant hand and was swatted clear of the dying raider's murderous sidelong advance. The tracks of the two ships diverged—but not fast enough, thought Grimes. He said urgently, "I don't care how you do it, Sandra, but get some of our sails trimmed to catch the light from Llanith. We must get out of here, and fast!"

"But we should board," said Sonya. "There may be survivors. There will be evidence. The fire will burn itself out once the atmosphere in the ship is exhausted."

"Not that sort of fire. Do something, Sandra."

Using the gyroscopes she turned the ship, at last getting the sails of the one surviving mast trimmed to the photon gale. Astern the wreck dwindled in a second to the merest point of light—and then, briefly, became a speck of such brilliance as to sear the retinas of those who watched. It had happened as Grimes had been sure that it must happen. The casing of the sphere of anti-matter had been warped by the heat of the fire—or, perhaps, had been buckled by an explosion. Contact with normal matter had been inevitable.

The pirate was gone, every atom of her structure canceled out.

The pirate was gone and *Pamir* was drifting, crippled. It was the time for the licking of wounds, the assessment of damage before, hopefully, limping into port under jury rig. Men aboard *Pamir* had been injured, perhaps killed. It had been an expensive victory. And, Grimes knew that it would not have been so expensive had he remembered to fire the guns of his broadside in succession instead of all at once.

He realized that Fowler, the gunnery officer, was saying something to him. "It was brilliant, sir, brilliant, the way you fought the action—"

He replied slowly, "We won. But—"

"But?" The young man's face wore a puzzled expression.

"But you can't make an omelet without breaking a few eggs," contributed Sonya rather too brightly.

"But you should be able to make one without blowing up the kitchen," was all that Grimes was able to manage in way of reply.

⪼ The Dutchman ⪻

GRIMES was packing his overnight bag without much enthusiasm.

"Do you have to go?" asked Sonya.

He replied rather testily, "I don't have to do anything. But the lightjammers have always been my babies and I've always made a point of seeing them in and seeing them out."

"But Coldharbor Bay? And in midwinter? There are times, my dear, when I strongly suspect that I married a masochist."

"If only you were a sadist we'd live happily forever after," he retorted. "And if you were a masochist you'd be coming with me to Port Erikson."

"Not bloody likely," she told him. "Why you couldn't have arranged for your precious lightjammers to berth somewhere in what passes for the Tropics on this dismal planet is beyond my comprehension."

"There were reasons," he said.

Yes, there were reasons, one of the most important being that a lightjammer is a potential superbomb with a yield greatly in excess of that of the most devastating nuclear fusion weapon. The essential guts of a starsailer is the sphere of anti-matter, contraterrene iron, held suspended in vacuum by powerful magnetic fields. In theory there is no possibility that the anti-matter will ever come in contact with normal matter—but history has a long record of disasters giving dreadful proof that theory and practice do not always march hand in hand. The terminal port for the lightjammers, therefore, was located in a region of Lorn uninhabited save by a handful of fur trappers. It would have been at the South Pole itself but for the necessity for open water, relatively ice-free the year around, to afford landing facilities for the ships.

The first of these weird vessels, *Flying Cloud*, had been an experimental job designed to go a long way in a long time, but with a very low power consumption. The most important characteristic of anti-matter—apart from its terrifying explosive potential—is anti-mass. A ship with a sphere of contraterrene iron incorporated in her structure is weightless and inertialess. With her sails spread to the photon gale she can attain an extremely high percentage of the velocity of light but cannot, of course, exceed it,

The crew of *Flying Cloud* had been, putting it mildly, a weird mob. Somehow they had become obsessed with the idea of turning the vessel into a real faster-than-light ship. (The conventional starship, proceeding under inertial drive and Mannschenn Drive, is not faster than light, strictly speaking; she makes lightyears-long voyages in mere weeks by, as it has been put, going ahead in space while going astern in time.) This desirable end they attempted to achieve by means of a jury-rigged rocket drive, using homemade solid fuel, just to give *Flying Cloud* that extra nudge.

Fantastically, the idea worked, although it should not have. Not only did it work, but there were economically advantageous side effects. The lightjammer finished up a long way off course, plunging down to apparently inevitable destruction on Llanith, one of the planets of the anti-matter systems to the galactic west of the Rim Worlds. But a transposition of atomic charges had taken place, She now was anti-matter herself, whereas that contraterrene iron sphere was now normal matter.

Flying Cloud had landed on Llanith and had been welcomed by the people, human rather than merely humanoid, of that world. She had remained on Llanith until the Llanithian scientists and engineers had worked out just what had happened and why. (The attitude of the scientists at first had been that it couldn't possibly have happened.) Then, after modifications had been made to her control systems and the makeshift rocket replaced by a properly designed reaction drive, she had returned to Lorn, carrying not only a sample shipment of trade goods but passengers from the Llanithi Consortium.

And Rim Runners, the shipping line of the Rim Worlds Confederacy, had a new trade.

Grimes sat in the forward cabin of the Rim Runners' atmosphere ferry that somebody had called—the name had stuck—the Commodore's Barge. He was not handling the controls himself. His old friend and shipmate Billy Williams, master of the deep space tug *Rim Malemute*, was piloting. Grimes was admiring the scenery.

The landscape unrolling beneath the barge was spectacular enough but cold and forbidding. Lake Misere was well-astern now and the craft was threading its way over and through the Great Barrens, skirting the higher, jagged, snowcapped peaks, its inertial drive snarling as Williams fought to maintain altitude in the vicious downdrafts. The big man cursed softly to himself.

Grimes said, "You would insist on coming along for the ride, Billy."

"I didn't think you'd make me drive. Skipper."

"Rank has its privileges."

"No need to rub it in. If it's all the same to you I'll take this little bitch down through the Blackall Pass. It's putting on distance, but I don't feel like risking the Valley of the Winds after what we've been getting already."

"As you've been saying, you're driving."

Williams brought the barge's head around to port, making for the entrance to the pass. The opening was black in the dark gray of the cliff face, a mere slit that seemed to widen as the aircraft came on to the correct line of approach. And then they were plunging through the gloomy, winding canyon—the tortuousness of which was an effective wind baffle, although the eddies at every bend made pilotage difficult. The echoes of the irregular beat of the inertial drive, bouncing back from the sheer granite walls, inhibited conversation.

They broke out at last into what passed for daylight in these high latitudes, under a sky which, on this side of the ranges, was thickly overcast. Only to the northwest, just above the featureless horizon of the Nullarbor Plain, was there a break in the cloud cover, a smear of sullen crimson to mark the setting of the Lorn sun.

They flew steadily over the desolate tundra through the gathering darkness. The lights of Port Erikson came up at last, bright but cheerless. Beyond them Grimes could see the tiny moving sparks of white and red and green that must be the navigation lanterns of the small icebreaker that, in winter, was employed to keep Coldharbor Bay clear of fast ices and pack ice.

"Too bloody much seamanship about this job, Skipper," remarked Williams cheerfully.

"No such thing as too much seamanship," retorted Grimes huffily. He pulled the microphone of the VHF transceiver from its clip. "Astronautical Superintendent to Port Erikson. Can you read me? Over."

"Loud and clear, Commodore, loud and clear. Pass your message. Over."

"My ETA Port Erikson is ten minutes from now. Over."

"We're all ready and waiting for you, Commodore."

"What's the latest on *Pamir*?"

"ETA confirmed a few minutes ago. 2000 hours our time."

"Thank you, Port Erikson. Over and out."

Ahead was the scarlet blinker that marked the end of the airstrip. Williams maintained speed until the flashing light was almost directly beneath the barge, until it looked as though they must crash into the spaceport's control tower. With only seconds to spare he brought the aircraft to a shuddering halt by application of full reverse thrust, let her fall, checked her descent a moment before she hit the concrete.

Grimes decided to say nothing. After all, he himself was frequently guilty of such exhibitions and all his life he had deplored the all-too-common *don't do as I do, do as I say,* philosophy.

Grimes and Williams waited in the control tower with Captain Rowse, the harbormaster. (In a normal spaceport his official title would have been port captain, but a normal spaceport does not run to a harbor, complete with wharfage and breakwaters.)

"She's showing up now," announced the radar operator.

"Thank you, Mr. Gorbels," said Rowse.

The VHF speaker came to life. "*Pamir* to Port Erikson, *Pamir* to Port Erikson. Am coming in. Over."

Grimes recognized the voice, of course. Listowel had been master of the experimental *Flying Cloud* and was now in command of *Pamir*. A good man, not easily panicked, one who would have been just as at home on the poop of a windjammer as in the control room of a spaceship.

The commodore moved so that he could look up through the transparent dome that roofed the control tower. Yes, there she was, her navigation lights bright sparks against the black overcast, white and emerald, masthead, port and starboard. (Her real masts were retracted, of course, and her sails furled. She was driving herself down through the atmosphere by negative dynamic lift, a dirigible airship rather than a spaceship.) Faintly Grimes could hear the throb of her airscrews, even above the thin whining of the wind that eddied about the tower.

The ship was lower now, visible through the windows that overlooked Coldharbor Bay. Grimes lifted borrowed night glasses to his eyes, ignoring the TV screen that presented the infrared picture. The slim, graceful length of her was clearly visible, picked out by the line of lighted ports. Down she came—down, down, slowly circling, until she was only meters above the dark, white-flecked waters of the bay. From her belly extended hoses and Grimes knew that the thirsty centrifugal pumps would be sucking in ballast.

"*Pamir* waterborne," announced Listowel from the VHF speaker. "Am proceeding to berth. Over."

Grimes, Williams and Rowse shrugged themselves into heavy overcoats, put on fur-lined caps. The harbormaster led the way to the elevator that would take them down to ground level. They dropped rapidly to the base of the tower. Outside it was bitterly cold and the wind carried thin flurries of snow. Grimes wondered why some genius could not devise earflaps that would not inhibit hearing—his own prominent ears felt as though they were going to snap off at any moment. But during berthing operations it was essential to hear as well as to see what was going on.

The three men walked rapidly to the wharf, breasting the wind—little, fat Rowse in the lead, chunky Grimes and big, burly Williams a couple of steps in the rear. The shed lights were on now, as were the position-marker flashers. Beside each of the latter waited three linesmen, beating their arms across their chests in an endeavor to keep warm. The berthing master, electric megaphone in his gloved hand, was striding up and down energetically. *Pamir* came in slowly and carefully, almost hidden by the cloud of spray thrown up by the turbulence induced by her airscrews. She was accosting the wharf at a steep angle at first and then turned, so that she was parallel to the line of wharfage. The wind did the rest, so that it was hardly necessary for Listowel to use his linethrowers fore and aft. She fell gently alongside, with her offshore screws swiveled to provide transverse thrust against the persistent pressure of the southerly.

She lay there, a great, gleaming torpedo shape, gently astir as the slight chop rolled her against the quietly protesting fenders. The hum of motors, the threshing of airscrews, suddenly ceased.

From an open window in his control room Listowel called, "Is this where you want me?"

"Make her fast as she is, Captain," called the berthing master.

"As she is," came the reply.

A few seconds later a side door opened and the brow extended from the wharf, stanchions coming erect and manropes tautening.

Grimes was first up the gangway. After all, as he had said to Sonya, the lightjammers were his babies.

Listowel received the boarding party in his day cabin. With him was Sandra Listowel, who was both his wife and his catering officer. Rim Runners did not, as a general rule, approve of wives traveling in their husband's ships in any capacity, but Sandra was one of the original *Flying Cloud* crew and had undergone training in that peculiar mixture of seamanship and airmanship required for the efficient handling of a lightjammer. Grimes often wondered if she had, over the years, become like so many of the wives of the old-time windjammer masters, a captain *de facto*—though he did not think that Ralph Listowel would allow such a situation to develop.

Captain Listowel had changed little over the years. When he rose to greet his visitors he towered over them. He had put on no weight and his closely cut hair was still dark, save for a touch of gray at the temples. And Sandra was as gorgeous as ever, a radiant blonde, not quite as slim as she had been but none the worse for that. Her severe, short-skirted, black uniform suited her.

Listowel produced a bottle and glasses. He said, "You might like to try this. You look as though you need warming up. It's something new. Our Llanithi friends acquired a taste for scotch and a local distiller thought he'd cash in on it. What he produced is not scotch. Even so, it's good. It might go well on Lorn and the other Rim Worlds."

Grimes sipped the clear, golden fluid experimentally, then enthusiastically, "Not bad at all." Then "You'd better have some more yourself to soften the blow, Listowel."

"What blow, Commodore?"

"You've a very quick turnaround this time. As you know *Herzogen Cecils* is tied up for repairs on Llanith—and I'd still like to know just how Captain Palmer got himself dismasted."

"I have his report with me, Commodore."

"Good. I'll read it later. And when *Lord Of The Isles* comes in to Port Erikson she's being withdrawn for survey. Which leaves you and *Sea Witch* to cope." He grinned. "As they used to say back on Earth in the days of sail, 'Growl you may, but go you must.'"

"But we're still in the days of sail, Commodore," said Listowel. "And as one of the sailing ship poets said, 'All I ask is a tall ship and a star to steer her by.'"

"Very touching, Ralph, very touching," commented Sandra Listowel. "But I'm sure that the Chief Stewards of the oceangoing sailing ships had their problems, just as I have." She turned to

Grimes. "Last time we were in Port Erikson, Commodore, we enjoyed our usual two weeks alongside—but even then we sailed without all our stores. How will it be this time?"

"Better," promised Grimes. "I'll light a fire under the tail of the Provendore Department back at Port Forlorn." He allowed Listowel to fill his glass. "Did you have a good trip, Captain?"

"Yes. Even so—"

"Even so what?"

"I think you might keep us informed, sir, of these other light-jammers, the experimental ones, cluttering up the route between Lorn and Llanith."

Grimes stared. "What are you talking about, Listowel?"

"We averted collision by the thickness of a coat of paint. Captain Palmer, in *Herzogen Cecile*, also had a close shave. His emergency alteration of course was so violent that it carried away his N and E masts with all their sails. He limped to Port Listowel on Llanith on S and W only."

"Why didn't he report it? The circumstances, I mean."

"He must have read your last circular, Commodore."

Grimes's prominent ears burned as he flushed angrily. But Listowel was right. He, Grimes, had written that circular under pressure from the Rim Worlds Admiralty—which body was, as he had put it, passing through a phase of acting like small boys playing at pirates. The fleet was out—or had been out or would be out—on deep space maneuvers. Masters and officers were reminded that the Carlotti bands were continually monitored by potentially hostile powers. Therefore no report of any sighting of Rim Worlds Navy warships was to be made over these channels, whatever the circumstances. And so forth.

"We are the only people with the Erikson-Charge-Reversing Drive," went on Listowel. "So we assumed that what we saw was an experimental warship. One of ours. Palmer assumed likewise."

Grimes made a major production of filling and lighting his pipe. He said through the swirling cloud of acrid blue smoke, "The Navy doesn't have any lightjammers, yet. They want some, just in case we ever fail to see eye to eye with the Llanithi Consortium. But the first ships of the line, as they are to be called, are still on the drawing board."

Listowel murmured thoughtfully, "Nevertheless we saw something—and it as near as dammit hit us. What was it, Commodore?"

"You tell me," said Grimes. "I'm listening."

LISTOWEL WAS SAYING, "We were bowling along under a full press of sail and the Doppler Log was reading point eight nine seven, so it was nowhere near time to light the fire under our arse—" He coughed apologetically. "That, sir, is the expression we use for starting the reaction drive—"

"I gathered as much," said Grimes. "But go on."

"We were just finishing dinner in the main salon. I had Llawissen and his two wives—he's the new Llanithi trade commissioner, as you know—at my table. We were making the usual small talk when I noticed that the little red warning light in the chandelier had come on."

"Sounds very fancy," commented Williams.

"You should have done more time in passenger ships, Billy," Grimes told him. "That signal is to tell the master that he's wanted in control, but for something short of a full-scale emergency. Carry on, Captain."

"So I excused myself, but didn't leave the table in a hurry. Still, I lost no time in getting to the control room. Young Wallasey, the third mate, was O.O.W. He said, 'We've got company, sir.' I said, 'Impossible.' He pointed and said, 'Look.'

"So I looked.

"We had company all right. She was out on the starboard beam, just clear of E topmast. She was only a light at first, a blueish glimmer, a star where we knew damn well no star should be, could be, hanging just above the distant mistiness of the Lens.

"'Anything on the radar?'" I asked.

"There wasn't—and these ships aren't fitted with Mass Proximity Indicators."

"No need for them," grunted Grimes, "unless you have Mannschenn Drive."

"So—there was nothing on the radar, which is what made me think afterward that this vessel must have been an experimental warship. The light was getting brighter and brighter, suggesting that the ship—I had already decided that it must be a ship—was getting closer.

"I got the big mounted binoculars trained on it. After I got them focused I could make out details, although that fuzzy, greenish light didn't help any. Some sort of force field? But no matter. I'd say that it—she—wasn't as big as *Pamir* or any of the other commercial lightjammers. She had an odd sort of rig, too. Instead of having four masts arranged in a cruciform pattern she had three, in series. And the sails—what I could see of them—had reflective surfaces on both sides instead of on one side only, as is the case with ours.

"And she was getting too bloody close on a convergent course. That was obvious, radar or no radar. Wallasey was calling her, first on the Carlotti set and then on NST, but getting no reply. There wasn't time to break out the Morse lamp. Whoever dreamed that we'd need it in deep space?

"So I said to hell with this and altered course, turning my W sails edge on to the Llanith sun. It was only just in time. That bastard was so near that I could see a line of ports with what looked like the muzzles of weapons sticking out of them. If she'd opened fire I wouldn't be here to tell the tale."

"Nor would any of us," commented Sandra Listowel.

"And only you and the officer of the watch saw this—thing?" asked Grimes.

"I'm not in the habit of throwing tea parties in my control room during emergencies, Commodore."

"Sorry. And presumably Captain Palmer saw something similar?"

"He did."

"But finish your story, Captain. What happened next?"

"Nothing. As I've told you, I altered course. And when next I was able to snatch a glance out of the ports she was gone. Like a snuffed candle, Wallasey told me."

Grimes grunted. He was thinking matters over. While he had discovered the anti-matter systems to the Galactic West he had never visited their worlds. And he had never sailed in the lightjammers—though these ships were his brain children. He could afford the time for a voyage to Llanith—although his best policy would be to make all arrangements for the conduct of affairs during his absence first and to inform Rim Runners' management afterward.

Not that this last mattered really. The Rim Worlds Navy would be interested in this story of alien light-jammers on the Lorn-Llanith trade route—and Grimes, as a Commodore of the Naval Reserve, had often in the past been called back to active duty to investigate strange occurrences. He had been called the Confederacy's odd-job man for reasons. And Sonya would be in this too—she still held her commission in the Intelligence Branch of the Federation Survey Service.

Grimes said to Rowse, "I'd like to borrow your office, Captain. I've a pile of telephoning to do. Oh, Captain Listowel, would you mind having accommodation ready for Mrs. Grimes and myself? We shall be making the next round trip with you."

"And what about me, Skipper?" asked Williams plaintively.

"I'm sorry, Bill, but there just aren't any senior masters kicking around loose at the moment. So, as of right now, you're appointed Port Forlorn astronautical superintendent, acting, temporary."

"Not unpaid?" demanded the big man.

"Not unpaid," agreed Grimes.

Williams's manner brightened.

Grimes called Admiral Kravitz first. The Officer Commanding Rim Worlds Navy was not pleased at being awakened from a sound sleep, but after he had listened to Grimes's story he was alert and businesslike. He glowered at Grimes from the telephone screen. "These reports. They're utterly fantastic. Can you trust these masters of yours? Couldn't they have been seeing things?"

"They saw something," said Grimes. "In the case of *Pamir*, the intruder was seen by Captain Listowel and his third officer, Mr. Wallasey. In the case of *Herzogen Cecile*, the chief and second officers were in the control room as well as Captain Palmer. All the stories tally, even to minor details."

"Is there any—ah—excessive drinking aboard your ships? Any addiction to hallucinogenic drugs?"

"No." Grimes's ears were reddening. He countered with: "Are you sure that the Navy hasn't any experimental lightjammers?"

"You know bloody well we haven't, Grimes. Oh, all right, all right. Have your free trip at the taxpayers' expense. Don't forget to send the bill for your fare in to the Rim Worlds Navy."

"And my commodore's pay and allowances, sir?"

"Take that up with the accounts department, Grimes. You know how to look after yourself. Call me again at a civilized hour tomorrow morning after you've got things organized."

"Good night."

Grimes allowed himself a small grin. He was in an if-I'm-up-everybody's-up mood. He called Sonya. She, too, exhibited extreme displeasure at being disturbed at, as she put it, a jesusless hour. But her displeasure was replaced by enthusiasm. By the time the call was concluded she had decided what she would pack for herself and for Grimes and assured him that she would be at Port Erikson within twenty-four hours.

There was another call Grimes would have liked to have made, but unluckily Ken Mayhew, one of the few remaining psionic communication officers in the Rim Worlds, was not on Lorn. He was spending a long holiday on Francisco, of which planet his wife was a native. A good PCO, Grimes often said, was worth his weight in Carlotti transceivers—but not all PCOs were good and in the vast majority of interstellar ships the temperamental telepaths had been replaced by the Time-Space-twisting Carlotti radio equipment. But

a Carlotti transceiver could not read minds, was incapable of that
practice, frowned upon by the Rhine Institute but exercised
nonetheless and known variously as snooping and prying. If *Pamir*
had carried a psionic radio officer much could have been learned
about the strange lightjammer. As it was, nothing—apart from the
details of her appearance—was known.

Grimes went to the guest bedroom that had been provided for
him in the Port Erikson staff accommodation block and settled
down to read the reports—Listowel's as well as Palmer's. He would
have liked to have discussed them with Rowse and Williams, but
the port captain was organizing the round-the-clock stevedoring
activities and Williams, who loved ships, was no doubt making a
nuisance of himself to *Pamir's* officers.

The reports told Grimes little more than he had already learned
from Captain Listowel's spoken account.

Grimes and Sonya were guests in *Pamir's* control room when
she sailed from Port Erikson at local noon, three days later. The
southerly had persisted, had freshened and was holding the ship
against the wharf. The pivoting airscrews would be hard put to it to
provide sufficient transverse thrust to pull her out bodily from the
berth. But the little icebreaker was also a tug and was given a
forward towline by *Pamir*.

Mooring lines were let go fore and aft, were swiftly winched
inboard. The pivoted offshore airscrews began to spin faster and
faster, their whirling blades flickering into invisibility—but they
were doing little more than holding the ship against the wind.

"Take her out, *Bustler*," ordered Listowel into his VHF microphone.

"Take her out, Captain," came the cheerful acknowledgment.

The towline grew taut, scattering a glittering spray in the thin
sunlight. *Bustler's* diesels thumped noisily and black smoke shot
from her squat funnel to be shredded by the stiff breeze. Grimes
went to an open window on the port side of the control room,
looked out and down. There was a gap now between the wharf fenders and the side of the ship forward, a gap that was slowly widening.

But what was happening aft? What about the projecting venturi of the reaction drive, the after control surfaces? Wasn't there a possibility—a probability—of their fouling the wharf gantries? But Listowel, standing in the middle of his control room, didn't seem to be worrying about it. And, after all, the ship was his.

The stern was coming off, too, under the tug of the airscrews, although not so rapidly. There was clearance between the tail fins and the nearest wharf structure—not much, but enough. And then the port propellers, unpivoted, whirled into motion, giving headway and accentuating the swinging moment. *Pamir* turned to starboard slowly but determinedly, a white and green jumble of brash ice piling up along that side. She came around into the wind and the starboard screws pivoted as she turned, giving headway instead of lateral thrust.

Astern the distance between ship and wharf was widening rapidly.

"Let go, *Bustler*," ordered Listowel and then, to Grimes, "I'm always afraid that one day I'll forget and drag that poor little bitch with me all the way to Llanith."

"Is there any market there for used tugs or icebreakers?"

"Button her up, Mr. Wallasey," said Listowel.

The third officer pressed buttons. The wheelhouse windows slid shut.

And about time. Grimes thought. Icy drafts had begun to eddy about the compartment.

"Dump ballast."

The ship lifted as the tons of water gushed out from her tanks, rising faster and faster, stemming the wind, until Coldharbor Bay, directly beneath her, seemed a puddle beside which a child had set a huddle of toy buildings—until far to the south the ice barrier, a coldly gleaming wall of pearly white, lifted over the black sea horizon.

She lifted like a rocket, but without noise and without crushing acceleration effects. She soared into the clear sky, the color of which deepened from blue to purple, to black. Below her the planet was no longer a vast, spread-out map—it was a globe, with seas and continents half-glimpsed through the swirling cloud formations, with the dark shadow of the terminator drifting slowly across it from the west.

The chief officer came into the control room to report all secured for space. Other reports came over the intercom. Listowel acknowledged them and then, smiling, turned to his guests. "Well, Commodore and Mrs. Grimes, how do you like it so far?"

"I envy you, Listowel. You've a fine ship and you know how to handle her."

"Thank you, Commodore." He said to the third officer, "Make the usual warning, Mr. Wallasey." Then, to Grimes, "Seats and seat belts, sir. I have to swing her to the right heading now."

The maneuver was routine enough in any interstellar ship, the turning of a vessel about her axes until she was lined up with the target star. Somewhere amidships the big directional gyroscopes grumbled, hummed and then whined, and centrifugal force gave the illusion of off-center gravity. The great globe that was Lorn seemed to fall away and to one side, and its sun drifted aft. Ahead now was only the blackness of intergalactic space, although the misty Lens was swimming slowly into view through the side ports. Then, coming gradually toward the center of the cartwheel sights, appeared the distant cluster of bright sparks that were the anti-matter stars. The gyroscopes slowed almost to a stop, grumbling, as Captain Listowel made the last fine adjustments. They halted at last.

The master looked up from his sighting telescope, murmured, "She'll do." Both hands went to the console before him. He said, "Look out through the side ports and aft, Commodore. This is worth watching."

It was.

From the control room—which, like the bridge of a seagoing ship or the conning tower of a submarine, was a superstructure— there was a good view astern. Grimes could see the engine pods, four to a side, their now motionless four-bladed airscrews gleaming in the harsh sunlight. He could see the stubs of three of the masts—W to port, N on the centerline and E to starboard. S, of course, was beneath the hull and not visible, except in the periscope screen. But those stubs were stubs no longer. They were elongating, extending, stretching like impossibly fast growing, straight-stemmed trees. And as they grew they sprouted branches, foliage—the yards and the sails. The royals at the head of each mast were fully spread before the process of telescopic elongation was completed.

There was disorientation then, visual confusion, upset balance as the star wind filled the sails. What had been up was up no longer. Aft was still aft, but it was also "down." Chairs swung in their gimbals, as did some of the instruments. Other equipment was cunningly designed so that it could be used from almost any angle.

Grimes realized what was happening but, twisting his body awkwardly in the chair, still stared in fascination aft and down through the polarized glass of the viewports. He had seen the sail plan of this ship, of course, had helped to draw it up; but this was the first time he had watched a lightjammer actually making sail. He mentally recited the names of the courses. He had insisted the old nomenclature be used. Northsail, lower topsail, upper topsail, topgallant, royal . . .

He turned away at last, asked, "Do you usually make sail all in one operation, Captain?"

Listowel laughed. "Only when I have guests in the control room."

Sonya laughed, too. "John would prefer to see all hands out in spacesuits, clambering in the rigging like monkeys."

"The good old days, eh?" Listowel unsnapped his seat belt. "Roll and go. Hell or Llanith in ninety days—and the sun's over the yardarm."

Grimes took one last look at that splendid suit of sails, black against the glare of the Lorn sun, before he got up to follow Listowel and Sonya from the control room. He realized that he would have to get his spacelegs back. In this inertialess ship, in spite of the already fantastic acceleration, the distinction between up and down was a matter of faith rather than of knowledge.

They enjoyed their drinks—more of the Llanithian whisky—in Listowel's comfortable day room, where Sandra joined them.

"How are the customers?" her husband asked her.

"There's only one this trip," she told him. She flashed a smile at the guests. "I don't count the commodore and Mrs. Grimes as real passengers."

"Who is it?" asked Grimes. "Anybody I know—or should know?"

"Perhaps you should know her, sir. She's a missionary."

"Why wasn't I warned?" demanded Listowel.

"I'm warning you now, Ralph."

"What's her name? What nut cult is she trying to peddle?"

"She's the Reverend Madam Swithin. Rather an old dear, actually. She's a missionary for the United Primitive Spiritualist Church."

"And she thinks she'll be able to convert the Llanithi?"

"She'll probably convert some of them. After all, given the right conditions you can convert anybody to anything."

"But United Primitive Spiritualism—" muttered Listowel disgustedly.

"They have something," Sonya told him. "I've had some odd experiences and so has John."

"I only hope she's not at my table," said the master.

"Where else could I put her, Ralph? After all, she is a person of some importance in her church. I couldn't put her with the junior officers."

"I'm sorry about this, Commodore," Listowel said.

"Don't worry, Captain. We'll survive somehow," Grimes told him.

The Reverend Madam Swithin was, as Sandra had said, rather an old dear, but the sort of old dear whose idea of conversation is asking endless questions. Yet it could be said in her favor that she enjoyed the excellent food prepared by Sandra and served by the efficient stewardess and that she did not belong to one of those sects that regard alcoholic beverages as sinful. It took her some little time to get things sorted out, however. She knew that a commodore is superior to a captain and so assumed that Grimes was master of

Pamir. She asked him why he wasn't wearing a uniform. Then she asked why *Pamir* wasn't named according the general Rim Runners principle, with the "Rim" prefix.

Grimes told her, "In these vessels we've tried to revive the names of the old sailing ships, the Terran windjammers. Unluckily most, if not all, of the most famous names are being used by Trans-Galactic Clippers—*Thermopylae* and *Cutty Sark* and so on."

"Are Trans-Galactic Clippers lightjammers like this one, Commodore?"

"No, Madam Swithin. But the original clippers were very fast sailing ships and long after sail had vanished from the seas the name 'clipper' was still being used by the operators of other forms of transport—road services, airlines and so forth. One of the first little ships to fly to Earth's moon was called *Yankee Clipper*."

"How interesting, Commodore. The usage gives one a sense of continuity, don't you think? And now, Captain, when do you think you're getting this clipper of yours to Llanith?"

"ETA is just three weeks subjective from now."

"You said 'Hell or Llanith in ninety days'," Sonya reminded him.

"Ninety days objective," He told her. "But only three weeks as we shall live them, Mrs. Grimes."

"And is there really any danger of the ship's getting wrecked? Not that I'm frightened, of course. I know that there is no death."

Sandra joined them at the table, bringing coffee. "Don't worry, Madam Swithin. That 'Hell or Llanith' is just an expression that Captain Listowel picked up from a book about the famous windjammers. There was a captain on the trade between England and Australia who used to say, 'Hell or Melbourne in ninety days!'"

"And as *I* was saying, dear, such a sense of continuity. So fascinating to think that you sailing ship captains are reincarnations of the old sailing ship captains. The wheel has come full circle and you have been reborn—"

Listowel was beginning to squirm uncomfortably in his chair. The junior officers at their tables—obviously listening—were starting to look amused. Grimes endeavoured to steer the conversation on to a fresh tack.

"And when, Captain," he asked, "do you start the reaction drive?"

"A week from now, Commodore, as soon as we have point nine recurring on the Doppler Log. Then we have a week of full acceleration and FTL flight. Then we have to decelerate. And then, all being well, we're there."

All being well, thought Grimes. *But if all is well, I shall have made this trip for nothing.*

SHE WAS A FINE SHIP, this *Pamir*, and most efficiently run—but, to one accustomed to a conventional starship, uncannily quiet. Grimes missed the incessant, noisy, arhythmic hammering of the inertial drive, the continuous thin, high keening of the Mannschenn Drive. Here the only mechanical noises were the occasional sobbing of a pump, the soft susurrus of the forced ventilation.

On she drove, running free before the photon gale. The Rim Stars astern were ruddily dim—the suns of the Llanithi Consortium blazed intensely blue ahead. And on the beam, mast and sails in black silhouette against it, glowed the great Lens of the Galaxy, unaffected by either red or blue shift.

The needle of the Doppler Log, after its initial rapid jump, crept slowly around its dial. *Point eight, point eight five, point eight seven five . . .* Grimes tried to imagine what the ship must look like to an outside observer, tried to visualize the compression along the fore and aft line. But to see her at all that mythical outside observer would have to be in another ship traveling in the same direction at the same speed—and then, of course, he would observe nothing abnormal.

And what would happen if *Pamir* hit something—even only a small piece of cosmic debris—at this fantastic velocity? So far the lightjammers had been lucky—but what if their luck suddenly ran out? The question, as far as her crew was concerned, was purely academic. They would never know what hit them—although after weeks or months or years the brief flare would be visible in the night skies of Lorn and Llanith.

At last came the time for the final acceleration—and the reversal of atomic charges. Again Grimes and Sonya were guests in the control room, watching with fascination. Listowel explained, "This isn't half as bad as that moment when the temporal precession field of the Mannschenn Drive is initiated. Oh, you'll feel something. We all do. Just a microsecond of tension and, at the same time—as the charges are reversed—what we call a scrambled spectrum. But there's none of the dithering about in and on alternate time tracks that we experienced when we first discovered the effect."

"Just as well," grunted Grimes. "Alternate time tracks are among my pet allergies."

Listowel was watching the log screen, which gave him far finer readings than the dial, to six places of decimals. Grimes and Sonya watched, too.

999993 . . . The crimson numerals glowed brightly. 999994 . . . 999995 . . . The 6 was a long time coming up . . . . Ah, here it was. 999997 . . . 999998 . . . There was another long delay. Then the final 9 appeared briefly but flickered back to 8.

"Go, you bitch, go," Listowel was whispering. 999999 . . .

"It's holding, sir," whispered one of the officers.

"I have to be sure . . . Now!" After the long days of quiet sailing the screaming roar of the rocket drive, carried by and through the metal structure of the ship, was startlingly loud. There should have been brutal acceleration, but there was not. There was not a physical sense of acceleration. Yet Grimes felt as though he, personally, were striving to lift some impossibly heavy weight. He felt as though he were pressing against some thin yet enormously tough film that stubbornly refused to break.

Then it burst.

There was real acceleration now, driving him down into the padding of his chair. He was dimly aware that Listowel—a strange Listowel, who looked like a photographic negative, whose shorts-and-shirt uniform was black instead of the regulation white, whose face had become oddly negroid—was doing things, explaining as his hands moved over the console. His voice, normally light, was a deep, grumbling bass. "Have to pivot the sails, Commodore. Edge on, or we'll be taken aback—"

Suddenly things snapped back to normal.

Color and sound were as they should be and the acceleration had eased to a fairly comfortable one gravity. Grimes took mental stock of himself. Yes, he was still Commodore John Grimes of the Rim Worlds Naval Reserve, astronautical superintendent of Rim Runners. And he was still aboard *Pamir*. He turned to look at his wife, who smiled back at him rather shakily. And Sonya was still Sonya.

So far so good.

And the log screen?

Blue numerals now—*1.000459* . . . *1.000460* . . . The final *1* flashed up and then, in steady succession: 2, 3, 4, 5 . . .

All my years in deep space, thought Grimes, *and this is the first time I've really traveled faster than light* . . .

"So . . . we are all anti-matter now, Captain?" asked the Reverend Madam Swithin that evening at dinner. She did not wait for a reply, but went on, "But what about our souls, our essential essences?"

"I'm afraid, madam, that that's rather outside my province," replied Listowel.

"And what do you think, Commodore?"

Grimes grunted through a mouthful of steak.

"But the Llanithi have souls," the missionary went on. "Otherwise I should not be traveling to their worlds."

A rather uncomfortable silence was broken by Sonya. "Tell me, Madam Swithin—do you ever, in your séances, establish communication with the departed spirits of non-human entities?"

"Frequently, Mrs. Grimes. One of our mediums has as her control a Shaara princess, who last enjoyed material existence five hundred standard years ago. And recently, during a service in our church in Port Farewell, a spirit spoke through the officiating medium and said he was—that he had been, rather—a people's marshal on Llanith. What is a people's marshal, Captain?"

"It's roughly equivalent to a police commissioner on our worlds, madam," replied Listowel.

Sonya sipped from her wine glass, then asked, "One thing has always rather puzzled me, Madam Swithin. One of the doctrines of your church is reincarnation. How does that fit in with that large number of disembodied spirits who are always present at your séances to say their pieces?"

The motherly little woman smiled sweetly at Sonya. "There is reincarnation, as we believe—as we *know*—Mrs. Grimes. But the soul is not reincarnated into a new body immediately after its release from the old one. In the case of ordinary people the delay is not a long one. It is the extraordinary people, the outstanding personalities, who often have to wait for centuries, or until a suitable vehicle for their rare psyches has become available—"

"In other words," said Grimes, who was becoming interested, "until the genes and chromosomes have been suitably shuffled and dealt."

"What a good way of putting it, Commodore. I must remember that." She looked at Grimes as though she were viewing him as a potential and valuable convert which, Grimes realized, he could be. *Why can't I keep my big mouth shut?* he asked himself. "You will agree, Commodore, that a special sort of character is required for the captain of a ship?"

Grimes made a noncommittal sound.

"And that an even more special kind of character is required for the captain of a sailing ship—"

"I did," admitted Grimes cautiously, "bear certain qualities in mind when I appointed the masters and officers to these lightjammers and not all of those I selected passed the rather rigorous training."

Listowel muttered something about bumbling around in blimps over the Great Barrens, but subsided when Grimes glared at him.

"And how many lightjammers does your company operate, Commodore?"

"At the moment, four. *Pamir*, *Herzogen Cecile*, *Lord Of The Isles* and *Sea Witch*. As the trade expands we shall require more tonnage, of course. *Preussen* and *Garthpool* are on the drawing boards. And the Rim Worlds Navy has the plans for at least three sailing warships."

"Four ships. And five more some time in the future. But what of the thousands of sailing captains who must have lived in the days when their vessels were the only long-distance transport on Earth? Many of those souls must still be waiting for reincarnation."

"One of my ancestors might be among them," said Grimes.

"Really, Commodore?"

"Yes. He was a Barbary Corsair—but before that he was master of an English ship in the Mediterranean trade. A forced convert to Islam who decided to play along and do as well for himself as possible—"

"Are you sure that he was never reincarnated, John?" asked Sonya. "Some of the less savory episodes in your past haven't been far short of piracy."

"I might be able to find out for you, Commodore," said Madam Swithin eagerly. "I am more of an administrator than a medium, but I do have powers—"

"Thank you," Grimes told her. "But I think I'd rather not know."

Pamir drove on, no longer scudding before the photon gale but riding the thunder of her rocket drive. Ahead was an impossible star cluster—the suns of the Llanithi Consortium blue-blazing, the Rim Suns sullenly smoldering embers. Astern was—nothing. On she drove, outrunning light, until the time came for deceleration.

The reaction drive was shut down and, at his controls, Listowel carefully pivoted his sails. Northsail, eastsail, southsail and westsail he turned, trimming them so that the radiance from the Llanithi stars was striking their reflecting surfaces at an oblique angle. Grimes, watching the Doppler Log screen, saw the numerals change from *25.111111* to *25.111110,* to *25.111109 . . .*

All four lower courses were now exerting full braking effect and the lower topsails were trimmed, squared. *23.768212 . . . 23.768000 . . . 23.759133 . . .* Upper topsails next. *19.373811 . . .* Topgallant sails *. . .* The log was winding down rapidly and ahead one of those vividly blue stars was a star no longer, was beginning to show an appreciable disk. Now the royals. *12.343433 . . . 11.300001 . . . 10.452552 . . . 8.325252 . . . 5.000000 . . . 2.688963 . . .*

So far there was no sensation. The ship was inertialess, her structure and crew protected from the forces that should have exploded them through the darkness and emptiness in a blazing flare of energy.

1.492981 . . . 1.205288 . . . 1.200438 . . . 1.113764 . . . 1.000009 . . .

The countdown was slowing.

1.000008 . . . 7 . . . 6 . . . 5 . . . 4 . . . 3 . . . 2 . . . 3 . . . 2 . . . 1 . . . 2 . . . 1 . . .

1.000000 . . .

As when the light barrier had been broken, there was the feeling of unbearable tension. Something snapped suddenly. The stars ahead diminished in number, although those remaining were still blue. Astern, dim and distant, the Rim Stars reappeared.

And the figures in the screen were now in red light: *999999 . . . 999998 . . . 999997 . . .*

"Sir." Willoughby, the chief officer was pointing. Out to starboard, just abaft the beam, was a star where no star should or could be—a point of greenish radiance that steadily brightened.

"Captain! Commodore!" It was Madam Swithin's voice. What the hell was she doing in the control room?

"Mr. Wallasey," said Listowel to his third officer, "please escort this lady down to her cabin."

"But, Captain," cried the missionary, "this is most important."

"So is that," he said, pointing. "I've no time to spare for—"

"That," she interrupted him, "is what is important."

"Mr. Wallasey—" began Listowel.

"Let her stay," said Sonya sharply. It was more of an order than a request. "Let her stay."

The young officer looked uncertainly at his Captain, at the commodore, at the commodore's wife. He looked again, questioningly, toward Listowel, But the master's full attention was on the strange light. It was closing on a converging course. And there was something solid, or apparently solid, in the center of that glowing circle of blue-green mist. A ship? Grimes had found a pair of binoculars, had them to his eyes. Yes, a ship.

Madam Swithin was speaking again, but the voice was not her own. It was male and had a strange, guttural accent. And the language was one that Grimes did not understand, although it seemed to be of Terran origin. German? No, he decided. Although there were similarities.

"Who are you?" Sonya was asking. "Speak so that we may understand."

"I cannot rest. I must not rest. Effer. To sail der seas vas I condemned, for all eternity, vhereffer and vheneffer dere are ships—"

The seas? wondered Grimes. *But space is a sea . . .*

He could make out the hull now through his glasses—high-pooped, with a tall forecastle. He could see the line of black-gaping gunports and the three masts with the square sails at fore and main, the staysails and the spritsail, the lateen sail at the mizzen . . .

This was no lightjammer.

"Kapitan!" that deep, urgent voice was commanding, "Starboard der helm! Starboard der helm!"

But an alteration of course to starboard would make a collision between *Pamir* and this apparition inevitable.

"Kapitan! Starboard der helm!"

And in the old days when the helm, the tiller, had been put to starboard both rudder and ship had turned to port, Grimes remembered from his reading. Even after the invention and introduction of the ship's wheel those topsy-turvy steering orders had persisted for quite a long while.

In the old days, the days of the windjammers . . .

And hadn't there been a legend about a Captain Van . . . What was his name? A Dutchman?

He laughed softly. "A ghost," he murmured. "A ghost."

Listowel laughed with him. "A bloody Rim Ghost. I should have known. I've heard enough about them. Phantom ships from alternate universes—"

A. Bertram Chandler

"Kapitan! For der luff of Gott, starboard!"

Listowel laughed again, contemptuously, "That thing can't hurt us. I'll not risk my spars and sails, my ship, for a silly, blown-away phantasm!"

A spurt of orange flame leaped from the archaic ship's forward gunport, followed by billowing dirty white smoke. The Dutchman had fired a warning shot.

"Listowel, bring her around to port at once," ordered Grimes.

"I'm not running from a ghost ship with ghost cannon, Commodore."

"Bring her around, damn you!"

"And you can't order me in my own control room—"

"Legally I can't—but I do order you." Had Grimes known how to handle the lightjammer he would have tried to push the younger man from the controls. But he did not know. The only thing in his mind that could be of value in this situation was his memory of the old sailors' tales.

"Kapitan! Starboard der helm!" It was a despairing cry in that strange male voice from the lips of the medium.

"He's warning us, Listowel!" cried Grimes. "The old legends— you've read them. I've seen your bookshelf. The appearance of the Flying Dutchman before disaster . . . The Vanderdecken ships were saved from disaster by a ghost ship's warning! Come to port, Captain! Bring her around to port!"

Realization dawned on Listowel's face. With a muttered oath he dropped his hands to the console. He worked fast now that it was almost too late—with desperate urgency. He trimmed the east sails, not bothering about precise angles, bringing all five of the great vanes around as fast as the trimming motors would let him, presenting their light-absorptive surfaces to the radiation of the Llanith sun. *Pamir* lurched as she fell off to port. The mast whipped violently and the royal was ripped from its yards, flapped ahead and away from the ship like a bat into hell. But the rest held as the ship pivoted about her short axis.

And Grimes, looking out to starboard, saw the Dutchman vanish like a snuffed candle—but not before he had glimpsed the tall figure on the poop, his long beard streaming in the wind (here, in interstellar space, where there were no winds but the star winds!), his right arm raised in a gesture of farewell.

"Well," muttered Listowel shakily. "Well—" Then: "Is it all right for us to resume course, Commodore?"

"I—I suppose so," replied Grimes. In a stronger voice he said, "I shall ground the lightjammers until a thorough survey has been made of this sector of space. There was something there. Something we just missed."

On the deck where she had fallen, where Sonya was supporting her head and shoulders, Madam Swithin began to stir. Her eyes opened, stared around her. "Where am I? What happened? How did I get here? I came all over queer and I don't remember any more—"

"Everything is all right," Sonya told her.

"Thank you, dear. Thank you. I shall be feeling better in a couple of jiffs. But I'd be ever so grateful if somebody could bring me a nice cup of—" The expression faded from her plump face and her eyes went vacant. That strange male voice—although now little more than a dying whisper—finished the sentence.

"—Holland gin," it said.

 The Last Hunt

I

GRIMES stood at the wide window of his office, which overlooked the Port Forlorn berthing apron, watched the starship *New Bedford* coming in. She was a stranger to the Rim Worlds. According to Lloyd's Register she was owned by the Hummel Foundation of Earth. The Foundation, Grimes knew, had been set up for the intensive study of xenobiology—its Interstellar Zoo, covering hundreds of square miles of Australia's Central Desert, was famous throughout the Galaxy. Almost equally famous was *New Bedford*'s master, Captain Haab. He was both master astronaut and big game hunter—an unlikely combination, but a highly successful one.

And what was Captain Haab doing out on the Rim?

Grimes could guess.

Slowly *New Bedford* dropped down from the clear sky—her arrival had coincided with one of Port Forlorn's rare fine days. She gleamed dazzlingly in the bright morning sunlight. As she gradually lost altitude the beat of her inertial drive rose from an irritable muttering to a noisy, unrhythmic drumming, frightening the snowbirds—which at this time of the year infested the spaceport—into glittering, clattering flight.

The commodore picked up binoculars, studied the descending

ship. He already knew that she was modified Epsilon Class, but was interested in the extent of the modifications. She looked more like a warship than a merchantman, the otherwise sleek lines of her hull broken by turrets and sponsons. Most of these seemed to be recent additions. She must have been specially fitted out for this expedition.

No doubt, Grimes thought, Captain Haab would be visiting him as soon as the arrival formalities were over and done with—it would be more of a business than a courtesy call. But everything was ready. The files of reports were still in Grimes's office, the spools of film, the three-dimensional charts with their plotted sightings and destructions. If Haab wanted information—which he almost certainly would—he should have it.

New Bedford was almost down now, dropping neatly into the center of the triangle marked by the brightly flashing red beacons. Already the beetlelike ground cars of the spaceport officials—port captain, port health officer, customs—had ventured on to the apron, were waiting to close in. But Haab, with all the resources of the Hummel Foundation behind him, would have no trouble in obtaining inward clearance.

New Bedford was down at last. Her inertial drive complained for the last time, then lapsed into silence. A telescopic mast extended from high on her hull, at control room level, and from it broke out a flag that fluttered in the light breeze. It was not, Grimes realized, the house flag of the Hummel Foundation, a stylized red dragon on a green field. This standard was white and blue.

Miss Walton, Grimes' secretary, had come to stand with him at the window. "What a funny ensign—what is it supposed to be? It looks like an airship, a blimp in a blue sky—"

The commodore laughed. "I think that the blue is supposed to represent sea, not sky. And that's not a blimp—"

"What is it, then, Commodore?"

"It could be a white whale," Grimes told her.

"Captain Haab to see you, sir," announced Miss Walton.

Grimes looked up from his desk where he had been blue-penciling the stores requisition sent in by the chief officer of *Rim Percheron*. "Show him in," he told his secretary.

The girl returned to the office followed by Haab. The master of *New Bedford* was a tall man, thin, towering over the little blonde. There was an oddly archaic cut to his tightly fitting black suit, to his stiff, white linen and black stock. His face was gaunt and deeply tanned between his closely cropped black hair and black chin beard. His eyes were a startlingly pale blue. He walked with a peculiarly jerky motion and from his right lee came a strange faint clicking noise.

Grimes rose to his feet, extended his right hand. "Welcome to Port Forlorn, Captain."

Haab took the commodore's hand in his own almost skeletal claw. "Thank you, sir."

"Sit down, Captain. Tea? Coffee?"

"Coffee if I may, Commodore. Black."

"Will you attend to it, please, Miss Walton? Black coffee for two. And did you have a good voyage out, Captain?"

"A quiet voyage."

"First time I've seen anybody from the Hummel Foundation out here. Of course, we haven't much in the way of exotic fauna on the Rim. Not on the man-colonized planets, that is. Most of our animals were raised from Terran stock."

"I'm not concerned with any of the lifeforms actually on the planets, Commodore."

A grin softened Grimes's craggy face. "I can guess what you've come for, Captain—" Miss Walton brought in the coffee tray, set it on the desk. Grimes said to the girl. "Would you mind having the projection room ready? You know the films we shall want—those that the admiralty lent me."

"The ones shot on the Lorn-Llanith route, sir?"

"Of course."

"Very good, sir. Oh, would you mind if I asked Captain Haab a question?"

"Go ahead, Miss Walton."

The girl addressed herself to *New Bedford*'s master. "I'm interested in flags, sir. What is the one that you have flying from your ship?"

Haab smiled thinly. "It's my own personal broad pennant. The Foundation allows me to wear it."

"But what is it, Captain?"

"A white whale," replied Haab.

"As I've already told you," grunted Grimes. "And now will you get those films ready?"

"And could you fill me in while we're waiting?" Haab asked Grimes.

"Of course, Captain. I'll start at the beginning."

"As you know," said Grimes, "we operate lightjammers on the run between the Rim Worlds and the Llanithi Consortium. The lightjammers are the only ships that can have their atomic charges reversed so that they can land on the anti-matter worlds without blowing themselves—and anybody else within ten thousand miles— to glory. The lightjammers had been running into trouble—a strange vessel kept appearing on a collision course, shoving them away to hell and gone off trajectory—"

Haab smiled. "You'll probably be hearing from the Rhine Institute about that. But the Hummel Foundation is concerned with living beings, not ghosts, not even such famous ghosts as the Flying Dutchman."

"Just as well. Since the navy started cleaning up the shipping lanes old Vanderdecken has been conspicuous by his absence. Maybe he's found a home on Atlantia. They still go in for sail in a big way there.

"Well, after the first reports came in I decided I'd better see for myself, so my wife and I took passage from Lorn to Llanith in *Pamir*. At that time it was thought that the Flying Dutchman was another lightjammer, a foreign ship snooping on our trade routes. But we had with us the Reverend Madam Swithin of the United Primitive Spiritualist Church, going out to Llanith as a missionary. Thanks to her we found out what the Flying Dutchman was and that Vanderdecken was warning us about something.

"So I grounded the lightjammers and sent a report to Admiral Kravitz, urging him to make a full-scale investigation. He did.

Luckily our fleet was out on maneuvers at the time so it all fitted in with the war games that were being played. Instead of the usual Redland versus Blueland it was the armed might of the Confederacy versus the Menace from Intergalactic Space. Mphm."

Haab registered strong disapproval. "Not a hunt," he growled, "but a military operation—"

"Of course. If one of our lightjammers had run into a herd of those things—or even a single one—there would have been a shocking mess. Don't forget that the Erikson Drive ships, unlike the Mannschenn Drive jobs, remain in normal Space-Time while accelerating to the velocity of light and return to NST when decelerating. The energy eaters—"

"Is that what you call them?"

"What else? The energy eaters were a menace to navigation and they were dealt with as such."

"I still don't like it."

"You're not master of a lightjammer, Captain. Oh, all right, all right, you're a big game hunter as well as being a shipmaster. But the EEs don't have nice, horned heads that you can hang on the wall. They don't have pretty pelts that can be made into fireside rugs."

"I want a living specimen."

"I doubt if your marvelous zoo in Central Australia would be able to accommodate it."

"A zoo need not be on a planetary surface, Commodore. The plans for an orbital zoo have been drawn up, with lines of magnetic force among a grouping of small artificial satellites forming the bars of a cage. If I capture a specimen the Foundation will have everything ready for its reception when I get it back to Earth."

"*If* you capture a specimen. The navy's doing a good job."

Haab inhaled deeply from the villainous black cigar that he was smoking as a counter measure to Grimes's foul pipe. He withdrew the thing from his mouth and his right hand, holding it, rested on his knee. Grimes sneezed. There was more than tobacco smoke in those acrid fumes.

He said hastily, "You're setting yourself on fire, Captain."

The other man looked down at the little charred circle in the cloth of his trousers, beat out the embers with his left hand.

Grimes said, "You must feel deeply on the subject. You didn't notice that you were burning yourself."

"I do feel deeply, Commodore. But this leg's prosthetic. I lost the original on Tanganore when a harpooned *spurzil* took retaliatory action. The Tanganorans fitted me out with this tin leg and, by the time I got back to Earth where I could have had a new flesh-and-blood one grown, I'd gotten used to it. In any case—I couldn't spare the time for a regeneration job."

"Tanganore? That's in the Cepheid Sector, isn't it? And what is a *spurzil*?"

"A sort of big armor-protected whale. White."

"And now you're hunting Moebius Dick himself."

"Moebius Dick, Commodore?"

"I thought that your private flag was supposed to represent the original Moby Dick."

"No. It represents the *spurzu* that took a piece of me. It's a reminder to myself to be careful. But *Moebius* Dick?"

"Wait until you've seen the films, Captain Haab."

Grimes sat with Haab in the darkened projection room and Miss Walton started the projector. Slowly the screen came alive and in it glowed words: OPERATION RIMHUNT. FOR EXHIBITION TO AUTHORIZED PERSONNEL ONLY.

The credit titles were succeeded by a spoken account of what was happening, by some quite good shots of lightjammers arriving at and departing from Port Erikson, by an excellent shot of *Herzogin Cecile* making sail. The voice of the commentator said, "But these ships, the pride of our merchant navy and the first vessels successfully to trade with the anti-matter Llanithi Consortium, discovered that all was not plain sailing." Grimes contrived to wince audibly. "A new menace appeared on the trade routes and only by taking violent evasive action were the lightjammers able to escape certain destruction."

"No mention of Vanderdecken," commented Haab.

"Our navy refuses to believe in ghosts," Grimes told him. "Their psychologists have a marvelous theory that the Flying Dutchman was no more than a projection of our own precognitive fears, a visual presentation of a hunch."

The commentator went on:

"Commodore John Grimes of the Rim Worlds naval reserve—also astronautical superintendent of Rim Runners—was a passenger aboard the lightjammer *Pamir*. He was in her control room when the master, acting upon a hunch, trimmed his sails in order to make a large alteration of course to port—"

"I like that!" snorted Grimes. "I had to bully the stubborn bastard into making that alteration."

"—deciding that there must have been some unseen danger ahead of the ship, Commodore Grimes made a report to Admiral Kravitz, recommending that a thorough survey be made of the trade routes between Lorn and Llanith. At the time the fleet was out on maneuvers off Eblis and the frigates *Rim Culverin* and *Rim Carronade* were detached to carry out investigations in the neighborhood of Llanith."

The last shot of a lightjammer under sail faded from the screen, was replaced by one of a conventional warship proceeding under Mannschenn Drive, obviously taken from a sister ship. In the background glowed the warped, convoluted Galactic Lens, an oval of luminescence twisted through and into an infinity of dimensions. The outline of *Rim Culverin* herself was hard and clear.

"Arriving at the position in which, according to Commodore Grimes's report, the danger was thought to exist, *Rim Culverin* and *Rim Carronade* reduced to cruising speed and initiated a search pattern. Both vessels, of course, had their mass proximity indicators tuned to maximum sensitivity. Eventually a target was seen in the screens, the indications being that it was something extremely small, with barely sufficient mass to register. It must be pointed out, however, that collision with a dust mote at a speed close to that of light could have serious consequences—"

"How do your lightjammers guard against that?" asked Haab.

"We don't. Cosmic dust is something that we don't have any of out on the Rim."

"What about hydrogen atoms? Wouldn't they be as bad?"

"We don't have any of those either—or the operation of light-jammers would be impossible. But look!"

"—inertial drive only, *Rim Culverin* and *Rim Carronade* approached the target with caution. Radar had been put into operation when the ships made their reentry into normal space-time and proved more effective than the mass proximity indicator had been. The original target was resolved into a cluster of targets, each presenting an echo in the screen equivalent to that given by a small ship, such as a scout. Furthermore, as the range decreased to a hundred kilometers and less, the targets could be seen visually."

In the screen was what looked like a star cluster, bright against the intergalactic nothingness.

"The cautious approach was continued—"

The effect now was more like a swarm of fireflies than a star cluster. The points of light were in rapid motion, weaving about each other in an intricate dance. The ship from which the film had been taken was approaching the shimmering display—probably magnification was being stepped up at the same time. If it were not—then the approach was far from cautious.

Each of the dancing lights possessed a definite shape.

"Haloes," murmured Haab.

"Not haloes," Grimes told him. "Look more closely, Captain."

Nonetheless, haloes they could have been, living annuli of iridescence—but twisted haloes. As they rotated about their centers they flared fitfully, seemed to vanish, flared again.

"What do they remind you of?" asked Grimes.

"The antenna of a Carlotti beacon or transceiver," replied Haab after a moment's thought. "But circular, instead of elliptical—that's what I thought when I saw the stills that the Survey Service passed on to the Foundation. It's more obvious when you see the things in motion."

"In other words," said Grimes, "a Moebius Strip. But watch."

The voice of the commentator came up again. "*Rim Culverin* dispatched a drone to make a closer investigation—"

There was a shot of the little craft—a spaceship in miniature, bristling with a complex array of scanners and antennae—pulling out and clear from the parent ship. *Rim Carronade*'s camera tracked her until she was too distant for details to be distinguished. Then this picture was replaced by the one seen by the probe's electronic eyes. The small unmanned craft was making a close approach to one of the whirling rings of light. The enigmatic thing was almost featureless, although flecks of greater luminosity on its surface were indicative of its rotation. It was a Moebius Strip made from a wide, radiant ribbon. It flared and dimmed like an isophase beacon with a period synchronized with that of its revolution. It could have been a machine—yet it gave the impression that it was alive. It filled the screen, spinning, pulsing—and then there was blackness.

The commentator said in a matter-of-fact voice, "The drone went dead. It had not been destroyed, however. Powerful telescopes and radar aboard both ships could still pick it up. But it was obvious that all its electronic equipment had suddenly ceased to function.

"It was obvious, too, that the cluster of mysterious entities was approaching the frigates at high velocity. Captain Laverton, aboard *Rim Carronade*, ordered a withdrawal from the scene. *Rim Carronade* and *Rim Culverin* proceeded west, first at normal cruising speed, then increasing to maximum inertial drive acceleration. But the hostile beings steadily decreased the range. *Rim Carronade* and *Rim Culverin* were obliged to open fire with their stern-mounted laser cannon—"

THE SCREEN SHOWED the false star cluster again, but its individual components were no longer dancing about each other, maintaining a globular formation—they were holding a steady trajectory. They were no longer alternating between light and darkness. Every now and again they would flare into increased brilliance, which did not diminish.

"Realizing that laser was an encouragement rather than a deterrent," the commentator went on, "Captain Laverton decided to take evasive action and ordered the starting of the Mannschenn Drive units aboard his ship and *Rim Culverin*, reasoning that once the frigates were out of synchronization with normal Space-Time the hostile entities would be unable to press home their attack. At first it seemed that these tactics would be successful, but after a lapse of no more than fifteen seconds the things reappeared at even closer range than before, obviously matching temporal precession rates. Captain Laverton returned to normal Space-Time briefly—and in the few seconds before he restarted his Mannschenn Drive, just as the entities reappeared off *Rim Carronade*'s quarter, launched a torpedo with a fission warhead fused for almost instant detonation. This defensive action was successful."

The screen displayed a fireball of incandescent plasma, expanding and thinning, the obvious aftermath of an atomic explosion in deep space. Through the cloud of glowing gases could be seen only a mere half-dozen of the entities—earlier there had been at least fifty of the things.

"Returning to NST, Captain Laverton observed that the majority of the creatures had been destroyed and that the few survivors were sluggish and—he thought erroneously—badly injured. Two were dispatched by laser fire. The remaining four retreated rapidly, eluding the frigates.

"The first phase of Operation Rimhunt was over."

"The next spool, sir?" asked Miss Walton.

"Not just yet, if you don't mind," replied Haab. Then, "I beg your pardon, Commodore. But I'd like to talk about what we've just seen first."

"Talk away, Captain." Grimes refilled and lit his pipe. "Talk away."

"As you know, Commodore, I've seen the stills and read the reports that your navy passed on to the Federation Survey Service, that the Survey Service, in its turn, passed on to the Foundation. I was present at most of the conferences of the Foundation's boffins. I didn't understand all they were saying, but I caught the general drift. The energy eaters, as they dubbed them, are just that. Their peculiar Moebius Strip configuration ensures that their entire surface is exposed to any source of radiation. According to *our* mathematicians they must be susceptible to magnetic fields—so the cage that our people are designing should work. The creatures are also susceptible to beamed Carlotti transmissions, which could be used to prevent a caged entity from escaping by desynchronizing with normal Space-Time."

Grimes grunted affirmatively.

"And as we have just seen—they can be killed. Killed by kindness." Haab chuckled dryly. "Throw the energy of a nuclear blast on to their plates and they're like a compulsive eater digging his grave with a knife and fork."

"Mphm."

"But *I* don't want to kill them. I want to capture one, or more than one, to take back to Earth. I want to save a specimen of this unique life form, probably not a native of this Galaxy, before the species is hunted to extinction."

"Then you had better get cracking," Grimes told him without much sympathy. To him a menace to navigation was just that. "At last report there's probably only one of the things left."

"Moebius Dick," murmured Haab.

They watched the remainder of the films of Operation Rimhunt, which could as well have been called Operation Search and Destroy. The use of fission weapons, stumbled upon by Captain Laverton, remained effective, but it had to be improved upon. The energy eaters were intelligent—just how intelligent no one knew, probably no one ever would know. After the almost complete wiping out of that first cluster they tended to run from the Confederacy's warships. Magnetic fields, set up by two or more vessels, were an invisible net from which not all of the entities escaped—and those that did so made their getaway by desynchronization. Time-Space twisting Carlotti beams were employed by the hunters and this technique seemed to inhibit temporal precession.

"Butchers," muttered Haab at last. "Butchers."

"Exterminators," corrected Grimes. "But both butchers and exterminators are essential to civilization. What about all the animals have killed in your profession? Can you afford to talk?"

"I can, Commodore. In the first place, I've gone after living specimens far more than I have dead ones. In the second place, the odds have never been stacked against the quarry in my hunts—as they have been in this operation of yours."

Grimes grunted. "I'm not a hunter. If I really wanted a dinner of grilled trout I'd be quite capable of tossing a hand grenade into the stream. If I have an infestation of rats or mice I go out and buy the most effective poison on the market."

"I seem to recall," said Haab, "that you once used a fusion bomb to destroy a rat-infested ship."

"Yes. I did. It was necessary."

"Necessity," murmured Haab, "what sins are committed in thy name? But let's agree to shelve our differences. Do you think I could see the charts of sightings and—ah—victorious naval actions?"

"Let's have them, please, Miss Walton," said Grimes.

Grimes later entertained Haab in his home. After the captain had returned to his ship Grimes's wife, Sonya, said, "So that's the great hunter."

"I hope you were impressed," said Grimes.

"Impressed? Oh, I suppose I was in a way. But the man's a monomaniac. Hunting is his whole life."

"But you can say in his favor that he's more concerned with capturing than killing."

"Is that so much better?" she demanded. "Have you ever seen the Hummel Foundation's zoo?"

Grimes had seen it many years ago when he had been a very junior officer in the Survey Service. He had thought at the time that those animals from Earth-type planets had been comparatively lucky, they had been allowed a limited freedom in the open air. The beings from worlds utterly unlike Earth had been confined in transparent domes, inside which the conditions of their natural habitats had been faithfully reproduced in all respects but one— room to run, fly or slither.

He said, "I think I know what you mean."

"I should hope you do," she replied. "I'd sooner be dead than in a cage."

"Haab's only doing his job."

"But he needn't enjoy it so much."

"Are we so much better?" he queried. "Here are these creatures, drifting in from the Odd Gods of the Galaxy know where. They may be intelligent—but have we tried to find out? Oh, no—not us. All we did find out is how to destroy them."

"Don't come over all virtuous, John. You were the first to start screaming about menaces to navigation on the Lorn-Llanith route. Now your precious lightjammers can come and go as they please. And that's what you wanted."

The following morning he received a call from Admiral Kravitz. "I'm putting you back on the active list, Grimes."

"Again, sir? My paperwork piled up when I made the voyage in

Pamir and I'm still trying to shovel my way through the worst of the drifts."

"I want one of our people along in *New Bedford* as an observer. You are the obvious choice for the assignment."

"Why me?"

"Why not you? You were keen enough to make a voyage in *Pamir* when it suited you. Now you can make a voyage in Haab's ship when it suits me."

"Does Captain Haab know I'll be along?"

"He has been told that he will have to have a representative of our navy aboard when he lifts from Port Forlorn. He has only one spare cabin in his ship—a dogbox—so you'll not be able to have Sonya along. Still, it should be an interesting trip."

"I hope so," said Grimes.

"With you among those present, it will be." The admiral chuckled. "But I have to ring off. I'll leave you to fix everything up with Haab. Let me know later what's been arranged. Over and out."

Grimes rose from his desk. "Miss Walton," he said to his secretary, "I shall be aboard *New Bedford* if anybody wants me. Meanwhile, you can call Captain Macindoe at his home—he's due back from leave, as you know—and ask him to come in to see me after lunch. He'll be acting superintendent in my absence."

"Not B—Not Commander Williams again?" asked the girl disappointedly.

"No. Billy Williams, as you almost called him, is better at looking after his precious *Rim Malemute* than keeping my chair warm. What the pair of you were doing when I was away in *Pamir* and on Llanith I hate to think."

He grinned, then made his way out of the office.

He looked with fresh interest at *New Bedford* as he walked briskly across the apron. His earlier curiosity about her had been academic rather than otherwise, but now that he would be shipping out in her he was beginning to feel almost a proprietorial concern.

He stared up at the dully gleaming tower that was her hull, at the sponsons and turrets that housed her weaponry, at the antennae indicative of sophisticated electronic equipment of a nature usually found only in warships and survey ships. But she was both, of course. Her normal employment could be classed as warfare of a sort and as survey work—also of a sort.

Grimes marched up the ramp to the after airlock. His way into the compartment was barred by an officer who asked curtly, "Your business, sir?"

Grimes's prominent ears started to redden. Surely everybody in Port Forlorn knew who he was. But this ship, of course, was not a regular visitor and her personnel were not Rim worlders.

He said gruffly, "Commodore Grimes to see Captain Haab."

The young man went to a telephone. "Fourth mate here, Captain. A Commodore Grimes to see you . . . Yes, sir. Right away." Then to Grimes, "Follow me, sir."

The elevator carried them swiftly up the axial shaft. Haab's quarters were just below and abaft the control room. The master rose from his desk as Grimes was ushered into his day cabin. "Welcome aboard, Commodore. Thank you, Mr. Timon, you may carry on." When the officer had left Haab asked, "And what can I do for you, Commodore Grimes?"

"I believe, Captain, that you've already heard from our admiralty."

"Indeed I have. They're insisting that I carry some snot-nosed ensign or junior lieutenant with me as an observer—"

"Not an ensign or a lieutenant, Captain."

"Who, then?"

Grimes grinned. "Me."

Haab did not grin in return. "But you're not—"

"But I am. I'm a reserve officer back on the active list as and from this morning."

"Oh?" Haab managed a frosty smile. "I'm afraid I can't offer you much in the way of accommodation, Commodore. This is a working ship. There's a spare cabin the mate has been using as a storeroom— he's getting it cleaned out now."

"As long as there's a bunk—"

"There is—but not much else." Haab's grin was a little warmer. "But I am neglecting my duties as a host." He walked to the little bar that stood against the bulkhead under the mounted head of some horrendously horned and tusked beast Grimes could not identify. "Perhaps you will join me in a sip of *mayrenrolh*?"

"It will be my pleasure." Haab filled small glasses with viscous, dark-brown fluid and Grimes accepted his, raised it. "Your very good health, sir."

"And yours, Commodore."

The drink was potent, although Grimes did not much care for its flavor. He said, "This is an unusual—ah—spirit."

"Yes. I laid in a supply when I was on Pinkenbah. The natives ferment it from the blood of the *mayren*, a big, carnivorous lizard."

"Fascinating," said Grimes, swallowing manfully. "I suppose your ship is well-stocked with all manner of foods and drinks."

"She is," Haab told him.

NEW BEDFORD lifted from Port Forlorn on a cold, drizzly morning, driving into and through the gray overcast. Grimes was a guest in her control room and, he was made to feel, a very unwelcome guest. Haab was coldly courteous, but his officers managed to convey the impression that they resented the presence of the outsider and were demanding silently of each other. *What is this old bastard doing here?*

New Bedford went upstairs in a hurry. Word had come through to Port Forlorn that *Rim Arquebus* was not only tracking what was believed to be the last of the energy eaters but had already made two unsuccessful attempts to destroy the creature. Haab had protested and had been told this sector of space was under the jurisdiction of the Rim Worlds Confederacy and that he, his ship and his people were only there on sufferance. The attitude adopted by his government did not make things any more pleasant for Grimes.

Haab wasted little time setting trajectory once he was clear of Lorn's Van Allens. He lined his ship up on an invisible point in space some lightyears in from the Llanith sun, then put his inertial drive on maximum acceleration, with his Mannschenn Drive developing a temporal precession rate that Grimes considered foolhardy. Foolhardy or not, the discomfort was extreme—the crushing weight of three gravities acceleration combined with the eerie sensation of always being almost at the point of living backward.

Apart from these discomforts she was not a happy ship. Her people, from the master down, were too dedicated. They lived hunting, talked hunting, thought hunting and, presumably, dreamed hunting. Grimes was allowed into a conversation only when it was assumed that he would make some contribution to the success of the expedition—and this was not often.

One night, at dinner, Haab did ask him for his views on the energy eaters.

"How intelligent do you think they are, Commodore?"

Grimes put down the fork with which he had been eating some vaguely fish-tasting mess, about which he had not dared to inquire. The implement clattered loudly on the surface of the plate—the high acceleration took some getting used to. He said, "You've seen all the reports, Captain Haab."

"Yes, Commodore Grimes. But you must have formed an opinion. After all, the energy eaters are in your back garden."

Grimes decided that he might as well talk as eat—he would not be missing much, "I don't suppose I need to tell you about the Terran shark, Captain. He has, however, been described as a mobile appetite. He just eats and eats without discrimination, often to his own undoing. He just hasn't the sense to consider the consequences. Right?"

Haab looked to Dr. Wayne, his biologist. Wayne grinned and said, "The Commodore hasn't put it in very scientific language, but he's not far off the beam."

"Then," Grimes went on, "we have human beings who are compulsive eaters. They often are far from being unintelligent—yet they cannot control themselves, even though they know that they are digging their graves with knives and forks. The energy eaters are more intelligent than sharks. They may be as intelligent as we are but we don't know. Intelligent or not, they are handicapped."

"Handicapped? Just how?" demanded Haab.

"Unlike human compulsive eaters they have no control over their intake. If there is raw energy around they absorb it, whether they want to or not. They know, I think, that the absorption of the energy generated by a nuclear explosion will be fatal—but if they are in the vicinity of such a blast they cannot help themselves. Sorry—they can help themselves, but only by exercising their power of temporal precession. And by the time they found this out they were almost extinct."

"Then Moebius Dick will give us a good fight," commented the mate. "He has survived in spite of everything that the navy has thrown at him."

"The commodore isn't very interested in fighting fish," said Haab. "He told me that he fishes for trout with hand grenades."

"I believe in getting results," said Grimes, conscious that the officers and specialists around the table were looking at him coldly.

New Bedford sped through the warped continuum, homing on the continuous Carlotti signal that Grimes had persuaded the captain of *Rim Arquebus* to transmit. The warship was remaining in the vicinity of the last sighting of Moebius Dick and had received orders from the admiralty to cooperate with Haab. Coded signals had been made to Grimes and, reading them, he had gained the impression that Captain Welldean of the *Arquebus* was far from happy. But Grimes's heart did not bleed for Welldean. Welldean was in his own ship with his own people as shipmates and his own cook turning out meals to his own taste. No doubt his feelings had been hurt when he had been ordered to abandon his own hunt and to put himself under the command of a reserve officer. But he was not an unwelcome guest aboard somebody else's vessel.

At last the tiny spark that was *Rim Arquebus* showed up just inside the screen of the mass proximity indicator. Speed was reduced and eventually both drive units were shut down. *Rim Arquebus* hung there, five kilometers from *New Bedford*, a minor but bright constellation in the blackness.

Welldean's fat, surly face looked out from the screen of the NST transceiver at Grimes and the others in *New Bedford's* control room.

"Have you any further information, Captain?" asked Haab.

Welldean replied in a flat voice, "The EE emerges into NST at regular half-hour intervals, remaining for ten minutes each time, presumably to feed on the radiation emitted by my ship. Pursuant to instructions—" he seemed to be glaring directly at Grimes— "I have made no hostile moves. Would the Commodore have any further orders for me?"

"None at the moment, Captain," Grimes told him. "Just stand by."

"*Rim Arquebus* standing by," acknowledged Welldean sulkily.

"When will Moebius Dick . . ." Haab was interrupted by a shout from his mate.

"There she blows!" The energy eater had appeared midway between the two ships. It was huge, brilliantly luminous, lazily rotating. Grimes paraphrased wryly, *He who eats and runs away will live to eat some other day* . . . This thing had eaten and run away, eaten and run away and it had grown, was a vortex of forces all of a kilometer across. It would never fit into *New Bedford's* capacious hold, a compartment designed for the carriage of alien life forms, some of them gigantic. But this did not matter. The cage of beams and fields would be set up outside the ship, but still within the temporal precession field of the Mannschenn Drive.

Grimes, a mere observer aboard a vessel that was not his own, felt superfluous, useless, as Haab and his officers went into the drill that had been worked out to the last detail. The mate, Murgatroyd, would remain on board in charge of the ship—and Haab, with the second, third and fourth mates, would go out in the one-man chasers. Haab was already in his spacesuit—the small craft were no more than a flying framework, unpressurized—and his prosthetic leg, through some freak of sound conductivity, clicked loudly as he moved. In his armor, with that mechanical noise accompanying every motion of his legs, he was more like a robot than a man, even though his chin beard was jutting through the open faceplate of his helmet.

"Good hunting, Captain," said Grimes.

"Thank you, Commodore." Haab turned to his mate. "You're in charge of the ship, Mr. Murgatroyd. Don't interfere with the hunt." Then, to Grimes, "Will you tell Captain Welldean to keep his guns and torpedoes to himself?" Welldean's heavy face scowled at them from the screen of the NST transceiver.

"Moebius Dick has gone," announced Murgatroyd.

"When he surfaces again, we shall be in position," Haab told him as he left the control room.

Murgatroyd looked at Grimes. *There's nobody else to talk to,* he seemed to be thinking, *so I may as well pass the time of day with you.* He said, "The Old Man always brings 'em back."

"Alive?" queried Grimes.

"When he wants to," replied the mate.

Then he laughed. "He hasn't much choice as far as that thing's concerned. If it's dead it's nothing." Even in free fall he contrived to give the impression of being slumped in his seat. An incongruous wistfulness softened the rough, scarred, big-featured face under the coarse, yellow hair.

"You wish you were out in one of the chasers," Grimes stated rather than asked.

"I do. But somebody has to mind the shop—and it always seems to be me. There they go, Commodore."

Four bright sparks darted into the emptiness between *New Bedford* and *Rim Arquebus*. As they reached a predetermined position they slowed, stopped, then slid into a square formation. Moebius Dick should reappear at the center of the quadrangle and then, at Haab's signal, each of the little crafts would become a fantastically powerful electromagnet and each would emit the beamed Carlotti transmissions, effectively netting the energy eater in time and space.

Murgatroyd and Grimes stared into the screen of the mass proximity indicator. Four little points of light marked the positions of the chasers, a much fainter one denoting the presence of the energy eater.

"Master to *New Bedford*," crackled from the speaker. "Check position, please."

"*New Bedford* to master," replied Murgatroyd. "You are exactly in position. Over."

"*Rim Arquebus* to Commodore Grimes," put in Welldean. "Do you wish me to take any action when the EE surfaces?"

"Haab to Grimes. You are only an observer. And that goes for your navy, too, Over."

"The old man gets tensed up," remarked Murgatroyd, with the faintest hint of apology in his voice.

"*Rim Arquebus* to Commodore Grimes. My weaponry is manned and ready," persisted Welldean.

"So is mine." Murgatroyd chuckled, waving a big hand over his fire-control console.

The minutes, the seconds, ticked by. Grimes watched the sweep second hand of the clock. He had noted the time of *Moebius Dick's* disappearance. The half-hour was almost up. When that red pointer came around to 37 . . .

"Now!" yelled the Mate.

Moebius Dick was back. The enormous circle of gyrating luminescence had reappeared in the center of the square formed by the chasers. From the NST speaker came the low-pitched buzz and crackle of interference as the solenoids were energized. The energy eater hung there, quivering, seeming to shrink within itself. Then it moved, tilting like a precessing gyroscope.

Haab's voice could be heard giving orders. "Increase to six hundred thousand gausses. To six-fifty—seven hundred—"

From one of the chasers came a bright, brief flare and from the speaker a cry of alarm: "Captain, my coil has blown!"

"Master to second and fourth mates—triangular formation."

Moebius Dick was spinning about a diametric axis, no longer a circle of light but a hazy sphere of radiance. The energy eater was rolling through the emptiness, directly toward one of the three still-functioning chasers. The small craft turned to run. *Rim Arquebus* stabbed out with a barrage of laser beams. In *New Bedford's* control room Murgatroyd swore, added his fire to that from the frigate. It was ineffective—or highly effective in the wrong way. The monster glowed ever more brightly as it absorbed the energy directed at it, moved ever faster. The chaser turned and twisted desperately, hopelessly. The other chasers could not pursue for fear of running into the fire from the ships. There was nothing that they could have done, in any case.

"The old man's boat—" muttered Murgatroyd. "I guess it's the way he wanted to go—" His hand fell away from the firing stud. Moebius Dick was rolling over Haab's small and fragile craft.

Grimes, on the NST VHF, was ordering, "Hold your fire, *Rim Arquebus!* Hold your fire!"

Welldean's voice came back, "What the hell do you think I'm doing?" Adding, as a grudging afterthought, "Sir."

The lights of the chaser flared briefly through the luminous, swirling haze that enveloped them, flared and died. But something, somebody, broke through the living radiance. It was the spacesuited Haab, using his personal propulsion unit to drive him back to his ship.

He broke through and broke away and for a second or so it seemed that he would succeed. Then Moebius Dick was after him, overtaking him, enveloping him. From the NST speaker came a short, dreadful scream. The globe of flame that was the energy eater seemed to swell, was swelling, visibly and rapidly, assuming the appearance of a gigantic, spherical fire opal. The three surviving chasers retreated rapidly.

Dark streaks suddenly marred the iridescent beauty of the sphere, spread, rapidly covering the entire surface. Where Moebius Dick had been there was only nothingness.

No, not nothingness.

Floating in the darkness, illumined by the searchlights of the three small craft, was the lifeless, armored figure of Captain Haab.

"They'll bring him in," muttered Murgatroyd. "I'll take him back to Earth for burial. Those were his wishes."

"*Rim Arquebus* to *New Bedford*," came Welldean's voice. "Do you require medical assistance? Shall I send a boat with my surgeon—"

"We've a quack of our own," snarled Murgatroyd, "and a good one. But even he won't be able to do anything. The old man is dead."

◈ Rim Change ◈

I'M A SORT OF EXCEPTION that proves the rule.

And that, oddly enough, is my name—George Rule, currently master in the employ of the Dog Star Line, one of the few independent shipping companies in the Federation able to compete successfully with the state-owned Interstellar Transport Commission. When I was much younger I used to be called, rather to my embarrassment, Golden Rule. That was when my hair, which I tend to wear long, and my beard were brightly blond. But, given time, everything fades, and my nickname has faded away with my original colouring. In uniform I'm just another tramp master—and the Odd Gods of the Galaxy know that there are plenty of such in the Universe!—and out of uniform I could be the man come to fix the robochef. It's odd—or is it?—how those engaged in that particular branch of robotics tend to run to fat . . .

But this exception business . . .

The space services of the Rim Confederacy are literally crawling with officers who blotted their copy books in the major shipping lines of the Federation and various autonomous kingdoms, republics and whatever, and even with a few who left certain navies under big black clouds. The famous Commodore Grimes, for example, the Rim Worlds' favorite son, isn't a Rim Worlder by birth; he was emptied out of the Federation Survey Service after the *Discovery* mutiny. (It was Grimes, by the way, who got *me* emptied out of Rim Runners, the Confederacy's state shipping line, many years ago.)

I am a Rim Worlder by birth. I'm one of the very few spacemen who was born an Outsider and who now serves in the Insiders' ships, the very opposite to all those Insiders who, for reasons best known to themselves, came out to the Rim. I was one of the first cadets to pass through the Confederacy's space training college at Port Last, on Ultimo. I started my spacegoing career as Fourth Mate of the old *Rim Mammoth* and then, after I gained my Second Mate's Certificate, was appointed Third Mate of *Rim Tiger*. Captain—as he was then—Grimes was master of her. He was a real martinet in those days.

Now that I'm master myself I can appreciate his reasons for wanting to run a taut ship. The affair aboard *Discovery* must still have been vivid in his mind and probably he was thinking that if he'd been less easy going the mutiny would never have happened. I didn't take kindly to the sort of discipline that he tried to impose. *Rim Mammoth* had been a *very* happy ship; the *Tiger* was far from it. Looking back on it all, any Third Mate of mine who tried to get away with the things that I tried to get away with would get a rough passage and a short one.

Anyhow—it was after I'd scrambled aboard at Port Fortinbras, very much the worse for wear, about two microseconds prior to liftoff—I was called into the Sacred Presence. Before he could start on me I told him what he could do with his Survey Service ideas. Then I told him what he could do with his ship. I told him that I wasn't at all surprised that *Discovery*'s officers had done what they did . . . And so on.

I don't blush easily, but the memory of that scene induces a hot flush from my scalp to the tips of my toes. I was lucky, bloody lucky, not to have been pushed out through an airlock without a spacesuit. (At the time we were, of course, well on our way to Port Forlorn.) Oh, I was escorted to the airlock after our landing on Lorn, taken to the Shipping Office and paid off, and told that it was extremely unlikely that Rim Runners would ever require my services again.

But I was lucky:

(a) I got a job.

(b) I got a job that took me away from the Rim.

(c) I got a job that exercised a certain civilizing influence (badly needed, I admit now) on me.

You may remember when Trans-Galactic Clippers used to include the Rim Worlds in the itinerary of their Universal Tours. One of their big ships—*Sobraon*—was in, and her Fourth Officer, who had incurred multiple injuries in a rented air car crash, was in hospital. The post was mine, I was told, until such time. as a regular TG man was available to relieve me.

I took it, of course, hastily affixing my autograph to *Sobraon's* Articles of Agreement before Captain Grimes could breathe a few unkind words into the ear of Captain Servetty, who was to be my new boss. And it was with great relief that I watched, from the Clipper's control room, the lights of Port Forlorn fading below us as we lifted. I decided, then, to make the most of this second chance. I decided, too, that I'd not return to the Rim Worlds, ever.

There was nothing to hold me; I was an orphan, and had never gotten on with the various aunts and uncles on either side of my family. I'd had a girl, but she'd ditched me, some time back, to marry a wind turbine maintenance engineer. This broken romance had been one of the reasons—the main reason, perhaps—why I'd been such a pain in the neck to old Grimes. As the Universal Tour proceeded everything that I saw—the glamorous worlds such as Caribbea, Electra and all the rest of them—stiffened my resolution. The Rim Worlds were so dreary, and the planets of the Shakespearean Sector were little better.

This was before Grimes, commanding *Faraway Quest*, had discovered the worlds of what is now known as the Eastern Circuit Tharn, Mellise, Grollor and Stree.

All that we had then were Lorn, Faraway, Ultimo and Thule— and, of course, Kinsolving's Planet and Eblis. But nobody ever went near either of those.

Sobraon knocked quite a few corners off me. There's a saying that you often hear, especially in star tramps, that Trans-Galactic Clippers is an outfit where accent counts for more than efficiency.

Don't you believe it. Those boys may convey the impression of taking a cruise in daddy's yacht, but they're superb spacemen. They play hard at times—but they work hard.

I played with them—and I like to think that I pulled my weight when it was time to work. I was genuinely sorry when I paid off at Canis Major—Dogtown to we Sirians—the capital city of the Sirian Sector. There was a new Fourth Mate, a Company boy, waiting for us there, so Captain Servetty had to take him on. He told me, though, that if I cared to fill in a TG Clippers application form he'd see to it that it received special consideration. I thanked him, of course, and I thought about it. I didn't have to think very hard about the repatriation to the Rim Worlds to which I was entitled. I took the money in lieu and decided to treat myself to a holiday.

It was while I was enjoying myself at New Capri that I met Jane. She too was on holiday—on annual leave, as a matter of fact. She was at that time a Purser with the Dog Star Line. It was largely because of her that I became a kennelman myself; I became a naturalized Sirian citizen shortly after we married. She gave up spacefaring when our first child was on the stocks.

Oh well, it's nice having your wife aboard ship with you—but it's also nice to have a home, complete with wife and children, to come back to. You can't have it both ways. And most of the time I got ships that never wandered far from Dogtown, and was contented enough as I rose slowly—but not too slowly—through the ranks from Third to Second, from Second to Chief and, finally, from Chief Officer to Master.

But now, after all these years, I was coming back to the Rim.

The Dog Star Line ships spend most of the time sniffing around their own backyard, but now and again, they stray. *Basset* had strayed, following the scent of commerce clear across the Galaxy. At home, on Canis Major, I'd loaded a big consignment of brassards and self-adjusting sun hats for Arcadia. I must find out some time how those brassards sold. They were made with waterproof pockets for smoking requirements, small change, folding money, etc. The Arcadians, who practice naturism all the year round, have always seemed to manage quite well with a simple bag slung over one shoulder.

At Ursa Major (the Arcadians have a childish love of puns) I filled up with the so-called Apples of Eden, a local fruit esteemed on quite a few worlds. These were consigned to New Maine. And what would one load in Port Penobscot? Need you ask? Smoked and pickled fish, of course, far less fragrant than what had been discharged. This shipment was for Rob Roy, one of the planets of the Empire of Waverley.

The cargo we loaded on Rob Roy was no surprise either. The Jacobeans, as they call themselves, maintain that their whisky is superior to the genuine article distilled in Scotland. It may be, it may not be; whisky is not my tipple. But the freight charges from the Empire of Waverley to the Rim Confederacy are far less than those from Earth to the Rim.

So *Basset* had followed the scent of profit clear from the Dog Star to the Rim, and now it looked as though the trail was petering out. On the other legs of the voyage Head Office, by means of Carlotti radio, had kept me well-informed as to what my future movements would be. On my run from Rob Roy to Lorn they had remained silent. And Rim Runners, my agents on Lorn, had replied to my ETA with only a curt acknowledgement. I didn't like it. None of us liked it: we'd all been away from home too long.

Probably I liked it less than my officers. I knew the Rim Worlds; I could think of far nicer planets to sit around awaiting orders.

We found the Lorn sun without any trouble—not that we should have had any trouble finding that dim luminary. Even if we hadn't been equipped with the Carlotti Direction Finder, and even if the Rim Worlds hadn't been able to boast the usual layout of Carlotti Beacons, we'd have had no trouble. There's the Galactic Lens, you see, and it doesn't thin out gradually towards its edges; the stars in the spiral arms are quite closely packed. (I use the word "closely" in a relative way, of course. If you had to walk a dozen or so lightyears you wouldn't think it was all that close.) And then there's that almost absolute nothingness between the galaxies. Almost absolute. . .

There's the occasional hydrogen atom, of course, and a few small star clusters doing their best to convey the impression that they don't really belong to the galactic family. The Rim Confederacy is one such cluster. There are the Lorn, Faraway, Ultimo, Thule, Eblis and Kinsolving suns. To the Galactic East there's a smaller cluster, with Tharn, Grollor, Mellise and Stree. To the West there's a sizeable anti-matter aggregation, with a dozen suns. So, as long as you're headed in roughly the right direction when you break out of the Lens, you have no difficulty identifying the cluster you want.

You have the Galactic Lens astern of you. When the Space-Time-twisting Mannschenn Drive is running it looks like an enormous, slowly squirming, luminescent amoeba. Ahead there's an uncanny blackness, and the sparse, glimmering, writhing nebulosities that are the Rim Suns seem to make that blackness even blacker, even emptier. And that emptiness still looks too damned empty even when the interstellar drive's shut down and the ship's back in the normal Continuum.

I could tell that my officers were scared by the weird scenery—or lack of it. I was feeling a bit uneasy myself; it was so many years since I'd been out here. But we got used to it after a while—as much as one can get used to it—and here we were at last, dropping down through the upper atmosphere of Lorn. The landing was scheduled for 0900 hours, Port Forlorn Local Time. We couldn't see anything of Port Forlorn yet, although we had clearance from Aerospace Control to enter and were homing on the radio beacon. Beneath us was the almost inevitable overcast, like a vast snowfield in the sunlight, and under the cloud ceiling there would be, I knew, the usual half-gale (if not something stronger) probably accompanied by rain, snow, hail or sleet. Or all four.

"How does it feel to be coming home, sir?" asked my Chief Officer sarcastically.

"My home's in Canis Major!" I snapped. Then I managed a grin. "If you'll forgive my being corny, home is where the heart is."

"You can say that again, Captain," he concurred. (He was recently married and the novelty hadn't worn off yet.)

I took a last, routine look around the control room, just to make sure that everybody was where he was supposed to be and that everything was working. Soon I'd have to give all my attention to the inertial drive and attitude controls and to the periscope screen; inevitably I'd have to do some fancy juggling with lateral and down-thrusts. Rugged, chunky Bindle, the Chief Officer, was strapped in the co-pilot's chair, ready to take over at once if I suffered a sudden heart attack or went mad or something. Loran, the Second, was hunched over the bank of navigational instruments, his long, skinny frame all awkward angles and the usual greasy black cowlick obscuring one eye. His job was to call out to me the various instrument readings if, for some reason, such data failed to appear on the periscope screen. Young Taylor, the Third, an extraordinarily ordinary looking youth, was manning the various telephones, including the NST transceiver with which we were in communication with Aerospace Control. In most Dog Star Line's vessels this was the Radio Officer's job, but I had found that our Sparks, Elizabeth Brown (Betty Boops, we called her) was far too great a distraction. Even when she was wearing a thickly opaque uniform blouse (she preferred ones which were not) her abundant charms were all too obvious.

We fell steadily, the inertial drive grumbling away in its odd, broken rhythm, healthily enough. We dropped into the upper cloud levels, and at first pearly gray mist alternated with clear air outside our viewports. And then, for what seemed like a long time, there was only dark, formless vapor. The ship shuddered suddenly and violently as turbulence took her in its grip. The changing code of the blips from the radio beacon told me that I was off course, but it was early yet to start bothering about corrections.

We broke through the cloud ceiling.

Looking into the screen, stepping up the magnification, I could see that there had been few changes during my long absence. The landscape, as always, was gray rather than green, almost featureless, although on the horizon the black, jagged peaks of the Forlorn Range loomed ominously. There were the wide fields in which were grown such unglamorous crops as beans and potatoes. There was the city, which had grown only a little, with the wind turbine towers and the factory chimneys in the industrial suburbs, each smokestack with its streamer of dirty white and yellow vapour. Yes, it was blowing down there all right.

And there was the spaceport, a few kilometers from the city. I could see, towards the edge of the screen, the triangle of bright red flashing beacons on the apron. They were well to leeward, I noted, of the only other ship in port. This, I had been told, was *Rim Osprey*. There would be enough clearance, I thought hopefully, although I wondered, not for the first time, why Port Captains, with acres of apron at their disposal, always like to pack vessels in closely. I applied lateral thrust generously, brought the beacons to the exact centre of the screen.

At first it wasn't too hard to keep them there, and then we dropped into a region of freak turbulence and to the observers in the Port Forlorn control tower it must have looked as though we were wandering all over the sky. An annoying voice issued from the NST speaker, "Where are you off to, Captain?"

"Don't answer the bastard!" I snarled to Taylor.

I had control of her again and, as well as maintaining a steady rate of descent, corrected the ship's attitude. We dropped rapidly and the numerals of the radar altimeter display were winding down fast. I was coming in with a ruddy blush—but that, I had learned years ago, was the only way to come in to Port Forlorn. I said as much to Bindle, who was beginning to make apprehensive noises. "Try to drop like a feather," I told him, "and you'll finish up blown into the other hemisphere . . ."

I heard Loran mutter something about a ton of bricks, but ignored him.

There was little in the screen now but dirty concrete and the flashing beacons, marking the triangle in the centre of which I was supposed to land—but only when my stern vanes were below the level of the top of the control tower did I step up downthrust. The ship complained and shuddered to the suddenly increased power of the inertial drive.

I was beginning to feel smug—but what happened then wiped

the silly grin off my face. I had been leaning, as it were, into the wind—and suddenly, as we came into the lee of the administration block, there was no longer any wind to lean against. Worse still, there was a nasty back eddy. I reversed lateral thrust at once, of course, but it seemed ages before it took effect. The marker beacons slid right to the edge of the screen, right off it. Then, with agonizing slowness, they drifted back, not far enough. . .

But we were down. I felt the slight jar and the contact lights came on. I cut the drive. *Basset* trembled and sighed as she sagged down into the cradle of her tripedal landing gear, as the great shock absorbers took the weight of her. With a steady hand—but it took an effort!—I fished a packet of Caribea panatellas out of my breast pocket, struck one of the long, green cylinders and stuck the unlit end between my lips. (I almost did it the wrong way round, but noticed just in time.) I checked all the tell-tales, saw nothing wrong and ordered quietly, "Make it Finished With Engines."

Nobody acknowledged the order. I looked around indignantly. All three officers were staring out through one of the viewports. "Gods! That was close! Bloody close!" the Mate was muttering.

I stared through that viewport myself. Yes, it had been close. Another meter over towards the administration block and one or other or our stern vanes would have torn down the side of the other ship, ripping her open like a huge can opener. I unsnapped my belt, walked a little unsteadily to join the officers at the viewport. We could look directly into our neighbor's control room. A junior officer, the shipkeeper, was staring across at us. His face was still white. It had reason to be.

"Port Forlorn Control to *Basset*," came from the speaker of the NST transceiver. "Do you read me?"

"Loud and clear," I replied automatically into the microphone.

"Port Forlorn Control to *Basset*. You are far too close to *Rim Osprey*. For your information, she is not a lamppost." *(Funny bastard*, I thought.) "You will have to shift. Oh, by the way, you also destroyed two of our marker beacons when you set down. Over."

I shrugged. It's a rare master who hasn't rubbed out the occasional marker beacon. And, after all, they're cheap enough. (But *Rim Osprey* wouldn't have been cheap if I'd hit her. But I hadn't hit her. So what?

Finally, after the ground crew had set out new beacons, I tackled the ticklish job of shifting ship. I managed it with no damage except for a slightly dented vanepad and a long scratch on the concrete apron. (*Straight as though drawn with a rule,* the Mate remarked. I forgave him, but it wasn't easy.)

When we had reberthed to the Port Captain's approval, Customs and Port Health boarded to clear us inwards. Both officials were quite amazed to find that my place of birth, as shown on the Crew List, was Port Forlorn. They had to say, of course, that I had gone to the dogs. My Agent—Rim Runners' Port Forlorn Branch Manager—made the same feeble joke. Finally we got down to business. He said, "I've nothing for you at the moment, Captain. My last instructions from your Owners were to try to arrange some sort of charter for you locally . . ."

I told him, rather plaintively, "But I want to go home . . ."

He replied cheerfully, "But you *are* home. Lives there a man with soul so dead, and all that. Don't you have friends or relatives here? And you were in Rim Runners once, weren't you?"

"I was," I admitted.

"Then you must know Commodore Grimes, our Astronautical Superintendent. He's in Port Forlorn now, as a matter of fact . . ."

"The commodore and I didn't part on the best of terms," I said carefully.

"Time wounds all heels," he told me. "Shall I tell him you're here?"

"Perhaps not," I said.

"He'll know anyhow, Captain. He always likes to look through the crew lists of strange ships that come in here." He laughed. "He could be looking for *your* name!"

"I should have changed it when I changed my nationality," I said. "But I doubt if he'll want to see *me* again."

‿✌‿✌‿✌‿✌

Oddly enough—or not so oddly—nobody went ashore that day. The weather was partly to blame; shortly after our final berthing a cold driving rain had set in.

Too, all the way to Lorn I'd been telling everybody how drab and dreary the Rim Worlds are, and they must have at least half-believed me.

And then, after dinner that night, a little party started in the wardroom. We were all relaxing after the voyage and we had a few drinks, and a few more, and then . . . You know how it is. And, as always, we finished up in full voice, singing our Company's anthem.

All the big outfits have one, usually some very old song with modern words tacked on to the antique melody. In the Waverley Royal Mail they have their own version of *Fly, bonny boat, like a bird on the wing.* In TG Clippers it's one of the ancient Terran sea chanteys, Sally Brown. *(Way, hey, roll and go!)* Rim Runners have a farewell song from some old comic opera. *(Good-bye, I'll run to find another sun/Where I may find! There are hearts more kind than the ones left behind . . .)*

And ourselves, the Dog Star Line? The choice is obvious.

> *"How much is that doggy in the window?*
> (Arf! Arf!)
> *"The one with the great big glass eyes . . .*
> *"How much is that doggy in the window?*
> *"I think she looks ever so nice*
>
> *"I don't want a Countess or a Duchess,*
> *"I don't want an Empress with wings . . ."*

(This, of course, a dig at the Waverley Royal Mail Line.)

> *"I don't want an Alpha or a Beta . . ."*

(The two biggest classes of ship in the Interstellar Transport Commission.)

> *"Or any of those fucking things!"*
> *"How much is that doggy in the window?*
> (Arf! Arf! Arf!)
> *"The one with the Sirius look,*
> *"How much is that doggy in the window?*
> *"Please put my name down in her book!"*

We were all happily arfing away, with a few yips and bow-wows, when the Mate noticed a visitor standing just outside the wardroom door. "Come in, come in!" he called. "This is Liberty Hall! You can spit on the mat and call the cat a bastard! But . . ."

We took the cue and roared in unison, "Beware of the dog!"

"That last," remarked a voice, familiar after many a year, "makes a very welcome new addition."

I turned slowly in my chair to look at him. At first I thought that the old bastard hadn't changed a bit.

Then I saw that his hair was gray now, matching his eyes, and that his face had acquired a few new wrinkles. Otherwise it was as it always had been, looking as though it had been hacked rather than carved out of some coarse textured stone and then left out in the weather. His ears were the same prominent jug handles of old.

"Don't let me interrupt the party, Captain Rule," he went on, slightly emphasizing the title. "I had some business with *Rim Osprey*, and then I thought that I'd call aboard here to see you. But it can wait until the morning."

I got to my feet, extended a slightly reluctant hand. He shook it. "Good to have you aboard, sir," I said in the conventional manner. "Will you join us in a small drink?"

He grinned. "Well, if you twist my arm hard enough . . ."

I introduced him around and found him a chair. If he was bearing no malice—and he had far more reason to than I did—then neither was I. He was very soon completely at home.

Betty Brown—wearing one of her transparent shirts and a skirt that was little more than a pelmet—and Sara Taine, my Purser, sat—literally—at his feet, getting up now and again to bring him savories or to freshen his drink. I didn't get that sort of service. I thought resentfully, and this was *my* ship . . . He had a fine repertoire of songs and stories, far more extensive than any of ours. Well, he should have done. He had been around so much longer.

At last he raised his wrist and looked at his watch. He said, "Thank you for the party, but I must be going . . ."

"The night's only a pup, Commodore," Bindle told him.

"It was a bitch of a night when I came aboard," he replied, "and probably still is. Raining cats and dogs . . ." He laughed. "Your Dog Star Line brand of humor seems to be catching . . ."

"Just one more before you go? One for the road?" urged the Mate.

"No. Thank you. I don't want to find myself in the doghouse when I get home. Goodnight, all. Goodnight. Goodnight . . ."

I saw him down to the after airlock.

He told me, "I'll be seeing you in the morning, Captain Rule, if it is convenient."

"Would you mind answering a question before you go, sir?" I asked him.

"I'll try. What is it?"

"I've always rather suspected, sir, that you were instrumental in getting me that berth in *Sobraon*. After all, Captain Servetty didn't have to take *me*, of all people. And he must have known why I was . . . available . . ."

"He did know, Captain. He asked me if he should sign you on. I told him that you had the makings of a good officer, but that he'd have to keep a close eye on you."

I said, "If I hadn't been such a self-centred puppy I'd have known that you were still getting over the *Discovery* business . . ."

He said, "Let's forget about it, shall we? It was all so long ago, and so very far away . . ." Suddenly he looked old, then recovered, equally suddenly, his appearance of ageless strength. "Goodnight, Captain Rule." Our handshake, this time, was really sincere. "I'll see you in the morning."

Wrapping his rather flamboyant cloak about his stocky figure he strode down the ramp, ignoring the wind and the rain, let himself into his squat, ugly little ground car, and then was gone in a flurry of spray.

"That Commodore Grimes isn't anything like the ogre you made him out to be," said Sara Taine when she brought me in my tea tray the next morning. "I'm looking forward to seeing him again. What time will he be coming aboard?"

I said severely, "He's married. Very happily, I believe."

She frowned. She had one of those thin, serious faces, under sleek, gleaming black hair, on which a frown sits rather well. She complained, "All the attractive men in my life are married. You, and Peter Bindle, and now your old pal Commodore Grimes . . ."

"What about the engineers?" I asked her. "What about the Second and Third Mates? Or the Quack?"

"Them!" she snorted, then grinned softly, "If I wasn't such a good friend of Jane's . . ."

"Don't tempt me, Sara. The way this voyage is dragging on I shouldn't require so very much tempting."

She had been sitting on the bed, sipping her own cup of tea. She got up, moved to a chair. "That will do, Captain Rule. As I've said, Jane and I are good friends. I want us to stay that way. But it is a pity that she has such archaic ideas about sex, isn't it?" She put her cup back on the tray with a clatter, got up and went out of the bedroom, leaving me to deal alone with the business of getting up to face the day.

Showered and dressed I made my way down to the wardroom for breakfast. There were no absentees; the Doctor had insisted that each of us take a neutralizer tablet before retiring. As you know, they're very effective—but by the time you need them you're in such a state you can't be bothered to take them. That's one of the beauties of having a party aboard ship; you have your own medical practitioner on hand to prescribe as required . . .

Canvey, the Interstellar Drive Engineer, asked what everybody else was intending to ask. He got in first. "Was that only a social call last night, Captain, or did Commodore Grimes have any information about our next loading?"

And then Terrigal, Reaction Drive Engineer, stated rather than asked, "He's coming aboard again this morning, isn't he?"

I told them, "The Commodore is Rim Runners' Astronautical Superintendent, not their Traffic Manager."

"But he still piles on a lot of gees, doesn't he?" said Canvey.

"I suppose he does," I admitted. I helped myself liberally from the dish of Caribbean tree-crab curry on the table, hoping that it would taste as good as it looked and smelled. (It did. Sara was as good a cook as she was a purser, and even the most sophisticated autochef—which ours wasn't—gives of its best only when imaginatively programmed.) I asked, "How is the crab holding out, Sara?"

"It isn't," she said. "This is the last of it."

"I tried to make a tissue culture," put in Dr. Forbes, who was Bio-Chemist as well as medical officer, "but it died on me . . ." He looked more like a professional mourner than ever as he imparted the bad news.

"Then I hope they send us home by way of Caribbea," I said.

"So there *is* a chance of our getting home," persisted Canvey. He was one of those little, gray, earnest men who always seem to be persisting.

"I'll believe it when we crunch down in Dogtown," said Porky Terrigal glumly, making sure of his second helping of the fragrant curry.

"You must have heard *something*, Captain . . ." went on Canvey.

"I'm just the Master," I told him. "Nobody ever tells *me* anything."

Breakfast over, I went back up to my quarters. Bindle brought me a morning paper; somebody in Rim Runners' dock office had been thoughtful enough to send copies on board. I lit a cigar, skimmed through it. It was deadly dull. (Other people's local rags are always dull—but this, *The Port Forlorn Confederate*, had been my local rag once . . .) I noted that *Basset* was listed in the Shipping Information column as having arrived. I noted, too, that the date of her departure was given as "indefinite". I knew that already.

I read that the Confederacy's Department of Tourism was thinking about reestablishing the holiday resort on Eblis. I read about the Burns Night party that had been thrown by the Ambassador of the Empire of Waverley. Obviously he couldn't have been waiting for our consignment of Waverley scotch. I read about the Rim Rules Football match between the Port Forlorn Pirates and the Desolation Drovers. I found it hard to raise any interest in the account of the game. Even when I had been a Rim Worlder myself I hadn't been all that keen, and on most of the worlds of the Sirian Sector *the* game is Old Association, the only *real* football. Finally I found the crossword. It wasn't one of the cryptic variety, just a collection of absurdly simple clues that a retarded child of five could have solved in four minutes. It only took *me* three and a half.

There was a knock at the door. I threw the paper aside, got out my chair to welcome Commodore Grimes.

He took the seat I offered him, pulled out of his pocket an ancient and battered pipe that looked as though it was the very one that he had always smoked when I last knew him. It smelt like it, too. Sara Taine came in with a tray of coffee things. She seemed disposed to hang around with flapping ears, and looked hurt when I told her, "That will be all, thanks, Sara."

Grimes said, "Quite comfortable quarters you have, Captain Rule."

"Yes," I agreed. "*Basset* and her sister ships are an improvement on the Commission's basic Epsilon design. We have our own yards now in the Sector, of course, and build our own vessels . . ."

"Passenger accommodation?" he asked.

"I can take a dozen, in single-berth cabins. More if people are willing to double up."

"Mphm." He looked at me through the cloud of acrid smoke that he had just emitted. I countered with a smokescreen of my own. "Mphm. You know, of course, that we have our own Survey Ship, *Faraway Quest* . . . ."

"I've heard of her, sir."

"Well, the *Quest*'s out of commission. Will be for some months yet. Oh, she's old, I admit, but even I didn't know that there were so many things wrong with her until she came up for Survey . . ." He relit his pipe, which had gone out, using one of the archaic matches that he still affected. "You know Kinsolving's Planet, of course?"

"I know of it, Commodore. I've never been there."

"I have," he told me. "Too often. The things that have happened to me there shouldn't happen to a dog. Well, the Port Forlorn University wants to send another expedition to Kinsolving. Normally I'd have been their bus driver, in *Faraway Quest*. But she, as I've told you, is grounded. And our Navy won't lay a ship on for a bunch of civilian scientists, psychic researchers at that. And all of our merchant tonnage, the Rim Runners fleet, is heavily committed for months to come. Do you get the picture?"

"I'm beginning to," I admitted reluctantly.

"Do I detect a certain lack of enthusiasm, Captain Rule? I can't say that I blame you. Oh, well, it shouldn't be hard to arrange a charter whereby we man the ship with our own personnel, while you and your boys and girls are put up in hotels at the Confederacy's expense."

"I stay with my ship," I told him. "And I'm pretty sure that all my people will be of the same mind."

"Good. I was expecting you to say that. So . . . *If* the charter is arranged—it's not definite yet—you'll be carrying half a dozen scientists, two qualified psionicists, the Kinsolving's Planet Advisor and his wife. The Advisor is me, of course. Sonya—my wife— doesn't like that world any more than I do, but she maintains that I'm far less liable to get into trouble if she's along . . ."

"What *is* wrong with Kinsolving?" I asked.

"You're a Rim Worlder born," he said. "You know the stories." Yes, I knew the stories, or some of them. Kinsolving had been colonized at the same time as the other Rim Worlds, but the colonization hadn't stuck. The people—those of them who hadn't committed suicide, been murdered or vanished without trace—were taken off and resettled on Lorn, Faraway, Ultimo and Thule.

They all told the same story—oppressive loneliness, even in the middle of a crowd, continuous acute depression, outbreaks of irrational violence and, every night, dreams so terrifying that the hapless colonists dreaded going to bed. One theory that I remembered was that Kinsolving is the focal point of . . . forces, psychic forces. Another theory was that around the planet the fabric of our Universe is somehow strained, almost to breaking point, and that some of the alternate Universes aren't at all pleasant by our standards. But you don't have to go to Kinsolving to get the feeling that if you make an effort you'll be able to step into another Continuum; that sensation is common enough anywhere on the Rim. But it's on Kinsolving that you know that no effort at all is necessary, that a mere sneeze would suffice to blow you out of the known Universe into . . . Into Heaven? Maybe, but the reverse would be more likely.

"Kinsolving," said Grimes softly, "is a sort of gateway . . . It's been opened quite a few times, to my knowledge. I'd as lief not be involved in its opening, but . . ." he shrugged . . . "it seems to be my fate always to be involved with the bloody planet."

There was a heavy silence, which I thought I'd better break. "The professional psionicists you mentioned . . . ?"

"Old friends of mine," he told me. "Ken Mayhew. One of a dying breed. He was a Psionic Communications Officer long before the Carlotti System was dreamed of. He still holds his commission in the Rim Worlds Naval Reserve. And Clarisse, his wife. A telepath and a teleporteuse. Both of them know Kinsolving."

"And does this Mayhew," I asked, "still cart his personal amplifier around with him? I can remember the old-time PCOs and how they used to make pets of those obscene, disembodied dogs' brains . . ."

"Ken used to keep his poodle's brain in aspic," said the Commodore, "but not any longer. He and Clarisse work as a team. She amplifies for him when he's sending or receiving, and he for her when she's teleporting."

"And the scientists? Any weirdos among them?"

"Oddly, enough, no. They study psychic phenomena without being in any way psychic themselves. They've cooked up some fantastically sensitive instruments, I understand, that can measure the slightest variations of temperature, atmospheric pressure, electrical potential and whatever. They have their own theory about

Kinsolving, which is that the planet is actually haunted, in the good, old-fashioned way. And for a ghost to appear and speak and throw things around it must get energy from somewhere. A drop in temperature, for example, indicates that energy is being used." He laughed, rather mirthlessly. "It makes a change from all the other ideas about Kinsolving—multidimensional universes and all the rest of it . . ."

"And what are *your* ideas about it, sir?" I asked.

"Kinsolving," he said, "is a world where anything can happen and almost certainly will."

The charter was arranged; our Canis Major Head Office was happy enough that profitable employment had been found for *Basset*. We, *Basset*'s crew, were not so happy. We were all a long way from home, and too long a time out, and this excursion to Kinsolving would inevitably delay our departure from the Rim Worlds for the Sirian Sector.

There was one slight consolation; we were not kept hanging around long on Lorn. One day sufficed for the discharge of our inward cargo. It was a matter of hours only to ready the passenger accommodations for occupancy. There was the routine overhaul of all machinery, which took four days, and while this was in progress extra stores were taken on and the crates and cases containing the scientists' equipment loaded. On the morning of the sixth day the passengers boarded.

Ken and Clarisse Mayhew I had already met at Grimes's home, where he and Sonya, his wife, had had us all to dinner. Ken was a typical telepath, one of the type with which I have become familiar in the days when the only FTL communication between ships and between ships and planet-base stations was through the PCOs. He was tall, inclined to be weedy, with mousy hair, muddy eyes and an otherworldly appearance. Clarisse was another kettle of tea, not at all conforming to the popular idea of a psionicist. She was a very attractive girl with brown hair and brown eyes, strong featured, although a mite too solidly built for my taste. Sonya Grimes, however, was the sort of woman for whom I could fall quite easily; tall and slim, with a thin, slightly prominent nose and a wide mouth, remarkable violet eyes, sleek auburn hair. Her figure? She could have worn an old flour sack and made it look as though it had been imported at great expense from Paris, Earth.

The commodore and his wife were guests in the control room during liftoff. Sonya was a spacewoman, I had learned earlier, and although married to a Rim Worlder she still retained both her Federation citizenship and her Survey Service commission. Grimes, I could see, was just itching to get his own paws on the controls. (He had confided to me that, at times, he found the life of a deskborne commodore more than a little irksome.) But he sat in one of the spare chairs, well out of the way, watching. I don't think that he missed anything. Sonya was beside him. She laughed when we went through our own Dog Star Line ritual after the routine checks for spaceworthiness.

The junior officer present—young Taylor, the Third—demanded in a portentously solemn voice, "What is the Word?"

We all roared in reply, "Growl you may, but go you must!"

Sonya, as I have said, was amused. She whispered to her husband, "I'm beginning to find out why this company's ships are called the chariots of the dogs . . ." I knew what she meant. That Twentieth Century book, *Chariots of the Gods*, is still regarded as a Bible by those people who believe in the Old Race who started all the present civilization extant in the Galaxy.

Aerospace Control gave us clearance to lift, wished us *bon voyage*. We climbed into what was an unusual phenomenon for Lorn, a clear sky. Soon the spaceport was no more than a huddle of model buildings far below us, with three toy ships on the apron. (*Rim Kestrel* and *Rim Wallaby* had come in before our departure; *Rim Osprey* was due to leave, for the worlds of the Eastern Circuit, later in the day.)

The little bitch was handling well. I took her up easily, not trying to break any records. I heard Sonya murmur, "George isn't like you, John. He doesn't show off using his auxiliary reaction drive when there's no need for it . . ." Grimes replied with a far from expressionless face.

Lorn, with its wide, dreary (even in the sunlight) plains, its jagged, snowcapped mountains, diminished below us, became a mottled globe, gray-brown land, green-blue water, white snow. Still we drove upward, through and clear to the Van Allens.

The inertial drive was shut down and the directional gyroscopes grumbled into life, swinging the ship about her axes, bringing her head around to point almost directly at the target star, the Kinsolving sun, a solitary spark in the empty blackness. On the ship's beam glowed the iridescent Lens of the Galaxy, spectacular and, to those of us not used to seeing it from outside, frightening. I steadied her up on the target, making a small allowance for drift. I restarted the inertial drive and then started the Mannschenn Drive, the Space-Time-twister.

As on every such occasion I visualized those gleaming rotors spinning, precessing, fading as they tumbled down the warped dimensions fading yet never vanishing, dragging the ship and all aboard her into that uncanny state where normal physical laws held good only within the fragile hull. There was the long second of *déjà vu* during which time seemed to run backward.

Inside the control room colors sagged down the spectrum and perspective was distorted, and all sounds were as though emanating from a distant echo chamber. Then all snapped back to normal, although the thin, high whine of the drive was a constant reminder that nothing was or would be normal until we were at our destination. And there was nothing normal outside the ports, of course. Ahead the Kinsolving sun was a writhing, multicolored nebulosity, and on the beam the Lens was a pullulating Klein flask blown by a drunken glass blower. It looked as though it were alive. Perhaps it was alive. Perhaps only with the Mannschenn Drive in operation do we see it as it really is . . .

I dismissed the uneasy thought from my mind. I said to Bindle, "Deep Space routine, Mr. Mate."

"But who will keep the dog watches?" asked Taylor.

"You're all watchdogs," I replied.

"More of your ritual?" asked Sonya interestedly.

"Yes," I admitted, feeling absurdly embarrassed. "I suppose it does sound rather childish to an outsider . . ."

Grimes laughed. "I remember one ship I was in when I was in the Survey Service. The cruiser *Orion*. We called her *O'Ryan*, of course, and everybody had to speak an approximation to Irish dialect, and *our* song, just as *Doggy In The Window* is your song, was *The Wearin' Of The Green . . .*"

"Still rather childish," his wife said, but her smile took any sting out of the words.

Grimes said, "Well, Captain Rule, are you coming down to meet the customers?"

I said, "I suppose it's one of the things I'm paid for."

The customers—the passengers—were in their own saloon. Ken and Clarisse Mayhew I had already met, of course; the others, until now, had been no more than names on the passenger list. There was a Dr. Thorne—I never did get it straight what exactly he was a doctor of—and his wife.

They were Jack Spratt and Mrs. Spratt in reverse, he a bearded, Falstaffian giant, she a gray, wispy sparrow. There were two, almost identical young men; mousey, studious, bespectacled. Their names were Paul Trentham and Bill Smith. The two young women could have been their sisters, but were not. One was Susan Howard, the other Mary Lestrange. They were friendly enough—not that they overdid it.

Sara, ever efficient, had seen to it that the bar in the saloon was well-stocked. Thorne took over as barman; the drinks soon dispelled the initial stiffness of this first meeting. I rather took to the leader of the expedition and he to me. I felt that I would be able, without giving offense, to ask him a question that had been bothering me slightly.

"Tell me, Doctor," I put to him, "why don't you have any mediums along? You have two psionicists, sure, but they are, essentially, communications specialists, and by communications I don't mean communications with the dear departed."

He laughed, a little ruefully. "One thing that our researches have taught us is this. There are many, many phoney mediums. Even the genuine ones sometimes, although not always intentionally so."

"What do you mean, exactly?"

"Look at it this way. A genuine medium is determined to deliver the goods. If the goods aren't forthcoming, because conditions aren't right, perhaps, then he or she would just hate to disappoint the customers. Quite possibly subconsciously—but now and again consciously—fake results are delivered. The main trouble, I suppose, is that the average medium doesn't have it drummed into him, all through a long training, that high standards of professional ethics must be maintained. A graduate of the Rhine Institute, however—such as Ken Mayhew—is bound by the Institute's code of ethics. He is therefore far more reliable than any medium."

"But you do believe in spiritualism, don't you?"

"I believe that there are hauntings. I believe that Kinsolving's Planet is haunted. I—we—want to find out by whom. Or what."

"I seem to be spending my life finding out," grumbled Grimes. "But every time I get a different answer."

"Perhaps you're a catalyst, Commodore," suggested Mrs. Thorne.

"And perhaps Captain Rule is a dogalyst," said Sonya.

I tried to laugh along with the rest at the vile pun—jokes about the Dog Star Line are all right when *we* make them, but . . .

The voyage was a relatively short one. It was like all other voyages, except that at the latter end of it we should not be landing at a proper spaceport with all the usual radio-navigational aids. There would be no bored voice coming from the NST speaker, talking us down. There would be no triangle of beacons to mark our berth on the apron. Come to that, there would be no apron. The spaceport had become a sizeable crater when *something* had destroyed the Franciscan ship *Piety* a while ago.

Grimes had brought his charts with him. Together we studied them. He advised me to make my landing in the old Sports Stadium, on the shore of Darkling Tarn, not far from the city of Enderston, the ruins of which stood on the east bank of the Weary River. Those colonists had shown a morbid taste in place names . . . That applied to all the Rim Worlds, of course, but Kinsolving took the prize for deliberately miserable nomenclature.

The commodore acted as pilot when we finally made our approach; he had been on Kinsolving before, more than once, and he possessed the local knowledge. I handled the controls myself, of course, but he was in the chair normally occupied by Bindle, advising.

We were making an early morning descent—always a wise policy when landing on a world without proper spaceport facilities. The lower the sun's altitude, the more pronounced the shadows cast by every irregularity of the ground. Too, when an expedition arrives at sunrise it has all the daylight hours to get itself organised. Left to myself, I'd have arrived when I arrived and not bothered about such niceties. It was Grimes, with his years of Survey experience behind him, who had urged me to adopt Survey Service S.O.P.

So we were coming down after a few hours of standing off in orbit. Already there was enough light for us to be able to make out details of the landscape beneath us. There was the Weary River—and with all the twists and turns it was making it was small wonder that it was tired! There was the Darkling Tarn—looking, Grimes said, like an octopus run over by a steamroller. Bindle loosed off the sounding rockets that, at Grimes' insistence, had been added to our normal equipment. Each of them, in its descent, left a long, unwavering smoke trail: there was no wind to incommode us.

Each of them released a parachute flare that drifted down slowly. As we ourselves dropped, the picture in the periscope screen expanded. We could see the city at last, a huddle of overgrown ruins. We could see the Stadium, an oval of green that was just a little lighter in tone than the near-indigo of the older growth around it. One of the flares had fallen just to one side of the sports ground and started a minor brush fire; the smoke from it was rising almost directly upwards.

At least it would be easier landing here than at the proper spaceport on Lorn . . . Grimes guessed my thoughts. "The ground's level enough, Captain Rule," he told me. "Or it was, last time I was here."

"Any large animals?" I asked.

"Just the descendants of the stock brought by the original colonists. Wild pigs and cattle. Rabbits. They'll all have sense enough to bolt for cover when they hear us coming down."

In the periscope screen the ground looked level enough. I maintained a slow but steady rate of descent, slowed it to the merest downward drift when there were only meters to go. At last the contact lights flashed on. I cut the inertial drive. The silence, broken at first by the sighing of the shock absorbers and the usual minor creakings and groanings, was oppressive. I looked at the commodore. He nodded, and said, "Yes, you can make it Finished With Engines." Before I did so I glanced at the clinometer. The ship was a little off the vertical, but only half a degree. It was nothing to worry about.

"So we're here," whispered Sonya. "Again." I didn't like the way she said it.

"Shore leave?" asked Bindle brightly. "Of course, we shall want an advance from the Purser first, sir."

"Ha, ha," I said. "Very funny." I looked out through the viewports. This didn't look like a world on which there would be any need for money. It didn't look like a world on which to take a pleasant walk.

Oh, the day was bright enough, and such scenery as was in view was pretty enough, in a jungly sort of way, but . . . It was as though a shadow was over everything, dimming colours and bringing a chill to the air that bit through to the very bones. The sunlight streaming through the viewports was bright, dazzlingly so, to the outer eye—but as far as the inner eye was concerned it could have been the rays of a lopsided moon intermittently breaking through driving storm clouds. I'm not a seventh son of a seventh son or any of that rubbish, and if I applied for admission to the Rhine Institute for training they'd turn me down without bothering with the routine tests, but I do have my psychic moments.

A premonition of impending doom, I thought. I liked the feel of it. I thought it again.

"If you don't mind, Captain Rule," said Grimes, "I'll assume command until such time as we lift off again. The ship is still your charge, of course, but all extravehicular activities are my pigeon."

"As you please, sir," I said a little stiffly. He was doing no more than to confirm, in front of witnesses, what had already been decided—but it was essential that my officers have no doubt as to who was boss cocky of the expedition. "Your orders, sir?"

"Please pass the word for everybody, ship's officers and civilian personnel, to assemble in the ward-room for briefing. I shall just be repeating what I have told you all time and time again during the voyage—but this is a world on which you can't be too careful. This is a planet on which anything might happen, and probably will."

I reached for the microphone and gave the necessary orders.

The wardroom was crowded with everybody packed into it, but there was seating for everybody. Grimes, nonetheless, remained standing. He said quietly, "Of all of us here, only Commander Mayhew, Mrs. Mayhew, Commander Verrill and myself have set foot on Kinsolving before . . ."

Commander Verrill? I wondered, then realised that he meant Sonya. "As we have told you," he went on, "this is a dangerous world, a very dangerous world. You have heard the story of what happened to the Neo-Calvanist expedition when an attempt was made to invoke the Jehovah of the Old Testament. I was among those present at the time, as was Mrs. Mayhew, and the crater where the spaceport used to be bears witness to the destruction of their ship, *Piety*. You have heard what happened when our own expedition, a little later, tried to repeat that foolhardy experiment. That time there was only one victim—me. And then there was the landing made by the Federation Survey Service's ship, *Star Pioneer*, aboard which Commander Verrill and myself were passengers. That time the pair of us got into trouble . . ."

"Of course," Sonya said sweetly, "I wasn't worrying myself sick about you the other times . . ."

"Mphm. Anyhow, this a smaller expedition than the previous ones and I therefore insist that when excursions are made from the ship there is to be no splitting up; nobody is to go wandering off by himself on some wild goose—or wild ghost—chase. Personal transceivers will be carried at all times. Ship's personnel, acting as escorts to the scientists, will be armed. Captain Rule and all of his officers hold commissions in the Sirian Sector Naval Reserve and are trained in the use of weaponry . . ."

Ha! I thought. *Ha bloody ha!* I remembered, all too well, our practice session at the Navy's small arms range shortly before our lift off from Dogtown. "Miss," the exasperated Petty Officer Instructor had said at last to Betty Boops, "if you *really* want to hurt anybody with that pistol creep up close and hit him over the head with it . . ." And most of the rest of us including myself, weren't much better. Only Sara, the Purser, made a fair showing.

"Compared to the rest of you," the P.O. had said, "she's Annie Oakley." He went on, turning to Betty, "And you, Miss, are Calamity Jane." Sara had been quite pleased . . .

Grimes continued, "You civilian ladies and gentlemen are not to set foot off the ship without your . . . watchdogs. Is that understood, Dr. Thorne?"

"Understood, Commodore," replied the scientist laconically.

"Good. I don't know about the rest of you, but my belly is firmly convinced that my throat's been cut. I propose that we all enjoy breakfast before getting the show on the road."

There were, as a matter of fact, two shows to be gotten on the road. One was the small party leaving the ship on foot to poke around the stadium and its environs, the other one flew to the city in the pinnace that we had on loan from the Rim Worlds Navy and that we carried in lieu of one of our own boats, which had been left in Port Forlorn. Like any ship's boat it was not only a spaceship in miniature but could be used as an atmosphere flier. Unlike a merchantship's boat, it was armed, mounting a heavy machine gun, a small laser cannon and a rocket projector.

Grimes and Sonya were in the boat party, as were Ken Mayhew, Dr. Thorne, Rose, his wispy wife, Sara Taine and myself. Sara was pleased at having real guns to play with—somehow she had appointed herself Gunnery Officer of the pinnace—and was hoping that she would have a chance to use them. I was hoping that she wouldn't.

We boarded the boat in its bay. The commodore took the

controls, the rest of us disposed ourselves around the small cabin. The inertial drive unit grumbled into life and we lifted from the chocks and then, with the application of full lateral thrust, shot out through the open port into the bright sunlight. Grimes took us round the ship in an ascending spiral. Bindle, who was minding the shop, waved to us from the control room. We were close enough to see his envious expression.

Grimes leveled out, headed for the city. It was not easy to see from this relatively low altitude; when we had been looking down on it the street plan had been obvious enough, but from a height of a mere one hundred meters it looked only like an unusually lumpy piece of jungle in the distance. Oh, there were a few ruined towers, prominent enough, but they were so overgrown that they could have been no more than freak geological formations.

I tried to enjoy the flight. I should have enjoyed it; the bright sunlight was streaming through the ports, the scenery over which we were skimming was unspoiled, I had enjoyed a good breakfast and my after-breakfast cigar was drawing well. And yet . . . For no reason at all—apart from a quite illogical feeling of unease—I kept looking aft. I noticed that the others—apart from Grimes—did so too. (But Grimes had his rearview screen above the console.) A fragment of half-remembered verse kept chasing itself though my mind. How did it go?

> Like one that on a lonesome road
> Doth walk in fear and dread,
> And having cast a glance behind
> Durst no more turn his head,
> Because he knows a fearsome fiend
> Doth close behind him tread . . .

Something like that, anyhow. And, in any case, there wasn't any fearsome fiend in our wake. I hoped.

Grimes tapped out his pipe and refilled and relit it for about the fifth time. Sara Taine checked, yet again, the pinnace's fire control panel. (But could you shoot at ghosts? I wondered. Had anybody had the forethought to substitute silver bullets for the normal machine-gun ammo?) Dr. Thorne cleared his throat and, speaking loudly to be heard over the irritable snarl of the inertial drive, asked Mayhew, "Do you *feel* anything, Ken?"

"I suspect," replied the telepath, speaking slowly and carefully, "that something out there doesn't like us . . ."

"A normal state of affairs on this world," grumbled Grimes.

"Are there likely to be any manifestations, Commodore?" said Thorne.

"Anything, no matter how unlikely, is likely here," was the reply. *Cheerful shower of bastards!* I thought.

Rose Thorne—people do tend to be given unfortunate names, although the lady's parents couldn't have been expected to know that she'd marry whom she did—had opened the case that she had carried aboard with her and was tinkering with fragile looking instruments. She was finding out, I supposed, if there were any variations in temperature, gravitational or magnetic fields or whatever. Presumably she discovered no anomalies. In any case, she said nothing. And Ken Mayhew had a very faraway look on his face, was staring into nothingness, a nothingness in which . . . something stirred. That was the impression I got. Cold shivers were chasing themselves up and down my spine.

"Cheer up, George," Sonya admonished me. "The first time here is the worst."

"Not for me it wasn't," grunted the commodore. "Although every time was bad."

"My first time was bad," stated Sonya.

We were over the outskirts of the city now, following a broad street through the cracked surface of which trees and bushes had thrust. On either side of us were the buildings, creeper-covered houses with empty windows peering like dead eyes through the tangled greenery. I found myself thinking of ancient graveyards—cemeteries in which the victims of massacre had been buried and commemorated, and then, after many years, forgotten. Something, disturbed by our noisy flight, scuttled below and ahead of us, finally diving into a doorway.

"Hold your fire, Sara," said Sonya sharply. "It's only a hen."

"Nothing wrong with roast chicken," I said. "The fowl in the tissue culture vats has long since lost whatever flavor it had . . ."

"There wouldn't have been much left for roasting if I'd let fly with the MG," Sara told me.

It was a feeble enough joke, but we all laughed nervously.

We came to a sort of square or plaza. There was a group of statuary—once a fountain?—in the middle of it, but so overgrown that it was impossible to see if the figures had been men or monsters. They looked like monsters now. Around the plaza were ruined towers, their outlines blurred by what looked like—was, in fact—Terran ivy. Those colonists had brought a fair selection of Earth flora and fauna with them, some of which had survived and flourished.

Grimes set the pinnace down carefully, very carefully, selecting an area that did not have any sturdy bushes and saplings thrusting up through the paving. We landed with hardly a jar. Reluctantly, it seemed, he turned off the drive. We could hear ourselves think again. This was not the relief that it should have been. The silence, after the arhythmic snarl and thump of the motor, seemed about to be broken by . . . something. By what?

"Well," said the commodore unnecessarily, "we're here."

"You know the city," said Thorne. "Wasn't there—isn't there—some sort of temple . . ."

"I don't want to go *there* again," said Sonya determinedly.

Grimes shrugged. "It's as good a place to start our . . . investigations as any. After all, we *are* here to investigate . . ." he remarked. He turned to Mayhew. "You're the psionicist, Ken. What do you think?"

The telepath seemed to jerk out of some private dream, and not a pleasant one. "The temple . . ." he murmured vaguely. "Yes . . . I remember. You told me about it . . ."

"Where is this temple?" asked Thorne.

"We shall have to walk," Grimes told him. "It's not on the plaza. It's in a little alley . . . I'm not sure that I'll be able to find it again . . ."

"I can lead you there," said Mayhew.

"You *would!*" muttered Sonya. So the telepath was picking something up, I thought. He would home on it, as a navigator homes on a radio beacon. I was beginning to feel as the commodore's wife was obviously feeling about it. Deciding to throw in my two bits' worth I asked, "Shall we leave somebody to guard the pinnace?" Sara scowled at me. She was the obvious choice. She would be no more keen on going outside than any of us, but she most certainly did not want to be left alone.

"It will not be necessary, George," said Grimes. "We will, of course, notify the ship of our intentions. And Ken will maintain his telepathic hook-up with Clarisse. And, before leaving, each of us will leave his hand impression so that the outer airlock door can be locked after us . . ."

This we did. The door would now open if any of us placed either hand—or only fingertips—on the plate set in the hull beside the entrance. One by one we jumped down to the mossy paving stones. There was an unpleasant dankness in the air in spite of the sunlight, a penetrating chill. Yet, according to the thermometer that Mrs. Thorne produced from her capacious shoulder bag, it was mild enough, a fraction over twenty six degrees, too warm for the heavy, long-sleeved shirts, long trousers and stout boots that we were wearing.

Mayhew took the lead, with Grimes, projectile pistol in hand, walking beside him. Sonya and I, immediately behind, followed his example, although she favored a laser hand gun. The Thornes followed us. Sara, carrying a submachine gun, brought up the rear. The telepath led us over the broken pavement, deviating from his course as required to avoid clumps of bushes and the occasional tree, but heading all the time to where a wide street opened off the plaza. It looked more like some fantastically fertile canyon than a manmade thoroughfare. The leaves of the omnipresent ivy glistened in the sunlight, glossy greens and a particularly poisonous looking yellow. There were other creepers too, native perhaps, or importations from other worlds than Earth, but they were fighting a losing battle against the hardy, destructive vine.

We walked slowly and cautiously into the wide street. It must have been an imposing avenue before the abandonment of the city, before burgeoning weeds blurred its perspective and obscured the clean lines of the buildings on either side of it. I tried to visualise it as it had been in its heyday—and succeeded all too well. Everything ... flickered, flickered then shone with an unnatural clarity. I cried out in alarm as I stared at the onrushing stream of traffic into which we were so carelessly walking. A gaudy chrome and scarlet ground car was almost upon on us, the fat woman driving it making no move either to swerve or to brake her vehicle. I grabbed Sonya's arm to drag her to one side, to safety. She cried out—and her sharp voice shattered the spell. Again there was the brief flickering and when normal vision returned I could see that nothing was moving in the street save ourselves. There was no traffic, no homicidal ground car. But there was a low mound ahead of us looking like a crouching, green furred beast. Freakishly, the lenses of its headlights had not been grown over and were regarding us like a pair of baleful eyes. And had I seen the ghost of the machine, I wondered, or of its driver?

Sonya was rubbing her arm and glaring at me. The others had stopped and were staring at me curiously.

"Did you *see* something, George?" asked Thorne.

I said slowly, "I saw this street as it must once have been, at its busiest. We were right in the middle of the traffic, about to be run down." I pointed at the derelict, almost unrecognisable car. "We were almost run down by . . . that. Or its ghost."

"The ghost of a *machine?*" demanded Thorne incredulously.

His wife, looking at an instrument she had taken from her bag, said, "The graph shows a sudden dip in temperature . . ."

"But a *machine?*" repeated the scientist.

"Why not?" countered Grimes. "Life force rubs off human beings on to the machinery with which they're in the most intimate contact. Ships, especially . . . And a car is, in some ways, almost a miniature ship . . ." He turned to Mayhew. "Ken?"

The telepath replied, in a distant voice, "I . . . I feel . . . resentment . . . In its dim, mechanical way that thing loved its mistress. It was abandoned, left here to rot . . ."

"Did *you* see anything?" persisted Thorne.

"I saw the same as George did," admitted Mayhew. "But I knew it wasn't . . . real."

We resumed our trudge along the overgrown street. Everybody, I noticed with a certain wry satisfaction, gave the abandoned car a wide berth. We walked on, and on, trying to ignore the brambly growths that clutched at our trouser legs as though with malign intent.

"Here," announced Mayhew.

We could just make out the entrance to a side alley, completely blocked with a tall, bamboolike growth with tangled strands of ivy filling the narrow spaces between the upright stems.

"Shall I?" asked Sonya.

"Yes," said Grimes, after a second's thought.

While Sara watched enviously the commodore's wife used her laser pistol like a machete, slashing with the almost invisible beam. There were crackling flames and billows of dense white smoke. Coughing and spluttering, with eyes watering, we backed away. I couldn't help thinking that a fire extinguisher would have been more useful than most of the other equipment we had brought along.

But only the bamboo burned; the surrounding ivy was too green to catch fire once the laser was no longer in use. At last the smoke cleared to a barely tolerable level and we were able to make our way forward. The embers were hot underfoot, nonetheless, but our boots were stout and the fabric of our trousers fireproof.

We found the church.

It was only a small building, standing apart from its taller neighbours. It was a featureless cube. Well, *almost* a cube. I got the impression that the angles were subtly, very subtly, wrong. Unlike the buildings to either side of it it was not overgrown. Its dull gray walls seemed to be of some synthetic stone. The plain rectangular door was also gray, possibly of uncorroded metal. There were no windows. Over the entrance, in black lettering, were the words, TEMPLE OF THE PRINCIPLE.

Grimes stared at the squat, ugly building. I could see from his face that he was far from happy. He muttered, "This is where we came in."

"This," Sonya corrected him, "is where we nearly went out . . ."

They had told me the story during the outward passage. I knew how they had investigated this odd temple, and found themselves thrown into an alternate existence, another plane of being on which their lives had taken altogether different courses. It had not been a dream, they insisted. They had actually lived those lives.

"Something . . ." Mayhew was muttering. "*Something* . . . But what? *But what?*"

"And what was the principle that they . . . er . . . worshipped?" asked Thorne, matter-of-factly.

"The Uncertainty Principle . . ." said Grimes, but dubiously. "You know, the funny part is that in none of the records of the abandoned colony is there any mention of this temple, or of the religion with which it was associated."

"The worshippers must have . . . left," Sonya said, "before the other colonists were evacuated."

"But where did they go?" asked Thorne.

"Or *when*," said Mayhew. "*To* when, I mean."

Grimes filled and lit his pipe, then almost immediately knocked it out again, put it back in his pocket. He pushed the door. I was expecting it to resist his applied pressure but it opened easily, far too easily. He led the way inside the temple. The others followed. I was last, as I waited until I had raised Bindle on my personal transceiver to tell him where we were and what we doing. He—always the humorist—said, "Drop something in the plate for me, Captain!"

I was expecting darkness in the huge, windowless room, but there was light—of a sort. The gray, subtly shifting twilight was worse than blackness would have been. It accentuated the . . . the *wrongness* of the angles where wall met wall, ceiling and floor. I was reminded of that eerie sensation one feels in the interstellar drive room of a ship when the Mannschenn Drive is running, the dim perception of planes at right angles to all the planes of the normal Space-Time continuum. Faintly self-luminous, not quite in the middle of that uncannily lopsided hall, was what had to be the altar, a sort of ominous coffin shape. But as I stared at it its planes and angles shifted. It was, I decided, more of a cube. Or *more* than a cube . . . A tesseract?

Rose Thorne was pulling instruments out of her capacious bag. She set one of them up on spidery, telescopic legs. She peered at the dial on top of it. "Fluctuations," she murmured, "slight, but definite . . ." She said in a louder voice, "There's something *odd* about the gravitational field of this place . . ."

"Gravity waves?" asked her husband.

She laughed briefly. "Ripples rather than waves. Undetectable by any normal gravitometer."

Thorne turned to Grimes. "Did you notice any phenomena like this when you were here before, John?"

"We didn't have any instruments with us," the commodore told him shortly.

"And what do *you* feel Ken?" the scientist asked Mayhew.

But the telepath did not reply.

Looking at him, the way that he was standing there, his gaze somehow turned inward, I was reminded of the uneasy sensation you get when a dog sees something—or seems to see something—that is invisible to you. "Old . . ." he whispered. "Old . . . From the time before this, and from the time before that, and the time before and the time before . . . The planet alive, alive and aware, a sentient world . . . Surviving every death and rebirth of the universe . . . Surviving beyond the continuum . . ."

It didn't make sense, I thought. It didn't make sense.

Or did it?

His lips moved again, but his voice was barely audible. "Communion . . . Yes. Communion . . ." He took a step, and then another, and another, like a sleepwalker. He paced slowly and deliberately up to—into—the dimly glowing tesseract. He seemed to flicker. The outline of his body wavered, wavered and faded. Then, quite suddenly, he was gone.

The metallic click as Sara cocked her submachine gun was startlingly loud. I still don't know what she thought that she was going to shoot at. I did know that in this situation all our weapons were utterly useless.

"We have to get Clarisse here," said Grimes at last. "She's the only one of us who'll be able to do anything." He added, in a whisper, "If anything can be done, that is . . ."

We had to go outside the temple before we could use our personal transceivers. Clarisse was already calling; she *knew*, of course. She was already in *Basset's* second boat, which was being piloted by young Taylor. Grimes told him to try to land in the street just by the mouth of the alley. There were more obstructions there than where we had set down, in the square, but speed was the prime consideration. I walked, accompanied by Sara, to the proposed landing site, my transceiver set for continuous beacon-transmission so that Taylor could home on it.

We heard the boat—the inertial drive is not famous for quiet running—before we saw it. Taylor came in low over the rooftops, wasting no time. He slammed the lifecraft down to the road surface, crushing a couple of well-developed bushes and knocking a stout sapling sideways. I shuddered. I didn't like to see ship's equipment—especially *my* ship's equipment—handled that way. The door midway along the torpedo-shaped hull snapped open. Clarisse jumped out.

She brushed past us, unspeaking, ran into the alley, clouds of fine ash exploding about her ankles. Sara and I followed her. Clarisse hesitated briefly at the temple doorway, exchanging a few words with Grimes and Sonya, then hurried inside. When the rest of us joined her we found her standing by the altar, motionless, her face set and expressionless. In the dim light she looked like a priestess of some ancient religion.

Then she spoke, but not to any of us.

"Ken," she whispered, obviously vocalising her thoughts. "Ken . . ." She smiled suddenly. She was getting through. "Yes . . . Here I am . . ."

"Where is he?" demanded Grimes urgently.

She ignored the question. Suddenly, walking as Mayhew had

walked, she stepped into that luminous shape, that distorted geometrical, multidimensional diagram. We saw the outline of her body through her clothing, her shadowy bone structure through her translucent flesh, and . . .

Nothing.

Thorne broke the stunned silence. "Did you observe the meter while all this was happening?" he asked his wife.

You cold-blooded bastard! I thought angrily, then realised that the scientists' instruments might provide some clue as to what had happened.

"No," she admitted, then stooped over the gravitometer, pressed a button. "But here's the printout."

We could all see the graph as she showed it to him. There were the slight, very slight irregularities that she had referred to as gravitational ripples. And there were two sharp and very definite dips. The first one must have registered when Mayhew disappeared, the second when Clarisse vanished.

So It, whatever *It* was, played around with gravity. A sentient planet, I reflected, ought to be able to do just that . . .

"Rose," said Grimes, "watch your gravitometer, will you?"

She shot him a puzzled look, but obeyed. The commodore brought something small out of his pocket. It was, I saw, a box of matches. He tossed it towards the tesseract. Nobody was surprised when it, too, vanished.

"The field intensified," reported the woman. "Briefly, slightly, but very definitely."

"So . . ." murmured Grimes. "So what?" He turned to face us all. "We must get Ken and Clarisse out. But how?"

Nobody answered him.

Having waited in vain for a reply he continued. "Twice, while on this blasted planet, I've been shunted . . . elsewhere. Each time I got back. I still don't know how. But if I could, they can." He gestured towards the altar. "That thing's a gateway. A gateway to where—or *when*?" He addressed me directly. "You've an engine-room gantry aboard your ship, George. And there are drilling and cutting tools in the engineers' workshop."

"Yes," I told him.

"I'd like them here. Mphm. But there'll be only a few meters of wire on your gantry winches. We could want more, much more . . ."

I remembered, then, something which had been a source of puzzlement to me for a long time. "In the storeroom," I told him, "are two funny little hand winches, with reels of very fine wire. There's a lot of wire. Nobody knows what those winches are for. But . . ."

"But they might come in handy now," said Grimes, suddenly and inexplicably cheerful. "I think I know what those winches are—although what they're doing aboard a merchant spaceship is a mystery. In the Survey Service, of course, we had things like them, for oceanographical work . . ."

"Your're losing me, sir," I said.

"I could be wrong, of course," he went on, "but I've a hunch that these will be just the things we need. I'd like one of them out here at once. The other one, I think, could be modified slightly. Your engineers can study the simple workings of it, and then fit it with a motor from your gantry . . ."

I suppose that he knew what he was talking about. Nobody else did.

We went outside the temple to use our transceivers to get in touch with Bindle, back aboard the ship. Grimes put him in the picture and then gave him detailed instructions. As well as the first of the odd little hand winches and the cutting tools he wanted a sound-powered telephone, with as much wire as could be found.

Then the commodore and myself went to the mouth of the alley to await the return of Taylor with the first installment of equipment. The boat came in at last and we boarded it at once and were promptly carried to the flat roof of the building. Under my watchful eye the Third Officer made a very cautious landing—but that rooftop, by the feel of it, could have supported the enormous weight of an Alpha Class liner. We unloaded the tools and the reel of wire, then Taylor lifted off and returned to the ship.

Grimes looked at the wire reel and laughed. He said, "And you really don't know what this is, George?"

"No," I told him.

"Was your ship ever on Atlantia?"

"A few times, I think, but never when I was in her."

"And one of those times—probably the last time—she over-carried cargo," went on Grimes. "And the good Dog Star Line Mate buried those leftover bones in the back garden, thinking that they might come in handy for something, some time. This is a sounding machine, such as the Atlanteans use in their big schooners, and such as we, in the Survey Service, use for charting the seas of a newly discovered world. But our machines have motors."

"I thought that all sounding was done electronically," I said.

"Most of it is," the commodore told me, "but an echometer can't bring up a sample of the bottom. . . Yes, this is a sounding machine, Armstrong Patent."

"Is that the make of it?" Grimes laughed again, obviously, amused by my ignorance. I rather resented this. It was all very well for him; he was one of *the* experts, if not *the* expert, on Terran maritime history. And not only that, he holds a Master Mariner's Certificate in addition to his qualifications as a Master Astronaut—he had actually sailed in command of a surface vessel on that watery world Aquarius.

"Armstrong Patent," he said, "is the nickname given by seamen to any piece of machinery powered by human muscle. And they're a weird mob, the Atlanteans, as you may know. They have a horror of automation even in its simplest forms. They pride themselves on having put the clock back to the good old days of wooden ships and iron men. But they do import some manufactured goods—such as this." He looked at the dial set horizontally on top of the winch. "And then two hundred fathoms of piano wire here. That's about three hundred and sixty five metres." He pulled a cylinder of heavy metal from its clip on the winch frame. "And here's the sinker. About ten kilograms of lead, by the feel of it."

"Oh, I see," I admitted. (Well, I did, after a fashion.)

"Mphm." Grimes was studying the legs on which the machine stood, the feet of which were designed so that they could be bolted to a deck. "Mphm . . ." He straightened up, then walked to the edge of the flat roof. I followed him. There was no parapet. I stayed well back; I don't suffer from acrophobia—I'd hardly be a spaceman if I did—but I always like to have something to hold on to. And it looked a long way down. The temple hadn't looked all that high from the ground, but in its vicinity perspective seemed to be following a new set of rules.

Grimes was shouting down to his wife after a futile attempt to use his personal transceiver. Apparently the inhibitory field was as effective on the roof as inside the building. "Sonya, we want some timber. Yes, timber! Two good, strong logs, straight, each at lost two metres long and fifteen centimetres thick . . . Yes, use your laser to cut them!"

When she had gone, accompanied by the others, he determined the center of the flat roof by pacing out the diagonals. Where these intersected he put down his precious pipe as a marker. I brought him the laser cutter—one with a self-contained power pack. He held it like the oversized pistol that it resembled, directing the thin pencil of incandescence almost directly downward.

At first it seemed the surface of the roof was going to be impossible to cut; the beam flattened weirdly at the point of impact, spreading to a tiny puddle of intense light, dazzlingly bright even though it was in the full rays of the sun. And then, quite suddenly, without any pyrotechnics, without so much as a wisp of smoke, there was penetration.

After that it was easy. Grimes described a circle of about one-meter diameter but left a thirty-degree arc uncut. He switched off and put down the cutter, then retrieved his pipe. When it was safely back in his pocket he extended a cautious fingertip to the cut in the roof. He looked puzzled. "Cold, stone cold," he whispered. "It shouldn't be. But it saves time."

I fetched the pinch bar and we got one end of it under the partially excised circle, then levered upwards. It came fairly easily, and did not spring back when the pressure was released. I took a firm hold on the smooth edge and held it while Grimes completed the cut.

When the disc was free it was amazingly light, even though it was all of four centimeters thick. I put it to one side and we looked down.

The altar—I may as well go on calling it that, although I was sure by now that it had no religious significance—was almost directly below us. Its alien geometry glimmered wanly. I'd been expecting, somehow, to find myself looking down into a hole, a very deep hole, but such was not the case. It was just as we had seen it from ground level, a distorted construct of slowly shifting planes of dim radiance. But we knew that if we fell into it we should keep on going.

Somebody was calling. It was Sonya, back from her wood-cutting expedition. We went to the edge of the roof. She and Sara were carrying one suitable looking log between them, the Thornes another. She shouted, "How do we get these up to you?"

Grimes did something to the winch handles of the sounding machine so that the wire ran off easily. He pulled as much as he needed off the reel, lowered the end of it over the edge of the roof to the ground. Sonya threw it around the first of the logs in a simple yet secure hitch. We pulled it up. It wasn't all that heavy, but the thin wire bit painfully into the palms of our hands. Then we brought up the second one.

We used the laser cutter to trim the logs to square section, adjusting the beam setting carefully before starting work. We didn't want to cut the roof from under our feet. Then we arranged the two baulks of timber so that they bridged the circular hole. We lifted the sounding machine and set so that it rested securely on the rough platform. Grimes shackled the heavy sinker to the end of the wire, left it dangling. "Mphm . . ." he grunted dubiously. He had found, clipped inside the frame of the winch, a small L-shaped rod of metal on a wooden handle. He asked, "Do you know how this works?"

I didn't. I'm a spaceman, not seaman.

"This," he told me, "is the feeler. Normally there's a good lead from the sounding machine so the wire runs horizontally from the reel to a block on the taffrail or to the end of the sounding boom. Whoever's working it holds the feeler in one hand, pressing down on the wire—and he knows when the sinker has hit bottom by the sudden slackening of tension. Then he brakes. Obviously we can't do that here. So you, George, will have to exercise a lateral pull with the feeler. Yell out as soon as you feel the wire go slack."

We took our positions, myself crouching and holding the feeler ready, he grasping both winch handles. He gave them a sharp half-turn forward and the sinker dropped, as the wire sang off the drum. It was plain that we hadn't found bottom on the floor of the temple. Out ran the gleaming wire, out, out. . .

I heard Grimes mutter, "Fifty. One hundred . . . One fifty. . ." And what would happen when we came to the end of the wire?

It went slack suddenly. "Now!" I shouted as I went over backward! Somehow I was still watching Grimes and saw him sharply turn the handles in reverse, braking the winch. When I scrambled to my feet he was looking at the dial. "One hundred and seventy three fathoms," he said slowly. "One hundred and seventy three fathoms straight down . . ." He grinned ruefully. "That was the easy part. Gravity was doing all the work. The hard part comes now!"

I didn't know what he meant until we had to wind up all that length of wire by hand. We waited a little while, hoping that Mayhew and Clarisse would be able to attach a message of some kind to the sinker, and then we took a handle each and turned and turned and turned. The pointer moved anti-clockwise on the dial with agonizing slowness. We had both of us worked up a fine sweat and acquired blisters on the palms of our hands when, at long last, the plummet lifted slowly through the hole in the roof. There was more than just the sinker attached to the wire. There was a square of scarlet synthesilk that, I remembered, Clarisse had worn as a neckerchief at the throat of her khaki shirt. And knotted into it was the box of matches that Grimes had dropped into the altar.

There was something wrong with it. It took me a little time to realise what it was—and then I saw that in order to read the brand name—PROMETHEUS—one would require a mirror.

The Thornes had a pad and a stylus among their equipment. We used the sounding machine wire to bring these up to the roof, then attached them to the sinker and sent them down to wherever

Mayhew and Clarisse were trapped. This time Grimes applied the brake when he had one hundred and sixty fathoms of wire down and walked out the rest by hand. Then we waited, Grimes smoking a pipe—his matches still worked in spite of the odd reversal—and myself a cigar. This would give the psionicists time to write their message and, in any case, we felt that we had earned a smoke.

We thought of asking Sonya to use the boat that we had left in the plaza to bring others of the party up to the roof to lend us a hand, then decided that, for the time being, it was better to have them standing by on the ground. To begin with, there was the problem of radio communication with the ship to be considered.

Our rest period over, we sweated again on what the commodore had so aptly called the Armstrong Patent machine. At last the sinker rose into view. Attached to it was a sheet torn from the pad. Grimes detached it carefully but eagerly, then grunted. Mayhew's handwriting, at the best of times, was barely legible, and a mirror image of his vile calligraphy was impossible. And nobody had a mirror. I suggested that Grimes hold the sheet of plastic up against the sunlight. He did so, then muttered irritably, "Damn the man! If he can't write, he should print!"

Squinting against the glare I looked over Grimes's shoulder. At least, I thought, we should be thankful for small mercies; Mayhew had written on only one side of the sheet. I could just make out: *Safe, so far, but no communication. It*—the "it" was heavily underlined—*will receive but not transmit. I can't get inside its mind. It wants to know about us but does not want us to know about it. It's draining us. Can you get us out?*

(It took us far longer to read the message than it has taken you.)

"This piano wire is strong," Grimes told me. "The weight of a human being is well below its safe working load, let alone its breaking strain. But I don't fancy winching Ken or Clarisse—Clarisse especially—up by hand."

I was inclined to agree.

Grimes wrote a short note to Mayhew, using the reverse side of the sheet on which the telepath's message had been penned. He printed in large block capitals: HELP BEING ORGANIZED. GRIMES. We sent it down attached to the sinker.

And then Taylor appeared with additional equipment, bringing the boat down to a landing almost at the edge of the roof. Also with him were Thorne's assistants—Trentham, Smith, Susan Howard and Mary Lestrange. The mousey quartet showed signs of pleasurable excitement. A few turns on the hand winch, I thought sourly, would wipe the silly grins off their faces. Betty was with them. She had brought a sound-powered telephone set, a large reel of light cable and a tape recorder. And there was the second sounding machine, to which a motor from the engineroom gantry had been attached. Porky Terrigal, the Reaction Drive Engineer, had come along with it to make sure that nobody misused his precious machinery. There were also thermocontainers of hot and cold drinks and boxes of sandwiches, a couple of coils of strong plastic line that Bindle had sent along thinking that they might come in useful (they did) and a spidery-looking folding ladder that would give us access from the roof to the ground, and vice versa.

The boat had to stay in position, as the power to the sounding machine winch would be fed from its fusion unit. Luckily the rooftop was wide enough to accommodate all the extra people and gear without crowding. Sonya and Sara came up to join the party, leaving the Thornes standing watch below.

Grimes turned the four young scientists to on the hand winch. By the time they got the sinker up to roof level they had lost their initial enthusiasm. The message was easier to read this time. To begin with, Mayhew had taken the hint and printed the words and, secondly, Susan Lestrange produced a small mirror from her shoulder bag. It said: *WOULD LIKE A LITTLE MORE TIME. CAN YOU SEND TELEPHONE? KEN.*

We sent the telephone, and with it some food and drink. Betty hooked an amplifier up to the instrument at our end of the line. We waited anxiously, far from sure that things would work. What if what had been happening to the written word also happened to the spoken word? Then, after what seemed an eternity of delay, we heard Mayhew's voice. "Thanks for the tucker, John! It's very welcome. All the others seem to have died of thirst and starvation . . ."

"What others?" asked Grimes.

"Clarisse here," came the reply. "Ken can't talk with his mouth full. We're safe, so far. But I'll try to put you in the picture. It feels like a huge control room, like a ship's, but much, much bigger. Only there are no controls as *we* know them, no banks of familiar instruments . . . This is a great, cavernous space with lights shifting and pulsing. . . We *know* that it all means something, that it isn't mere random activity, but what? But *what?* Maintaining stasis over uncountable millennia . . . Staying put in Time-and-Space while the Universe around it dies and is reborn . . ." A note of hysteria crept into her voice. "*It* . . . *It* has sucked us dry, of all we know, even of knowledge that we did not dream that we owned."

"And now *It* isn't interested in us anymore. We can take our places with the . . . others . . ."

"What others?" demanded Grimes.

Mayhew came back on the line. "There are bodies here. Not decayed but . . . desiccated. Sort of mummified. Some human. Some . . . not. There's . . . something not far from us with an exoskeleton. Something not from *this* Universe. And there are two things like centaurs . . . The arthropod thing is holding a machine of some kind . . . It could be a complicated weapon . . . And there's all the time the slow, regular pulse of the coloured lights washing over everything, and there's something that's like a gigantic pendulum, but not of metal, but of radiance . . . I can *feel* it rather than see it . . ." He paused. "It's like being a tiny insect in the works of some vast clock, only the wheels and the gears and the pendulum aren't material . . ."

Clarisse cried, interrupting, "But can you imagine a clock ticking backwards?"

Thorne had climbed up the rooftop. He said, "I heard all that. We must try to bring up some . . . specimens."

"All that I'm concerned with," Grimes told him, "is bringing our friends up."

"It would be criminal," said the scientist, "to miss this opportunity."

"It will be criminal," said Grimes, "to risk two lives any further. How do we know that the . . . gateway will stay open? No; we get Clarisse and Ken out of there *now*."

The wire of the hand-powered sounding machine had been reeled in by this time and, under Grimes's supervision, the one with the electric motor was set up in its place. To the sinker the commodore attached one of the coils of light plastic rope. He said into the telephone, "You remember that book of mine you borrowed on bends and hitches and knots and splices, Ken? You should be able to throw a secure bowline on the bight with the line I'm sending down to you . . . Yes, you sit in it . . ."

"But can't he send up something, *anything*, first?" pleaded Thorne.

"No, Doctor." Grimes was adamant.

"I overheard some of that," came Mayhew's voice. "I think we should. That lobster thing, and the contraption it's holding in its claws . . . I could carry it up with me . . ."

"Mayhew is speaking sense," commented the scientist.

There was a long wait. Then, "It's heavy," came the voice from the speaker. "Damned heavy. We can't shift it."

"Then leave it," Grimes ordered. "The sinker and the plastic line are on their way down to you now. I'm using the electrically powered machine, so I'll have you and Clarisse up in no time."

"You have *two* machines?" asked Mayhew.

"Yes. Why?"

"I'll send Clarisse up first. Send the wire down again, and I'll have made a sling with what's left of the line and put it round the . . . *thing*. Then you bring *me* up with the hand-powered winch, and you can use the stronger one to lift the specimen . . ."

"Well?" demanded Thorne.

"All right," Grimes agreed reluctantly.

It took no time at all to extricate Clarisse. Grimes had sent Taylor down to the temple, accompanied by the two girl scientists, to pull her clear of the altar and then down to the floor as soon as she emerged. She joined us on the roof. I looked at her and tried to remember on which of her cheekbones that beauty spot had been . . .

We sent the wire down again. Mayhew telephoned that he had

the end of it, was making it fast to the sling that he had managed to get around the body of the weird alien. We then shifted the electric winch to one side, replacing it with the hand-powered one. Grimes was worried that the two sounding wires might become entangled, but the sinker dropped with the same speed that it had done on the prior occasions.

Mayhew said that he was seated in the bowline and ready to come up. Trentham and Smith manned the winch handles. It was brutally hard work; the winch was not geared. After a while Grimes and I had to spell them. And then Thorne and Terrigal took a turn. Mayhew was bringing his end of the telephone up with him and was keeping us informed. "Like swimming up through a sort of gray fog . . ." he said. "I'm putting my hand out, but there's nothing solid. . I can see the other wire . . . I can touch *that*, but it's all that I can touch . . . Looking up, I can see a sort of distorted square of white light . . . It's a long way off . . ."

Yes, it was a long way. A long way for him, and a bloody long way for those of us who were doing all the work. I hoped that Dr. Thorne was enjoying his turn at the winch; it had been his idea that a specimen be brought up. If he hadn't insisted Mayhew would have been whisked to safety with the same speed as Clarisse.

We heard Taylor's shout from below at last, just as Mayhew himself reported that he was being lifted into the temple. We came back on the winch after the Third Mate had caught his swinging feet and was lowering him safely to the floor. Once he was out of his harness he came up the ladder to join us on the rooftop.

Now that the operation was almost over I realized, suddenly, how time had flown. It was almost sunset, and a chill breeze was blowing from the east. In a matter of minutes it would be dark. Kinsolving has no moon and here, on the Rim, there would be precious little starlight.

Grimes said, "I think we should defer any further operations until tomorrow morning."

Thorne said, "But there are lights in the boat. A searchlight . . ."

Mayhew said, "John, do we *want* that . . . thing? I've a feeling that the gateway may be closing again, at any second."

"Oh, all right," said Grimes resignedly. He turned to me, "Let's get the electric winch back on to the platform."

We did so. Then he told me, "It's your equipment, George, operated by your personnel. Over to you."

I thought, *You buck-passing old bastard!* But what he had said made sense. I gestured to Terrigal at the winch controls, made the Heave Away! signal. The piano wire tightened. I looked over Terrigal's shoulder and could see the pointer on the dial begin to move. I visualised that bundle of—something—being dragged across the floor of the . . . Cavern? Control room? The winch hadn't got the weight yet.

Then it took the strain and almost coincidentally the sun set. The light breeze was chillier still and there was almost no twilight. Somebody switched on the lights in the boat, including the searchlight, which flooded the rooftop with a harsh, white radiance. The winch groaned. Terrigal complained, "I can't be held responsible for any damage to the machinery . . ."

"Keep her coming!" I told him. I was more concerned about the baulks of timber upon which the sounding machine was resting than with the machine itself. But engineers, in my experience, always tend to be slaves to rather than masters of their engines.

There was an acrid taint in the air from overheated metal and insulation and the wire, a filament of incandescent silver in the searchlight beam, was beginning to sing. But the pointer on the dial was moving—slowly, slowly, but moving.

I asked, "Can't you go any faster?"

"No, Captain. I'm on the last notch now. And I don't like it."

"Better get people cleared away from here, George," Grimes told me. "If that wire parts it's going to spring back . . ."

"And what about *me*?" demanded Terrigal.

"If you're scared . . ." I began.

"Yes, I am scared!" he growled. "And so would you be if you had any bloody sense. But I wouldn't trust any of you on this winch!"

All right, all right—I *was* scared. And it was more than a fear of a lethally lashing end of broken wire. It was that primordial dread of the unknown that has afflicted man from his first beginnings, that afflicts, too, the lower orders of the animal kingdom. The darkness around the brilliantly lit rooftop was alive with shifting, whispering shadows. Most of our party, I noticed, had already taken refuge in the boat, a little cave of light and warmth that offered shelter, probably illusory, from the Ultimate Night that seemed to be closing around us. Only Grimes, Sonya, Sara and myself remained in the open—and, of course, Terrigal at the winch controls.

The winch was making an eerie whining noise. The smell of hot metal and scorching insulation was much stronger. And the wire itself was keening—and was . . . stretching. Surely it was stretching. Surely that shining filament was now so, thin as to be almost invisible.

"Enough!" ordered Grimes "Avast heaving!"

The engineer brought the control handle round anti-clockwise, but it had no effect. He cried, "She won't stop!"

"Mr. Taylor!" shouted Grimes into the boat, "Switch off the power to the winch!"

"The switch is jammed!" came the reply.

"She won't stop! She won't stop!" yelled Terrigal, frantically jiggling his controls.

The light was dimming, sagging down the spectrum, and outlines were wavering, and frightened voices sounded as though they were coming from an echo chamber. The thin high keening of the overtaut wire was above and below and through all other noises. Sonya and Sara were wrestling with the power cable, tugging at it, worrying it like two dogs fighting over a bone, trying to drag it out of its socket in the boat's hull. It resisted all their efforts.

"Let's get out of here!" snapped Grimes. "Into the boat, all of you!"

Terrigal abandoned his winch, but not before aiming a vicious kick at the control box. He scurried into the little airlock. The two women followed. Grimes and I made it to the door in a dead heat; he pushed me inside then followed hard after me. As soon as we were all in, Taylor, forward at the controls, slammed the inertial drive into maximum lift, not bothering to close the airlock doors first. We started to rise, then stopped with a jerk, heeling alarmingly to port. The power cable to the winch was holding us down. But it would soon part, I thought. It must part. It was only a power cable, not a heavy-duty mooring wire.

It didn't part. It . . . stretched. It shouldn't have done, but it did. And we lifted again, slowly, with the inertial drive hammering like a mechanical riveter gone mad. I clung to the frame of the open door and looked down. I saw the sounding machine dragged up and clear from the circular hole in the roof, with the shining filament of wire still extending straight downwards.

Terrifyingly the city around the temple was coming to life—but it wasn't the city that we had explored. The human colonists had laid out their streets in a rectangular plan; these streets were concentric circles connected by radial thoroughfares. And there were the tall, cylindrical towers, agleam with lights, each topped with a shining sphere. Unsubstantial they seemed at first, but as I watched they appeared to acquire solidity.

Grimes saw it too. He shouted to Taylor, to Terrigal, to anybody who was close enough to the fusion generator to do something about it, "You have to cut the power to the winch! We're dredging up the Past—and we shall be in it!"

"Just show me how, Commodore!" cried the engineer. "Just show me how! I've done all that *I* can do—short of stopping the jenny!"

And if he did stop the generator we should fall like a stone. *If* he could stop it, that is.

An aircraft came slowly into view, circling us warily. It was huge, a cylindrical hull, rounded at the ends, with vanes sticking out at all sorts of odd angles. It was like nothing that I had ever seen and possessed a nightmarishly alien quality. There were tubes protruding from turrets that could have been, that almost certainly were guns, and they were trained upon us. What if the alien commander—I visualized him, or *it*, as being of the same species as the lobsterlike being whose body we had been attempting to recover—should open fire? What would happen to us?

Nothing pleasant, that was for sure.

❧ ❧ ❧ ❧

But we had weapons of our own; we could, at least, defend ourselves if attacked. Sara, I was sure, would enjoy being able to play with her toys. And Sara, I suddenly realized, was beside me in the cramped little airlock, holding her sub-machine gun. I said to her, "What use do you think that will be? What's wrong with the heavy armament?"

She replied obscurely, "I can't bring it to bear." I couldn't see why she couldn't. That blasted flying battleship was staying well within the arcs-of-fire of the laser cannon and the heavy machine gun, and a guided missile would home on her no matter where she was relative to us.

Sara opened fire. Bright tracer flashed out from the muzzle of the gun, but not towards the huge flying ship. It may have been the first round of the burst that hit the power cable, certainly it was one in the first half-dozen. There was an arcing sputter of blue flame and the boat, released from its tether, went up like a bat out of hell.

And below us the weird city out of Time flickered and vanished.

I turned to Grimes. "You said sir, that the things that happen or Kinsolving's Planet shouldn't happen to a dog. And they shouldn't happen, either, to respectable employees of the Dog Star Line."

He managed a grin, then went, "Arf, arf!"